The Mistress of
Beulah Land

was many things. She was daughter of one of Georgia's proudest families. She was wife to a man willing to give her anything if she did not interfere with his unbridled sensual pleasures. She was lover to a man who asked her to give up all the prejudices of her race and class. But above all she was mistress of the lush plantation that was the home of romance and passion and a sense of endless time, where white and black, master and slave, lived together in an intimacy never revealed to any outsider, where sex was as easy as laughter but love took strange and hidden twists . . .

. . . the great plantation that you will come to know with all your senses and never forget, flamboyant and doomed in all its splendor, pride, and corruption . . .

Beulah Land

BEULAH LAND

Lonnie Coleman

A DELL BOOK ·

To Gordon Reekie

Published by
DELL PUBLISHING CO., INC.
1 Dag Hammarskjold Plaza
New York, New York 10017
Copyright © 1973 by Lonnie Coleman
All rights reserved.
For information contact
Doubleday & Company, Inc.,
New York, New York.
Dell ® TM 681510, Dell Publishing Co., Inc.
Reprinted by arrangement with
Doubleday & Company, Inc.
Printed in the United States of America
First Dell printing—October 1974

Thou shalt no more be termed Forsaken neither shall thy land any more be termed Desolate: but thou shall be called Hephzibah, and thy land Beulah: for the Lord delighteth in thee, and thy land shall be married.

Isaiah 62:4

PART ONE

One

Savannah was one of the South's great ports, acting as goods and culture broker between the land mass behind it and the world beyond its shores. Many roads led from Savannah to other, smaller centers. One of these, a town called Highboro, fifty-three miles northwest of Savannah, had its own roads leading to other, smaller towns, and to farms and plantations. The main road out of Highboro was red clay with veins of blue-black. In fair weather it was hard as stone to the hoofs of horses and mules, but when rain fell in more than a brief shower, it became a slippery bog. Two roads led from the main road to the plantation called Beulah Land.

A back road ran through cotton and corn fields that claimed the choicest of the sixteen hundred acres, through the neck of a wood of cypress, oak, and pine, watered by a creek. The road ended with barns, smoke houses, chicken yards, water wells, a kitchen garden, and the forty cabins that housed the Negroes who worked the plantation. These numbered a hundred and fifty, more or less, depending on births and deaths rather than sales, and were never referred to by Arnold Kendrick as slaves, although the phrase he used, "my people," spoke ownership as well as a kind of kinship.

The front road to Beulah Land curved over a hill through an orchard of plum and peach trees until it settled to a straight, dignified avenue bordered by cedar and oak trees all the way to the front door of the house that was its end and reason for being. The house was a large one, built mostly of wood, and owed whatever distinction it possessed to size rather than design.

Fronting it was a broad porch with squared wooden columns lifting the full two-story height of the house to support the roof. The house was painted gray, its shutters dark green. The work buildings out in back had been left to weather gray and were a softer, warmer shade than the house. The slave cabins were whitewashed, as were the lower trunks of the trees nearest the big house.

The front porch opened directly into a wide center hall, off which, on either side, were living and dining rooms. The stairway to the next floor was in the front left living room, leaving the center hall a clear passage for whatever breezes stirred through the house and the roofed but open-sided breezeway to the kitchens and store rooms where Deborah Kendrick spent much of her time.

Although Lovey, who was about her own age, acted as her deputy, it was Deborah who had trained, or retrained, the house servants and who indeed knew how all the male hands on the place were occupied: who plowed and hoed, who chopped and sawed, and who cared for which animals. Deborah and Lovey were a strange pairing, if anyone thought about it, but no one did, because they had been for so long the pair who ran the house.

Deborah was an erect, quick-stepping woman whose face, because it seemed ever to be scrutinizing and weighing, held no softness or humor. Her dark red hair was parted in the middle and caught at the back of her neck in a bun that grew heavier and larger every year.

Lovey was shorter than her mistress and ampler in bosom and behind, but equally quick-stepping. Unlike Deborah, she laughed frequently. Her gestures, like her laugh, were quick and nervous, by temperament rather than reason, for Lovey was afraid of nothing and no one. Her independence of spirit was the thing Deborah had first noticed about her when she came to live at Beulah Land following her marriage to Arnold in 1800.

In the bill of sale that had brought *her* to Beulah Land a year before Deborah's arrival, Lovey's name was given as Laverne La Vey, but this was too fancy to be endured by her new fellows, who soon converted La Vey into Lovey and dropped Laverne altogether.

Laverne La Vey had been plump and attractive, and her temper delighted the other slaves, for their only entertainment was in each other and the turn of events on the plantation. One after another the unattached men made approaches to the girl, who slapped them away like so many flies, declaring that she had no time or mind for men, that, in fact, she despised every one of them and was determined that her distant but eventual grave be virginal. This was taken as an amusing display of spirit, even rebellion, since it was understood that a woman's function, in addition to performing whatever work she was set to, was to bear the children who would replace her and her man, when their time of usefulness was over. Besides, it was so obviously absurd. How could a girl as pretty and lively as Laverne hope to hold out against the pressing ardor of the young men?

Yet hold out she did for two years until, where youth had failed, age prevailed in the person of a quiet man named Ezra. He was the blacksmith, but more than that. Jobs were assigned, of course, but a man's aptitudes governed his eventual occupations. Ezra's understanding of animals other than horses and mules grew as the years passed until, in addition to being blacksmith, he was Beulah Land's animal doctor. He remembered every remedy he heard about, discarding the ones that failed to work for him and venturing to experiment with local herbs. Ezra's word was law on the treatment of all animal ills at Beulah Land, and, in time, since the bodies of men and women have much in common with those of beasts, he was consulted on human ills by the other slaves, and sometimes by the Kendricks too; and he began to be called, inevitably, Doctor.

Ezra's knowledge was held in awe and superstition by his fellow slaves. It was supposed that he knew even more than he did, and field and house gossip made legend of his spells and predictions, although his predictions were always based on clever diagnosis, and he had nothing at all to do with spells.

His attendance on the ill meant that he was sometimes present at deaths, and this led to further duties of "laying out" the dead for burial. Treating thus with the dead made him a further object of awe and superstition, set him apart. It might not have been so had he married, but he had not at the time Laverne La Vey was brought to live and work at Beulah Land, when he was near forty and had long been considered one of those whose concerns turned them away from an interest in women. Ezra was, in truth, lonely, in spite of the busy life he led. The rare times there was no call on his services he spent fishing on the creekbanks or sitting in the cabin that he tended himself. He had not even a pet dog or cat, for when every animal is a man's concern, he is unlikely to single out one for special attention.

Ezra along with the others noted Laverne's prettiness and her temper, and found himself pleased as well as

amused by her when, alone in his cabin at night, he
thought of her—something he had heard her say that day,
her laugh, a shout of sudden, transient rage.

Lovey could not say when she first began to notice
Ezra, but when she did, it was as though she had always
known and trusted him. By that time she had been picked
as special helper by the new bride and mistress. Since
most of her waking hours were spent with, or within call
of, Deborah Kendrick, and since Arnold Kendrick often
found himself consulting with Ezra when the work day
was done and he and Deborah drew closer for night company, so Lovey and Ezra became accustomed to each
other and found themselves easy together.

On more than one dark night Ezra escorted Lovey from
the big house to the cabin she shared with Widow Jane
and her ugly unmarried daughters, Posie and Buttercup.
When he saw that she accepted him as a familiar, that is,
that she could be still in his presence, evidently feeling no
need to strain and buck and break away as she did in the
presence of others, he began to give her such things as
were in his power to give: a perfect peach, a nicely
trimmed quill to pick her teeth, and once a remedy for
earache made of crushed camphor leaves and oil of
cloves.

As she grew aware of him, Lovey knew what had happened and what would happen, and to her credit she did
not tease the man with vagaries and protestations. Her
awareness showing in her eyes emboldened Ezra to speak;
and when she listened quietly, to take her hand; and when
she did not withdraw, the thing was quickly settled between them.

Deborah and Arnold saw them married in the living
room of the big house one Sunday in September 1801.
Ezra's cabin became Lovey's, and together Lovey and
Ezra were those closest to the Kendricks of all who
dwelled at Beulah Land. Before her marriage, which to her
raucous delight astonished the other plantation hands,
Lovey had been in a position of growing, if undefined,
power. After it, Ezra's own maturity extenuating her
youth, she was recognized as the mistress of the house—
after the Mistress.

Lovey was honest to the bone; it would not have
occurred to her to be otherwise; it was part of her independence. Never shy, she found perfectly natural her new
role as household harrier. She abominated dirt and laz-

iness and understood that they came together in the persons of bad workers; so her duty was clear to her. She harried, she scolded, she trotted about seeing that work was properly done. Deborah found ease and comfort in her noisiness and nervous good humor. The work got done, and its accomplishment was the satisfaction Lovey took and gave. The girls and women who worked under her supervision resented her, of course, and occasionally, briefly, hated her. But they could not hate her long, because even the dullest of them saw that she was as just as she was relentless. Deborah might now and then choose to appear not to see a piece of slovenly work for what it was; Lovey, never. The house was hers. It would be clean.

And to comfort the sullen and the slovenly, Lovey offered one ridiculous flaw: she was a bad cook. Every other woman on the place took pride in her ability to cook certain dishes better than others could or did, for herself and her family, sometimes for the Kendricks. But Lovey knew and admitted her failing. She said herself that if she stepped through a kitchen door where cake was baking, the cake would fall. Laughing, she declared that the sound of her voice soured cream, encouraged rice to stick and burn. Her not being able to cook, and her generous appreciation of the good cooking of others, made her almost, sometimes popular.

Two

Time went by, and the two principal families of Beulah Land remained childless. Lovey conceived and miscarried three times, and gossip offered several explanations: Ezra had so long denied himself a woman that when he got one, the mysterious ways of flesh and spirit would not acknowledge and accommodate each other. Their blood refused to mix; what each was, canceled the other. He old, she young; he silent, she turbulent.

As for Deborah and Arnold, none on the plantation had ever seen them touch, not a hand on hand or arm, so there was less wonder at Deborah's being barren. Yet both Deborah and Arnold wanted to have children; not because they were a loving pair, but because children were needed to inhabit and sustain Beulah Land. For all their need and wanting, they remained two, alone each and together.

The land flourished, with plenty and to spare. There was increase in the yield of cotton and corn, of cattle, pigs, and fowl. Old slaves died, or became so feeble they were good for nothing but sitting in doorways as flies walked undisturbed over the backs of their hands and they wondered when the next meal would be ready. But babies were born: kicked, cried, lived.

Then, in the spring of 1805, both Deborah and Lovey found themselves with child, but waited to tell each other until their figures told for them. As they went about in tandem, their bellies poking out as if in some slow, absurd competition, they were the subject of whispered jokes. The fact that they were never came to Deborah's attention, of course, and when it came to Lovey's, she flew into such a rage that nobody dared again to laugh or even smile in her presence until she was delivered of her child.

Deborah's boy was born on December 24, 1805, and named Leon. Lovey's boy was born on January 2, 1806, and named Floyd. Neither delivery was complicated, although Deborah's took longer. She tried in vain to nourish her babe, whereas Lovey's breasts soon plumped with milk that sometimes seeped from her nipples and made damp patches on the bib of her dress.

Floyd ate and slept. The little milk Deborah produced upset Leon's stomach and made him fret and cry. Nursing their babies one morning in Deborah's bedroom as they talked over the day's duties, Lovey studied poor Leon squirming and kicking against Deborah's meager bosom; then, without a word, she took him from his mother and gave him her free breast. Both women stared as the two babes sucked life from Lovey's body. White and brown, they fed until content. Their jaws and mouths relaxed; their fists and feet pushed against Lovey's soft flesh no longer; they slept. Lovey smiled down at them with pride and satisfaction. Deborah covered her bosom and never offered it to Leon again.

Thereafter Lovey fed both boys at the same time. Her doing so became one of the familiar sights of the plantation day. Deborah was casually grateful to Lovey for freeing her to attend her main concerns as mistress of Beulah Land. There was an epidemic of influenza that winter, and she was more often attended by Ezra than Lovey as she went from cabin to cabin feeling heads and necks for fever and administering a liquid medicine for coughs which Ezra had concocted of peach brandy and sulphur.

When winter ended and spring came warmly on, the plowed, sown fields were fragrant with loamy promise, and the two boy babies were together for most of the day. When they were not feeding side by side, they were set on a quilted pallet which was moved from one place to another as Lovey moved from one activity to another.

The Widow Jane's daughter Posie was assigned by Deborah to assist Lovey with the little boys. Afraid of them, she found eager assistants in the adolescent girls who were suddenly discovering the wonder of birth and babies and who, when Lovey was out of the room where they were, found entertainment in undiapering the infants and tickling their genitals until erection occurred; whereupon the girls, shrieking with laughter, declared that all males, young and old, had but one thing in mind. Then rediapering the boys with suddenly harsh, punishing hands, they sang them lullabies half remembered and half invented.

That summer Ezra rigged padded pillow cases as swings on the thick-limbed fig tree that grew near the kitchen door. Floyd and Leon, when other matters claimed Lovey's attention, were set safely upright in the padded swings, swaddled like papooses. They slept and woke, and seeing each other, laughed, as the wind swung them to and fro in the fig-scented air.

Three

Deborah's second, and as it transpired, last child was born in March 1808, and named Selma for Arnold's mother, long dead. There were five fingers on each of the infant's hands and five toes on each of her feet. Her legs were two, eyes two, arms two. Head and trunk were what is expected of a baby. Yet from the first she seemed an alien creature. In a lap, on a bed, in her cradle, she did not move or cry. Picked up, she appeared startled. When the time came that she should smile, she would not. She looked at every face that drew close to hers as if it had materialized from the spirit world.

Deborah gave her mainly into Buttercup's care, but that one was afraid of babies like her sister Posie, especially when she was alone with the little girl.

Lovey miscarried twice again, but in 1809 conceived, and in June of 1810 bore a daughter she named Pauline. Pauline's tiny hands closed like traps on whatever finger

came within their range, and her unblinking wet eyes were
dark with distrust. Lovey laughed and shrugged and said
she must be Ezra's, for she could see nothing of herself in
the baby, and could not fathom her mystery. Ezra laughed
and forgot about her most of the time, Floyd being more
glory and wonder than he had ever dreamed possible.

Four

"Floyd! You *Floyd! Le*-on! Where you hiding? Come when
I call!"

Lovey fidgeted, one foot tapping the stone step that led
to the kitchen. She had been gathering eggs, a morning
occupation that put her in good humor because, although
some hens laid their eggs properly in nests that had been
built for them, others dropped them in odd corners of
yard and barn, indeed, wherever spirit and flesh moved
them, thereby making the finding of them something of a
game. Her apron, caught tightly in one hand, held seventeen hen's eggs, white and brown and speckled, and four
guinea eggs, which she decided she would keep for brooding.

"Come here this minute, *both* of you!"

They appeared, by magic it seemed, and stood staring
up at her. "You hongry?" she asked, nodding her head affirmatively, although it was only an hour since they had
eaten. She went into the kitchen, holding the aproned eggs
carefully, and they followed her. "Posie! Untie me!" Posie
left her butter churn and with one deft yank untied
Lovey's apron and caught the eggs in a basket that sat
empty on the meat-chopping table.

Frowning, Lovey went to the stove and opened the
oven door. Half a dozen biscuits left over from breakfast
lay hardening in a flat baking pan. She took two of them,
poked a finger in their sides and filled the holes she made
with syrup. Each boy grabbed a biscuit and ran out the
doorway. But once around the corner of the house they
whistled to old Belle, queen of the hounds, who waddled
toward them, teats sagging and swaying, tail lifted in expectation. Leon flipped his biscuit in the air, and she
caught and swallowed it without knowing what had gone
down her throat. Floyd flipped his, and the old dog held it
in her mouth briefly before swallowing. Her tail quivered
in gratitude, as they laughed and ran away.

Five

One of the several qualities that fitted Arnold Kendrick for his role in life was a genuine interest and pleasure in watching other people work, his absorption the keener when he understood and respected the skill of the work being done. This quality drew him often to Ezra's blacksmith shop. On the same small, hot fire of his foundry Ezra might be stewing an experimental brew of herbs and heating a bar of iron to bend into horseshoe or pot handle or wall hook. Moving unhurriedly and speaking no greeting, Arnold sidled into the open-sided shed and slouched peacefully, like a waiting horse, as he watched Ezra work. The two might be together an hour without acknowledging the presence of each other. Sometimes Arnold, after watching his fill, sidled out again, having spoken no word, his departure as unacknowledged by Ezra as his attendance had been.

However, sometimes they spoke, as when:

"Man came last night," Arnold said. (Ezra knew this.) "A free man looking for work. Paper to prove he belongs to himself. Been in Highboro a little time; before that, Savannah, he says. Name of Roscoe Elk." Ezra took pincers and lifted a strip of red-white metal from the fire and began to hammer it as delicately as if he feared to wake an invalid. "*Says* he knows something about smithing. Want to give him a try?"

Ezra looked up from his work seriously. Then he started to hammer again, more lightly and meticulously than before. When Arnold had turned his back to go, Ezra said, "Try him."

Six

Roscoe Elk claimed to be half Indian, and it is possible that he was. It is also possible that he had invented the background to give himself mystery. His claim accorded with a slightly hooked nose and with coarse black hair that showed no kink. He cultivated near silence, which contrasted tellingly with the volubility of the slaves around him. There was no telling his age. The young thought him old; the old considered him mature, but still young.

It is never hard for a clever man to rise, no matter how low he is born, for the world is full of lazy people, and Roscoe had learned early that if he stood ready to do a portion of another man's work, take on some of his responsibility, he gained power.

Ezra was not at all lazy, but he was not jealous of his position either, having much to do and an active mind that was forever expanding his knowledge and activity instead of narrowing them. Within six months of his coming Roscoe was acknowledged blacksmith. His work brought most men to him, and it was among the lazy ones of them he accrued power. "Just leave it there . . . I'll do it . . . Never mind . . . Don't worry."

He had not been a year on the place before it was common to hear people say, "Ask Roscoe; Roscoe will know." From blacksmith he became in logical sequence general mender and maker. Since it involved hardware, he tended the scales that weighed the work of the slave hands. While not paid in money for what they did, the more productive were rewarded with privileges and bonus goods. Knowing how to figure and how to write, he presently found himself—or rather, others found him to be—keeper of records and accounts. No one but the ambitious enjoy the nitty-natty of daily life, but Roscoe never complained. Once power was his, sloth in others would no longer, of course, be tolerated.

Seven

Then as now many of life's events turned on the matter of convenience. It simplified things if a man chose a wife from among those he had long known. Strengths and weaknesses of various families were known as well as their property and as carefully weighed. As a credit to his own possible future need as much as from friendly concern and generosity, neighbor helped neighbor. Rain may fall on one acre while that lying next goes parched. Families were often large, death in them more commonly expected than nowadays. If a man fancied a woman and walked or rode out to court her, it was not unusual for his

brother to accompany him and court a sister of the
woman. So it happened more often then than now that
brothers married sisters.

Arnold and his younger brother Felix had in that way
ridden from Beulah Land three miles into the town of
Highboro to court the Singleton sisters, Deborah and Nell,
and to marry them. Arnold and Deborah settled at Beulah
Land. Felix read law, argued cases in court, bought town
property, and became a thorough town man, settling with
Nell in the house her parents had built, but adding a wing
to it and an acre to its grounds to set his mark of ownership.

Felix was a gay, convivial man, needing the faces and
voices of his fellow creatures more than his brother did,
and he might have been entirely happy except for the fact
that his wife Nell possessed little energy for life and was
altogether weaker fibered than her sister Deborah.

Nell's overriding consideration was not to be bothered.
To attain and sustain this plateau of inaction was her true
vocation. Everything else bent to it. Her principal tool and
weapon was what she called her delicate constitution.

"I declare I have to actually *think* about it in order to
draw the next breath. If I didn't, I'd just go out like a
candle."

On her wedding night Felix innocently and enthusiastically set about to claim his marital rights. Nell fainted,
which dispelled the physical ardor Felix felt for her. His
next attempt at conjunction resulted in her throwing up
her supper. After waiting a fortnight he tried again. She
engaged in a fit of weeping that would have melted the
lust of Tarquin, and Felix was no Tarquin.

When he realized he was to be denied children as well
as "home pleasure," he looked about him and made do
with what he found. Had he been given to depression, he
might have despaired at the chancy improvisations and
half measures he was forced to, but being a cheerful man,
he made a virtue of the impromptu and woke each day
with feelings of anticipation and adventure. If he accepted, as he did, Nell's declaration of delicate health, so she
also accepted, with eyes open and willfully blind, his minor and major infidelities. A mating, if such it may be
called, begun as a convenience to both, continued and endured as one. They were in their way perfectly loyal. Neither would hear a word against the other, and in time
their very thoughts agreed with their public behavior.

"Well, Nellie," Deborah exclaimed, as the carriage she had watched all the way up the front road rolled to a stop at the door, "you're here at last. I expected you earlier."

"I woke feeling so poorly I despaired of coming at all, except that I wouldn't disappoint Felix." Nell sat still with her eyes nearly closed and her hands drooping in her lap, as Felix hopped out of the carriage and gave his sister-in-law a hug. Laughing, he trotted past her into the house, calling back, "Where is Arnold? Out with the hands, is he?"

Deborah helped Nell down from her seat as Plumboy, a skinny, grinning child who worked in the stables, held the horses until the lady had got out of the carriage and he could guide it around the house to the barn where the horses would be unhitched and attended to.

"How are you, Deborah?" Nell asked plaintively as she allowed herself to be guided up the steps onto the porch.

"Entirely fit," Deborah said, "as I am happy to see you are too."

Nell smiled forgivingly. "Would it were so. But we must all, I tell myself, bow to God's will."

"Fiddle, Nellie. You're as strong as a team of oxen."

Their mutual greeting accomplished, and it varied little from one time to the next, they linked arms and entered the long hall, turning left into the room that would take them upstairs to the front bedroom habitually used by Nell and Felix. As they climbed, they heard from the kitchen wing a chorus of laughter, then Lovey's voice raised in fierce complaint: "Mister Felix, I told you, I told you, I tell you again—keep your hands in your pockets and your pockets tucked inside your trousers! You, Buttercup, hush that giggling and catch little Selma before she falls! Am I the only one with eyes?"

Unheeding as if unhearing, Nell glided up the winding stairs, Deborah following.

Eight

The Davis plantation, called simply Oaks, shared no boundary with Beulah Land, but the Davises were the nearest considerable family in the county, and so there were frequent social occasions that brought the two families together. Indeed, the intervention between them of two small farms, each of less than a hundred acres, made for a closer feeling between them perhaps than if they had shared a boundary line.

Benjamin and Edna Davis were plain as potatoes, Deborah said privately, but goodhearted. Both were stout, florid, and open-faced, and might have passed for brother and sister had their true relationship not been known. Both had big red hands that when empty looked like idle farm tools. Arnold and Benjamin hunted together, consulted with each other about slaves and crops and animals. Deborah and Edna exchanged vegetable and flower seed and cuttings, recipes and patterns for sewing.

The Davises had two sons, Bonard, who was three years older than Leon, and Bruce, nicknamed Rooster, who was a year younger than Leon. Rooster was clearly his parents' son, a jolly, easy, earthy boy. Bonard was like no one else in the family: dark, handsome even as a child, haughty, and sly.

At a barbecue the Kendricks gave one Fourth of July, the boys, who had known each other all their lives and therefore never thought about each other, got into a fight while playing a game of marbles. Leon, who was eight years old at the time, accused Bonard of cheating and of thereby stealing a beautifully flecked green glass marble that he treasured particularly. Bonard called Leon a liar and gave him a hard push that made him trip and fall to the ground.

He was up quickly and flew at Bonard with his head down, butting the older boy so hard in his midsection that Bonard gasped for breath. Seeing his brother attacked, Rooster, who was somewhat short for his age but already well fleshed, began kicking Leon's legs from behind. Recovering his wind, Bonard grabbed an ear with one hand and used the other to shove Leon's chin upward. Floyd, who had been watching the game of marbles but not playing, although he and Leon played the game together when there was no company, leaped on Bonard's back and began choking him.

Rooster left off kicking and tried to pull Floyd from Bonard's back. All happened in seconds and without words except for the accusations of thief, cheat, and liar that had occasioned the fight. Within seconds it was over, as Felix and Benjamin, who stood nearby smoking cigars and talking about the building of a new courthouse in Highboro, separated the tangle of bodies.

"Dirty nigger!"

"Thief! Cheat!"

Felix passed Floyd to Ezra, who had come up quickly as the fighting began, and Ezra took his son away. Arnold arrived, looking mildly puzzled at the affair, told Leon that he was host to the Davis boys and that he must apologize instantly. While Leon protested, Bonard pocketed the green marble as Rooster, who saw him do it, stared at him, astonished at even his boldness.

Rooster's helping his brother had been triggered by a simple feeling of family solidarity, not particular regard, for, although he was four years younger than Bonard—a difference in age that might have been supposed to keep them tolerably well disposed toward each other, the younger admiring and imitating, the older encouraging and teaching—they were frequently at odds at home. Bonard was a bully. He gave orders to his younger brother and smacked him when they were not obeyed. Rooster was an amiable child, but he frequently, healthily rebelled. Unable because of his inferior size and strength to beat his brother physically, he contrived jokes to puncture Bonard's haughty dignity. Once, having suffered a beating for no reason other than Bonard's bad temper, he bided his time until Bonard slept and poured a pitcher of cold water over his face and head. He was beaten again, but it was worth it to him.

Seeing Bonard now pocket the green marble, Rooster unhesitatingly changed sides. While Arnold was repeating the obligations of a host and urging his son to shake hands and be friends with his recent opponents, Rooster marched up, took Leon's hand and shook it as if he would like to shake it off, beaming at Leon the while in the friendliest way. Bonard took advantage of the general approval voiced at this demonstration of good fellowship to slip away and subsequently follow and spy upon a group of young girls who, after whispering together, had gone to a secluded part of the grove where the barbecue was being held to squat in the bushes and pee.

The attention of the parents having been called to their sons, a plan was settled about their future education before the day was over. Up to this time Leon had received instruction in arithmetic, reading, writing, and the Bible from Deborah who, although certainly no scholar, at any rate knew more than her son did about those subjects. The Episcopal parson in Highboro had been giving Bonard instruction in Latin and mathematics twice a week, and Bonard was supposed to pass on this instruction to Rooster: teaching himself by teaching Rooster. But the arrangement was unsatisfactory, and just the week before Benjamin, on a business trip to Savannah, had engaged a tutor to come out in late August to live at Oaks and instruct both his sons in Latin, algebra, English grammar and composition, and ancient history. It was arranged on the spot that Leon should join the Davis brothers in their home schooling, and that Arnold should pay half of the tutor's fee.

The tutor, a Mr. Jeremy Bartram, arrived at Oaks in early September, the year 1814. Coming as he did directly from Savannah, he missed the civilized amenities of that city and gave himself certain patronizing airs until he was driven by loneliness to seek civil comfort of the country folk he lived among, and thereafter made it his serious concern to impart some knowledge to those whose ignorance had brought him there. In addition to a trunk packed mainly with books and maps from which he was to teach, he brought a flute. Now and then he took it out and sounded notes on it, but he never was able to teach himself to play it, and finally forgot all about it and his romantic notion of composing melodies in the Arcadian scene.

Each weekday morning Plumboy saddled a horse for Leon to ride alone to Oaks for his daily lessons. On Tuesday of the second week Leon refused to go unless Floyd were allowed to accompany him. Deborah spanked Leon and had Ezra set him on the horse. As long as she stood and watched, he let himself be carried down the drive to the main road that would take him to Oaks, but as soon as she went back into the house and about her morning work, he returned. He did not dismount, but sat on the horse in the shade of a tree, in the branches of which Floyd sat swinging his legs and staring down at his friend. Arnold found them when he returned from the fields for his noon meal. He ordered the boy down from the horse after ascertaining that he had not come home sick. When he tried to reason with him, Leon clenched his jaw and would not answer.

Arnold took him into the front parlor, hoping to daunt him with formality, for this was the place they had their rare serious talks. And this is where Deborah found them after she had rung the hand bell in the dining room and found herself still sitting alone after some minutes had passed.

Soon after her came Lovey, who stood in the doorway frowning and watching her master and mistress talk to the boy. As their voices grew colder, her frown made deeper ruts in her face. Leon looked at her miserably, and when he saw her shoulders rise and fall in a sympathetic sigh, he ran to her and hid his face in her apron front. Her arms went around him automatically, and she said to the two who turned, "What harm? Him and Floyd used to one another. He'll learn better with Floyd along. Besides, he's young to go all that way by hisself. What if a snake jumped out and scared the horse?" The expressions of Arnold and Deborah relaxed at this unlikely supposition. "I hear there's a band of Indians camping in the eastern part of the county. We all know they go out stealing from their camps, a horse, a chicken, whatever they find. Like nothing better than to find a little boy alone on a fine horse. Never see that horse again, maybe not the boy. Take both and vanish like smoke, the way Indians do. Think about that."

On Wednesday, when Plumboy saddled the horse and Leon mounted him, Floyd mounted too and sat back of the saddle, his legs straight out at the sides and he giggling until everyone present smiled—Lovey and Deborah and Posie and Plumboy.

Rooster thought the whole thing a great joke. Mr. Bartram made no demur at the presence of the Negro boy in his classroom. Other young men had colored attendants, he reminded himself. Bonard, remembering the incident of the marble dispute and the boy's part in Leon's attack, insisted that Floyd, if he were allowed to stay at all, sit on the floor.

Nine

Selma was six years old, a quiet, private child who responded politely enough when noticed but seemed not to require the attention of her elders. Some are born strangers to their world, time and place wrong, feeling no fiber or drop of kinship with those called family, no affinity for the larger circle of the local order. Such a one was Selma.

Sensing from the beginning that she was alien, she accepted it, as she accepted herself. She took what she felt and saw in her own way. The older she grew the more she was pressed to leave or reject her true self as she knew it and to accept the world about her the way its other inhabitants accepted it. She knew they were wrong, but who can fight alone and unfriended when laughter and love, or professed love, are used to bring one into line with the others?

As a baby Selma had seen ghosts and strangers wherever she looked, and no face or eye that recognized and accepted her as she was. No one was cruel, but no one understood her. She had no social manner, and most people have, or affect to have it, even in infancy. The majority are born with a talent and taste for adapting. Selma was not.

At the very first she was suspected of being "simple." She stared back wonderingly at those who picked her up and smiled put-on smiles and jounced her and pulled her dress aside to look at her small, perfectly formed hands and feet, that even in her infancy did not twitch and clutch like most babies', but were still when exposed, like birds surprised to caution.

She took interest and pleasure in things without needing to share or to perform her reactions. Warm sunlight, the touch of soft cloth soothed her. The chatter of birds absorbed her as if she knew their language. The trickle of water on a hand was pleasure. In early terrorizing Buttercup, she assured herself as much privacy as an infant can have.

Pauline failed of acceptance in the opposite way. Losing, or perhaps suppressing, the distrust her eyes had early evidenced, the reaching, clutching baby fists described her temperament. Perhaps it had to do with her circumstance. Born in summer, she was in her early months always dressed lightly, although never left naked as some babies were. She knew air and sun on her skin, and the touch of other skin on hers. Her hands opened, her feet twitched obligingly. Her amiability at first charmed, then bored by its excess.

Lovey played with her, but never lost herself in the child. She always remembered when it was time to do something else. Deborah pronounced her a good-natured baby, held her, bobbing her playfully up and down in the air until she cried, then passed her on to Buttercup's hands.

The first year of her life Pauline lived on pallets when she was not being held or carried. Selma lived the first year of hers in the large cradle Leon had used before her and which still had a smell she found disagreeable, although she did not know it as his. Both little girls were early ambulatory. The one bored, the other mystified those who would pay her attention, and so both were left largely to develop as they would on their own.

At six Selma was independent. She loved the kitchen garden, and since its season was long, she played in it often, touching, looking, smelling. Tomato leaves and okra pods were like a cat's tongue. The blossoming peas, the curling tendrils of bean vines were of such delicate and tender beauty she could bear to touch them only with fingertips. The squash and cucumbers, bumpy as a frog's back, the clean, dry, rough rind of cantaloupe, the surprise of pulling a stalk and having a radish or an onion come up out of the ground—these drew her to the garden and held wonder for her.

In the early morning the garden was damp, and her dress would catch stickily on the wet plants as she wandered about, ignoring the kitchen girls who had been sent to gather the day's vegetables while the dew was still on them. The plants, most of them, were a size she could feel easy with, but people were too large.

Seeing that she did no harm and caused none to be done to herself, Deborah let her alone. Now and then she talked to her, but when she did, she found herself—not herself at all, and wondered why, and forgot, or accepted it as merely one of life's stray ends of which there are so many. Her voice sounded to her ears overemphatic and false, increasing her dissatisfaction with both herself and the child. She felt that Selma was simply waiting for her to be done with whatever she had to say, and there is nothing an adult so little understands, or wants, from a child as patience.

With her father Selma came closer. She recognized his shyness, and while it was not possible for them to feel intimate together, nevertheless their encounters were graced by an affection, almost unindicated except for a look in the eyes and the occasional touching made consciously, playfully formal by both of them in order to assure each other that there was no wish to trespass on private preserves.

Leon was as strange to her as she to him. She knew the

meaning of the words "brother" and "sister," but they carried for her no emotional bracketing. The children were seldom together except for meals. Anyway, there were always so many people about. And Leon had a friend, Floyd. He and Floyd seemed always to be together when they were not eating and sleeping.

From the time she could walk, Selma had a sense of the dimensions of her world. She went everywhere, more often than not alone, because Buttercup was not by zeal or temper a firm attendant. Everyone on the place knew her, of course, and if she grew tired where she wandered, she had only to ask to be taken home for arms to reach down and pick her up, cradle her as she rested head comfortably against a sweaty shoulder. True, untaught aristocrat, she accepted a physical familiarity from those who served her she would not have tolerated from her peers. There was safety even in the jarring walk that carried her.

Pauline's world was more proscribed. She had no desire to wander. She stayed wherever she was put and hoped people would find and notice her. When they did, she was happy, and when they did not, she was lonely.

Most of the cabins had a patch of garden, a few turnips or cabbages or stalks of corn, indicative of whim more than need, for all ate from the common supply, although the selection depended on what was left after the choicest went to the big house. Lovey and Ezra's cabin had no garden, for neither had time to work in it. There was only an umbrella chinaberry tree that gave in spring a lovely smell of its purple flowering, and in summer a blessed shade. As soon as she had the strength, Pauline climbed the tree. It was not big, although it seemed so to her when she was four, but its foliaged branches gave her a feeling of delicious privacy. (If she could not have company, then privacy would have to do.) She observed the passing world as secretly as a cat hiding in a hedge.

It was from this perch she first became familiar with the sight of Selma on her solitary wanderings. She watched her without revealing herself. Although it was her nature to offer herself too freely, when Selma came along, she drew into the foliage cautiously. She knew that Selma was the daughter of the mistress. Seeing her, unseen by her, Pauline hungered fiercely to know her.

A little older, Pauline followed her mother to the kitchen of the big house. It is easy enough for a quiet, respectful, obliging child to be tolerated in a big kitchen,

and Pauline was soon at home there, passing a cooking
fork before it was needed, alert to pick up a dropped dishcloth, graduating soon enough to peeling and scraping,
learning to wait, learning to judge.

The summer Pauline became seven, Selma was nine.
The two knew each other by sight, but had never spoken
directly to each other, only as part of a general audience.
It was that summer Selma developed a passion for lemons.
Her father brought a large supply from town so that the
family might enjoy lemon in their tea and make lemonade
on a hot day. These uses held no special attraction for
Selma.

Then, one morning, Lovey complained of toothache,
and Ezra advised her to suck a lemon. Selma happened to
be in the kitchen when Lovey cut a small round hole in
the stem-end of a lemon and pressed its sides, letting the
juice drip into her mouth and onto the aching tooth. Her
eyes watered, her mouth watered, she moaned softly, comforted.

The smell of lemon seduced the child. She asked for
one. Humoring her, but telling her she would not like the
sour taste, Lovey cut a hole in another lemon and handed
it to Selma. Selma put it to her lips, pressed the oily, aromatic skin, and found earthly delight that was near-heav-
enly.

After that she often begged for a lemon, but only of
Lovey, instinct telling her that such an appetite would not
be understood by her mother. Unquestioningly, Lovey
obliged her when there were lemons. When they were
scarce, she was denied them.

One such time when Selma had been denied and lan-
guished in the midday, dew-dried, sun-hot kitchen garden,
Pauline found her and wordlessly presented her with an
entire lemon she had stolen from her mother's small, secret trove.

Ten

The position of Roscoe Elk increased until it could increase no more under the prevailing circumstances. He
was paid a wage. He lived alone in a cabin, cleaned and
attended by the wives of those men who owed him special
favors. Knowing how to be amiable when it suited his

purpose, he sometimes obtained other favors of the women. Everything had a use, and favors got favors, and who would not smile at a solemn wink?

The very ease with which Roscoe made his way at Beulah Land made him despise those who allowed his growing power to thrive, but he never thought of moving on to another place.

He did not know who he was or what his parentage had been, but there was in his head a faint memory of Indians and Creoles and New Orleans, too vague for him to credit seriously himself, but serving to suggest his mystery to others.

His first real memory was of traveling with a man called Alfonzo, a half-and-half black and white, who pretended to be, maybe was, a real gypsy, and had a cart and a mule he drove all over everywhere, sharpening knives and scissors, soldering pots and pans, affecting, when he thought he could get away with it, a knowledge of water divining.

When he was thirteen, Roscoe ran away from Alfonzo. Alfonzo had beaten and buggered him for a year before his escape. It was summer, and he slept in woods during the day and walked at night.

Eventually, he found himself in Jacksonville, and having by then shed his fear of Alfonzo's following him, he begged work on the docks of the St. Johns River, and presently was earning enough to feed and clothe his body. Nothing else was required. A tired boy can sleep anywhere.

He made friends with the Negro cook of a shacky restaurant near the waterfront. The cook, who was called simply Cuz by everyone, was a free man. Living with him in the back of the restaurant—there was no sexual demand, only loneliness and generosity on the part of the cook—Roscoe grew to manhood and obtained, through his friend's resources, a paper proving that he was himself a free man.

After that he went from one job to another, first in Jacksonville while still sharing quarters with Cuz, then moving up to Savannah where he found work easily, and after Savannah venturing into the countryside, finally drifting to Highboro, Georgia, where he worked for a few weeks as a porter in a hardware store. Having heard that it was the most considerable plantation thereabouts, he decided to try his luck and fate at Beulah Land.

During his travels Roscoe had learned to despise black slave and white master alike. He thought himself superior to them. The feeling that it was Deborah Kendrick who would eventually decide his future grew stronger in him, and he courted her regard in many quiet ways.

He did not underrate her shrewdness, nor overrate her self-interest. But as she went about her daily business, and a conscientious mistress of a plantation was busy all the day, he had seen a restlessness reaching out to expand and command. He was content to bide his time and wait for his chance, confident that he would recognize it when it came.

The only flyspeck on his future was the question of Leon and Floyd. They were not part of the order; he did not know how he would fit them in.

His ascendancy over the slaves was accomplished and needed tending only here and there, and now and then. He weighed their work, he kept their small accountings. A frown, a nod, a pause in speaking were all the discipline necessary, for people are ever ready to see themselves in the worst light, to know their own weaknesses better than anyone else can know them.

Roscoe understood that there are many shadings of character and relationship, and that these are always changing, however imperceptibly. His ordinary observation told him which slaves he could deal with hardly and which were best handled softly, and those few not to be handled at all. Of the last, when he had been there three or four years, he knew only Lovey and Ezra to be immune to his power. They baffled him, because they were neither self-seeking nor self-excusing. They could not be despised as he despised the white-loving willies and janes of his earlier experience who knew their place and accepted its lowness, who feared God and had no greater hope than to go on serving their white folks in Heaven.

Floyd was their son. Floyd was the—he would not use the word friend, he could not say servant—companion, the everyday, no-kin brother of the son of the lord and lady. While the boys were young, this was not a problem, but as they grew older it became one that plagued his mind at odd times. Children of slaves were set to work early. Heavy demands were not made of them, but they worked alongside their fathers and mothers in the fields and woods, house and barns and pens. They took a childish pride in learning the work that would occupy them all their lives, and were praised and rewarded for any sign of quickness or excellence.

As an extension of his record-keeping, Roscoe had come to be something of a director of workers, with a good eye for assigning men where they were most needed, which Arnold Kendrick was quick to appreciate and confide to Deborah, although she would have already seen it for herself. All Arnold had to say was, "Send some men to dig up the potato hill," for Roscoe to know exactly the job to be done, how many hands were required to accomplish it, and how long it should take.

Floyd was a bright, fast-growing boy, always a little too big for his clothes, and Roscoe could not see him without wanting to set him to work. Floyd did work sometimes; he was not lazy. He could hoe corn, chop cotton, pick cotton, pull fodder, cut sugar cane, all before he was ten years old, and he often did such work. But as often he left it without a word of permission to go off with Leon to the woods, or wherever the mood of the day and hour suggested. Floyd was a slave boy, but he felt free, and that was what Roscoe could neither understand nor abide.

Remembering himself as a boy, he hated Floyd. Gradually and carefully he brought up the question with Arnold, who seemed surprised that there was such a question at all, gave him no satisfaction, no authority to deal with the boy.

"Of course he's to work," Arnold said slowly. But even as Roscoe's mind-wrinkle relaxed, he added, "He has a lot to do, you know, with Leon. He's Lovey and Ezra's boy." He thought that over a bit. "Not to be treated just like anybody, you understand. But when he isn't obliged to be with Leon or doing what his ma and pa tell him, let him work."

Boys are smart in knowing who is against them, and Floyd and Leon knew that Roscoe was against them. He never overstepped his authority to the point where Leon wanted to complain to his father. Leon was not one to make decisions and take action anyway. He liked to let life happen, and if trouble came, not hurry or hassle it, but wait and see if it would solve itself or run its course. Roscoe was so often there, it seemed, asking questions, not waiting to hear them answered, furrowing his brow and talking of who was too sick to work and how shorthanded they were in the hollow where the sugar cane grew. Behind his back they teased one another about him, but the idea of Roscoe as a menace to them grew in their minds, just as Roscoe meant it to. When a fly is noticed and not brushed aside, he gains confidence.

Eleven

Clovis had not been a virgin since she was four years old, and by the time she was fifteen she was tolerably well acquainted with the ways of men, and knew something of how to manage them. Although he had made no straight approach, she was aware that Roscoe wanted her. Her mother dead, her father unknown to her and she to him, she lived in a cabin of single women of various ages, including Posie and Buttercup, whose mother Jane had recently died. She'd heard about the women who did for Roscoe, one way and another. Gossip declared that he had the biggest dick they'd ever seen, that he did it longer than other men, and that he sometimes required funny things of them that surprised and hurt. She knew that if, when the time came, she managed him cleverly, it would be to her future advantage.

She did not incline to him. For a while she thought it might be to do with the gossip. Then she decided it was because he was old. Then, as she herself grew older, and months at such an age as hers are like years at another, she realized that he was not old at all, and what seemed age was something else, the way he set himself remote from others.

Leon and Floyd were fourteen, a year younger than she, when she got both of them on her mind. There they were. She didn't know why. Maybe it was because a prophecy of their future manhood had begun to show in their bodies. Similarly big of head, feet, and hands, with knee and elbow joints that looked swollen, they moved quickly but without grace, or even much precision, and they considered themselves the center of the universe.

Their voices were alike because they had always been together. All his life Leon would sound a little Negro-ish to white people, and Floyd would sound to other Negroes not quite like they sounded to each other. They shared the same humor at that age, although Leon was jokier than Floyd, while Floyd was more often pensive than Leon and less likely to act on whim. Their being together was accepted by everyone with no question, only the feeling: what is, is.

Mindful of her curiosity and inclination, Clovis wondered if there might be something for her in them rather than Roscoe. She watched. One Monday morning in midsummer Floyd caught her at it.

It was a clear, hot day with promise of getting hotter, and not a cloud in the sky, a perfect washday. Clovis was at a tub scrubbing clothes, her sleeves rolled up, her face sweaty with exertion, her skirt damp from water she had sloshed out of the tub onto herself. She and four other women were at work, and they would be at it for most of the day. The big, round, black pots were fired and boiling linens and clothes from the big house.

Presently, when she finished the tub she was working on and passed it to the next woman to rinse, she stirred a pot with a long, wooden paddle, then used the paddle to lift out a wet load to a stump. Taking a stouter stick, she beat the clothes, loosening their dirt. Then she put them into her washtub with fresh water and soaped and scrubbed, enjoying her own rhythm of work, her body tuned and in harmony with the effort she made and her pleasure in using muscle.

Floyd was supposed to saw logs that day from two old trees that had been struck by lightning and removed from the edge of a corn field earlier that summer. He and Leon had worked together for a while, playfully, but getting the work along. Then they had been quiet a few minutes plotting together, Floyd at first shaking his head, then laughing and nodding agreement.

Leon then went away to dig worms for the fishing they had decided to do. Their bait bed was near the old gnarled fig tree that grew near the door of the kitchen to the big house, the same tree from whose branches they had swung as babies.

The spot got the wet slops thrown from the kitchen door, keeping the ground damp even in dry weather and making a natural home for earthworms. Leon required only minutes to fill a jar with earth and worms enough for their purpose. A hundred yards away Floyd sawed logs with a regular, unconcerned rhythm, as if he intended to be at it all day. Not by an eye's flick did he appear to notice when Leon went into the near barn and presently emerged with two fishing poles, held so close together they might have looked one at a distance.

But when the saw had cut through the log he worked on, Floyd paused to rest a minute, wiped his face lightly with his shirt sleeve and sighed. Leon was going away. Already he was across the wash-yard area and entering the safer ground of the outhouses, which were screened by huge, stalky sunflowers, all in full, protective bloom. Floyd then set the saw casually to one side and looked about. No one appeared to pay him the least mind.

Then as he strolled past her, Clovis looked at him and smiled in a way that made him know she had watched the whole game. Laughing, he ran into the sunflowers and was gone. Leon waited a little beyond and handed Floyd his pole as they set off for the thick woods.

As soon as they entered, they paused to enjoy being there. Both boys were barefoot. They savored the cool of the sudden shade on their bodies, the cool of damp, black ground under their hot feet. Setting off suddenly with unspoken agreement, they took a winding path well known to both of them, Leon carrying his pole in his right hand, and Floyd his in his left, both poles maneuvered more or less parallel to the ground so that they would not catch in the foliage above.

They walked fifteen minutes before coming to the fishing bank they currently preferred to others, having paused on the way once to urinate carefully off the path. Another time they lingered to watch butterflies hovering over a plant that looked to be sickly festering, its top leaves having turned a pulpy white that evidently created a smell that drew the pretty insects, whose wings beat the hot still air caressingly.

There was no sand bar on the place they chose. The bank dropped straight down to dark water. No plants growing on the bottom reached above the surface. The water looked indeed bottomless, although they knew exactly how deep it was, having tested it frequently over the years with poles. They stood quietly for a bit, listening. A humming-singing sound began that might have been from one voice or a thousand.

Leon found a pebble, stretched his arm back in an aiming motion, and let the pebble fly across the creek and into the bush. The humming-singing abruptly ceased. Floyd took up a stick and trailed it along the top of the water as if writing, before dropping the stick and letting it float away downstream.

Setting the bait jar steady between two roots, the boys

checked the lines and sinkers on their fishing poles before
baiting the hooks. Kneeling on the leafy bank, Leon
swung his line lightly through the air and let it drop into
the water. Floyd frowned and strolled a few paces along
the bank before deciding on a spot to drop his line. The
humming-singing started up again across the creek.

Finishing the tub of clothes she had been working on,
Clovis did not go to one of the boiling pots and repeat her
earlier procedure. She emptied the tub and left it on the
old work table that had been in place so long its leg ends
disappeared into the ground, seeming to grow there.
Theresa, the senior washwoman of the group, saw her
wander off, but did not question her, as Clovis had known
she would not. Clovis had the reputation of being a good
worker who never shirked her share like some of the others.

Following the way the boys had gone, she passed the
outhouses and continued to the woods. Inside the woods
she paused briefly, as they had done before her, then
guessing at which path they might have taken, she went
along it. A few minutes later, however, some instinct told
her she was wrong. She went back to her starting point
and took another path, confident this time, although she
did not know why she was.

She walked, making no noise at all, stopping now and
then to cock her head sideways and listen before continuing. The farther she got, the slower she walked, and the
more often she paused. Finally she stopped and stood
without moving for several minutes, statue-like, as the
multitude of woods activity went on about her, mostly unseen and unheard, but nevertheless known by her to be
transpiring.

Now she bent almost double and inched along. Finally
she stopped altogether, knowing she was there, although
no sound told her so, and she had not yet seen them. She
found a dry seat on a fallen log that had lain there so
long all its bark was gone, and green moss covered its
lower sides. Cautiously, she pushed aside a leafy, supple
twig cluster and saw them.

They sat on dry leaves a few yards apart, so still they
might have been sleeping. Leon's back was to her, but
Floyd sat in clear profile. She gave them a thorough
going-over with her eyes, gradually relaxing her body into
a more comfortable position as she savored finding them.

She didn't know why she felt so, but simply looking at

them, it was as if she had won something or been given something. She felt her throat thicken with silent laughter which she quickly repressed. Whatever did they think they were doing, she wondered, just sitting there like that? They were not even holding their fishing poles. Instead, each had secured the big end of his pole in the giving leafmold earth and sat, Leon with his hands slack in his lap, Floyd with hands loose at his sides. Leon's back was supported comfortably by a stump. Floyd had his against the trunk of a tree that grew close to the water's edge.

Neither bored nor diverted, she sat watching them for a quarter hour. Suddenly Floyd's pole bent at its thin end, and instantly, as if he were part of the pole's action before he touched it, Floyd was on one knee and one foot, the pole in his hands. Leon got to both feet as Floyd brought up and swung onto the bank a broad-tailed, broad-bodied bream. The fish flopped briefly in the dry leaves before Floyd, with Leon now beside him, unhooked it. He held the thrashing fish by the gills.

"Big one," she heard Leon say.

Floyd trotted along the bank and returned with their earlier catch, four bream of various sizes strung on a thin, forked tree branch Leon had cut after landing the first fish of the morning nearly an hour ago. Floyd added the new one, which was still twitching, and replaced the forked branch in the water a little way away.

"Let's smoke," Floyd said then.

Each boy felt in his pockets and found a corncob pipe. Leon drew a cloth sack from his hip pocket, and they filled the pipes with what Clovis almost certainly knew was not real tobacco, but what was called rabbit tobacco and grew wild. Floyd held both pipes while Leon searched again in his pockets and found a flint and an old Indian arrowhead. Even at her distance Clovis knew what it must be; plenty of arrowheads were turned up whenever a field was dug or plowed, and they were commonly used to strike fires.

Leon got a blaze of leaves going and nursed it, keeping it small. Each boy lighted a dry twig from which he then lighted his pipe. The rabbit tobacco burned unevenly, and the pipes often had to be relighted. The sweet, pungent smoke drifted toward Clovis and caused her stomach to jump, making her realize she was hungry and that it must be getting on to the noon dinnertime.

When they were done smoking, Leon smothered the

small fire he had built, and they tapped out their pipes, cleaning the bowls with fresh leaves. They checked their bait, and Leon replaced his, finding that most of the worm had been nibbled off the hook while they smoked. Then both stuck their poles firmly into the ground and slouched down again on the creekbank a few yards apart.

Hunger told her to go, and by now Theresa would be wondering where she had got off to. She'd have to make up a story—not too much of one, the shorter the better, and the more likely it would be accepted as true. Still she sat there, as if she knew that as soon as she took leave, something interesting would happen.

As casually as he might reach for pipe and tobacco, Leon unbuttoned the front of his trousers and rested his hand inside a few seconds before drawing out his dick. Shaking it to erection was a matter of seconds. He stared down at it seriously and pulled the foreskin up over the head. When he let it go, the head throbbed and bobbed like a creature separate. He tapped the stiff thing from side to side and back and forth, then let it alone to arch and subside.

Clovis watched unblinking, wondering what would happen next. Glancing at his companion, Floyd did not change expression. He too watched with as serious a face as Leon's. Then he undid his lower buttons and brought out his own dick. It was already hard. Clovis stared first at one, then the other.

Looking every few seconds at each other's actions, but not looking into each other's face, the boys began to masturbate.

The impulse Clovis had was to step out and show herself, to say, "You boys don't have to do none of that, for here I am." But the automatic reserve and consideration animals accord each other's sexuality kept her where she was. She boiled inside. She trembled and took hold of the log on both sides of her seat. She hated them! How could they do that and leave her out?

Common sense reminded her they did not know she was there and available, but she let her passionate resentment of what they were doing blaze away and consume her mind.

It was not long before both boys achieved orgasm with involuntary, unchecked body twitching. After resting, they shook their limbering dicks matter-of-factly, and put them back inside their clothes. Leon wiped his hand dry with leaves, Floyd his with a bunch of Spanish moss he reached up and pulled from a tree limb.

What would they have done, Clovis asked herself furiously, if a fish had gone for their baited hooks while they were doing that? As her mind pictured the conflict, it became ridiculous, and she found relief in silent laughter.

They were both standing now. Leon stretched and yawned. Floyd picked up his fishing pole and swung the line in to shore. Leon stretched again, then did the same thing Floyd had done with his pole.

"How come you ain't done it to a girl yet?" Leon asked.

"I don't know. How come you?" Floyd answered.

"It's easier for you than me," Leon said. "How can I even try to when everybody'd know? You're different. Nobody would think a thing."

"Bet my mama would!" Floyd laughed. "Swim before we go?"

Both shed their clothes in a minute. Clovis watched them dive into the creek and thrash about, churning up the dark water they had earlier been at pains not to disturb. Heeding a sudden alarm that swept her nerves, Clovis got up from the log and made her way back along the path rapidly, no longer constrained to caution and quiet.

The boys swam about and yelled, ducked each other, dared each other to stay longer under water, finally tired. Contentedly, they slipped into their clothes without waiting for their bodies to dry. Floyd took up his pole and the fish they had caught.

"You want 'em?" Leon asked.

Floyd shook his head. "Give 'em to Old Maggie."

Where the woods met the fields they stopped. Without having to talk about it, Leon now took both fishing poles and the bait jar which Floyd had emptied, and carried the twigged fish in the same hand as he carried the jar. Floyd went off at a trot. Leon followed, alone.

Old Maggie was glad to have the fish. She dearly loved a fish, she told Leon, in the same words and same way she had told him a hundred times before, as if she feared hers was a peculiar fondness he would find it hard to comprehend. Whenever he had a fish he didn't need, she would be proud to have it. Saying so, she loosened the blunt-bladed knife stuck into the wooden side of her cabin door and began to scale the largest of the bream. Leon left her and made his way toward the big house.

Floyd would be there before him, eating in the kitchen.

Lovey would scold him and tell him he was too late, that
his mother and father had long since finished their meal.
And when he followed her into the kitchen, she would
load a plate with boiled peas wrinkling in their juice, roasting ears, and sliced tomatoes, and let him sit down and
eat with Floyd, maybe on the back door step, because it
was too hot to eat in the kitchen, and besides, the girls
were busy there. Helping the girls would be odd little
Pauline.

Twelve

Deborah told Selma she was too old to go barefoot, that
she was indeed almost a young woman, and it was time
she learned to behave like one. Selma said that shoes were
not sensible for the places she walked; they were blockish
and clumsy. When they got wet, they creaked and smelled
and took days to dry out. She often found herself standing
in the shallows of the creek to catch a water bug or to
skim a cobweb from a tree limb that dipped to the water's
edge.

Lovey solved the problem with compromise. She made
slippers from an old canvas weather screen and dyed the
slippers red. They were pliant enough to please Selma and
protective enough to satisfy her mother.

At twelve Selma was still happiest alone. She had sub-
mitted to her mother's teaching her to read and write and
do simple figuring, but she refused to learn any more, and
Deborah did not press her, for gentlewomen had no need
of education beyond the subjects fitting their basic gump-
tion. Selma was at ease with all the Negroes on the place.
She was uncomfortable with her kin and kind—even her
father now. She loved him, but knew, alas, there was
nothing she could do about that. He loved her, but never
lost his shyness with her. Indeed, his shyness with everyone deepened as he grew into middle age, so that he
found it hard to make decisions that involved people. The
two who more and more often stepped in to make these
decisions for him were Deborah and Roscoe.

Lovey was Selma's friend. Ezra was almost a god. She
followed him about until he learned to ignore her, which
made her worship him the more. She watched the way he
touched things, the plants he plucked leaves or flowers or
stems from, the ones he left alone. Deborah was a big,

uninteresting thing called a mother. Leon was a boy. Everything about him seemed to remind her of that. He smelled funny. He made noise. He had shorter hair. His clothes forked—why? Didn't her trunk go into two legs too?

No one told her anything she needed to know. Her father was shy. Her mother was dull as corn bread—everything she said was dull, everything she did was predictable. Lovey was busy. Ezra didn't notice she was alive. Aunt Nell was insane. So much for her family.

If she had no one, she did have things. She could watch ants by the hour, but embroidery and the Bible made her wish she was dead. She was company to herself, but she was alone, and she felt both loss and lack, although they had been caused largely by the way she felt and was.

Once for a period of several days when she was eleven, she had felt she had no capability except to hear. Visual impressions were only enough to give her physical guidance, no pleasure, no pain. Food had no taste. Fingers might have frozen and broken off for all the good they were for touching. But her ears were agonizingly acute. She heard vapor rise. The sound of feet on earth was thunder. And thunder was the end of the world. It all happened on a fiercely hot day that ended in a storm, and when the lightning stopped blinding her and the thunder no longer tore her apart, she was as she had been before. She tasted, she touched. Her hearing was only normally sensitive.

She had forgot that strange time until today. She felt odd. In the morning her ears pounded as if each had a giant's heart beating just inside the drums. Her face flushed with the first fever she had ever known except the temporary one sun sometimes gave her. That came from without; this fever, from within. Her vision blurred and melted. She rubbed her eyes and then saw halos around every object she singled out to gaze upon.

These sensations, or hallucinations, ceased abruptly, and she felt that she was herself once more: Selma in the garden, Selma on the porch, Selma running, Selma running across the yards and scattering a flock of strolling guineas, running across the fields, and into the woods. She quieted when she came to the creek. She picked a green leaf and chewed it, and when it set her teeth on edge, spat it out. She followed a snake that wriggled away from her until she found herself caught in a tangle of brush. By the time she extricated herself, he was gone. She went to the creek's edge in something like a daze. It was happening. She would die, that was all, that was it. She looked down at the blood between her feet on the sand bar. She'd known it would be there before she looked. It was an expected horror, she did not know why, like the ugly gaps in her mouth when she lost her first teeth, worse than the boils she'd had everywhere the summer she was nine that disappeared as mysteriously as they had appeared when cooler weather came on.

She went home. When she got there, she walked quietly and steadily, not with her usual dartings and quick halts, across the last yard, into the kitchen wing at the back of the house, through the covered breezeway, through the wide hall of the big house into the front room where the stairs began.

Deborah was talking to her Uncle Felix. She ignored them. They seemed unaware of her. Maybe she had become invisible. As soon as the thought occurred, she believed she had. Climbing the stairs, she heard Uncle Felix say, "Talk to him, Deb. Make him see. If his is the biggest investment, it will all come back to him and more, much more. It'll put Highboro on the map. We'll get all the ginning of the county. He'll get his own done and make a profit on the others. There'll be no more wagon trains of raw cotton to Savannah."

Halfway up the stairs Selma began to cry and ran the rest of the way to her room. Felix and Deborah looked at each other. Deborah said, "I'll talk to him. You know I will. It's so hard to get him to answer. What you say is mere logic. Why won't he see it?"

There was silence. Then Felix said, "Is the child all right?"

Deborah looked surprised. She had seen her daughter but not thought about her at all. Now she left her brother-in-law and went up the stairs. She opened the closed door of Selma's room and went in. Not seeing the child, she stopped stock still and looked about. Tilting her head, she heard breathing, looked down and saw the red of one canvas shoe projected from underneath the high, canopied bed. Going over, she pulled the child out roughly. Selma would not look at her, lay stiff on the floor, and when Deborah tried to pick her up, turned to jelly.

"What have you been doing you shouldn't?" Deborah demanded. "What ails you?"

Gathering herself to herself, Selma stood, weak but in

control of her body for the moment, anyway. "I'm dying. Give my dolls to Lovey. Goodbye."

Deborah looked down and saw evidence of what had happened. "Oh, dear Lord," she said, "am I to be spared nothing this day? Stay. Wait. Don't you go anywhere. No one is to see you; you hear me?"

Selma wasn't about to go anywhere. All she wanted was to be let alone to finish dying. She stood waiting for the Lord to claim her. She only hoped He would not sing, as they did in church.

Deborah marched past Felix without acknowledging that she even saw him. A few minutes later Lovey ran panting and angry up the stairs. Deborah returned and sat on a chair beside Felix. She did not let her eyes go toward the stairs. "And how is Nell?" she asked.

"Not strong," Felix responded. "There are times I fear for her."

Deborah received this observation gravely.

Upstairs Lovey found Selma and gathered her into her arms, big though she now was. She sat on the side of the bed, holding the frightened child in a fierce embrace. Selma could not at first make any sense of what Lovey was saying, but gradually she got the idea that what had happened to her happened also to others, that it was not, as she had been sure, the first time it had ever happened in the world.

"Why?" she asked and cried again, in relief and anger.

"Law' knows," Lovey answered, and rocked and kissed the child.

Thirteen

A day has relatively few hours, but an extravagance of minutes and a multitude of seconds; and most of life's events happen in seconds and minutes, not hours. With so many people and so many acres, a great many events were bound to occur on the plantation every day.

On the Wednesday after washday Clovis and a girl named Myrtis were in the peanut patch pulling up peanuts to feed the hogs. They pulled up the plants and shook earth off the nuts which budded from the underground roots. The work was easy. The day was hot. Myrtis told Clovis a dream she said she'd had the night before in which she had floated over Beulah Land like an angel. Actually, she'd had no such dream, but she wanted to make herself interesting, so she repeated a dream she'd heard her mother once tell: "Do it mean I gonna die soon?"

Clovis paused briefly to consider. "Yes."

Shock held her quiet for only a moment; then Myrtis screamed with laughter. Clovis felt clever and pleased. Laughter bubbled up in her and increased that of Myrtis; and from the boredom of circumstance and the liveliness of their youth both became hysterical. Clovis hit Myrtis on the hand. Myrtis grabbed Clovis, embraced her, still shaking and squeaking with laughter. When Myrtis loosened her grip on her friend, Clovis became the friendly aggressor, pushing Myrtis —"Go *on*, girl!"—then catching her in an embrace. They fell, and that made them laugh even harder, and when they had exhausted themselves laughing, when even the forced continuance of one did not set off a like response in the other, they sat without getting up and wiped their eyes and noses.

Myrtis pulled a peanut off a plant, opened the damp, soft shell and ate the two peas inside.

"That won't get you calico for Christmas."

They looked up, then stood up, not hastily, but not slowly either, Myrtis first, then Clovis.

Roscoe Elk sat on his mule named April and looked down at them.

"We just cuttin' the fool; you know?" Myrtis said.

Roscoe was looking at Clovis, and it flattered her and made her uncomfortable. Sassily, she said, "Don't fancy calico for Christmas, but might like silk." He almost, not quite, smiled. "You fancy peanuts, Mister Elk?"

"Never had to eat 'em."

"They good. Chillun love 'em. After we give most of these to the hogs, I'm gonna boil some in salt water for the younguns. You welcome to come eat some, if you so mind."

Roscoe looked at her steadily almost a minute before turning his mule and riding away at a steady walk. April had an open sore near her ass hole and carried her tail arched, which seemed to set both comment and question mark on the encounter.

When she thought he was out of earshot, Myrtis said, "Did you see?"

"Did I see what?"

"Did you see what I see?"

"What you see?"

"That man got a big bone in his britches whilst he sat on that mule talkin' to us!" Myrtis laughed shrilly. "Enough to make a pussy pucker! Don't it? You reckon it were cause of me or cause of you?"

"You," Clovis said. "You the one gone die soon."

Myrtis giggled, then laughed with her mouth open, then bellowed with her whole body shaking. It was hot, and life was boring, and anything could pass for an event with her. "You—girl!" she screamed, and gave Clovis a slap and a shove.

Clovis straightened herself and said, "Stop pushing me. I got things to think about."

Myrtis turned sullenly and began to pack the dying plants into a torn sack. "Wish I had."

Clovis thought about him with interest but with her pores closed. She did what she said she would do: she boiled a mess of the fresh peanuts in their hulls in salted water. And she sat, the center of a crowd of children, late in the afternoon on the ground beside the cabin where she lived with the other single women. A big bowl of peanuts rested in her lap. Clovis took one, broke it carefully, let salty water in the hull drip into her mouth, then ate the peas and sucked the damp shells until their salt taste was gone.

Roscoe Elk walked by. He did not stop, or speak, or even look at her. The children, who might have acted as a natural bridge between the non-communicants, were too absorbed in trying to eat the peanuts in exactly the way Clovis had, to notice Roscoe, or the way Clovis now looked angrily at his back.

She had wanted him to stop, to speak; not because she favored him, but because by not doing so he denied that he favored her. That was the moment she knew she could have him. The knowledge did not soothe her, but turned her mind to Leon and Floyd. She was aware of the children's chatter without attending to it. Instead, she ate another peanut, letting its salt water seep under her tongue.

Fourteen

It was a day of lassitude. People worked, but in an automatic way. No one hurried. No one raised his voice in anger or joy. Nothing that could be still moved, except the young in whom the heat and quiet bred boredom and kindled its antidote, lust. Even Roscoe, ordinarily unaffected by the weather, forgot to assign Floyd special work, and Floyd decided not to join the general work crew who were picking cotton that day. In the hot, late July weather the cotton had popped out of its bolls like exploding stars.

Instead, Floyd went to the woods with Leon. They carried a round watermelon, each taking his turn to hold it on his head or under an arm, because it was heavy and made a clumsy burden.

By midafternoon nothing much was going on in the big house. After the midday meal and a short rest Arnold had headed for town to see Felix on the business of the proposed building of a cotton gin. He would not have considered going in such sultry weather except that he had told Felix he would come yesterday and put it off to today.

Deborah retired to her room, undressed to her petticoat and rested herself on the bed. Selma sat under a tree in the peach and plum orchard. The ripest fruit was picked every day, but some inevitably was overlooked and dropped naturally to the ground, rotting and fermenting. The smell had made Selma drunk and sleepy. Even the bees moved slowly.

In the kitchen wing Lovey had thrown a large thin cloth over the food left from the midday meal, so that the flies could not soil and spoil it; and she had gone then to her cabin to rest for an hour, as long a time as she was ever able to lie down during the day, such was her restless nature. She left the kitchen girls, Clovis and Myrtis, to finish the dishwashing and to put things away.

Clovis dried as Myrtis washed. Both were mainly house and yard workers. They washed and ironed clothes, and often added their hands to those regularly employed in the kitchen. They were seldom called farther into the main part of the house than the dining room. Their work in the fields was occasional and light, such as the gathering of peanut plants to feed the hogs.

Finishing the dishes, Clovis spread the last of the wet cloths over the windowsill to dry. Cook, having deserted the kitchen as soon as the noon meal was served, now returned, and saw that all was in order. She had brought from the smoke house one of the last of the hams they had cured the winter before. She set it on the large, bare table she used to prepare food, took a dry cloth and began

to wipe the ham free of its white and green mold. When
it had aired and its smoked skin had sweated, she would
wipe it again, then cut slices for Pauline to fry for supper.
Pauline had a nice way with ham, managing to keep it
juicy while letting it crisp on the outside.

Myrtis yawned and stood watching Cook work on the
ham. She pretended more interest than she felt, because
she hoped to be promoted from washwoman to general
kitchen helper. Clovis drifted toward the door. Slow
movement attracts attention as much as quick movement,
so she moved at a carefully calculated normal speed, instinctively slowing it a little because of the lassitude of the
day. She did not want Myrtis to ask if she might go with
her, or worse, simply to follow without asking.

Clovis had taken from the pantry a clean gallon bucket,
the kind used to store cane syrup, and when not required
for that, handy for berry picking. The buckets accumulated in the pantry as the syrup was used during the winter and spring and summer, to be filled again when the
autumn cane was ground and its juice boiled to make syrup.

If anyone asked where she was going, she could say she
had seen a growth of late-ripening blackberries in the
branch and thought she would gather them for a pie.
The best lies use truth. There were ripe blackberries in the
woods, and if she did not find Floyd and Leon, whose direction she had noted from the kitchen window, then
maybe she would gather some of the berries. They'd been
red just turning purple when she saw them. They would
be ready now.

Because of the heat, and because she had seen the
watermelon, she knew they must plan to swim and cool
the melon at the same time, so she took the pathway she'd
last used when she followed them. But on the way, reflect-
ing that swimming and fishing were seldom done in the
same place and that Leon and Floyd's doing both at the
same spot the other day was probably a special circumstance, she veered below the place she had found them before. By swimming below the fishing area their noise and
activity would not disturb the fish.

She was dead right in the way she had figured. When
she came off the path to the creek, she heard them
shouting. Pleased with herself, she crept through the brush
along the stream. She calculated carefully. She wanted to
be able to hear their noise, but she did not need to hear

what they actually said. She found a likely spot, took off her dress, which was all she wore, and draped it over a bush, hoping the red bugs would not find it and infest it before she reclaimed it. They bit and itched terribly. She left her berry bucket by the bush and waded naked into the creek, delighting in the feel of water, cool enough to cool her but warm enough not to make her shiver and jump as it came up over her feet and calves and knees and thighs. As she walked, it rose above her navel and touched the bottom of her breasts. She bent her knees and floated her body. When she found the bottom again with her feet, she splashed water over her face and neck and hair. Finally, she made herself weighty and sank entirely beneath the surface, then bobbed up feeling clean and listened for the voices around the bend of the creek. Cautiously, she set her feet down and began the slow walking water dictates. The sandy bottom of the creek stayed with her as she moved toward the sounds they made.

Before she was in their view, she turned and floated on her back, having to kick under water to propel herself, since she was downstream of them. She knew they had seen her when they stopped talking. She made herself turn slowly onto her stomach and began to swim before she saw them and acted surprised.

As she began to swim away, Floyd called, "Hey, girl! Saw your head and thought you was a turtle!"

She touched bottom with her feet and swung around. "Didn't mean to bother you none. Didn't know you was here."

Since people seldom hear their own noise, they accepted that. She floated away, and Floyd shouted, "Where you going?"

"Oh," she said vaguely, again finding the bottom with her feet, "ain't it hot today? Thought I'd die in that kitchen. Come down here to cool off some, but didn't know you all were—"

"You don't have to go," Floyd said. Leon had not spoken, but his eyes had been on the girl since she appeared, leaving her only for brief looks of encouragement to Floyd.

She gave a full amused laugh. "Yes I do got to go!"

"How come?"

"I got nothin' on me!" She floated farther downstream, and the boys splashed after her.

"You covered by the creek," Floyd assured her.

She stopped, waiting for them. "That is so," she said, modestly folding her arms. Although her smile acknowledged him, she made no sign of recognizing Leon.

Floyd laughed. "You know something funny? *We* got nothin' on neither!"

She laughed as if it were the funniest thing she had ever heard said, until Floyd, longing to touch her, found a way: he pushed her head under water. Bobbing up she sputtered and caught her breath and pretended to be offended. "That ain't fair!" She made again as if to swim away.

Floyd, with Leon close behind him, dived and caught her by one ankle. She jerked away and turned to slap and splash water at Floyd. "Stop it, stop it, I say, you better stop it!" she said and let herself laugh to show she was not really troubled.

Leon, grinning now, splashed water lightly at her face. She giggled and splashed him back. All three were laughing and splashing, the boys toward the girl, and she toward them; and when she finally pretended, shrieking, to be bested, the boys began to splash water at each other. To interrupt them, lest they forget her, she cried, "Ain't this a whole lot of fun?" She turned to float on her back, her breasts and the rounding of her belly projected boldly above water. Their silence told her they saw, and presently Floyd swam up beside her, and Leon swam up on her other side.

They floated quietly downstream, the boys face down, the girl face up.

Floyd reached a hand and touched a teat, and when the girl did not demur, cupped it. Leon watched and followed and stopped when the girl suddenly put her feet on the bottom of the creek and stood, looking at both of them solemnly, the water just touching under her breasts and seeming to float them. After looking at Leon, she focused her attention on Floyd. Her look left his face and went deliberately down his neck and chest, and saw beneath water, which wasn't dark enough really to hide a body, that his thing was hard. She moved her eyes quickly away, as if startled, and took a step or two toward the creekbank.

Leon grabbed her arm. "Clovis!" Surprised at himself, he let her go.

She turned not to him but to Floyd. "He know my name," she said.

Floyd laughed. "We know the name of every gal on the place."

She walked away. "Well, you go bother 'every gal'— don't bother me!"

He caught a foot as she clambered up the bankside. She kicked, but lightly. He was up on the bank with her, beside her, over her, on her. Shrieking and laughing, she pretended to fight him, but the blows of her hand were soft—they had none of that strength she used to pound dirty clothes—and her wriggling was not such as to discourage him. Indeed, it merely whetted the sensitivity of his now full-blooded dick.

She sighed. She closed her eyes and waited. His hands closed over her breasts, and then he drew back and away. She opened her thighs and raised her knees, and then his thing was touching hers, both gently slimed. She helped him in, keeping her eyes closed until he was hilted. He withdrew and returned, and began a steady in-and-away movement, slow away, faster and faster in. When she opened her eyes, she saw Leon sprawled on the bank beside them, his white body glistening with water, his dick hard and red, thrusting out from a sparse sprouting of blond pubic hair. Closing her eyes again she reached to touch him on his thing, felt him quiver, and drew her hand away. Floyd was panting and pumping faster and faster. She held herself back, letting him get well ahead of her, the creek wet of his body mixed now with sweat wet, and him choking out sounds like a bullfrog in spring. She relaxed and lay loose when he shot into her; she was pleased, gratified, but nowhere near satisfied. After slumping briefly over her, he put his hands to the ground and supported himself, pulling out of her. Arching his behind, he turned and fell away to one side, resting on his back and gradually breathing more quietly.

Leon, on her other side, gazed at them both, until she turned her body slightly toward him in invitation. He touched a breast. It was hot, its nipple hard. She took his hand and guided it back to his dick, making his hand touch it before hers did. When hers touched it, he was suddenly, all of him, one muscle. He swung over her, and she set his dick on a straight, smooth course. The fever and excitement of his coming made her come too, and they locked together, their sweaty cheeks clenched, their lips not having touched at all.

The grateful weakness of having given himself up overcame him. For a few seconds he almost slept, or almost

fainted, until the thought shocked him awake: she's black.
He slipped out of her, as if by doing so he might deny he
had been there. Lying on his back with his eyes closed
tight, he covered his limbering dick and slack balls with
both hands.

He heard them whispering, but he pretended to sleep,
and when their voices went away, he did sleep. When he
woke, it was only a few minutes later, but he had no notion of what time had passed. Floyd was standing on the
bank looking at the water. Suddenly he turned and smiled
at Leon, a smile so warm and fond, Leon lost his terror,
and sat up, and stood.

"Come on," Floyd said. "Race you for the watermelon!"

They dived flat and shallow, hitting the water at almost
the same time, its impact shocking and burning their
bodies. They raced upstream around the bend, and when
they stopped, they found themselves where they had started, and swam about in a leisurely manner until they had
put enough time between now and then to look openly at
each other without embarrassment.

Floyd swam over to a cypress tree, the roots of which
grew down into the water. Between branches of its
watered roots he found the melon he had wedged there.
He rolled it onto the bank and swung himself up after it.
Leon followed him. Raising the melon into the air, Floyd
dropped it to the firm ground, splitting it into four pieces.

Each boy took a piece and scooped a hand into the
ripe, mealy meat, and spat small black seeds into the
creek as they ate. When they finished, their hands were
sticky wet, so they swam again, and then walked back and
forth on the bank as the shady hot air dried them. "We
did it," Floyd bragged delightedly. "We sure enough did
it!"

Clovis had long since found her dress and put it on.
She had no need to talk to anybody. She was very pleased
with herself. Leon was her first white boy, and she
shrugged, thinking how he did it just about like everyone
else. She took the tin bucket by its wire handle and swung
it as she walked off to find the berry patch. The berries
were just right. She ate almost as many as she picked, but
gathered enough to make a pie, and she walked back
home thinking how good it was to be a girl.

Fifteen

The secret they shared had the effect of separating them. It did not occur to Floyd that what had happened would come between them, but when Leon closed up and wouldn't talk about it, Floyd withdrew in hurt puzzlement. He showed himself plainly to Roscoe, who promptly assigned him work along with the others. Floyd went off with them, hoping Leon saw him go.

Leon had thought of Floyd only as Floyd, who had always been there and would always be there. He had never tried to put a word on what they were. But awareness of the blackness of Clovis gave him awareness of Floyd's color and station in a way that made him miserable. He and Floyd had shared everything, even the tutoring at Oaks, which they had continued until a month ago when Mr. Jeremy Bartram made up his mind to go back to Savannah and see what the future held for him there. When he packed his maps and books, he gave the flute to Edna Davis who had been kind to him in her motherly way. She proudly set it on a mantelpiece in the living room.

Bonard was already away at college, and Rooster had absorbed about as much of Mr. Bartram's teaching as he was able to. He stoutly declared that he wanted nothing but to learn farming and that he would refuse to follow his brother away to school no matter what threats or promises were made. In truth Edna and Benjamin were pleased with their younger son for this staunchness of resolve, and they made no protest when Mr. Bartram told them of his decision to return to the city.

Nothing had been settled about Leon's future education.

Now this had happened. No one had taught Leon how to feel about Negroes; he had absorbed and accepted what those around, black and white, did and felt. He knew that white men fucked black women and that, generally speaking, no one thought the worse of them for it, and certainly no one could call them to account. In the stories Bonard told them before he went away to college, the idea was a constant. A common joke of the time was, "Hell, I didn't know white women had pussies till I was twenty years old." There was even a word for black sex: poontang. White boys had their first sexual encounters with black girls, who were always said to be compliant, if they did not actually seek such encounters. It was supposed that their compliance was partly the pleasure of their earthy natures, partly a hope of favors and advancement for themselves and their families.

Leon wanted to forget about Clovis, and let things be as they'd been before her; and at the same time he wanted to do it with her again. He thought not of her but of her titties and pussy, her heat and motion. In a sweat of repulsion and lust he thought of her. With Floyd's drawing away from him, he was lonely and ready for any plan that popped into his mind. The simplest and most obvious one did.

One day, seeing Floyd go off to the fields with the others after noon dinner and a rest under the trees, Leon took care to walk past the kitchen window where Clovis was working. He stared in until she looked out, and then he walked off to the woods, looking back one time meaningfully before he disappeared. He waited, desperate with fear and desire, for almost an hour before she came. When she found him, they took off their clothes and fucked without a word said. But when it was over, he put his clothes on quickly, resolving to take them off again and wash himself in the creek with sand as soon as she had gone away. But she lay there staring at him sullenly.

Finally he asked her if anything was the matter, and she said, "You ought to give me something."

"What can I give you?" he replied, offended.

"I don't know. Something." She turned her head away.

After a minute he said to placate her, "I tell you—I'll bring something next time." It was the first he'd thought of meeting her again, and he was instantly both sorry and glad.

"You promise?"

"Yes," he said, wanting to be rid of her. What if someone came along now with her naked?

"When?"

"Tomorrow."

"What you give me?" she teased, smiling for the first time.

"Don't worry. I'll bring something."

The next afternoon they met at the same place at about the same time. He brought a handkerchief with pretty embroidery on it that he had taken from Selma's room. Aunt

Nell had given it to her along with others last Christmas, and he doubted that one would be missed.

"What's that?" she said rudely, when she had asked what he had to give her and he had produced it from a pocket.

"It's Selma's. Isn't it pretty? I thought you'd like it."

She shook her head, laughing. "I wash and iron her clothes; Lovey do her fine things. What I gone do with this? Anybody see it, they say I stole it." She handed back the present, and he put it into his pocket again, mortified. "You have to give me something better than that."

"Who says I have to give you?" he said.

"If you don't, maybe I tell on you."

"You wouldn't do that!"

"How come I wouldn't?"

"Just don't—please don't, Clovis."

She appeared to consider. "Well—I think about it. Tell you what: I won't tell—yet. Hey—you want to do it?"

Her boldness, far from repelling him, excited him, coming as it did just after she had put them on a commercial footing. He stripped himself quickly. She took off her dress only when he slipped his hands under it and urged her to hurry.

The next day he brought her a gold piece he had been given by his Uncle Felix last Christmas. He hated to part with it, but he thought as he did so how little Uncle Felix would disapprove of the use it was put to, if indeed he disapproved at all. At fourteen going on fifteen Leon already knew about Felix and his black women; and he didn't know how he knew, because such things were accepted but not very much talked about.

She met him three more afternoons in a row, which he had told her she owed him for such a good present as the gold piece. The fifth day after their first meeting alone was a Saturday, and Leon went into Highboro that morning with his father. They jogged their horses back side by side late in the afternoon, bringing mail and town news and an invitation from Nell to eat dinner with her and Felix tomorrow after church. Sunday Leon rode with his mother and father and Selma in the carriage to Highboro where they attended church services and visited on the church porch with county neighbors and friends who had also driven in.

After a large afternoon dinner with Nell and Felix, they journeyed home again in the covered carriage in a light,

cooling rain that was uncharacteristic of the season. July
more often brought thunder and lightning and torrents of
rain, sometimes a storm of hailstones.

That evening after supper they all sat on the porch. Deborah and Arnold argued over the question of the cotton
gin, Deborah urging that they put money enough into it to
assure Kendrick control, Arnold veering from the idea of
cautious participation to none at all. He didn't want any
more responsibility. They went to bed with nothing
resolved, leaving Leon alone with his thoughts. Selma had
already gone off to her room.

In the distance, from the slave quarters, Leon could
hear gospel singing and hand clapping, and then it ceased
and all was quiet. He remembered a story Bonard had
told, about a plantation he'd heard another boy tell about,
where the young man on that place was given his own
Negro girl when he was fourteen years old, and that he
was free to fuck her any time he wanted to. Thinking
about it and envying that unknown boy gave Leon an
erection. He got up and walked about the yards a while,
but he encountered no one, only a couple of inquisitive
hound dogs who came to see who was stirring in the
night.

Sixteen

One person had knowledge, and another strong suspicion,
of the meetings of Leon and Clovis.

Although much alone, Selma was surrounded by creatures. She had also stayed, now and then, a day or two in
town with her aunt and uncle in order to attend a children's party at Christmas or on a birthday, so she had the
acquaintance of other young girls, most of whom knew or
pretended to know more about "life" than she did. Their
whispers and snickerings, inaccurate as one was and disgusting as the other, nevertheless bore out what she had
inevitably observed of animal behavior on the home plantation. She was fanciful, but she was logical too, and too
natural a lover of truth to be a romantic. So she knew
about male and female things, and the whole business appalled her. It was so very close and violating.

The woods of the plantation were as familiar and
known to her as they were to Leon, and, unlike her

brother, she had an inclination to privacy, which made her early wise in ways of quietness. They had often been near each other, with her observing him and him not knowing she was within a mile of him. And so one day curiosity made her follow—not Leon but Clovis—to the woods and to discover her with Leon, the two of them naked and behaving like hogs in a muddy pen.

It did not occur to her to tell anyone. She had no feelings of human behavior's being moral or not. She only knew what she instinctively approved and what she did not. She did not approve of her brother.

She had never liked him. She had been troubled by his smell without knowing it was his in the cradle she had succeeded to. This early aversion was merely the foundation of her feeling about male things in general. The brusque, graceless way male creatures moved about—those additional things of theirs hanging loose were untidy and unnatural, she thought.

The Sunday they all went into Highboro to church and then to Aunt Nell's, she had ignored Leon, keeping to the opposite seat of the carriage on the way, although she liked to move about and pay close attention to the passing view. When conversation between her mother and father grew lively and she feared some effort might be made to draw her into it, she opened her Bible and pretended to read and ponder on a passage, she who had no interest in the Bible. She had, however, long ago learned the practical use to which it might be put. Seldom, if ever, will one sitting with a Bible open and seeming to read it be interrupted.

She had seen her brother and the girl Clovis and despised them for what they did. Her disgust on the occasion did not strike her as excessive, even though she knew from observation that the behavior she had witnessed was not uncommon, and she had heard that it was necessary in order to continue all animal species.

Another person had no direct knowledge of what had occurred, but he made a surmise based on accident. April, the mule Roscoe most often rode on his rounds of the fields, had gone lame one afternoon in the highest acres where cotton grew and where Roscoe had gone to judge the readiness of the cotton there for picking. He remembered that the horn on her hind hoofs had been growing longer and more ragged and that he had been intending to trim them but had not. They had doubtless become ten-

der. Since he had taken on more of the management of
the actual farm work, he had, naturally, given up most of
his blacksmithing. The assistant he had trained, a feckless
young man named Ebenezer, had strength enough and
more for the work, but he had no initiative and little judgment one could rely on. Roscoe had made a mistake in
bothering with him at all, but sometimes a man was
clumsy at a job and suddenly became skillful when he got
the hang of it. Not Ebenezer. Roscoe would have to train
someone else. Ezra, of course, was getting too old and was
too much a personage on the place to be asked to resume
the work. But thinking of him, he suddenly thought: Why
not Ezra's son?

As soon as the thought came, he knew it was logical
and right. The boy was young, but he was quick and intelligent. He had hung around and helped with some of the
blacksmith jobs as long as his father worked in the shed.
And the last few days he had shown himself willing to
work on a steady basis without running off to be playmate
for Leon. He would set Floyd to work in his father's old
place. No one could object to such a logical arrangement.
Ezra would naturally wish to train the boy, which would
leave Roscoe free for his other tasks. It was a fruitful
idea.

Roscoe would not have admitted to fondness for anyone
or anything, but because April had served him depend-
ably, he did have a certain consideration for the beast, so
he now dismounted, not wanting her to bear his weight on
her tender hoofs, and led her down the gently sloping
fields toward the main cluster of work buildings and barns
behind the big house. He walked her through one of the
corn fields that had given most of its yield early. The fodder was ready to pull; he would set men to it soon. The
only ears of corn remaining were stray ones that had been
overlooked and had grown to such grossness and hardness
in the shucks they were good for nothing but feeding hogs
in winter or, shelled off the cob, might do to fatten turkeys. Perhaps some of it might even be used to make lye
hominy, a staple in the winter diet of the slaves.

The corn stalks stood high and thick-leafed, and the
rows grew to the edge of the woods. That was how he
happened to see Clovis the day she came away from a
meeting with Leon. As she stepped into the open, the sun
hit her. She stopped, opened her palm, and stared at a
small object that sparkled in the sun. She looked at it with

obvious pleasure and pride, and she was beyond the child stage of being pleased at the sight of pretty stones. Then, as if to hide, preserve, and enjoy it the more, she put the object into her mouth and walked away to the shade of the trees that grew by the outlying cabins.

Instinctively, he waited and watched the edge of the woods. April turned her head and gazed at him soberly, as if to ask why they paused. When the man made no move, she lipped a long leaf of corn and pawed the earth lightly. That failing to get a response, she shat hugely. The offal was hardly out of her before it was covered by huge, noisy flies. Still the man stood waiting.

Then Roscoe saw Leon. Looking more like a man than a boy, something in his way of walking being prideful and masculine, he came out of the woods and looked after the distant figure of Clovis. His eyes did not have to find her, but knew exactly where to aim. He shrugged and smiled, as if enjoying a joke with himself, or reminding himself of something pleasurable that had recently happened. Then he opened the front of his breeches and pulled out his dick. He looked down at it shook it indulgently, stroked it two or three times, and put it back into his breeches.

Roscoe knew that Clovis and the master's boy had done it. He waited until Leon had walked on out of sight, taking the same way Clovis had taken into the shade of the trees near the cabins. He thought: slut.

A day or two later Leon decided that diddling with Clovis was too dangerous to continue. That is why he had welcomed the Saturday and Sunday excursions into Highboro. And although the Sunday evening on the porch had found him in a mood to backslide, daylight renewed his resolution to have nothing more to do with the girl. Just as one action leads to another, so does inaction encourage itself.

A week later, if anyone had said her name to him suddenly, he would have been able to hear it without a start of guilt. He felt almost chaste again, and in his chastity lonely. He missed Floyd. Still a boy, he had a sudden piercing nostalgia for his own boyhood.

When he made approaches to his old friend, Floyd was agreeable enough, but there was no longer between them the unthinking sense of trust and spontaneous intimacy they had known all their lives until recently. Floyd spoke with enthusiasm of learning blacksmithing from his father. Leon stood and watched them working together one day in the old shed, but that made him feel even more alone and outside.

Out of boredom he even made an effort to be friendly with Selma, but she rejected him so quickly that he withdrew, surprised and offended. It was like a gift when one day, the middle of August, Bonard and Rooster Davis rode over to visit. Leon greeted them as if they were his oldest, dearest friends, and pressed them to extend their visit to include supper, and flattered Bonard by asking for stories of his experiences at college. When he'd finished the last winter session, Bonard had gone to Macon to stay with a friend and fellow student, which had disappointed his mother and father. He had only recently returned to Oaks to see them for a few weeks before returning to Savannah to continue his studies.

Were the masters stern and demanding, Leon wanted to know, or lenient? Were the students agreeable fellows? What were the living quarters like? What games were played? What other pleasures were available?

Bonard responded generously, bragging and lying and even telling a little of the truth, and making both of the younger boys laugh. Rooster heard the stories without any feeling except his own entertainment at hearing them told. But Leon, caught as he was in limbo, envied Bonard and began to yearn to have such experiences of his own. When he walked them down to the creek late in the afternoon and suggested they might swim, Bonard shook his head. Since deference to Bonard was the pattern of the afternoon, they did not swim. But their remoteness from the house helped them to feel private and independent and adult, and Bonard began to speak of his experiences with girls in Savannah.

There was a woman calling herself Mrs. Allendale who kept a house with several girls, and Bonard knew them all. One could go there and have something to drink, and talk, and arrange with Mrs. Allendale to have more private dealings with one of the girls in her room. Once he had had two together! Leon listened and thrilled with envy and admiration. "Are they white girls?" he asked.

"Certainly," Bonard said lazily, expertly skimming a flat stone over the surface of the creek so that it broke water twice before sinking. Then he looked at the younger boy and smiled indulgently. "You been getting poontang?"

When Leon blushed, Bonard dug him in the side with a bony elbow. laughing hugely. Rooster looked at both of them as if they were crazy.

At supper, which they were pleased to stay for when Deborah added her urging to that of Leon, they renewed their acquaintance with Selma. She was still a child, dressed and looked like a child, but something about her appeared to challenge Bonard, for he paid her more than polite attention. When he saw that it was beginning to make her shy and abrupt in her replies, he began to speak to the whole table about a company of actors that had come to Savannah last winter and performed several plays of Shakespeare. Everyone except Rooster listened with interest. Rooster was bored, knew his brother was putting on airs, and absent-mindedly smacked his lips as he consumed his food. Selma followed Bonard's account closely, looking at the food on her plate the while, but eating little of it, ever attentive to the handsome visitor. She had decided that he was indeed handsome, and that his dark, lean face was sensitive. Something of her reaction was noticed by Deborah, who reflected, not for the first time but for the first time with more than idle hope, that the alliance of the two plantations by marriage would be as natural an occurrence as it could be advantageous.

When there was a pause, she addressed herself to Bonard. "What does your father say to the building of the cotton gin in Highboro?"

Bonard laughed. "He's all in favor, ma'am—as long as someone else puts up the money!"

Only Leon and his father smiled at that. Rooster stared at his brother uncomprehendingly. Frowning, Deborah said, "Indeed? Mr. Kendrick has all but decided to make a considerable investment in the building of it."

Rooster grinned, relieved. "So has Pa. It's Mama that's holding us back. She's against anything that takes money off the land."

"But surely," Deborah said, "she can see the logic of having a cotton gin in Highboro? Think of the cost and time of wagon-freighting the raw cotton to Savannah to be ginned. If we did it here, one freight wagon might carry several bales of ginned cotton. To say nothing of—" She was suddenly aware as she looked down the table that no one cared about what she was saying, except Rooster who nodded his head eagerly in agreement. Arnold was looking at her with near anger, the humiliated-man look he got sometimes when she expressed herself forcefully on business matters, instead of pretending to take her lead from him, like a flower facing and following the path of the sun. She reached for the silver hand bell above her

plate and rang it loudly, as much from irritation as to
summon the servingmaid. "Won't anyone have more
chicken? Or ham? Mr. Davis?" Bonard declined with a
shake of his head and a smile. "Rooster, surely you—?"

"No, thank you, ma'am," he said.

"If you're certain—" Had she been looking at him,
she'd have seen his willingness to be pressed further, but
her look had already passed on to her husband. "Mr.
Kendrick?"

"No, Deborah. Thank you."

She let a questioning glance suffice for Selma and Leon,
waiting for no answering word or gesture, but turning to
the door that now opened from the wide center hall.
Lovey appeared instead of Myrtis who was serving at table that evening. "Excuse me, everybody, but, Miss Deb,
you better come with me. That girl Clovis crying and carrying on. I don't know how to say it."

Before anyone could rise and pull back her chair, Deborah was out of it and swept from the room, Lovey close
behind her.

Leon sat mummified with fear.

Bonard looked about and laughed. "Something always
stirring with the nigras!" Selma decided that Bonard was
ordinary after all. He laughed too often, and his laugh
was common. But he *was* good-looking. With his hair
worn long and his slim, graceful hands, he might almost
have been a girl.

When Deborah and Lovey reached the kitchen, they
found only Cook and Myrtis and Pauline. "Where is she?"
Lovey demanded.

Cook spoke. "Said she felt sick, so I told her to go on,
and she went."

Lovey turned in astonishment to Deborah. "Hollering
her head off, she was, about how she gone take an ax to
Roscoe Elk, and he never to my knowledge so much as
looked her way!"

"Well, whatever was wrong is apparently over," Deborah said. To Myrtis she said, "Clear the table and serve
the blancmange."

Myrtis and Clovis had been sharing the serving the last
few days because Flossie, the woman who usually attended to the dining room, had cut one of her hands on a
broken fruit jar as she worked with Cook and Pauline
putting up peach preserves. The appearance of Clovis in
the dining room embarrassed Leon, especially as it seemed

to him she paused overlong after serving him from a dish before going on to the next place.

Her pauses were not so marked as to attract anyone else's attention, but they were deliberate. She'd been surprised when he stopped meeting her. Her pride was hurt, and besides, she had enjoyed their times together. She put herself in his way a time or two, but he ignored her. The pauses were meant to punish him as well as tempt him again, but they had gone unheeded, and she had begun to look about for another likely partner.

There were always those she might have, but after the master's son, and being rewarded with money too, she was vain and looked higher than the ordinary buck who worked in the fields and seldom bathed. It was therefore natural for her to recall the response she had seen in Roscoe's eyes.

That very afternoon, after the hands had come in from the fields and Roscoe had made notations in his record book of the weight of cotton each man and woman had picked that day, they drifted off chattering to their cabins, the younger children who were not required to work trailing after them. The weighing and recording provided the main event of the day, and the children liked to be present to share in the suspense of rivalries and the jokes that were shouted. ("Strong-Tom picked two hundred and fourteen pounds yesterday, but Strong-Tom must have had a night that weakened him, because he picked only a hundred and eighty-three today. What you got to say about that, Lottie?")

When almost everyone had gone from the entrance of the barn where the cotton was stored, Roscoe sat and added up the day's total yield. As he was about to close his book, checking the total one more time against yesterday's, Clovis walked by him and into the barn. He looked at her with surprise, knowing that she was usually helping in the kitchen at this time of day. He glanced around. There was no one but the girl. "Can I help you find something?" he called. Appearing not to hear, she made no reply but went farther into the barn where it was now darkly shadowed.

Roscoe followed and found her lying on her back on a pile of cotton. Without speaking he sat down beside her and began to handle her, hold her, press her. Clovis responded, partly at the novelty of being touched by a man she did not truly fancy, of whom she even felt a certain physical revulsion, a flesh-crawling that was not unpleasant because it was new to her.

One thing led to another, as she had expected it would, but when finally he turned her over, and after slicking his dick with spit, tried to penetrate her behind, she cried out and began to fight him. He was strong and held her, but when he penetrated her with a brutal push of his hips, the shock of it set her to whimpering and then screaming. He clamped a hand over her mouth, keeping his position, but she fought more fiercely, and he was put off the mood and suddenly let her go.

As fast as she could she tugged her clothes on, running and weeping. In that state she had appeared in the kitchen; and when Lovey, who was debating with Cook the meals to be served tomorrow, could not calm her, or even make sense of what she said in her increasing hysteria, she had felt compelled to go to the dining room and summon her mistress. Realizing that she was about to be confronted by the mistress, Clovis fled to her cabin where she bathed her face and hands, still weeping angrily.

With a pretty, prissy mince, Myrtis went into the dining room and served the blancmange.

Seventeen

The last scattered cotton, that which had come to fullness after the first picking, was at last gathered, and the crop was finished for the year. A wagon train regularly made its way between Beulah Land and Savannah with the cotton to be ginned and baled and sold.

Arnold Kendrick and Benjamin Davis used to go together to the port city, but in recent years had taken turns, each acting as the other's agent on alternate years. That summer of 1820 Arnold went for both of them.

When the first wagons left from Oaks and Beulah Land, Arnold traveled with them, camping on the way when night fell, and sleeping under the wagons alongside the drivers who were always his most trustworthy men. The wagons went back and forth until the entire crops of Oaks and Beulah Land had been freighted, ginned, and sold, some of the bales to be shipped to northern ports, others to England.

According to the plan they had earlier agreed upon,

Deborah traveled by carriage just ahead of the last wagon train and met Arnold in Savannah. He kept on at the inn where he boarded whenever he traveled alone to the city. Deborah had accepted an invitation to stay with a spinster who was an old friend, the two having been at school together. Miss Penelope Pennington had a small income from various properties she had inherited from her father—she was an only child—and she had recently assumed the guardianship of her Cousin Beufort's two orphaned daughters, Lauretta and Sarah. Cousin Beufort had died of the fever in June.

Lauretta Pennington was eleven years old and her sister Sarah was nine. They were pretty little girls with nice manners, Lauretta lively, Sarah somewhat subdued. Used to Selma, whom she considered eccentric, Deborah found them charming and in her mind compared them to their advantage to Selma. She spent the greater part of each day inspecting and ordering the supplies that were the main object of her journey to Savannah. These included such items of wear as the plantation did not provide for her family as well as the slaves. She also ordered nuts and raisins and other Christmas treats for everybody—and chewing tobacco, snuff, and certain medicines Ezra would need for his patients during the winter.

Usually, Arnold dined with them at Miss Pennington's house, while keeping residence at the inn; and Deborah frequently commented on the expense and inconvenience of the arrangement and declared how much simpler life would be for them all when there was a cotton gin in Highboro. Arnold, who rather enjoyed the adventure of being away from home, seldom bothered to answer her.

At Beulah Land, Lovey kept the house and its servants in strict order, using the absence of the master and the mistress for a thorough autumn cleaning, beating rugs, sweeping ceilings, airing and sunning mattresses and pillows, and taking quilts down from shelves to see that they were fit for the winter. One of her more satisfying occupations each autumn was checking the apples and peaches they had dried on flat boards in the sun, afterward packing them tightly in thick cotton bags and hanging them high in a dry place where air might circulate around them and keep them from molding. The quart and half-gallon jars of pears, peaches, plum jam, strawberry and blackberry preserves, watermelon rind preserves, honey, tomatoes, snap beans, pickled cucumbers and beets were counted and stored, and a record was made of their numbers and precise location.

Without anyone's having clearly deputized him as such, Roscoe Elk acted as general overseer of all that was not Lovey's domain. During this time Leon stayed with the Davises, and Selma with her Aunt Nell and Uncle Felix in Highboro. The minister at St. Thomas's Church had promised that he would set up a schedule to teach Leon and Rooster algebra, map-drawing, Plato, and Caesar's Gallic Wars.

Bonard went off to college in Savannah very soon after Deborah and Arnold returned to Beulah Land. Leon was sorry to be home again, having enjoyed the company of Rooster and Bonard, particularly the latter, since neither of them shared Rooster's interest in farming matters. Selma was glad to have the fields and woods to walk over again. She felt easy enough with her placid Aunt Nell, but the hearty joviality of Uncle Felix more often than not distressed her. She was glad too to see her father again.

She was to go into Highboro with Leon during the winter to attend classes at a day school for young ladies, where she would receive instruction in French, drawing, music, and English composition.

Selma took no pleasure in schooling, although she did interest herself in the illustrated books at Beulah Land having to do with natural history. One morning in October she waited for Leon to drive them in the pony cart to Highboro, sitting in the little front parlor just where her mother and Uncle Felix had sat the day she thought she was dying. She had a book open on her lap, and when Arnold came in from an early hunt—he had started at four—with their good neighbor Benjamin Davis, she said, "Papa, have you ever seen a Chinaman?"

He paused at the stairs. "No, Puss, I haven't."

"I'm not sure I believe there is such a thing," she said gravely.

He smiled down at her. "Oh, yes. There are Chinamen and Japanese, who are much the same, from all report. There are Russians and Turks and Eskimos—all quite wild and different from us, I believe."

"I am happy they are not here, then," she said with a frown.

"Don't worry it so, Puss." He cupped the back of her head with his hand and bending, kissed her on the brow.

"You smell of fur," she said. "What did you kill?"

"Only a very old stag—half blind, and a crippled turkey gobbler. I assure you it was a favor to them to be helped out of this life."

"You're teasing me because I don't like your killing things."

"There'll be roast venison for supper. Ezra is dressing the stag now."

"Papa, I worry about you."

"Do you, Pussy?"

Leon came flying down the stairs, stopping abruptly when he saw his father. After greeting him, he turned to Selma. "We'd best go, we're late."

"I'm ready. Plumboy brought the cart around quite some time ago."

"Go on, both of you," Arnold said. "And behave yourselves. Try to learn something. I want to hear each of you recite a new poem tonight."

A week or so later Flossie performed the disservice to the household of marrying a man named Monday Kendrick who belonged to Oaks. Monday's father had been a slave of Arnold's father and therefore taken his last name, being sold to Oaks when he married one of their kitchen workers. The slaves of the two plantations sometimes married each other, and when this happened, Arnold and Benjamin arranged an exchange, so that a married couple would not be separated.

The marriage took place in the dining room of Beulah Land, and Arnold Kendrick read the marriage service as he had done before when any of the house servants or other favored slaves were married. Because Monday Kendrick was a man Benjamin did not want to lose, it had been decided that Flossie would go to Oaks in exchange for a seamstress whose skills Deborah had long coveted.

Flossie was married in a new dress bought and sewn for her by Deborah, who had trained her and had a special regard for her. They both cried when Flossie rode away with Monday in the wagon he had brought from Oaks. She carried ten dollars Deborah had given her as a present, a coop of twelve chickens Arnold had presented to the couple, her clothes, pots, pans, and quilts and an uncut wedding cake, one of the dozen that had been baked to celebrate the event. The others had been eaten with fresh sugar-cane juice, the main quantity of which was even now cooking into syrup, giving the crisp air a sweet smell. There had been much joking and laughter before the tears as the couple rode off to Oaks in the wagon.

Eighteen

Fruit cakes were baked, sprinkled liberally with brandy,
wrapped in cloth, and stored in round wooden cheese
boxes until Christmas. As the weather cooled, beef cattle
were slaughtered and dressed. Then one cold day in late
November, when the ground was hard and icicles hung
from the windmill, and dead grass and hedges were stiff
and white with frost, there was the first hog-killing of the
winter. There would be another in January, but this was
the more exciting and festive one, because it was such a
long time since everybody had tasted fresh pork: chops
and backbone, chitterlings, souse, blood pudding, trotters
and ears that were boiled and brined, fresh sausage, and
link sausage and hams that were hung in the smokehouse
to cure.

It was a hard-working day, but a happy one too, and
everyone on the plantation either participated or watched,
bundled into heavy sweaters, with wool stockings or caps
to keep heads warm. Thirty large, fat hogs were killed and
dressed. The air was heavy with the smell of woodsmoke
and boiling fat being rendered into lard and cracklings in
the washpots the laundresses used for their work in more
ordinary times. Bladders were made into balloons by the
children, who raced about to keep warm, laughing and
shrieking, glad for once to do whatever mean chores were
required of them, for it was a happy thing to be employed
that day; it gave even the children a feeling of importance.

Cows bawled balefully at the smell of fire and blood,
and barnyard fowl were quiet as on a cloudy day. Dogs
hung about, careful to keep out of the way but ready to
grab at whatever was discarded and dropped to the
ground.

In the kitchen of the big house Deborah and Lovey supervised the grinding of sausage meat and the blending of
seasonings for it. Pauline watched them carefully, learning
and remembering everything she saw. Cook made souse
and blood pudding with the help of Clovis and Myrtis.
Every man, woman, and child would eat fresh pork that
day, and sleep well that night, tired from the long day's
work and excitement.

Next morning Clovis, who had known it for some time but denied the knowledge, admitted to herself that she was pregnant. She went to Maggie, who was so old she did no work except what pleased her in and about her own cabin. Age had brought her a reputation for knowing certain witchy ways to foster love, to tell the future, and to get rid of a baby. Maggie smoked her pipe and listened to the girl, but said nothing until Clovis handed her a paper sack of sugar she had sneaked from the kitchen. Everyone knew Maggie's craving for sugar. When supplied with it, the old woman sometimes ate it straight from its bag with a spoon.

She told Clovis to come back that evening. When Clovis did, she cooled a stinking brew that had cooked all afternoon over her fire and gave it to the girl to drink. It tasted so vile Clovis felt the mere drinking of it should absolve her of the pregnancy. But all that happened was that she woke in the night and had to both vomit and shit.

But the mornings following that, she knew the other life was still within her. She also knew that when she began to show, her condition would be observed by Lovey and the mistress, who would ask her who the father was so that a marriage might be made. Deborah was firm about that: all babies born on the plantation should have a father who acknowledged them. When she was asked who begat her child, what could Clovis answer?

However, another event was to fill all minds and hearts before anyone knew or cared about the prospective motherhood of Clovis. It was an event that touched the lives of everyone on the plantation—indeed, of everyone in the county, an event that was to have infinite reverberations, like a sound that echoes and echoes, and can never be said to cease.

It began ordinarily enough. Felix and Nell had come out from Highboro for a few days' visit after the late November hog-killing. For one who concerned herself so little with the pleasure of the flesh, Nell had a particular regard for blood pudding and fresh backbone.

With company in the house, Arnold grew bored by the small social demands on his attention and manners and rode over to Oaks one afternoon to engage Benjamin for hunting on the following day. There was no need for game as provender; the only notion was to have some sport.

Benjamin, with Rooster, who was becoming a good marksman and loved to go hunting with his father, saddled horses and trotted over to Beulah Land next morning. By five o'clock they and Arnold rode off to the bleak fields and woods, followed by three of Arnold's best dogs. Finding no game in the fields, they dismounted, tied their horses, and went on foot into the woods.

As they walked, they separated, at first keeping in sight of each other, and then not. Rooster was drawing a bead on a bushy squirrel that thought he was hidden in a clump of mistletoe, when he heard the report of a gun. He recognized it as Mr. Kendrick's. Silence followed, no outcry of pleasure, no curse of disappointment at a missed shot; nothing.

Rooster lowered his gun, forgetting the squirrel that had in any case raced fast as a lizard around the limb of the tree and down its trunk when the gun sounded. Rooster walked in the direction the shot had come from and encountered his father who looked at him as quizzically as the son looked at the father.

Without a word they advanced together. One of the dogs whined. The others joined him. Benjamin and Rooster hurried, and presently they found Arnold Kendrick, who had evidently slipped or tripped and set his gun off. He was dead, his head blown nearly off his neck, his blood soaking into the carpet of leaves he had collapsed upon.

Nineteen

Arnold Kendrick, who had been the shiest and mildest of men, was the subject of extravagant, almost gross mourning, his death a veritable gleaning of grief, satisfying some winter need of the Negroes at Beulah Land. It was as if they both looked back over the years he had held them in servitude and celebrated his destruction, and saw into the future and knew that his going meant harder times for them. He had been a kind and considerate master as masters go. His gentle virtues in life were magnified in death to heroic proportions, to satisfy the need for legend and pride in the people he had owned.

His true kin were less hardly struck except for Selma, who had lost something that had not proceeded to its full realization, and now never would. Deborah and Leon and Felix, after initial surprise at the tragedy, thought more of how it might affect the future than of what was lost. The first look between Deborah and Felix was one of shock, but when that subsided, and the news was nibbled to absorption between them (Nell having taken to her bed), they looked at each other again and without putting it into words, understood the new cotton gin would be built in Highboro and that Kendrick money would control it.

Arnold had been brought home over his horse by the practical if not sensitive Benjamin and Rooster. They carried his body into the hall and put it down on a long table where newspapers and hats were usually dropped.

Simple, stark words had passed swiftly from cabin to cabin, and the people had come outdoors from their bedrooms and kitchens, half dressed, hastily drawing their clothes about them, whispering wide-eyed in their shock, gathering gradually into a crowd at the back of the kitchen wing. They wept and exclaimed prayers and blessings, parting to clear a way for Lovey and Ezra when they hurried to the big house, followed closely by Floyd and Pauline.

When Deborah and Felix had been summoned by the girl who had come in early to start the kitchen fires, they appeared to find the facts hard to comprehend, as if their minds were still asleep. Ezra understood quickly enough and left Benjamin and Rooster with his mistress while he went to the back door and summoned Skeeter and Bozo, two of the most reliable men on the place, head drivers of the cotton wagons by whose side Arnold had slept on the trip to Savannah in September. The men entered shyly and carried Arnold's body upstairs to his and Deborah's room. Ezra followed them; he knew it was for him to bathe and dress the master for his coffin.

Lovey had gone quickly to Selma and Leon. Pauline stopped at Selma's door to wait until her mother had first told Leon. Floyd went with her into Leon's room, with which he was long familiar but which he had not entered for several months. Leon had heard the commotion outside and downstairs and was awake, his expression a mixture of the fearful and hopeful which princes ever have worn as they waited for news of the death of kings and their own ascension. Lovey told him what had happened. When he sat up in bed in his night gown, she leaned automatically to hug him, and then let him go, seeing that he did not grieve.

Floyd waited inside the doorway, looking and feeling,

for the first time in Leon's presence, like a servant. Leon did not appear to notice him at all but got out of bed, slipped the night gown over his head and began to dress. Floyd went out with his mother and crept downstairs and out of the house, while she went on to Selma's room, where Pauline stood guard at the door.

Selma was entirely under the covers, holding the edge of the top quilt over her head, herself a shivering mound. Her senses told her some calamity had come, although the murmurous sounds of the people outside the house and the clamorous comings and goings on the stairs had not told her the precise nature and size of the calamity.

Lovey pulled back the quilt gently, and before she said anything, gathered the girl into her arms. Sitting on the side of the bed, rocking and comforting the child in her arms, she told her that her father was dead. Selma lay stiff in Lovey's embrace, her eyes glassy. When Pauline, made bold by sympathy, crept close and reached out a hand to touch and comfort, Selma cried out and kicked her away, collapsing on Lovey's bosom and lap with terrible sobs, wailing, "I wish it was Mama!"

Downstairs Felix had assumed formal charge of things, although it was Deborah's voice that quietly directed him in what he said and did.

Laura-Lou, the new seamstress who had come from Oaks in Flossie's stead, was put to work immediately. With one apprentice, and working with only what she found in the sewing room, she adapted certain clothes of Deborah's and Selma's to traditional mourning costumes. All decoration was stripped from everything black or gray, and the garments threaded or bordered in black, making black on gray and black on black. Cloth violets were allowed to remain on the bosom of one of Deborah's gowns, since they were dark and drooping enough to suggest an emblem of despair.

Selma was appalled by the ritual of the tragedy. When she finally accepted her father's death in her mind and marrow, she wanted to go away, flee to the fields and woods in order to think about him and come closer to him. Instead, she was required to stay in the house, to remain silent, to see no one but her mother and aunt, neither of whom understood or cared what she was feeling, although Nell assured her that she herself would certainly never be able to smile again.

Pauline, who had been so rudely dismissed, went to the

family cabin and cried, both for what was and what was
not. Floyd found the place in the woods where the accident had happened. He was glad it was not close to the
part of the creek he and Leon had once found so congenial.

Leon attended his mother quietly for the most part. He
was learning: the more happens, the less required of one.
Outdoors the cows lowed to be milked. The chickens
clucked and scratched. Like a sneeze that goes on repeating itself, a cock crowed again and again, heralding a
new day.

The first one to ride from Highboro on hearing the
news was the St. Thomas's minister who taught Leon and
Rooster a little Latin and less Greek. He comforted with
one hand, as it were, and planned with the other. By the
time he took his leave, eyes were dry, breathing normal,
and what are called "suitable arrangements" had been
made.

Attendance at the funeral was large. People kept saying
to one another it was lucky the clear weather held, although whether a man prefers to be buried in fair weather
rather than foul would seem debatable. In addition, after
the hard work of the summer and autumn, a sober event
between Thanksgiving and Christmas was not unwelcome.

Every slave on Beulah Land attended the funeral, even
the oldest and most feeble. The place was left to dogs and
cattle and hogs and fowl. Every horse and mule was
hitched to everything that had wheels—cart, wagon, or
carriage—to transport the mourners. Those who were not
so accommodated walked. A large section of pews was reserved for the family and the plantation people. White
and black faces were about equal in number inside and
outside the church.

At the last moment Selma refused to sit with her
brother and mother, and slipped away to be with Lovey
and Ezra, Floyd and Pauline, who sat together in the first
row of the pews reserved for the Negroes of Beulah Land.
She had rested when tired in their arms, and been carried
home safely by the least known of them, and so she chose
now to endure this awful hour with them, a spot of white
in a curtain of black.

When the service in the church ended, the ones inside
joined the ones who had been forced to wait and listen
outside, and all went together to the final ceremony at the
grave. The last words were read and spoken. The coffin

was lowered into the ground. As the first earth was shoveled over it, the song of the Beulah Land slaves started as a moaning hum and then broke into worded song. They sang out their despair at death and hope of resurrection—their own as much as Arnold Kendrick's. But everyone took the singing as a sign of devotion to the dead master. Ritual serves more than one purpose.

They got back to Beulah Land late in the afternoon. They fed and milked the cows, fed the horses and hogs and fowl. Then they built fires and cooked, and when food was ready, ate hugely, comforted in the knowledge that they were not the new ghost in the night.

Twenty

After the funeral Deborah took full charge of Beulah Land. Having so often chafed as she observed the convention of deferring to her husband and being guided by him, she now gloried in her true self. She more than enjoyed command; it was what she had been born to do. She could not, of course, see to everything but—so far, at any rate—she and Roscoe Elk worked well together. He saw her mettle, and while assuming new authority, was careful not to presume or encroach on hers.

Everything he did must appear to serve her wish and order. Let cruder men beg or jostle for power; Roscoe knew subtler, surer ways. There was the question, not a superficial one, of what he was to be designated and called. Titles are important to those who wear them and those ruled by them. He brought up the question himself and suggested "Overseer"—a title the slaves would immediately understand and accept after the initial pause in their minds to register his being a Negro like themselves—or half Indian, as he claimed. But Deborah, being new to real authority and jealous of delegating it, suggested that he be called "Deputy." The word came to have a special meaning at Beulah Land for the little while it was used. "De Deputy" was a phrase spoken and heard hundreds of times a day, and it was uttered in complete submission, although the slaves knew that Roscoe worked for a wage, owned little of value, could move along elsewhere if the mood took him—or be told to move along at Mistress Deborah's discretion.

Before she could ask, he showed her his record books, and she praised them for their completeness and neatness while resolving to herself to gradually take back some of the authority Arnold had let go. He waited each morning for her to command him, and when she did not, he shifted easily to the role of commander himself.

Although the real test of their joint management would come in the more active seasons of plowing and sowing, tending and harvesting, the plantation now settled into smooth working order.

Arnold's death had occurred only a few weeks before Christmas, but not wanting to disappoint her people who looked forward to Christmas festivities from one year to the next, Deborah made it clear that Christmas at Beulah Land was to be observed in as much the traditional way as accorded with decorum. The only prohibitions were large parties, to which half the county were accustomed to come, and house guests other than Felix and Nell. This dampened spirits enough, for the slaves loved having guests and parties. For one thing, it relieved their boredom, and it gave them a chance to see old friends and to make new acquaintances among the servants brought by the visitors to the big house.

Deborah, however, distributed the new clothes and special holiday treats she and Arnold had ordered in Savannah back in September, and the slaves were encouraged to have their own parties in their own quarters. Almost every night the sounds of fiddle and banjo, clapping hands and dancing feet could be heard distantly by those in the big house, and Selma slipped out two or three times to join parties, at least as listener and observer.

Lovey and Ezra did not allow the playing of music and dancing in their cabin, because they considered themselves, second only to the Kendricks, to be in mourning. But they attended occasional gatherings for an hour to be sociable, and permitted Floyd and Pauline to go or not as they pleased. At one of these parties attended by Lovey and her family, Selma suddenly crept into the cabin and slipped over to Lovey. Standing in the yard listening, she had seen her through the doorway, then waited to make sure when the door opened to let someone else out.

Lovey tempered her surprise with a kiss and a soft exclamation: "Merry Christmas, Angel." Ezra smiled at her and touched her on her long, blond hair. Made thus welcome Selma looked at the circle of children dancing on the side,

away from their elders. When she saw her, Pauline broke
from the circle and, emboldened by the Christmas spirit,
went to Selma. Taking her by the hand, she led her back to
the circle, which opened to include her. All then joined
hands and danced.

After smiling at them and deciding to allow Selma to
stay and dance a little while—she still was enough child to
be unconventionally present—Lovey turned back to observe
the larger group. Floyd was dancing with Clovis, and as he
swung her around to the gibberish whine of the fiddle and
the cheery pecking of the banjo, Lovey saw that the girl
was pregnant. Old Maggie, who was happy with her hoard
of peppermint sticks, her own Christmas treat from the
mistress, chortled, seeing Lovey's surprise.

Leon had ridden over for a party at Oaks. Bonard was
home for the holidays and had promised to show Leon
"how to get next to the girls." Deborah and Felix were
having a glass of claret before the open fire in the big
drawing room that looked so unfestive, in spite of small
hangings of holly and mistletoe. Nell, sitting bolt upright,
pretended to nap so that no one would address her, and
wondered if she might make an excuse to slip off to the
kitchen for another bit of fruit cake before bedtime. She
belched silently, parting her lips only enough to let the gas
out. Deborah and Felix talked with satisfaction about the
building of the cotton gin, which would be fully operative
by the time cotton was ready next summer.

Twenty-One

Lovey let the question of Clovis abide until after the start
of the new year, and then she took the girl aside and asked
if she knew she was pregnant. Clovis admitted that she
did, and Lovey asked, "Who is the father?"

"I can't tell you," Clovis said.

"You will," Lovey said.

"Don't make me, Miss Lovey," Clovis whined.

"You know Miss Deborah's word on this, girl, and her
word is law."

"I won't tell!"

Lovey grabbed Clovis by the wrist and pulled her
across the yard to the woodpile where she selected a long,
thin stick, and brandished it in the air. The girl was larger

than she, but such was Lovey's strength of character, none
of the other slaves had ever rebelled overtly against her
will. "You see this stick?" Clovis's eyes rounded in alarm.
"You are going to tell me who the man is, if you know.
I've seen you sneak off with this-one and that-one, but I
disremember who they were. You are going to tell me
right now, girl, or after I beat you half to death with this
stick. Which will it be?" Clovis tried to pull away, but
Lovey held her and glared at her with contempt. When
the girl still made no reply, Lovey whacked her hard on
her plump rump with the stick.

Clovis cried out, "Miss Lovey, stop it now! Don't do
it!"

"Tell me!" Lovey raised the stick again.

Clovis wept to dramatize her next words. "Mister Leon
and your Floyd!"

Lovey was so shocked she hit the girl again harder than
she had before. She continued to beat her, until Clovis
wept in real pain and wailed, "It so! It so!"

Lovey let her go, and Clovis ran off to the slave quarters, a hand comforting her burning behind. Lovey threw
the stick aside furiously, as if it were the thing that had
offended her. She walked around the big house three times
before she was calm enough to go inside. Cook and Myrtis, busy preparing the noon meal, saw her mood and kept
silent. Lovey only appeared to watch what they were
doing before going out again. She went directly to the
blacksmith shed where she found both Ezra and Floyd.
Seeing her stern expression, they stopped work.

To Floyd she said, "Clovis is pregnant. She say she lay
with you and Leon. Is it so?"

Ezra looked at his boy, stricken. Floyd swallowed as if
his spit had suddenly turned to sand, and stared at his feet
without seeing them, unable to meet his mother's eyes. He
whispered, "I was with her one time."

"One time?" Ezra said. Floyd nodded his head.

Lovey and Ezra exchanged looks. "You sure and positive?" Lovey said to Floyd.

"Yes, Mama."

"You swear?" Ezra said.

"Yes, Papa," Floyd said in a stronger voice.

"You won't tell on Leon?" It was question and statement.

Floyd shook his head.

"Very well, sir!" Lovey said with more energy. "You

know the stand Miss Deb takes on bastard babies!"

Ezra said to Lovey, "I don't think it can be his. I wouldn't let him marry her if it was."

Lovey's eyes filled with tears. "My baby Leon too?" She folded her arms and rocked back and forth, grieving.

Ezra said, "Floyd will not marry her."

"No," Lovey said after a moment. "I couldn't stand that." Floyd had begun to cry, ashamed of having distressed his mother and father. He fell to his knees between them and embraced their legs. "I'm sorry, Mama, Papa!" His forehead touched Lovey's shoes.

Ezra looked down at him with love and anguish, and then touched his shoulder. Floyd stopped crying, although he was still too embarrassed to look up. Clumsily, he caught his father's hand and kissed it.

"I'll go see Miss Deb," Lovey said. Her voice and face were bitter as she marched back along the cold, hard path to the main house.

She found her mistress in the sewing room upstairs conferring with Laura-Lou about the new night gowns for Selma. She made herself be still and patient until the conference degenerated into a series of repetitions on both sides.

"You understand what I mean about the width of the hem and the buttons *here* so that a neckband may be attached in really cold weather?"

"Yes'm. Button *here,* just to side of this panel of embroidery—?"

"That's right. Here and here too, remember—"

"Yes'm." Vigorous head nod. "Here and here—"

At that point Lovey cleared her throat in such a firm way that Deborah looked over at her. Seeing Lovey's grim face, she merely directed an automatic last word to Laura-Lou before leaving the sewing room. With Lovey following, she walked quickly down the second-floor hallway and into her own room. Already it had lost its look of dual occupancy. The wardrobes contained only Deborah's clothing, Arnold's having been given, not to the people on the plantation, but to the minister of St. Thomas's in Highboro to distribute to whatever needy white men might apply to him for help. His brushes and razor and strop had been put away for Leon's future use.

Following her mistress into the room, Lovey closed the door behind them, and the two women looked straight at each other.

"Miss Deb," Lovey began, "you know the girl Clovis works in the kitchen, sometimes serves at table—"

"Yes, yes." Deborah nodded impatiently, seeing that Lovey brought trouble and not wanting to endure her gradual approach to it.

"She is pregnant."

Deborah's tension relaxed a little. The problem was serious, of course, but not unfamiliar. "And not married."

"Yes'm. Not married."

"You've talked to her."

"Yes, Miss Deb."

"Who is the father?"

There was a long pause. Lovey heaved a heavy, aching sigh.

"Tell me, Lovey," Deborah insisted, carefully controlling her voice, but wondering instantly if it could be Felix.

"I had to beat her with a stick before she'd say." Deborah waited in growing alarm. It was not the simple problem she had guessed. "She's a trifling girl, Miss Deb—she go with this-one, that-one, but when I scared her good, she say—she say Floyd!"

"Floyd is still a boy."

"I already question Floyd with his father there, and Floyd say one time—"

"I find it hard to believe, and harder to understand. We surely can't let him marry this girl."

"No, ma'am. I couldn't stand that, nor could his papa. But that ain't all. I don't know if I ought to say or not, or even if I can."

"For Heaven's sake, Lovey, say." Deborah was so completely alerted by now to an expectancy of bad news that her mind had leaped beyond Lovey's revelations.

"She must be lying, Miss Deb," Lovey mumbled, "but she say—she say she been with our Leon."

Nothing like it had ever before happened at Beulah Land. Deborah opened the door, and Lovey followed on her heels, although she stopped short at the door to Leon's room when Deborah opened it and entered without knocking.

Leon was sitting at his desk with a shallow wooden tray full of arrowheads that had been turned up over the years by the plantation plowmen. They had turned up hundreds, and these were only the best he had saved. Lovey waited in the hall, her ears cocked to the crack of the door.

Turning and seeing his mother, Leon rose from his

chair. "What is it, Mama? Is anything wrong? You look
so—"

"*You* must tell me if anything is wrong."

Leon, who had all but forgotten, or put out of his
mind, the late summer's adventure and its possible consequences, knew instantly that this must have to do with
Clovis.

His feeling was justified when Deborah said, "You
know the girl, Clovis?"

Leon nodded, unable to speak. She had *told*. The bad
girl had told on him.

"Lovey tells me she is pregnant." Leon stared at his
mother's hands. "Clovis has been persuaded to name the
possible father." He could look at nothing but her hands,
each rapidly and cruelly massaging the other. "Floyd has
admitted that he was with the girl, but she says that you
also have been with her. Is it so? Tell me the truth. If
what she says is a lie, I shall sell her instantly, and that
will be the end of it."

"Did Floyd say I had?" Leon asked.

"Tell me!" Deborah demanded.

"Yes."

Deborah slapped the boy so hard he almost fell. At the
sound of it Lovey rushed into the room and went straight
to Leon. Although he was now taller than she, she put her
arms around him protectively so that he seemed smaller
than she, a child again. "Don't hit this boy again!" she
said angrily. "He needs helping, not hurting!"

Looking numb with shock and anger, Deborah turned
and left the room. The last thing she heard as she made
her way to her own room was Lovey's voice, scolding,
consoling, blaming and forgiving, deploring and loving.
Although it wasn't certain—how many others had the girl
lain with?—it was possible that a bastard, one that could
be her grandchild, would be born at Beulah Land.

Twenty-Two

Word of what had transpired and rumor of more had
spread over the plantation like oil on water. Having been
found out, Clovis knew no restraint. For all her world to
hear she wailed the general outline of her predicament
and the actions that had brought it to a head.

In her room in the big house Deborah wrote a note and put it herself under Leon's door. It read: *I cannot bring myself to speak to you as yet, but you are to remain in your room until I instruct you otherwise.* Leon and Lovey read the note together, after which Lovey crumbled it in her hand and went to Deborah's room. She knocked on the closed door and called, "It's Lovey." After a moment Deborah's voice asked her to come in.

"What am I to do?" Deborah said, not as an appeal, but as an expression of outrage.

"Floyd is all mine, and I consider Leon part mine, so what are *we* to do, you better say."

Deborah clapped her hands together until they were red. "How *could* Leon? How could Floyd? That common kitchen girl!"

"Miss Deb," Lovey said impatiently, "you don't leave a honey pot open and expect the flies to eat salt. Turning it in my mind, I'm surprised that girl wasn't pregnant a year or two ago."

"I'm not thinking about her."

"I know it, and I'm not either, except in passing. I said it to show how our boys are unlucky, that's all. Of course, there's the other thing. It ain't nice to say, but it's a fact—she could have been fooling with ten at the same time and only named Leon and Floyd because they give her some tone and expectation. There's no proof either one fathered the child she carries."

"No. I see that. She can't hope that Floyd will be made to marry her, but she can hope that by naming him, her chances of an advantageous marriage are better than they would be otherwise."

"If the Lord was just, He'd take her unto him, or send her to the Devil."

"Let's not go into that. What about the boys? There's bound to be gossip. Here at least. Hopefully, not in town."

"Oh yes there will be, too."

"I suppose we'll have to put up with it and ignore it," Deborah said.

"Nothing else we can do." Lovey blinked rapidly, her mind working. "Send Leon to town, Miss Deb, to stay with his Aunt Nell and Uncle Felix."

Deborah frowned, her mind busy too. She picked up from a commode an old snuff box she used for pins and stared at the likeness of General Washington on its lid.

Then putting it down without having been aware she had picked it up, she nodded vigorously and clapped her hands again. "You're right, Lovey. Of course you're right!"

Lovey sighed. "Out of sight, out of mind, they say. No use for him to stay here and be shamed."

"I don't care about his feelings," Deborah said, "but I don't like the idea of our people seeing him without respect. He will be their master one day."

"Just so," Lovey said grimly. "Floyd can siphon off their disrespect."

"I didn't mean it that way, Lovey."

"I know you didn't. I want Floyd to swallow his medicine and learn his lesson. Short of marrying her."

"Leon will be closer to his tutor. But he can't stay in Highboro forever. Still, I should like him to be away from here a long while." Deborah walked back and forth, worrying the problem. Lovey waited. Deborah went to a window and looked out over bare trees to the gray fields beyond.

Lovey stirred, bored with inaction. "It's nigh time for dinner. They'll soon be ringing the bell."

"When they do, I shall go down and eat, no matter that every bite will stick in my craw. But I don't want Leon there. Go and tell him he is not to come down when he hears the bell. He can do without his noon victuals. Then ask Plumboy to saddle a horse. Tell Leon to pack clothes enough for a few days in Highboro, and to go. I don't want to see him. I have nothing to say to him. You may tell him that."

"I won't have to; he knows." Lovey moved to the door.

"Don't you aggravate me too, Lovey!" Deborah exclaimed.

"No'm!" Lovey said huffily and went out.

Leon packed his clothes and rode away to Highboro to stay with his aunt and uncle, taking with him a short letter Deborah had written and sealed with candle wax before going downstairs to the dining room to eat her silent and solitary meal. Selma did not appear. Deborah wondered vaguely where she was, but the child sometimes chose not to come to a meal, so she didn't worry about her. Her mind was too full of Leon to accommodate another concern. The male sex, she thought with disgust.

She would like to be rid of Leon until he became a man and developed a true man's sense of responsibility and obligation. She chewed her way doggedly through the food on her plate, carefully courteous to Myrtis when she appeared to serve a dish, but not genial. She never was anyway, so her preoccupation today should raise no special comment. Slowly, as if self-generating, a plan presented itself to her.

Bonard had not yet returned to Savannah to continue his education; he had extended his Christmas visit beyond its first allotment. He should, however, be leaving soon. Why not have Leon go with him? Leon was fifteen. There would be tutors at the college willing to coach him if he were discovered to be not yet fully qualified to attend regular classes. That would assure his being away for months, well beyond the time when Clovis would have her child. "Out of sight, out of mind," Lovey had said, and it was so. If the plan worked reasonably well, Leon would be absent from Beulah Land, except perhaps for short vacations, until he was indeed a grown man.

When she finished the unwanted and untasted meal, she found Lovey, whose eyes were red from the tears she had shed on seeing Leon off to town. Deborah asked Lovey to send Ezra to her. She sent for Ezra because he was already involved in the affair, and because he was a man of dignity and discretion.

When he attended her, she asked him to ride over to Oaks and tell Mr. Benjamin Davis that she needed his advice and help most urgently and would be ever obliged to him if he could ride back with Ezra, or follow him soon after, to receive her confidence. Ezra listened gravely to Deborah, nodded to indicate that he understood her instructions, and took his leave.

As Ezra rode to Oaks, Leon was making his way in the opposite direction to Highboro and a future that would keep him away from Beulah Land, except for those short visits Deborah had grudgingly allowed to herself might be necessary, for a long time. His eyes smarted, and his nose ran until he wiped it with his jacket sleeve. It wasn't cold, but he felt cold as he wondered what would happen to him next.

High up in the hay barn, warm in a hill of loose hay, Selma reposed with a copy of *Robinson Crusoe*, one of the few story books she knew to be to her taste. She liked it because she felt a kinship with Crusoe's aloneness, and she shared his interest, in his case enforced, in what is called natural history.

She had not forgotten the noon meal, and she had heard the bell heralding it; but being a sensitive child, she had been aware of all the comings and goings, the raised voices and solemn faces in the big house, as well as the nervous excitement that had spread all day among the Negroes. So she had taken her book and two apples and gone off to the barn to read and think and be alone. The place she chose was near a window.

Although the shutter was closed, it admitted a generous crack of light, enough to read by on the bright winter day, and she had chanced to see both Leon and Ezra ride off the place without knowing the destination of either.

Late in the afternoon Benjamin Davis came over, and between them, he and Deborah settled that in a few days he would escort both Bonard and Leon to Savannah and make arrangements for Leon's lodging and education. Deborah was satisfied to leave details entirely to her friend and neighbor. For his help she promised him that his next year's cotton crop to be processed at her gin would cost him nothing. He said, "Tut," but did not refuse the offer. (As it turned out, Deborah took a share of Benjamin's cotton for the ginning of it, but less than she would have if she had not felt herself to be in some degree indebted to him.)

She was drafting a letter to her old friend in Savannah, Miss Pennington, to tell her that her son would presently take up residence there and ask if he might be permitted to call upon her and her nieces for the benefit of refined company of true ladies, when there was a knock at the door of the small sitting room that now served as her office, and where she now kept a work desk.

She said, "Come in," and in walked Roscoe Elk. He was dressed formally for plantation business, she thought automatically: shirt collar buttoned although he wore no stock, suit jacket on and buttoned, hat carried in the crook of one arm. Deborah did not at first acknowledge the importance his dress gave the occasion, but said merely, "What is it, Roscoe?"

He bowed his head, then lifted it. His voice was more than serious when he spoke; it was solemn and sonorous. "Madam," he said, "you are aware of the perturbation that has afflicted the people on this day when it became known that the girl Clovis was with child?"

Astonished at these words as well as his manner of speaking them, Deborah at first merely stared at him.

Then she nodded once, abruptly.

Roscoe took a breath. "I," he then said, "and none other, shall marry her. I shall be the father of her child."

The pause between them lengthened, grew in solemnity. Finally Deborah said, "Is she ready to marry you?"

Roscoe nodded. "I have told her how it is to be, and she has agreed."

"Has she!" Deborah's relief burst forth before she could think to hide it. Here was the solution to her problem, and the girl did not lose either—was not Roscoe the most important man on the plantation? She was more than lucky; she was blessed. A thought intruded. "But you are free, and she is not."

Roscoe nodded. "It is my hope for you to agree," he said carefully, "that should the time come for me to leave here, you will sell her to me."

"I agree, of course," Deborah said. "We have never separated husband and wife at Beulah Land." Roscoe bowed his head again briefly, as if to set his seal on their understanding. Deborah stood. "We shall have the wedding in the dining room, and I shall have a parson come out from Highboro to say the marriage words over you."

Again Roscoe nodded, then apparently feeling that enough had been settled for the moment, he turned to take his leave. His hand was on the doorknob when Deborah's voice stopped him. "I think, Roscoe, that you must be called 'Overseer' from now on."

He turned slowly and looked at her. "So be it," he said, and then went out, closing the door quietly.

PART TWO

1828

One

Rooster, it happened, was the first of his generation to marry, and it came about in a simple and natural way. At twenty-two he was a man in body and mind. He had held to his resolve to avoid more schooling than Mr. Bartram provided, and he had become a keen and knowledgeable farmer, gradually taking on more and more of his father's work and responsibilities, so that when Benjamin, in 1825, suffered a stroke of paralysis, Oaks was not without a master. Benjamin was fortunate enough to keep, or to regain the use of, his faculties, but he never walked again.

Monday Kendrick, who had married Flossie of Beulah Land and taken her to live at Oaks, assumed personal charge of his master. Monday was a giant of a man, six and a half feet tall, and he moved Benjamin from place to place as easily as another might move a child. The two men, who had always had a high regard for each other, became good friends. Without telling anyone but Rooster, Benjamin signed a legal paper which Felix had drawn up for him that gave Monday and Flossie and whatever children they might produce between them their freedom upon Benjamin's death.

Because Bonard had no taste or talent for farming, Rooster became in all practical ways master at Oaks. Belying his nickname, which nevertheless clung to him as such have a way of doing, although changing meaning in people's minds, Rooster was a quiet and sober man without in any way suggesting coldness. Heavy-shouldered and deep-chested, he was always to feel a little out of place and to move a little awkwardly indoors.

He loved his land and tended it well, and he had earned the respect of everyone, including now even his brother, for Bonard was sensible enough to see that, although the elder and natural heir, he would have made a mess of the management of Oaks. He was content to leave the work and responsibility to his brother, with the understanding that when their father died, he would be provided with a

fair portion of the profits of the plantation. He had at the
time of his father's stroke begun to read law under the supervision of Felix Kendrick in Highboro. He did not work
very hard, and Felix was certainly no hard taskmaster; the
two shared amusement in each other's philandering and
enjoyed telling tales over their cigars, each encouraging
the other to exaggeration in the most amiable way. People
in the county, who always had opinions on such matters,
and whose opinions counted with those concerned, agreed
that the Davis brothers had arranged things very well between them.

In all seasons there was a good deal of riding about and
discussion among the farmers, and Rooster did his share
of both. He was highly regarded by Deborah, who valued
his opinions. Roscoe Elk sometimes made a third in their
talk of crops and livestock. In his riding about Rooster
had naturally become friendly and easy with the farmers
of the two small estates that separated Beulah Land from
Oaks. Both the Cokers and the Andersons had sons and
daughters, and Rooster found himself eventually with
warmer feelings for Gertrude Coker, called Trudy, than he
entertained for any other young woman of his acquaintance.

Trudy pleased Rooster in every way. She was always
cheerful and often jolly, which made him less sober with
her than he was with others. Their temperaments made a
good balancing seesaw. And she was a true farm girl.
Casual but not careless in her dress, she forgot to wear a
sunbonnet most of the time, or discarded it; her arms
were frequently bare, dress sleeves rolled above the elbows. The summer sun made her arms as tan as Rooster's,
and sprinkled her face with freckles, and bleached her
brown hair with streaks the color of straw.

Rooster first became aware of his feeling for Trudy
when he saw her dancing with another man at a Christmas party at Beulah Land. He fidgeted uncomfortably,
then found himself, unreasonably, becoming angry at the
sight of her laughing and dancing with such evident enjoy-
ment with Clarence Anderson, whom he had hitherto
liked well enough. There was, Rooster had observed earlier that evening, a full moon in a clear sky, and he took
his first opportunity to ask Trudy to join him in admiring
the pretty sight. Before they returned to the wide hall
where the dancing was done, he told her he loved her and
asked her to love him. She laughed and threw her arms
about his neck and kissed him full on the lips; and they

were engaged to be married to each other. Rooster actually hurt with happiness, it had come so suddenly. His
scalp tightened and prickled, the flesh of his arms crawled
beneath his sleeves, his loins were hot and achey with the
fullness of blood that rushed there.

Rooster refused to allow Trudy to dance with anyone
else for the remainder of that evening, and when this
roused comment, the blushing, laughing pair found themselves encircled by friends who demanded to know if they
were lovers: They admitted they had become engaged
within the last half hour. As soon as it was said, before
the applause of friends subsided, Rooster dragged Trudy
by the arm into the dining room where his father sat, with
Edna in attendance on one side of him and Monday the
other.

He told his parents what had happened and kissed them
both, as then did Trudy, before she urged her fiancé away
to repeat the performance with her mother and father.
Both sets of parents were pleased, and presently the
Cokers sought out the Davises to exchange approval,
share satisfaction. Edna, who had always wanted a daughter, was to have one she knew she could love, a girl who,
when the time came, would be completely capable of re-
placing her as mistress of Oaks. All she lacked was an experience of managing servants, and Edna would soon
teach her that.

The wedding in February attracted a larger gathering
from all over the county than the church could hold.
There was no need to send invitations to those near at
hand; everyone assumed rightly that he and she would be
welcome. People were truly glad at the event, and no one
was spiteful in pointing out the superior match Trudy had
made, for her virtue and goodness were known and admired as much as Rooster's worthiness of them.

Two

The wedding of Rooster and Trudy, while giving such general pleasure, set Deborah to thinking again about the future of her own children. Although Rooster was her favorite of the Davis brothers, it seemed to her appropriate to
promote as much as she was able the prospect of a marriage between her daughter Selma and Bonard.

Bonard was, after all, the elder brother, and would

eventually come in for a good share of the profits of
Oaks. He appeared to be settling down to a regular pursuit of a career in the law under the sponsorship of her
brother-in-law. Whatever might be said of the frivolous
side of Felix's nature, no one could dispute the fact that
he was a first-class man of business affairs. Had he not
been the first to see the advantages of a cotton gin built
with Kendrick money? Between them Deborah and Felix
owned the gin; it paid for itself over again each year, and
they had added a warehouse at his suggestion to the original structure. Felix bought the bales of cotton the smaller
farms produced and stored them until he could command
the best price, with none of the possible haste the farmers
might have felt to make a sale. Bonard would do well under the tutelage of Felix.

And as he settled down, she hoped in marriage to
Selma for whom he had always evidenced a particular regard, so, she had no doubt, would Leon. Leon was considered a little wild by the county folk. His father's death
might have provided an opportunity for early maturing,
but it had done no such thing, because of the scandal concerning the girl Clovis.

Deborah's suddenly made plan of sending him to school
with Bonard in Savannah had been followed. The Samuel
Holt Academy for young men was not a college, although
those attending it were accustomed to refer to it as such.
First-year boys were required to live on the premises of
the Academy, but in his second year Leon persuaded his
mother and the Academy authorities to let him take lodgings with Bonard in the town.

No one thought Bonard wicked, but he was said to be
haughty and pleasure-loving, and if expedience had not
dictated Deborah's sending Leon away with him, she
surely might have found safer guide and mentor for her
son. Leon was an agreeable boy who liked to be liked
even more than do most; he was therefore malleable. He
had no strong ambition, no special bent toward the study
of law for a possible future in politics. He was bored by
talk of business, although he was polite enough to hide it
in the company of his elders.

He should have found, and probably would have found,
interest and employment on Beulah Land which, after all,
would be his one day, but for the fact that Deborah and
Roscoe Elk were too jealous of the management of the
plantation to allow him any scope there. A young man of
firmer character might have forced his way, made de-

mands to assure himself a place, but it was Leon's amiability again more than weakness that kept him from assert-
ing himself with his mother and her overseer. Deborah
complained that he took no interest in the estate at the
same time she denied him opportunity.

And with Roscoe, Leon had a special and peculiar relationship. Roscoe had relieved an embarrassing and poten-
tially scandalous situation when he married Clovis and became in name at least father of the child who, when born,
had obviously been fathered by a white man. It would be
ingratitude to use the man on that occasion, and to withdraw the position he held as a direct result of it, now that
Leon was of an age to assume his responsibilities.

Like many other strong people Deborah wanted things
both ways. She wanted Leon to interest himself in the
plantation, while keeping her own powerful position and
continuing to use Roscoe Elk for her convenience and the
prosperity of Beulah Land. The fact that the situation was
largely, although not entirely, one of her own making did
not prevent her complaining that Leon, if he did not
change his ways, would become a wastrel.

Her scheme to nurture a future match between Leon
and one of Penelope Pennington's nieces had not come to
anything. Soon after his arrival in Savannah, Leon had
dutifully called upon Miss Pennington in her house on
Broughton Street to make her acquaintance and that of
the Misses Lauretta and Sarah. Lauretta had quite taken
his fancy, but there was no way for him to get ahead with
her. Miss Penelope and Sarah were always there. Lauretta
was attracted to the handsome young man and used him
to practice her flirting, but nothing serious grew out of it,
because Miss Penelope was so very insistent on keeping
the tone one of "family." Leon was the son of her old
school friend; therefore, he was treated like a nephew,
and Lauretta and Sarah were encouraged to look on him
as a cousin.

It was not that Miss Penelope, or "Aunt Pea" as her
nieces called her, was insensible of the advantage of a future alliance between the Kendricks and the Penningtons.
But she was a spinster who knew and cared nothing for
matchmaking. Her very presence was a dampener to any
feelings that might have gone beyond convivial banter.
With the right kind of encouragement, affection might
have budded and grown, but Miss Penelope was not the
one to supply a congenial atmosphere for such a develop-
ment of young romance. And, too, Sarah was always

there, a nice, quiet child, pretty in her way, but lacking the liveliness of her older sister—indeed, sober.

Without despairing altogether of an eventual match that would join Leon to the older Pennington girl, Deborah let it slip out of her mind for the time being, leaving it, as it were, a matter pending.

Just as Bonard had gone off to school first and set up a pattern of life which Leon later joined and became a partner to, so did Bonard return home after his studies at the Academy and set up a kind of life Leon later made himself partner to when *he* left the Academy and returned to Beulah Land. The two young men were friendly in a junior-senior way perfectly understood and honored by both of them, without their being real friends. The participation of each in the mild debaucheries of drinking and womanizing they practiced encouraged and excused the other.

Leon was, at least, discreet enough to take his pleasures away from Beulah Land. He never showed himself when drinking to anyone there. He was, indeed, seldom what might be called "drunk," although both he and Bonard liked wine and whiskey and the lift and release from boredom they attained through them. They also enjoyed—not "affairs" which neither had the experience of—but relatively uncomplicated sexual relations which were found easily enough with whores. Leon was on these occasions of mild debauch a cheerful drinker and a cheerful fucker. Bonard tended to become quarrelsome if he drank beyond a certain stage, but since his belligerence never included Leon, only strangers and stray acquaintances, Leon took no special notice. Bonard had also occasionally found pleasure in rough treatment of his whores. One of them once had him barred for a time from a house she worked in because he blacked one of her eyes and so brutally savaged one of her breasts with his teeth she was unable to show herself to another customer for a fortnight.

Never did Leon allow his eyes to linger overlong on the dark girls at Beulah Land. The experience of Clovis had taught him a lesson. Master's son though he was when it happened, she'd had the upper hand. She had separated him from his friend Floyd, she had embarrassed and shamed him, and she had finally driven him from his home. The babe she bore, which everyone knew was his, was born misshapen. Light of skin when the birth redness faded, he was not regularly formed. There was something odd about his back that came to be a hump when he grew, and one leg was shorter than the other, which caused him to walk with a limp when he finally learned to walk.

Deborah wrote Leon in Savannah of the child's birth: *Clovis has had a son and named him Roman. He is lighter in color than she or Roscoe, and he is deformed. We do not expect him to live.*

When he came home on his first visit from the Academy, Leon was careful not to venture much about the plantation, spending most of his time indoors, or over at Oaks, or riding and driving about the countryside with Bonard.

Three

When Clovis was well along in her second pregnancy, Roscoe found a moment during one of Leon's vacations from the Academy to ask for an interview with the mistress when she and "the young master" might find it convenient to be present together, since the matter he wished to broach was one of importance and general concern.

Deborah and Leon received the Overseer in the little sitting room which, in spite of having to accommodate the traffic of the stairs to the second floor, had become Deborah's business office. When Roscoe knocked at the door, and Deborah asked him to enter, he did so. He was dressed in Sunday clothes, and his manner suggested the ceremonial, partly perhaps because he carried under one arm a box or casket with closed lid, the whole lacquered peacock blue. He bowed his head after he had briefly engaged Deborah's eyes and said formally, "Mrs. Kendrick." She nodded, and he appeared to be on the point of going into the business that had brought him to seek audience when he suddenly seemed to see Leon for the first time.

Turning to the young man, he bowed his head again, then addressed himself to Deborah. Leon flushed uncomfortably.

Roscoe said, "I have come to ask the mistress—and the young master—if I may buy my wife Clovis, seeing that she is with child."

Deborah required a moment to go beyond her initial surprise, and when she had done so, she thought about it another few moments and then said, "I believe we can come to an agreement on the matter."

"What would the mistress—and master—think a reasonable sum for me to pay?"

"I think that is for you to suggest. Clovis was not, as you know, ever bought or sold; she was born on Beulah Land. We do not sell our people, unless they ask it."

"I propose that she be valued at one thousand dollars," Roscoe said. "I have enquired, and that appears to be the price of a woman her age and strength at this time."

Deborah managed to say with an appearance of calm, although light sweat had come out on her forehead, "That is then perfectly reasonable. And is it your wish—I hope not—to take leave of Beulah Land?"

"No, Mistress." Deborah smiled her relief. "I merely want Mrs. Elk to live as a free woman, and for our child—our children to be free born."

"Yes, I understand that. Let us say that we are agreed, and that you may pay when and how you choose."

"I am prepared to pay now." He took the casket in both hands.

"But I shall have to ask Mr. Felix Kendrick to draw up a paper to this effect—"

Roscoe nodded. "I wish to pay now if the mistress please. The legal paper will come, and young Master Leon Kendrick will be witness that I have paid the agreed-upon sum of money."

"Very well," Deborah said, and resigned herself to what must follow.

Roscoe held out the casket to them and opened the lid, revealing an interior packed with coins. "I ask mistress—or master—to tally the amount in case I have made an error."

"I am sure you have counted accurately," Deborah said. "I shall give you a receipt."

"Please, Mistress. I cannot accept a receipt until the money has been counted," Roscoe said. "That is not proper business. If the young master—"

Deborah and Leon exchanged looks, and Leon took the casket of money and sat down at Deborah's desk. She stood on one side of the desk, Roscoe on the other, both attending and watching.

Leon began to count. He made small notations on a sheet of paper provided by Deborah. Three quarters of an hour later he was finished, and he added the various columns of figures—the money was in both American and English denominations—he had made during the counting. Finishing, he passed the figures to Deborah. She looked them over carefully, nodding now and then as she paused to register a certain sum. Presently she said, "I find that correct."

"The receipt we spoke of?" Roscoe said.

"Certainly."

Leon got up from the desk, giving the chair he had sat on to his mother. Quickly she composed a receipt for the amount, giving the purpose for which it was paid, signing it, then handing it to Roscoe.

Roscoe read it carefully and nodded, then turned deferentially to Leon. "If Master Leon will also sign?"

Leon took his mother's pen from her, dipped it nervously into the inkpot she had left open and scribbled his name below hers, handing the paper to Roscoe without allowing time for the ink to dry.

Roscoe looked at the paper again, and at Leon's signature with obvious satisfaction. "Now," he said, "my children will be free born."

"That is so," Deborah said, "but what about Roman?"

As soon as she had spoken, she realized that she should not have. Leon, standing, felt himself go numb with shock at her thoughtless question, even before Roscoe said, "The child named Roman may remain a slave. He was born to that state. Perhaps that is his fate."

Four

Lovey said often enough that she wanted her children to marry, and that she longed for grandchildren, but such declarations are common and in this instance were an exaggeration, if not a downright untruth. Most of the young men on the place who were Floyd's age were married or bespoke, and most of the girls Pauline's age were married, or hoping soon to be, or had at least an unsatisfactory love problem to brood over and complain about. Many of them regularly begged old Maggie for advice and potions.

Pauline had no intention of marrying. When she said so, people remembered Lovey when she was a girl and her similar resolution, and so gave little or no credence to the daughter's. Pauline worked mainly in the kitchen, but her duties were what she made them. No one stood over her in any sense. She had no desire to succeed Cook when that worthy one decided to hang up her apron and go to her heavenly reward, or, losing her skill, was encouraged

to sit by the stove on winter days and gabble about the
grand meals she had prepared and seen eaten a decade or
five ago. It was settled in Deborah's mind that Myrtis
would take over the kitchen when Cook was ready to
leave it. Myrtis was already a more than competent cook
of regular, plain fare, which was all that Deborah could
think was required by any reasonable household.

Pauline was an inspired cook. She made occasional
dishes when the mood struck her. She would take endless
time and pains to get a dish just right; her instinct was
sure, her taste sophisticated. Her special talent was for
sweet things. No one else had her way with cakes and pies
and more refined desserts. She did not, would not, bake to
order and every day. Leave that to Myrtis—her apple pie
or peach cobbler always seemed to consist mainly of
damp dough and thin syrup, and her cakes usually fea-
tured one layer that had been burned and scraped and icing heaped on thickly to hide the inward slope of the
cake's architecture.

Pauline's cakes and pies and tarts and custards and jellies and candies and cream confections were always received in the dining room with respect, gratitude, even
joy. They were gifts, not something to be taken for granted, or commanded. She worked truly by inspiration, and
she took special pains with lemony concoctions, hopeful
of pleasing Selma. The feeling of a bond is not always a
welcome or comfortable thing. Selma knew that some
strand linked her and Pauline, but she was not ready to
acknowledge it, and indeed she had no perception of its
nature and quality.

Almost a side occupation for Pauline was her interest in
and talent for remedies, which she learned from her father. Again: it was not for her to set up as doctor or
veterinarian or nurse; but she had used many hours to
watch Ezra at work over his mixings and brewings, and
she learned his skill of remembering just how things
would go differently with the veriest shade of difference in
the preparation. Common ills might wax or wane by common cures; her only interest was in the odd, the special.
She was happy in her way, and if she had secret dreams
and longings, she shared them with no one.

Floyd shared himself with any and everyone. He, too,
was happy enough. If anything, he had too much of company. Someone was always in his blacksmith shed. He was
a clever and conscientious workman. He had no patience
with what "would do." Everything must fit, be right, or it

was wrong. He worked hard, and still found times to fish with his father, make a horseshoe-nail ring for a child, mend a pot, sit and talk or listen to an old man or old woman who sat alone.

Nor did he lack for womankind. Without brag or swagger he attracted women and needed them. He took favors offered when the offer was without strings, and he gave his own favors in a way that involved him only temporarily. He never sought or took an advantage, would not touch a girl who fancied herself in love. Open and amiable to all as he seemed and indeed was to a certain degree, he was a man of privacies and shades of feeling he himself had not begun to sort and understand.

The most solid emotion he experienced was his friendship with his father. It was during this time they came to know each other best, value each other most. It was the time Ezra was most father, and Floyd was most son. It had little to do with words they spoke. There was a thing about being together, a trust, a comfort, a sudden explosion of love more like pain than laughter. Sometimes, as they sat on the creekbank where Floyd used to sit with Leon, it seemed to Floyd that he had never been as close to anyone outside his own self and never would be again. Saying nothing, sitting, watching the water, or the cork on a fishing line, listening to that mysterious life-hum of the creek, an understanding would come to Floyd that this was perfect love. He would never be worthy of such a father; his knowing that Ezra loved him above all others in the world was holier than God and angels. He wanted his father never to get older than he was at this moment. He wanted them always to sit thus side by side. Knowing it could not be only heightened the intensity of the love he felt, so that he had to be careful how much he showed to this man who was now visibly getting old, lest Ezra say, "What is it, son? Is anything troubling you?" There was no answer to that except, "No, Papa. I love you."

For all her free talk of wanting marriage and grandchildren from Pauline and Floyd, Lovey was perfectly content to have things go on as they were. Neither of her children, she thought, was likely to give her any serious trouble. Without understanding them, or wondering whether or not she did, she trusted them.

She worried more about Selma and Leon, whom she thought of as her other two children. She feared for Selma; she feared for Leon; and she distrusted Deborah and her plans for them, because Deborah's plans were not based on the needs and natures of her children, which she did not in any case comprehend, but rather on what Deborah herself thought might be most appropriate and advantageous. Deborah would scheme and make plans for those who should be left to take their own directions. Lovey could not prevent her, but she could continue to watch and perhaps interfere when a time came that made interference necessary and possible.

Five

Selma had lost her purity. No one who has it keeps it, and few even know when they have it, much less care about losing it. Selma held on to hers as long as she was able, but there were many things to corrupt and bend and fragment it, the strongest being, for Selma, a concern for people and things outside herself.

For a time she had been largely sufficient unto herself. For a time Deborah and what Deborah wanted her to be did not bother her for more than a passing, inconvenient moment; she was better and stronger than that. But her disregard, rather than active dislike, for her brother Leon was involvement of a kind. Her complex feelings about her father represented a truer and deeper involvement. When he lived, she wanted to love and to avoid him at the same time, to say in essence: "I love you, leave me alone." When he died, the love and avoidance became grief and anger and guilt. No one dies without someone living feeling guilt. Whatever; another loss of purity.

Then there was what she had seen between Leon and Clovis, and what had happened after—Leon's being away at school which, she knew, was only another way of keeping him away from home because of what he had done. There was the child Clovis had after her marriage to Roscoe, a pale, twisted thing, standing in Selma's mind for the wrongness of what she had seen happen between the two whose physical union resulted in his creation.

There was Aunt Nell and the way she made her body and mind lie to accommodate social conventions that offended her nature. There was Aunt Nell's very kindness—not, to be sure, a thing that ever put her out very much or that she allowed to get the upper hand of her. Still, it was there. Aunt Nell could not, Selma saw, be as selfish and private as she would have liked. And part of the reason for that was that Uncle Felix who, although a scoundrel by ordinary standards of behavior, was other things besides a scoundrel: a disappointed husband, a kind and foolish man with needs that had to do with nothing and no one but himself. So, Aunt Nell, with an almost perfect selfishness, could not be entirely true even to her own selfishness. Why would people interfere? Why would they interpose their qualities, good or bad, that made it impossible for a woman to be true to herself? Better the isolated selfishness than the meaningless involvements that turned aside honesty, fragmented the true self.

There was the school Selma had attended in Highboro: her experience there complementing her growing knowledge of her Aunt Nell and Uncle Felix. The girls she came to know had learned so early, so eagerly and automatically to deny they were themselves, or had a true, private self, they would now deny such a denial had been made—and believe they spoke truth in doing so. Is a girl born thinking the color pink, or a soft curl, or a mincy walk, or a put-on tender smile, or an affected giggle is feminine and to be desired? Who made such rules? Why is it wrong, if it is, to think more about rain than a mother? Would the world end if she burnt her Bible and never thought of it again? If she denied that music (the only kind *they* understood) was music at all to her ear?

At the first doubt or hesitation, purity and innocence begin the slow rust into what is called "experience" and "learning about life." And when one is totally corrupted and compromised, one may then be considered "mature."

In desperate need of some touch, some reassurance, Selma fell in love with a young schoolmate whose name was Elizabeth-Ann Malone and who was everything Selma was not—conventional, accepting, approving, hopeful. Even as she scoffed at her, as she scolded her young love for bowing to false idols, she herself began to accept those idols and in time found that she was able, if she tried very hard, to behave like the other girls: to shriek in seeming terror at an unexpected noise, to giggle at any small bit of dull news, to pretend a concern for clothes and cooking and sewing and even babies—to, indeed, "grow up," betrayed and betraying all the purity and innocence and good, true selfishness she had been born with.

Bonard's was another, and a different self-deception. Having been self-seeking and self-satisfying, he now felt a hunger for purity and innocence, and thought he saw these exemplified in the person of Selma. For all her re-

cent seeming collaboration with convention, she was still
unusual and original enough in appearance and conversation to delight by her freshness anyone who considered
himself as jaded or sated with conventional society as
Bonard considered himself to be.

Between them and not knowing it—in fact, they would
have denied it had it been stated—both Selma and Bonard
were ready to play parts in Deborah's scheme of an alliance between them.

Haughty though he was to his inferiors, Bonard was
lively and charming when with Selma; and she who could
be odd to the point of eccentricity became in Bonard's
company the mild, shy maiden, a Sleeping Beauty to be
quickened to life again by the kiss of the Prince.

Bonard looked a prince. He set great store on personal
cleanliness, both of his person and apparel, so there was
nothing about him to offend Selma's sensibilities. Smitten
by the young girl, Bonard looked all alert, and his mere
alertness looked like sensitivity to the young girl.

Deborah's hints to Selma were clumsy and obvious,
which perversely only served to set off Bonard's sensitivity
in a stronger and more sympathetic light. But it was
Rooster's marrying Trudy that put the cap on the doll.

There were parties at which Bonard regularly heard,
"Appears to me, Bonard, your young brother has beat you
to it."

There were female parties for Trudy at which Selma
heard repeatedly, "What a fine family the Davises are, to
be sure!"

And there were parties attended by both Selma and
Bonard where it seemed to fall naturally that they were
together, or placed together by name cards, and they fell
into a joking way of comparing experiences and exchanging mockeries about those around them. Eager to please
her, Bonard had little more to do than nod and smile for
Selma to believe that he thought and felt as she did, that
there truly was a special bond between them.

Never really alone, they affected to treasure the brief
pauses they shared in society when someone by chance
left them, before someone else came in. One time—had it
been a more humid day, it might not have happened, or
would have happened differently—caught alone, they
chanced to turn at the same time to face each other and
something in their look of surprise at this coincidence,
sharpened by the electricity of the dry air, gave the moment importance. That moment persuaded Selma that she

could love Bonard. Quick to see in her eyes what had
happened, he took her hands in his, and a minute later
they were engaged to be married.

Six

There was brief talk of a double wedding, but Bonard's
pride would not sanction that; he could not seem to follow and join his younger brother. So Trudy and Rooster
were married in February, and Trudy was pregnant before
the wedding date of Selma and Bonard was finally set for
the middle of May.

Curiously, having given her promise and allowed it to
be made public, Selma did not back away. Once they were
engaged to be married, Selma and Bonard were even less
often alone than they had been when unpromised. They
allowed themselves to be taken over by others, to become
puppet dolls for all the hands and wills about them.

Laura-Lou, the seamstress who had come from Oaks to
Beulah Land when Flossie married Monday Kendrick and
went to Oaks, excellent though she was, would not do for
the finer wedding apparel. Surprisingly, Nell commanded
the energy to escort Selma to Savannah, where they stayed
with the three Misses Pennington, and Nell and Selma
chose the wedding clothes, or rather, Nell chose them,
with passionate opinions given by the Misses Pennington,
and considered and rejected or accepted by Nell, for
Selma did not care at all what she would wear. A cloth
rose at the wrist band was the matter of debate for days,
its final approval a triumph for those who had championed
it, a rout for those who had opposed it.

Nell showed herself at this time to be tireless, not at all
the languid lady she was satisfied to be at home. She was
sharp and shrewd with clerks and seamstresses, firmly
argued this ribbon against that, looked with cold and
knowing eye on crochet and embroidery, glared at lace
to discover its dishonesties, demanded always and often
received near perfection.

And still Selma remained calm and uninvolved. She enjoyed the experience of Savannah, where she had never
been before, but thought it far too large and bustling. Its
population, including slaves, was said to be between eight
and nine thousand! She could not conceive of there being
that many human souls anywhere in one place on earth,

and remembered in a shallow wrinkle of her brain a question she had once put to her father: "Papa, are there Chinamen?"

Most of what she saw was from the carriage that took them about to shops, and less often to pay calls. And twice they found energy and inclination enough to attend plays performed by a stock company at the Savannah Theatre in Chippewa Square. Selma quite liked the oldest Miss Pennington and quickly adopted the habit of the nieces of calling her "Aunt Pea." She found Lauretta a little daunting—so pretty, so sure of herself, so much a city girl. Sarah was less forbidding. In contrast to her older sister she seemed almost mousy. Having decided that, Selma realized with a flash of perception that she was wrong. Sarah was a girl who kept her own counsel, guarded her privacies, waited for a worthy occasion. Selma liked both girls, and she liked their aunt, and for the first time in her life thought there might be taste and judgment in her mother for having made such a friend as "Aunt Pea," however long ago it had been done and however much her mother had changed since.

Impulsively, she asked them to come and stay at Beulah Land when she was to be married; but Aunt Pea would not commit them to such a spontaneous proposal and replied that they might all enjoy a time in the country when things were less hectic than they were bound to be in the course of wedding preparations.

During the busy time Nell and Selma were with the Penningtons, Bonard and Leon made a sudden, brief raid on the city. Their trip had been spur of the moment, initiated by Bonard, eagerly agreed to by Leon. They were noisy and mysterious about the reason for their coming, both at home and at the Pennington house during the three hours they allowed themselves to be persuaded to dine and visit. Most of the visit was the occasion for Lauretta to charm the young men. Those three hardly allowed attention to veer to anyone else for even a moment; the others became audience. After the young men had taken their leave, Lauretta exclaimed delightedly that Mr. Davis must be as shy as he was enamored, seeing how he had insisted on talking to her because he was evidently too embarrassed to talk to his beloved in company; whereas Mr. Kendrick clearly, she avowed, had a preference for her sister Sarah, because it was well known that young gentlemen avoided talking to those they favored, and chattered easily only with those present they would scarcely recognize were they to meet them again.

Sarah made no comment on this diagnosis of the evening, but Selma looked sharply questioning at her Aunt
Nell, who yawned. If there was one thing, Nell allowed,
that she had no knowledge of, it was the ways of young
men and what went on in their minds to dictate their perverse behavior; at which they all laughed and felt more
friendly toward one another.

The reason for Bonard and Leon's trip to Savannah was
no mystery at all. They had come for a good time, for
what Bonard called "a last spree." They took lodgings at
an inn, avoiding their old landlady who would have
treated them like schoolboys again. They ate richly, drank
immoderately, and went every night to the whorehouse
they had known and often patronized during the years
they attended Samuel Holt's Academy for young gentlemen.

They returned home, a shaky and pale Bonard who, it
was supposed, had been so bereft when his bride-to-be
was absent in Savannah choosing clothes to please him
that he had followed her there to make the best of whatever glimpses or brief periods of her company she could
afford him; and a Leon who appeared to be amused and
pleased with life, and himself most of all. After them
came a preoccupied Selma with her proud Aunt Nell, the
repository and giver of all knowledge about the dozens of
garments that had been commissioned, designed, made, fitted, and finally approved.

And then began the time when the two principals of the
coming event hardly saw each other at all, except in the
company of a dozen or so others. Supposedly the center-
piece of each party, they were actually treated more like
dolls now than before. The only demand on them was that
they be present and look happy. The courtiers ruled the
castle. The convenience and feelings of the dottiest great
aunt or most uncivil cousin were considered over theirs.

Ritual and regimentation are strong anti-aphrodisiacs.
When they had done their work, Selma and Bonard might
have been mere gingerbread figures. no longer even dolls,
so blank did they feel toward each other.

Seven

The log Selma sat upon lay half in, half out of water.
Trailing the fingers of a hand in the creek, she was hardly
aware of what she did, for the water was as warm as her
blood on the May morning of the day she was to be married.

She had waked early even for her, having retired to her
room early the evening before after telling her mother and
Aunt Nell she wished to be alone. Bonard, with Rooster
and his cheery, pregnant Trudy, had been guests of the
Kendricks for the evening supper, and Leon had ridden
back beside the carriage that conveyed the young Davises
home to Oaks, after Selma had wished them all a quiet
good night. The homegoing party was thoughtful and content. Only Leon now and then trotted his horse close to
the carriage and made a mild, agreeable joke with his
friend Bonard. As they turned off the main road to the
narrow one leading to Oaks, their sudden laughter at
Leon's latest quip, accompanied by a homecoming whin-
nying of the horses, flushed a flock of birds that had gone
to roost for the night in roadbank shrubbery.

Alone in her bedroom, Selma made a last inspection of
the odd things left in her wardrobe. A trunk was packed
with her new clothes, its lid left open to accommodate any
late decision or reconsideration. At the bottom of the
wardrobe—how had she not seen them before?—she
found the old red canvas shoes Lovey had made for her
long ago. Trying them, she discovered that they still fit, although a little snugly and stiffly.

So she wore them this morning, leaving the house so
early the smoke from breakfast fires was only beginning
to curl from the cabin chimneys as she picked her way
through the rows of the corn field and into the woods, finally stopping here to rest on the log that had fallen in a
storm two winters ago and settled naturally into mud and
sand.

Frowning, Selma removed the slippers and then sat like
a child with her feet in the water. She arched her feet
slowly and stared at them with fascination. They might
have been pale fishes there just beneath the surface. Then
she drew them out of the water up onto the log, making a

high angle of her knees and resting her arms and head on them.

The wedding was to be at noon. The only house guests at Beulah Land were her Aunt Nell and Uncle Felix. Others, who had come from a distance and required lodging, stayed at Oaks; and there was a large family of cousins who had temporarily taken over Nell's house in town. The rector of St. Thomas's, the Reverend Curtis Lamont, was to marry Selma to Bonard. He and his wife, even now, readied themselves to drive in their new buggy the three miles from Highboro to Beulah Land.

The ceremony would take place in the wide center hall which yesterday had been cleared and lined with great pots of Boston fern, and this morning would be further furnished with chairs at the sides for the elderly and infirm (others would stand), and decorated with fresh cut flowers of all the kinds the gardens of Beulah Land afforded, as well as branches of the waxen-leafed magnolias that seemed appropriate to every special occasion, summer and winter.

The kitchen had for the last several days been a tense and temperish center of activity where cakes were baked and hams were boiled, and where this morning chickens would be fried, salads prepared, jars of various delicacies opened and set out ready for consumption after the wedding had been performed. Though a Friday, it was a holiday for the people of Beulah Land; they would feast on fried chicken and cake, corn and melons.

Selma closed her eyes and tried to bring to focus in her mind an image of her lover's face, but it would not be summoned, and presently she opened her eyes to look about her. She would be going soon. She must, or they would wonder where she was. The notion of causing her mother worry pleased her.

Deborah had long wanted this day, and now it was come. She had for so many years made observations on the suitability of such a union, the blessings and convenience that were bound to ensure if it were effected; and now it was to be.

Did she love him? Yes, she loved him, if she knew what such love was. She believed that it involved more of a willingness to be receptive to him than a more passionate and active emotion. Did she know him? Yes, she had always known him, never remembered when he was not trying to please her. When she was a child and he had seemed to her already a grown man, he had given her such special looks, and a softer consideration than he gave to anyone else. It was that particular kindness he evidenced toward her alone that had finally disposed her to have him, and not Deborah's unceasing advocacy of his suit.

Nothing could have persuaded her to accept him if she had not decided that, whatever he was to others, to her he had always been and would always be gentle, a gentle man. She was ignorant, and she knew it. The only knowledge she had of the private side of the relationship of a man and a woman was from the shocked observation she had once made of her brother and the Negro girl Clovis, such ages ago she should have forgot it. *They* were mere animals. It would be different for her, she knew; but she did not know how. She tried once to open the subject with her Aunt Nell, but that lady only looked at her in a mild, puzzled way and suggested to the girl that preliminary speculation was of no value in her opinion, and that as for her, she believed she could say that she and Selma's uncle had shared a long and near-perfect bliss—their joy marred only by their joint concern over the delicacy of her health. Perhaps that could not be considered a flaw in their happiness. Did it not, after all, bring them closer in the most loving regard and consideration? Was it not perhaps even the very flower instead of the thorn in their union? In any case, Selma was not to worry. She would be happy; Nell assured her she would be.

Over the rank reek of mud slime that always emanated from the creekbank, there was a scent from the woods of flowering blackberry and honeysuckle and scuppernong that gave such a fragrance to the day as declared it special and blessed. Without consciously deciding to, Selma suddenly brushed the canvas slippers off the log into the stream, as if in doing so she brushed her girlhood away and became a woman. The unexpectedness of the action provoked her to laughter. Watching the red canvas shoes float away and sink to the darkness of the creek's depth, the girl stood up, bracing the sides of the log with firmed toes, and laughed until tears came; and then frightened a little at the unusual display she had made, she turned to go home.

Lovey was at the back door, Lovey worried and waiting. It was Deborah she had been pleased at the notion of fretting, not Lovey. The girl began to run, and running, opened her arms. Seeing her coming, Lovey's relief became anger. "There you are! Where *have* you been? No shoes! Child! Child!"

By then Selma had found and enfolded her. They both chuckled and cooed in the warm security of their love for each other. Conspirators, they ceased all sound as they left the breezeway and entered the wide hall. They tiptoed past the dining room where Deborah and Leon, Nell and Felix were having breakfast—the air rich with the smell of biscuits and fried ham and gravy and coffee—and into the office-stairwell room. As they ascended, arms about each other's waist, they lost the smell of the breakfast food. Two of the house servants had brought in large baskets of fresh cut roses, white and pink and yellow and red, that would be arranged later by Nell, who was considered to have a special way with flowers.

"It smells like a summer funeral," Selma observed.

"Don't say! Don't you!" Lovey said fiercely as they came to the top of the stairs.

Eight

While Selma bathed in the hat-shaped tub that was moved from bedroom to bedroom depending on who required it, and had been an hour ago set in hers and filled with heated water, Lovey went down to the kitchen and brought up a tray with coffeepot and cups and a plate of thin-sliced pound cake. In her other hand she carried a kettle of boiling water, which she added to Selma's tub after she had set down the tray. When Selma screamed and stood in the bathtub, Lovey gave her a towel for her face, and using another towel for her back, helped dry the girl, giving her neck and head the brisk rubbing which Selma always protested but which always relaxed her.

Selma looked about the room. There was her wedding dress, spread as carefully as an altar cloth over the counterpane of the made-up bed she supposed she would never sleep in again. "Where is my trunk?" she asked.

"Skeeter come and got it while ago," Lovey said. "Put it on the wagon for Plumboy to carry to Oaks. It be there, or nearly, by now." Selma frowned but did not speak. "Something else you want to take? Ain't the end of the earth. I expect things to be going back and forth every day, if not every hour."

Selma shook her head. "It seems funny, my things over there."

"Better get used to it." Lovey handed her underclothes, and then poured a cup of coffee, adding a lot of cream the way Selma liked it.

Selma sat on a stool and accepted the cup Lovey offered her. "Drink coffee with me, Lovey," she said.

Lovey paused to look at her. Selma was like a child again as she sat on the stool in her underclothes. Lovey poured herself a cup of coffee, leaving it black. She picked up the plate of cake and offered it to Selma, who took a slice and ate it greedily in three bites that were so quickly consecutive as to appear almost one bite. She took another piece before Lovey set the plate down on the sewing table beside the stool, so that it was within Selma's reach. Lovey pinched off the corner of a cake slice and tasted it critically. "Lemony," she said.

Selma nodded. "Pauline did it for me, because she knows." She ate a third slice and licked her fingers, greasy from the butter in the cake. "I don't know, Lovey."

"Of course you do!" Lovey said, frowning and drawing in her chin. There was a knock at the hall door. "Who is it?" Lovey asked crankily as she went to the door and opened it, revealing Nell Kendrick's personal maid, brought out by her from Highboro.

"It's me, Bianca," the woman said. "I come to do the hair." Bianca was complacent about her skill in dressing hair. She carried her special comb and brush, although similar items were to be found on Selma's dresser top, and Bianca knew it; but she knew, too, that it added to her reputation if she insisted on using her own tools. In a large apron pocket she carried a special pair of scissors and curling irons, and behind her stood Buttercup with a kettle of hot water and a deep, wide china bowl. Buttercup put her burdens down on a side table and went out.

Bianca set her equipment on the dresser, and then with scant grace told Selma to sit down on a straight-backed chair she had dragged over to the dresser, and to be so good as to move and talk as little as possible. Mercilessly, on the common theory that what hurt was good, Bianca combed and brushed, pulled, twisted, and fluffed Selma's hair until she had tamed it. Presently Buttercup returned with her sister Posie, who carried an oil lamp that had been lighted with a straw from the kitchen stove, and which Bianca needed to heat her curling irons.

When the tongs were hot enough, she withdrew them

from the lamp chimney and wiped off the smoke film on her apron before gripping a rope of hair with the tongs and rolling it over the tongs to cook until a curl was made and held. Then Bianca loosened the tongs and slipped them carefully out, leaving a stiff, unnatural curl to be admired by those who stood watching.

Lovey stood to one side scowling. She maintained authority over the preparation scene by being the only one who sipped coffee, setting the cup back into the ridged circle of the saucer with a clank that made Buttercup and Posie start, although Bianca appeared not to notice her at all.

Selma stared into the looking glass over the dresser and saw her hair being tortured into the general lineaments of her Aunt Nell's on other formal occasions.

After the hair was curled and arranged, the petticoat and the wedding dress were put on the girl as tenderly as a cook will mold whipped egg white. The dress, which had been made in Savannah, was simple but fine: white satin with an outer covering of lace, the neckline dipping to the top of Selma's bosom, the waist gathered in to further emphasize the rounding of the bosom. The lace and satin skirt billowed generously and fell to the top of Selma's white satin slippers. There was no train and no veil, but when the time approached for the actual wedding, Lovey would set on the crown of Selma's hair a tiara-shaped three-quarter circle of lace fern and the small white flowers they called snowdrops.

As Posie knelt to guide Selma's feet into the satin shoes, Nell knocked at the door and came in without having been acknowledged. Behind her came Myrtis carrying a tray with a pitcher of lemonade and glasses, a task she was now too important to perform except on such a special occasion. She had wanted to see the young mistress close up in her wedding clothes so as to go back to those in the kitchen with a fresh sensation. Even as Myrtis stared at the nearly bride, Nell went to Selma and put a prayer book into her hands.

"Something borrowed, old, and blue," she said. "Carry it and think of me." She kissed Selma's cheek and fled the room as if pursued by satyrs.

As she left, those attending Selma heard the noise from downstairs. The guests having assembled now moved closer as the important hour approached.

Lovey poured a glass of lemonade and sipped from it as a royal taster might have before handing it to Selma.

"Sour," Lovey pronounced it.

"Pauline knows," Selma answered automatically.

The shoes on, Posie rose from the floor with an important groan, Buttercup helping her both to rise and to groan. Those two then blotted with thin soft cloths Selma's exposed face and neck and bosom and arms and hands, and applied to them a mixture of cornstarch and scented powder with cotton puffs.

After them Bianca came with a small chamois cloth she had dipped in oil and now applied to Selma's lips; then quickly wiped each of her fingernails so that they shone pinkly. Selma stared curiously at her image in the looking glass.

Another knock at the door was followed by Leon's entrance. Eager, smiling, face flushed and hands nervous, he took from his waistcoat pocket a brooch pin and held it out for Selma to see. "Something new," he said. "Do you like it?" Against a taupe oval rimmed with gold was a delicately wrought profile in ivory of a young girl's head that might have been Selma's own.

"Yes, I do. Thank you, Leon. Thank you," Selma said, as if caught dreaming. "Where is Mama?"

Leon looked surprised. "With the guests. I am to escort you downstairs when you are ready and give you away. Are you? Ready, I mean? It's time."

Selma looked about, confused, the vague smile fading from her face. She turned her body, keeping her feet in place as if they were weighted to the floor. "Am I ready, Lovey?"

Without looking at the girl Lovey said to Leon, "Is everything down there ready?" Leon nodded. Lovey turned to Posie. "Go see." Posie started out of the room, but Lovey overtook and stopped her. "I better." She went out, leaving the door open. The buzzing sound from downstairs was stronger now than before. Presently, after a signal from Lovey had been relayed down to the pianist and singer below, music began, at first the piano, tentatively, gathering authority; and then after a pause, a soprano sang of love eternal.

As she sang. Lovey returned to Selma, and when her eyes met the girl's, she nodded. She took the tiara of fern and snowdrops from the damp cloth where it had waited and fixed them on Selma's crown of curls.

Before Lovey's hands could drop to her sides, Selma grasped and kissed them in such a fierce way as surprised all except Lovey. Leon offered his arm to his sister, and

Selma put a small hand into the crooked elbow which Leon then pressed hard against his side. Lovey placed the prayer book Nell had brought, now with the stem of a white rose separating its closed halves, into Selma's free hand. It served to steady and occupy the hand.

Gradually becoming more aware of the music as it gained in volume and they left the bedroom, went into the upper hallway and on to the stairs, Selma and Leon adjusted their walking to its rhythm. When they were seen from below to start their descent, the song ended, and the piano began the Wedding March. Down the stairs they proceeded, and when they came to the bottom, walked out to the wide hallway. Selma had known it all her life, had walked or run through it a dozen times a day. Now it was like entering an arena of wild beasts.

The older guests were sitting on the chairs provided at the sides of the hall, and they turned to find her, the ones who did not see so well asking each other, "Is she there? Is she coming now?"

The others, standing, turned too, and their faces were all strange to Selma. There was no face she knew, only masks from nightmare. She stopped, but Leon held her hand in his arm, her body against his, and when he stepped again, she found herself forced to step with him.

There was Deborah, her back stiff, her head round as a melon—and Aunt Nell who, having arranged for all the clothes, now affected to be fainty-weak; Uncle Felix, an arm supporting Aunt Nell; Benjamin Davis in his wheeled chair, attended by his wife Edna and the ever-present Monday; Trudy alone because Rooster acted as Best Man; Selma's old school friend, Elizabeth-Ann Malone, looking as if she might at any moment succumb to laughter.

There, finally, was Bonard with his brother. Bonard's face was turned to her, his lips set in a grimace that might have begun as a smile, his eyeballs moving only a little, and that with seeming effort, as though to keep from freezing in their sockets.

Beyond Bonard was the Reverend Curtis Lamont, looking solemn as a crow, and beyond him, crowding the breezeway, were the dark, entranced faces of the Negroes of Beulah Land, made suddenly anonymous in their mute curiosity. Jesus on the cross, Joan at the stake and feeling the flames climb her legs, could not have felt more forsaken than Selma, putting one foot before the other until she stood beside Bonard. As he took her hand and her brother stepped back and away, Selma picked out one

face from the otherwise unrecognized dark tapestry of
faces on the breezeway behind the rector. It was Pauline,
who looked back at her as if her heart had broken.

Nine

After the period of eating and drinking that followed the
wedding ceremony, the married couple, the bridegroom's
father and mother, the father's attendant, the brother and
sister-in-law had finally taken their leave and made their
way in two carriages to Oaks, where they found another
celebration party in progress. Fatigued nearly to hysteria,
Selma yet found strength to walk smiling among the
slaves who were so energetically rejoicing in her marriage.

Seeing how she was, and remembering his and Trudy's
feelings at the time of their still recent wedding, Rooster
took matters in hand. His father was tired, so Rooster
urged him to go to bed, which he did, helped there by Monday. Rooster and Trudy and Edna remained at the party,
mingling and talking and smiling and clapping their hands
with the rhythm of the dancing, while Bonard and Selma
slipped away upstairs to begin their honeymoon.

Bonard closed the door of his bedroom, shutting out
the sounds of celebration that came from belowstairs. He
then pried off his shoes, using his own feet to serve each
other, and ripped the cravat from his throat.

Except that the floral tiara which Lovey had placed on
her hair was now lost, Selma was dressed as she had been
for the wedding, but there were stains on the lace and
gown, made when champagne spilled from the glasses of
guests who had pressed too close to offer wishes for her
happiness.

Perfectly confident, Bonard went to her and crushed
her to him. Presently, she pushed him away. "No, Bonard." He looked at her surprised, and took her to him
again. After a moment during which his hands moved and
groped her flesh, she pulled away and slapped his face,
not having calculated to do so, but being tired and taking
offense at his insensitivity, and finding his face close at
hand. The slap shocked him to alertness. He was tired
too, and he had drunk beyond his usual capacity to absorb and use the alcohol he took in. He reached with both
hands.

"Don't! Please don't, Bonard!"

The dress began to tear at the neck where he had caught it. She slapped at his hands, and he moved them down to her breasts and squeezed hard. She pushed him away. He lost his balance and fell to the floor; then panting and angry, got to his feet and threw himself at her, outraged at her rejection.

Close, body to body, face to face, hands engaging hands, they struggled, equally at first, but his strength, now inspired by anger, outlasted hers.

"Your father will hear—" she warned desperately.

He shook his head. "He sleeps downstairs by the kitchen now—"

"Trudy—your mother—" she said, to threaten him, but also as if she hoped for help from them. Bonard went to the door to the hallway and opened it a crack. The sounds of music and dancing came from below at such a steady pitch it was obvious the celebrants would hear nothing beyond their own clamor.

Bonard closed the door and turned to Selma. They stared at each other. He caught her by the arm as she began to move away, and she cried out, but his free hand slapped and then held her mouth tightly so that she could only moan. In clumsy fury he ripped her dress away in shreds and great, hanging pieces. When she freed herself enough to scream again, he held her from behind with one hand slapped again over her mouth. They both breathed heavily, as much from exhaustion as from emotion. Bonard, still holding her mouth closed, said, his voice puzzled and pleading, "What's got into you, Selma? You're supposed to *let* me!"

She struggled.

"Don't you know anything? Didn't anybody ever tell you?"

She struggled again and then was still. He took her stillness for surrender and turned her to face him. "I *love* you, Selma—this don't mean I don't. I've wanted to fuck you ever since you were a little girl so pretty and proud you wouldn't look at another soul. Now, you going to be good?"

She drew her head back and spat into his face. His left hand wiped his face with almost as much rage as his right hand slapped hers. "God damn you, girl! You can't do that to me—" He grabbed both her arms and shook her hard. "Now, you going to be good and do your duty by me? Then everything'll be all right. You going to be good? It won't take long, and I promise not to hurt you more than I can help."

She said nothing, her breathing hard and irregular, her chest rising and falling in spasms.

"Selma, honey, I don't want it to *be* this way! Won't you be sweet to me?" He dropped his hands from her arms.

"I hate you, Bonard."

"Selma, don't. Don't you talk to me that way. I reckon you are just about the most ignorant girl for her age I ever saw. Don't you know when a man and woman marry, they take off their clothes and lie down together and do things—or he does, and she lets him?" When she remained silent, he shook his head despairingly and said, "You don't understand a word I'm saying, do you, Honey?"

"I hate you."

His heart and mind closed against her only a second before his eyes showed it. She drew away, genuinely frightened for the first time. Again he was quick. He grabbed her by one wrist and then caught the other and held her. "You not going to let me?"

She drew her chin in and her face back as far from him as she could.

"You not?"

She shook her head.

"You not even gonna let me kiss you?"

She stared at him unblinking.

"Let me kiss your pretty little mouth?"

She shook her head.

"You never gonna let me kiss you? That what you saying?"

She shook her head, her eyes hating and frightened.

"You must think you something, don't you? You don't know nothing. Not one damn little thing, you hear me?"

She made a pause in her breathing. "You're drunk and crazy."

"If you don't let me like you supposed to, I'll have to just make you." Quickly he undid his trousers and stepped out of them when they dropped to the floor. Pulling his genitals free from his drawers, he cupped his balls with one hand and shook his penis with the other. "Your education begins now. You see this, gal? This here is a big, hard dick—this here is *me*. Understand? This is the best thing there is, and whether you want to or not, you're

going to have it shoved up your little pussy. It'd be easier
for me and you both if you acted nice, but however you
act, it's gonna be my way."

She backed away from him, shaking her head quickly
again and again in total rejection of him and of all he
said.

"Don't you run from me," he said, his voice mean
now. "Don't you holler, neither—don't you squawk like
no chicken!"

She sprang toward the door with what strength she had
left, but he caught her as she opened it. The sound of music and shuffling feet came up the stairwell. He pulled her
back and shut the door, shutting the world out, shutting
them in together.

"I was wrong, Bonard. I was wrong to marry you. I'm
sorry, but you've got to let me go now. I didn't know
what it all meant. I can't do what you want. Let me go,
for pity's sake!"

He held his penis again and stroked it. "Now that's a
pretty thing, don't you think so? It's give me a lot of pleasure, and it could pleasure you too, were you willing."

"Please, Bonard. Please. I'm begging you. Please—"

"You sure you not going to let me do it?"

She shook her head in terrified jerks.

"You not? You right sure you not?"

Ten

She woke herself moaning and choking on her own
phlegm. As consciousness returned, she raised her head
from the floor where he had left her. "Thank God," she
breathed, telling herself that she was at least and at last
alone. Knowing only that, needing only that for the moment, she kept her head up from the floor, although to do
so was an effort, and her head swayed, nodded, and
drooped, as if seeking a pillow to rest on. He was—somewhere in the room. She could hear him breathing and
snoring. He, him.

She raised herself to lean on an elbow. Her elbow was
skinned raw from the coarse rug. Her crotch was fiery
and aching. She opened her legs a little to ease its fever,
then closed them automatically in a self-protective grip.

Another two or three minutes, and she knew he was on
the bed, and that he continued to sleep. Her mind would

not go back over the earlier part of the night, but it did register a fact or two. She was at Oaks. She had been— He was now asleep. She looked toward the sound of his snoring, her head nodding with fatigue that looked like a gesture of dumb assent.

If she remained very still for a while, perhaps she would be all right.

No, she would not be all right. She should go to the bed and kill him where he slept.

She let herself droop back upon the floor, her head resting on the rug, its dust touching her nostrils as its coarse weave touched her cheek.

A great effort was required for her to sit. A quarter of an hour later she stood with the help of a chair. She was too tired to stand. She let herself down carefully to the floor again, and then she crawled slowly to the door.

Reaching up she found the knob and turned it until the door swung open—silently, she thanked God. On all fours, she crawled into the hallway where she lay resting for half an hour before she thought she was capable of trying the stairs. The party was long over. She heard not a sound. Finding the stair railing, she pulled herself erect and, holding the railing with both hands, crept down the stairs and out of the door of the house, vowing that she would never enter it again.

Eleven

As he'd grown older, and he was now sixty-eight, Ezra had become a light and restless sleeper, as a result of which his family had changed their sleeping arrangements. Lovey and Pauline shared the largest bed in the biggest room, which served as both bed and sitting room. Ezra slept on a cot in the kitchen, so that he could brew his medicines on the stove at any odd hours he chose, and go in and out the back door day or night without troubling anyone. Not many meals other than breakfast were cooked and eaten in the cabin. Lovey and Pauline ate from the kitchen of the main house and sent a basket of select victuals to Floyd in the blacksmith shed, where Ezra often joined him to eat. Floyd himself slept in a lean-to he had built onto the cabin, which was intended mostly for storage and to shelter the smaller sick animals Ezra wanted near him during the night. Only when the weather was coldest did Floyd spread a pallet on the kitchen floor near his father's cot.

As Floyd woke now in the lean-to, it was still dark; no light came through the crack in the wall just above his eye level; but he knew it was day, or nearly so, and when a moment later he heard the first crowing of a rooster, he smiled and rolled over on his back, raising his knees to make a tent of the single sheet that covered him. It was a new day, and he woke ready for it.

He was glad the wedding was over and hoped that things would quickly settle back into normal order. Unlike most of the others on the place, he did not like holidays or special events that for him disrupted, for them broke up in a welcome way the steady rhythm of life at Beulah Land. He was master of his work, and although much of it was routine, he found interest in a good many things that came his way to do or to mend or make. He was his own man, slave or not. No one told him what to do, not even Roscoe, and he was, if unfulfilled and sometimes restless to find or do something he could not have named, he was not an unhappy man.

When he had dressed, he stepped into the kitchen where he found Ezra at the stove waiting for him. The two men did not speak, but they nodded to each other, and Ezra poured out two cups of coffee, which they drank slowly, remaining standing, each engaged by his own morning thoughts.

Finishing the coffee, Floyd set cup and saucer down on the kitchen table and said, "Going to check my lines."

"Come with you," Ezra said. They heard a stirring in the bedroom, and presently Lovey showed herself at the door in her long nightgown that fell to the floor and covered her feet, so that she had to hold it when she walked.

"I'll get breakfast directly," she said.

"No hurry," Ezra told her. "I'm going with Floyd to check his lines."

She nodded and went back into the bedroom.

They stepped out the back door, leaving it open to let fresh air into the house. By now it was light, although the sun had not yet risen. A friendly hound on his morning tour of the grounds trotted over and sniffed inquisitively at Floyd's hand. When he nuzzled Ezra's side as if asking for food, Ezra gave him a not unkind kick, and the two men proceeded on their way.

The sky was high and clear; in the east it had brightened and reddened. A light breeze ruffled the leaves of

the high sunflower stalks, and when the men got beyond
them into the corn field, they paused and peed, Ezra taking longer about it than Floyd because he was old and his
controls were not as responsive as his son's.

They went into the woods and to the creek, following
no path but picking a way that brought them in a straight
short line to the water. They came out just where Floyd
had set his first line the evening before, when he had wanted to get away from the dancing and drinking and general celebration that continued long into the night. There
would be no further call on him that night, he knew, for
all the wedding guests had gone, except Felix and Nell
Kendrick, who were to stay on for a few days so that Nell
might, as she said, regain a little strength after all the
physical and emotional exertion she had endured.

There was nothing on the first line. When Floyd drew it
up, they saw that all but a small bit of bait, that just
around the hook, had been nibbled away during the night.

They looked at each other briefly and smiled. "Smart
old catfish, bet you," Ezra said. "Like he was taunting us."

Floyd dropped the line back into the water. He would
reset it tonight, perhaps moving it along the bank to another location. The next two lines each yielded a catfish,
and Floyd removed them from the hooks carefully to
avoid their spiky fins.

"Be good for breakfast," Ezra said.

After they followed a bend in the course of the water,
they stopped stock-still, not knowing at first what it was
they saw, then knowing and hurrying toward her, for it
was Selma. She had apparently gone to sleep with her
head against the log that rested one end on the sandy
bank and the other on the sloping muddy bottom of the
creek.

Her dress, what was left of it, was rags. Her feet were
bare, their tops and her ankles crisscrossed with blood
scratches. Her bosom was uncovered and bruised, as were
her upper arms. Her hair was a tangle, her face white as
death. They feared that she was indeed dead, but when
Ezra dropped the fish he carried and knelt beside her and
touched her flesh, he nodded his head, and then gingerly,
with both hands, lifted her to a sitting position, whereupon she opened her eyes.

For a few seconds her eyes and mouth were wide, as in
a silent scream, until she seemed to remember or to see
and comprehend where she was. Then she made clear that
she recognized him. As she had many times when a little

girl, tired from her wanderings over the plantation, she now said, "Take me home, Ezra," and closed her eyes as she said it.

Floyd picked her up in his arms, and Ezra led the way to a main path that was wide enough so that the foliage would not slap their sides as they made their way. They went quickly, Ezra ahead, Floyd carrying the girl in a sometimes clumsy and stumbling run, until they came back to the kitchen door of the cabin.

Lovey needed only one look. "Lord God," she breathed, and went into the big room where Pauline had just finished making up their bed. Floyd followed and set Selma down on the bed and stood back. Pauline stared. Lovey dismissed Ezra and Floyd with a brief head motion, and they returned to the kitchen. Ham was frying in a skillet, and Ezra took a fork and turned it, to be doing something while they waited. Pauline came in, grabbed a tin washpan from its nail on the wall and a kettle of hot water from the stove top and returned to her mother and the girl.

The two men waited again, standing, not looking at each other. They heard the soft, shocked, angry exclamations of their women and the fierce tearing of a sheet to make cloths to clean the girl's wounds. In a little while Pauline came out with the washpan, now filled with dirty, bloody water. She stepped to the kitchen door and threw the water into the yard, and then she faced them.

"Papa, you go tell Miss Deb, Mama says. Floyd, you come and carry her to the house when we get her wrapped in a quilt." Ezra left instantly.

Before she could go ahead of him into the room, Floyd said, "Is she awake? Can you tell how bad she is?"

Pauline's eyes spoke her fury before her words did. "She look like she's been chewed by dogs."

Twelve

And so, Beulah Land provided another sensation for the town and county. There was no possible way of keeping the affair secret. Word of Selma's return from her new husband's house and of her condition on that return spread rapidly among the Negroes of Beulah Land. They were, with the exception of Roscoe and his wife, fierce partisans of Selma's. They loved her and accepted her as she was in a way her family never had done, and they knew that she loved and accepted them too as they were. Wrong done to her was wrong done to them. They pitied her and were angry for her. When all was known, Deborah was wise enough to tell Roscoe, not that he needed such prodding, to be particular that day to keep all hands hard at work, even though it was a Saturday, so that they would have less time for fretful gossip.

Floyd rode into Highboro to fetch Dr. Chester Porterfield, whose wife Mamie was not bound by the same professional discretion as the doctor. Bonard rode over to Beulah Land an hour after they had settled Selma in her room. He was unshaved, and his clothes showed the haste with which he had dressed after waking to discover that his bride had left him. He was near hysteria, his mind in a torment of shame and offended pride. He had, from overdrinking and the heightened emotion of the occasion, behaved cruelly. That he knew, but he also asserted to Deborah and Felix, who received him on his arrival, that he had been sorely provoked.

Deborah was cold and reserved and said that he must return to Oaks alone for the time being, but that when Selma was recovered, she would certainly see the reasonableness of returning to live with him. In the meantime, they must all be as cautious and silent as possible and hope that neighbors would soon forget what had happened, their further curiosity being unsatisfied. When Bonard sat still and frowning, he was persuaded to return to Oaks by Felix, who, alone of those who knew some details of what had occurred, felt any sympathy for the young man. He had, after all, but to remember his own wedding night. Although the years had built a convenient fiction between them, neither he nor Nell would, of course, ever forget what had happened to them.

Nell had, indeed, taken to her bed—or rather, kept to it when she heard the news from Felix. Before she was equal to the effort of rising that morning, he entered her room and told her in a careful way enough of what had happened for her to imagine the rest of it.

As for Pauline, her anger increased as she absorbed the event. After Bonard arrived at the house, Lovey, who knew more of her daughter's passionate nature than anyone else even if she did not understand it, intercepted Pauline in the breezeway and disarmed her of a butchering knife she carried concealed in the folds of her long skirt. As Lovey wrenched the knife from her daughter's hand and hid it in the folds of her own skirt, she said, "You want it worse? You want to kill me? You want to make them have to kill *you?*"

Pauline fled from the breezeway to the family cabin where she remained alone until she had grown calm enough to return to the main house and go about her usual work.

Leon was very much of a solitary that day. No one needed him, there was nothing for him to do. His mind was in a state of thorough confusion. Bonard was and had always been his friend. (Long ago he had forgot their fight at the Fourth of July barbecue over the green marble.) He and Selma had never been close to each other. Neither knew why, but both accepted the fact of it. And yet he felt now suddenly unfriended, unbrothered, even in some way unmanned, for he and Selma *were* kin, however little value they had put on kinship, were of the same flesh and blood. So he was bound to feel the offense of what had happened even though not wanting to blame his old friend. Late in the morning, after Bonard had ridden away, having had his interview with Deborah and Felix without asking for Leon, Leon went outdoors, hoping to find occupation in observing the work of others. It was a warm day, as perfect as it had promised to be when Floyd and Ezra had first stepped out the door of their cabin that morning.

Leon meandered without his attention's being engaged through the yards of the barns. It was too hot, even this early, to walk or ride into the fields, so he strolled down the front drive into the fruit orchard. Pausing beneath a pear tree to mop his forehead with the kerchief he carried loose in his hands, he suddenly heard laughter over his head, laughter quickly smothered. Startled and annoyed, feeling that he was spied upon, he looked upward and there discovered, perched in the crotch made by two branches, the strange child of Clovis and Roscoe they had called Roman.

Not theirs. His. His child.

Roman was embarrassed at being so discovered, and after remaining still for a minute on his perch while the young master stared at him, he dropped down to the ground and scampered away through the trees. "Boy!" Leon cried. "Come back, boy!" But the child was gone.

Dr. Porterfield came and made his examination of Selma, then frowned and talked gravely to Deborah, and to Lovey, who insisted on being present. He prescribed quiet and rest, a light diet, and laudanum if the patient happened to become agitated. There was, he assured them, nothing seriously wrong with her, certainly nothing that time would not heal.

Late in the afternoon of that same day Rooster Davis rode over to see Deborah alone. They were old friends who easily bridged their difference in age by a common interest in the land, but the half hour they now spent together consisted largely of pauses and silences. Neither smiled nor ever looked directly at the other. Rooster conveyed to Deborah his parents' distress and concern, and said that he had been most particularly commissioned by his wife Trudy to offer her services in any way she might be useful. After the longest pause, Rooster got up from his chair and took his leave, without anything's having been achieved.

Bonard came over every day and begged to be allowed to see and talk to Selma, but when Deborah endeavored to persuade her to this, Selma became morbidly excited and ran about her room like a bird trying to escape its cage. Lovey was at last sent for and succeeded in quieting the girl by promising her that she would never be forced to see Bonard again unless she herself wished it.

The invalid's body healed itself, but Lovey slept on a cot in her room every night, because Selma had dreams and woke screaming or sobbing, or worse, did not wake, but whimpered fearfully in her sleep until Lovey shook her awake and then rocked her in her embrace to calm her enough to try sleep again.

It was a busy time of the year, and the Negroes worked long and hard every day in the fields except Sunday. In the course of days, although they did not forget her, they naturally spoke of her less often than they had at the beginning of her trouble, and accepted the fact that she kept to her room, not even venturing to take her meals in the dining room with the family.

Selma may have grown stronger in body, but she seemed to be no healthier in mind. Nell, whom she refused to see, wailed pitifully that she was sure she had done all she could for the child and then ordered Felix to have her conveyed back to their house in Highboro. As she and Deborah parted at the front door, Nell gave expression to a sudden notion. "Why don't you ask Miss Pennington and her nieces to come and visit? Perhaps they might distract Selma from her grief and painful memories." Deborah said she would think about it, and

waited to watch the carriage drive away through the orchard and on to the main road.

Selma always knew when Bonard paid his calls to the
house. Although she refused to see him, his very presence
at Beulah Land made for too much agitation for her, and
finally Deborah, prompted by Lovey, begged Bonard to
space his visits farther apart, if not to give them up altogether, to come only when she sent to him to say it was
all right.

Felix provided a temporary solution when he suggested
to both families that it might be salutory for all if Bonard
accompanied him to Savannah where he was obliged to go
in a day or two on business that concerned the cotton gin
and the marketing and shipping of Beulah Land cotton
later that summer. Leon wanted to go with them but
thought he might appear frivolous if he suggested it. And
so Felix and Bonard departed, to everyone's relief.

Selma avoided her mother's company and would not respond sensibly when Deobrah insisted upon talking to her.
She continued despondent, to have bad dreams. One afternoon of a day that had been quiet and ordinary enough,
she tried to stab herself with a pair of scissors, but they
were only sewing scissors and old ones and luckily too
dull to inflict real damage before Lovey took them away
from her.

It was then Lovey presented to Deborah what Deborah
should have seen for herself: the necessity for Selma to be
attended day and night by someone who was truly concerned for her well-being.

Deborah admitted that the need was beyond Lovey's capacity to satisfy it. If *she* attended Selma, who would su-
pervise the house and servants? No one else was prepared
to do that, nor was Lovey prepared to allow anyone to su-
persede her if such a suitable person were discovered.

Pondering the matter, Deborah observed, "I know. Yes,
I know; I do, I know. But who is willing to attend her
constantly? Who can be trusted? Indeed, whom would she
allow to attend her?"

"Pauline would like to try."

"Pauline?"

That night Pauline, not Lovey, slept in Selma's room.
Pauline comforted her when she woke crying in the dark
morning hours. When day came and Selma woke again,
Pauline lay beside her on top of the bed covering, and it
seemed natural to Selma that she was there.

Thirteen

"Come away from the window, Lauretta. You are standing right in the light where people passing can see you.
Whatever are you waiting there for, a knight on a white
charger?" Lauretta did not turn until she heard her aunt
leave the room, her shoes tapping four times as she
crossed the bare stretch of polished floor between the carpet and the throw rug separating the family parlor from
the dining room.

It was an evening in late May. The day had been hot,
as May days could be in Savannah, and the Misses Pennington, the one old, the two young, had enjoyed ice in
their tea at their evening meal.

"Oh, how nice, Aunt Pea!" Sarah said, when Clarice
brought the tea in to them.

Penelope nodded acknowledgment of her niece's pleasure, at the same time managing to include in the nod a
reminder that they were poor and getting poorer, that the
house they lived in, which she had inherited from her father when he died unexpectedly of yellow fever ("Not in
an epidemic year; he never did anything common"), was
too large and expensive to keep up for three women, or
one woman and two girls.

"Five cents a pound it costs," Penelope said, "and half
melted before they get it home. We'll have to do without
this summer, except for the most terrible occasions. I declare I don't know where it will end."

Lauretta drank from her glass in a gulp, caught a small
piece of ice in her teeth and chewed it loudly.

"Do stop that vulgar noise," Penelope said. "You sound
like a Geechee Negro chewing rock candy, and furthermore you'll break your teeth, and I cannot afford to buy
new ones for you, so you'll have to go about with your
mouth closed and never smile. And further—furthermore,
it's like chewing money. It was meant to cool the tea, not
freeze your tongue."

The meal over, Penelope had wandered restlessly about
the house, doing nothing constructive, interrupting the servants at their work in the kitchen, picking at threads that
then unraveled, hoping it would rain and settle the dust,
but doubting aloud to herself that it would ever rain
again. All of this was prologue to her snappish remark to

Lauretta as she trotted through the family parlor where
Sarah sat contented, or appeared so anyway, making patient, small stitches in the fabric held taut on her lap by
round embroidery frames.

When the girls were alone again, Lauretta turned to her
younger sister, and seeing her freshly, as Lauretta always
tried to see everything, often declaring that she could not
bear repetition, she laughed and said, "Honey, wake up!
You look like something that's been pressed in a Bible."

Sarah smiled without pausing at her sewing or looking
up at Lauretta. "And you," she said with dry deliberation,
"are full of schemes. You are never so giddy after supper
unless you are planning mischief."

Lauretta giggled and turned back to the window. She
looked out again around the curtain, and seeing nothing
yawned, although the sound of it was more like a sigh.
"*The Merchant of Venice* is not my favorite play by Mr.
Shakespeare. However—" She paused, to dare and encourage her sister to finish the thought for her, as if it
were a game.

"However," Sarah said obligingly, "you feel that Bas-
sanio is being acted brilliantly by the handsome Mr.
Douglas Savage."

"The company moves to Atlanta in two days," Lauretta
said.

"And, in Atlanta, Mr. Savage will doubtless attract to
himself the admiration of another multitude of silly girls,
even as he has done in Savannah."

"I am not silly, and I am nearly twenty."

"You are nineteen—barely," Sarah said.

"I am a hundred, and nothing has ever happened in
Savannah, nor ever will. How can you stand it, Sarah?
How can you sit there sewing as if it were your destiny,
when we are at the time of life that should be gay and full
of enchantment?"

"I don't require enchantment," Sarah said. "Only a little
sense now and then—and ice in summer."

"Girls." Penelope was back from her latest cricket-hop-
ping tour of the downstairs. "They are almost done in the
kitchen, and I have told them nothing more is required.
Do you want anything, either of you?" She looked briefly
at each, and when neither spoke, she continued, "If it
would only rain. I have my headache. I know it's from
not raining. If it would rain, my head would run clear as
spring water. It always does when the air is light. When
the air is heavy, as it so often is from April right on to

November, then I am heavy too. I shall go to my room and try to distract myself by remembering the first bars of every opera I have ever heard sung."

"Is there anything I can do for you, Aunt Pea?" Sarah asked.

"No, dear child. Only see that your sister does not fly to the moon. I count on you. Good night, and I pray that neither of you is ever afflicted with my terrible headaches, although they do say the Lord sends trials to those He loves."

Sarah rose, holding her embroidery, and kissed her aunt on the cheek. "Good night, Aunt Pea."

Lauretta kissed the other cheek and echoed her sister's "Good night, Aunt Pea," saying it with a modesty that from her was almost a mockery. They waited until the aunt had gone upstairs and they heard her door close before they relaxed their expressions. Sarah sat down again. The clock in the hallway chimed its full-hour cycle of simple melodies and then sounded nine strokes. Lauretta turned to the sound at the last stroke and curtsied.

"Now guess," she then said to her sister, "guess what I am—" She broke off as Clarice entered from the dining room.

Clarice said, "Miss Pea say that's all for tonight. Is she gone to bed?"

"To her room," Sarah said. "She has one of her headaches."

"Poor soul. I am sometimes similarly afflicted," Clarice said. "It happens to those of us with the nervous temperament. Is there anything you want, before I go get off my feet?"

"No, thank you, Clarice. Good night," Sara said. "Rest well."

"Good night. I'll try, although—"

As Clarice, shaking her head, went back through the dining room to the kitchen and her room beyond it, where her daughter Ricey had just gone, Lauretta said in her bright, mocking way, "Good night. And that is the end of the world. Nothing happened, but good night, and *selah*."

"I know that trick," Sarah said. "You are trying to make me feel sorry for you and sympathize so that I shall agree with your next suggestion. What is it? That we slip out and walk around the block when we hear Aunt Pea begin to snore?"

"Are you content with so little?"

Sarah smiled. "That's the next part of the trick, wistful

appeal couched as question-accusation. I am content, yes, and what we have and are is not 'so little.' "

Lauretta held up her hands. "Do not, I pray you, lecture me on Christian gratitude."

Sarah took up her sewing, having to study it to find her place as she would have a book, so little was her mind on the embroidery. "We have a good home, for which I *am* grateful."

Five minutes later Lauretta said, "I wish I were like you."

"No, you do not," Sarah said.

"Yes, I do. Sometimes."

"Only when something frightens you." She looked up at her sister with quick concern. "Has anything?"

"No, Sarah. Dear Sarah."

Sarah loosened the wooden hoops and reset them to include a new, undone area. "I can't decide between blue and lavender there, so I shall come back to it. I know this must be green."

"Not frightened."

Sarah looked up again, half anxious, half suspecting that her sister was at her familiar game of making drama. "Not frightened," she said as a statement, and waited with seeming unconcern.

Lauretta went into the hallway and stood listening for a few moments, then returned. "Asleep," she said and smiled. "So noisily asleep it is a wonder she does not wake and tell herself to be quiet so that she can sleep."

"Would you like to walk around the block?" Sarah asked. "There'd be no harm in that."

"Do you remember," Lauretta began, smiling, "do you remember when we were girls and first came to live with Aunt Pea? Sometimes we filled an old stocking with rags and hid in the hedge and dragged it across the front walk when the night watchmen made their rounds?"

"I do remember." They laughed without making much sound.

"Sarah, I must tell you. I have met Mr. Savage."

"Yes, dear," Sarah agreed calmly. "We both enjoyed his performance last Friday evening, and you contrived it so that we were in Chippewa Square the next afternoon at the time he was likely to arrive at the theatre for the special matinee performance. He smiled, I remember, seeing us, but that is not remarkable, since you are so very pretty. And Mr. Savage is, I should think, used to smiling at admirers who contrive 'accidentally' to be in his way. I

know your penchant for romantic dreaming. It is harmless. so long as it remains romantic dreaming."

"I have seen him twice since."

"By chance, naturally," Sarah said after a brief pause.

"Arranged. I have met him. He knows me. We know
each other. He knows about you, about Aunt Pea, where
we live—"

"Lauretta!"

"Sh!"

"Lauretta," Sarah whispered, and then spoke in her
normal low tone. "You are 'joking' me, aren't you?"

"Dear Sarah—I am in love."

"But he is an actor. And you cannot really know him?"

"I do. Yes, yes. I do."

"Lauretta, this is—beyond absurdity. You cannot tell
me that you actually have so far forgotten yourself—and
Aunt Pea as to—"

"Sh!" Both listened. "I thought I heard—" There was at
first no sound, then came the faint, far sound of their
aunt's snoring. They both relaxed visibly. "I said I would
meet him tonight . . . Now. I must go."

"You shall not!"

"Sarah, you do not command me! Dear Sarah, don't be
unhappy with me?"

"Where are you going?"

"Only to the corner by the pump under the lamp. I said
if I could get away, I'd see him there as soon after nine as
I could."

"He must be at the theatre surely."

"They're playing *Macbeth*. He is Banquo and out of it
by now. Only the leading actors come out and bow at the
end." Lauretta was at the window again. "There he is! I
think it is he—" She moved into the hallway.

"You mustn't go! I cannot allow you—"

Lauretta embraced her sister briefly. "Sarah, you are a
child of seventeen. I am a woman of twenty."

"Nineteen, and what if Aunt wakes? What will I tell
her?"

"She never wakes. Doomsday might trumpet and she
would yet outtrumpet it with her snoring."

"She had the headache. She sometimes wakes with that.
If she asks for you?"

"She never asks for me. Besides, I shall return in five
minutes."

"Five?"

"Or ten."

Lauretta had opened the front door and, leaving it open, gone down the path to the gate and out onto the walkway. Sarah went out the front door too and pulled it nearly but not quite to behind her. She had left her sewing in a jumble on the floor where she dropped it, left her mind there with it too. Lauretta had this time taken her genuinely by surprise. She'd had no inkling at all of what had gone on—if what Lauretta said was true and not a romantic fiction, if Lauretta were not "joking" her again.

It was not a night of moon and stars. The thick, heavy clouds that Penelope had hoped would bring rain and relieve her headache lay over the city as they had done all the day long, and might tomorrow, unless a wind blew in from the sea. Not knowing what to do, Sarah went out into the front garden and sat down on a stone bench beside the sun dial. After ten minutes she could see through the dark like a cat. The nearest light was at the intersection where the pump and the oil lamp were, but she could see neither from where she sat.

It seemed an hour, but it was little more than half that before Lauretta returned. When Sarah rose from her seat, Lauretta halted on the path, startled. Then she recognized Sarah and kissed her on the cheek and said, "Don't ask me anything, and promise me you will honor my confidence. I am in Paradise!"

Together they walked into the house. Sarah shut the door behind them and latched it. Each lighted a candle, and Sarah blew out the last lamp, carefully waiting until the red portion of the wick went black. With the final smoke of the lamp in their nostrils and the newly lighted candles in their hands, the girls made their way upstairs. They parted at the door of Lauretta's bedroom, with a quick kiss on the cheek, each to the other, and restrained agitation.

Sarah set her candle down on the bureau and opened the curtains which Ricey had closed earlier that evening while her mother finished the kitchen work. The candle guttered and went out, and Sarah decided against lighting it again. A few moments later the candle smell was gone, and her eyes were again used to the dark. She undressed and put on her nightgown and stood at the open window brushing her hair. And gradually she grew calm. She had paid her dues of being Lauretta's sister and Aunt Pea's niece. She loved them dearly, but it was good to be alone now and be only herself.

As she brushed her hair, the curtains billowed with a sudden breeze, then blew into the room with such force as to overturn a small piecrust table. She left it where it fell. There had been nothing on it but a book. Without any more warning, lightning flashed, and seconds later thunder boomed and shook the room as if that room were its single object. And the rain fell, at first violently, and driven by the wind. Then wind and rain assumed a calmer, gentler attitude. When Sarah got into bed, she did so without closing her shutters, and she hoped that in her sleep, Aunt Pea's head would lighten even as the air did so.

Fourteen

When the Arden Bledsoe Company of Shakespearean Players concluded their engagement at the Savannah Theatre in Chippewa Square on Saturday night, Sarah sighed with relief and also with pity for her sister; for during that Saturday and the day following Lauretta gave evidence of much distress of soul. She sighed and shook her head and looked abstracted; she paced about; and often she did not respond if a question was put to her.

When the three ladies had retired to their rooms on the Saturday night and Sarah had prepared herself for bed and blown out her candle, she heard sounds of weeping from Lauretta's room, which was next door to her own. She went quickly on tiptoe into the hall, not needing a light, so familiar was the way, so often had each gone in the night to visit the other on errands more trivial than serious.

When she went in, Lauretta was startled into stopping her crying and blowing out her candle in the same breath.

"Lauretta dear, I heard you through the wall. Are you unhappy?"

"I am sorry I disturbed you," Lauretta answered in a voice unnaturally loud with the effort of her response.

"You didn't disturb me; I wasn't asleep. Is it about Mr. Savage?"

"If you must know, Sarah—"

"Not 'must.' I want to know because you are dear to me."

"Yes; Mr. Savage," Lauretta said curtly.

Sarah moved toward her in the dark. "You are still dressed."

"I was just going to make ready for bed."

"Let me help you." Sarah put an arm around Lauretta's shoulder in a sisterly way, but Lauretta shrugged free.

"I am capable of going to bed without assistance."

"I am sorry," Sarah said meekly. "I haven't meant to intrude. I only felt concerned for you . . . Are the Bledsoe Players now to move on?"

There was a pause before Lauretta answered. "Earliest tomorrow morning, I believe. They are to begin the journey to Atlanta at six o'clock, by stages."

"Dear Lauretta. I can imagine how you feel, but surely it is best that you—"

"Don't, Sarah!" Lauretta exclaimed. "I cannot, I *will* not discuss it further with you. Not now."

"I am sorry. I have been clumsy." She went to the door but before opening it said, "If you should want company, or if you require anything at all during the night, you have only to call. I shall hear."

"Good night, Sarah!"

Lauretta's tone was so vehement that Sarah went out quickly, closing the door behind her. Immediately, she heard her sister commence weeping again. She yearned to re-enter the room and comfort her, but she dared not. She had been rebuffed. She had been clumsy, no doubt, as she had said, however well her actions were intended. Lauretta would want to be alone, of course, feeling herself to be in love and knowing that her lover was, although now perhaps shouting lines upon the city's stage, soon to abandon the city that held her.

Sarah went to bed and wept a little in sympathy. She fell asleep after listening hard and hearing no sound from her sister's room.

She woke early but made herself stay in bed. After a while, hearing voices through the window that faced the back yards, she got up and went to look out. It was a misty, gray day. Uncle Joshua, who acted as butler and general manager of the house and its grounds, was walking from one flower bed to another in the back garden with Ichabod, the man whose main work was outdoors, planting and tending plants, although he performed miscellaneous chores as necessary. He was not dignified by the title "gardener," being allowed no opinions, simply directed by Uncle Joshua to do this, that, and the other.

Sarah heard Ricey's voice raised in the kitchen just below her bedroom, and then Clarice's voice, loud and scolding. She bathed quickly after pouring water from the pitcher into the bowl on her washstand. Ricey brought water to the three bedrooms every night. During the winter months, at the time they had asked to be called, she carried up kettles of hot water which they mixed with the cold from the pitchers. In severe weather they had to break the ice that had formed overnight at the top of the pitchers before using it to cool the water from the kettles.

Bathed, she dressed simply. She would dress again before going to services at St. John's. Leaving her room, she paused at Lauretta's door, but hearing nothing, proceeded downstairs and on to the kitchen. When coffee was brewed, she helped Ricey set two trays, one for Aunt Pea, and the other with two cups and saucers, which she carried up to Lauretta's room. Lauretta could not mind; they often had their morning coffee together, the first to wake going down and bringing it up.

She knocked and entered to find Lauretta sitting by her window. She was still in her nightgown, but her eyes looked stark and staring with the skin darkly puffed beneath them, as if they had not closed all night.

"Good morning, Lauretta." Sarah set the tray on a table and poured coffee into the two cups, adding sugar and cream in the amounts they liked.

When she handed coffee to her sister, Lauretta took it, sipped from the cup, then set cup into saucer and saucer on her lap. "Thank you." Her eyes blinked rapidly as if fevered and in need of cooling. "You would oblige me greatly, Sarah, if you told Aunt Pea I am not well enough for church."

"Certainly," Sarah said, "but won't you dress and come down for breakfast?"

"Oh no, I cannot do that."

"I shall send Ricey up with a tray. Is there anything special you think you might fancy?"

"Nothing at all. No tray. Nothing, please, Sarah. Sarah dear."

Her shaking hands, her distracted eyes, moved the younger sister deeply, and Sarah rose and went downstairs, strengthened in her resolve to be her sister's protector. She would honor her need for privacy and see that others did so.

Penelope accepted word of Lauretta's indisposition

casually. After routine expressions of concern and sympathy, she put Lauretta out of her mind. Sunday would be easier without Lauretta's pertness.

The morning mist evaporated, and the day turned fine and sunny. Sarah and Penelope opened parasols to hold between themselves and the blinding sun, and walked to St. John's in South Broad Street. Arriving when it was still early for services, they strolled in the cemetery and looked on the graves of their fathers and mothers.

Lauretta did not come downstairs for the midday Sunday dinner. She did, however, dress herself and walk in the garden when the sun went down; and she came in to join her sister and aunt for their usual early Sunday supper. Clarice had baked fresh rolls. Otherwise, the food was what had been left over from dinner, pieced out with relishes. Clarice offered a dessert of gingerbread and apple sauce, traditional for Sunday night cold supper, but only Sarah ate it.

After supper, Lauretta asked to be excused, as she thought she would be better quiet in her room. Penelope was so pleased by her subdued manner that she gave Ricey a glass of sherry to take to her when Ricey went upstairs to refill bedroom pitchers with water for the night, and to draw curtains.

When Sarah and Penelope retired an hour later, there was no light under the door and no sound from Lauretta's room. Another half hour and Penelope was asleep and snoring. Sarah heard the sound of it across the hallway, even though both their doors were closed. Feeling lonely, she blew out her candle and then went to the window to look out. The mist of the morning that had been dissipated by the day's sun had now returned, spreading mystery over the garden below where she had seen Uncle Joshua and Ichabod walking that morning. The smell of jasmine set her mind to dreamy music until she remembered her sister's sorrow. Saying a prayer for Lauretta, Sarah went to bed and to sleep.

Next morning she woke and rose, bathed herself and dressed, went downstairs and subsequently carried a tray upstairs to Lauretta's room. She knocked on the door cheerfully and went in without waiting to be invited. Lauretta was not there, and her bed had not been slept in. The sherry glass Aunt Pea had sent up brimming full the evening before was now empty and served as paper weight to the letter Lauretta had written.

Fifteen

Dearest Sarah.

As I write this, you and Aunt Pea are at church. When you read it, I shall be married to Mr. Douglas Savage. You have been so good and kind, dear Sarah, and I have not meant to deceive you, although I admit that I allowed you to misread my own state of mind. What you saw as my distress at losing Douglas was in reality my distress at knowing I should soon lose you and be leaving the safe harbor of my girlhood. How tenderly I shall think of you! You most of all, but Aunt Pea too, and Clarice and Ricey and Uncle Joshua and yes even Ichabod and all our funny acquaintances. And won't they be jealous of my marrying before them and going away to live an exciting life far from Savannah!

But I must be more serious (although not solemn, please!) because I am so soon to be a married woman, and you must not think my responsibilities sit lightly on my shoulders, for they do not. When the Company ended their engagement here, they were to go on this morning toward Atlanta by stages, but Douglas has separated himself from the Bledsoe Players, something he has long wanted to do, feeling himself ready for larger challenges of Thespis. He has gone to nearby Port Wentworth to arrange for our marriage this night. When you are all asleep, and the house is quiet (always early on a Sunday evening, you know), I shall creep away with one traveling bag. Douglas has said he will be waiting in a hired buggy near the waterpump at the corner intersection of streets. We shall return to Port Wentworth, to take our marriage vows before the minister who will be waiting, and to stay the night. Then tomorrow morning—it will be *now*, or even an hour or so ago when you read this!—we shall travel on to—guess!

North? South? West? We cannot go East, can we, because there is the Atlantic Ocean! Unless we are to take a sloop or packet boat—and I shall not say as to that!

This is meant—this silliness as you may call it—deliberately, to confuse you. I know you will think I enjoy that because of what you declare is my romantic nature and my tendency to dramatize; but I do not, dear Sarah. I earnestly wish I might tell you all. I wish I knew all myself! No, I do not wish that. I want to go to a new life, to the unexpected, to have each day reveal itself and its events freshly to me. What I mean to say is: Please persuade Aunt Pea not to send after us, for it will be no use. I am a grown woman and may marry as I please. I wish particularly not to hurt or embarrass her. Tell her—I cannot bring myself to write anyone but you!—that I love her, and thank her for caring for me, and entreat her to remember me kindly.

I shall write to you again when we are far (or near?) away. You may have anything of mine I leave that you want and find yourself capable of wearing. I am sorry that my shoes will be too small for you, but your feet have been somewhat precocious in their growth!

Remember ever and continue to love,
Your loving sister,
Lauretta

P.S. I may become an actress. Douglas says I am very beautiful although I know he is blind where I am concerned. However, I intend to practice reading aloud to myself by way of preparation, should opportunity arise, with particular reference to the characters of Portia and Rosalind. I believe I might engage to play them without total discredit! Adieu.

When she had read the letter four times, each repetition with diminishing speed and agitation, although her toes crimped in her slippers when she reread the reference to her feet, she wondered how she should present it, and the fact of Lauretta's departure, to her Aunt Pea.

As she stood debating the matter with herself, the bell was rung in the dining room downstairs, the bell that had summoned her and her sister to so many thousands of meals from the time of their first being orphaned until yesterday. Sarah folded the letter hastily and put it into the waist pocket of the morning dress she had put on earlier, and hurried out of the room and downstairs.

She found her Aunt Pea seated at her usual place. She wore a flowered cotton dress with a ruffled cap of the same material. Ricey was just setting before her a large bowl of early dewberries.

"Good morning, Aunt Pea," Sarah said as she slipped into her chair.

"Good morning, Sarah dear. I hope you have slept well. These look like excellent dewberries. Will you have some?"

"Yes, please."

As she served them, adding cream and sugar to both servings withour further consulting her niece, Penelope said, "I gather that Lauretta will not be joining us?"

Sarah caught her breath in panic, then managed to say, "Yes, Aunt Pea. I mean to say—she will not." Her answer was true as far as it went, but Sarah blushed, knowing she deceived the trusting old lady, who even now was so cheerfully beginning to eat her berries.

"Such a nice taste," Penelope said. "A little sharp because it is still early for them, although the recent heat has brought them along quickly. Perhaps too quickly."

Sarah spooned berries into her mouth and managed a vague "Mm" that could mean anthing or nothing, without violating good manners by talking as she ate, nor the truth by making a direct statement, for in reality she tasted nothing, so preoccupied was she by the event she had so recently discovered.

"Poor Lauretta," Penelope said charitably. "She loves a good dewberry as much as I do. Do your think she might try a bowl of them if Ricey carried them to her?"

"No! I know she would not, Aunt."

"Is she so poorly? Ah—" On this comfortably plaintive note the old lady subsided, accepting with a nod Ricey's offer of coffee from the large pot she had just brought in, and whose spout was steaming delectably. At that moment the door of the kitchen opened, and Clarice entered with a basket of freshly fried and sugared doughnuts nested in a crisp towel.

"Here!" Clarice triumphantly offered the basket to Penelope.

"Oh, Clarice!" She took a doughnut and bit into it. "You spoil us, you really do. God in Heaven cannot eat as well as we do."

"Yes'm. You ready for one, Miss Sarah?"

"Thank you."

"You may leave them," Penelope said. "They are so very good! I declare I have tasted none better ever, no, not even of your own making!"

Clarice responded with a pleased gruffness. "Anybody want eggs? Grits? Sausage? Ham? Bacon?"

"Nothing! Delicious! Unless you, Sarah?"

"No, Aunt Pea. Thank you, Clarice."

"I declare I think hot cinnamon must be my favorite flavor!" Penelope said.

"So is sage dressing with a fat baked hen!" Clarice rejoined, and chuckled to encourage good humor.

"You shame me! You make me appear greedy!" Penelope said in an unashamed and perfectly satisfied way. "Well, I am, I suppose, and I don't mind admitting it."

Uncle Joshua entered from the parlor, announcing his presence with a portentous and extended clearing of the throat. When this failed to get the attention of his mistress, who took a certain pleasure in teasing him, he said loudly and gravely, "Miss Penelope, I do not wish to interrupt your breakfast. However—"

"If you did not, you would not!" she responded gaily.

"Miss Pea!" the old man thundered in the way that had sometimes cowed her when she was a girl and he already a grown man, a man of dignity and consequence in her father's household.

She allowed herself to appear a little cowed. "Yes, Uncle Joshua?"

"I have just come from speaking with the yard man, Ichabod. He had been speaking earlier this morning with the yard man next door, whose name is Isak."

"Yes, Uncle Joshua," she said. "That is very interesting, but are you certain it requires my immediate attention?"

"Isak had the toothache last night and could not sleep." Penelope nodded absently and took another doughnut from the basket. Redolent of sugar and spice, the doughnut occupied her attention as she consumed it, interspersing bites with sips of coffee, which aided her chewing as well as adding an attractive variation of flavor.

"Walking the floor with his toothache," Joshua continued inexorably, "he observed, or says he observed, in the early hours of the morning, a figure leaving these premises, a young female leaving these premises."

Penelope finished chewing and swallowed, presenting then a countenance more worthy of his serious scrutiny.

"Absurd," she said. "*I* am here of a certainty. Miss Sarah is here; and Miss Lauretta is indisposed and resting in her room."

"Is she, Miss Pea?"

The old man looked at her, a look heavy with doubt and gloomy insinuation.

"Aunt Pea," Sarah said hastily, "I haven't had the

chance to—I don't really know how to tell you—" Uncle
Joshua and Aunt Pea stared at her with a fearful intensity. Sarah took the letter from her pocket and unfolded it
and put it into her aunt's hands.

Penelope read without pause or exclamation, but her
eyes moved nervously as wasps around a threatened nest.
"Well," she said when she came to the end, then turned
the letter back to its beginning and read it through again.
She had left an unfinished doughnut beside her coffee cup,
but when she finished rereading the letter, her fingers
remembered, if her pride did not, and presently had
stuffed into her mouth the remains of the doughnut she had
seemed to abandon in the air of emotion. "Well. And
how is it I have known nothing of this?"

"You remember our going to the play, Aunt Pea—you,
Lauretta, and I?"

"Shakespeare is better ignored than read, better read
than seen performed; I have always said so. The words
made flesh are—" She shivered and pursed her lips.

Sarah told her everything she knew, blaming herself to
the point of boasting, for what had happened. Penelope
made her tell it all again. When the story was twice told,
she declared that she should never as long as she lived
recover from the blow, that Lauretta had lost her good
name and by now must have sailed from Port Wentworth
to Boston or New York, that she and—her husband (she
steeled herself to use the word, and then hoped that it was
true) had gone by stage coach to Atlanta. The next second she decided they had traveled west toward Alabama,
or north into Carolina. Or perhaps they were still in Port
Wentworth.

What they knew—and they now consisted of Penelope,
Sarah, Joshua, Clarice, Ricey, and Ichabod out of sight
beyond the window—was that they knew nothing at all of
where she was. Sarah blamed herself aloud and silently,
which gave them all a certain satisfaction, since the real
culprit was not present to be scored.

"Uncle Joshua," Penelope said, "will you send Ichabod
to enquire if Judge Truebody is free to come and talk to
me?"

"I won't send, I'll go myself."

Judge Horace Truebody was Penelope's old and especially valued friend, having been her father's lawyer and
entrusted with the management of his and subsequently
her estate. Penelope had always consulted him before
making any important decision. He had advised her to

take the nieces into her house and care when they were
orphaned—not that she needed to be told her duty—but
he had felt that the living arrangement might benefit her
as well as them. And so it had, providing companionship
for the spinster and guidance for the girls.

On the present occasion he came to her side within the
hour, and within another he had set off to Port Wentworth to make enquiries. Before night fell he was again at
the house on Broughton Street with news. He had found
the minister who had married the young lovers and so was
able to reassure Penelope that "the worst" had not transpired. Her niece Lauretta, however foolishly, was truly
married. People might laugh; they could not scorn. As to
her present whereabouts, he could give less comfort. A
sloop had sailed that morning from Port Wentworth to
Baltimore, and a young couple fitting the general description of Mr. and Mrs. Douglas Savage had taken passage.

"What must I do?" Penelope asked.

"That which is most difficult," Judge Truebody replied.
"Nothing. Wait and see. The young woman has been in-
considerate, perhaps rash, but only time will tell. The only
sensible and practical advice I can give you is to let a little water flow under the bridge and see if it runs clear or
muddy. What cannot be helped must be endured." Judge
Truebody was given to such familiar old sayings. He had
learned early in life that they gave his listener as much
comfort and reassurance as did his name.

Miss Penelope bowed her head, to Judge Truebody and
to fate. She thanked the old man who was obviously tired
from his efforts on her behalf, and he went away.

Sarah and her aunt had kept to the house all day long
as if waiting, without quite hoping, for a message from
Lauretta. The next morning when they sat down to a plain
breakfast of grits and fried eggs after a night during which
each had paced the floor of her room more than she had
slept in her bed, a message of another sort and from another source, totally unexpected, arrived.

It was from Deborah Kendrick to her friend Penelope
Pennington. After polite greetings and general courtesies,
Deborah told briefly of the wedding, and even more
briefly of her daughter's coming home after it. She used
the expressions "much perturbation of spirit" and "we
none of us know what may happen next," and then she issued an invitation that was more in the form of an appeal: Would Penelope and her nieces consider coming to
Beulah Land to visit, as soon and for as long a time as

they might be able to spare? She thought, Deborah wrote, she hoped that the company of the young Misses Pennington might encourage Selma to throw off her despondency which hung like a cloud over the heads of all in the house. She, Deborah, would be much and forever obliged if her old friend found it in her heart to accede to her request.

The letter immediately eased the tension in the household. Trouble loves trouble, and Penelope admitted that hers was, all things considered, less severe and pressing than Deborah's.

There were other advantages to be gained if they accepted the invitation than a no doubt pleasant residence in country air during several weeks of summer heat. There would be a certain saving of money of which Penelope was not insensible. Her household expenses would go on with the servants left behind, but Uncle Joshua would see that all was done economically. There was—of course—the advantage of obliging her friend. There was the advantage of avoiding gossip in their Savannah circle, simply by being absent. When there is an absence of the principals and little or no information about them, speculations are likely to be so many and varied as to cancel each other's credibility.

And there was the chance, however slight it seemed when she remembered the particular geniality that had existed between Lauretta and Leon, with Sarah pretty much left out of it—still, there was the chance of—let it be called "friendship" developing between her niece Sarah and one or both of the Kendrick children.

It was not too much to hope. In a hopeless time, nothing is.

Only minutes were required for Penelope's mind to receive and digest the contents of the letter and to jump ahead to speculation on the future. She discussed the letter with Sarah, and in less detail and confidence with Uncle Joshua and Clarice. They all agreed that a visit to Beulah Land at this time was a desirable thing. Uncle Joshua promised to be vigilant to receive and pass on any word, letter, message, or even serious rumor that came to them at home. Judge Truebody was consulted, and it was decided that as soon as they left Savannah, he would issue a simple announcement of Lauretta's marriage.

Penelope wrote to Deborah accepting her invitation. Forty-eight hours later Penelope and Sarah had packed a trunk with what was thought to be required for a country

visit in the season. Ricey would accompany and attend
them. On their last evening at Broughton Street before
setting off the next morning, Penelope and Sarah sat together in the family parlor. Penelope held on her lap a cat
named Prudence, and a copy of *As You Like It* in one
hand, lowered to the circle of light provided by the oil
lamp. She was reading the play again with particular attention to the part Rosalind played in it and trying to
think of Lauretta's acting it. It was absurd, of course, but
then one never knew. Lauretta certainly had a flair for the
dramatical. The large arc of gesture, the full tone, a tendency to hysteria in all her feelings which is the heightened mood of drama surely—yes, it might be. Sarah sat,
the embroidery firmly in her lap, the two locked wooden
hoops solid and definite as doomsday and resurrection.
Sarah worked, Sarah silent, mild and meek. Looking at
her, Penelope thought: *Very well then—and the meek
shall inherit the earth.*

Sixteen

The members of the two households of Oaks and Beulah
Land felt themselves to be waiting, at least for some sign
of the future, if not a good clear word of direction. Felix
and Bonard had returned from Savannah without, of
course, having called at the Pennington house on
Broughton Street. Staring at Selma's trunk which remained at one side of his bedroom Bonard could, depending upon his mood, tell himself that if Selma rejoined
him—and he had every confidence that she would in
time—her clothes were already there; and if she did not,
the clothes were packed and ready to go and could be out
of the house in five minutes. It was a fact that Selma was
the only virgin Bonard had ever lain with. When he
thought of that hour, he tried to remember detail, but
never was able to. If he thought of it with wounded pride
and something akin to shame, he thought of it also with
excitement that pushed him to lust, and one night when
he retired to his room and saw the trunk suddenly as he
entered from the hall with his lighted candle, he paused
and set the candle down on top of the trunk. His mind
seemed to follow his actions, as one may watch oneself in
a dream, for he had not thought what he was going to do
until he had actually loosened his trousers and pulled out

his dick and masturbated it until his semen shot out over
the trunk in insult and homage.

Rooster and Trudy, his father and mother, behaved
toward him very much as they had before his marriage,
with the difference that they never seemed to find mood
or occasion to touch him. He was not treated like a leper,
but he was not treated like a beloved brother and son either, and they had always been a family for touching in
easy, comfortable ways they were scarce aware of.

Selma did not sit and brood, not did she cackle or sob
in corridors after midnight, as those reckoned to be of disturbed mind are supposed to do. She wanted little to do
with anybody. She ate in her room, one of the kitchen
girls bringing trays for her and Pauline. She most often
appeared calm, both because for her the thing was over
and done, if not resolved, and because Pauline had a quieting effect upon her. Pauline was the only person in the
main house at Beulah Land who might be said to be
happy. She had loved Selma all her life, and now she was
with her every minute of the day and night.

They did not talk very much, but Pauline was always
conscious of Selma, could follow the slightest alteration in
her mood without a word having been spoken: by a gesture, a way of sitting, or getting up from a chair, the
tempo of her breathing, the tensing and relaxing of a
hand. These were obvious and easy indicators of mood
which anyone attentive to Selma might have read.
Pauline's knowledge went further than that, through the
subtlest realms of perception and intuition; it was
awareness that included but went beyond what is called
"love." Perfectly satisfied with the way she spent each
day, Pauline's contentment created a healing atmosphere
that Selma could not but take strength from.

Leon did not see Bonard during those days, for Bonard
once again rode or drove a buggy into Highboro to "read
law" at the office Felix kept more as a private retreat than
as a place of business, although his law books were there,
and there business was sometimes transacted.

At Beulah Land people went about their business, if
they had any, and sat or wandered bored if they did not.
Leon was one of the latter until he took to hanging about
Floyd's smith shop. The new closeness of Selma and
Pauline may have had something to do with suggesting it.
Kinship and blood are even more complex than is gener-
ally supposed.

Floyd did not welcome Leon, but he did not seem sur-

prised at his frequent presence. Enough time had elapsed
since their closeness and subsequent estrangement, which
neither had ever explained to himself, for them to meet as
friends again. As Leon learned to appreciate Floyd's skill
in his work, their pleasure in each other's company increased. Not much was said, but there was after the first
few visits a feeling of "I didn't know you could do that"
and "you'll see more," of pride and approval. Without
their charting the progress of renewed friendship, Leon
began to hand Floyd things the second before he reached
for them himself, and they began to work together almost
like master craftsman and apprentice, Leon never forcing
his way, Floyd never excluding him. If Floyd felt resentment over the fact that Leon, by the nature of things, was
able to seek him out when he needed him, whereas he
must wait to be sought, he was generous enough to smile
over the fact.

And Ezra—Papa to one, Uncle Ezra to the other—was
in and out, his visits small, bright punctuations in a long
day. The young men began to talk to each other again,
about little things at first, then about little and big things
alternately and together. Leon felt himself growing toward
a kind of health and acceptance of himself not unlike that
his sister was experiencing from the attendance of
Pauline. When Deborah received Penelope's letter saying
they were coming and when they expected to arrive, that
was her sign that past events might work themselves out
as best they could; and that the future was now to commence.

Seventeen

Leon drove the carriage in to Highboro on the afternoon
the stage was expected to bring the Misses Pennington.
Skeeter followed with a wagon. Leon smoked a cigar with
Bonard and his Uncle Felix in the latter's office, and then
he went to the house and drank tea with his Aunt Nell.
Skeeter arrived just as they were about to set off for the
post office where the stage would arrive. Nell and Felix
had engaged to spend a few days at Beulah Land at the
beginning of the visit of the Penningtons. Nell would go
out with Leon and the guests; Felix would go out later in
the afternoon, as Bonard went home. Skeeter set Felix
and Nell's hampers and one small trunk on his wagon and

followed the carriage as Leon drove down to the post office.

In good time the stagecoach arrived, and Nell and Leon welcomed Penelope and Sarah. Skeeter took onto his wagon the belongings of the guests, including Ricey.

The three ladies were settled in the open carriage, and Leon took the driver's seat and off they went. Nell and Penelope engaged each other in comfortable conversation that mentioned without going into the two unsettling marriages the ladies' families had been party to since last meeting in Savannah.

It was a warm day, but clear and dry. There had been rain recently, so the foliage along the way had its own fresh color, yet the clay road was hard enough to be driven upon without creating clouds of dust. Leon felt good, and somehow, suddenly important. He sat erect in the driver's seat, conscious of his muscle and that of the two horses that drew the carriage along to Beulah Land. They moved at a nice clip, not so fast as to blur the passing scenery and jostle the occupants of the carriage, nor so slow as to bore and tire them.

Sarah found herself surprisingly relaxed after the journey they had made, and ready to enjoy whatever came next. As the two older women found much to talk about, she was left pleasantly to herself on the other seat. She looked about and liked what she saw of the country the clay road cut through. Fields of cultivated land on both sides alternated with wooded areas and a bridge over a branch of the creek.

At one point Leon turned briefly, keeping his eyes on the horses and his hands on the reins, to say, "Beulah Land begins here—everything we pass until we get to the door is Beulah Land!" It was more than information, it was happy boast, and they all laughed with pleasure in him. Having laughed, the two older ladies resumed their conversation about back pain, and Sarah looked about, from one side of the road to the other, up, and once back, and then far to the horizon, and thought: *Beulah Land, all of this is Beulah Land.*

The fullness of its impact, that of the earth itself with all its promise, caused her to look at Leon in a new way. This Beulah Land would be his. Her thought was neither ambitious nor calculating. She saw that the land was beautiful, and that driving over it, Leon took on a presence, a personal importance she had never felt in him when they met in Savannah, where he had always appeared to be somewhat frivolous, somehow furtive or secret, and often bored. Here he was at home in all ways.

There was something else Sarah felt, and that was that she was the young woman present, something she had never felt before her sister left them. A new discovery: she did not have to feel, or pretend to feel, of second importance. She was first for the first time in her whole life; and her sudden realization of the fact made her a little drunk, along with the warm day and its dry air with a thousand fragrances making one to her, and the spacious land stretching over fields and hills, through woods to the horizon.

And Leon, sitting there on the high seat alert, erect, and handsome, was not merely a part of this; he *was* Beulah Land.

As for Leon, life had been dim for him of late; he had been second to others and to the events that centered about them. Now suddenly he felt himself a whole man, the master, not just "young master," the courtesy title which was sometimes used, he knew, in a scornful way; he was in fact master of the estate they drove through.

And Sarah—how had he not noticed her before in Savannah? She was not only pretty. In the open air and light where he had seldom seen her before, she was far prettier than he remembered Lauretta as being. She was real and alive and of the moment, without patina and without need of it. He felt himself delighted with her, eager to press the advantage of their earlier acquaintance. How glad he was Lauretta had done whatever they said she had done. Sarah here, Sarah now, was natural and right.

When he turned the horses in from the main road to the private road that went through the orchard to the front circle drive of the house, he saw Floyd, who had put new shoes on a young mare and was accustoming the horse to them by riding her along the side of the drive.

Leon's and Floyd's eyes met at the same instant.

"Hey, Floyd!"

"Yee-oh!" Floyd called, laughing. And Floyd, perhaps because of the fine weather and seeing his friend sitting proud and important, felt like a boy on his first horse, and let go the bridle rein for an instant to slap the mare's flanks with both hands. Grabbing the rein again, he galloped up the drive toward the house laughing and

shouting, "Company coming! Company coming!" which
the guests declared was the finest welcome they could
imagine to Beulah Land.

Eighteen

Deborah was at the steps to greet them, Lovey behind her
on the porch, as Leon hopped off his seat and helped the
ladies from the carriage. Penelope was first, and she and
Deborah embraced with a new intimacy because of their
parallel troubles. Then Leon brought Sarah down, his
hand strong over hers and holding hers just enough longer
than was necessary to give the moment an emphasis he
hoped she would remember later. Deborah took Sarah
gently by the shoulders and looked at her directly before
kissing her on the cheek and bidding her welcome. When
Leon had helped her out, Nell joined Lovey on the porch,
and then together the women went into the house.

Leon stayed behind with Floyd, who had dismounted.
Plumboy was there to take care of the carriage and
horses, so Leon walked with Floyd and the mare around
the house to the stables.

"You appear mighty pleased with yourself," Floyd observed in the smiling way Leon knew was meant to tease
him.

"I think she's the best girl in the world! She's changed
some since I last saw her."

"Or you have," Floyd suggested.

"Maybe I have," Leon agreed happily.

Side by side Deborah and Lovey led the way up the
stairs, the others following. They proceeded to the largest
and most lavishly appointed guest room, which Nell and
Felix usually claimed when they were at Beulah Land because of its two big comfortable beds. (Years ago Nell
had said, "I am sometimes restless in the night because of
my uncertain constitution, and fear to disturb poor Felix
who sleeps like a blessed angel.") Nell had been the first
to insist that the Penningtons have the room. They were
very special guests, she allowed, and besides, they were to
be there for a long visit and must be made as comfortable
as possible. Both Sarah and Penelope exclaimed at the noble proportions of the room and its handsome furnishings.
Besides the beds, each of which had a table handily at its
head with its own oil lamp, there were two large ward-

robes, two bureaus with deep, wide drawers, a full-length looking glass on a floor pedestal that could be tilted in its walnut frame to afford the viewer a thorough self-examination. There were comfortable chairs and further tables holding books and vases of flowers, dishes of pins and odd buttons, and a useful pair of scissors on a stand with various threads looped over pegs, and needles stuck into a red velvet cushion shaped like a heart. The curtains were thin and white for summer, freshly washed for the visitors and breathing a fragrance of soap and sunshine.

After a few minutes Lovey went downstairs to see if Skeeter had come yet with the trunks, and to look over the girl Ricey if he had, in order to decide her sleeping accommodation. If she looked decent and agreeable, Lovey would ask her to stay with her, since she had the space, now that Pauline spent every night in Selma's room. Skeeter had not arrived, so she told Buttercup to let her know the minute he did. Then she went back upstairs and into Selma's room, the door of which Selma had closed on first hearing the commotion downstairs of the visitors arriving. Selma stood reading by the window, with Pauline seated nearby, sewing on her lap.

"Miss Penelope and Miss Sarah have come," Lovey announced. "You must go and speak to them."

Selma looked frightened for a moment; then her eyes cleared and she closed and put down her book. "Yes, I must," she said. "They were kind to me. They are good people."

As Lovey and Pauline stared at each other with pleased surprise, Selma left them and went to the room she knew the guests would occupy. The door was open, so she walked right in. The four in the room stopped talking at sight of her. Selma went to Penelope and took her by the hand. "Welcome, Aunt Pea," she said.

Penelope kissed the girl and hugged her briefly. "Thank you, my dear."

When she was released, Selma turned to Sarah. "I am glad that you have come," Selma said simply.

Knowing of Selma's nervous condition and recent avoidance of society, Sarah was touched by her words and appearance, and had to exercise control not to show too much sympathy in her eyes. She took the girl's hand and pressed it. "I am happy to see you again. I hope you will help me to make the acquaintance of Beulah Land."

"Oh," Selma said, "there will be plenty to help you do that."

"I hope particularly for you to show me about, if you will be so kind, when you feel the strength and inclination."

Selma said uncertainly, "There are perhaps one or two places the others might not think to show you, which I know, and which you might like."

"I shall be grateful."

"Will you excuse me now?"

They nodded to each other as if there was understanding between them, and Selma turned and went out of the room, her mother staring after her astonished, Nell smiling with something like triumph because the visit had been, after all, her idea.

Deborah was immensely encouraged when Selma later came downstairs for supper with all of them. But she did not know Selma, would never indeed have the smallest understanding of her. What she looked upon as a sign of Selma's recovery had nothing to do with that. Selma had every intention of continuing her life much as it had taken form during the last several weeks. But she did regard the Misses Pennington highly, and wanted to be courteous to them, and so she made the effort, no small one, that first day to make them feel welcome.

After supper she again excused herself and retired to her room, where she was glad to find Pauline waiting. Sarah was disappointed at her leaving them, but Leon instantly offered himself as escort over the gardens.

He included Penelope in his invitation, but she declared that she would be more comfortable with Deborah and Nell on the wide porch where the three sat rocking contentedly back and forth in large, cane-bottomed and cane-backed chairs. Felix had gone out by himself to smoke a cigar and "to look over the stock," a standard ploy of the menfolk to get away from their women, who were glad enough to see them go, preferring, as they did, the easiness of one another's company.

It was not yet dark. There was an insect hum over the gardens like the echo of a held note of a cello, full and warm and ripe with the completion of a fair summer's day. The flower gardens were lush with color, fragrant with rose and petunia and jasmine. The graveled walks had been newly raked. A white peacock, out to catch the last rays of the evening sun, made a procession all by himself as he stepped out from behind a hedge.

"Look at him!" Sarah marveled. "Like the king leaving his palace to open Parliament."

"He is; oh, he is!" Leon laughed delightedly.

They talked then, as they strolled, of Savannah. It had, in truth, already acquired a nostalgia and glamour of the past for Leon, although it was not so very long since he had lived there as a student. But part of the special status he now accorded it in his affectionate references was meant to please Sarah, whose home it had always been.

"Are the Pride of India trees blooming on South Broad?" he asked.

"We call them chinaberry," she said with a smile.

"My name is grander."

"That is just the point. Chinaberry will do for me."

"You are not romantic," he accused.

"I am!" she protested, then quickly turned her face to look up into the dark foliage of a huge magnolia tree, her eyes drawn by the dazzle of sun on a perfect, creamy bloom. "How lovely it is. I don't believe I have ever seen such a large magnolia."

Leon nodded, pleased and proprietory. "It was here when the house was built, and long before. There were a lot of them. Some were in the way and had to be cut down. This place was known as Magnolia Garden before we owned it, although they were not a garden, they grew wild. My grandfather built the house in 1783."

"Did he?" Sarah said with intense interest. "That means it is—oh, nearly fifty years old. Think of it!"

"Yes," Leon agreed, although he did not care about its age except as it appeared to please his guest.

They paused to watch a hummingbird suspended in a whir of wings, his beak in a blossom. "Do they never rest?" she asked.

"They mustn't, or they die," he said.

They walked on, made thoughtful and a little sad by the hummingbird. But when they came to the orchard and strolled in and out among the trees, their hearts and talk grew lighter, and they laughed, and although Sarah protested that he must leave them alone until they were fully ripened, Leon squeezed peach after peach until he found one whose sides gave enough for him to pull it for her.

She took it from his hand and smelled it and held it against her cheek. "It is still warm from the day." Then, "Look!" she exclaimed, pointing toward a child who seemed to bend double as he ran helterskelter in and out of the patterned lines of trees. "Did we frighten him, do you think?"

Leon shrugged.

"Is it a child you know?"

"No," Leon said, although he had recognized Roman.

"Surely you must know, at least to recognize, everyone on the place," she said. "Even the children."

"It's getting dark. Look." He pointed. "A star." He looked about the sky. "Yes, it is the first. Let us make a wish on it."

She nodded.

They stared intently at the star glittering sharp against the blue sky that was darkening to night.

"What did you wish?" he said when she relaxed her expression.

"Too many things. I should have concentrated my wishing all to one goal."

"I wished—"

"Don't tell. It's bad luck, they say."

They turned to walk back.

Before they reached the house they heard music from the group of Negroes who had turned out to serenade the visitors. They lingered by the blossoming wisteria vines at the dark end of the porch until a song ended, and then joined the three ladies, who had stopped rocking and were listening appreciatively. At the conclusion of the song the ladies applauded, and Felix, who had stood behind the little band, and had indeed been the instigator of their performance, stepped forward and joined the ladies in their applause.

"Now something to dance to!" Felix sang the words.

Immediately, violin and banjo began a jiggy, jouncy tune. Felix clapped his hands in time, and Deborah, surprisingly, got out of her chair and made gliding, dancing steps as she joined her brother-in-law. Penelope and Nell laughed and clapped encouragement as Felix and Deborah began to dance.

"Where are the young'uns?" Felix demanded. "They should be dancing!"

Leon stepped from the shadows and assumed a caricature of the male dancing posture. Sarah came forward and curtsied and joined hands with him. They danced country fashion, the hearty, somewhat vulgar movements given charm and innocence by their youth. Deborah and Felix left off and clapped their hands in time to the music, as did Nell and Penelope.

Upstairs, Selma and Pauline leaned over the windowsill of Selma's room to hear better. Remembering the occasion long ago when her father died and Christmas was celebrated by the Negroes, but meagerly in the main house, and she had gone out to the cabin where they were playing music and dancing and had been invited by Pauline to join a circle of children—remembering that time, Selma now reached her hand to Pauline's, not in need but in gratitude and affection.

Nineteen

Lovey was her instant champion, though she needed none. Myrtis invited her to come and go in her kitchen as she would, which astonished everyone who overheard, for since old Cook had died, Myrtis had changed from a simple, amiable girl to a fierce and jealous queen of her domain. Ezra showed Sarah his sick animals and explained what was wrong with them and what he was doing to heal them. Without effort or calculation, she struck the right note with everyone. So in tune was she at this time, she became what anyone sought or thought to see in her.

Deborah found her "sensible and practical, with right attitudes toward things that mattered." Nell discovered that she was particularly sympathetic to the afflictions of others. Felix pronounced her "a capital girl, so very free and jolly."

Even Selma accepted her and acted to please her, guiding her into the woods to her secret places. There was a bend of the creek where a narrow branching of water ran shallow and swift and cold over white pebbles. To hold one's hands in it calmed the blood and reconciled the spirit, Selma told her. There was a trellis of scuppernong vines that fell in one place near to the ground and was strong enough to climb and swing upon. Both were still child enough to enjoy that. There was her private blackberry patch known to no one else. She was certain of this, because when the berries were ripe, they rotted and fell or made food for the birds if she did not herself pick and eat them. Now they were hard and green. She told Sarah how every year at the same time she found the shedded skin of a snake there. She had never seen him, and yet she felt she knew him, because they shared the patch without strife or formal treaty. They walked through the woods and recited the Sonnets to each other, and returned to the house arm in arm, tired and content.

When they came to the door of Selma's room, Selma

always took her guest's hand in a friendly but formal way, indicating by the gesture that their adventure was over, for the time being at any rate, and that she would go into her room alone. There she always found Pauline waiting, and Pauline was almost not jealous of these excursions, which was her tribute to Sarah. Pauline had observed Sarah closely when she first came to Beulah Land and understood that Sarah was one who gave trust and affection without demanding tribute.

Leon knew every day in a surer way that she was "the best girl in all the world." He took her with him to watch Floyd work, and Floyd made a ring for her out of a horseshoe nail, just as he did for the children. When the ring cooled, he handed it to Leon, who polished it on his trouser leg before slipping it on her finger. She declared that she would always wear it. Floyd warned her that it would turn and rust. She said that if it did, she would ask him to make her another, and the three laughed at that companionably together.

And so as Sarah learned to love Beulah Land, nearly all, but not all, of Beulah Land learned to love her. The child Roman, she discovered, followed her about. He never came close; he did not always follow her, and he never made a nuisance of himself by japing for her attention, but she was aware of the boy. A time or two she turned and endeavored to talk to him, but he was shy. At first he ran away. Then he stayed, but was silent. She feared briefly that he was a "natural" in addition to his other afflictions, but soon decided from the intelligence of his eyes and his quick expressions that he was not a "natural"—was perhaps even "unnaturally" clever. Unable because of his shyness to talk to him, she smiled when they met to show she recognized him, and now and then she addressed him softly without giving any appearance of requiring an answer. She was, she declared one day to Lovey, "quite intrigued" with the child, at which Lovey looked startled and said, "No, don't do that!" Sarah stared at her astonished. For a moment Lovey hesitated as if she were about to say more, and then she shook her head and walked away.

On the day after that, teased by the mystery of it, Sarah, during the course of an ordinary solitary walk, turned and saw the little boy, who immediately stopped too. With sudden decision she walked toward him, but he read the decision plainly in her face and gait, and turned and ran. She laughed and ran after him, calling, "Roman, wait!" She had learned his name from Posie. He would not stop, though she called his name again, ran faster than she did, although she kept him in sight, across the field, and across the back yards where people turned to stare at the two, and on to the slave quarters. Having started the game, she would not stop, but followed him all the way. The one leading the other they ran to a cabin where a big-bodied woman sat on an open porch no more than half the size of a bedsheet. The woman caught the boy and held him as he tried to wriggle away. Sarah stopped on the single stone step, smiling and breathing hard from her exertion. The woman slapped the child hard. Roman did not cry, but stood rigid before her, his face flushing with shame and the force of the blow.

"Oh, please!" Sarah cried out in dismay.

The woman turned her face to her. "Surely he has done something wrong, if you were chasing him?"

"Not at all! I merely wanted to speak to him so I called—it was like a game—we ran—"

The woman looked at the child. "You hear the lady? Why didn't you stop if she called you?" She slapped him again. He did not, would not cry.

"Please don't do that!" Sarah demanded.

Her tone seemed to please the woman, who turned to face her again. "I am his mother. My name is Clovis Elk. I am the wife of the Overseer."

"Yes?" Sarah felt that she was being told more than she comprehended.

"You are the young visitor," Clovis said.

"I am Sarah Pennington."

"Roman babbles about you." She moved her hand from the boy's arm to his back. "He says how pretty you are. He likes pretty things because he is so ugly." Roman blushed agonizingly, bringing to Sarah's attention the fact that he was lighter than the woman, lighter than she remembered Roscoe Elk as being.

Ignoring the woman as if she were not there, Sarah said, "I like you, Roman, and I would like to be your friend."

Clovis threw back her head and laughed. "Say 'thank you' to the lady!" Clovis shouted, breaking her laughter. Two smaller children, dark as she was and far darker than Roman, ran past Sarah onto the porch and clutched at the woman's skirt and arm. "Mu-dear! Mu-dear!" they said together.

"These are Roman's brothers," Clovis said, holding the

small boys against her as if wanting to draw attention to the fact that she and they were the same color. "Their names are Alonzo and Roscoe."

"Mu-dear!"

"Mu-dear!"

"Except for Roman, we are what you call in Savannah 'F.P.C.' Is it so?"

"Free persons of color?"

She nodded. "The young'uns were born free after I was bought and paid for by my husband, who is part Indian. Only Roman is a slave." Clovis laughed again and hugged the small boys. Roman ran into the house without looking at anyone. Angry and disturbed, Sarah turned and left them without another word.

Twenty

Nell and Felix had gone back to their house in Highboro. Beulah Land was its everyday, working, living self. The Negroes under Roscoe's supervision hoed corn and cotton, and suckled tobacco, which they were trying as a new crop at the suggestion of Felix. Rooster had not planted any. He was waiting to see how the Beulah Land experiment turned out, thinking that it might not be worth the careful tending required and the building of a special barn in which to cure the crop.

The men also cut trees in the woods, those that had been struck by lightning or were dying naturally and inhibited the free growth of a younger timber. The trees were chopped or sawed down, then trimmed or dragged out by mule teams, and cut into usable lengths of wood for winter warmth and for cooking.

Leon had been inspired by Sarah's visit to work on the plantation more seriously than he ever had before. He was knowledgeable about livestock from being so much with Floyd and Ezra as they worked, and now his frequent presence at the stables and stalls and pens gave weight and authority to the opinions he voiced. The first time he automatically, without planning to do so, contradicted an opinion of Roscoe's and gave a contrary order about the use of a team of mules, Plumboy's eyes opened wide, and he looked from one to the other until Roscoe struck him on the shoulder with a little tasseled whip he had recently taken to carrying, more as a plaything for his idle hands

than an object to use. "Do it, man!" he ordered and
strode away, leaving Leon to finish the matter his own
way.

When he was not offering his arm and company to
Sarah, who found much to do and now needed no guide,
Leon went wherever the largest force was employed,
walked or rode among them, or stood watching, much as
his father before him had, enjoying the sight of men and
women working. Now and then he abandoned his role of
spectator and joined the work, borrowing a hoe or an ax
or a knife or a bucket or a spade, as the work demanded.
He was quick and adept and would for short, concentrated spells work harder and with more skill than anyone
about him, not trying to set an example, but doing it for
the sheer pleasure and interest of doing it. He had the
aristocrat's ease with dirt and the use of his hands,
whereas Roscoe was seldom seen to use his hands, except
to guide the reins of his mule. He abhorred direct hand-
dirt contact, as a man who had been forced by early circumstance to work at any kind of labor he could get.

Roscoe was seldom present when Leon joined the work
force. He left on-the-spot supervision largely to his lieutenants, men chosen because they were afraid of him and
who owed him some debt or personal allegiance, and who
would therefore get the most out of the workers that
could be got.

The workers, men and women alike, were pleased with
Leon's joining them if he did not stay too long. It made a
welcome break and novelty in a boring day. But a long
stay merely underlined the drudgery of what they had to
do. Roscoe's odd, surprise visits accomplished more in getting work done than Leon's spur of the moment visits that
sometimes were overextended both in the time he spent
and the unwanted intimacy he enforced by joining the actual work. A man found it easier to keep his own hoe
than to lend it and take it back. The different angle of another's swing could dull its cutting edge.

There was much visiting back and forth among the
women of Beulah Land and Oaks and the two farms between them, and between all of these and the people of
Highboro, who often rode or walked into the countryside
during the summer months to sit and lounge and gossip,
to sample a peach or pear, to share a melon and a story.
There were frequent impromptu country frolics, an evening of dancing perhaps that had not been planned but
grew out of a sudden stopping-by or chance suggestion. If

there was pleasure and relaxation to be had, word would spread mysteriously, and others would presently arrive in a wagon or on a horse or on foot to join the party. Selma, of course, attended none of these gatherings, and since it was understood there would not likely be any confrontation between estranged husband and wife, Bonard frequented such as he pleased. There was courtesy between him and Sarah, friendliness between him and Leon.

At one such light summer frolic, which the older people attended, indeed, would not miss, Bonard paid his respects to Miss Penelope and asked if she had recent news of her married niece.

"Her second letter came this very day from Baltimore," she was happy to inform him. "She and Mr. Savage are moving to Philadelphia shortly, where Mr. Savage expects to appear in a fall and winter season of theatrical productions with a new company."

"How very interesting it must be for—Miss Lauretta, I was about to say—Mrs. Savage, I should say."

"Ah," she said warmly, "you knew her as Lauretta and may still call her so. Little did we know when you and she and Leon and Sarah used to have such lively times together on Broughton Street that she—and you, of course!—that all of you—oh, dear!"

"May I fetch you a glass of punch, ma'am?" Bonard asked to relieve her embarrassment.

Uncle Joshua wrote from Savannah to say that all was well on Broughton Street, that the use of whale oil had been almost eliminated during their absence, and that the largest single item of expenditure was for sugar for Clarice's jellying and preserving. She was taking advantage of the absence of her mistress and the cheap abundance—it was all but given away—of seasonal fruit to put up a good supply for the winter. Uncle Joshua also wrote that the townspeople, with the stern if not threatening example of himself and Judge Truebody, had quite accepted the fact of Miss Lauretta's elopement and marriage.

Penelope received letters from Judge Truebody in which he conveyed the sentiment that Savannah's loss was Beulah Land's gain, and advised concerning Lauretta's future that one must hope for the best but be prepared for the worst—and managed, in short, to remind Penelope that she was away from home, and that however well her niece took to country life, she herself had had a bate of it, that she missed Savannah—and Uncle Joshua and Clarice and yes even Ichabod, and most of all she missed her own dear house on Broughton Street.

It was now the middle of July, and they had been visiting for nearly six weeks. Penelope had long since exhausted every confidence she wished to share with Deborah. There were moments she could do nothing but despise her for her dull sense of duty and her countrified preoccupation with weather and crops. There were mornings it was all she could do to eat her breakfast cantaloupe and batter cakes with the others before escaping to the quiet of her room. She had come to abominate country air with its wretched fresh smells of fruit and bloom and animal excreta. She could not cross the kitchen yard without pressing a kerchief to her nose; yet Deborah could scrape chicken filth from the bottom of a shoe on a step as she calmly talked of rain and neighbors. The morning milk was too warm, with too intimate a taste of the inside of a cow where it had too recently been. She thought if she were asked to enjoy another ear of corn, no matter if it were boiled, baked, or roasted, she would take it and throw it at someone or something. She longed for the close, stale smell of the indoors in Savannah. No matter how one opened windows and aired the house, there always remained a good house smell of furniture and oil and attic must. It never, thank goodness, could be mistaken for a garden or a pasture. She longed for the sour, put-upon look of Clarice, the frowning disapproval of Uncle Joshua, the cheerful, idling idiocy of lazy Ichabod.

"It is time for us to go home," she said to Sarah one night when they had retired to their room.

Sarah looked surprised, pained, and then resigned.

"We must go home to Savannah," together they said to Deborah and Leon and Selma the next day.

"Oh, no!" Leon said.

"Please stay!" Selma begged Sarah.

"You've only just come," Deborah grumped to Penelope.

Firmly, Penelope said again, "We must go home to Savannah."

After a week of hearing this repeated, the large family of Beulah Land and its neighbors began to believe at last that the Pennington ladies were going to leave them. A sweet, romantic sadness then seemed to come over them all. Selma escorted Sarah to all her private places to say goodbye. The blackberry patch was full of ripe fruit, which they ate as they wept and declared they should never, never forget this time they had spent together.

Rooster and Trudy came over for what was expected to be a last supper. Trudy was getting larger every time they saw her. When Sarah left her room, Leon was like her shadow, indoors and out. He was in love, and he fancied himself even more in love than he was. He remembered (Floyd had mentioned her, and Leon had said, "Good Lord, is she still up and about?") that Sarah had not yet met old Maggie, so one day he took Maggie a present of a pint of liquor and Sarah. The old woman, who had ever loved a drama and initiated not a few, and who had felt snubbed because the guests had paid her no visit, was instantly won to the young girl when she saw her, saw the pretty face and soft eyes and smiling lips and understood why the reports that had come to her had all been so alike and so good. She said she would tell her fortune, and she took a long straw from a sage broom and stirred the cold ashes in the fireplace, where she had cooked earlier in the day.

"You will travel," she said frowning, "but you will return." She dropped the straw, rose from her chair, which rocked and creaked by itself without her weight to steady it. She raised her hands, the fingers spread apart for emphasis, and said as if she were repeating words she had received in confidence from Heaven: "Who comes to us in love, let her abide here. Praise be the Lord!"

As they walked thoughtfully back to the house, Leon stopped and took Sarah's hand. "Don't go, Sarah. Be my wife. Marry me. I and Beulah Land need you!"

Leon was late in his proposal, and Sarah accepted it quietly. The very moment Leon drove the carriage from the main road into the private drive through the orchard, when Floyd met them and galloped then ahead, calling, "Company coming!"—she had decided, she knew now, that she must one day be mistress of Beulah Land.

Twenty-One

Oh, there was rejoicing!

Yet the reaction that followed immediately was the declaration by almost everyone that he had known it would happen. How could it be other? Sarah belonged so clearly to Beulah Land that Leon seemed almost the incidental agent of her permanently abiding there. The departure of the visitors—no longer just visitors, not yet family—was put off a week so that everyone might congratulate everyone else. But plans and dates were settled at last, and leave was finally taken.

Discretion as well as etiquette dictated that the wedding be in Savannah. By having it there, the society that Penelope belonged to was satisfied, perhaps rather, mollified, having been deprived of Lauretta's wedding.

There was no embarrassment over how to accommodate neighbors of Beulah Land, nor need to solve the persistent riddle of how to both acknowledge and ignore the marriage of Selma and Bonard.

Since the wedding was to be in Savannah, the only people from the country who made the journey to attend it were Deborah, Nell, and Felix. A bridegroom's backers are notably less fulsome in their attentions than a bride's. Selma had said she would go, but on the day before the family party was to take coach, she declared that she was not, after all, fit enough to travel.

Sarah and Leon took their vows to each other in the presence of a large and interested section of Savannah society at St. John's Church. Judge Truebody gave the bride away, and Felix Kendrick acted as his nephew's Best Man. Deborah and Nell sat alone in the front pew on the right-hand side of the church. The one surprise of the ceremony occurred when Leon took the ring from Felix to place on Sarah's finger. To it he added, intending it as a sweet and private joke, a new ring Floyd had fashioned for him from a horseshoe nail. Sarah smiled when she recognized what had been done, and cupped her hand over the two rings on the same finger, making her own meaning out of it.

Twenty-Two

On the night of the wedding day Selma and Lovey and Pauline sat together after supper in Selma's room. They had eaten there—no point in setting the dining room for Selma alone—Lovey joining her daughters, as she called them both, to make a little celebration. Each enjoyed a glass of wine before having supper, and the atmosphere was genial, that of three old and trusting friends together, knowing that no one would break in of a sudden and ask any to play the part she usually played, but was relieved of playing tonight.

They had begun to yawn, although it was early. The day had been a warm one, but Lovey pulled the curtains nearly to, for it was October, and she had observed signs all day that told her the night might turn cold for the time of year. A sweetness that was almost sickliness hung in the air. The last of the sugar cane had been ground that day and boiled into syrup, the scent of which lingered and reached everywhere.

It was then, as their minds drifted toward sleep, that they heard the galloping of a horse on the drive, followed by knocking on the front door downstairs. Lovey froze as she considered the possibilities; then shook her head and went out, not bothering to close the door after her. Pauline went to the door and pushed it not quite to, so that she could listen. When Lovey opened the door downstairs and the sound of the caller's voice came up, Selma closed the window quietly and stood with her back to it, watching Pauline.

Lovey knew from Bonard's eyes when she let him in that he had been drinking. His quick breathing might have come from excitement and hard riding, but the shining eyes were from liquor and a conviction that he had been done ill.

"Mister Bonard, nobody home; they all gone to Savannah," Lovey said. When he tried to walk by her, her hands met his chest and pressed lightly. "Everybody in Savannah—"

He pushed her aside. "I know who's not!" he said and ran down the hall into the stairwell room. "Selma!" he yelled. "Selma! I come to claim you! You got to come with me now, you hear? Home to Oaks! Your clothes are there waiting—come and wear them like you ought!"

Pauline closed the door upstairs and bolted it. Lovey was beside Bonard downstairs, waiting to see what he would do next.

"You hear me, Selma?" Clutching the banisters with both hands gave him strength of body and purpose, and he took a breath and plunged up them. After him went Lovey. Seeing that Selma's door was closed, she made no move to interfere. Bonard had often in the old days been on this floor visiting Leon in his room, so he knew which was Selma's and went to it directly to knock on the door, then to try the knob, and when he found it ungiving, to pound hard on the door with open palms.

"Mister Bonard—go home!" Lovey pleaded.

"You *in* there, Selma?" He paused. There was no word or movement behind the door. "Selma!" He shook the knob and kicked the wall. Then making himself quiet, he spoke through the closed door as if he knew she was just on the other side of it, an inch away. "Don't you love me one bit?"

Lovey grasped his arm. "Go home, Mister Bonard. Best to, like I say."

He pulled away from her and pressed his body and arms and face as flat against the door as he could, as if to embrace his love.

There was a sharp click; he drew back. Then there was the sliding of the bolt, and the door opened; but the woman there was not Selma.

"Hit me, if you will," Pauline said. "You'll not touch her again."

Bonard frowned. "Who are you?" He turned to Lovey. Lovey slammed the door in her daughter's face and took him by the arm and led him to and down the stairs, as if he were a sleepwalker and she were guiding him back to the warmth and safety of his bed.

Floyd stood at the foot of the stairs, not smiling or stern. Lovey did not know what had brought him—perhaps he'd heard the horse galloping when Bonard first came—but she was thankful to see him.

"Floyd?" Bonard said. "I seem to be—" Bonard shook his head, started to speak again but could not make words, looked enquiringly into the other man's face.

"I'll ride with you back to Oaks," Floyd said.

And he did so. Rooster came down to the hall when he heard Floyd and Bonard come in. Bonard was near fainting with tiredness and leaned heavily on his escort. Rooster gave Floyd a thanking nod and took his brother away to his room. Floyd got back on his mule and rode home.

Twenty-Three

By unspoken agreement Sarah and Leon, save for a simple goodnight kiss, did not become intimate, although they slept in the same bed, during the time on Broughton Street. Two days after the wedding, when it was agreed that the bride had had sufficient rest from the exertions that had led up to the wedding, they took coach to Beulah

Land, arriving on the afternoon of the second day, after pausing to rest at an inn overnnight.

Leon did not take Sarah to his room, but rather joined her in the room she had earlier occupied as a visitor. Because of the room's largeness and comfortable furnishings, they had decided to take it as theirs, leaving Leon's old room for guests.

Sarah's sadness at parting from Penelope was dissipated upon her arrival at Beulah Land, for it was a coming home; and if she had not felt it so surely, the feeling might have puzzled her. But that was the way it was with her and Beulah Land: they took to each other in a way that could not be denied.

By now Sarah and Leon were beginning to be easy and familiar with each other's small personal ways. They found it comfortable to be together. They touched hands, arms, cheeks easily. It was, Leon marveled, as if they were innocent girl and boy, or brother and sister. Then he laughed at himself for the thought. Yet it was so for him.

Sarah began to wonder when their relations would alter and progress further. She'd had a sister less reticent than she and knew what she might expect. So gently had Leon treated her, she was certain that whatever came now must be kindly effected. She was eager for him to go ahead. She wanted children. She had not thought of it until she came to Beulah Land to visit, but seeing all of the people living and working together, she knew herself to be a strong woman for family. What better father could children have than Leon, good and handsome, who held her hand and patted it, who put an arm about her waist or shoulders, who held her affectionately, whose lips were warm and sweet. She began to feel that she must have fallen in love with him since, not before, their marriage, and from this thought she took joy.

On a night soon after their homecoming, when they blew out their candles and went to bed, she turned to him. He opened his arms to her, and she pressed herself against him. Only their night clothes separated them. Her heart began to beat fast—or was it his she felt? She did not know, but she lost her girl's reticence as he kissed her, and kissed him with increasing ardor.

Leon fought panic. After his first encounters with Clovis, all the girls he had been with were girls who made themselves available, girls with whom one might be easy and playful, taking what one pleased without concern for their feelings. The whole thing of *fucking* was that you did it with women like that. Now—he was a fool not to have thought of this moment—he could not feel passion for the girl in his arms. To do so would have seemed incestuous.

It was only when he closed his eyes tight as a child praying or making a wish that panic subsided. His mind called up and fixed on that summer day when he and Floyd had gone to the woods to fish, and then swam, and Clovis came around the bend of the creek to be with them. He saw Floyd; he saw Clovis; he felt what he had felt then. Sarah's willing and wondering body accepted his. But he was not Leon, she was not Sarah.

PART THREE

1835

One

Between them they owned three hundred slaves, but every
year now, in January, June, and October, Edna Davis and
Deborah Kendrick took brooms and shears, shovel and
rake to the cemetery in Highboro to attend to the graves
of their husbands. (After two further strokes that came
five days apart, Benjamin Davis had died on July 17,
1831.)

It was Edna who had initiated the companionable grave
tending. Deborah would have been content to leave the
job to Ezra, but she could not very well refuse to accompany her old neighbor when she was asked. And she had
soon come to enjoy and look forward to the occasions. It
was, for one thing, a time the two women, different as
they were from each other but sharing so many problems
and experiences, could talk without thinking how they
sounded to family and friends.

Their plots in the cemetery, like their plantations, were
separated by smaller plots, but they were yet close enough
for the women to talk without raising their voices unduly;
and sometimes, when conversation became intimate, they
worked together first in one plot and then in the other.

Arnold Kendrick's gravestone told his name and the
dates of his birth and death, nothing more. That of Benjamin Davis added to the dates enclosing his span of life
an inscription: *Over in the summer land.*

Edna stood back from her husband's grave, staring at it
intently but without apparent sorrow, before breaking her
own gaze and pointing with the toe of one shoe. "This is
where I will be," she said with satisfaction.

Deborah nodded. Edna sketched the future map
routinely each time they worked there together. Moving a
few steps along she said, "Over here Rooster and Trudy
and their children. Leaving a lot of space for them; don't
know how many will come, do I? Now here is where I
have in mind for Bonard. On the side. With us, but giving

him a little privacy. And there's room for his wife too."

"I don't think you need plan on that," Deborah said.

"Do you reckon they'll never come together again?"

"I fear not," Deborah said, and after a pause added, "Alas."

"A shame and a pity," Edna agreed.

"The waste," Deborah said. "It's waste I mind."

"You did your best, and I did too; but the Lord had his own plan that wouldn't be denied."

"I suppose so," Deborah said, as if she were not sure she agreed and harbored resentment at any alteration of her plans, even if instigated by the Lord.

"I do hate things left unfinished."

"I do too. But what we mind and what we want—" Deborah shrugged. "Well." She walked back to her own plot, took the rake she had left propped on Arnold's tombstone and picked the dead leaves from its prongs.

Edna whipped her heavy shawl in the air and pulled it over her shoulders and back, tying the ends in a loose knot as she joined her friend. "I think we've done enough for this time, don't you?"

Deborah nodded.

"It looks real nice. Where are you having them put you?"

"I don't much care," Deborah said, and Edna looked shocked. Gathering the tools they had used, they walked away toward the horse and buggy they had left in the lane that ran through the middle of the cemetery.

Because it was her buggy this time, Deborah put away their tools in the back box. She climbed into the driver's seat and undid the reins she'd tied together and around the side railing of the seat. The horse twisted his neck to look at her, then faced front again, shaking his head.

Edna pulled her tired, heavy weight up into the seat beside Deborah and fumbled briefly for a bundle she had brought along and tucked under the seat. Finding a pint fruit jar, she unscrewed the top of it and shook it invitingly. "Some of our peach brandy Rooster put up last summer," she said, holding it out. "Take a swallow or two. It helps against the cold."

Deborah took the jar and drank from it, then wiped the rim with the heel of her palm and gave it back. "Oh, my." She blinked watering eyes. "That does taste good."

Edna nodded firmly. "I say we need it on these January trips. You try to pick a mild day, but it's still winter, and ͏ceptive."

"We're not as young as we used to be."

"Do you feel the cold more?" Edna asked encouragingly. "I sure do."

"Yes, I do."

Edna drank from the jar, rested it on her knee a moment, then drank from it again before wiping the rim with the end of her shawl and handing it to Deborah. Deborah held it without drinking, then took a sip and followed it by a swallow.

"Keeps the cold out, that's so," Deborah observed sociably

"I'm glad I brought it," Edna said, as if she did not always bring a jar of something or other, summer or winter. "How *is* Selma nowadays? I didn't see her all through Christmas at the various things."

"She won't go anywhere. Seldom even comes to meals with the rest of us."

"Stays in her room?"

"Walks, or stays in her room. Walks a lot, even bad weather. Comes home, bottom of her dress and cloak muddy, and her looking half frozen and not caring."

"Walks—by herself?"

"No, no. There's the—Lovey's daughter."

"Pauline?"

"Yes, Pauline. Devoted."

Edna accepted the jar Deborah held out to her. "Don't she mingle with Sarah and Leon even?"

"Not with Leon. She won't let a man come near her, no white one, anyway; although she's easy enough with Ezra and such. Sarah, yes. Not to mingle exactly, but likes her. Lets her come sit in her room sometimes. Only Selma doesn't seem to need her. Or need anyone, except Pauline maybe. That's always been her way. You know, I've never blamed Bonard—"

"I know you've never. I suppose I have, being a woman who lived most of my life in a house of men and thinking it would be nice to know another woman in the house. I blamed Bonard because I felt he scared Selma, and I wanted her to be with us."

Deborah looked brooding for a moment. "She writes poetry."

Again Edna looked shocked. "Poetry?"

"Scribbling. Things that rhyme sometimes but mostly don't. Sarah calls them her poems."

"Oh," Edna said, the word sounding stark although she had meant it to comfort.

"Sarah says she understands them. I don't. I like a poem to rhyme, if there has to be a poem. What else is it for?"

Edna nodded, but her next words showed that her mind had veered off from Selma. "Sarah needs to have a baby." Deborah's stillness told her she had gone too far; she had encroached on privacies. "I talk a lot," she apologized.

"Our children—will we ever understand them!" Deborah exclaimed, taking that way to excuse her friend's presumption.

"Surely Sarah is a comfort to you," Edna said.

"Oh, yes. When she isn't busy with her school. She's teaching the children to read and write and figure a little. Funniest thing I ever saw, a whole line of pickaninnies saying the multiplication table."

Edna pursed her lips before commenting, "Too much of that and they won't be so ready to take hoe in hand when the time comes."

Deborah shook her head. "They're all too lazy to stick at it. Soon as they learn to write their names and do a little basic adding, off they go." She took another sip from the jar, then gave it back to Edna without bothering to wipe the rim. "That's good, and that's enough. Are we ready to go?" She took up the reins, slapped them slackly across the horse's rump and said, "Giddap, Napoleon."

Without turning his head or switching his tail in acknowledgment, the horse picked up his feet and moved along the lane.

"We stayed longer than we thought," Edna said. "It's starting to get dark."

"January days are short. But I'll have us home soon. Come to Beulah Land and take supper with us. Leon will drive you home later."

Edna laughed appreciation. "I thank you, but I better not. I want to see my grandchildren. Adam and James and Annabel and Doreen—their very names comfort me when I think how everything is and how little of what we want turns out."

Deborah drove the buggy through the main road of Highboro at a conventional trot, but as soon as they left the town, she slapped the reins hard on the horse's rump, surprising him into a faster trot and then a gallop. Edna and Deborah gripped the side rails of the buggy and giggled like girls as the horse galloped along through twilight toward Oaks and Beulah Land.

Two

Another death had been that of Maggie. She did not die naturally of old age, but was the victim of one of her innocent appetites. She had tried to eat a small, fried perch without removing its head and bones, thinking them soft enough to pass, and had choked before she or anyone near her could stuff corn bread down her throat to clear it. The manner of her departure provided interested comment and speculation, and so prevented any chill of sadness from attending the event. Besides, there was her age. Although no one could say how old she was, it was agreed that she had been the oldest person living at Beulah Land. Their astonishment at her living so long was matched by satisfaction that she had at long last died, natural causes or not.

Her cabin stood empty—she had no living relative on the plantation—until Sarah asked Deborah if she might use it for her school. Deborah agreed that she might, until it was needed. The few sticks of furniture, the quilts and pans and one kettle were given to the first who asked for them. Floyd had the floors and walls scoured clean, and built benches and set up sawhorse tables of a height to suit children.

Her school had begun with Roman.

Before she married Leon, Sarah had taken notice of the boy, in spite of Lovey's efforts to discourage her. After her marriage, she sought him out. Again, Lovey tried to discourage her interest. So did Deborah. So, furiously—it was the first time they quarreled—did Leon. So, certainly, did the child's mother, Clovis. And twice, in warning and insult, Roscoe struck the boy in Sarah's presence.

It was that that made her realize the reason behind all of their putting obstacles in the way of her knowing Roman. Leon was, of course, his father. She saw it all in a second. It explained everything in that strange first meeting with Clovis. After first shock she realized that she was not even surprised.

Considering that he was Leon's son and she hoped that she herself would conceive, she might well have hated the sight of him. Instead, she began to love him, seeing his hunched-back, which made him seem to crouch, seeing

one leg bent at the knee to accommodate the shortness of
the other, seeing his unwavering eyes with their look of
complete awareness of what he was.

She did not ponder it or try to understand it further.
She asked him to walk with her, and he did. They talked
to each other, without either of them at first making very
much sense of what the other said, understanding only
that they needed each other's company.

After Leon had admitted the truth of being Roman's father, he said, "Now surely you see that it, to say the least,
embarrasses me."

"I'm sorry," Sarah said.

"The people are laughing. They think it's your ignorance."

"I'm sorry."

"Then leave him alone!"

"No. I won't do that."

"Why?"

Deborah took her into her office one morning and said,
"My dear Sarah, it isn't suitable. I'm sorry you had to find
out about all that, but he *was* a boy, and there was no
more to it than a foolish mistake, a summer misfortune.
You do see that you must let him alone now?"

Sarah shook her head stubbornly.

It was the first time Deborah had not found her submis-
sive. She narrowed her eyes and stared at the girl, who
met her look evenly; and she wondered if it might be a
good thing in the long run, this unexpected strength that
allowed her to say no to all of them.

Roscoe's hitting the boy in her presence, on the pretext
of punishing him for his slowness at responding to a simple question, but really to warn Sarah away from him, did
not turn her away. After the first time, Sarah did not even
listen to the exasperated pleading of Leon, or the scolding
of Deborah, or the emotional advice of Lovey.

Roman was teased and taunted by his younger, darker
brothers, Roscoe and Alonzo, slapped and screamed at by
his mother, and beaten by his nominal father. But it made
no difference.

She took him by the hand, and they walked together
through the orchard when spring came and it bloomed;
beyond that, through the woods and fields. Once, early on,
she asked him in a brisk tone, "Does it hurt you to walk?"

"No," he said, and she let that settle it.

Sometimes she went too fast in her eagerness to explore, and had to stop and wait for him. Sometimes she even chided him. "Come along! You can walk faster than that." Now and then they raced short distances, as if both of them were children and rivals. She did not make the mistake of letting him win, which might have discouraged his trying to pit his strength against hers.

"What do you dream about?" she asked him one day.

"You sometimes," he answered readily.

"Do you?" She was pleased.

"And I dream I'm like everybody else. It's a funny thing, but in my sleep, I'm straight and tall."

"You won't ever be, Roman."

"I know," he said.

"You have other things. You *think* better than practically anyone else I know. Except Aunt Pea and Uncle Joshua."

He laughed. By then he knew about her Aunt Pea and Uncle Joshua. She talked about her life in Savannah to him sometimes when she found herself missing it. "Better than your sister?"

"She doesn't think at all. Poor dear would be better off if she did. Or maybe not. She likes not to know things, she says, until they happen."

"Ask me a question."

"What is nine times seven?"

"Sixty-three," he said instantly.

"That was always one of the hardest for me to remember."

"You've told me," he said. "That's why I never forget it."

"What's the population of Savannah?"

"Ten thousand."

She shrugged. "That isn't thinking, you know. That's merely information." They walked on. After a little time Sarah said, "Do you know that in addition to thinking well, you are also a handsome boy?"

He stopped, and his face registered denial, anger, and embarrassment. He turned away from her and ran. She ran after him and caught him. "Have I ever told you a lie?" she asked, her tone vexed.

"I was little when Mama first stood me in front of the mirror and said, 'Look at ugly you!' "

"Your mama is wrong." Sarah turned and walked away from him. When he followed, she stopped and waited, not smiling. He came up, and she put out her hand. He took it, and they walked back to the house.

Seeing a child with a grown person makes other children curious. Those at Beulah Land began to hang about when Sarah and Roman sat together on the back steps looking through old schoolbooks she'd had Aunt Pea send her from Savannah. The brighter ones picked up words and facts and figures, and began to chant them in imitation of Roman, both for the fun of it and to get Sarah's attention.

Sarah invited them to come closer, and that is how her school evolved. It was never a school in a formal sense, with regular classes and schedule. Roman fell into the habit of waiting for Sarah on the back porch after breakfast, and when she was not required to be occupied otherwise, she joined him, and they walked about together, through the yards of the slave quarters, through the kitchen garden and orchard, along the edge of a field, into the woods. Soon, instead of their being just Sarah and Roman, they were more often a troop.

Rainy days provided a problem, and that is why when old Maggie died about six months after Sarah came to Beulah Land a bride, she asked for the cabin and was given the use of it. The very old people who were beyond work and for whom any diversion was better than none sometimes came to sit and listen, and a few of them learned to write their names and the year of their birth, of which they were very proud.

Ezra came in and out because he loved Sarah and enjoyed watching her with the children, but he never stayed for very long at a time. At seventy-five he was still busy with his herbs and healing potions. His hands were still firm in their understanding of where and how to touch an animal to give comfort. Floyd came to watch and listen too, because he liked being near Sarah.

But mainly it was the children. Some came for a certain time, and then dropped out, and came again when whatever work or interest had deflected them was satisfied. Two who never came were Roman's half brothers, Alonzo and Roscoe. Their father taught them, as he had taught their mother (but not Roman, never Roman) before they were born.

Probably none of this would have happened, or it would have happened in a lesser or different way if family demands on Sarah had been greater; but there was little for her to do. The running of the house was managed so efficiently by Lovey it could provide no occupation for Sarah. Deborah and Roscoe ran the plantation jealously. Indeed, they kept things pretty much to themselves again. After Leon's fly at applying himself to the working affairs of the place during the time he was first in love with Sarah, his efforts had slacked off.

He was too proud to pretend he was needed where he clearly was not, too shy or weak to take authority from Deborah and Roscoe, who would surely have resisted any such effort on his part. And he took too much pleasure in idleness to be able to continue consistently any effort he began.

For the first year of their marriage, but with decreasing frequency, he and Sarah had applied themselves to becoming a loving couple. Familiarity did not quell Leon's feelings of embarrassment at fondling sexually an innocent woman. His self-consciousness made him awkward and ineffective, and so he never roused Sarah to any genuine passion. She wanted to feel it, and she wanted a child. But she felt nothing except his awkwardness and embarrassment and responded in ways that mirrored and compounded them, believing that she failed him in some manner she was too ignorant to know. Eventually, her own shyness and sense of decorum prevented her trying to approach him physically except for the most innocent gestures of affection. She was genuinely fond of him and felt certain that Leon was fond of her, but there was no physical desire in the feeling on either side. Finally accepting that it was so, they slept in separate beds in the large room they shared.

Sarah told herself that it was not perhaps for everyone to know the storms of the blood certain poetry had led her to expect of loving. In any event, she had Roman and her school. And Leon renewed his old friendship with Bonard. More and more often he rode with him into town, and they sometimes went together to certain sisters who lived alone beyond the edge of town in the other direction from their plantations. Their names, or the names they had given themselves, were Florabel, Pansy, and Annette, and Leon felt robust and easy with them and was happy to enjoy his fucking again.

Leon and Bonard also began to do business together. Bonard was firmly established with Felix now, and Felix was glad to welcome his nephew into their business dealings. Presently, Leon was taking a larger and more confident part in the actual money end of the running of Beulah Land. Felix gradually turned over to him the matters he had previously handled for Deborah, including all those pertaining to the cotton gin and the storage warehouse, which they owned jointly, and which up to now had been left entirely to Felix to manage.

Given a sheet of figures, Leon understood them—better than Deborah, it turned out, although he would never have her shrewdness in understanding how those figures were translated from acreage and barn, from good husbandry of land and livestock. Roscoe knew every detail of the sweat work. Leon soon learned the pen work. Deborah knew less of both than either of them, but more than either knew of each other's realm of activity. If it was not a happy arrangement, there was the advantage that it worked.

Had she been wholly dependent on her marriage for fulfillment, Sarah would have perhaps turned melancholy and morbid. But she had Beulah Land and its people. As the years passed and she came to know them better, she gradually accumulated a score of their grievances against Roscoe and Clovis. When she was purchased by her husband, Clovis ceased working as maid and laundress and, in fact, in any way for the Kendricks, which left her with time to cultivate her talent as a dressmaker.

Laura-Lou did all of the sewing for the white family at Beulah Land, but Clovis had developed a considerable following among the slaves. They made their own common clothes, but Clovis was much in demand to buy the materials and to plan, cut out, and sew their best, especially wedding and funeral dresses. No girl on Beulah Land would think of marrying now without a dress from Clovis. They paid in money or promises or both. Although not given wages, the slaves were allowed to raise and sell chickens and garden produce, and most of them earned bonus moneys for special work done.

Sarah knew from what the women told her and her own acquaintance of town prices that Clovis charged extravagantly for the dress materials and such trimmings as buttons and ribbon, as well as her own skillful sewing. She was able to set whatever value she pleased on these things because she was willing to extend credit. Of course, the elderly women who commissioned their burying dresses from her had to pay in advance. Some of those dresses were made and folded away for years, with paper between folds, before they were used; and they were brought out and displayed on special occasions.

Sarah learned also that Roscoe had frequent money dealings with the male slaves. How extensive they were, she could only surmise, but what she heard and put together led her to believe that most of the men were in debt to Roscoe. She asked Leon if he knew about this. He said vaguely, "Oh, yes."

When she pressed him to declare his opinion of its rightness and fitness, he replied that it did not concern him one way or another and that if she were really determined to pursue the matter, she should consult Deborah. "Although," he added with a smile, "you had better watch how you interfere between Mama and Roscoe. That's dangerous ground for meddling."

She did, finally bring up the matter with Deborah. "You may leave Roscoe to me," Deborah said shortly. "I pay his wages."

"But, Aunt Deb—" Sarah had never changed from this polite form of address, used on Sarah's earliest acquaintance with her as her Aunt Pea's old friend, and continued when acquaintance become family relationship. "Is it right that our people should be in debt to a man who himself works for wages on Beulah Land?"

Deborah caught her breath with exasperation. "Roscoe works for a decent but moderate wage, and he has my permission to deal with the men as he deems fit, so long as the work is done on time. I do not concern myself with how he accomplishes this. Nor must you, my girl."

Feeling "in for a penny, in for a pound," Sarah plunged ahead. "Are you also unconcerned, since I assume that you must be aware of the fact that Roscoe sometimes has men beaten? He doesn't touch them himself, but he has trained the man called Big Tom to use the lash at his direction."

Deborah waved a hand. "Slave gossip."

"More than that."

"Have you been witness to such punishment?"

"No, ma'am, I have not."

"Well then."

"Aunt Deb—"

"I do not intend to continue this discussion! It was impertinent of you to introduce the subject."

"I am sorry. I only beg that you—"

"Discipline must be maintained among the people, and Roscoe has my approval of whatever means he has found necessary."

"Please, Aunt Deb, won't you—"

"Cease!" Deborah marched angrily from the room, leaving Sarah to feel unhappy with herself and unsatisfied as to the situation she had sought to discuss.

She reported the encounter and the gist of the conversation to Leon that evening after supper as she helped him pack his traveling bags. He and Bonard were going tomorrow by the stagecoach to Savannah for a week or so of business dealings.

"You are tenderhearted, dear Sarah, and so the people are bound to exaggerate their woes, seeing that you are sympathetic."

"No, Leon. They don't lie to me."

"Perhaps not lie, but they love the dramatic, you know. You've been to some of their church services and funerals."

"It isn't like that when they talk to me."

"A thing grows in their minds, until they don't know themselves how far they're stretching it from the truth."

"There was no 'drama' in the way it was told. There was fear."

The word made him pause, because he admitted it to be true. He himself, ever since he was a boy, had felt an emotion close to fear when he thought of, or had dealings with Roscoe. "Do you know of any case of downright injustice?"

"Is flogging ever justified?"

Frowning, he took particular care in the folding of the cravats he intended to take with him. "Let's talk of it again," he finally said, "when I return. Until then, try to be still about it. Please? It really doesn't do to push Mama too hard when it comes to Roscoe."

She busied herself at a drawer of his bureau. "These kerchiefs are worn nearly through," she observed.

"Never mind. I intend buying a new supply in Savannah."

"You will remember all of my messages to Aunt Pea?"

"Oh, yes, yes." He smiled.

"The poor darling is always a little despondent late in the winter."

"Bonard and I shall take supper with her one evening and make her laugh with funny stories. And I shall ask her to do the shopping for you, which will please and occupy her."

"I wish you were staying with her."

"It's easier to go about our business from the hotel."

"I suppose it is. I know you have said so. You think to be no more than a week or ten days?"

"About that," he said cautiously. "If it must be more than that, more than a day or two longer than that, I shall send word. But no, I expect to be back at Beulah Land in a week or so."

"I wish I were going."

He made no reply, but turned his back and took a waistcoat close to an oil lamp to examine the front of it.

She allowed herself a private smile before saying in a lighter tone, "Do you think they will really build the railroad all the way from Savannah to Macon?"

"They say so, and I hear they are ready to begin, if indeed they have not already commenced."

"What a difference it will make to us all!" she said cheerfully. "In a few years we may take a simple stage— even a carriage—to Dublin, and there take the train to Savannah!"

"It will be something for the cotton and timber too, you know," he observed teasingly. "It isn't actually being laid out only for you to visit Broughton Street, or for Aunt Pea to come to Beulah Land."

"You will press her to come this spring for a long visit? Urge her to return with you."

"I shall, my love." He took her by the shoulders and kissed her gently on the forehead. They looked at each other with true affection. "Now let us go downstairs and have a glass of wine before the fire with Mama. I'm sure she too will want to repeat all of her commissions." She laughed and took his arm, and they left the final packing for later, when they would need some occupation to keep them together and apart before bedtime.

Three

Although she kept herself busy, she missed Leon. There are different ways of being husband and wife, and while the way of Leon and Sarah fell short of complete fulfillment for each, it was seldom marred by disagreements, never by real strife, and their weddedness had grown more solidly important to both over the years, as their trust in each other grew, strengthened by deeper and deeper affection. The awkward moments would be between them as long as they lived, but even those were not without tender feelings. And there was so very much they could share. Sarah loved Leon's lightheartedness, his readiness to laugh, to see the fun of a thing; she loved his lively intelligence and his handsome appearance.

More and more she understood the difficulties that must have attended his youth and maturing, as she considered his father's early death, his mother's strength and pragmatism, her absence of any sympathetic knowledge of and sensitive concern for either of her children. Such was Sarah's honesty of mind and warmth of heart, she could feel protective of Selma at the same time she sorrowed for Bonard in his bleak, unhappy situation of life. He was married, and therefore not free to seek a wife; yet he had no wife.

Even when he left her, his heart lightening boyishly with the contemplation of pleasures he and Bonard would seek in Savannah after their business had been done each day—even then he knew he should be glad to return to her when the time came. Regretting sorely not giving her a child, he was her child, as well as her husband. The jouncing coach, working together with the snug fit of his trousers and lively thoughts, brought him to partial erection. Yes, he loved her; and oh, he cherished her, even as every mile and hour that separated them made him a happier, freer man.

The day after his departure Sarah kept her school in the morning as usual, and walked with Selma and Pauline in the early afternoon, it being mild and near windless then. She had supper with Deborah, and after it, while Deborah met with Roscoe in her office, Sarah went with Ezra on his rounds of the sick. They were joined by Floyd, and she accompanied them finally to their cabin, where they found Lovey, and all talked as they sat and drank coffee around the kitchen table.

When Sarah rose to go, Floyd rose with her; but Sarah said she would go alone, and she did, although Floyd stood in the dark yard and followed her progress as long as he could. Two of the hounds trotted out inquisitively to see who was stirring, and she petted them and talked to them as they escorted her to the back door of the big house.

The next afternoon Sarah accompanied Deborah, who drove her own buggy, to Oaks. Sarah spent most of the time there talking to Trudy, whom she liked, and playing games with Trudy's children, who delighted her. Rooster joined them for tea and cake, and Sarah was interested to observe Deborah with him. Deborah became almost girlishly intense in both her heavy humor and her seriousness. Sarah understood—it was not a new thought—more clearly than ever before that Rooster was the son Deborah wished she had had. She was touched by the light play of jealousy between Deborah and Edna, as both endeavored to please and claim the attention of the young man.

Driving them home, Deborah had nothing to say, although by the look of her face, her mind was not idle. She flicked the reins loosely against the back of the horse until Napoleon had enough of it and stopped abruptly in the middle of the road, turning to look at her as if to ask if she had taken leave of her senses. Deborah stared back at him mildly, as though half asleep, and after a moment, Sarah took the reins from her hands and drove the remainder of the distance to Beulah Land. Someone waved from the front yard of the Anderson farm, but it was nearly dark by then, and Sarah waved back without knowing who it was. Glancing at Deborah, who sat still with her own thoughts, Sarah felt lonely and wished Leon were home again.

She had begun to conjecture hopefully the time of his return when she received a letter.

> My dearest—
> I am delayed, just as I hoped to be on my way to you. We had more or less concluded our business arrangements here when this morning Aunt Pea summoned me to her house and entreated me to make a journey for her.
> You will never guess!
> An unsigned broadsheet has come to her in an envelope in the mails. It advertises performances of a certain Roderick Conyngham Shakespearean Company in Charleston, South Carolina, for the coming week. Among the performers listed there is a Mrs. Lauretta Savage!

Aunt Pea is agitated with hope and eagerness for me to go there and to discover if it indeed be—she has every expectation that it will be—your sister, her niece: and she also asks that I ascertain exactly what are her present circumstances. So you see, I shall have real news when next we meet!

A sloop is set to sail from Lower Rice Mill Wharf this very evening, and I have bought passage aboard it.

If his family asks, Bonard wishes to say he will remain here at the City Hotel until I return, and then we shall come home together as originally planned. It is but a short delay.

Until then, my beloved, I am your devoted husband,

Leon

Four

Leon had been to Charleston only once before, and that as an escapade with Bonard when they were students at the Samuel Holt Academy. He recognized Sullivan's Island on the right and James Island on the left as they came in, but when he stepped ashore and followed the porter with his luggage to a hotel, he found that he remembered little else beyond the amiable atmosphere of the waterfront and the pleasant smells of cooking food that filled the air, of which he could easily identify coffee and fish and garlic and chocolate and hot pepper.

He relaxed and fancied himself a mysterious and romantic figure as he went along behind the porter he had engaged to conduct him to a hotel "suitable for a planter there on business." The man turned his head now and then to be sure Leon did not lose him. He had told Leon it was a short distance to the Palmetto Island Hotel, and so it proved to be. He now told Leon as they arrived at the entrance that it was one of several in Charleston owned by a colored man, a Mr. Bruton. It looked to be a comfortable place, and he understood how it might suit as accommodation to gentlemen whose business brought them occasionally to Charleston's dock area.

When he took his room, he showed the broadsheet he had taken from Aunt Pea. The solemnly refined clerk told

him the theatre was in King Street and that there was to
be a performance that evening of *Julius Caesar*. Leon
remembered it as a play that did not offer very much opportunity to its female characters. Portia and Calphurnia
were dull ladies, both. Would Lauretta, if she proved to
be one of the company, appear this evening at all?

After a rest in his room, Leon called for hot water, and
bathed and put on fresh linen. He then went out and
walked about, beside the walled gardens of rich private
dwellings, then back into the docking area where he entered a public house and dined on a dozen oysters and a
beefsteak. He enjoyed a cigar, excellent coffee, and a last
glass of wine, and arrived at the theatre in plenty of time
to secure a seat with a close view of the stage.

The single program sheet told him that Mrs. Savage
would take the role of Portia. The theatre filled, and the
play began. He knew that Portia must appear in Caesar's
train of attendants in the early scenes, but the stage was
not so well lighted that he could find and recognize the
actress who played the character. It was not until the second act that she appeared with importance in her own
right. Yes, it was she, Lauretta! Leon could hardly contain
his excitement on discovering her, and smiled broadly
during her first scene, which was hardly appropriate to the
content of that episode. She was older, but so were they
all, of course. She was more beautiful, a woman now, not
a girl. How fluid and spirited were her movements, he decided. With what passionate dignity did she scold Brutus:
"Dwell I but in the suburbs of your good pleasure?" Brutus was played by Roderick Conyngham, the company's
leading actor and manager.

Leon followed the play in a sort of daze, resulting from
the close atmosphere, the wine he had drunk, and the very
novelty of watching actors, one of whom he knew, upon a
stage. When it was over, he went out with the rest of the
audience, but enquired of one of the attendants the way to
the door backstage. When he found it and knocked and
got no answer, he turned the knob and stepped inside. He
found himself face to face, much to their mutual surprise
and to Leon's amusement, with the cadaverous old man
who had so recently performed the role of Casca. He still
wore his toga. Spitcurls were sculptured about his forehead and cheeks. Covering his laughter with a cough,
Leon asked if he might be directed to Mrs. Savage.

The old man looked him over suspiciously and instructed him to wait where he was. As he scuttled away, Leon looked about. He had never before been in the working part of a theatre. He stared up into the dark flies above the stage. He touched a rope. Its tautness warned him to let it alone. He peered at a desk with slanted top, finding manuscript pages upon it with large markings, which he correctly took to be the cue script.

He took a step toward the stage when he was stopped by a severe-looking matron's appearing at his side. She too wore toga and sandals, although she had contented herself with a simpler hair arrangement than had the old man. Leon remembered her as Calphurnia and bowed. "I am Mrs. Roderick Conyngham," she informed him. "How may I help you, sir?"

"I have come to see Mrs. Savage," Leon answered.

"We do not encourage strangers to call upon female persons of the company, sir. We are a respectable assemblage of artists. My husband, Mr. Conyngham, has indeed performed before crowned heads of Europe. You have, no doubt, heard something of his renown?"

Leon bowed again. "I am, madam, a provincial planter, and therefore ignorant of his fame. However, I am not a stranger to Mrs. Savage. I have the honor of being, indeed, her brother-in-law, having married her sister."

"Indeed, sir!"

"Indeed, ma'am."

"Please wait."

Leon was enjoying himself. The whole incident was like a play, he thought, feeling himself clever and important, and anticipating Lauretta's surprise when she discovered him. He was not disappointed. Mrs. Conyngham returned presently, followed by Lauretta, already in happy flutter before she saw him.

"It isn't! It is! Leon, my lamb, my brother, my old friend!" Her sudden tears providing authenticity for her greeting, their chaperon, the company's manageress, nodded to both and left them. Leon had taken her hands, and she kissed him heartily on the mouth, leaving a taste of lip rouge. "Is Sarah with you? How have you discovered me!"

He began to explain about the broadsheet in the mail, but when she put on a puzzled look, he left off.

"Never mind!" she exclaimed. "Come and talk to me while I clean my face—" She pulled him after her by the hand, and they entered a small room at stage level with no furnishings other than a couple of chairs, a table with a mirror stand that served as her dressing table, and a smoky oil lamp.

Lauretta sat him down in one of the chairs and herself down in another and began to smear a light, clear oil into her face skin. He watched her in smiling fascination, the smell of the oil she applied so quickly and with such careless skill mingling with the fumes of the smoking lamp.

"And where is Sarah?"

"Beulah Land, of course!"

"Of course! How is she?"

"Well. I left her well. Very well, in fact."

"Why do you have no children?" When he flushed, she laughed and said, "Please believe that was more unthinking than naughty and more naughty than cruel." She turned from the mirror briefly. "I have written, you know."

"Sarah shows me your letters."

"Of course." She had not yet made the transition from thinking of them as flirting young people to the adults they were with different lives and responsibilities. Or perhaps she was punishing him, not for anything he had done, but for what he had, or she thought he had, that she had not. "I so seldom have a dependable address I can ask that letters be sent to. It is—oh—two years—nearer three since I have had a letter from Sarah."

"Then how did you know we still have no child?"

"It is true then?"

He nodded.

"Perhaps I find it difficult to think of Sarah as a mother. My fault. I think of her as a child still, though I know I am not, and of course I know she cannot be either." She took a towel and began scrubbing her face free of oil and powder and rouge. "I do love her so. And how is Aunt Pea?"

He told her that she too was well, and that it was her anxiety and curiosity after receiving the broadsheet in her mail that had led her to ask Leon to come to Charleston to see if he might find her.

"Who could have sent it?" she asked herself, but aloud, then shook her head, dismissing the question. "I'm sure I've heard Aunt Pea mention acquaintances who live here, but I forget who they may be. They, however, would have heard gossip about my elopement at the time it occurred and would have remembered the name. Some people have nothing better to do than to store up information for future tattle."

"Is your husband one of the company also?" Leon asked.

The towel covered her face for a moment, before she dropped it to the floor beside her chair and stood. "I am famished! Will you take me to supper somewhere?"

"I shall be delighted."

"I hope you are hungry too, or I shall be ashamed, for I am truly perishing. I never have more than a bite before a performance. I'm too nervous, and one must be at one's best. We never know who may be out there!" She laughed and touched him quickly on the hand. "You haven't said: Did you enjoy the performance at all, or was it agony? Tell me truly: Was I quite, utterly bad?"

"I liked it," he said, aware of how little his answer measured the vehemence of her questions. "I liked it very much!" When she smiled and waited, he said with a shrug, "How can I say as to the performance? I could not take my eyes from you when you were on the stage; and when you were not, I waited."

She smiled brilliantly, and he knew he had managed to say the right thing. It was half manners, but half meant, too. "I am better in other things," she said modestly. "Mr. Conyngham is rehearsing us in *The Merchant of Venice*. He will do Shylock, of course. I shall try very hard to be good as Portia—another Portia altogether!"

" 'Dwell I but in the suburbs of your pleasure?' " he quoted, pleased with himself to remember the line. She applauded and laughed.

"You," she declared, "should make an excellent Portia, no doubt of it!" She rose and walked around her chair. The scent of her sweat and perfume made him feel that he was expanding, his wrists thickening to fill his cuffs, his neck bulging to burst his collar, his whole body straining at the seams.

Using both hands, she turned his head. "You must continue to look that way," she said behind him, "and not into the mirror, mind! While I—" Her pause suggested the action she was taking, which she then described. "Fold the toga so and so and so. Sandals off—there. I suppose you never have been in a room where a woman was dressing, excepting for Sarah. Or have there been—occasions?" She laughed. He heard the slippery sound of fabric, and disobeying her, looked into the mirror and saw that she had slipped a dress over her head and was pulling it down into place.

Before they left the theatre Lauretta stopped briefly at the Conyngham dressing room backstage. Through a crack of the door Leon saw the manager's wife, still wearing her toga, but with her coarse, graying-brown hair now hanging in two long braids on either side of her head; she was seated at a table counting the receipts from the evening performance. Lauretta mentioned him by name as well as relationship, and assured her employers that she should be quite safe, and that although they were going now to supper and should doubtless have much news to exchange, she would return to their lodgings in due time.

She then led them to a tavern not far from Leon's hotel, and they supped adequately, Lauretta enjoying a winter crab gumbo, which the very black and shining-faced Negro cook dipped from a large, aromatic pot onto a bed of freshly steamed rice. Leon was content with cold ham and cheese, which he ate on toasted biscuits. They drank wine with their food, and Leon noted that Lauretta, without seeming in the least affected by it, emptied her glass faster than he, and without apology or indeed any comment at all allowed him to refill the tumbler at her plate until they were well into a second bottle.

While she ate robustly and he fiddled his victuals about his plate, only now and then taking a bite, he told her about Beulah Land, and about Sarah there: how she loved the place and how those on it loved her. He spoke of Selma and Bonard. She remembered Bonard, of course, and listened to his story attentively, then demanding to know why Bonard had not also come to Charleston to see her upon the stage, "—So that I might say I have two stage-door beaux!"

That set them to laughing, and when they subsided, their hands touching their glasses in a companionable way without needing to lift them very often, Leon said, "You did not answer my earlier question, although the answer is perhaps partially given in the fact that you did not."

She looked at him quietly.

"Douglas Savage is not one of the company," he said.

She smiled and lifted her glass and drank from it. Setting it down, she said, "He seems to have happened to me such a very long time ago."

"Is he no longer your husband?"

"No longer—nor ever was." Seeing his shock, she add-

ed, "I thought he was, but it seems that I was mistaken."
She looked into her glass which was still half full, and
twisted it by the stem. "He was a sweet man," she said in
an unforced, worldly way that both shocked Leon again
and thrilled him. "Weak, I suppose, but charming and
handsome too. We were happy. It was really so romantic
and exciting for me at first." Her eyes narrowed thoughtfully. "Without being a very good actor himself—he
hadn't the temperament to rise to the top of the profes-
sion, and that counts for more than native talent or
learned skills, I have come to believe—he was a remark-
ably good teacher. He showed me how to stand and move,
how to use my voice, how to accommodate myself to
other actors in a scene—and that is very important . . .
not to lose yourself, but to use what they are doing, and
even to help them, in an interesting way."

"You are serious about acting, about it—all." He
laughed. "I sound absurd even to myself."

She slapped his hand lightly. "Never—you must never
again call yourself absurd. People take us so much at our
own evaluation. Yes, I'm serious about it, because it is the
way I earn my living. What else can I do?"

"Come home," he said impulsively, covering her hand
with his. "There is a place for you at Beulah Land."

"No," she said consideringly, "although you are kind to
ask me."

"Are you ambitious then to become a—well, a great
and famous actress?"

She frowned and gripped the hand he had left on hers
with brief intensity before withdrawing hers. "I don't
think so. I do have the temperament. I could be anything
I really wanted to." She smiled at herself. "But that is the
trouble. I don't want very hard to be anything. *I* am more
important to me than are any ambitions."

"What happened to you and Mr. Savage?"

Deliberately taking the question another way, she said,
"We went, after we were married, to Baltimore, where
Douglas found a place in a new acting company that was
just forming there. After a time the company traveled
north, not playing in the big cities, because they had available more famous companies than his, but playing in the
smaller cities that were yet large enough to provide considerable patronage. I did not act—other than in private
with Douglas, as he taught me some of the things he
knew. We traveled through Pennsylvania and New York

State, and east from there. I began to act in occasional performances, matinees usually, when someone was ill and unable to play—or drunk."

When his eyes went automatically to her glass, she laughed. "Don't worry. Not I. I like the taste of wine and the way it 'unknots' me, if you understand that."

"I do, very well."

"I thought you might." Her eyes mocked him briefly. "Anyway—some of this you'll have known from my letters to Sarah, although I never told her about Mr. Savage's leaving."

"Go on, please."

"We drifted up and down the East Coast. I played more and more often, and so in time became a regular member of the company. I learned how to apply cosmetics to my face to suit it to different roles. Were you quite disgusted, seeing me remove the evidence at the theatre?"

"Not in the least, although you are more lovely with your own skin."

She smiled, accepting the compliment. "Two years after we were married we found ourselves giving performances in New Bedford, Massachusetts. My name, along with that of Douglas, appeared on the bills and broadsheets—mine listed merely as 'Mrs. Douglas Savage.' One evening when Douglas and I arrived at the theatre to prepare ourselves for the performance, there was a woman waiting beside the stage door with a female child of five or six years. She—the woman, I mean—threw herself upon Douglas and began to weep and accuse him of treachery and desertion. The child wept too, hysterically." She frowned. "I do not like children very much, but I moved instinctively to comfort the little girl. Holding her in my arms I witnessed Douglas's breaking away from the woman, who was loudly proclaiming herself his wife. He kept repeating furiously—and ridiculously, it seemed to me even then—'But you live in Salem!' And she answered him, 'No longer, villain! I have tracked you down at last!' "

"What a dreadful thing to have happened to you," Leon said.

Lauretta laughed. "Yes, I suppose. But I rather enjoyed it too, you know. Remember my romantic disposition, my insistence that life be constantly new and surprising! Well, it certainly was so on that day. To go back to the scene: Douglas freed himself of the overwrought woman and streaked out of the theatre like a scalded cat. The child wrenched herself from my arms and went to her mother, thereby engaging her attention until Douglas had sufficient time to make his escape—from all of us."

"Do you mean to say you have not seen him since?"

"I mean that precisely!" She laughed.

"Good God!" he exclaimed, and laughed, and said, "I don't know why I laugh."

"Because it is funny," she said. "Not amusing, mind. Funny! I managed to quiet the woman and the child after a quarter of an hour and walked them away from the theatre. The woman—I should call her Mrs. Savage, I suppose—took me to her lodging rooms and gave me tea, after showing me documents that proved beyond question that my Douglas—and hers too—had indeed married her and was the father of that terrible, squalling brat she had in tow!"

"Amazing. It is simply amazing," Leon declared.

"Knowing well that Douglas had made an escape from both of us, I left the mother and child. But mischief compelled me to say, even as I did so, that whereas I was obviously not legally 'Mrs. Douglas Savage,' it was also possible that neither was she—that there may have been a cornucopia of 'Mrs. Douglas Savages' before either of us!"

"How could you do anything but faint or weep?" Leon said admiringly.

"And wouldn't that have been ridiculous?" Lauretta observed.

"Perhaps you are right."

"Of course I am."

"And since then?"

"I have been an actress. I left that company and joined another in Boston—after a series of small adventures—" She stopped to laugh at herself, which made him jealous and curious to know what adventures she remembered. "I shall not trouble you to hear them related. This is my third company. I changed again after the Boston one. I now feel quite shriven of the past. I don't call myself 'Mrs. Douglas Savage,' but I have assumed the privilege of being known as 'Mrs. Lauretta Savage.' With actors, the respectability of the marriage appellation is so very important."

He stared at her, saying finally, "You are wonderful."

Five

Leon remained in Charleston that night, the next day, the next night. He and Lauretta were together every hour except for the times she was performing at the theatre. She appalled, amazed, delighted, and depleted him. She did not wait to be approached: her hands were on him as much as his were on her, stroking where he had never been stroked, pinching impishly, holding him loosely, gripping him violently. She taught him what she said actors called "the European way of kissing." In the midst of one of their lovemakings—both seemed starved for each other's flesh—she rolled him over and straddled him and pumped herself up and down on him so vigorously that he slipped out of her just as he came, and she swung herself about on top of him and lipped the head of his penis as it continued to shoot, and until it began to subside, her knees pressing his head between them until he thought he should die of completion.

She *was* wonderful, he told himself; and he had never been so glad to leave anyone as he was to leave her on the morning of the second day. She walked with him to the landing, and just before he went aboard the sloop that would carry him to Savannah, said, "Tell Sarah—tell Aunt Pea—anything you like, but nothing that will hurt them. Goodbye, Leon." She took his face in her hands and kissed him, there in the bright winter sunlight, not caring who saw them. "It was I who sent the broadsheet to Aunt Pea. I was so close, I missed you all and hoped that she would send someone to see me. Thank God it was you and not Judge Truebody!" Laughing, she walked away without turning to wave, although he stood watching her until she disappeared. He went aboard the boat, as thankful to be rid of her as he had been to have her. She was too much for him. He almost wept with relief, thinking how it would be to see Sarah again, and his occasional, complaisant, undemanding whores.

Six

Deborah was dead before Sarah's letter arrived at
Broughton Street telling her aunt that her mother-in-law
was "ill with pneumonia and we fear for her." Sarah
urged her to do whatever she could to hasten Leon's return
home. Penelope sent Ichabod to the City Hotel with an invitation to Bonard to sup with her that evening. They and
Judge Trueboy were just finishing their evening meal
when Leon returned from Rice Mill Wharf where his
sloop had put in. Not having known just when to expect
him, Penelope saw his arrival as providential.

She told him of his mother's illness, and after consulting together, they decided to set off by stagecoach the following morning. Penelope was hopeful of being some use
to her old friend. She knew at any rate that she could offer counsel and support to the younger women of the
household. When the men took early leave, Penelope and
Clarice set about choosing clothes for the journey and the
visit. Ricey finished cleaning the dining room and kitchen,
while Uncle Joshua waited for his mistress to come back
downstairs so that he might tell her how well he intended
to care for things on Broughton Street during her absence.
He sat on a side chair in the dining room, his large, wrinkled hands folded on his lap and his gray head nodding
on his shoulders. He had turned the lamp down low. It
was seldom now that he ventured above the ground floor,
because the stairs were hard on his rheumatism, particularly during the damp winter months. Penelope's old cat
Prudence was curled asleep in the side chair by Uncle
Joshua.

The travelers did not learn of Deborah's death until
they arrived at the post office in Highboro. Nell had sent
Felix to meet every coach, even before Leon could possibly have taken one.

Deborah had not suffered terribly, nor had she suffered
long. She allowed one morning when she decided to keep
to her bed that she had felt "weaky" ever since she and
Edna Davis had spent an afternoon working on their husbands' graves. At noon, when Lovey herself carried a tray
up to her, she would not eat, and asked Lovey to please
tell Ezra to come to her. This Lovey did immediately.

Ezra was still the medicine man for the plantation. After talking to his mistress a little while, he left the room, Lovey staying behind. Going to look for her, he met Sarah on the stairs and told her to send for Dr. Chester Porterfield. She took his hand, her eyes lifting toward Deborah's room. Guessing her thought, he said, "Lovey is with her. No need for you. Let her rest."

Together they went downstairs, and a few minutes later Floyd was galloping down the front drive to summon the doctor. Ezra returned to Deborah's room with a herb gruel which he coaxed her into eating. He also brought a small padded cloth into which other herbs had been sewn. When it was steeped in hot water and held under Deborah's nose, it gave off a sharp, penetrating odor that he hoped would allow her to breathe more easily; and so it did.

Then the portly Dr. Porterfield arrived, delighted to see Deborah on a sick bed at last. In all the time they had known each other, she had never asked that his knowledge be put to her aid, and it gave him special pleasure to be sent for now, until she made it perfectly clear by her surprise and annoyance at seeing him that it was not she who had asked him to come. The first thing the doctor did after taking command of the sick room was to order "that mess" as he called Ezra's remedies, to be taken away. He gave the patient calomel for her fever and said that a mustard plaster was to be applied to her chest "as hot as she can bear it." Then he felt her pulse, looking gravely at the large watch he drew from a pocket of his waistcoat.

Deborah's condition worsened by the hour. Dr. Porterfield returned that evening. When he had examined her and then spoke in private to Sarah, he used the dread word "pneumonia" for the first time, which prompted Sarah to write the letter to Penelope asking that she speed, if she could, Leon's return. Floyd insisted on taking the letter himself to the stage at the post office next morning, and on the same trip to town, gave Nell her first real news of Deborah's illness, no longer called "an indisposition." Having got a promise from Felix that he would meet every coach coming from every direction—"He may have detoured for reasons we cannot know, or started back before he received Sarah's message."—Nell packed a trunk and had herself driven to Beulah Land.

So, when the party from Savannah arrived and were met by Felix, who now had the knowledge to convey that is the solemnest that may be conveyed about a person, they immediately went on to Beulah Land in the livery coach Felix held in readiness. Sarah and Nell stood on the porch waiting for them, having been alerted to their approach by Lovey. Leon leaped out before the coach stopped, and Sarah met him with an embrace that combined sympathetic tears and love, but in which sorrow was less than the joy she took in their reunion. Felix went to comfort Nell who, having borne all bravely until now, declared that she was prostrated by a grief she surely could never survive.

Penelope greeted her niece warmly and quietly. Bonard whispered a few words to Sarah and Leon, and when Sarah assured him that Selma was in her room and had taken the tragedy calmly but had better not be visited, Bonard bowed and got back into the coach which, now driven by Plumboy, carried him home to Oaks.

Sarah saw that they all appeared to be waiting, so she turned and led them indoors. Deborah had been washed and dressed by Lovey and Ezra, with Nell the calm and rather curious witness. Sarah had gone into Highboro, attended by Floyd, in the buggy that had been Deborah's own favored means of conveyance. She chose a coffin at the hardware store and directed that it be taken immediately to Beulah Land. She then called upon the Reverend Curtis Lamont, who saw his duty clear and plain, and saddled his horse to follow the buggy back to the plantation.

Deborah was put into the coffin, and the coffin was set on sawhorses that had been draped with black cloth and set up in the little sitting room that had been for so long her business office.

That is where Sarah now led them. Ezra, who had taken it on himself to attend the body, stood when they entered the room and escorted them to the coffin, where they looked down on the mortal remains of the woman who for thirty-five years had been mistress of Beulah Land. Looking at her, the declaration of the burial service went through Penelope's mind: *We brought nothing into this world, and it is certain we can carry nothing out.* The words seemed singularly impertinent ones to apply to Deborah.

Looking at her, Penelope was suddenly informed with a sense of her own mortality. Deborah had been so much and done so much, had been so definite and solid a person, had so long commanded and been obeyed. Yet there she was, what was left of her, brought low at last, and not a tear in a single eye.

Her gaze shifting then to her niece, Penelope remembered that she had had little time or inclination during their journey from Savannah to Highboro to ask Leon about his visit with Lauretta. They would all hear it told later, no doubt. But just now the subject of Lauretta seemed a remote if not trivial one to intrude upon the attention of the new mistress of Beulah Land.

Seven

The Reverend Curtis Lamont was in the house a good deal from the time of Deborah's death until she was buried beside Arnold in the family plot in Highboro. He came and went with the arrogant authority of one who knows himself the bridge from this world to the next. Sarah was courteous and thoughtful of his comfort. Nell favored him with a description of her unassuageable mourning. Emboldened by what he assumed to be their grateful deference, he sought to enter Selma's room to offer consolation, but was met by Pauline at the door; and when her firmness failed to persuade him that his help was not needed there, Selma rose from her chair, where she had sat writing, and went to the man.

"I cannot see you. Please go away."

The reverend, who had managed to insinuate himself inside the doorway, smiled painfully and decided to interpret her curtness as grief. "We must accept and bow to God's will."

She looked at him quizzically. "Do not presume to speak for me, I beg you. I decline and veto the inclusive 'we.'"

Such license in behavior should be admonished, he decided, and not pardoned as mere eccentricity. "Do not forget, madam, that it was I who gave you religious instruction in your childhood, who united you in the sight of God and man to the husband you chose then to abandon."

"I do not forget. That was a day's work for which you deserve hanging. Good day, sir."

"*Sir?*" She put a hand on the door, but he stood fast. "You dare to be impudent to God?"

"No, sir. God and I are on the best of terms; and He has never mentioned you to me."

"Have you quite given in to madness, my child?" he asked in tones of murderous pity.

"I am not your child. I am my father's—and, of course, my mother's too."

"Why then do you not weep for her?"

"Perhaps God has seen fit to comfort me. Again I say: Good day, sir."

"Wait."

"No, sir. Do not you wait—upon me, that is." She opened the door wide, and when he continued to ignore the gesture, she shoved him, which so surprised the man that he did actually allow her to propel him from the room, after which she slammed the door and bolted it.

Selma did not extend such behavior to her family; nor, it is true, did they provoke her to do it. She went on her walks with Pauline just as she had long done. She nodded politely to those she passed. But she would not stop in her mother's office to look upon her mother's corpse. When Lovey insisted that she must, she said, "No, Lovey. I must not."

"You're an unfeeling child!" Lovey said passionately.

"She was wrong," Selma answered simply. "She was very, and always, wrong. You look at her if it gives you comfort or amusement. It gives me neither."

Sarah went to Selma's room and talked quietly to her, asking her to attend the funeral. She listened politely and then shook her head. "If I cannot be true, I shall at any rate not be entirely false."

"Please, dear Selma. You don't have to do anything. Simply be there."

"Being there, or anywhere, is not simple for me. Let them think me 'simple.' They do anyhow. That is our joke." She turned to Pauline, who looked up at her and smiled. Selma went behind Pauline's chair and, bending, hugged her and the chair she sat in. She looked back at Sarah. "Pauline is no longer a slave, you know. Mama freed her when she died."

Sarah showed surprise. "I made her promise. Soon after that time they took the scissors away from me. Before you came. Dear Sarah! I'm glad you came. I hope that you are still glad. I hope that you will never, never be sorry that you married Beulah Land."

"Do you mean to say Aunt Deborah really has made Pauline legally free?"

"Yes'm," Pauline said. "I saw the paper it's on."

"She can come and go as she will," Selma said. "Now we shall see if she goes, or if she stays."

"I'll stay—you know I'll stay!" Pauline addressed the words to Selma hotly, even harshly, as if it were something they had argued, and as if she had forgotten that Sarah was present.

Selma turned to Sarah again. "Ask Uncle Felix. He will tell you so. He drew up all the papers she signed. Pauline is free; Lovey and Ezra are free. And so is Floyd free. They may all go, if they choose. Or stay, if they love us."

Sarah went out and downstairs, where she found Felix and Leon. She related briefly her conversation with Selma, and Felix said, "Yes, it's true. I was not going to bring it up until after the funeral. She signed papers for Lovey and Ezra and their children, Floyd and Pauline."

Sarah looked at Leon. "Will they leave us?"

"I don't think so," he said, but he looked troubled.

Felix shrugged and laughed. "Where would they go?"

"Why, anywhere," Sarah said, and went off then to find Lovey.

When Sarah had put the matter to her, Lovey grunted.

"Are you glad? What will it mean, Lovey?"

"I been my own all my life," Lovey declared firmly. Her bosom rose and fell irregularly as she strove to hold onto her emotions. Then she let go. "How come she try to make me less than I am by giving me back to myself?" She shook her head angrily. "I will never forgive her. Everything else she did, I tried to forgive. That I will not. I knew her thirty-five years and never knew her at all. Nor she me. That is a loss. That is all loss."

"Will you and Ezra stay?"

"Beulah Land is our home," Lovey said, her voice sounding cold to Sarah for the first time.

"Will Floyd and Pauline stay?" Sarah persisted.

Lovey studied a while over that, not because she didn't think she knew, but because she had to be careful how she put the answer. She said at last, "They got ties, you see. I wish to God—ah, well."

Eight

Perhaps the only true mourner at Deborah's funeral was
Rooster Davis, who sat for the service in a pew with his
wife Trudy, their children Adam and James and Annabel
and Doreen, his mother Edna, and his brother Bonard. In
the front pew, of course, Leon and Sarah sat with Nell
and Felix and Penelope.

Nell was pleasantly surprised at the small turn-out, and
later explained it charitably by saying, "It was the
weather, not at all clement." It had been a gray day, but
neither cold nor raining. People from out of town and, indeed, the whole county were there, but they had not come
in large family groups as they had when Arnold Kendrick
died. Rather, one person of a family attended, to represent
the whole. It was the end of winter, and people had had
their fill of winter dyings, of which there were always so
very many. They longed for spring. Early plowing and
sowing had been done. The earth having been turned and
opened to air, would teem again with life. It was the
wrong time for dying. Alive, Deborah had been a force.
Dead, she was of no consequence, beyond that decorum
required. It was not that she had been bad or hated; but
she had not been loved.

Even the Reverend Curtis Lamont did not seem to have
his mind on Deborah. The funeral sermon was aimed
rather at one absent, whom he epitomized as "the
thankless child of a dutiful parent." Those who listened to
his words were mildly disconcerted, but few listened. At
the end of it they said it had been a nice funeral and
cleared the church without lingering on the porch to exchange reminiscences of the dead.

Not many went to the cemetery for the interment, and
there was no spontaneous outpouring of song from the
Beulah Land slaves who had attended. Strong emotion of
any temper was lacking. Edna had kind thoughts, remembering the afternoon not so very long ago that she and
Deborah had worked together there. She remembered Deborah's saying she didn't care where they put her when
her time came. She remembered the end of the afternoon:
the gathering of tools, and Deborah's putting them away
in the back box of the buggy; of her finding the peach

brandy where she had left it under the seat. She remembered their taking the homely comfort of the brandy together, and then riding through town and on home in the twilight and falling night. But who was there to tell of all that?

Nine

What is called love may not be such at all, and that which is never called love may sometimes be the very essence of it. Lovey would deny that she had loved Deborah. She had done her duty by her. She had often been made uneasy by her. She had disapproved of her, now and then briefly hated her. She had spoken *to* her, though, more often than to anyone else in her silent monologue that, sleeping and waking, provided the running commentary on her life. Now that Deborah was dead, she missed her. That made her angry, and that was a kind of love.

Bad-tempered as a moulting fowl, she scolded Myrtis in the kitchen, noisily abused Posie and Buttercup until they wept and fled to their cabin. She criticized Pauline. She nagged at Floyd. Both her children were suddenly unsatisfactory to her. Why did they not marry and give her grandchildren?

Pauline had never favored men, as she herself had not when she was young. Nor had Pauline been favored by men, and there the parallel stopped, or its double lines collided. Men had always been after *her*, Lovey recalled with angry satisfaction. Pauline, they seemed not to see, or else to see through. Very well then. Pauline was fixed, set. If she wanted her life to be Selma's, that was at least something, because Selma needed her.

But what of Floyd? Why did he not marry? He was alone. He had her, and he had Ezra, and that was good enough for both of them, and more than enough for Ezra, but it should not have been for Floyd. Floyd ought to have a wife. She knew he was not a man who does not need a woman.

There is always something you do not have, she reflected. If you have freedom, you no longer have the need of it.

Ten

When he was born, Roman's face was like that of a sad
old man. It was only as he grew older that he began to
look like a child. In April of 1835, when he was fourteen,
he had taken over entirely as teacher of the younger children, and he and Sarah were more like colleagues than
boy and woman as they worked together in the one-room
cabin that served as their school. If he had a problem in
the work, it was that he was too gentle to impose discipline, and his younger pupils, who were naturally restless
anyway, were quick to take advantage of him when Sarah
was not present.

She was usually there when school was in session, but
recently her attention had been diverted to other quarters.
Leon had not, since his mother's death, taken a firm hold
as master of Beulah Land. He'd had to wait too long for
independence and responsibility to exercise them naturally. Where he should have been firm, he was uncertain
and self-conscious. He continued to work mainly with,
and to know most about, the bookkeeping end of oper-
ating the plantation, and Roscoe moved to absorb more
and more of the authority that had been Deborah's. When
Leon was in town with Bonard and Felix, as he often was,
matters needing the master's care were referred to the
mistress. Sarah soon lost her shyness and learned to make
decisions. She also learned that any hesitation or attempt
to let a matter settle itself simply meant that Roscoe would
settle it. She occasionally made poor, even wrong decisions, but she taught herself to indulge in self-reproach
only in private. It was better to be wrong than to let more
power slip into Roscoe's hands.

There was no beating of slaves now, whatever they had
done—stolen, or been disobedient, or feigned illness to
avoid certain hated jobs, such as building a fence in the
swampy area of the woods to keep cattle from venturing
where they might cripple themselves and drown. The first
time she heard of a beating after Deborah died, she begged
Leon to send for Roscoe, and in her presence tell him that
the practice was to be discontinued.

"There must be discipline," Roscoe answered in a reasonable tone.

"Of course," Leon said with a glance at Sarah. They had discussed this probable objection, and she had suggested the answer he now made. "If there is any question of physical punishment, however, it should be referred to me."

Roscoe bowed his head, veiling insolence in a quiet and earnest voice. "The master is often in Highboro when a man must be dealt with. The memory of slaves is short, like that of children. Punishment must quickly follow the error for them to understand and benefit."

Leon looked disconcerted until Sarah said, "When Mr. Kendrick is not here, the matter will be referred to me."

Roscoe nodded, as if relieved to settle this small but vexing question.

Soon after that interview, however, he made his first direct move against Sarah. One morning when she had finished her breakfast and chatted a while with Lovey about the day's routine, she went off to the school and found no one there but the youngest children. When she asked, "Where is Roman? Is he sick?" there was a tittering. She clapped her hands to quiet them and said, "Where are the older children?" There was no response. "Cannot anyone tell me?"

Otis and Lotus, the five-year-old twins of Myrtis, stepped forward hand in hand. Otis said, "It Mister Elk." Lotus nodded, frowning seriously to support her brother.

"What do you mean? What is Mister Elk?"

Their courage expended, Otis and Lotus looked at each other and turned and ran out of the cabin. As if that were a signal, the dam broke, and out ran all the other children. After a moment Sarah followed them and stood at the door perplexed, watching them scatter. Without thinking more about it, she followed the general direction they had taken to the slave quarters, where she presently found herself at the Overseer's house. Arms folded, Clovis stood in her front yard in an easy slouch, watching her two youngest sons playing at marbles.

"Good morning," Sarah said. Clovis turned a bland face to her without speaking, her eyes acknowledging her, just. The boys stopped playing and stood watching their mother with knowing looks. "Is Roman sick?" Sarah asked.

Clovis shook her head briefly.

"Is he here?"

Clovis widened her eyes, managing to look both blank and mocking. The boys began to giggle. She did not know them well, because they never came to her school.

"Where can I find your husband?" Sarah asked.

Clovis gave a sharp barking laugh and again shook her head, at which the boys doubled up with laughter. Letting their knees buckle, they fell to the ground and whooped and hollered and rolled about in a parody of uncontrollable mirth. Ignoring them, Sarah turned and walked to the big house, entering the back way. Seeing her agitation, Lovey followed her into the office, which continued to be used as such after Deborah's death.

"What is it?" Lovey asked.

Sarah told her what had happened. Lovey nodded, as if she were not surprised. "So," she said, and waited.

When Sarah had given herself a minute to think about it, she said, "Tell Plumboy to go find Roscoe and ask him to come here to me directly."

Lovey went out. Sarah took a book and tried to read to pass the time of waiting, but she could not attend to it. The ticking of the clock seemed unnaturally loud, as it always did when her nerves were in discord, and she looked at it too often. Five minutes, ten, thirty—fifty minutes passed. She had not turned a single page when she put the book down and went hurrying through the wide hall and breezeway to find Lovey. She saw her in the near distance standing in the kitchen garden talking to Tobey, whose sole work was the tending of the vegetables and the herb garden. Lovey broke off when she saw Sarah and came to meet her. "Well?" she said.

"Did you send for him?"

"Of course I did."

"Yes. But it is an hour since, and he has not come."

"Tobey!" Lovey called. The man came over quickly. "Find Floyd and tell him I want him." Tobey went off at a trot in the direction of the blacksmith shed. Sarah returned to the house and the office where she tried to read again and failed. She had passed from puzzlement through anger and embarrassment and was feeling dead calm when the knock came at the door forty minutes after she had last spoken to Lovey.

"Come in," she ordered.

The door opened and Roscoe entered, his face showing nothing. "Floyd said you wanted me."

"Did Plumboy not find you earlier?"

"He found me."

"Why did you not come then?"

He paused. "He didn't say there was a hurry about it."

She allowed a pause to be her comment. "When I went to teach the children this morning, only the youngest were there. Where are the older ones?"

"Working," he said without hesitation.

"We've never expected the children to work."

"They're needed. Twelve and thirteen years old is getting beyond 'children.'"

"And eight and nine and ten?"

Roscoe shrugged. "They wanted to go with the older ones. I got them chopping cotton. The rain made weeds. Every hand is useful today."

Sarah let another moment pass. "Is Roman chopping cotton and weeding too?"

Roscoe took his time. He knew how to use a pause too. Fixing his eyes on her soberly, he nodded.

"Why?" she said.

"He's fourteen. Others that age do the work of a man."

"Roman has been working with me in the school."

Roscoe smiled.

"That is work too, you know!" As soon as she said it, she regretted letting her anger show.

Roscoe lowered his voice as if he were about to share a secret with her. "I decided he was getting to be too much of a gal-boy and a man's work would be good for him."

"You took him away without consulting me."

Roscoe smiled a rebuke. "Mistress has kept him a child."

"He has been doing a man's work for me."

"Mistress may say so."

"I want him to continue with that work," she said in a measured way.

"Surely not!" He laughed, as if what she said was so obviously beyond reason there was no thinking she meant it to be taken seriously.

He continued the laugh until her silence forced him to acknowledge a disadvantage. "Are you telling me that as Overseer I may not assign work to the hands as I see the need?" His voice betrayed him. She had observed him and listened to him carefully during her years at Beulah Land, and she understood that it was only when he was angry that he fell into a way of carefully overenunciating each word and saying it separately, as if he were translating literally from a foreign language.

She kept her voice cool. "I am telling you the children

are not to work. Let them go through today, but tomorrow give them no order."

He turned to go, but at the door he stopped. "Roman is mine. He will do as I direct." He started out, but her voice again stopped him.

"You and your wife are free, and of course your children too, except for Roman."

"Would Mistress like me to remind him he is still a slave?" Roscoe held the doorknob, turning it slowly one way and then the other before he went on. "I believe the time has come for me to buy the boy," he said softly.

"He's not for sale."

"The old mistress made a promise to let me buy his freedom."

"The old mistress is dead."

"I shall speak to the master then."

"It will make no difference."

"I will not have a child who is encouraged to disobey me living in my house."

"Then I shall arrange for him to live in my house."

Roscoe hesitated, wanting her to say more, to give him the advantage again with a show of temper, but she did not. "Mistress—we have spoken in haste."

She forced a smile. "I had some time to reflect before you came. Roman belongs to Beulah Land. Send him to me. I shall tell him where he is to sleep in future."

Roscoe left, closing the door firmly but not in a way that admitted anger or defeat. A minute later Lovey entered without bothering to knock.

"There will be no school today, Lovey. But tomorrow it will be kept as usual. Is there a place in one of the store rooms off the kitchen for a bed, do you think?"

"Who for?"

"Roscoe says he does not want Roman to stay in his house if Roman continues to work in the school."

"You see now? Let the boy stay where he is—let him alone! I told you, everybody told you!"

"Yes, you all told me, seven years ago, and I wouldn't listen." Sarah let her shoulders relax. When she did so, her hands untensed of themselves, curled naturally in her lap, and she smiled a genuine smile. "I did not invent Roman, nor did he create himself. He has as much right to life at Beulah Land as I or you—or, indeed, his father."

Lovey might frown, and she did, but she knew Sarah's strength and accepted her authority. "There is a little room," she said grudgingly, "back of the kitchen; but Myrtis keeps her flour barrels and lard tubs there."

"I know the one. It won't do. It has no window. There's a bigger room beyond it with a window."

"That has the extra stove for baking! Myrtis will never give it up! It's where we dry clothes when it won't stop raining—"

"Leave the stove where it is. It will warm the room in winter. Tell Myrtis. No—I shall."

"No!" Lovey thundered. "I will tell her! You are doing everything you can to make everything worse! Everybody has forgot, or all but—now, moving that boy into the house, they'll remember, and there'll be all the talk again."

Sarah's voice sounded tired when she answered. "I can't help that, Lovey."

"What will Mister Leon say to it?"

"I'll explain it to him."

"You shame him!"

"It will be all right."

"No, it will not!"

"Lovey, now that is enough. I will not have even you tell me what I may do."

Leon did not return from town for noontime dinner, nor had Sarah thought he would. He did not ride into Highboro every day, but when he did, she knew not to expect him until late afternoon, and sometimes not until well after supper. Ordinarily, since she was the only one to be served, she would have insisted on taking her noon meal at the kitchen table with Lovey and Myrtis. They had been surprised and uncomfortable the first time she did that, but they had accepted her company when she pointed out impatiently how absurd it was for her to sit alone in the big dining room, with Selma eating in her room, and Leon in town. That they felt a little sorry for her too made it easier for them; and she was so very friendly about it, it would have been rude of them to make further objection.

Today, however, knowing Lovey to be angry with her, she allowed her place to be set in the dining room, and she ate alone. Then, seeking comfort, she went out to find Ezra. He was not in the barns with any of the ailing, non-working animals. He was not in the kitchen of his and Lovey's cabin where she often watched him making his medicines. She found him with Floyd in the smithy

shed. She greeted both with a nod and sat down on a bench
as they continued to work.

Floyd finished sharpening a plow blade that had been
dinted by rough stones turned by the plowmen. Setting it
aside, he looked at her and finally acknowledged her
presence.

"Mama told me about Roman," he said drily. "Myrtis
and her girls are clearing out the room. I'll set up the bed
in a little while, so he can sleep there tonight. Better if
he's out of Roscoe's way quick, if he's going to be."

"I didn't plan it; but the way it happened, it was the thing
to do."

Floyd looked at her as seriously as she spoke to him.
Unlike his mother, he did not bring automatic disapproval
to every unexpected turn in the day's events. He also
remembered that Roman might have been his own son instead of Leon's. Still, he said, "He might have had his bed
in the school."

"That would put him entirely on his own, and he's too
young for that. I wanted to bring him *in*."

They heard the sound of running, and, looking out, saw
Roman approaching. When Roman saw them, he stopped
and stared, as if undecided, and then backed away. Having missed the first chance, no one spoke a greeting until
Sarah called to him.

"Roman, are you looking for me? Here I am. Come in."

He made no answer and showed no evidence of having
heard her.

"I was just about to go and look for you."

He began to edge away, but Sarah stepped out of the
shed and took his arm. They stared at each other before
he said, "I was working in the field. I'm clumsy with my
hands. Even the little ones do it better than I can. Then
my papa came and told me I was to stop—and I wasn't to
live at the house any more. The ones that heard him
laughed, like they knew why, but I didn't know. He said
come and find you."

Sarah looked at Floyd, but he looked away and turned
to his work again. Ezra had stopped working the forge
and stood facing her, but his eyes were closed and he
frowned as if remembering an old pain.

"Come with me," Sarah said. "I want a walk."

She took Roman by the hand and together they made a
wide circle around the big house. It was early afternoon,
and most of those who were not working in the fields

BEULAH LAND 207

were indoors taking an hour's rest. Sarah guided them to
the orchard, where the blossoms had given way to small
knotty fruit, and the foliage was thickening to provide
shade for the fruit to ripen without undue forcing by the
sun.

She suggested that they sit under the peach trees and
found a patch of tufty grass to drop down upon. Roman
sat down carefully beside her. He was a thin boy. The
bones of his head and hands were prominent; his elbows
and knees showed a sharpness that clothes did nothing to
soften.

"You are fourteen," she said.

He looked at her and waited.

"You know who your mother is."

He nodded. The way she put the question was formal,
as if they were strangers.

"Do you know who your father is?"

"Yes. No." She saw the rush of blood under the warm
brown skin of his neck and face. "Roscoe Elk is supposed
to be, but I don't see how he can be. I've been made fun
of. I used to think it was account of my legs and hump.
Then I thought it was because I'm lighter than most of
them. I looked at her and him, and knew I couldn't be
his."

"Did the ones who made fun of you say who your father was?"

He did not answer immediately, and she waited. "How
could I believe that? He's married to you!"

"It's true. He is your father."

The boy looked away, wondering about it.

"How old are you?" she asked, as if they were going
over a lesson to make sure he understood a point that had
been unclear.

"Fourteen," he answered mechanically.

"How old am I?" she asked, echoing something of his
mechanical tone because it helped her to keep her voice
steady.

He brought his mind quickly back to her. "You're
twenty-four, ten years older than I am."

"So you see, he could not have been married to me
when you were born. He wasn't so very much older than
you are now. Nor was your mother."

It took a long minute for him to absorb that. "I bet she
knew what she was doing! She never did anything she didn't
know!"

She took his hands and shook them roughly as if scolding him. "Your mother is free, Roscoe Elk is free. Your brothers are free."

"They're not my brothers!"

"You have the same mother."

"They're niggers! I'm half white—you said so!"

"They are free," she repeated. "You are a slave. Do you know why?"

"Because nobody wanted me," he said.

"That may have been so," she agreed, "but it's no longer true. You're a slave because I want you." He stared at her, not understanding what she meant. "Roscoe Elk tried to buy you today," she continued. "I told him you were not for sale."

"He'd have made me free?"

"No, he would not have. Buying you would have made you *his* slave."

For the moment during which he considered what that would have meant he looked terrified. Then he said, "Instead, I'm your slave."

"I wish," she said, "that you were my son."

"You'll have white children; you won't want me!" he shouted at her, drawing back and away as if to rise from the ground and leave her. She did not touch him to make him stay, so he stopped himself. She did not answer him, which made him feel better than if she had tried to. After a time she said, "As soon as you're old enough so that he can't claim a father's legal rights over you, you'll get papers to show you're free. I promise. Then you can go anywhere you please, do and be what you want to do and be."

He thought for a time before replying. "Yes'm? And till then, who am I?"

It was late when Leon came home that night, and he was sorry to find her waiting for him on the front porch, because he was a little drunk, and he smelled faintly of sex and the perfume of whores he and Bonard had been with. She had fallen asleep waiting, but woke when she heard his horse coming along the drive. She called his name. He did not answer, but walked his horse around the house to the barn, where one of Plumboy's young stable hands roused himself from his hay bed and took the bridle reins from his master.

Turning to the house, Leon was surprised to find Sarah beside him and became immediately defensive. "Why are you still up?" he said accusingly.

"I wanted to talk to you." She put her hand under his arm, and they walked toward the house as she related what had happened that day. They paused on the breezeway and looked out over the moonlit land. He laughed finally. "You *have* had a day of making mischief," he said.

"How do you mean?"

"What I say." He yawned. Under his own sweetish sweat smell she caught the odor of his whores and his drinking, as she had so many times before; and she said nothing about it, as she had not so many times before. Yawning again, he began to laugh. "Sarah, Sarah! There are times I wish you were more like Aunt Nell, leaving people alone and complaining about the ways of the Almighty. Just don't drive Roscoe away. Overseers are hard to find, good ones anyway. Don't expect me to go to the fields with the hands every day and count the hoes every night. Whatever you do—and you'll do it—remember Beulah Land needs Roscoe. Maybe more than he needs us."

"Leon, what do you mean? Leon!" He had gone ahead of her and was climbing the stairs without a light.

Eleven

Having tested each other's mettle, both Sarah and Roscoe drew back, were careful to behave casually when they met and to keep the key low when they dealt together, as they were required by circumstance to do several times every day. It was a busy summer, and there were always problems and decisions, but neither she nor he allowed himself to show any emotion to the other.

She watched for him to show resentment about her having taken Roman into the house, but he did not. It was as though the boy no longer existed for him. They never met. Roman saw to that. Floyd painted Roman's room and built him a rough desk and a case for the books Sarah had taken to ordering from Savannah to give him. When he was not occupied with Sarah or with reading, Roman often fell into talk with the kitchen women, being so near to them. He entertained them by telling them things from his reading. They took pride in his smartness and were grateful in an easy, laughing, teasing way for his attentions to them. They often made special treats for him. Otis and Lotus followed him everywhere.

Leon was in town almost as much as ever. The school no longer kept, and would not again until the fall. The children were in the fields, not by Roscoe's orders, but because that is where everyone else was now, and therefore where they wanted to be, even for their playing.

Selma, accompanied usually by Pauline, walked early in the day, but after retiring to her room in midmorning, seldom ventured forth again. Leon brought lemons and ice from town almost every evening, but there never seemed to be enough lemons to make a pie or cake, so many did Pauline take for Selma's pleasure.

After the long visit she had paid to Beulah Land in late winter and spring—the grass had grown over Deborah's grave before she made her departure—Penelope was content to keep to Broughton Street in Savannah. *As I grow older,* she wrote to Sarah, *the old home is dearer to me than ever, and even a day away from it seems a day lost. Prudence surprised us all by having five kittens. As soon as their eyes have opened and cleared, and before we grow too fond of them, I shall put them into a basket and tie a ribbon on the handle, and have Ricey take them about among the neighbors offering them to whoever at the time may need a good cat. I trust the books arrived safely.*

It was an abundant summer. The corn was fat and milky, coming on early and lasting long. Watermelons almost split open of themselves, needing only the touch of a knife point. The cotton grew thick and heavy in its bolls even before the bolls popped open. Just as it was ready for picking, on Sunday, August 2, 1835—Sarah would remember the date as long as she lived—an unexpected visitor arrived.

Leon had driven himself and Sarah into Highboro for church services, because they had not been since June, and Sarah thought they ought to see county people again and ask how their crops were coming along. It was a hot day, but dry enough so that they were tolerably comfortable.

Nell had visited Deborah's grave before church services and put on the tombstone a fruit jar filled with fresh water and with roses that had been cut for her house only yesterday and could be said to be almost fresh. Anyhow, they were good enough for a grave, and who would see them after this morning, when others too strolled among the mounds of their dead? Nell sighed, meeting Sarah on the church porch to tell her what she had done, adding that Deborah had dearly loved a rose. If she had said that Deborah dearly loved a bale of cotton and therefore she had put one on her tombstone, that would have accorded nearer honesty, but such self-complimenting stories as that of Nell's visit to her sister's entombed flesh are seldom listened to, and may be as extravagant as the speaker cares to make them. To that end: Deborah dearly loved a rose.

By earlier agreement, Felix and Nell drove their buggy back to Beulah Land after services, alongside Leon's where the road was wide enough, just behind where it was not. Birds chirped and sang in roadside hedge and tangle, and ungathered blackberries hung dusty in their briary vines along the way, not needed even by the birds, who found plenty to feed on in the fields.

At Beulah Land, after a suitable interval of rest for the ladies and business talk for the gentlemen, the family, including Selma today, who had had a mild disagreement with Pauline and so decided to leave her for an hour to grow more tractable, gathered in the dining room for the Sunday dinner Myrtis and her helpers had provided.

There were platters piled high with fried chicken, deep bowls of potato salad, plates of sliced tomatoes and cucumbers, a tureen of roasting ears of corn, fried okra, fried squash and onions, boiled snap beans with ham hock, rice, two boats of thickened, greasy chicken gravy, a dish of pickled peaches studded with cloves, another of pickled beets, plates of hot biscuits, and jars of hot pepper sauce and cucumber pickles and chowchow. There were large pitchers of iced tea with lemon slices floating in them. And on the sideboard, covered with a thin, light cloth so the flies could not get at them, were a chocolate pie and a peach pie, both with high, perfectly browned meringue, and a large, cut-glass bowl of strawberries.

Before the family came in, Otis and Lotus, who took their responsibilities seriously, had been stood on the seats of chairs and given long, tasseled plumes to move to keep the flies from lighting on the food. Now that the family was there, Myrtis herself, leaving the serving to her helpers, stood with both plumes doing what she could to keep the flies and air in motion.

Nell had ceased to talk of the dear departed dead and

was enjoying her third pulley-bone. ("The white meat at the breast is the only part that agrees with me—thank you, dear Leon.") and wondering if the potato salad had gone a little rancid in the heat when Lovey entered, and going directly to Sarah's chair, announced that her sister waited upon her in the little office.

Sarah was out of her chair and running from the room before anyone could help her. When Leon and Nell made as if to follow her, Lovey stopped them by saying, "Finish your dinner first. They haven't seen each other a long time."

"That's so, Lovey," Nell said, content to postpone her participation in the interesting surprise. She asked for a pickled peach, declaring that everyone knew that their combination of sweetness and tartness was an excellent tonic for nerves. Leon sat down again too.

Lauretta stood at a window looking out as Sarah entered, but turned hearing her sister. "Dear, dear Lauretta!" Sarah cried, rushing to her—weeping, embracing and kissing her, laughing like a child whose greediest dreams have come true on Christmas morning. Lauretta laughed and wept too, although with less fervor. The occasion was not, after all, one of surprise to her, as it was for Sarah.

"You are the same!" Sarah exclaimed. "No! You're more beautiful than you were as a girl. Look at you! Oh, how good it is to look at you!" Suiting action to words, Sarah drew back from Lauretta and did indeed look at her. Her face went blank, and then her mouth opened in astonishment. "You're—Leon told me that Mr. Savage had gone away—"

"It's true. He did."

"Did he know when he left you that you—"

Lauretta shook her head. "Nor did I."

"Even so, he is a villain!"

"Others have called him that."

"And so he is! The scoundrel! Leon told us only that he had gone. He did not say that it was recently, or do I recollect it wrong? Never mind; let us sit down." Sarah drew her sister onto a sofa. "You will not have known, but Leon returned home to find his mother dead and in her coffin. So you see, it was a confused time for everyone. Leon said that he left you in good spirits and that you were determined to continue with the acting company—"

"Yes, that was so."

"Did you know when you saw Leon that you were with child? Brave, misguided Lauretta! Did you, knowing, not tell him? Oh, my poor darling!" Lauretta wept again. It was certainly the easiest scene she had ever been called upon to enact, but it did not altogether please her. She was happy enough with Sarah's reactions, but it was, after all, her scene, as she had envisioned it anyway, and Sarah would let her get hardly a word in edgewise. "If he had known!"

"I assure you he did not!" Lauretta then declared. "He did tell me, however, that I was welcome at Beulah Land at any time, so I do not arrive quite uninvited."

"Of course you are welcome! No one more—ever. Never anyone so much! When I think what you must have endured! Have you seen Aunt Pea? Does she know?"

"No. I thought first of going there, but I could not cause her such distress as my appearance in this condition must surely have done. We are so well known in Savannah, and I left it in such a— So many friends and others to whom explanations would have to be given."

"You were right to come here. But then, under that romantic disposition of yours is a practical mind, and always has been! Here no one will be curious—no more than in a friendly way. There need be no explanation. You will be to everyone my dear sister who has decided to visit me in the country until your child is born. Your husband having—gone abroad for some months on business matters!" Sarah clapped her hands happily at her invention, and Lauretta decided not to comment on its lack of freshness and credibility.

"So be it," Lauretta said, smiling on the other fondly.

"We must have Leon pursue the villain immediately!"

"No! That cannot be done, I assure you!"

"Did he behave so monstrously to you? Poor darling! However did you manage to get here on a Sunday?"

"Yesterday I came as far as Dublin. Exhausted, I stayed the night at an inn, having arranged before retiring to have a livery rig bring me here this morning. The driver knew the way. Everyone appears to know where Beulah Land is situated. You are famous!"

"Had I dreamed you were as close as Dublin! Why did you not write to say you were coming, so that I might have had happy days of suspenseful waiting!"

"I should have written," Lauretta said meekly, "but I

was not entirely certain, until I came off from Dublin this morning, that I was selfish enough to impose my misfortunes on your love." Her words were no less felt for having been thought over earlier. They moved both sisters to more tears.

"Oh, my dear sister—Beulah Land is yours!"

"Perhaps your husband—"

"Do not say so formally 'your husband'!"

"Leon—"

"Leon!"

"—may not be so welcoming as you."

"Oh, he shall be, depend upon it! But I am mistress of Beulah Land," Sarah said, and the authority with which she said it was not lost on Lauretta. "What I say do, is done."

Lauretta blinked her eyes rapidly, in admiration, gratitude, and irritation. "My little sister—" Her voice wavered.

Sarah was up from the sofa like a shot. She marched straight to a marble-topped credenza and poured out claret into two glasses. Bringing them back to the sofa, she gave one to Lauretta. "This will quiet our nerves," she said, and drank, and sat again, holding glass in one hand, caressing her sister with the other. That is how Leon and the others found them a quarter of an hour later when Lovey preceded them into the room with a tray of glasses filled with iced tea.

Twelve

Everyone was kind, but summer is an uncomfortable time in which to be pregnant, and Lauretta was not of the best disposition as she waited for motherhood. Everything at Beulah Land reminded her of Sarah's importance and of her dependence on her sister. Before coming, she had thought herself the central figure in the drama. She had anticipated Leon's initial astonishment, followed by concern for her well-being. He was hardly more than civil, treating her not at all as one for whom he felt a special tenderness and responsibility, but rather as an embarrassing, unwelcome, and even boring reminder of past indiscretion.

He sought no moment to speak to her privately, although she dropped sufficient hints at the dining table of her intention of walking in the orchard or along the drive or in the woods, at such and such an early or late hour in the day, when it was not too hot for her to enjoy gentle exercise. Not once did he apprehend her under an arbor or as she rounded a bend; and pretty soon she left off taking walks altogether.

Edna and Trudy Davis made the time to come over and pay their respects, but after courtesies, they addressed their attention entirely to Sarah, making it clear that they considered Lauretta of no particular interest, except as the older sister of their friend. They did not behave at all as if she were a figure of mystery and importance, and when she declared to them how fortunate she felt herself to be to have a sister as good as Sarah who was eager to look after her at such a time, they merely nodded their heads as if what she said was only the simple truth and had nothing in it of special grace or modesty.

Everyone, in fact, was forever consulting Sarah, waiting for Sarah to express an opinion or preference, deferring to Sarah. It rubbed Lauretta's fur the wrong way. The household women were obliging, but not in any personal sense. Lovey saw to it that she had every comfort the plantation could provide, but she never spoke to or looked at her as if she mattered of herself at all.

Selma paid her respects by joining the family group for supper in the dining room on the Sunday evening of Lauretta's arrival, but after that she went about her routine very much as she usually did. As the days passed, Sarah spent as much time as she could afford with her sister, and it was a good deal in dibs and dabs, but it was not enough to satisfy Lauretta. Sarah was forever bustling into Lauretta's presence, but they seldom settled down to a really good quiet talk without Lovey's, or someone else's, interrupting to say that Sarah's attention was required yonder, there, and everywhere but where she was. Always, Sarah apologized, begging forgiveness for these interruptions, and always she allowed them and went off to attend to whatever had been brought to her notice. She seemed to have little curiosity about Lauretta's life upon the stage, whereas Lauretta had thought they would spend many hours together with Sarah envious and sighing as she, Lauretta, told her of her travels and experiences in and of the larger world.

"Oh, yes, tell me, please!" Sarah would implore, and

seem to mean it when Lauretta dropped an allusion to her other life; but soon enough Sarah would be up and away, begging Lauretta upon leaving her to be *certain sure* she remembered exactly where she had left off, so that they might pick up there at the earliest opportunity.

Aunt Pea wrote anxiously on being informed of Lauretta's arrival and condition and intended sojourn at Beulah Land, but it seemed to Lauretta that she was easily reassured, writing very soon to Sarah that, "As much as I long to see and be with Lauretta, I think I should not travel in this heat unless I am really needed."

Nell—"Aunt Nell," as Lauretta promptly called her on their renewed acquaintance—was friendly, but she was far too self-absorbed to evidence true sympathy and interest. When Lauretta spoke with her on any but the most trivial concern, Nell's eyes wandered to a cameo brooch pinned to her own breast. It was a likeness of General George Washington that had belonged to Deborah, and she studied it as though she had never seen it before, unpinning it to look upon it the more closely, and now and then making a remark or asking a question that really had nothing to do with whatever Lauretta was saying.

It was, then, small wonder that Lauretta felt wronged by Leon and took a self-annealing satisfaction in the reflection that it would cause a sensation were she to tell Sarah the truth of her recent past. That she did not, made her feel virtuous. It would, after all, ruin Sarah's marriage. What sort of marriage was it anyhow, she asked herself, that produced no child in seven years? Even as she wondered, she could not but observe between Sarah and Leon evidence of an affection she did not understand but could not discount.

The only relief she had from her many physical and emotional discomforts was the occasional company of Bonard. He did not stop at Beulah Land for dinner or supper, but he would come by to find Leon on some business matter, or he would return from town with him and pause a few minutes on the porch where Lauretta spent so many of her hours, with little to claim her attention other than a bee's progress from one flower to the next, or the usually vain hope that a breeze would stir the ropey wisteria into a cooling motion.

Bonard would dismount if he were on horseback, or step out from buggy or carriage, and come onto the porch as if eager to speak with her, or sometimes merely plant a foot on a step, companionably propping an elbow on his knee as he talked. What cheered and entertained Lauretta was that, notwithstanding her condition, he treated her as a man does a woman he thinks beautiful, desirable, and consequential. Indeed, at their first meeting, his was no polite sympathy, but the sly and amused attitude of one who guessed without having been told what had transpired on the occasion of Leon's journey to Charleston.

She was so surprised—she had not remembered Bonard as in any way amusing, only as somewhat grim and sinister on his visits to Broughton Street—that she laughed outright when he took her hand the first time and, bowing low over it, spoke his respects. Soon, with no private meeting or word, it was as if they shared a secret joke. They looked at each other in such an ironic and particularly interested way that Lauretta could feel that she was not negligible as a woman who might create pleasure or discord, as she pleased.

Thirteen

The two farms that lay between Beulah Land and Oaks were the one owned by Trudy's family, the Cokers, and that of the Andersons. Clarence Anderson, who had survived his older brother Walt, buried his mother and father too, then saw his two sisters, Bessie and Emily, married to men who worked at jobs in Highboro. Bessie married a clerk in the hardware store, and Emily became the wife of the manager of the post office, whereupon she put on airs of superiority with her sister.

As for Clarence, he was a sporty, glib, teasing kind of man. It was, in fact, he with whom Trudy had been enjoying a jolly dance when Rooster, watching jealously, had determined to seize the first chance to invite her outdoors to look at the moon with him, and subsequently to ask her to be his wife.

Clarence Anderson had not married, but lived on the place he now called his with half a dozen slaves who worked the land for what little it produced. By nature a sport and a gambler, he would bet on anything: a dog fight, a horse race, a fishing catch, the amount of an acre's yield of corn or cotton. And so he was in debt. That in itself was not surprising or unusual. But Leon had recently discovered that Clarence was in debt to Roscoe Elk.

With patience and care, a profit can always be made on those who are said to be poor, to have nothing, but who actually do now and then borrow small amounts for special needs or vanities and eventually repay somewhat larger sums. Roscoe had maintained his traffic in these small loans, but gradually over the years he had extended his sphere of activity to the town of Highboro and the surrounding county. His name was passed from one profligate to another as one who would lend money discreetly, with none of the bother of going to a bank or a lawyer, and conferring and signing papers with official stamps on them, although the signed papers Roscoe held proved to be none the less legally binding in the end, for all that they had seemed to be casually written out and agreed to.

Since all gamblers who borrow fancy themselves suddenly winning large sums and being free of debt at a sweep, Roscoe did not lack debtors. And so, naturally, one of them was Clarence Anderson. It was this which Leon had in mind when he cautioned Sarah not to press Roscoe too closely. Clarence Anderson's farm shared borders with Beulah Land.

Fourteen

"What you thinking about?"

"You, Mama."

She had hoped to surprise him into revelation, but he was on his guard and would not be trapped. They sat, Lovey and Floyd, in the late, lingering light of an early September day, she on the back step of the family cabin, he on a short, upended log he would chop into firewood before winter came on. He peeled a length of sugar cane, notched it, offered a piece to his mother which she took and chewed absently, took a piece himself and chewed the juice out of it.

"Hum," she said.

Floyd spat out the dry fiber and then bit off another notch.

Lovey shook her head dramatically. *"I'll* never have a grandchild. Not you nor Pauline—"

"Mama, hush."

"Don't tell me 'hush'!"

"Hush." He said it softly, wiped his knife blade on his trousers and stuck the knife into the side of the log he sat on.

"Your papa is old," she said.

Floyd laughed at her. "No, he ain't. He's young as that crow he found in the field this morning with his wing broke by Roscoe Junior and his slingshot."

"Your papa will make him fly again. Your papa has healing hands. But he can't heal you."

"Mama, stop. Give up."

"He's got that crow on the kitchen table now, rubbing his wing with tallow and turpentine to strengthen it, the crow looking at him all the while like he would kill him, was he able."

"Mama, don't talk to me in parables."

"I won't talk to you at all. You don't talk. Only dodge and deny."

"All right. Try me now."

"You've got papers that say you can go and come anytime you please. F.P.C. papers you've got."

"He's old. You said so."

"Better he be lonesome for you than find out how you feel. You can't stay on, feeling the way you do. You know that."

"I won't leave Papa."

"I don't want you to—"

"You don't care."

"That ain't so: you know it."

"I don't know it."

"Floyd?"

"Yes, Mama?"

"Don't you sigh to make me sorry for you!"

"No, Mama. No."

"How could you let yourself? Boy!"

"Me and Leon, born together, boys together. Maybe it's to do with that."

"They would kill you for what you got in your heart."

"No one going to kill me, Mama. I'm not one of your niggerish niggers to get drunk and give myself away."

Her voice held wonder as well as outrage. "How do you think of her?"

"Mama, don't. Don't you now."

Lovey put her head down on her folded arms and knees and cried.

"Oh, Mama," he said, somewhere between compassion and exasperation.

She rose and flew at him, arms and hands swinging and flailing. "Don't you! Don't you!" She beat him about the head and shoulders until he was forced to move back and hold up his arms to guard his face. Inside the cabin the crow gave an angry, anguished cry at taking help from a man. Floyd turned, unable to deal or to reason with her, and ran into the falling darkness, because there was nothing more he could say.

Could he go? How could he stay?

As long as no one else knew, it was all inside him, and if it hurt, no matter; and if now and then it made him happy, no accounting. Alone on his cot at night, eyes opened or closed, he dreamed, and she was there, although not realized at first. If he had been fanciful, he might have admitted her in fantasy or symbols, but he thought and felt in clear images, and there were two taboos he could not transcend, one of color, the other of brother code. She was white, and married to his brother. It changed nothing that they had gone their different ways; when they were babies and boys, he and Leon had been brothers, and so they would always be. They had lain in Lovey's arms side by side and drawn sustenance together from her breasts.

He went farther into the darkening woods, his eyes adjusting to the changing light, and he knowing the way anyhow as well as any creature the woods were home to. He had walked every path a thousand times over, with Ezra, and Leon, and alone. Here he had been happy and unhappy, slow and quick, thought good and bad.

Lovey knew, and that changed it, because she considered what it could mean and do to everybody, whereas he had held it private, so that it affected no one but himself. No good to ask how and when she had seen. She had seen and known, and he would have to go; but he would put it off as long as he could.

Fifteen

"Leon?"

He turned, frowning.

"Here I am."

It was not late, but it was dark. He had just ridden home from town, parting with Bonard at the main road and jogging his horse quietly along the drive. Even so, Sugar, who was Plumboy's best stable hand, had heard and recognized the sound of the master's horse and was ready at the steps to lead the animal away to his stall and make him comfortable for the night. Leon had then mounted the steps to the porch and been stopped by Lauretta's greeting.

"Come and sit with me. I'm all alone. Sarah has gone off with Ezra to tend to one of the ailing hands—Skeeter, she called him. Chills and fever and is 'sarten sure' his time has come!" She laughed brightly. "You know how they are—I swanee it's been an education being here these last few weeks and seeing all she does! I used to think it was the darkies took care of the white folks, but it seems to me to be the other way round!"

His eyes adjusted to the darkness of the porch, which was more deeply shadowed where Lauretta sat because of the wisteria vines. The leaves were dying, but had not yet let go. She was alone, as she had said. She sat in a high-backed rocking chair that had been a favorite of his mother's, and she had a woolen shawl around her shoulders, such as Deborah might have worn against the chill of an autumn evening.

"I should go in, Lauretta. There are some figures I want to set down in the books while they're fresh on my mind."

She smiled, and although he could not read her eyes, he could see her teeth white in the darkness. "My goodness, how you treat me like a leper! I am not, you know. I am a perfectly normal woman in a—what they call a natural condition, if not quite a natural situation."

Leon bowed stiffly. "You will please excuse me." He turned to go.

"No! I do not excuse you, sir; come back!" Leon stopped. Her voice both threatened and cajoled. "Stay and talk to me. I am all alone, as you see." She lifted a hand, palm up, to beckon him. "Come here; sit beside me." He went toward her cautiously, but did not take her hand, and after a moment she let it fall to the arm of her chair.

"Well," he said, "what is it?"

"Sit down."

He did so, on a chair out of her hand's reach.

"I fear you are heartless."

"I hope I am not that," he said irritably.

She settled herself back in her chair, as if having brought him to her, she now had no fear of losing him. "We have not talked at all since I came."

"I don't know what you mean."

"Oh, Leon." She laughed intimately. "Your voice bristles with fear. You're not at all the free and happy cavalier you appeared to be when we met in Charleston!" She smiled without humor, for her satisfaction alone.

"Am I the father of the child you will have?"

"What a very cruel and insulting thing to say to me! If you were not, do you think I could accept your hospitality? Reluctant though it has been."

"It has not been reluctant, Lauretta."

"Well then, nervous."

"I ask you again: Will it be my child?"

"Do you suggest that it was sired by that great and shining Thespian light, Roderick Conyngham, admired of kings? Will it, do you think, enter the world declaiming, 'To be or not to be'? And what will your answer be to that?"

"Don't be flippant, Lauretta. You are quizzing me."

"I shall stop, if you show that you have something still of the regard for me I believed you to have in Charleston."

"What happened in Charleston has nothing to do with here and now."

"Oh, it has everything to do with here and now!"

"You cannot accuse me of seducing you," he said.

"By saying the which, you accuse me of seducing you!"

"No."

"What then?"

She waited. He tried to sort and order his thoughts. It was several minutes before he spoke, and by the time he did, she had consciously relaxed her tension, sitting easier than she had before, one hand curled on her lap, the other reaching idly to touch a drying leaf.

"I blame myself," he said at last. "How could I have been such a fool?"

Since no woman is flattered at being told that loving her was fool's work, she said, "You are detestable!"

"Yes, I am," he agreed. "Married to the dearest, best woman in the world—and to forget it in a moment of weakness, to allow myself to—"

"To what, sir?"

He shrugged.

"To fuck, sir! Is that the word you could not say? Do not spare my sensibilities. They are sturdier than your own."

"Why did you come here?"

"Where was I to go? You had invited me."

"Yes. I had done, yes."

"I came to deliver myself of your—possible heir. Why has Sarah not given you a child?"

"Don't speak of Sarah."

"Oh, certainly," she agreed. "I am not good enough to speak of 'the dearest and best,' having corrupted her husband and brazenly come to ask asylum for a time—only for the time it will take to unburden myself of an unhappy and unwanted load."

"You are wonderful," he said, with a different meaning than he had said it their first evening together in Charleston.

"I consider that a frugal accolade from one who made it impossible for me to continue the life I was content to follow—as my own mistress, not yours or any man's."

"Spare me the concept of yourself as victim. You are my victim as a greedy king is the victim of his appetites."

"Well said!" She clapped her hands in mock applause. "Fear sharpens your wits."

"I am not afraid of you."

She pretended surprise. "Then am I free to tell Sarah it is your child I carry? One that she cannot herself conceive?"

"If you want to destroy her happiness," he said bleakly.

"Is she, then, happy?"

"I believe she is."

"Not merely busy?"

"I don't consider that I have known you at all before tonight," he said slowly.

"You don't know me now. If only you understood," she added.

"I should like *you* to understand something, Lauretta. Sarah and Beulah Land are the best things in the world. You cannot threaten them, you can only threaten me."

"I revise my earlier estimate and take you at your own evaluation. You are not merely detestable—you are, indeed, a fool. I cannot express to you adequately the loathing I feel when I think that I am to bear your child."

Leon stood. "We have insulted each other quite enough

to satisfy even your hunger for theatrics. Good night, ma'am."

Her hand reached swiftly, found, clutched, and twisted the bottom of his jacket. "I shan't let you get away with despising me."

He pulled away from her. "Don't think, Lauretta, I haven't seen you making faces at Bonard. You cannot win anything there, you know. He is not free to take and grant favors."

"You are jealous!" Her voice rose in a happy, singing moan. "You are jealous! Admit it, sir?"

"Again I bid you good night, ma'am."

Sixteen

At eleven o'clock in the morning of October 5, 1835, Lauretta's child was born. It was not an easy or a quick birth. On the day before, after the customary large Sunday dinner at midday, Sarah and Lauretta retired to their separate rooms to rest for an hour. Lauretta occupied the bedroom that had once been Leon's, and was converted into a guest room when Leon and Sarah married. Lauretta had made it hers since her arrival on the second day of August.

Having dozed, Sarah woke slowly to a sound she instantly recognized: the surprised protest of a woman commencing labor pains with her first child. Slipping from her bed, not yet fully awake, she ran in her petticoat to her sister's room and found Lauretta sitting on the edge of the high bed, hands on either side of her low-bulging belly, eyes staring down fearfully, as if at last realizing the strength of a mortal enemy.

"I am here!" Sarah exclaimed, going to Lauretta and sitting beside her to put an arm about her.

Lauretta shrugged her away. "Get someone to help me," she whispered, her face pale with fear.

"Will it be better if you lie down? Try to relax."

"For pity's sake, go and fetch someone who *knows!*"

"I'll get Lovey, and send to town right away for the doctor."

She ran from the room and down the stairs, not pausing to dress. Leon was not in the office. From the breezeway she saw him in the yard talking to Floyd.

"Leon!" she called. then went to the kitchen and poked her head in. "Is Lovey here?"

"No'm," said both girls who were washing the dinner dishes.

Having been alerted to her alarm by the way she called to them and then rushed on, Leon and Floyd met her at the steps. "Floyd," she said first, "find Lovey for me and send her to my sister's room. She thinks the baby is starting." Without a word, Floyd ran off toward his family's cabin.

Leon was looking quite as pale as Lauretta had when Sarah left her. "I'll go for the doctor."

"Send Floyd when he comes back."

"No! I will go myself."

She kissed his cheek quickly. "You are good."

As he stared at her, she turned and ran back into the house. He went toward the barn calling, "Sugar! Where are you, god damn it? Plumboy! Saddle my horse!"

Leon rode hard into Highboro, more as one fleeing than as one going for help. He found Dr. Chester Porterfield at home, sleeping after his own heavy noonday dinner. When roused by his wife, he was at first reluctant to go for yet a while, and when she scolded him, he began to dress, but sullenly refused to hurry. He had, of course, known his services would be called upon and had made the acquaintance of the mother-to-be a month ago. The thought that went through the doctor's mind on that occasion as he enjoyed coffee and cake was, "Pretty woman. Big hips. Should have no trouble." Now, as his wife urged him to "make haste," reminding him of the importance of the Kendricks, he stuck out his tongue at her and made a childish sound before telling her to have their manservant hitch up the horse and buggy. He then went out to the front porch and, yawning, talked a minute or two with Leon before suggesting that Leon get along back home, promising him that he would follow shortly. "There is time, God's own plenty. You'll see."

He was right in saying there was time and wrong in saying that Leon would see, because Leon went straight from the doctor's house to his uncle's office. It happened that Bonard had been the dinner guest of Felix and Nell, and that after dinner, as was their custom, Felix and Bonard left Nell to her rest and digestion and went off to the office to drink a little whiskey slowly, to smoke cigars, and to talk about all manner of things men could only talk about in each other's company.

Leon was as happy to find them as they were surprised to see him. When Bonard had given him a cigar and helped him light it from his own, and when Felix had found a glass for him and poured whiskey into it, the three settled back, tilting their chairs onto hind legs, and talked.

"Is she now!" Bonard said after Leon told them what had brought him so unexpectedly into town. "Go easy, friend. You're nervous enough to be yourself the father!" Bonard rolled his cigar in his fingers appreciatively, raised it to his mouth and drew on it deeply. He held the smoke warm and pungent in his mouth and then exhaled it in voluptuous clouds. Looking at Leon, he narrowed his eyes and finally smiled. "She'll be slim and pretty again," he said. "And seasoned. There's nothing like a seasoned woman to set a man to his best." Bonard looked at Felix, and they laughed together, candid reprobate and remorseless old sinner. Leon looked from one to the other to see if they were laughing at him, and then he laughed with them, without having decided.

At Beulah Land matters that could, progressed quickly, and those that would not, took their time. Lovey was with Lauretta five minutes after Floyd found her having an after-dinner nap on her bed. As she drew outer clothes over the petticoat she had, like Sarah, rested in, she told Floyd to find Myrtis and send her along to her.

As soon as she entered Lauretta's room, Lovey ordered Lauretta to undress, and then she and Sarah helped her to do it. Presently, Myrtis arrived and knocked on the door and came in without waiting for permission. Occasions of childbirth always embolden women to assume authority. Lovey asked her to stand by in the kitchen, and to post Plumboy as lookout for the doctor's buggy, and to send the brighter of her two kitchen helpers, Juanita, to assist them as she might be needed.

Unasked, Buttercup and Posie arrived soon after, in clean, starched dresses and aprons, wearing serious looks with an air of knowing which the old give themselves often with no justification other than their own proven survival. As the audience in the room increased, so did Lauretta's demonstration of discomfort and pain. She whimpered, she moaned and groaned, she beat her hands upon the bed's sides. She twisted and arched her body. She did everything she could to concentrate attention

upon herself, except actually giving birth. Buttercup and
Posie whispered together before Buttercup slipped up to
the foot of the bed and tied a knot in the corner of the
sheet Lauretta lay upon "to help ease the pain."

Dr. Porterfield arrived and examined the patient—or
rather, glanced at her—with more contempt than concern,
chuckled, advised everyone to relax and at the same time
to stand ready, and then went downstairs to the dining
room, followed by Sarah, who wanted to question him,
but who presently found herself ringing the bell for Myrtis and asking her to bring the doctor some coffee and
cake. She wondered where Leon was, what kept him in
town; but she would not let herself ask the doctor if he
knew her husband's whereabouts. She could guess well
enough—with his Uncle Felix and Aunt Nell, in all likeli-
hood. Watching the doctor gobbling up pecan cake, the
crumbs of it falling to his chin whiskers and sticking there
briefly until they fell to the table and the floor, she asked
how long he thought it would be before the child came.
He winked at her, chewing his cake, and said to her when
his mouth was free enough to deliver speech, "Patience.
All we may do is wait until we are needed. In the meantime, don't worry; try to rest."

It was twenty-two hours from the time Sarah heard
Lauretta's first cry until she heard the first cry of the
child. Lauretta slept briefly, but her body continued to
work even while she slept. Sarah lay down toward midnight on a hard sofa that was seldom used even for sitting; it was only something to keep the upper hall from
looking bare. She wondered before she fell asleep why
Leon had not returned, and woke to wonder again why he
was not there with her.

No one ate a real supper, although the doctor did very
well with the cold victuals Myrtis assembled and set out
on the dining table. Myrtis also saw to it that coffee was
hot and abundant. The kitchen chimneys smoked all night
that night. Every now and then those in the house were
startled out of their fatigue by the sound of Lauretta's
screams, which had long since ceased to be mere girl-fear
and self-dramatizing apprehension. They knew her pain
was real when she began to rend the very air with profane
curses, some of which they had never heard before in
their lives, but recognized as if they had always known the
words and phrases.

Sarah was herself exhausted, and the doctor was red-faced and droopy-eyed after eating a whole pound of cheese, although not at one time, and having consumed various sweets and cold biscuits and glasses of brandy since early breakfast.

Then late in the morning, after long hours of tired bustle, the house went suddenly quiet. Lauretta had fainted. The doctor was working the child from her body. A reek of sweat and blood hung in the air of the room whose windows had been closed to guard Lauretta against chill. The cry of the newborn child sounded, angry and terrified, and Sarah was there. The clock in the upper hall struck and chimed, and she counted eleven.

"She's a baby girl," Juanita said as she smoothed the baby clean with hands that had been buttered as if she meant to pull syrup candy. Sarah stood looking at the squalling child, whose cries diminished, from exhaustion or acclimatization to the outer world. Lauretta slept, even as Lovey cleaned and tidied her and her bed. In their room, from which Selma had not stirred since hearing Lauretta's ordeal begin the day before, Selma slept too, at last, Pauline holding her in her arms as if she were the child that had just been born.

Roscoe saw to it that work continued that day in areas he was accustomed to ordering it done. Lovey and Myrtis kept the household going, slipping away for cat naps when they could. Dr Porterfield went back to Highboro with a rumbling belly and a tale to tell his waiting wife. After seeing her sister comfortable and asleep, Sarah went to her room, fell on her bed, and was asleep before she could bring herself to remove her shoes. Looking in on her a little while later, Lovey removed them, and lifted Sarah's head to slip a pillow under it, and drew the curtains against the light of day.

When Sarah woke, she found daylight nearly gone. She was still tired as she went to the washstand to bathe her face and hands. After brushing her hair and pulling it back in a knot, she went off to Lauretta's room. When she entered, the room was shadowed, and Lauretta appeared to be asleep. Juanita, sitting beside the cradle that had rocked Selma and Leon in their infancies, smiled at her and put a vertical finger to her lips.

Sarah went to the cradle and looked down at the sleeping child. "Is she all right?" she whispered.

Juanita nodded importantly. "Lovey brought up that Fedora. Had her baby two weeks ago. Fedora fed her, and she didn't even spit up once. This gonna be a good baby."

"Oh, that's good," Sarah said gratefully. "Have you been to bed at all?"

"No'm."

"You must be so tired."

"Well'm. I'm a little tired, but I had to see you to ask you something." Sarah looked at the girl, waiting for her to go on, but Juanita was suddenly shy. "Well'm. I wondered if. I wanted to ask you can I be this baby's nurse?" It was said, and Juanita looked at Sarah as if much depended on the answer she was given.

"I see no reason not," Sarah said consideringly. "Why do you want to be?"

Having the matter settled, Juanita looked down at the child. "Oh," she said vaguely, "I don't know'm. I love a baby."

"You may certainly look after her—unless her mother wants to herself." Seeing alarm spread over Juanita's face, she added hastily, "But I don't think she will, and in any case she'll need someone to help her."

Reassured, Juanita said, "What's her name?"

"Why—" Sarah laughed, forgetting to whisper. "Do you know, she never, my sister, talked about naming the child, never talked about boys' names or girls' names! I'll ask her when she wakes."

The hall door opened, and Lovey entered with a tray, followed by Fedora, a stout and very black woman, who went straight to the cradle. Lovey set the tray down on a table beside Lauretta's bed. To Juanita she said, "Open the curtains so air can come in. This room stinks." Juanita obeyed, and went anxiously back to Fedora who had picked up the baby, waking her and causing her to cry. Juanita hovered over the two—Fedora had taken her chair—as Fedora bared a breast and offered it. The child stopped crying when she found the nipple. Fedora gave Juanita a dazzling smile of superiority.

"Wake up, miss," Lovey said at the bed, where Sarah had joined her. "Time for you to eat."

Lauretta opened her eyes. "I'm awake," she said faintly. "I haven't slept at all."

"You slept," Lovey assured her, "some hours."

"How can you know?"

"You snored."

"I don't snore."

"Yes, you do. Raise your head up a little."

"I don't want food."

"You need it. Gruel made with squirrel stock. It'll strengthen you." She lifted the inverted top bowl off the gruel, picked up a spoon, and began to spoon it into Lauretta's mouth. Lauretta soon was eating greedily, and finished the bowlful. Lovey handed her a glass of milk, which she began to drink.

It was only then she saw, or at any rate acknowledged, Sarah. As soon as their eyes met, Sarah bent and kissed her cheek. "You've a pretty daughter," she said.

Lauretta frowned. "All babies are ugly."

"Juanita has fallen in love with her and insists on being her nurse! She also wants to know what to call her." The sisters looked at each other, Sarah smiling, Lauretta blank-faced, not yet realizing, it seemed, that her ordeal had produced a human life.

Sarah laughed. "Fedora is feeding her again. You may see her when she has taken her nourishment."

Lauretta shook her head against the pillow. "I don't want to."

"Of course you do, but not until we decide upon a name."

Lauretta shrugged.

Waiting another moment, Sarah said, "If you haven't settled on one, may it be Mama's?"

"If you like," Lauretta said absently.

Lovey looked down at her frowning, then at Sarah, frowning harder. "You can close the curtains, but not all the way." She picked up the tray and went out.

The mother, fed, closed her eyes and slept again. Sarah moved over to Juanita and Fedora. The baby's mouth had relaxed, her eyes were closed. She too had eaten; she too would sleep. Juanita took her gingerly from Fedora and cradled her in her arms. Fedora buttoned her dress and left them.

As Juanita held the baby close, looking down at her and swaying her gently, Sarah whispered, "Her name is Rachel."

Juanita smiled and nodded, as if she had been reminded of something she had known all along.

Sarah took a candle to light her way through the hall and down the stairs, but when she closed the door of Lauretta's room behind her, Leon, who had been waiting at the cracked door of their room, called, "Sarah?" and she hurried into the room with him.

"Are you all right?" she asked, closing the door.

He leaned forward and kissed her on the forehead, taking the candle from her and setting it down on a side table. " 'Are you all right?' " he repeated her words self-mockingly. "Oh, Sarah, why don't you scream and curse me for a weak fool? It's I who ought to ask, 'Are you all right?' If only you were not so good, if you would punish me a little for all the poor things I do!"

By this time she had observed that he needed to shave, and that his clothes were untidy. If he had not slept in them, they nevertheless showed evidence that he had worn them for two days. However, he appeared to be quite sober.

"The child was born this morning. Lauretta has had a bad time, but seems to be resting now, although in depressed spirits. We have only now given the little girl a name—Rachel, for our mother who died when we were so young."

"Sarah!" His voice choked on her name, and he wept.

"Leon, my dear—" She put her arms around him, and he let her, taking comfort in her strength and closeness, surrendering to the luxury of remorse.

"It should have been your child!" he said.

"Well," she said softly, at a loss.

"If only it were!"

"Well, she isn't, and we must see that she has good care. I speak of her as 'she' not 'it,' you see? She is already real to me."

Leon drew away from her, in control of himself again. "I know," he murmured.

"I have slept all afternoon," she said gaily. "And you are home—I am so glad. I am only now going downstairs to see how things have been today. Supper will surely be ready very soon. Freshen yourself if you like, and then join me. I think we might have a glass of wine to toast the new child, don't you?"

Leon nodded. "Very well. But remember, Sarah, I tried to tell you—I am sorry for what I have done and been."

"You are home. What else matters?" She hugged him briefly and in a continuing motion picked up her candle and went out.

Glancing about her on her way downstairs and through the house, she saw that all was in order, as she had expected it to be. Trust Lovey. On Doomsday Lovey would see to it that the yards were swept. In the kitchen she found her with Myrtis and Sallou, the other kitchen helper. She bade them all a good evening and said, "Mister Leon is home. How near is supper? What are we having to eat?"

"Scraps," Myrtis said glumly. "That doctor et everything wasn't moving. Chicken pie and sweet potatoes. Turnip greens and pot dodgers. I had the time so I made some peach tarts."

"Nobody will starve," Lovey said.

"No," Sarah agreed, and then hesitated before turning to Myrtis again. "You'll need to find another helper for the kitchen work. Take whoever you want. Juanita asked if she could be the baby's nurse, and I said she could."

Sallou, who Sarah had thought before to be perhaps a little simple, began a high-pitched giggle, and Lovey said to Myrtis, "I told you," and Myrtis ordered Sallou to hush her fuss if she didn't want her sassy face slapped. Sarah smiled uncertainly at them all and said, "Well," which could mean anything or nothing. Sensing that she had been somehow inadequate if not downright unsatisfactory, so far as Myrtis was concerned, she went to the big stove, sniffing, and when she saw the platter of peach tarts keeping warm on the back of the stove, she asked Myrtis, "May I have one now? I shouldn't, but I am starving."

Her dignity and authority restored, Myrtis took a fork and deftly served one of the tarts to her mistress on a fresh napkin which a chastened Sallou whisked before her.

"Oh, I thank you!" Sarah crooned appreciatively, picking up the tart in her fingers and beginning to eat it.

"Don't burn yourself!" Myrtis scolded her.

"I won't," Sarah promised and went out to the porch from the kitchen, wanting to be away from them. She walked decisively, as though she left on an errand and knew precisely where she was going, although she did not. As she went out the back door and down the steps, she saw Roman, and guessed from his face that he had been waiting for her.

"Roman! It is good to see you." She took his hand and squeezed it.

"You woke at last!" he exclaimed, smiling, but a little accusingly too. "Lovey told me you were up all night and I wouldn't see you till tomorrow."

"Have some peach tart."

He shook his head.

She broke off a piece and conveyed it to his mouth.

which opened and received it. She ate the rest and wiped her greasy fingers on the napkin. They chewed together, eyes rolling, shoulders shaking with laughter kept silent, lest they choke.

"I heard it's a little girl!"

"Name is Rachel."

"Rachel?"

"My mother's name."

"Ah." He nodded.

"You know," she teased him. "I kind of forgot what you look like, Roman, the last day has been so strange, like a day out of time."

"I look like me!"

"Yes," she agreed happily. "You look like you!" But even as she said it, she remembered Leon and her suggestion that they have a glass of wine together to celebrate the new baby's safe arrival. She said good night to Roman and went into the house again.

Seventeen

Felix and Nell came to look at the child. Nell shook her head and said, "Poor mite; a lifetime of suffering ahead, born as she is a female into this vale of tears." Juanita, who had assumed full charge of the baby, asked "Miss Nell" if she would like to hold Rachel a minute, but the offer was declined with a sad smile.

Others were more cheerful on their visits. All of the Davises came, including the youngest. Their stay was short, friendly, and a little noisy. The four children, who had obviously been instructed not to touch the baby, stood solemnly, hands held behind them, as Juanita lowered Rachel for them to see closely. The two older ones— Adam was six and Annabel five—had seen their brother James and sister Doreen when they were babies, so it might be assumed that the viewing of this new child could provide no sensation. Yet it did, perhaps because she was not one of them. They stared, they gawked. Annabel cupped a hand over Adam's ear. He frowned and whispered back to her. Then he said, "Annabel says can we see her toes."

Everyone laughed, and Juanita obligingly slipped off one of Rachel's bootees. Annabel counted the toes care-

fully, her lips moving, but no sound coming from her.
Adam was staring at Rachel's head, and when Annabel
had satisfied herself in her count, he exclaimed, "Look at
her little ears!" They all did, and no one laughed, although only Juanita seemed to be unsurprised at the boy's
having picked the baby's ears for special comment. They
were perfectly formed. Juanita, who knew the baby better
than anyone else, beamed at the boy and suggested generously, "You can touch one if you be gentle."

Adam pointed his index finger carefully, closer and
closer to the baby's head. Finger touched ear. The boy
stared at the baby. The baby suddenly cried, as everyone
else laughed, and the party broke up. Sarah walked out
with them and saw them cram themselves and each other
into one large carriage, with much laughter and shouting
and a heated discussion of who had sat on whose lap on
the way over and what promises had been made of lap-
space for the return.

As they drove away, Sarah called after them, "You all
look like a big basket of puppies!" Their laughter at this
came back to her until the carriage rounded a curve in the
drive. Alone in the front yard, Sarah missed and envied
the good cheer of the departing family party. Even Bonard had been jokey and lighthearted, and charming with
his young nieces and nephews. When she went into the
house, Sarah heard from Juanita that Lauretta had gone
off to her room "with the headache."

Most of their county neighbors made a visit, or at least
a casual stopping-by on their way to or from town. Late
autumn was not a season when work pressed. After a
busy summer there was time for people to lift their heads
from their hands and look about them, to remember
friends, enemies, and acquaintances, and even to talk to
them of matters nothing to do with crops and livestock.
There were dances, planned and impromptu, and all manner of other country frolics, such as cane grindings and
syrup making, candy pullings—and one hasty marriage to
accommodate a surprise pregnancy—all these were occasions of social exchange, which included old quarrels as
well as new flirtations. Because of Lauretta's advanced
pregnancy when she arrived at Beulah Land, the menfolk
among the Kendrick acquaintance were not expected to
come calling before the child was born, and the women
were too busy preserving foods and dealing with other
matters related to harvest time. They all came now to pay

their respects to mother and child.

The women of the Coker family walked over from their farm one mild morning after Trudy had given them a report of her own visit, and even Clarence Anderson came from his place, although his introduction to Lauretta and his glimpse of Rachel were incidental to his interview with Leon in the office, during which Leon agreed to extend more or less indefinitely the due-payment date of a sum of money he had lent Clarence earlier in the year. Clarence's money dealings with Roscoe Elk were not mentioned when he dealt with Leon, or with any of his peers, although a vaguely worded argument he used with Leon made reference to the common boundaries they shared and of the "undesirability of a stranger's coming into possession of the old Anderson Farm."

Penelope made ready to visit Beulah Land as soon as she had news of Rachel's birth, but before she could set out on the journey, Judge Truebody died of pneumonia—suddenly, people said, although death from pneumonia of men his age was always said to be sudden, in spite of the familiar jingle: "Ailing Monday, bed on Tuesday, bad on Wednesday, dead on Thursday, sad on Friday, buried Saturday, forgotten Sunday."

Penelope put off her traveling for almost two weeks. There were not merely the sad events, mainly social, attending the death of her old protector. After the judge was gone, certainly to his earthly and hopefully to his Heavenly rest, Penelope had several meetings with officials of the Bank of Georgia, into whose care the judge had arranged that she submit herself and her affairs, should he himself prove finally mortal.

It was November when Penelope arrived, attended by Clarice's daughter Ricey, who had performed the same function on every visit her mistress had made to Beulah Land since their first seven years ago. She had quite as many friends there as did Penelope. Sarah began immediately to press her Aunt Pea to remain at least until the New Year. Penelope said no initially, and then went through a period of seeming to weigh the matter, but she had brought with her clothes suitable and adequate for the whole winter.

Although she greeted her aunt and once-guardian affectionately enough, and even made a properly dramatic display on their first meeting after seven years, Lauretta quickly fell back into the alternately depressed and dis-

tracted moods that had been her portion since attaining
motherhood. Whereas once she had sat waiting and
hoping for almost anyone to join her and talk a little
while, now she showed reluctance to settle into any pro-
longed discussion, and was not even free with small chat.

She recovered her strength quickly, which made her
restless and eager to be up long before the ten days of bed
rest women of her class considered obligatory. She gave
Rachel only perfunctory attention. Fedora continued to
feed the child; Juanita did everything else required for her
care and well-being. Lauretta used words such as "pretty"
and "sweet" and "dear," but the baby did not recognize
her mother and was indeed fretful when Lauretta now and
then grabbed her up to show her off to company. The
child's response to such whimsical attention was not flattering. Soon, when company arrived, Lauretta would re-
tire to her room. Although certainly willing to take center
stage, she had seen quickly enough that people came not
because of her but in deference to Sarah and to the Kendrick position.

A room smaller then Lauretta's bedroom and next to it
was cleared of Laura-Lou's sewing equipment and made
into a nursery, with the baby's cradle, various tables and
chests, and a bed for Juanita. Except with those early visitors, Lauretta did not dissemble her feelings about the
child. She ignored her, and when reminded of her existence gave her as little time as she could manage without
exciting comment. Sarah put it down to the baby's reminding Lauretta of Douglas Savage and the pain of his
desertion. She excused her sister and lavished attention on
the child, who very soon began to recognize her and respond to her presence and voice and caresses as an infant
usually does only to its mother, whoever's hands may perform necessary functions when the mother is absent.

Lauretta was regular in her attendance at meals in the
dining room, as a result of which meals were more regularly taken there than they had been since Sarah became
mistress of Beulah Land. It was not for Lauretta to share
the quick meal at a kitchen table with servants. And, Penelope's arrival put the cap on the old formalities of bell
ringing and sitting down and being served and eating with
social conversation. Penelope especially enjoyed the ritual
of breakfast. She liked her meat and eggs, her grits and
gravy and hot biscuits, with coffee and sweets to prolong
the meal as a comfortable and agreeable family occasion.

The fresh air of a new day, the morning energy and bustle, fresh gossip that had somehow been spawned overnight, gave Penelope a reassurance of life itself that became more important to her every day of her life. She
woke with a clear head and a sharp appetite for food and
for people, and she kept them the whole day long.

Lauretta was anxious to regain her condition as an attractive woman and spent many hours of her days in intense self-grooming. She had picked up from her acting
acquaintances a certain amount of reliable information as
well as an uncertain amount of rumor and superstition,
but aside from these, she had an instinct for doing what
made her look and feel better and younger, and more the
early Lauretta. She cultivated cleanliness as if it were the
godly virtue it is reputed to be; but she did not entrust
herself entirely to Heavenly care. She spent time before a
glass with scissors and curlers and carmine and corn
starch, testing, staring critically, changing here a lock of
hair and there a blending of rouge and powder.

She spent other hours thinking about her past life and
vowing to make that ahead better. She did not know yet
what she intended to do with herself but, bored with the
country, she gave in to glorious daydreams. On the solitary walks she had begun to take as the only way she
could be sure of being quite alone, she dreamed of the
outside, of the far and future world she would make.

On one of her walks in early November she met Bonard, who was walking too, but whose horse, it turned out,
was tethered nearby. It was not coincidental that they
met, for Bonard's interest in her had sharpened since her
arrival at Beulah Land in August, and peaked since she
delivered her child. He remembered the way she had flirted with him and Leon on their visit to Broughton Street
when Selma was in Savannah to buy her wedding clothes.

When they met, however—and it was the third day in a
row he had paced and lingered in that particular lane,
having heard Leon casually refer to her walks and the fact
that she walked out of the ordinary ways to avoid people—he was, or appeared to be all surprise and gallantry,
at any rate as long as he could maintain the attitude.

"Miss Lauretta! You are out alone? Pray take my arm
and lean as you step up to and over that log. You walk
without even a dog to companion and protect you? This is
monstrous neglect on the part of your hosts at Beulah

Land! What if some churlish fellow were to apprehend you? Some fellow like me?"

Lauretta had begun to laugh, and when he paused in his speech, she threw back her head and let her laughter ring forth joyously to reward him for amusing her. He watched her with satisfaction, finally lifting his shoulders in an exaggerated gesture of acknowledgment that she had caught him out.

"You scoundrel!" she said delightedly. "How glad I am to see you! I have been so bored."

After this they continued to meet, not at first by arrangement, but rather by hint and sigh. The weather remained fine through November, as it often did. (One year, when they were boys, Leon and Floyd had swum in the creek on Thanksgiving Day.) Without asking or offering secrecy, neither spoke of their meetings to another living soul.

Eighteen

Sarah and Roman kept their school again, sometimes out of doors, indoors when it rained or "turned off cool."

Roman held up a large card for the youngest, who had just started to attend. "A," he said.

"A-a-a-a-a-a-a-a-a," they sang together.

"B."

"B-e-e-e-e-e-e-e-e!" they echoed with increasing confidence.

"What's this?" He held up another card.

"C-e-e-e-e-e-e-e-e!"

"No!" Roman said sternly. "It's a G!"

"You trick us!" a young one accused, experiencing his first betrayal in the process of formal education.

Roman held up both cards. "This is a C. This is G. Now tell me what's the difference?"

One child chortled boldly, not having yet learned fear, "That right! What difference do it make!"

Listening with one part of her mind, Sarah smiled as she read simple poems to a circle of seven older boys and girls. The rhyme and rhythm made it easy for them to follow and understand and sometimes even to remember after one hearing. Sarah was careful never to go on for too long a time, because then the sound inevitably became lullling and could make the children sleepy.

Another day she watched Roman take a class through a spelling lesson. She was always pleased to see that he did not ever scorn or make fun of them when they got a word wrong. Especially when two words sounded alike but were spelled differently and had different meanings, he was slow and patient, able to go over the same ground again and again without seeming bored.

Geography was often a part of spelling lessons, as every subject blended into or sparked off every other. All, even the youngest, knew how to spell their names and "Beulah Land" and "Highboro" and "Georgia"—although "Georgia" was not as easy to learn to spell as "Mary-land" and "Ala-bama." Some of the states were all but impossible for them to learn to spell, or learn anything else about. Distant though it was, "Vermont" was all right. It was spelled just the way it sounded, and there was a certain connection between "mont" and "marble." But "Rhode Island" made no sense. There was obviously no reason for an "h" in "Rhode," and how could there be an "s" in "Island"? And why was it called an island when it clearly from the map was not?

When eyes clouded with suspicion and worry lines were deep on dark young brows, Roman had a sure way of breaking up the tension and making them laugh. He would point suddenly with comical sternness to Otis and Lotus and demand to know how they spelled "Mississippi." Those two serious children would instantly spring up from their bench and, holding hands, they would solemnly pronounce and spell out: "Mississippi! M-i-s-s-i-double-s-i-p-p-i!"

Their earnestness combined with the droll suggestiveness of the last four letters spoken separately never failed to convulse the other children with laughter. The only ones who kept straight faces were the twins, who looked questioningly at Roman, and Roman who met their look with the quiet assurance that they had spelled it right.

The country children also found nursery rhymes hilarious, a special favorite being:

"Hey diddle diddle,
The cat and the fiddle,
The cow jumped over the moon!"

Sarah was happy in her school, happy with Roman and with the children. Aunt Pea's curiosity was roused only after Sarah had several times slipped away from the breakfast table, claiming that she must attend her own school and be on time. Penelope finally asked to be allowed to join her, and when on one occasion a young boy asked her a question, supposing her to be a teacher since she was obviously not a pupil, she answered, "Ask me no questions, I'll tell you no lies!" which the children had never heard, and which they picked up and repeated immediately and so many times that Penelope's head was quite turned by her success. After that she felt bound to go to the school for a little while every day that Sarah went. She sat quietly, always interested— How could she not be?—often entranced. To observe young ones learning is headier wine than Omar's.

Juanita came too, bringing Rachel with her, Rachel her excuse as well as her reason. She would sit there and absorb as much as she could understand, and she found that she understood more all the time, without fear of being asked to answer questions, to perform—the thing indeed that had made her shun the school as much as she could when she had been of an age to attend.

Sarah was happy.

Sometimes—not often—Selma and Pauline would come and sit just outside the classes, whether they were being held in or out of doors, but they never gave evidence of seeing the others, and never admitted to being seen. Solid as a block of sugar or salt, they would sit there silently, everyone conspiring with them to accept them as invisible guests. This too was a useful lesson for the children, and one they learned quicker than multiplication tables, or how to spell "Rhode Island." Their sensibilities were acute, and they loved making believe.

Lauretta did not come to the school. Nor did Leon. Ezra continued to look in and to go away with the appearance of being refreshed and absorbed in new thoughts. Floyd came with him now and then, but stopped coming altogether when he found himself unable to move his eyes away from Sarah.

For the time, Sarah was happy.

Nineteen

On Monday morning of Thanksgiving week Edna Davis drove her buggy from Oaks to Beulah Land, went along the drive to the front of the house and, seeing no one, did not pause there, but continued around the house. She had got down from her seat and whipped the reins around the stock before Sugar came from the barn to help her.

"Where's your mistress?" she asked, and Sugar gestured toward the cabin they had long since come to think of as "the schoolhouse."

"I'll fetch her, ma'am," Sugar offered.

"I'll go myself," Edna declared and marched off.

Sugar looked at the horse and buggy, feeling that he had failed in his duty somewhere, but the reins were perfectly secure, and no one had told him to expect a visitor. The horse turned his head briefly to look at the young man, then faced forward again, shook his head harness as if to jingle it deliberately, pawed the earth twice, and then lifted his tail daintily before dropping two round, dry turds.

Sarah spied Edna at the door and went to greet her. "Miss Edna!" she said in a welcoming way, taking one of the older woman's big red hands into both of hers. "Have you come to see me by yourself?"

"Yes, I have," Edna said seriously.

"I'm glad to have you. Let's go up to the house where we can sit comfortably."

"Can we just walk a little? I want to talk to *you* without any of the others, if you'll let me."

"Certainly," Sarah said and put her arm through Edna's and guided her away from the school.

They walked silently until Edna said, "I don't know what's unsettled me, truly I don't. But I have been so downhearted I haven't known what to do. You wouldn't think it, big, everybody says jolly old thing like me, would you?"

Sarah squeezed her arm and hand but said nothing.

"I hate to let on to Trudy, she's so busy, or to Rooster, he's busy too, especially when I've got no real complaint. Just worry. Do you ever just *worry?*" She stopped to look at Sarah. Sarah looked back at her quietly. Edna sighed. "When you expecting to kill your first hogs?"

"First cold weather after Thanksgiving," Sarah said, without appearing to find the question odd or out of place.

Edna nodded. "Us too. First real freeze. If there's a little time between Thanksgiving and that, will you do something with me?"

"Of course I will, Miss Edna."

"I sound foolish, even to me. You remember me and Deborah used to go to the cemetery to look after our graves?" Sarah nodded. "Well, I haven't been since I went last with her, first of the year. It's over time. I don't want to go by myself."

"I'll certainly go with you," Sarah said. "I should have thought of it myself. But my sister—"

"I know!"

"And Aunt Pea has been here—"

"And there's your school," Edna said fulsomely to further excuse her of any possible slacking or self-blame.

Sarah patted her hand. "You just tell me when you want to go, and we'll go. I promise nothing will stand in the way. And we'll go by ourselves, just as you and Aunt Deb used to go, unless Trudy wants to come with us."

"Oh, you are a good girl!" Edna said, patting Sarah's hand gratefully. "You've got a good heart as well as a good head. No, let's not ask Trudy. She has so much to tend to, and she'd be in some hurry or— I wish Bonard could have married a girl like you. Oh, I don't mean to speak ill of Selma, but she's always been something strange in her ways, and that isn't what Bonard needed. It would have made all the difference if he'd— There I go." She laughed at herself unconvincingly. "They do say it's a sign of getting old when folks start saying 'if only this, if only that.' Well, there's no 'if only,' there's only what is."

They had made their way slowly around the house and come again to the back door. "Come in and sit," Sarah said. Edna shook her head. "Wouldn't you like a cup of coffee? Or sassafras tea to be a change?"

"No, dear, really not. I'll go." She looked down at her woolen dress and pulled the heavy shawl she wore over it closer, as if to hide the everyday shabbiness of the old dress. "I didn't think—just came the way I was. I don't want anybody to see me."

"There's no one likely to, except Aunt Pea and Lauretta if she's in, and they're family."

"Oh, but they're city!"

"Come in, do?"

Edna shook her head firmly. "I must hit the grit." She went to the buggy and stepped up into it as lightly as a girl before Sarah could help her. Once again, Sugar emerged from the barn too late to be of any assistance. Seeing Edna in her seat, he merely stood there, watching her with his mistress. "How are you, Sugar?" Edna said, as if seeing him for the first time.

"Just fine, Miss Edna."

"That's good. Violet tells me you're coming to spend the day with her Thanksgiving. That right?"

Sugar was overcome with mirth. Nodding his head and laughing heartily, he ducked back into the barn.

Edna took up the reins and made a short turn of the buggy. Then she paused, holding the reins. "It's made me feel s'much better coming to see you!" she said gaily with a good show of her more customary spirit.

"Come any time, Miss Edna. And come soon now for our—for our cemetery drill! You hear?"

Edna nodded, smiled, slapped the reins lightly on the horse's back, and started him off at a walk. Sarah followed for a few paces until Edna turned in her seat and called, "How's the baby? I meant to ask earlier!"

"She's well and fine! Rachel is fine!" Sarah called back.

Edna laughed her pleasure and approval and set the horse, who knew her ways at least as well as she knew his, into a quick trot down the drive.

Twenty

The two days before Thanksgiving were busy ones. Eighteen turkeys were killed and dressed and roasted in the ovens of the main house, along with scores of pumpkin pies. These were for the slaves' holiday eating, since most of their cabins had no oven to accommodate a big turkey.

On Thanksgiving Day the family's turkey and a ham were cooked before and during the time the family drove in to church in Highboro. The old coach was used as the only vehicle large enough to transport with dignity Leon and Sarah, Selma and Penelope and Lauretta. There was more room than they expected to have, because half an hour before they were to set off, Lauretta called Sarah into her room and told her she did not feel well enough to go along. She had a headache, and she thought her heart was beating too fast. In any event, she had better lie down while they were gone, she said, and hoped to feel well enough to join them at the dinner table when they returned. She wanted no assistance or attention, she declared, when Sarah offered first to stay with her, and when that was refused, to ask Lovey to look in on her.

So, off to church went the family, leaving Lauretta behind in her room. Juanita watched them drive away, standing at the window of the nursery with Rachel in her arms and lifting and waving one of the baby's hands at them as they rolled off. They did not see her, and as if to console her, Juanita said to Rachel, "Never you mind, one day you be riding in that old coach, big as anybody!" Lauretta continued to lie down in her room for about an hour, and then quite suddenly, as if having received a cue, she got up and began to move around the room, briskly sorting clothes.

Lovey saw her leave the house and go off toward the woods with a bundle in her arms, but she registered merely the sight, without trying to explain it to herself, having a good deal too much, she thought, on her mind already. She—so far only she—knew that Floyd had made his decision. She knew too that she would have the hardest thing of all to do: explain the leaving to Ezra.

"I can't, Mama," he had said in a tight, quiet voice. "Going is hard enough. I can't both go and lie too. Not even to Papa."

"Come back," she had said, "when you get over it."

"What will you tell them?"

"I don't know. Something. Do me a favor? When you're ready, just go. Don't tell me again, I'll know." She had seen the little signs, and she knew that he was ready.

After church services, which were short but not short enough, because every woman present was thinking more about her dinner than of giving thanks to the Lord, the Kendrick family with Penelope, gossiping with old friends and county neighbors, went into the grove where the coaches and buggies, and a few wagons with improvised cross-board seats, giving them the function of buckboards, had been left. The Kendricks and Penelope settled into the coach comfortably with Leon on the driver's seat this time, and Sugar, who had driven them in, riding to Oaks on the outside back frame of the Davis carriage. The oldest boy, Adam, had insisted on riding there with him. Sugar had long been courting the girl named Violet at Oaks, with the permission of the masters of both plantations. All the Davises had come in except Bonard. Felix drove his buggy, with Nell on the seat beside him and a light trunkful of their necessaries on the buggy box behind. They were going to Beulah Land for dinner and, as Sarah had asked them, ". . . for a day or two anyway after?"

The dinner they ate was truly a feast, and when they all, including Lauretta who felt much, much better, she said, went in to the dining room, the very sight of the table full of food made Selma feel that she had already eaten. Suddenly, she could not, she decided, sit down and watch them eating, and listen to their exclamations about the tastiness of this and that and their polite arguments about whether the ham or the turkey was better. Taking one look at the table, she said "You must all excuse me," and went away quickly to her room, knowing that her name for eccentric behavior would allow them to accept her action without surprise or hurt feelings. Anyway, she had missed Pauline, and Pauline would sulk during the first hour of her return.

Those remaining laughed and sat down and were very soon indeed debating the merits of the ham as opposed to those of the turkey.

Twenty-One

The family dinner thus honored and celebrated, as all such rituals must be, the various participants walked about a very little while before retiring to their rooms for rest.

Later, Lauretta excused herself from joining the others for supper, declaring that she was not unwell, as she had feared herself to be earlier in the day, but that she believed it would do her good to be quiet in her room until morning, if they would forgive her. They did forgive her, and with spirits freshened by the afternoon rest, Sarah and Leon rejoined their relatives and guests in a quiet but still enjoyable cold supper. Nell had declared that she would only sit with them and take nothing, but Leon, and then Sarah, and indeed Penelope and Felix too, so pressed and encouraged her that she found she was able to eat a morsel or two after all.

In conclusion, after much urging, she allowed Sarah to set a wedge of pumpkin pie before her. Even as she protested that she would not touch it, Leon tilted a pitcher of thick cream over the whole, and when she had done exclaiming her objections, she sighed, picked up a spoon, and saying, "Waste not, want not," began to consume it.

When they had finished eating, they sat for a little bit of time in companionable stupor, until Sarah began to edge her chair back, and Felix half rose to help her from it.

"Wait!"

Surprised, all turned to Penelope whose command had halted them in their various actions.

"I have only just remembered something," Penelope said shyly. "Papa—on Thanksgiving Day, offered prayers before every meal, of course, but at the end of the last one, he said another. 'We thank Thee, Lord, and mayest Thou teach us to be just to ourselves, even as we are to each other.' " When they looked at her smiling, as if waiting for her to conclude, Penelope said, "That's all of it; I sometimes think he meant one thing; other times, another."

Nell said, sounding for her a touch impatient, "The directive words would surely seem to be 'even as'?"

"Ah, who knows," Sarah said mysteriously, controlling her laughter.

After that everyone hastily scraped chair legs—there was never carpeting in the dining room—and gradually said good night. Nell declared for a period of meditation in her room before sleeping. She would, she allowed, read a chapter or so from the Bible, without which she never moved from home, "not knowing when the Lord will call me to Him." Perhaps one of the Psalms; they were so comforting when read in the proper spirit. She took a candle from the hallway into the office room and thence up the stairs.

While the others' attention was upon her leave-taking, Felix drifted into the shadows and down the wide hall and breezeway, and quickly out of doors. There was a lively sound from the slave quarters. The big house might be going quiet for the night, but it was early yet, and not a Sunday, and in spite of the somewhat religious cast of the day, it was one of celebration, and even Deborah had given permission for "orderly dancing," and certainly neither Leon nor Sarah had abridged any leniency enjoyed in Deborah's time of command.

Felix knew well how to sidle, and sidle in he did to the house where the music was being made. By the time anyone registered the fact of his presence, he had made himself appear so easy and natural a member of the festivities that no one spoke of noticing him, and his white presence was no dampener on the dark frolicking. From that stage of acceptance it was easy for him to speak first to this one, then that, then to three or four together, and then to stand alone smiling and tapping a foot to the music. It wasn't necessary for him to play the game out that way, because everyone knew what he was about, but he did it.

The ending of the day's events was as much ritual as had been its other, earlier events. Stella, a black woman in her middle thirties, whom he fancied and who in her way occasionally fancied him, was there, and he winked at her as he talked to others, and then watched her dance a little, and then saw her slip out the door alone.

A minute or two later he went out also and found her waiting. When she saw him, she giggled, and he giggled too. Neither did so in any derisive way, but rather as friendly conspirators. Soon after, they went into one of the barns and up a short, easy-slanting ladder to one of the haylofts.

Felix was neither a sly nor a subtle man in the act of sex. He was a thumper and a humper even as he grew older. So it was tonight. He humped, and the sound thumped through the hay to the boards it rested on, raising dust below and waking a cow, who stood up awkwardly in her stall. When she was firmly on all four legs, and only then, she lowed, the sound moody and accusing. Ever since he was a boy in this same barn, although then with girls whose names he had now forgotten, the sound of a cow's lowing in just that way had been a powerful aphrodisiac for Felix. The cow's lowing, the hot, wet, working flesh below but encompassing him gave him a pleasure nothing else ever had or would.

Afterward they talked a little and touched each other and lightly slapped each other's flesh here and there. "Stella," Felix said with a sigh, "that's the best piece of pussy I ever had in my life."

This made her laugh. He always said it, and she always laughed. "Fact," he said solemnly, which set her off again. Felix dressed—undressing and dressing in the dark were old skills for him—and after some whispering together, he gave Stella some money, which pleased her but which was not the whole reason she met him. "I don't mean to encourage you to do this kind of thing for money, you understand."

"No, sir, I don't."

He made a show of astonishment. "You mean everybody is free except me?"

"What you mean by 'everybody'?"

"I don't flatter myself you make do with one old man."

"Don't you throw off on yourself, Mister Felix. You fuck as good as anybody, and that's the truth."

"Well, it's nice of you to say so, my dear, even if it isn't true. You're a good girl, Stella."

When he left her, sometimes he paused in the back yard before going indoors, to look up at the sky, perhaps to light and smoke a cigar before bed. Tonight he did so, and was barely a quarter into the cigar when Floyd stepped out of the darkness and said, "Evening, Mister Felix."

"That you, Floyd?"

"Yessir."

"Getting some air—heavy food all day, you know. Needed a little walk around. Everybody seems to have gone to bed. You been—ah—up to something or other?" As he grew older, Felix discovered that he liked to tease younger men about their sexual adventures. It gave a pleasant edge to his own wilting lust.

"No." Floyd smiled, understanding and not minding. Felix looked at him again more closely.

"Floyd?" Floyd did not answer, stood waiting for Felix to register the implication of his present appearance. He was dressed in his best every-day, and beside him on the ground was a good-sized canvas-covered bundle, neatly tied, in which were his other clothes. "Well now," he said slowly after a minute or so, "has everybody except me known you plan to leave us tonight?"

"Nobody knows," Floyd said. "Mama knows I am, but not when."

"And you've decided it's now." Felix drew on his cigar while he studied it over to himself. "Nothing to stop you. You're a free man. You have papers; I signed them myself." Again Floyd waited, not expectantly, but knowing where Felix's train of thought would lead him. "You just going to go off without any word to them? Or *do* they

know; have you hinted any?" Floyd shook his head. "So."
Felix waited, and Floyd let him wait a little longer and
finish his own thoughts to himself. When he did and then
looked a first vague but genuine question to Floyd, Floyd
said, "We didn't happen to meet. I wanted to see you before I went." Felix nodded, the lawyer and man of business.

"I have the right," Floyd said, merely to make the point
again.

Felix nodded.

"I have papers, and I can travel with them without
trouble."

Felix thought about that and then nodded slowly. "I
should think so. You're not the kind of man who attracts
attention or gets in trouble anyway. But you were born
here, Floyd. Why, when you and Leon were boys, they
couldn't separate you. I remember they couldn't even get
him to go to that tutor over at Oaks until they let you go
with him. You can't leave Leon without telling him."

"I want you to tell him for me," Floyd said. "I can't."

Slowly Felix nodded and frowned, but there were still
questions in his eyes that showed back of the glow of the
cigar when he drew deeply on it.

Floyd said, "I'm not gone forever." Felix exhaled a big
billow of smoke. "I couldn't leave Mama and Papa like
that." Felix nodded, his chin hardly moving, but his eyes
expressive.

"No," he said. "I know how Lovey and Ezra feel—I
know some, that is to say." He looked at Floyd quietly,
studying his face. "That's why you waited for me, so I
would tell them. Quite right, Floyd. We all can do a lot
for each other in ways that don't cost as much as they
give. Everybody will be half dead tomorrow anyhow, I'll
tell them you've gone, but I bet they don't believe it till
next week."

"Thank you, Mister Felix."

Felix put out his hand and Floyd took it, pressed it,
and let it go.

Floyd turned to leave. "Hold on," Felix said, suddenly
unwilling to let him go. "You move so fast. How are you
going? Have you got it all planned?"

"Walk to Highboro. Isn't far. From there I'll borrow a
ride on a wagon. I know folks all the way from here to
Savannah from going times with Skeeter and the cotton
trains. When I get to the coast, I'll decide where next."

"By God," Felix said, "I envy you, starting out from here tonight your own man, nothing to hold you." Floyd's smile held irony, but Felix did not see it. "Floyd, let me help you a little. No need for you to walk all the way into town. I have always—don't ask me why—wanted to help somebody 'get away.' You come with me now. We'll wake up Sugar, and I'll tell him to saddle my horse, and then she's yours. When you got no more use for her, sell her. That'll put a dollar in your pocket and keep you from starving. Godalmighty, I do envy you."

Floyd saddled the horse himself, saying there was no need to wake Sugar. He left at a walk down the drive toward the main road. Felix stared through the darkness long after he had lost sight and sound of the departing man. Then he went in and upstairs and found Nell asleep, the candle on the mantel burned down and nearly out. He blew it out and again undressed in the dark.

Twenty-Two

Sarah woke in what was for her a rare mood; she felt irritable and apprehensive and put it down to the rich food of the day before. The sound that had waked her was that of the maids in the upper hall, bringing first-coffee to the sleepers, as and at the very time they had been directed to do so. Whatever the excesses of the day and evening before, Myrtis was evidently in proper command downstairs.

Sarah slipped out of bed and threw a dress over her head, casually pulling it into place as she stepped into shoes without bothering with stockings. She opened the door into the hall just as Sallou raised her hand to knock on it. Smiling automatically, she said good-morning and that she would take the coffee tray, which she did. Unexpectedly free, Sallou looked blank a moment before going off to be bossy with the helper who had taken Juanita's place, a girl named Sharon, who was still awed by the big house, and nervous at being so close to the intimate living arrangements of the white family.

Sarah set the tray on the table beside Leon's bed. She was about to speak his name and touch his shoulder when her own feeling stopped her. She was a feeling woman, but one who was usually in command of what she felt, who seldom caught herself in any sudden welling of emotion. But now her eyes smarted and her throat thickened, and the very surprise of it made her want to howl with grief and rebellion, she did not know why. She looked at her husband's sleeping face. The reddish blond hair that framed it was matted and dull, and the overnight growth of stubble-beard showed darkly. But the lips were rounded, rosy, and sweetly curved, the nose straight and strong, the chin full but clearly indented. His eyes were closed, the lashes darker than his head hair, the color, she remembered, of his pubic hair. Thinking of this, she saw that he had an erection that showed under the cover. The one hand that showed outside the quilt that came nearly up to his chin as if he would hide in it was relaxed, but it was a firm, man's hand, with nothing soft about it, and none of the scaly look she had seen on the backs of some other men's hands. To Sarah his face looked innocent and vulnerable and sad.

She blinked her eyes dry and shook his shoulder. "Leon?"

His eyes opened gradually.

"Coffee's here. I don't want any. Will you get up and see them all through breakfast? I don't think I feel up to it."

He pulled the quilt up, and when he let it fall again, his erection was gone. His eyes were now not only open but awake, and he took one of her hands. "Are you ailing?" he said.

She shook her head and smiled. "No!—only a little off for humoring everyone."

He yawned. "I'll get up and go down," he said. He threw off the bedcovers as she stood back, and swung himself up to sit on the side of the bed, his feet just touching the floor, his night gown caught and bunched under him in such a way that the bottom hem cut across his thighs. "I'll make Aunt Nell eat a dozen batter cakes and half a dozen slices of ham."

Sarah laughed and turned toward the door.

"Won't you have coffee?"

But she was at the door, and smiled and shook her head and left.

In the hall she found Sharon frowning and knocking at Lauretta's door. "She don't answer," Sharon said timidly, as if it might be her fault.

"She may be sleeping still. Just leave the tray on the floor outside."

"Yes'm."

Sarah went quickly downstairs. In the kitchen she asked Myrtis to make her a pot of sassafras tea. When it was ready, she drank it in deep, healing draughts. Then she went straight outdoors. For once she was glad that Roman did not wait for her. There was a chill of winter on the air, but no wind, so she was comfortable walking briskly.

As she cut across the back yards of a row of slave cabins, she saw Felix sitting on a stump near the kitchen door of Lovey's cabin. She stopped to wonder why he was there. By his attitude—leaning forward comfortably, elbows on knees, chin in hands, eyes set on the cabin door, he had been there a while, and not accidentally or without purpose. As she stood watching, the back door opened, and Ezra came out. He seemed surprised to find Felix there. Felix stood up. The back door opened and closed again, letting Lovey into the yard. Ezra might be surprised. Lovey, obviously, was not. She strode directly to Felix. He spoke—Sarah could not hear what he said, only the sound of words—and Lovey turned and went to Ezra, who was moving forward toward Felix.

Sarah began to run. Lovey's arms were around Ezra, whose face had frozen in stark disbelief and whose body seemed to shrivel and fade like ice melting in summer sun. She stopped short of them as Lovey supported Ezra to the door and inside. Felix turned and saw her.

"What's wrong?" she asked. "Why are you here?"

Felix frowned, shaking his head. "Took it hard. Knew they would, especially Ezra. He and the boy so close."

"Will you for God's sake tell me what has happened to make them feel so?"

Felix looked at her without his usual manners and humor, and his voice was sharp, as it was only occasionally in court. "Floyd has gone away, of course. What else could upset them?"

"Floyd?" She did not understand, her tone said.

"Yes," he said impatiently. "He left last night. I helped him on his way—gave him my horse, in fact. Good horse. He'll get a nice price for her if he has to sell her. I must say you look astounded. Why? He was free. He should have gone before. Wasting himself here, not enough to do with either his body or his mind, and he obviously didn't have his heart set on marrying any of the freshening heifers on the place. Leon's age, you know. Oh, he said he might come back one day, but for his sake I hope he doesn't. Don't you?"

The wail she had earlier controlled poured forth from her open mouth now, with a grief so sharp it shocked her to silence almost as soon as it began. After a moment when her body rocked and she had to catch her balance, she could say, "Leon's heart will be broken."

"There," Felix said, forgiving her for puzzling him, and hugging her lightly now that he thought he knew the tenor of her thoughts. "He'll get used to the idea. He'll soon see it's the right thing for Floyd to have done. He wasn't sneaking away, you know, by not telling everybody first; he just didn't want to have to argue about it. I saw that, and so should you, knowing Floyd as you must have." His head jerked toward the cabin. "It's them I worry about. He was the sunrise for Ezra."

Sarah's tears came then, but quietly, and so she found, if not comfort, at least a release.

Felix said, "Lovey was not surprised. She's the one who will make Ezra see."

"Should we send Pauline to them?" Sarah said a moment later.

Felix shook his head without making a comment. "Do you want to tell Leon?" As they looked at each other, the sound came over the grounds from the house of the bell for breakfast. "Let's go to breakfast now and bide our time. When they've eaten, I'll tell everyone at once. Will you allow me?—since I was, if not instrumental in his going, at least in full and sympathetic knowledge of it."

Sarah had got herself in better control. "Yes. Do it just as you say, only without me, please. I am not myself this morning. I had told Leon before I came out, and he said he would be at breakfast and explain that I would not be coming." She urged him with her eyes toward the house.

"Are you all right now?"

She nodded her head rapidly in a way he had never seen her do before, plainly telling him she was not all right, that she was even on the point of hysteria. "Yes," he said for her falsely, seeing that she wanted him to leave her.

"Do let Leon have his breakfast first!" she called after him. He did not turn, or pause in his going, only nodded his head up and down.

She did not walk in the direction he had taken, because she did not want to have to put on her manners. Her manners were not usually put on, but this morning they would have to be, if they were required, so it was best, she thought, to keep out of everyone's way.

She walked nearer to the house, but not near enough
for anyone inside to see her and join her, or to press her
to join them inside. Presently, she knew by the sounds
that came through windows and by the hurrying of Sallou
and Sharon back and forth through the breezeway with
platters of steaming food that the family party had
gathered for morning food. She went carefully through
the side yard where she was sure nobody would be. Nobody was. She straightened, gaining inches in her neck
and legs as she merely relaxed and began to look around
her.

The peacocks were molting, although it seemed to her
they molted year round. They were such nasty creatures,
she really did not know why they continued to have them.
It was Leon's father who had started them, and no one
had seen fit since to stop them. The front yard had not
been swept, nor had she thought it would be yet. It would
take a day for things to come back to normal. She bent
and picked up a feather that one of the peacocks had
dropped. Holding it against the light, she looked at its unlikely color blendings and thought that Rachel might fancy
it, so she took it indoors with her.

Having decided to bathe her face and hands and to
dress more conventionally now, she went up the stairs,
aware as she did so of the dim but cheerful sounds from
the dining room. At the top of the stairs, before she
turned off to her and Leon's room, she saw that Lauretta
had not taken in her coffee tray. She shrugged. Lauretta
was lazy and sleeping. Let her be. Or perhaps she had gone
directly downstairs to join the others and not thought to do
anything about the tray.

At the washstand in her room she took the towel Leon
had used and wiped the bowl clean of its film of soap and
a hair or two he had left. She poured water from the
pitcher into the big bowl, and after taking off the few
clothes she had put on earlier, she bathed herself quickly
with soap and rag all over. She then dressed carefully but
without dawdling, feeling better now, more herself, but
still unsettled. She would hope to catch the family party
toward the end of their breakfast and somehow in the
general talk and speculation dilute and disperse the intense
feelings she had been surprised by earlier. She went into
the hall, leaving the door open so that the room would
air.

The sight of the tray outside Lauretta's door made her

pause irritably. It was absurd, she thought. Lauretta was
not a famous actress upon the stage, to be encouraged to
loll in bed until noon. She knocked sharply on the door.
There was no answering voice. For the first time, she became alarmed, wondering if her sister was sick, and felt
remorse for those few hard thoughts of a moment ago.
The door opened easily enough. She entered and closed it
behind her, looking about. The curtains had not been
opened, and the light in the room was dim. As she went
closer to it, she saw that the bed had been lain upon but
not slept in. Truly alarmed now, she drew the curtains,
letting bright light in, and then she saw the letter propped
against the cold and empty brass candlestick on the mantelpiece. With a strong sense of having done it all before,
as indeed she had, she reached for the letter. Lauretta had
written one word across it in her bold hand:

SARAH

She ripped the folded sheet from the envelope and read
rapidly, only certain passages really hitting her mind
clearly: . . . *know you will be surprised, but Bonard has
long nurtured a strong regard for me . . . exactly where
we have not yet decided but Bonard says first to New Orleans to have a taste of adventure and fancy living which
have been denied us both for so long* . . . Sarah's eyes
raced on to the end. . . . *but if you think me totally heartless at leaving my only child, then I tell you, and nothing
else could bring me to reveal this, the child is Leon's, and
so yours in a way. Take her as your daughter, for she
cannot be mine, and perhaps she will make up to you the
absence of children of your own* . . . *Ever with love,
Lauretta.*

Sarah could not stand it. At first, finishing the letter,
she told herself she must keep in control. She must remain
calm, for there would be trouble enough, soon enough,
anyhow. Rooster would be over to see if they knew. Even
as she told herself to be quiet, her ears were shocked and
savaged by a sound of screaming she only gradually realized was her own. It brought Leon on the run. He had
just been told of Floyd's leaving and felt on hearing this
strange cry from his wife upstairs that the world must
truly have gone mad this morning. He found Sarah in a
faint on the floor: by the time he had lifted her onto
Lauretta's bed, others were there.

She came to herself very soon. Penelope and Nell
ceased being mild old ladies and took over firmly, getting

Sarah back into her own room and bed half an hour later, comfortably undressed and pillowed. She would not talk other than to say yes or no to questions they put about her physical condition and comfort, and they carefully refrained from pressing her. The room was darkened a little, and Penelope settled down in a chair to sit with her, Nell deciding to leave because, as she said to Penelope, "If I stay, we'll talk."

Leon had gone back into Lauretta's room after moving Sarah to her proper bed and there had found the letter on the floor where Sarah had lain when he first entered. He snatched it up and read. Coming out into the hall from the invalid's room, Nell saw Leon through the open doorway and said, "Where is Lauretta?"

He looked up from his reading. He looked at her without seeming to see her at all. "My God," he said.

Twenty-Three

Sarah slept until noon, and woke only when Leon entered the room followed by Sharon, who carried a tray. She felt as though she had slept a long time, and that it was another day, but that feeling was merely an extension of hope. Young though she was, Sarah had known other troubles and unhappiness, and her wish had always been a simple one: for time to pass—not that she might forget, for there was no chance of that, but because she knew time had a way of blunting sharp points and changing the light on a subject; and the intervention of other events, in particular minor ones, between It and Now gave her perspective. Or perhaps it was only another way of repeating the immemorial "time heals."

She saw him speak to Penelope, who promptly got up from her chair and went to the door, followed out by Sharon. When they had gone, Leon brought the tray to the table beside her bed and set it down. He had looked her way, of course, but he had not looked at her, and he did not until he drew up a chair and sat down in it close to her.

"I've brought you something to eat," he said then. She shook her head. "Maybe later. Did you sleep?" She nodded. He reached into his pocket and brought out the letter. She looked at it in his hands. He looked at her face.

"It's true, and I have nothing to say to you about it. Shall I destroy this?" She nodded once.

He went to the fireplace and struck fire with the Tinder Horn, igniting a corner of the opened letter and holding it until it began to burn his fingers before dropping it into the grate.

When he had returned and sat down again, he said, "It is not, of course, as simple as that. Beulah Land and Oaks have between them made another scandal. There is no hiding it, two people like that—they've left a trail a mile wide. Bonard was quite open, it seems, in tidying up his business affairs and making cash and banking note conversions. I got this both from Uncle Felix and from Rooster, with whom I have talked this morning. Although neither knew what he was up to, they knew he was up to something, but when they came near to asking a question, he always stopped them by saying they would find out soon enough." He was silent a minute or two, although his face worked with his thoughts. "As for Lauretta, I can only tell you that I never loved her, any more than—" He shrugged and looked down at his hands, the palms of which he was wiping against his trouser legs.

"Any more than Roman's mother," she said.

He blushed, slowly and deeply.

"I'm sorry if that was cruel," she said, and there was another silence between them. Then she said, "No, I am not sorry for saying it. I am not a Christian saint to take the arrows meekly. I hate and resent what has happened! I despise Lauretta! If she were here, I would try to scratch and tear her to ribbons!—and feel no shame or regret if I succeeded!" She subsided weakly, dropping her head against the pillows again, closing her eyes. Without opening them, she said with self-mockery, "I talk so fierce—and, oh, I shall act so mild."

"Sarah!" he said with anguished concern, taking her hands, closing his over them and pulling them toward his breast. "I love only you! I have loved only you!" His head was bent over his hands and hers, and she felt his moist breath on her fingers.

"I cannot say the same," she said. When he looked up at her, she returned his look steadily, but the words she spoke were a mutation of the truth in her heart. "I must love Roman and Rachel. They are my children too. We shall christen her Rachel Kendrick, and make no bones about it. Let anyone who dares, question me."

He looked toward the tray on the table and lifted a covering napkin. "There's a turkey broth—very good for you, Myrtis says—and some cold ham and bread and butter. Won't you eat something?"

She smiled for the first time. "Yes, if it will make you feel better."

Eagerly he spread a fresh napkin and picked up the bowl of broth and spoon. It would have been easier for her to feed herself, but she saw how much he wanted to do it, and so she allowed herself to be fed. But when they had got through the broth, dripping as much as was safely conveyed from bowl to lips, she declared that she felt stronger and would sit up for the ham and bread. She did so, and he packed extra pillows behind her and set the plates about her on the bed so that she might reach them easily.

She found that she was hungry. Between bites she thought, and now and then exclaimed a fragment of what went through her mind. "Poor Aunt Pea . . . Uncle Felix will miss Bonard, they were almost like father and son . . . Is Lauretta merely vain and reckless, or downright wicked? Romantics always feel romantic about themselves, never about other people. That's the point about romantics . . . Poor Bonard! . . . And dear old Edna, how she must feel! . . . Has anyone told Selma? I don't suppose it will matter to her, will it? . . . Oh, I'd all but forgot! It had gone right out of my head. Floyd! . . . Lovey, Ezra, they have a real grief! . . ."

She finished the last piece of ham and ate the last bit of bread and butter. Leon gathered the dishes and put them back on the tray.

"If I go down for coffee, will you drink some with me?"

"You haven't had your dinner," she said.

He smiled and went out the door. Soon he returned with coffee and cups and saucers, and served them. He found her out of bed, having opened the curtains and put on a robe over her bed dress.

They sat down with their coffee by the window. When they had drunk the first cup in silence and Leon had poured fresh, she observed, "I've felt sorrow and rage, I've pitied everyone except you. Yet you have lost two friends. You'll miss them both, Leon."

His face went very still, almost stiff, as if she had trespassed on an area that was not hers to make a concern.

He finished his coffee and was patient without seeming to
be, as she finished hers more slowly. Then he stood and
said, "I think I must go downstairs. They will begin to
wonder about us."

"Tell them I shall be down in a little while, and not to
come up for me."

He nodded. There was a pause during which either
might have reached kindly toward the other, but neither
did, and the moment was lost. Leon went out and left
Sarah alone again without anything's having been really
changed between them.

Twenty-Four

The freeze they needed came as it almost always did each
year, a few days after Thanksgiving. It held, and on Tuesday they butchered hogs at Beulah Land and at Oaks, and
on smaller farms nearby sharing the same weather. So, it
was well into the second week of December before Sarah
and Edna were given their mild day to drive into Highboro to the cemetery. Edna used her buggy for the trip.
She remembered, and told Sarah, that it was her turn. She
drove over and had dinner with Sarah before they set out,
and they had close to three hours of daylight to work together.

Edna was a helpful teacher and guide. First, she explained the layout of the cemetery, leading the younger
woman about as comfortably as if she were showing the
rooms and furnishings of a house. Sarah had been there
often before, but she had never noticed very much or
thought about it. As they walked, Edna talked, and the
cemetery became something like the family tree of the
town and county. Although most of the country people
buried their dead in country church yards, families like the
Davises and Kendricks were buried here, so that there was
a continuity that would have been otherwise lacking.

Edna did not know it all by any means, and some of
the details she offered were only guesses, and she said so,
but the longer Sarah listened and connected this name
with that, without trying to hold and remember it all, she
got a sense of lives lived and remembered—at least into
this generation. A hundred years from now, she thought,
others might stroll here and read, *Sarah, wife of Leon,*

born—. And the thought was not morbid. Nothing of the afternoon was. It was a day in which she learned to think of past and future equally as "family."

The two women raked and trimmed and smoothed, sometimes talking, sometimes not, and as she worked, Sarah began to understand and share the particular satisfaction she knew Edna found in the work.

The middle of the afternoon Edna looked up and saw with consternation Trudy and the four children approaching. The children ran ahead to her, delighted at her obvious surprise. Trudy followed, looking about her curiously. Sarah was working in the Kendrick plot, and did not come over, although she looked up and smiled and waved.

"We surprised you, didn't we, Grandma?" Annabel said.

"You certainly did." Edna turned her face and voice from the child to Trudy. "What are you all doing here?"

Trudy laughed. "I must say that isn't much of a welcome—"

"Nor meant to be," Edna said. "You children!" she called to the young ones who had darted away. "Behave yourselves!—and don't you run across anybody's grave, or I'll skin you!" She addressed herself to Trudy again. "You didn't say you planned on coming to town today."

"I didn't plan to, but it turned out so mild, just like you said it would. I decided it was the best time to bring the children in to look at all the Christmas things in the stores. They want everything they see."

"Of course they do." Edna snorted and waved a hand dismissingly. "Just get 'em a box of raisins and a sack of niggertoes." She had gone back to work; she was scraping earth mold from the edge of Benjamin's tomb.

"Well," Trudy said, "you really did come to work, I can see."

"Mm," was all Edna gave her.

"Adam!" Trudy called loudly. "We're going now! You hasten and make the others come along to the gate!"

Instead, Adam and Annabel and Doreen and James came bounding back to say goodbye to Edna. "You coming with us, Grandma?" Doreen asked.

"No, I'm coming later by myself after I drive Miss Sarah home. Call goodbye to her as you go."

"Is that Grandpa?" Doreen asked, looking at the gravestone where Edna knelt.

"Of course it is," Adam said. "I told you."

"You going to be right next to him?" Doreen persisted.

"Yes, I am," Edna said. "Now go on."

They called goodbye to Sarah, not once but several times, together and separately, and Sarah lifted her head to smile and a hand to wave.

"Well," Trudy said, and followed the children away.

An hour later when they had gone back and forth comparing their work and admiring what each other had done, they talked of what they would do next time they came, "around midspring," Edna suggested. Then they cleaned their tools and took them back to the buggy. The tools stored, the two women climbed tiredly into the buggy, and Edna found and opened a jar.

"Time for a little blackberry wine," Edna said, and offered the jar to Sarah, who took it. "Got no glasses; we can drink from different sides."

"Edna, you think of everything." There would be no more "miss" between them in direct conversation. Sarah drank. "That is so good!"

Edna smiled and took the jar back and drank carefully from her side of the rim. "Rooster has a nice hand at making wine and brandy, especially as one who doesn't care much for them himself. His daddy taught him."

Later, when they turned from the main road into the drive that would take them to the front door of Beulah Land, Edna said, "I wouldn't take anything for Trudy's having married Rooster, but she's—well, not got a lively mind. Doesn't think beyond house and children, poultry and preserves."

They had not spoken all afternoon of Bonard and Lauretta, Sarah realized, after she had got down from the buggy, and Edna had driven away home. But thinking this, albeit thankfully, she remembered Rachel and hurried into the house.

PART FOUR

1837

One

The Anderson farmhouse had once been a pleasant enough place when the whole family—Clarence, his mother and father, his older brother Walt, and his sisters Bessie and Emily—lived there; not overcommodious perhaps, and claiming no distinction of architecture or furnishings at all, but comfortable, more than adequate. Now the parents were dead, and so too was Walt; the sisters, who despised country living, had prudently married town men and taken themselves to live in Highboro.

Clarence, the sporty, jokey Anderson son, known to all as one ever ready to make a bet, share a jar of liquor, to play a game of cards, or chase a woman—although the latter pursuit had gained him naught but the occasional whore, who did not run very fast anyway—this Clarence, who had been surrounded by family, then in a space of eighteen months freed of its bonds by death and marriage, decided one morning early to kill himself, and did so. He was not sober when he did it, but he was rational. He had been alone and awake all the night, and before daylight, which he had vowed to himself not to see again, he loaded a pistol, turned it on himself, and blew his head all but off his neck.

The year 1837 was one of disquietude for the country. Money was short. Loans were called in. The Federal government had over-extended itself, particularly in the West. The wheat crop of 1836 was a failure, and the price of cotton had dropped to half of what it had been.

Clarence Anderson was not ruined by the Panic of 1837; he was destroyed first by his own fecklessness and finally by his own hand. Money short? He had only to mumble for friendly pocket and purse to open. It had seemed so simple, until he saw that he embarrassed old friends, which sent him to such men as Roscoe Elk, who could not embarrass him because he was so much above him. But came a time when Roscoe turned arrogant and

hard to deal with, and notes were signed for past and current loans, long, detailed notes which he did not read
then, drawn up and executed by a lawyer named Guthrie
in Kitesville, a close-by largish town, so that there would
be no gossip in Highboro to agitate his sisters.

Now, in the early spring of 1837, there was no money
and no way to plant a crop, for which there would be no
profit anyhow, because of low prices and what was already owed. The once-sporty, once-gay young man had
nothing, and no one to turn to, and so he did what he
could do, took the one action left to him. The gun, the
cold predawn, the despair that was complete, not at all romantic or comical now as it once had seemed to him—
combined to make an explosion and mark an ending.

On the mantelpiece were two letters he had written and
sealed with wax streaked with soot. The various notes he
had signed were in a jumble, but all together at least, in a
wooden casket on the table that held the lamp, and the
bottle. He had once been carefree, even careless with
the contents of a bottle, but he had learned frugality at the
end. He deliberately finished the bottle of corn whiskey
before he clenched the pistol to his forehead above and
between his eyes.

The sound woke the half-dozen slaves in the two mean
cabins near the house, but they did not leave their beds.
They guessed the truth, but were afraid to confirm it, and
so decided to let it wait till morning. In a curious kind of
relief, they slept again. Whatever the future, it would not
be the same as the past. The shame of a slave was compounded when he knew himself the chattel of a poor man.
If he feared the rich, he despised the poor.

The fire Clarence had set to blaze the evening before,
and sat in front of during his last hours, was now dead.
The room grew cold as he grew cold. A sudden gust of
wind skirled through the cracks around a window frame,
stirred, lifted, and carried a fine gray and white ash from
the hearth into the room and around the feet of the dead
man. The clock ticked. It would not stop until twelve minutes after seven the following evening, at which time
Bessie noticed it and told Emily, who wound and started
it again, the last thing they did before leaving again for
town.

On cold nights the Anderson children—Walt and
Clarence, Bessie and Emily—had used to get into woolen
night gowns that reached to the floor and run to the fire

to warm themselves before bed. Standing before the hearth they would chatter and giggle and tease as their mother smeared tallow over their raw, chapped knuckles and knees; and then they would flee to cold dark rooms, promising to say their prayers in bed. More often than not, they had done so.

> "Now I lay me down to sleep.
> I pray Thee, Lord, my soul to keep.
> If I should die before I wake,
> I pray Thee, Lord, my soul to take.
> Amen."

Two

Leon had the news from the letter with his name written across its envelope just after he finished his breakfast. He and Sarah had eaten together and been cheerful and amiable. Juanita had brought Rachel down before they finished, and taking the nurse-privilege, had drawn out a chair and sat down with the baby, whose special trick at that time was "rubber-knees, marble-knees." She would stare at her audience—anyone would do—with leering intensity, bouncing the while on bent, rubbery knees as if she intended to go on forever. Then quite suddenly the knees would stiffen; a frown would come to her face and freeze. Her body rigid, she would stand like a slab of marble before tilting and falling into arms she knew would be there to catch her. Then she would collapse into a delirium of vain and joyous laughter, celebrating her own cleverness. She knew herself to be irresistible, and so everyone thought that she was.

This morning Leon left his chair to catch her, although it was more often Sarah. Both loved her dearly, and while they could not think of her as "our" child, each thought of her as "my" child.

"Crazy pussy!" Leon exclaimed, holding the happy child over his head and looking up at her, as Sarah and Juanita sat by beaming.

It was into this family scene that Lovey walked with the letter. The laughter stopped, except for that of the child. Juanita stood quickly, without thinking what she was doing, and assumed a slightly servile pose. Lovey had been more severe than ever since Floyd's departure had brought on Ezra's decline. The old man was in fact old at last, although he had appeared for most of his life to be so to the others because of his dignity and special occupations.

Lovey said, "Man they call Turnip from over at the Anderson Place brought this. He say—Juanita, take the child away."

Leon handed the still-gurgling baby to Juanita, who went out with her hastily. Sarah and Leon, both standing waited for Lovey's explanation. "Clarence Anderson has put a gun to his head and killed hisself. He left this letter for you." She handed it to Leon and left them.

Sarah sat down and waited as Leon opened the letter and read rapidly. He finished it and went back to the beginning and read again more carefully, although he had understood it the first time. "The poor bastard," he whispered. Nodding to himself he said, "Well, this is a day. This is a day, to be sure." He went to her and gave her the letter. "If he has indeed killed himself, we will share boundaries with a new owner of the Anderson Farm."

In the midst of her reading she exclaimed, "Roscoe Elk! How can it be? Surely it cannot be so."

Leon nodded. "Clarence borrowed from me, he borrowed from everyone who would lend to him. But when it's all sorted, it won't surprise me to find that it's Roscoe who holds the signed notes—I certainly don't, and I doubt that his other friends do—and that it's Roscoe who has the strongest claim on whatever there is to claim."

"What of Bessie and Emily? Surely they—?"

"There's no 'surely' nor even 'maybe.' The farm and the hands were Clarence's. They had no part of it. Clarence's letter begs me to settle his affairs the best I can. I'll go over there right away to see who's in charge and what I can do. Then I'll go to town and do whatever's next. Before the day's out I want Uncle Felix and me to ride to Kitesville to see this lawyer Guthrie, Clarence says see in his letter."

"Let me go with you. To offer help to Bessie and Emily?"

"Let me offer for you and send word. You stay here. I'd like to know you are here. They both have husbands, you know."

"Yes. Very well."

Leon went upstairs to choose a coat of sober appearance. Sarah went to the window and looked out. Selma was just crossing the yard, accompanied by Pauline. They might be going anywhere—simply to walk about the yards, or to the fruit orchard or fields or woods, wherever their fancies led them.

Selma wore black, which she had done ever since Bonard and Lauretta went away together nearly a year and a half ago. Told what had occurred, she had said calmly, "Then I am a widow. I shall wear weeds." And so she had done. Making one of her rare trips into town she had ordered black in all weights and styles of cloth to suit her and to accommodate the seasons. Laura-Lou made the black dresses, and Selma wore them every day. At first people—the few who saw her spread the word—were merely astonished. Then they laughed and whispered. Then they settled into a nervous acceptance of this newest mark of Selma's eccentricity.

—She was crazy, of course. Look at the way she left her husband on the very wedding night. Look at how she had hidden ever since with nobody knowing what went on between her and that uppity darky Pauline. If Selma was a man, they'd know beyond question what to think, and raise a row, their business or not. But she was a female, and she was a Kendrick, so whatever she did was allowed her.—

Sarah watched them now, Selma and Pauline, marching along side by side, keeping in military step, their eyes straight ahead and they seeming oblivious to other activity around them. There was Sallou scattering crumbled biscuits from a pie pan to the pea and guinea fowls, that alone of the fowl had free run of the yards.

And there was Roman walking between Otis and Lotus, holding a hand of each. His room being back of the kitchen and pantries, he saw Myrtis's twins often, even when they were not in school. Their father had died the winter before. Though still a young man, he had cut his foot on rusty iron, and although Myrtis had tied it up with a kerosene-drenched rag holding a copper penny, he had got the blood poisoning anyway and died of it. Feeling sorry for the twins, and fond of them too, Roman gave them more of his time, a surrogate father.

Roman, during the last year, had suddenly, mysteriously grown quite handsome. Sarah had always said he was, but she was the only one who saw it before now. He was still hunchbacked, he still limped—of course. But the features of his face were becoming his own and clearly defined, with no pudginess or vague line or awkward angle. The tone of his voice had lowered and deepened without losing its musicality. His hands, the fingers still knuckly with adolescence but long and finely formed, were as eloquent in expression as his face, whether in motion or repose.

Sarah watched him as he lifted Lotus to sit on the bare old table that lived outdoors in all seasons and was used to support the washtubs on the one or two days of every week washing was done. Otis clambered up by himself to sit beside her. Sarah smiled as she saw Roman's head go back in laughter at something Lotus must have said, for she had drawn her head down on her short neck and was obviously laughing too. Even as she saw in the clear molding of nose and lips and chin proof that he was Leon's son, Sarah loved him. And she saw someone else who did not.

Roscoe Elk came up from the barns walking in a hurry. But he stopped when he saw Roman and the children; after staring at them briefly, he came on toward the house.

Sarah left the window and went into the hall and breezeway a moment after she heard Leon pass along them. She had got to the breezeway and paused to look out as Leon emerged from the back door and found Roscoe waiting for him.

"I just heard about Mister Clarence Anderson," he said in a sober voice.

"I too," Leon said. "I'm going over there and to town."

"Mister—Kendrick," Roscoe said, his uncharacteristic hesitation arresting Leon. "Would you think it a good thing for me to go too? With you. I have—I am as shocked and surprised as you can be—still, I have—interests over there."

Leon stared at him. "Yes, come along. It may save time." They walked away from the house together toward the barns. "Why would you lend him money?" Leon asked with an abruptness that sounded like anger.

The Overseer's answer came without pause or special inflection. "Why, because he needed it and asked me. I never thought it would go beyond my lending and his paying me back in time."

"But he signed notes to you, or so his letter to me says."

"That is true." Roscoe shrugged, not obsequiously, but as if explanation were unneccessary. "The question of promissory notes may be ignored between those who are equal. But Mr. Anderson did not, of course, consider me his equal."

Sarah went back along the hall. Sharon was in the dining room clearing the table. She picked up the oval bowl that had held hot grits. The remaining grits were cold and had congealed. Taking a spoon, Sharon turned the molded grits upside down in the bowl and said to herself but aloud, "Slice it, fry it, eat it in redeye, that's what Mama used to do." She saw her mistress and ducked her head. "I was just talking to myself, ma'am. For company."

"I do that too." Sarah patted her hand and then pressed a finger to a platter to catch a shred of fried ham that had stuck there. Putting it to her tongue, she found it salty and bitter.

Three

The other letter Clarence had written and left on the mantelpiece was to his sisters, Bessie and Emily, telling them he was a failure, which they knew in spite of his recourse to a lawyer in Kitesville, and wishing them a happy future life in sentimental and lugubrious language that changed style at the end to advise them in plain words that Leon Kendrick (and not either of their husbands, they were resentful and thankful to discover) would bring his earthly affairs to the best conclusion possible.

Leon found Bessie and Emily when he arrived at the Anderson Farm and went into the house. The body had been removed from the living room to a bed in the parent's old room, and a sheet spread over it. As Leon talked to them quietly in the living room, Emily's husband, Amos Mooney, arrived from town, sensibly bringing with him both the sheriff and the man who generally prepared the dead for burial.

An hour later Leon was ready to leave, having said and done as much as he could there. He found Roscoe, who had spent the waiting time looking over the barns and talking to the only male slave who seemed sensible and intelligent. Together they rode into Highboro.

As the day wore on, Leon adduced that the main reason Roscoe had wanted to accompany him was not fear for the validity of his claims on the estate of Clarence An-

derson, but the craftiness to gain for those claims respectability and acceptance, with a hint that Leon endorsed
the involvement of his overseer in Clarence Anderson's affairs, that he was even perhaps using Roscoe Elk as proxy
to secure the Anderson Farm as a part of Beulah Land!

The Kitesville lawyer, Mr. Guthrie, turned out to be
perfectly honest. Later, Leon was to acknowledge to himself that Roscoe would, of course, have sought the most
reliable and unchallengeable legal services he could find.
Mr. Guthrie and Felix Kendrick talked lawyer points to
each other while Leon and Roscoe stood solemnly by pretending they understood the exact meaning of what was
said.

The upshot was that Roscoe would have it all—land,
house, slaves. Whatever the claims of anyone else, be they
written or spoken, Roscoe's notes were specific and denied
all other claims and agreements that might come later or
that might be put forth as having come before. Mr.
Guthrie suggested with some sternness that Roscoe allow
the sisters Bessie and Emily—and without their knowing
he "allowed" them—to take whatever they wanted from
the house. The law was the law, but public feeling had to
be considered too. Roscoe agreed instantly, and Mr.
Guthrie said he would, with the two Mr. Kendricks, un-
dertake to explain the general situation and disposition of
the property to the surviving sisters.

Riding home finally, late that night, Leon could think of
no dignified way to ask Roscoe the largest question in his
mind. Would Roscoe now leave Beulah Land?

There is, generally speaking, a quick if not easy acceptance of the worst and a sensible dealing with its exigen-
cies, and so it proved in the present unhappy instance. It
would seem that tragedy seldom destroys people, that, in
fact, as is so often said, it "brings out the best" in them
and that more often than tragedy it is the boredom of
humdrum everyday that has power to drive men mad.

However that may be, Clarence was bathed and dressed
and put into a coffin that was then closed and not opened
again. Turnip, the head man of the slaves, who had taken
charge the morning of his master's suicide, maintained order on the farm by keeping everybody at work.

The funeral took place without causing any real stir. It
was the time of late-winter, early-spring plowing, and
none of the county people came merely in search of diversion. Some of the townspeople attended, but not very

many. Embarrassment prevailed for once over curiosity. The church was less than half filled, and the brief ceremony in the cemetery could boast only a single row of mourners. The sisters and their husbands were there, but none of the husbands' families. Leon and Sarah stood together, and next to them were Edna Davis and Rooster. The children had come with them, but Edna had sent them to wait in the buckboard after the church service. She did not consider it good for them to stand in the cold cemetery before an open grave while final prayers were said. It was too soon after their mother's death. Trudy had died last November in the winter's first epidemic of influenza.

When the final pieties had been droned out, they turned from the grave and walked away. Edna put her arm through Sarah's, and Rooster fell into step and conversation with Leon. Edna looked younger and ruddier than she had in years, the result of her being needed and important again. She steered Sarah to the Davis plot and paused.

Looking down she sighed. "Her grave still looks so new, even with the nice stone. Well, time will make it more natural, like my Benjamin's." As they then turned and walked back to the main path, they saw Leon and Rooster waiting at the gate, talking earnestly together— "about the new crop." Edna guessed, and chuckled.

The important question that had so concerned Leon on the day of Clarence's suicide was not asked. As day followed day, Leon decided that it would be as well not to show his concern, to let Roscoe come to it when he had to. And just so, it happened. Roscoe sought an interview. The occasions of Roscoe's "seeking an interview" had been rare, the most memorable being those on which he announced his intention of marrying Clovis and of buying her.

Sarah was with Leon in the office to receive him. After bowing his head briefly and formally to each of them, he began to speak.

"I have been Overseer at Beulah Land for a large number of years, and I believe I have given satisfaction." Both Leon and Sarah blinked assent, as the smallest gesture they could make consistent with good manners and the truth. "I have just come into possession of a property— done legally and with no objections having been raised— as there could not have been, legally and logically." He paused again but had to do without even the smallest gesture of comment from the Kendrick husband and wife, as he privately thought of them. "I have been long familiar with the problems as well as the best possibilities of the land and hands and livestock that constitute Beulah Land. Have I not?" Leon and Sarah nodded their heads once, in such near unison they might have been Otis and Lotus in the schoolroom. "The new property I have been but recently possessed of is, as you know, that which has been known as the Anderson Farm, or the Anderson Place. As you know also, its borders are, in part, Beulah Land's. Therefore, I say it will be logical and practical for me to continue to be the Overseer here, and manage my own adjoining property too, with no sacrifice of attention to my previous duties and obligations."

Sarah and Leon looked at each other, Sarah without changing expression, Leon smiling his relief. Watching, Roscoe noted the difference in their reactions and understood perfectly well what lay back of them. After allowing a pause to endure for a suitable dignified time and a little beyond, he said, "If you have confidence in my capabilities, I shall continue here in my present situation. But— with your agreement—I shall live, my wife and children and myself, at the new Elk Place."

Leon and Sarah looked briefly startled on hearing his name for the old Anderson Place, but after a questioning glance at Sarah, Leon said, "Where you live is as you please. The house you have here is yours for as long as you like."

"I no longer require it," Roscoe said with satisfaction; and because he had observed Leon's growing relief during the course of the interview, he allowed himself the pleasure of adding, "Mrs. Elk and myself and our children will be more comfortably positioned in the new house over there."

Leon nodded, impatient to end the interview now that he was assured of Roscoe's staying. "Very well."

"We are then in agreement and accord?" Roscoe said.

"Certainly," Leon said.

"Then I thank you and bid you good day." Roscoe repeated his earlier head nods. "Mrs. Kendrick. Mr. Kendrick." They nodded back at him, and he found the door and went out.

As soon as he had gone, Sarah said, "If Floyd had not left us!"

"What?" She had surprised him.

"Floyd could be Overseer, and we could tell Roscoe Elk to go and be damned."

"Floyd?"

"Yes, certainly, Floyd. He knew every bit as much as Roscoe."

"He couldn't have managed the people."

"He wouldn't have driven and beaten them, but he would have managed them. Oh, I know we told Roscoe not to punish them without permission from either you or me, but he goes his own way, you may be sure, and the people are either in debt to him, or too awed and frightened of him to complain. If only Floyd *were* here!"

"Well, he isn't," Leon said, nursing still some of his own old hurt over Floyd's having left Beulah Land.

"No, he isn't. And you have made it all too clear to Roscoe how much we need him."

"I'm sorry my behavior—my expression of attitude, if you will, fails to meet your requirements and expectations."

She laughed shortly. "Don't talk like a play, Leon. You sound like Roscoe with the hifalutin balances and repetitions he fancies are so elegant. Nevertheless, he knows he has the upper hand of us."

"Upper hand! He owns a few miserable acres and a clutch of ignorant slaves who are probably not worth their keep. Be reasonable."

"You will see," she said maddeningly, and went out to find Juanita and Rachel, or Roman, or even sour Lovey— any real friend who might cheer her up after the interview she had found degrading.

It was nearly three weeks later that the move took place. Emily and Bessie had the day after the funeral taken the few items from the house they wanted. Being townswomen now, they laughed at country things, calling them tacky and old-fashioned. Roscoe's own wagon, drawn by Roscoe's own mule, came over to carry back to the new Elk Place the clothes and other personal belongings of the Elk family. Soon after it, Turnip drove a horse and carriage over to transport in style to their new home Clovis and her sons, Roscoe and Alonzo, who were now fourteen and eleven.

Clovis was dressed in one of her own-sewed best dresses, a deep purple woolen. The boys were clean and shiny black, wearing white shirts and good gray trousers and coats.

"Y'all ready?" Turnip asked after he had helped Clovis—which he had been instructed to do—into the carriage, and the boys had climbed up after her.

Clovis nodded regally; Turnip climbed back into his seat, clucked to the horse, and they moved off at a walk. Peeping from windows and doors and from behind tree trunks and outhouses, their old acquaintances watched them, and all was well and quiet until Sallou, standing at one of the kitchen windows, lost control of her senses and began to laugh hysterically. The sound set others off, who had observed before in mere tense curiosity. As the carriage went past them and around the house to the front drive—Turnip had also been instructed that he was not to take the back road—it was more than Clovis could bear. Her face burned, her mind and heart raged within her, and without willing it, she stood in the carriage and twisted her body to look back at the laughing Negroes who had come out from their hiding places. Shaking both fists in the air, she screamed. "Ignorant slaves!—*I* got slaves of my own now!—See me? See!"

In a panic that told him to move, Turnip whipped the horse into a trot, and the carriage was soon out of sight of those in the yards. Roman sat in a crotch of limbs in an apple tree in the orchard and watched them pass. As the dust rose from the drive and drifted in waves over him, he said to himself, "Now, I am free." But there were tears in his eyes. He knew she hated him. But she was his mother, and he would never forgive her.

Four

In April, Roman was sixteen, half the age of his father Leon, and only a little beyond the age Leon had been when he fathered Roman. Yet the two of them, in the sixteen years both had been on earth together, had exchanged no more than a hundred words, all of them impersonal. Leon had always avoided the boy, and often did not speak when they met by chance. He disapproved of and ignored as much as he could Sarah's friendship with him. He admitted his paternity, but only as a physical fact, and privately. Roman was more a stranger to him than was any other human soul on the plantation. To Roman, Leon was a total mystery, and one that fascinated him.

He could not conceive of Leon's ever having desired his mother Clovis. His mental discord at imagining their bodies linked together even in blind lust was such that he could not think straight. That was because he could not imagine his father and his mother ever having been the age he now was, and feeling the things he now felt.

His mind was lively, and he enjoyed and employed its energy, but he was not ambitious. He had been supplied with books, and further books that those first books suggested; but he had never known a real teacher. Sarah had been friend, mother, sponsor, advocate, protector, playmate. She had pointed and encouraged, but she had not really been his teacher except at the very beginning. And at least one inspired, mad, total teacher is necessary to change a life, to charge a good mind with ambition and appetite for the world beyond.

Much is observed of the violent changes in the body of an adolescent boy, but the chaos of mind and heart is at least as extreme.

Knowing that he was the first boy who had ever felt this way, Roman experienced the things every boy does—celestial elation and suicidal depression, lust a thousand times more throbbing than the wildest beating of a heart, and asceticism cold enough to chill a Siberian saint.

His hands groped the flesh of his body everywhere they could reach, not only his genitals, but there too. He gripped his biceps, his calves, the rounds of his behind. He kissed his shoulders, smelled under his arms, licked the insides of his wrists and elbows, admired the curving of thigh and chest, fearfully explored with his fingers the hunched back, and finally decided that he was not altogether repulsive. Although he did not think of her—how could he, when touching his own body?—Sarah's having told him that he was handsome made it possible for him to accept his body the way it was.

And when hands did not grope and explore, he lay on the bed of his room back of the kitchen and pantries, blessedly isolated from the whole world; and he lay there like a holy man, as unaware of his body as if he had been true disembodied spirit.

But he burned; more often than not he burned. His special kind of childhood had not deprived him of the knowledge of sex that is the common lot, and so he made the usual bridge between his sexual feelings and the idea of the female body. Actually, there did not seem to Roman to be any connection. But the notion of a breast brings to mind a curve, and a curve is sensual; and a woman's face, more often than not, wears a soft look, and that is sensual too. Forcing his vague impulses and impressions into a kind of unity, Roman fixed his mind on Sallou.

Everything encouraged his hopeful fantasies. She was there, working nearby, and so, practically, it would be possible for him to find an occasion to have sex with her. She was friendly and flattered at his attention when he chose to give it, recognizing as she did his special position on the plantation. The deciding factor was that for her age she had big fat titties, which were the only truly female thing to have authentic flesh attraction for Roman.

And so, inevitably, he brooded and sweated and planned, and finally managed to get Sallou into his room one hot afternoon in early May during those hours when nobody stirred about the main house. She had come to him after Myrtis had gone home for her rest. She had offered to finish up the dishes by herself, an offer Sharon was not about to question.

In Roman's room, Sallou quickly took off her dress and stood naked before him, giggling, with her hands clenched together like a weapon before her crotch, as if ready to stun the balls of the horniest bull, if she were so minded. He took off his trousers but kept his shirt on, shy of her seeing his back. When he went to her and cautiously touched one of her breasts, his dick hardened and rose, and he felt proud and manly to be doing what he was doing. Making cups of his hands, he gently lifted both her breasts. Quiet now, she took his dick and balls into her hands. No one had ever touched them before, except during the infancy he did not remember, and he almost fainted with this newly discovered sensation. She skinned him back and then, since he made no move to take the next step, she began too roughly to masturbate him. When she felt him good and hard, she pushed herself against him, standing on tiptoe and stretching her legs open to push his dick into her. It had hardly touched her when he came. His ejaculation leaped like a fountain, and she stepped back from him as if threatened by vileness.

And she laughed. It had never happened with her like that before. In her innocence and wounded vanity, she laughed at him. Now his hands, spread open like a fan,

screened his genitals. She watched him a minute as he
stood there uncertainly, not knowing what to do. Presently
she said, "It's all over, I spect," and threw her dress over
her head, pulling it down matter-of-factly to fit her body.
She smiled. "You got to learn some more before I come
to you again, boy."

He looked so sick and unhappy she took pity on him.
"But that's all right. Everybody have to learn." She moved
to the door and stopped. "How come you keep your shirt
on?" she teased. "Fraid I see something?" She came back
to him. "Ought not to be shamed of that, you can't help it
anyway. My mama tole me it was a punishment for the
sin of your mama. It's good luck to touch it, they say."
Before he knew what she was about, she had run her
hand under his shirt at the back and grasped his hump.
"Oh, my God! That ought to luck me forever!" He
wrenched away from her and began to strike her wildly
across the face and head, and she ran bawling from the
room.

Five

Since going away with Bonard, Lauretta had written to
Sarah only once, from their first major stop, New Orleans.
She wrote to say what a good time they were having, and
that they were talking of moving westward when they
tired of the old city. As the months passed, Sarah was
pleased that she did not hear again from her sister. She
hoped that Lauretta was gone for good.

Being the younger sister, Sarah had, during their childhood, always been second, alternately Lauretta's scorned
and petted pawn. Had Lauretta loved her? Well, she had
used her. Sarah suspected that "love" for Lauretta was a
word to say rather than an emotion to know. Had she
loved Lauretta? She thought hard about it, and decided
that she had, at times, but not in an everlasting way.
Lauretta had always been selfish, but it can be gratifying
to indulge selfishness in those one cares about. Still, no
whole person can forever love another who is wholly selfish. Sarah admitted to herself that she had had good times
with Lauretta. She had admired her beauty and laughed at
her wit and spontaneity, even as Lauretta's wit made her

seem dull and her spontaneity made her feel plebeian and responsible.

That was what she could not forgive Lauretta: the making her feel responsible and dull and "good"—but not pretty, never pretty. Lauretta had, wittingly or not, made her appear to be those things to others too. Because of Lauretta she would never believe that she could be truly interesting to a man. As a child—she remembered with increasing anger—she had seldom considered what she liked or what she wanted. Once a year, on her birthday, Lauretta had graciously insisted, "No, you say, you choose. Today you are first." The other 364 days of the year Lauretta said and chose and was first.

Always she had deferred to Lauretta, as though it were the natural law of the universe that she do so; and that is exactly how Lauretta, without any self-consciousness, had accepted deference, Sarah's and everyone else's. Beautiful Lauretta. Witty, charming, unpredictable Lauretta! Sweet Sarah. Gentle Sarah. Good Sarah.

All of her past resentments, unadmitted at the time of origin, indeed unsuspected, now worked in Sarah's breast. No, she did not love Lauretta; she did not even like her. Likable and lovable she might be to men, but no woman would ever think of her without a frown or a curse. Pleased with this thought because it absolved her a little of her uncharitable resentment, Sarah smiled.

Then she heard Rachel laughing upstairs, and she flew through the hall and up the stairs and into the child's room. Juanita was holding her in her arms at the window, although Rachel could perfectly well stand and walk by now. Sarah did not snatch at her impulsively, but smiled at Juanita and held her arms out to the eager baby who continued to laugh as she leaned from Juanita toward Sarah to be taken.

Sarah took her, and rocked her in her arms, looking down at her face. "Whose baby are you?" she asked, and answered, "Mine!" At which the child and woman laughed their approval of each other. It was only half an hour later, when Rachel had demonstrated vigorously her standing, walking, and running abilities, and used her favorite words, but without making sentences, that Sarah gave her back into Juanita's keeping and returned to her duties. Rachel laughed and cooed and flirted as long as Sarah was in sight. Juanita held her hand as she peered through the stair railings at the woman she clearly considered her mother. In the downstairs hall, heading for the kitchen, Sara thought: *Poor Lauretta, what her foolishness has given me!*

Floyd had written more often than Lauretta. To Lovey and Ezra he sent long, detailed letters telling where he had been, where he then was, and where he thought of going next. When he left Beulah Land that Thanksgiving midnight a year and a half ago, he did go on to Savannah, just as he and Felix had talked of his doing, and he sold the mare with saddle when he got there. From Savannah he worked his passage as common seaman on an English merchant ship carrying lumber and bales of cotton to Liverpool. A January passage on the Atlantic is more likely to be bad than good, and Floyd's ship wallowed through a winter storm the whole way, from which he concluded that he hated the sea.

The food was poor. The men's quarters were mean and disgusting, the air there being fetid. Nothing ever dried, not his feet, nor his skin, nor a particle of his clothing for the entire voyage. The ship's master was not a tyrant nor a sadist; he was merely a dull man of business; and while he sought no devices to make his crew miserable, neither did he practice care and kindness on their behalf. He knew most of his crew would be new every voyage anyway. Any suggestion of casting bread upon the waters would have got from him an uncomprehending stare.

Floyd wrote to Ezra and Lovey from Liverpool, and the letter reached them only two months later. From Liverpool he made his way across the country into Norfolk, where he labored as a farm hand during the spring and early summer of 1836. Later that summer he worked his passage from Yarmouth to Holland. After Yarmouth, from which he had also written, they heard nothing for a while. Their next letter, four months later, was written in Marseilles, from which he said he was taking ship to Egypt and the Levant. For one who did not like the sea life, Floyd yet found it the easiest way to get about and to avoid the decision of settling down in one place.

The waits between letters, instead of making Ezra despair, kept him living. He had to know what happened next to his son. After the longest gap in news, there was finally a new letter that summer of 1837, from England. Yes, he had been to Egypt and the Levant. He had seen Jerusalem and Antioch and other ancient places he would tell them about when he returned. For the first time he wrote of coming home in a definite way. He sent seeds he had gathered on his voyages and wrote: *Papa, I want you to plant all of these seeds just how and where you feel is right. Nobody could give me clear directions considering the differences in climate and season and soil. But plant them, and when I come home in a few months' time, before this year is out, I want you to tell me all the things about these seeds I cannot tell you now. Promise me, and do it. Your loving son, Floyd.*

Ezra's pride had not allowed him to stay in bed in his weakness, but almost from Floyd's leaving he had spent most of his waking hours, and they were near twenty every day, in a rocking chair in his kitchen, or sitting on the back step in warm weather. He doctored no one, and if any came for advice, he had little to give, and that so desultory no one believed in the efficacy of it enough to follow it.

But on receipt of this letter with the seeds and the promise, he got up from his lame repose, put off dying, and became something of his old self again. He looked long at the different seeds, holding them in his hands, rubbing them gently between the tips of his fingers as if they would give up their secrets to him by touch. Perhaps they did. He planted all of them, and most of them came up and grew, and the tending of them, not knowing what any would turn out to be, gave the old man reason to live, beyond his real reason, which was, of course, the promise that Floyd would return.

That letter, which turned out to be the last, was not passed about, but it was read to others, or its news was told. Sarah saw the letter, because she went every day to visit Ezra. Roman had taken to accompanying her on the visits, for he had long admired the old man's knowledge. Then, too, Ezra was the father of a man he had known, although not well, who was colored and free, and who had traveled on his own to England and Holland and France. "And Egypt and Antioch," he repeated softly when Sarah again read this last letter aloud, to please Ezra, who never tired of reading it, or hearing it read.

And so that summer of 1837 Ezra planted the seeds and tended the plants that grew from them; he made careful observations; and he waited.

Six

Adam asked Edna, "What is this, Grandma?" At eight he was tall enough to see everything on the high mantelpiece of the living room, and confident enough to pick up the object of his current curiosity and hold it out toward her.

Edna looked at it, puzzled herself, until her eyes showed that she remembered. "I declare! I must have looked at that a dozen times a day since I put it there, twenty and more years ago. It's a flute left—given to us—by your papa and Uncle Bonard's teacher who lived with us, Tutor he was called. Mister Bartram. Jeremy Bartram. A very nice young man once he settled in. Your Uncle Leon used to ride over every day for lessons too. What a long time ago that is."

Adam took the instrument back and examined it. He then put it to his mouth and blew through it without making any intelligent sound. He practiced fingering the holes of the flute, blowing lightly, but achieving no improvement.

Violet fluttered into the room. "They coming! I seen the wagon in the distance and heard Sugar holler!"

Sugar of Beulah Land had courted Violet of Oaks successfully, and they had been married to each other in the dining room at Oaks. When offered the arrangement that had been made on such matters in the past between the two plantations, the choice of their living together at one or the other, they demurred. They were perfectly happy living as they were, they said. They saw each other quite enough as present occasions provided. Each delighted in meeting the other, and neither sorrowed at parting.

The occasion of the meeting today was a family picnic for the children of Oaks and Beulah Land. Sarah had said to Edna that it would be pleasant to spend a day not thinking about the serious working of the two plantations. Edna had promptly suggested that they—and Adam and James and Doreen and Annabel, and Rachel and her nurse Juanita—spend a day in a pine grove they all knew, between their plantations and town, a piece of land that belonged to neither family and was considered common ground because there was a small, old, now-abandoned burying ground on it.

Edna said to Violet, "Gather the children; I'll go see the baskets are ready."

There was no hurrying. It was summer, everything planted and coming to fruition in God's time, nothing yet harvested except for the table fruits and vegetables that were taken every day from garden and orchard, but had not yet appeared in such abundance as suggested preserving for winter use. All there was to do was tending, checking the grass and weeds and insects, watching the sky and hoping for the impossible; no rain on this field of cotton, a fair rain on that of corn to keep it juicy and sweet, and a lot of rain on the sugar cane, alternating with hours of hot sun, to best mature it.

Two mules drew the large wagon, the largest Beulah Land boasted. Sugar sat on the driver's seat with Sarah beside him. She wore a comfortable cotton frock open at the neck, and a crisp starched sun bonnet to shield her head and eyes from the heat and glare of the day. In the main body of the wagon were half a dozen cane-bottomed chairs, on one of which Juanita sat primly, hands folded in her lap, as she consciously enjoyed her outing. The other chairs were empty. Roman sat at the open back end, or tail gate, dangling his legs; and beside him Rachel sat dangling hers, although there wasn't much of them to dangle. Rachel had refused to leave Beulah Land without Roman.

Under the wagon for its shade, keeping to the exact pace of the mules, walking or trotting, was one of the hound dogs. Only Juanita recognized him and knew that he was called Bone. He had come along because he was bored and because no one had stopped him from joining the party. There was nothing for the hunting dogs to do at that season but beg a biscuit at the kitchen steps—although well fed, hound dogs are greedy—or to rush barking in mock attack at a hen or two, and this only when there were no people about to kick them for their mischief.

Because it was a family picnic, Sarah had told Sugar to take the wagon around to the back door of Oaks, and he did. By the time he called, "Whoa!" there was no need for it. The mules had stopped by the kitchen door of their own accord, and the dog Bone had smelled a bitch in heat and trotted off, following his nose. Edna and Adam and the other children were waiting there for them, having been fully alerted by Violet.

A little time was pleasantly wasted by the social calls of:

"Well, get down and come in for a while!"

"Are you ready? We have a good day for it, don't we?"

"Hot!"

"Oh, not so bad!"

"You're right, could be worse. Hotter later, though."

"Well—"

Sarah took off her sun bonnet and loosened her hair to cool her head.

"I've got a horn," Adam said.

Roman hopped down from the back of the wagon and lifted Rachel down beside him. "Let's see it."

Adam politely handed the flute to Roman. Although no one cared about the flute, they all crowded around because it made a focus for their initial getting together. Aside from Sugar, who had got down from his driver's seat and begun to talk teasingly to Violet, who was pretending to look coolly over his right shoulder into the horizon that had never interested her before, the others surrounded Roman: Sarah and Rachel and Juanita, Adam and James and Doreen and Annabel. Even Edna hesitated a moment in her checking of the contents of the food baskets. "Play it," she said to Roman.

After looking it over and fingering it, Roman put the flute to his lips and sounded several notes. He played the same notes again, more quickly and surely, the repetition giving authority to his improvised performance. Then he ventured new sounds, and when he was out of breath, he took the flute from his lips and looked around him. The others sighed, as if gratified by the music he had produced. Edna nodded her head decisively. "Roman," she said, "the flute is yours."

Roman looked quickly at Adam, but Adam's manners were too good for him to show that he wanted to keep possession of the instrument. He even managed to smile at Roman, as if adding his giving to the grandmother's: and Roman held the horn in his hands a little more firmly. "Thank you," he said, looking at Adam as he said it.

Hoisting her baskets into the back of the wagon, Edna enquired frankly of Sarah, "What's in yours?"

"Peach pickles, cucumber pickles, a gallon of tea, a gallon of lemonade, a gallon of water, two chocolate pies and two lemon pies and a coconut cake so sweet it makes my teeth ache to think of it!" They had talked it over beforehand, of course, and agreed on what each of them would provide. "What's in your old baskets?"

"Six fried chickens, two dozen light rolls, eighteen deviled eggs, and enough potato salad to choke a Baptist choir at a camp meeting."

The women laughed and hugged each other lightly. The children squealed and jumped with greed and anticipation. Presently everyone had climbed or been lifted into the old wagon, and they set off for the picnic grove.

They found it shady and cool and deserted. Everyone piled out of the wagon, leaving the food baskets. Sugar unhitched the mules and led them to a shady place of their own to stand dreaming and attracting flies until they were needed again. The children ran about, eager to explore the new place. None of them had come here before, although all had passed it on the way into town. It was a place Edna had brought Bonard and Rooster sometimes when they were boys. Finally the children settle into games, not too seriously, yet ready to amuse themselves and each other.

Rachel was enchanted by everything and everyone. It was the first real party she had been to. She toddled and ran about, frequently sitting abruptly and unintentionally on the slickly needled ground under the pine trees, and laughing when she did so. That was the day she also, when she wandered off by herself, discovered ants. When she cried out, Adam rushed to find her and slapped the insects off her bare feet.

Being the oldest of the children, Adam could afford to pay attention to the youngest without loss of station, and he was never far away from Rachel after that. Doreen and Annabel found her boring, since she was both female and younger than they were. After a while, rebelling at Adam's insistence that she be included in every game, they flounced away to the small burying ground and made up stories about who was buried there. James went off by himself to another part of the grove where he found interest in sitting quietly and observing Violet and Sugar, who thought, if they thought at all, that they were alone. Violet was half asleep, or pretending to be. Neither talked. A bee buzzed in the sweet, dusty air, and Sugar sat beside Violet with a hand under her dress and between her legs. James stared at them, wondering if they were sick, they looked so funny.

Adam had entirely assumed the role of courtly nurse-brother to Rachel, whose energies and invention doubled as she took the measure of his interest and patience. Roman watched the two children, feeling himself a very grown man, but acknowledging his affection for both of them. Rachel was everybody's darling, but she was particularly his. He watched them now unjealously. Although he had seen Adam occasionally for all the boy's life, he saw young-manly beauty in him today for the first time. Making up the story of their lives, he decided that they would grow up friends, fall in love, and marry! It was just what would happen, and one day long away in the future he would tell them he had thought of it on this day. He sounded notes on the flute, not trying to make a special tune, just putting music into the air.

"I declare," Edna said, "it's like he already knows how to play that thing. I'm glad he has it. He's a teacher, and it was our teacher, Mr. Bartram, who brought it here in the first place. Poor soul, I wonder whatever happened to him. I don't suppose you came across him in Savannah? He wanted to compose 'airs for Arcadia,' he said. But he never could put two notes together that sounded any better than a goose's honk. Now, Roman has a touch with it. Children! You stay away from those graves, you hear me, or else the people in them will come to haunt you tonight when you go to sleep in the dark! Anybody hungry?"

This question brought them on the run. Juanita was commissioned to pour lemonade for them to drink while Edna and Sarah set out the food. Bone, who had trotted about the grove sniffing uninterestedly, returned to the center of activity and sat patiently waiting his chance, knowing that it would come.

All of them, including Juanita and Violet and Sugar, ate and said they could eat no more, and then ate more. They were talking of lying down on the ragged old quilts that had been brought along as underlining for the tablecloths, when they heard a horse approaching. Presently, they saw that the man riding him was Roscoe Elk. They stared at him. He returned their look with less surprise.

"Good day!" he said. "You are having a children's outing. A nice time and place for it too. I am glad to see you enjoy yourselves on my new, small property."

"Is it yours?" Sarah asked.

"I don't remember it belonging to anybody," Edna said.

Roscoe shook his head, smiling. "I took it as a favor from someone who needed a little ready money. It is useless to me. I shall not think of disturbing the old graves. There is nothing to do about the grove anyhow, except to be gratified that such as you come here and find it a pleasant place to sit and enjoy yourselves. You are welcome. Perhaps my sons will like it too. I shall tell their mother to bring them one day."

He bowed from the saddle and turned the horse's head away with the bridle and left them.

The children played again, but Edna and Sarah watched Roscoe go, and continued to stare at nothing when he disappeared from view. The children were too tired for games, and their stomachs were too full for exercise, and so very soon they subsided on the quilt pallets and slept. Edna leaned her head against the trunk of a tree and slept too, leaving Sarah to muse on the growing affluence of Roscoe Elk.

When Edna woke, they called to the children to say they must soon be going. Juanita and Violet helped Edna and Sarah load the depleted baskets and dirty dishes and glasses into the wagon, while Sugar hitched up the mules. Finally, they all settled themselves in the wagon, some sitting on the rush chairs, others on the bare floor boards. Roman again sat at the tailgate, trying notes on the flute, now and again glancing back at Adam. He did not envy the boy or want anything of him; he wanted to *be* him.

Bone, deciding not to travel home on his own feet, pretended to love children; and so a place was made for him, and he was made much of, as the old wagon creaked along the hard clay road back to Oaks and Beulah Land.

Seven

That summer Roman was always in love, although the object of his love changed. His encounter with Sallou, prompted by flesh need, still had something of love in his anticipation. Sensitive males are no more intelligent than other kinds at judging the females who attract them, often seeing in the dullest of these, qualities that exist only in the lover's imagination. And so, before their private adventure, Roman had imagined Sallou lively and even witty, hearing her chat and joke in the kitchen with Myrtis and Sharon and the occasional extra helper. After their meeting he ignored her altogether, to punish her for his

mistake in judgment, as well as her crude impertinence at
touching his back and teasing about it.

For a few days after the picnic he thought of Adam
Davis with an intensity that was a kind of love. Reliving
that day in his mind, he altered detail. Now, it was Adam,
not Adam's grandmother, who had made him a present of
the flute. "Here, Roman, I want you to have this."—
"Thank you, Adam, I shall make music for you." He did
not fancy touching the boy in any carnal way, but he daydreamed situations that made contact between them necessary. Walking in the woods he found Adam sitting on a
log, having just sprained his ankle by jumping a stump
and landing off-balance. Adam was too brave to cry, but
his face wore a look of pain and fear until he looked up
and saw Roman approaching. Roman quickly assessed the
situation and in a minute had Adam laughing. His love
giving him strength, he picked the boy up and carried him
in his arms all the way home. He felt Adam's head
against his shoulder. After Adam had been put to bed,
and the doctor had come and gone, saying the boy must
not walk for a month, Adam had been restless and called
for Roman. Roman sat with him and read aloud for hours
every day; they became friends, and remained friends after Adam's recovery. A variation of the dream had Adam
forgetting Roman when he could walk again, but finding
nothing contenting in his activities and former friends until he suddenly remembered, reclaimed, and asked to be
forgiven by his best friend, Roman.

Such dreams comforted Roman's restless sensibilities
only briefly. He remembered that Adam was a child and
that none of the dream was true, nor likely to become so,
and his fancy moved on, lighting next on one of the slave
girls, who was called Roxy. She had been, or seemed to
be, an ordinary enough girl until her mother died a few
months ago. Her father, it was rumored, forced himself
on her and afterward beat her, and then ignored her entirely and let her run wild. She was said now to go into or
back of the barn with any stud who signaled to her. She
was careless of her clothes and never bathed, not even her
face and hands, and her hair went undressed, standing up
and around her head like overripe cotton popping out of
the boll. She was scorned and ignored by all the women
and girls.

It was then that Roman, knowing her history, real and
rumored, and seasoning it with romantic sentimentalities,

decided that he could love her. Where others jeered, he
would be kind. Seeing him notice her, Roxy would begin
to bathe herself again, and to mend and wash her clothes,
and wait for him to smile on her new, changed self. When
that daydream had taken him to the point of actually
speaking to her, she laughed at him and declared she
"wasn't going to fuck no humpback."

Roman kept to his room the rest of that day, feeling a
fool and ashamed of his foolish romancing. There were
others he loved briefly. If none were as absurd as his
dreams of Roxy and Adam, their appeal was not as potent
either, and they came and were forgotten in a day's du-
rance.

Many of the nicer, shier slave girls would have been
pleased at Roman's notice, but he never saw them. When
his fancy had exhausted the impossibilities, it seemed almost natural that he should find himself thinking of Leon.
No other had as powerful a claim on his imagination. He
knew beyond question that he was Leon's son, and he
knew that their relationship would never be acknowledged
more than it presently was. There was romance in the
very degradation of the kinship, encouraging boldness.

One day when Rachel followed him out of doors, he
took her hand and led her about the grounds as he often
did, showing her things and talking to her. He loved the
way she would let go his hand and march straight up to a
thing and stare at it—a rock, a bush, a flower pot, empty
and overturned, anything—and then come back and take
his hand again as casually as she had let it go. That day
he showed her figs growing on the gnarled tree near the
kitchen door, the same tree whose limbs had supported
the swaddled babies, Leon and Floyd, once upon a time.
He took her around the house and showed her a small
pomegranate tree, and picked a fruit. When he opened it,
revealing its multitude of tiny pink jewels, she was astonished, and wanted to eat them. But he would not let her,
afraid she would swallow the seeds, and so distracted her
by teaching her to feed the fleshly pellets of fruit to the
guineas that came pod-racking up to them.

They were laughing together when she suddenly spied
Leon coming around the house from the barns. She
dropped what remained of the fruit in her hands and ran
squealing toward the man Roman did not know was her
father as well as his. If he had known, what further romantic flights he would have flown!

Instead, he watched as his darling girl-baby ran across the grass. Seeing her, Leon dropped to his knees and opened his arms to catch her. They laughed and hugged and looked at each other. Leon stood, swinging her up into his arms and taking her off to the house, not even noticing—and Rachel forgetting—Roman standing there with half a pomegranate in his hands and the guineas around him noisily demanding that he give it to them.

It was right: the man and the child, both so beautiful and so intent on each other that all else was forgotten.

Before sleeping that night, Roman thought again of the incident, seeing Rachel less and less clearly in his mind, because she was the more familiar to him, and seeing Leon more clearly than he usually did, his face a little flushed with the heat of the day, sweat running down the sides of his cheeks from the line of his golden-reddish hair. Alone in his bed, Roman groaned, knowing it was Leon he loved. He could not claim him as father; yet would he find a way to love him.

Eight

Felix ailed. He had not been his truly well self since last autumn when he suffered a bout of chills and fever. He recovered—that is, the chills and fever diminished and finally ceased altogether, but he did not get his strength back fully before he was brought to bed with influenza during the same early-winter epidemic that took Trudy Davis to her grave.

He admitted, to himself at least, that he had rushed his convalescence from that bout of illness, so impatient had he been to enjoy the normal pleasures of Christmas. But early in the new year he had been worried by pains in his chest, so sharp and localized that he was certain the trouble was with his lungs—or no, his heart. He woke another morning feeling nothing but hungry and a little tired, well enough to decide there was clearly nothing at all the matter with him.

Yet when he began to eat and drink and smoke in what was for him a normal, moderate way, he did not digest his food so very well; and when he woke now and then in the night, he discovered an arm or a thigh to be "asleep," and even felt that something else was there, some hovering malignant spirit on watch to catch him at his weakest hour and point him toward oblivion.

His urine burned like brine first thing every morning, four days running, and then troubled him no more. One midafternoon he went suddenly deaf in one ear, and his eyes did not focus just as they should. Another day he felt brief nausea, followed by a pounding pain in his lower gut when he rose in court to make a standard plea.

In short, Felix was concerned about his body for the first time in his life. He had taken it for granted, but now, of a sudden, it seemed a miracle that one heartbeat followed another with measurable frequence, that he drew breath in and blew it out, that his bowels moved, that he sweated, felt heat and cold, knew hunger and satiety, sneezed, farted, had hiccups, and that his hair and nails grew in a perceptible enough way to need trimming now and then.

The days he felt all right he was aware of feeling all right, instead of merely accepting it as his natural state of being. Feeling well, he dared his body, forced it to drink and smoke a little more than was usual for him, fucked twice in one day as a test—and then was gloomy when his body reprimanded him with tiredness, or odd aches and pains.

Was he merely getting old? he asked himself. He was not far from sixty; many men were dead before this time of life. He told himself to be careful. Nell did not notice any difference in him, for which he was thankful, but then he was quiet about his ailments when he could be, and she was long conditioned to a peaceful contemplation of her own state of health to the exclusion of anyone else's, although she could be kind and solicitous when her attention was focused on a genuine need.

It was Leon who saw and felt the difference in his uncle. Born nephew, Leon had long looked upon his Uncle Felix as good companion, the more so since sharing the particular easy comradeship that had developed between Bonard and Felix during the time Bonard had studied first the law and business affairs with the older man, and then how to enjoy life, though married to a woman who regrets you.

It is not possible to say with any certainty that the pleasures Leon had learned to share with Bonard and Felix had doomed his marriage to a lack of intimacy; but it is certain that fulfillment in his marriage would have made his intimate acquaintance with Felix and Bonard's pleasures an absurdity. It was an illustration of the fact that our lacks often point us to more pleasures than our strengths.

Shorn of Bonard's friendship—and in such a particular way too: his sister's husband running away with his wife's sister, who had borne him a child—Leon was confused, and resentful, and afraid. Had Felix been himself at that time, Leon might have weathered events more sanely. But Felix was uncharacteristically thinking of himself. He did not seek to tempt and divert his nephew to their usual light debaucheries, and Leon felt little appetite for pursuing them alone, without male companionship.

He loved Sarah, of course; and more than "of course" he loved Sarah. She loved him. But he was not strong enough to upset the delicate balance of accommodation they had reached by suddenly pressing her to join him in an attempt to make their marriage a more complete one. She was happy with Rachel and Beulah Land. Nor could Leon suddenly take into his hands the management of Beulah Land. He had for too long watched others manage the place: his father, his mother, Roscoe Elk—and now Sarah. He could not assume a responsibility he had no thought of continuing. He had been taught to leave it to others; he was content to do so. If things went a little wrong now and then, how much did it matter?

He knew that Floyd had written to say he was coming back, but his return was merely speculative. He had not been really close to Floyd since the summer of 1820 when they were boys coming to young manhood, and had been suddenly estranged by an almost mutual experience. Without Bonard, more than not without Felix, Leon was lonely. Young still, but old enough to know that being young is in itself no guarantee of joy, he was lonely. He remembered days when burdens were lighter. He remembered Floyd and the pleasant, natural things they had done that summer of loafing, swimming and fishing in the creek, not caring if they were missed, and having the contented feeling that it would all go on just that way forever.

Now uncompanioned, he visited some of the old places, as nearly as he could judge them to have been, with the creek gradually changing its geography as time brought, alternately, flood and drought. Giving himself up to nostalgia, he picked a melon on his way and continued

into the woods to the creek where he and Floyd had
fished and swum. The underwater cypress roots between
which he fixed his melon to cool might have been exactly
those Floyd and he had used for the same purpose when
they were boys. He took off his clothes and left them on
the gray, dry nubs of branches of a tree that had been
struck by lightning and died.

After swimming he stretched himself on the bank of the
creek, which was hard-packed sand and ground moss that
was almost like grass. Lying on his back, he looked up
through the branches of trees to blue sky, and then hearing the buzz of summer swamp, familiar all his life,
turned face sideways, and saw butterflies that looked like
the same butterflies he had seen and forgotten seventeen
summers ago.

Across the creek, crouched low, sitting on a log, Roman
watched. He had watched for the last several days as
Leon followed the same general pattern of activity and in-
dolence.

Today he had come here before Leon. Eventually, Leon
came strolling along. Roman watched him put the melon
on the ground, and when it rolled and Leon said,
"Whoa!" and set a twig to secure it on the bank, Roman
shared the minor suspense and smiled as the man smiled.
Having balanced the melon, Leon immediately took it up
and found the holding nest for it in the watered cypress
roots.

He took a stick and trailed it in the water, then seemed
to be writing with it on the surface, finally dropping it
into the creek and watching it float downstream. From the
rise and fall of Leon's shoulders, Roman surmised a sigh.

Leon walked along the bank a few yards, and Roman
wondered if he would be forced to get up from his shel-
tered watching post and follow along on his side of the
creek to keep the man in sight, a desire that had become
necessity during the last minutes. But Leon stopped, tilted
back his head and belched hugely. The homely sound was
shocking on the quiet woodland air.

Leon squatted on the bankside and stared into the water
as if he saw a turtle or a fish moving just below the surface in the gray-brown shallows. Leaning forward, he began to lose his balance. To correct it, he reared back so
abruptly that he fell on his behind and sat laughing at
himself, as Rachel had done on the picnic in the grove.

Roman followed every move the man made with atten-

tion so total he was unaware of it himself. Leon drew his
knees up, leaned folded arms on them, bent head to arms.
Sitting on the low log across the creek, Roman did the
same thing. Presently, Leon pressed his face into his arms
so that it was hidden from the boy. Was he crying? Roman speculated with alarm and hope. No. He raised his
head and yawned. Roman relaxed, disappointed. He wanted
his idol to be despondent this day.

Minutes later, Leon stood and began to undress himself,
evidently thinking so little of what he was doing that his
gestures were clumsy, fingers fumbling buttons, hands
pulling too weakly or too vigorously at shirt sleeve or
trouser leg.

Roman watched with increasing involvement. The man
was his father. Roman's flesh was Leon's. *That is me* is
what he felt, knowing both that it was, and was not, true.
Leon's body was sparsely haired, none visible on his chest,
that on his arms and legs hardly visible, and that around
his genitals darker than the red gold of his head hair, as a
man's mustache and beard may sometimes be.

He scratched his thigh. He slapped both hands on his
bare chest, and then with no warning hint or gesture he
dived shallowly into the creek, surfaced like a leaping fish,
flinging water from his hair and head, and yelled like a
happy child, "Wa—hoo!"

He submerged slowly, perpendicularly, and emerged the
same way, breathing water out of his mouth and nose vo-
luptuously. Then he swam. He swam in a large circle. He
lay on his back and thrashed his arms and legs, shouting
now like a wild Indian. Roman watched with total com-
mitment and total admiration. Had a man ever been as
beautiful as his father?

Even when Leon tired of swimming and walked out of
the water, his movements slow and awkward because of
the unevenness of the bottom and the draw of the current,
Roman found every motion he made a matter of wonder.

Discovery is basic to first love; everything Leon did was
a revelation of beauty for Roman. What he did was right,
had always been right, just as all that his mother did and
had done had been wrong. Roman's body was in a fever
of love for the man there, and he knew what he must do.
He would go a little downstream where the creek narrowed and a fallen tree spanned it from bank to bank.

Leon lay on his back. He was not sleeping, but he had
dreamed, half awake, when he heard a stir he knew in-

stantly was human-, not creature-made. He raised his head
from the ground and saw Roman who had just emerged
from the woods, letting a tree branch he had turned aside
for easier passage slap back to its natural place: that
sound had wakened Leon's attention.

Leon knew their meeting was not an accident. However
it had come about, it seemed to him a natural consequence of his own thoughts that day. The boy glared at
him in what looked like anger, but Leon was certain Roman had come here now because he wanted them to meet
this way.

"I'm sorry," Roman said, his voice lilting falsely. "I
didn't know you were here. I didn't think anybody would
be here."

Leon looked at him. If Roman had turned and gone
away, the lie might have been accepted by both, however
much each knew it was a lie. But Roman paused, and
paused until it looked like staying. Only then, too late, he
turned to go. When he had taken four steps, Leon said,
"It's all right. You can stay. Stay. Please."

Roman did not pretend not to hear, but he did not look
back at Leon when he turned and walked to the bank a
few feet away from the reclining man, then squatted as he
had seen Leon do earlier, then fell back abruptly and
laughed.

Disturbed, Leon laughed an echo of Roman's laugh.
Even when it is not honest, laughter can make a bad moment easier. Theirs now made it possible for them to look
quickly behind its cover, and to look away blank-faced,
having seen more than they could admit. Leon closed his
eyes and made a play of relaxing his body. He stretched
his legs and spread his toes, arched his chest, showing his
body in tension on the pretext of relaxing it.

Even then, Roman might have left, but he did not. Leon
might have turned over on his belly and stopped it, but he
did not. When he opened his eyes a quivering slit, he saw
that Roman had moved nearer. Closing them again, he
hardly breathed. Presently, he felt the boy's hand touch
the side of his chest. He breathed again; the hand crept to
the navel and paused there, one finger gently exploring, as
if reaching back for the secret of Leon's own birth. Leon
felt his dick harden. He did not will it, but sex thinks
without the brain. He felt the boy's lips kissing his dick.
Narcissus had found his image, and was gladly lost.

Nine

Sarah looked up from the ledger as she closed it and handed it back to Roscoe Elk. "The accounting is accurate, all quite in order," she said. Taking the ledger, he nodded. "However, there is one thing not accounted for in the ledger."

Lips firming, he frowned patiently.

"The man Pojo," she said. To give him a moment to adjust to her turning the conversation, a matter of manners she had not yet learned to put aside, she added what they both knew, "A shortening of the nickname 'Poor Joe,' I understand, given to him when he was a boy."

"Yes?" he said gruffly, refusing her delicate pace.

"You had him beaten."

Roscoe looked quickly around the office, as if to remind her that he should be dealing with the master of the plantation, not his wife. Abruptly bringing his eyes back to focus on her face, he said without any concession, "He stole."

"He took corn from the barn to feed his pig, which I gave him last Christmas along with permission to eat it then or raise it and sell it, keeping whatever money he got for his own use."

"He stole," Roscoe repeated coldly.

"They do not consider it stealing to take from the family supplies, because they are part of the family. They think stealing is only when they take from each other."

"Stealing is stealing."

"Does Pojo owe you money?"

That made him hesitate, but only for a moment. "I would have to look in my record book to say."

"You remember that Mr. Kendrick and I gave you instructions that no one was to be dealt physical punishment without our knowledge and approval?"

He said nothing.

"You do remember, then."

"If I might speak to Mr. Kendrick, I'm sure I could make my position clear so that he would understand and not disapprove of what I have ordered done."

This was open insolence, for they both knew that Leon, two days ago, had saddled a horse and ridden off without speaking to a soul. There had been no word of him since.

"You may speak to Mr. Kendrick as much as you like and he allows—when he returns. In his absence, you answer to me, as does everyone else who works here."

He looked at her long and hard before nodding curtly. "To be seen running to the owners to clear every point of discipline for mischief and error would destroy my authority. I cannot manage one hundred and sixty-two slaves without authority. They are like mules, not to be reasoned with, but told to gee and haw."

"They are people, Mr. Elk. Our people."

"May God make them grateful for that," he said drily. She flushed. "Where is Pojo's pig now?"

"With the general lot."

"You took the pig from him?"

"Because he was fattened on stolen grain, he belongs to the plantation. That is how I figure to right his wrong."

"You did that on your own authority?"

"I did not actually carry the pig myself from Pojo's pen to the main pens—no."

She held onto her temper. If she admitted to him that she saw his impertinence, the thing would have to go further than she wanted it to go—or rather, further than Leon would let her go. "See that the pig is returned to Pojo."

"I don't think I would recognize the pig."

"I'm sure Pojo would. Let him take him back."

"Perhaps if he is left to choose, he will take another, larger, fatter."

"Give him the pig, I say!"

"They look on such generosity as weakness. If they get away with it one time, they'll try another."

"You have my instructions. That is all."

"The working day is over. Tomorrow—"

"Send Pojo to me here. I shall tell him."

"I shall be glad to send someone to send Pojo to you here. Mrs. Kendrick. As for me, I must go to my own little farm now and close the day's work there."

"Very well, but send—see that Pojo comes to me."

Roscoe nodded carefully, holding his contempt within reasonable bounds.

A quarter of an hour later Lovey entered the office without knocking and said, "Pojo's here and says he's been sent for."

"Yes."

Frowning at her mistress, Lovey muttered, "Thieving scoundrel," and went out the door.

A minute later the man entered, smiling hugely, nervously, falsely. Sarah had seen him often enough before, but only at a distance. She had never had occasion to speak to him. "Are you all right, Pojo?" she asked.

"Whassat? Whassat, ma'am?" His face was a mask of grinning, calculated stupidity.

"I asked if you were all right," she said sharply.

He considered. "Yas'm. Yas'm. Tolerable." He nodded his head vigorously, as if agreeing with himself.

"You are to have your pig back, Pojo."

"Yas'm!" He nodded again.

"I know that Mr. Elk took him from you, but you are to have him back again. He is yours, to raise and sell or not, just as you please. He belongs to you. Do you understand?"

"Yas'm. He is a moughty skinny ole hog. Not worth much, not ever gone be worth much, I reckon."

"Well, he is yours." Sarah smiled, trying to coax the man into relaxing and speaking to her naturally. "I'm sorry you were punished. It should not have happened. I did not authorize anyone to have you beaten."

"Yas'm. They say they caught me at it. But it was just our own corn."

"Yes."

"Our corn I was taking to feed him, skinny ole bo' hog."

"I understand how you thought about it when you did it."

"They whipped me for it."

"I know. I'm sorry. That is what I have been saying. It shouldn't have been so."

"Yas'm. But they did. What do Mistress want to see me about?"

Ten

"I declare I don't know what you carrying on so for, honey, calling yourself a monster. Less I got it wrong— did I? Some little nigger boy sucked your peter when you was lying buck naked and half asleep after swimming in the creek. Sugar, that kind of thing must happen all the time, them being the animals and all they are. If nothing worse ever occurs to you, you better think yourself lucky."

Leon, who'd had no sleep for two days except for odd half hours, lurched to his feet and slapped the woman across the face.

When she grabbed his hands, he immediately subsided into his chair. "That will be enough! I have—we have all of us been patient seeing how you're an old friend, but my patience for one has come to an end! You have been here two days, drinking our likker and eating what vittles we could get you to eat, and you've been welcome. But you will not strike me, sir, nor anyone else. And you will leave here now. Don't come back to this door until you can show a decent Christian face. God alone knows what that Miss Priss of a wife will say when she sees you. But you're her problem, not ours, not now." She took him by the hair and pulled his head up so that he was forced to look at her. When she spoke again, her voice had lost its anger and shaded into pity. "You are a mess, sure enough. Go on home like I say; and when you get yourself straightened out—but not before, remember!—you are welcome here again."

It was Florabel Bixby who spoke, eldest of the three sisters who lived in a house behind a hedge just outside of Highboro and were kind enough to entertain gentlemen of the neighborhood who lacked certain comforts in their family arrangements. Florabel was past her bloom, and more often than not assumed the role of motherly hostess to vistors, while her younger sisters, Pansy and Annette (now asleep, it was early morning), attended to the bedroom business. Florabel occasionally agreed to initiate a young man brought along by an older one, often his father or uncle, but the older men themselves preferred one of the younger sisters for their more active pleasures.

Leon thought about what Florabel said and nodded. He closed his eyes. Thinking he might drift into sleep again, she was on the verge of shaking his arm and speaking when he cleared his throat, then coughed to clear it better, opening his eyes. Getting to his feet, he steadied himself and walked to the living room wall that boasted the biggest mirror in the house. Unable to see, he stepped to a side table and picked up an oil lamp, holding it to his mirrored image. After studying himself quietly, he said, "My God," and set the lamp down again. "If you will be so kind, Miss Flora as to give me coffee, I'll be on my way."

She nodded and went to the kitchen, he following, knowing she would allow him to use the indoor pump to wash his face and hands. Half an hour later he saddled and mounted his horse, but he did not turn the horse toward home. Instead, he rode to Felix and Nell's. When the servant answered his knock at the front door, he asked that Mr. Kendrick be told he waited for him at his office. Felix found him there and gave him a drink, seeing that his hands shook and his knees had no strength. Then Felix talked quietly to his nephew a few minutes before taking him home to breakfast.

Nell treated his appearance as perfectly natural, ignoring his soiled clothes and unshaved face. Later in the morning Nell and Felix drove to Beulah Land in their buggy, Leon trotting his horse alongside them Sarah welcomed them as though nothing in Leon's absence nor the trio's unannounced arrival were out of the ordinary.

The visitors stayed the day, Felix walking about the fields with Leon, after Leon had bathed and put on fresh clothes, speaking with Roscoe Elk at length, and being seen by all hands; Nell, enjoying her visit with Sarah, which included short times with Rachel and Juanita and the consumption of quantities of lemonade and tea and fresh farm edibles. After supper she and Felix took the buggy home, carrying a hamper of new peas and corn and tomatoes. Nell encouraged Felix to smoke a cigar, the smell of which she rather liked out of doors, although she would not tolerate it in the house.

Alone, Sarah and Leon made their peace by talking of Beulah Land. She told him the trouble she'd had with Roscoe about Pojo. She was careful to tell it just as it happened. "What makes me furious," she ended by saying, "is that even when we were talking, I could see that he was right in a way, and I was wrong—but I was right really, wasn't I? We can't let him bully the people, even when they do wrong."

"Dear Sarah." He put his arms about her, and she rested her head against his neck. "I am so very sorry I put you in the way of dealing with that."

"My dear!" Her arms tightened about his waist; then she let him go. "Listen!" They cocked their heads in listening attitudes, and the sound of Juanita's loving-scolding voice drifted down the stairs. "Rachel has the wide-awakes because of the visitors and your return. Otherwise, she'd have been asleep an hour ago. Since she isn't, shall we go in to see her? It won't make any real difference, and she'll like it so, even if Juanita does not."

Leon shook his head. "I'll walk a little in the night air."

"I'll go in for just a minute."

"Good night, Sarah."

She paused a second on the stairs. "Good night."

Presently, he heard a door open and close, and the sound of voices behind it happy and muffled. He took a cigar from the box on the desk, rolled it between his fingers, sniffed it, bit off the pointed end, and lighted it with a candle flame. When it glowed evenly, he went out and walked the grounds as he had done times without number, in an effort to understand himself—not in a total, long-enduring way, just enough to not loathe himself, enough to be able to sleep and rest and wake again and say, "This is a new day."

Eleven

Roman had observed Leon's return with Felix and Nell, and Rachel's running out of the house to meet them, followed by Sarah and Juanita. He had, since parting with Leon three days ago on the creekbank, lived in his own hell which was the more confusing for revealing flashes of joy and revelation.

He hardly remembered (he told himself) what had happened. (Oh, but he did, he did!) The way it ended, he would never forget and never understand. His hands and lips had been on his father's flesh, taking like from him again as he had taken it at the moment of his conception, when Leon had come, his body arching and thrashing as if in a mad fit. Crying out, he had turned face and body to the ground.

Roman sat beside him. The hidden face, the naked back and shoulders heaving against the creekbank were an accusation as well as a refusal. He did not understand; he did not understand any of it. What had brought him there today? What had moved Leon finally to accept him after years of denying him, only then to turn away? What was *wrong?* No one had taught him; instinct had bid him do what he had done. Was instinct then wrong? The new idea was to trust it, doubt reason when reason put feeling aside. But sitting there beside the despairing man, he wanted only to go, to be gone, to hide.

He scrambled up from the ground; standing, hesitated. Left alone, would the man be all right? He knelt, touched the man's head at the back. Leon jerked aside, his whole body quivering. Roman stood again, walked a few steps, paused, then ran, and ran.

When at last he felt safely alone, he stopped by the creek at a place it flowed almost even with the bank. He bathed his face and hands and slapped water on his hot ears and the aching muscles at the back of his neck. Leaning on one elbow, he felt deathly tired. The supporting elbow slid out straight, and Roman slept.

When he woke, it was dusk. The woods were moist and dense in their own shadow the instant the sun set. Insects and other woodland creatures that had been daunted to silence and near immobility by the sun's light and heat found voice and movement again. There were brief scuttling sounds in the brush, a song of insects different from the day music, a mood of cool ooze in which a snake might slide, a turtle ponder walking without fear of surprise and rout. Roman rose guiltily, like a guest who knows he has overstayed. Making his way out of the woods as quick as he could, he found a narrow road bordering a field, no more than wagon tracks with grass and weeds growing between them.

Pausing at the back door when he got home, he heard the women in the kitchen preparing supper. Sallou said slyly, "Do I set the whole table, you reckon?"

Myrtis answered, "Yes."

Sallou said, "The mister went off like he was never coming back. Will the missus want to sit there all by her lonesome?"

"Set the table and quit acting biggety and know-all. Sharon, slice them tomatoes more even. Where did I set down the vinegar bottle?"

That, three days ago.

Today, Leon had returned. He walked now in the dark, but not alone. Roman was nearby watching, aching to show himself and speak, but not daring, knowing he and his love were despised.

Twelve

As grain and fiber of the larger fields came to ripeness and were harvested by gangs of Negroes, who sometimes sang, more often from boredom than jubilation, so too Ezra's planting of the foreign seeds Floyd had sent him grew and revealed themselves as pod and stalk and vine and gourd shapes. Here a row five feet long of something, next a row of something else, next to third and fourth and fifth, all planted with different seeds, often a single row accommodating two or more specimens.

For one row he had mixed sand with the black soil; for another, dry powdered clay. He watered one and left another to natural rainfall. He pruned this one, permitted that to sprawl and run as it would, doing all this by guess and instinct. Trusting no rake or hoe, he tended the plants with one rusted kitchen spoon and his own ten fingers.

On an afternoon she found him in his miniature farm staring at a delicate-leafed plant, Lovey laughed out loud, for Ezra was shading the plant with her old parasol that she used only for churchgoing on the hottest Sundays. He looked up at her with surprise. "I won't lose any. I'll show the boy every one grew."

"He may not come till winter, if then."

"He'll come soon and see with his own eyes how they look in the ground."

She left him kneeling, still holding the parasol.

For all the business of late summer harvest, Sarah usually found time to drive into Highboro for church on Sunday. She was not deeply religious, her mind being more on this world than the next. She neither accepted nor rejected with zeal; she accepted quietly, doubted courteously and privately, and speculated in a moderation. But she liked to see people and to hear news, so she went to church. News was crops—cotton, corn, cane—and it was people—who died, who married, who gave birth, who came to live or visit. Church service also provided opportunity to talk to Edna. During the busiest weeks of harvesting and preserving, they heard of each other through the grapevine of their servants but had no time for casual visiting, and so depended on Sundays.

On the first Sunday of September she drove her own buggy into Highboro, her passengers, Rachel and Juanita. Rachel was too young for church, but she liked change and movement, so Sarah had begun to take her and her nurse with her for company when Leon did not go, leaving them in the buggy or at Nell's to pass the time she spent in church. Leon was not a regular worshiper, and this Sunday he and Felix had ridden over to the other side of the county to look at a stand of timber they were thinking of buying together. The production of lumber and selling it on the foreign market were matters of growing interest to them, especially in years as lean as this one promised to be.

Sarah left Rachel and Juanita sharing a basket of peaches and chattering together in the grove where other rigs and wagons waited for owners who were presently engaged in giving God his weekly nod. Sarah saw Edna on the church porch for only a few minutes before they were surrounded and separated by other women of their acquaintance. Edna called to her friend, "Rooster wants particularly to speak to you—remember!"

After the singing and sermon, they met again on the porch and walked with Rooster to their buggies in the grove.

"When do you and Roman start your school again?" Rooster wanted to know.

"As soon as the heaviest work is finished. Soon now," Sarah said. "I've missed it."

"When I go to Savannah with my cotton, I'm going to bring back a tutor for my boys," Rooster said.

"Like him and Bonard had," Edna supplied. "And we're wondering if you'll take the girls at your school when you start teaching."

"Oh, of course I will!" Sarah said. "I wish I'd thought of it. Rachel is too young, but she sits with us anyway, and Doreen and Annabel will certainly be welcome. Will you promise to send them every day?"

"We surely will!"

"It's so important that they come regularly," Sarah said.

"It's most kind of you, Sarah," Rooster said warmly.

"I've wanted to know them better," Sarah said, "and for Rachel to know them. Edna, you come with them."

"I'm too old for lessons and school."

As they laughed, Sarah turned to Rooster. "You must see Aunt Pea when you go to Savannah. She'll help you find your tutor, and she'll glory doing it. It's just the kind of problem she loves. You will also do me a favor by helping her make up her mind to come see us for a long visit. She always comes about this time of year—has—but every year she says she isn't coming *this* year and has to be coaxed, so I hope you'll help me."

"Gladly. I coax good." Rooster laughed, and so did she.

"Very well, I count on you, Bruce! Will you just look at my child?"

They had come into the grove. Their buggies, it turned out, were separated only by a buckboard and a wagon with improvised plank seats. Rachel stood in the middle of

a circle of children, four of whom were Rooster's. They
had run out with their friends the instant church was
over, making the most of the few minutes a week they
could be together. Rachel was singing for the group and
they were, at least temporarily, quiet. As the adults approached, though, the circle broke, the older children running away together, leaving Rachel surprised and alone,
her song interrupted.

Sarah knelt and hugged the child. Rachel then curtsied
to Edna and Rooster, both of whom paid her kind notice
before going to their buggy and calling for their scattered
young ones. Sarah and Juanita settled themselves and
Rachel into the buggy seat, Sarah talking the while to
Edna and Rooster. The owners of the buckboard and the
wagon had not yet appeared, having lingered to gossip in
the church yard. It was sometimes close to an hour after
Sunday services that the grove was finally cleared.

Edna called again to the four missing children, using
their names: "Adam! Annabel! Doreen! You James!
Come running!" When they did not appear, Rooster raised
his voice to add a threat: "We're leaving right now!
You'll have to walk all the way home!" Untying the reins,
he slapped them lightly on the horse's flanks and moved
his buggy along after Sarah's. The children suddenly appeared, screaming in delighted panic, "Wait! Oh, wait for
us, Papa!"

Rooster slowed the horse without stopping, while Edna
helped Annabel up on one side and he pulled Doreen up
on the other. The two boys hopped up to the back seat
over the hay box. And so the two parties rolled away
home, the adults smiling and nodding when they caught
each other's eyes, the children calling mysterious inanities
back and forth. The buggies would for a time maintain an
equal pace side by side; then one would give way so that
another buggy might pass.

Once, when they had been parted and Sarah's buggy
was several lengths in the lead, Edna said, "She called you
'Bruce' back yonder." He nodded. "Nobody else does."

"Well," he said equably, "it's my name, the very one
you gave me."

Half an hour later and well past noon the buggies went
separate ways after their inhabitants had exchanged a
dozen "last" goodbyes. Sarah drove briskly along the drive
from the main road, through the orchard and around the
house to her back door, where Sugar met her to take the
horse and buggy off to the barn. Dinner was ready, she

was certain, and she didn't like to make Myrtis wait. She hoped Leon had come home and that Felix was with him.

She had started in—Rachel and Juanita had gone before her to tell the kitchen girls of their adventure in town— when her eye was caught by the un-Sunday sight of a dozen men who had evidently been working, since they carried pitchforks on their shoulders. They were just approaching one of the barns. A minute later she found them inside putting their tools away. Addressing herself to the one named Rex, a man she knew to be intelligent and responsible, she asked where they had been working. He glanced at the others; all shuffled and appeared uneasy. "Over to the Elk Place, missy," Rex said.

"Doing what?"

"Pitching late scattered hay."

"You don't work on Sundays; it's your time off."

"Well'm," Rex said, "that's it, you see. It's time off for us here, but Mr. Elk he needed this work done, and we was paying out a little debt we owed."

"Have you done this before?" she asked, keeping her voice even.

"Now and again, yes'm. Mr. Elk lets us work it off when we can't pay it off."

"Did you see him?"

"Yes, yes," Leon said impatiently. "I saw him and talked to him. It's all right."

Leon was tired and irritable. He had come home midafternoon from the timber inspection trip with Felix, who had left him at the main road and gone home, saying Nell hadn't been pert that morning and that he was eager to see her. Leon had had no dinner, and as soon as he got into the house, Sarah flew at him about the men who'd worked that morning for Roscoe Elk. While he ate cold leftovers, she made him say he would ride right over to Roscoe's for an explanation.

"Why is it all right?" she now said. "They are our men."

"They worked for him because they owe him money, and they were working on time we left them free; so how does it hurt us?"

"Don't you see?"

"No, I don't," he said impatiently.

"More and more they'll get the feeling they work for Roscoe Elk, answer to Roscoe Elk. In time they may very well come to think they do us a favor to work the fields of Beulah Land, that it is time taken from—the 'Elk Place.' "

"You are talking foolishness."

"You will see."

"I don't think you know how galling it is to hear you playing at Overseer yourself and assuming that you know more about running Beulah Land than does anyone else. Every day you grow more like my mother!"

"Leon—where are you going?"

"Where I will not be treated as a child!" he exclaimed, having decided to go only when she asked him. "Where I may be allowed to sit and take my ease—and yes, my pleasure—and not be sent galloping about on errands for the 'mistress!' "

"Leon!—Leon?"

If she had not followed him through the house and breezeway to the back door, he might have stayed. He might have walked about, dissipating his bad temper in movement, and joined her again at supper, in however taciturn a mood. But in her guilty feeling at badgering him—maybe he was right that she was overtouchy about Roscoe Elk—she followed, and so he had to get back on his horse and go where he did not really want to go, not at just that time, anyway—to the house behind the hedge beyond Highboro where the Bixby sisters, Florabel, Annette, and Pansy, waited to console and entertain the lusty, the lonely, and the misunderstood.

Thirteen

Roman had gone far beyond the self-dramatizing despair that is common enough among those his age. His self-pity was not sweet and consoling, but bitter. Having little to do, he had therefore done too much. Keeping the school was his only work, but it was not kept in summer and harvest time. His lovings may have been fanciful, but his rejections had been real. His love for Leon had been, was, real. His rejection by Leon, after the briefest hope of acceptance, had been brutal.

Roman did not approach Leon directly, but he watched him, hidden or from a distance. When one day Roman could stand his limbo-purgatory no longer, he put himself directly in Leon's way, and privately too, so that there could be no excuse to himself later of "Well, he couldn't because others were there." Roman plotted the meeting; he came around a corner directly in Leon's path and stood wordless, however much his eyes and attitude pled for acknowledgment. When Leon stared at him, his face going red and registering nothing more than pity and contempt —why then, right then, Roman might have killed him. But after he stepped aside, head bowed in humiliation and anger, he decided to kill himself instead.

It was not a sudden thought. Dreams of death are as common as dreams of love with the young, and Roman had reasons for both, if ever youth did. He loved Rachel, he loved Sarah, and they, he could admit to himself, cared about him. But his caring for them was not as important to them as their caring for him was to him; and that inequality of need he could no longer admit and live on. He despised his mother, and she had forgot him. He disliked his half brothers without ever having known them. Roscoe Elk was his enemy. Leon, the smallest crumb from whom would have sustained the boy, too obviously wished him dead—or worse, unborn.

So, on the 19th of September at four o'clock in the afternoon, Roman went to one of the barns, cut a length of strong new rope, looped it under his shirt to hide it, and went off toward the woods. He felt himself watched, even though he was not. But when he got into the woods, he knew himself alone, without audience, idle or eager. He wasted no time going over it all again in his mind. He went directly to the small open space on the creekbank where he had been for the first and only time intimate with his father.

He found a tree strong enough for the deed—the same tree through whose leafy limbs the naked Leon, nostalgic for his own youth, had looked at the blue sky before Roman appeared. Roman climbed it, and it was not easy. He scraped the skin of one palm raw on rough oak bark, and winced to see it bleed, only to smile bleakly at how superficial that was compared to what would be.

He had left his shoes at the bottom of the tree so that it would be easier to climb, and he achieved the first strong high limb sweating and panting. He worked a long time fitting and knotting the rope around the limb where another, small limb branched, making a natural brake for the rope. He had no knowledge of knots and rope, and he had to make very sure it would hold. Finally, with equal care, he invented a noose that looked reliable, and certainly was. He put it around his neck and drew it close to fit. Closing his eyes, thinking no tortured farewell, no anything, he slipped off the limb and dropped.

His feet did not kick empty air, and he did not at first comprehend what had happened. Then he realized that he had been caught and held in arms, although the body the arms belonged to staggered and shifted its feet to find a firm foundation. Incredulous, Roman thought and said, "Leon!" Opening his eyes, he looked into the angry face of Floyd.

Floyd rapidly loosened the noose and freed the boy's neck and head of it. Having him safe, he set him on his feet, and seeing that he was unharmed, grasped his shoulders in both hands, shook him roughly and cried, "What are you up to, hey?" Floyd let him go, stood and stared at him, letting his own thoughts settle. When he had collected himself a little, he said as if just discovering the fact, "Roman?"

Roman's head drooped. He trembled from the shock of what he had done, and not done.

Floyd pulled his chin up. "Look at me! What *damn-fool*, *fool*-thing were you trying to do? Tell me!"

Roman stepped back from the man. "You shouldn't have stopped me."

Floyd grabbed him and held him until he was still; and then Floyd said, "First thing, climb that tree and untie that rope and drop it down to me."

Roman shook his head and pushed free. Floyd shrugged and began to climb the tree himself. Even in his agitation, Roman felt pleased in a small part of his mind at the man's finding the climb difficult. It made him feel less clumsy and inept. Floyd made his way up the trunk, slipping a time or two and having to grab hard, and after inching along to the rope, untied it. The untying took him several minutes, and he muttered over the task, finally calling down to the boy, "With this many knots, you could have hung a horse!" When the rope was at last free, he dropped it to the ground where it fell in an impotent coil at Roman's feet.

Floyd took his time coming down the tree. Looking at his palms when his feet found the ground, he said, "Bleeding. You put me to a lot of trouble. There I was, cutting off from the main road the back way because I wanted to see this place before I got home. I used to play here when

I was a boy. Fished, sat around." He frowned, remembering. "All kinds of things we did, Leon and me. You thought I was Leon. Why?"

Roman's lips parted and trembled. "Hoped."

"Hoped." Floyd shook his head. "God, hoped." He picked up the rope, looped it over a fist enough times to make a tight coil, and then swung his arm and let the coiled rope fly high over the creek, landing with a splash. They both watched as it took water and sank.

"How's my papa?" Floyd said everyday-like. "I asked the first person I met when I got to Highboro this morning. The man said, 'Oh, he's well. Or let me think now: Did he die?' "

"He's well." Roman found it easier to talk about someone else. "He got the seeds you sent. It was already summer when they came and he planted them, so they were late growing, and he's left them in the ground, saying you'd be here in time to see them."

Floyd nodded, as if this only confirmed what he had known. "Mama's all right." It was more statement than question, but a statement that contained query.

Roman smiled for the first time. "Still telling everybody and God how to do right."

"That's my mama," Floyd said. "Sit down. I'm all-sudden tired. Ever since I left, I've been coming back; now that I'm here, I need to stop and catch my breath." He found a dry place on the bank and sat. Roman sat near him, and they looked at the creek until Floyd said, "I've thought about this very place many-a-many time." He studied the boy's face. "You've changed a lot in two years, nearly come to a man. You favor him now." Roman did not answer, but looked steadily back at Floyd. "I want you to tell me everything that's happened on Beulah Land since I've been gone. Don't leave out a baby's birth or one old folk's dying." They had never until now had occasion to look at each other closely enough to learn anything. "You're Leon's son, all right," Floyd said. "But did you know you might have been mine instead?"

The question surprised Roman, but somehow lifted the yoke from his back and mind. He began to talk. The more he talked, the more there seemed to be to tell. He told Floyd about Sarah and Rachel, about Ezra's getting feeble, about Roscoe Elk and his owning the Anderson Farm now, and moving there. He talked about his school. He talked about the Davis family. And he began to talk

about himself. He even told Floyd about the girl Roxy,
but not about Sallou and her coming to his room that
time. He came up to telling, but then could not, about
Leon. It was dusk when, without having said they would,
they got up and walked together out of the woods and
across the fields toward the plantation buildings. Supper
fires had been lighted, and their smoke drifted thinly on
the evening air, like spirits of the past fading into the forgotten.

Fourteen

It was a homecoming; oh, it was. Even Selma and Pauline
came down from their private shelf to touch and smile
and listen. Lovey was a woman reborn. She walked with
youthier spring; her speech was crisp and crackling once
more; and she laughed like a girl when she showed off the
combs Floyd had brought to her from Greece, and the
shawl from Spain. Ezra put on, and never again put off, a
look of such quiet joy it made those who saw him shy, as
though to speak to him of his son's return were an impertinence, as superfluous as a compliment to a saint.

Myrtis sang and dreamed in the kitchen, wondering if
she were too old, although she was just his age, to appear
agreeable to a man who had seen half the women in the
world. Her twins Otis and Lotus were owl-eyed when he
admitted that he had been to Mesopotamia and begged to
be told what he had seen there. Felix came out from
Highboro and laughed and shook his head, and shook
Floyd's hand, and said he was both sorry and glad to see
him again.

Leon, that first evening, after giving him two hours with
Ezra and Lovey, took him into the office where they sat
and smoked cigars together and drank a glass of claret.
Sarah came in to greet him. She took both his hands in
hers and looked as if she would have done more, but did
not. Leon smiled his regard on both as they smiled theirs
on each other. She left, making Floyd promise he would
come to Roman's school soon and tell all the children together of the places he had been.

Floyd and Leon talked on, leaving the office after a
while and walking over grounds of Beulah Land they had
shared their whole lives. They may have been closer as

boys, when they did not appraise or question closeness, but they had not felt closer to each other as men. The admission and expression of old friendship had had to wait, it seemed, on Floyd's going away and coming home again. As they talked, Floyd became increasingly aware of the ways Roscoe Elk loomed large in Leon's recital of the fortunes and misfortunes of the last two years, although he made no comment on the fact.

It was not late, although it seemed so by plantation habits when they said good night and Floyd found his way back to the family cabin—and found Ezra on the back steps waiting for him. Ezra, who had already shown Floyd the growing plants, began to "show" him again in the dark. For the first time Floyd understood that his father was an old man.

The stir of Floyd's return had hardly stilled, and the pleasure of his presence had only begun to seem unremarkable when Rooster returned from his business trip to Savannah. It had, he confessed to Leon, been a disappointing one. Because cotton prices were low, he had decided to sell only what he needed to get ready cash. Part of the remainder he had stored in a Savannah warehouse; most of it he had sent back to Highboro, where he knew Leon and Felix would hold it for him in their warehouse. Penelope came from Savannah with Rooster, and the tutor they had chosen together for his sons. Driscoll Proctor was a solemn man of thirty-two whose manner was deliberate, even awkward, in a way that was not unwelcome. He was said to be especially "strong" in Latin and geography.

Penelope settled in to what had come to be considered "her old room." Nell and Felix came for a day to welcome her and stayed a week. Edna brought Annabel and Doreen on the first morning they were to attend Roman's school, and spent the day, taking the girls home to Oaks in the buggy late in the afternoon. Henceforth, they would be accompanied by Violet, who was thus allowed to see her husband Sugar more often now that she was pregnant and not so casual as she had been about her marriage."

It was that time of year just before people settled into their winter routine, which was so much slower and easier than plowing and planting and growing and harvest times. This year harvest energy had grown near to frenzy, because the rewards for the year's labor were so uncertain.

The price of cotton being half what it usually was, Leon and Felix found themselves, having ginned the cot-

ton of the smaller farms of the surrounding county, stor-
ing it free in their warehouse with their own, waiting for
the price to rise, and in the meantime extending credit or
guaranteeing payment for goods bought at local stores, acting, indeed, as agents. When the gin finally shut down its
operation for the year, the warehouse was full. Rex was
excused from his winter work on the plantation and sent
to live in a shanty back of the warehouse and act as
watchman, taking his main meals in Nell's kitchen.

Although times were hard and people said so, they did
not worry overmuch. The harvest was in, their winter
provisions were assured, seed waited for spring—and next
year prices were certain to rise. Since everyone was poor,
no one felt poor. And the usual parties and dances were
enjoyed, as well as such diversions as quilting bees, corn-
shuckings, livestock judging and selling, now and then
horse racing. People began to feel a comfortable anticipation of Thanksgiving and Christmas.

In spite of the poor-mouth everyone talked, it promised
to be very much like other winters, even after word
passed around that more than one farmer of small private
acreages had "lost" his farm to the bank, because of this
year's price failures; they had proved decisive and fatal
when added to accumulated small debts and loans of years
past.

In one such case, a family named Ralston—man, wife,
a son and daughter not babes nor grown—lost their place,
but it was over on the far edge of the county, and no one
seemed to know them, although everyone knew of them.
The bank put their farm up for sale, and Roscoe Elk
bought it. Mr. Guthrie, the lawyer who had managed his
interests in the Anderson Place before it became his, stood
for him in sale. People might feel and whisper that it
didn't seem quite right somehow, but no one could call it
suspect legally. In any event, it was not the surprise the
Anderson affair had been. And what on earth, they asked
one another, would Roscoe Elk do with a farm way over
yonder?

The Ralston house stood empty, the family having
loaded what they were able to in a wagon and set off west
for Alabama, it was said. A week after their departure,
the old house burned to the ground, no knowing by whose
hand, if any hand had done the deed. The next time Roscoe rode over to look at his new property, only the black

chimney remained of the house where Ralstons had lived for three generations.

Fifteen

One day soon after, Roscoe asked Leon to see him on particular, private business, and Leon set a time for him to come to the office. After some hesitation, he told Sarah and suggested that she join him at the time appointed, before she could suggest it herself. However he might chafe under the strong opinions she held on the running of the plantation, he knew that her presence would prevent him from being too easy in the matter of whatever it was Roscoe wanted. It would also make later explanation unnecessary, thereby avoiding a quarrel. It was certain Roscoe wanted something, or he would not have been so formal. In the general way of things, they might see each other half a dozen times a day when any ordinary question could be put and answered on the spot.

Waiting, Leon checked over accounts in one of the record books on the desk. All his figures were in, but such had been the pressures of the autumn season, it would take a time to bring accounting matters up to date. While she waited, Sarah stood at a window, from which she presently saw Roman and Floyd walking with Rachel between them. Rachel and Floyd had quickly become friends and, Sarah was glad to observe, so had Floyd and Roman. She had been aware all the summer of Roman's troubled spirits, but she had not known how to help him, and she had, besides, been so very busy with other affairs, she put off thinking about him seriously from one day to the next.

Now Roman seemed to be himself again, sure and lively and content. He had needed more than attention from her, she realized: he had needed friending by a man he could like and admire, and from whom he could learn how to be such a man. In all but physical fact, he'd had no father.

At the appointed hour of four, there was a knock on the door. They turned from their separate preoccupations to look at each other, a look that only asked, "Are you there?" Reassured, they faced the door, and Leon requested the knocker to "Come in!"

Sarah had sat down at a little distance from Leon, so

that when Roscoe entered, he did not at first see her. He came in briskly, closing the door with a firmness that made its own small comment. It was only when Leon said, "What is it you wish to tell us, or ask us?" that Roscoe turned his head and saw her. The assurance of his step diminished a little as he went to a point in the room almost equidistant between them, favoring Leon just enough to indicate that it was intended. Sarah smiled so faintly only she knew she smiled.

"Yes!" Roscoe said. After one of his calculated pauses he began, "Mr. Kendrick. Mrs. Kendrick. As our work at Beulah Land has more or less ended—or slowed down, let us say, for this year—I have found my mind turning to certain problems and possibilities of my own affairs—without, however, neglecting in any way my larger responsibilities here."

He paused.

"Let me say, indeed, that to think of one is to think of both. All are one, at least in my thinking, if not in actuality—as we all know, of course." He opened his mouth and his eyes crinkled in what he intended as a display of good humor, but no sound of laughter issued from the open mouth, and the eyes behind the crinkled edges were bare of expression. "You will have heard of my acquiring a new property." He shrugged. "A negligible place some miles away. The soil is so rocky and poor I hardly know what to do with it. I think of not farming it at all, but letting it go to grass and clover and putting cattle on it—after I fence it, of course."

Leon nodded. Sarah kept her stillness, waiting now a little more alertly, for she knew that at some point in these formal utterances, however circumlocutory, Roscoe did finally come to a point.

Roscoe sighed, studying the carpet, or seeming to, sighed again more heavily, like a man who may regret, but knows he must accept, the advent of new responsibilities. "I am, in short, forced to look about me for help, assistance—that is to say, dependable, reliable *new* help and assistance. The man called Turnip, who came into my ownership with the Anderson estate, is the best of a sorry lot. I consider putting him on the new property—the house burned down, did you hear? But the barn is still there and he can sleep in one of the snugger stalls if the winter is not too severe. He and the cattle can keep each other warm."

He paused now to look from him to her and back to him. His eyes crinkled again in an affably meant expression, but his mouth remained closed.

"However that may be—"

Leon leaned a little forward in his chair at the desk. Sarah leaned back in hers.

"I clearly have, as you will have perceived, a problem to solve. If I put Turnip to look after the new Elk property, I will need another man or two—indeed, I am ready to consider acquiring more."

He paused to allow this intelligence to have its effect.

"Over the years—so long as none are bought or sold— the slave population of a plantation will generally remain at about the same number, what with the births balancing off the loss of those from age and various fevers and other malignant conditions of the flesh. On Beulah Land we have done better. None have been bought or sold in the time I have presided over their work. And because of the care you yourself"—he cocked his head briefly toward Sarah—"and perhaps notably Mrs. Kendrick have given them, their numbers have increased. From the one hundred and forty-eight I found here originally, the count has risen to one hundred and sixty-two, and that does not include those slaves who were given their freedom, notably Lovey and Ezra and Pauline and Floyd—who has recently returned, seemingly to live here, but whose occupation has not been clearly defined to me. Nor does it, of course, include Mrs. Elk whose freedom I purchased."

The pause this time was a short one.

"Nor does it include the slave Roman, who does no regular plantation work. So the increase is substantial. The crop, we might say, has been good. The care you and Mrs. Kendrick have given the slaves has paid handsome dividends. I have ever thought it unwise of owners to deny their slaves proper food or to house them badly or to ignore their illnesses. Those owners would not think of doing so with hogs or mules or cattle, yet slaves are a more valuable property than are those.

"I offer to buy from you, and not at the reduced value level this year has brought on goods of all kinds, but at the evaluation that held true a year ago—I offer to buy two—or four, if you will, male slaves, and one female for Mrs. Elk to train for the house. The two women from the Anderson settlement are not fit for work in a respectable house; they will serve merely as field hands."

Leon stared ahead as if in a trance, but he was far from any state of sleep; his mind was, rather, intensely active. The money from selling two or four men and one woman, negligible though it might have been in other years, would not be so in this. Every penny had become important. He thought of the credit he had extended to the small-farm owners, the guarantees he had made, all in the, of course, natural expectation that the price of cotton would rise next year. Also, it was true there were more people on Beulah Land than were needed for the work. Two men often were set to a task one could easily accomplish. The loss of five would not make even a small difference; it would make none. Roscoe's proposal was not merely a temptation. It was logical and fair—more than fair, he decided.

Roscoe knew, or guessed, perfectly well what Leon was thinking. "May I hope," he said, after allowing Leon as full a pause as he himself often inflicted, "and may I understand that my proposal be considered in as practical a light as I have myself considered making it, and that soon I may anticipate an answer that will do something toward solving my problem?"

Sarah also guessed what Leon had been thinking. She had known before this hour that she hated Roscoe Elk, but she had not hated him with a hundredth the ferocity she did now. She acknowledged to herself that part of her hatred was the result of his logical reasoning. It was not true—if truth is what is in the heart of the doer, then it was not true that Sarah had cared for "her people" because it meant accretion of them as property. But it was true, as Roscoe had reminded her, that they were not, or not merely "her people"; they were slaves, property, hers and Leon's. She might not so think of them, but the law saw them as plantation slaves. She was suddenly aware that Leon was staring at her in hope and dread. She returned his look with one of complete rejection of Roscoe's proposal.

Slowly, Leon's face reflected his acceptance of her stand. He nodded, knowing what he must do. "Not in my lifetime have we sold our people," he said, "although we have swapped about to accommodate them when marriages occurred that involved those not belonging to Beulah Land. I am afraid, very afraid, we cannot consider selling any now. Although I am glad you came to talk to me first. I see and understand, of course, that you do need other hands, more assistance, as you expressed it."

"Surely—" Roscoe pronounced the word earnestly. "Surely, each time we live in must decide its own arrangements and not merely take the pattern of the past? Surely my buying such a very few is not like offering them on the auction block in Savannah or Atlanta? They have worked under my supervision and know me as I know them. I do not believe they care much who they call master. If I buy only those willing to be bought by me, can you see wrong in that?"

Sarah stood, not in hauteur but wanting to end the interview with some dignity. "Mr. Elk, it is useless to continue this discussion," she said. "I believe we understand your problem, but I am afraid we cannot help you toward a solution."

Roscoe, who had looked directly at her with a mask of courteous deference while she spoke, turned his eyes questioningly toward Leon, who rose from his chair somewhat jerkily, as if he had sat too long and his legs were surprised to be suddenly supporting him. "Just so, just so," he said lamely. "You see the position."

Roscoe Elk almost, not quite, smiled a genuine smile before bowing his head. "I am sorry we cannot come to a happier conclusion. However, I shall hope to be luckier elsewhere."

"Very proper of you to ask me first," Leon said in a conciliatory tone, "but you see how Mrs. Kendrick and I feel about such matters."

The gesture of bowed head was further enforced by a slow bowing of Roscoe Elk's body, after which he withdrew, closing the door softly after him. Sarah turned to look out the window. The only moving creatures she saw were half a dozen guinea fowl stepping slowly along together, their feathers ruffled against the coolness of the autumn afternoon.

"Confound it, Sarah!" Leon said behind her. "Was it necessary to dismiss him without our consulting further on what he proposed?" She turned from the window. "I know. I know it's not been done since early in my father's time as master of Beulah Land, but we need the money. This a hard year."

"I know that," she said.

"What Roscoe says is true; we have more people than we want for the work there is to do—particularly during the winter. We feed them all year, but they work productively only a few months of the year. It is a stupid system."

"Have you become an abolitionist?"

"Damn it, Sarah, don't make a joke of it. It's very well for you to stand high with your principles and scorn profit, but I know what the account books tell me."

She went to him, took his hand and kissed him quickly on the cheek. "I'm sorry. I haven't meant to provoke you. It is Roscoe Elk who has provoked *me*. That man knows so well how to turn the truth to show its ugliest face."

"He only wanted to—to buy a field hand or two."

"He wanted that, but that is not all he wanted."

"You imagine devils that don't exist, like ancient theologians. There are devils enough, God knows."

She touched his hand again. "Are we really so poor?"

"We are not poor at all," he said irritably. "It is only that we are not rich enough to ignore the chance of money coming to hand."

After a moment she said, "I do know that. I'm sorry if I have seemed to speak frivolously. You know I am not."

He put an arm around her waist and walked her back to the window. "Let us not fret and worry it. All will be well—next year. In the meantime—what the deuce is Rachel doing out there alone?"

She followed his gaze, and sure enough, there was Rachel, standing still in an open space, looking this way and that. Then all became clear. From behind one of the big oaks Roman stepped and called to her something they could not hear. From behind another oak where he had hidden to make their game, Floyd stepped. She ran to Roman, who squatted so that she might hug him; and then she ran to Floyd, who caught her and lifted her high in the air, the starched pinafore she wore over a wool dress billowing about her as she shrieked her pleasure.

Leon flung open the window and called, "Bring her here to me!"

Floyd nodded his head to show he had heard, still lifting and lowering and swinging the child through the air to her delight, as he brought her to the window. Floyd pretended to throw her through the window, although his hands did not let her go until he felt her taken by Leon's hands. All laughed together except Roman, who had not come up, but stood in the distance smiling in a formal way. Noticing him, Sarah called, "Roman! You've only a thin shirt on your shoulders—you mustn't take a chill!"

This released him, and he turned to go. Floyd elaborately pantomimed a farewell to the child as he said, "Bye, Bye! Goodbye, Rachel! Bye!" Then he turned and went off after Roman.

"Who do you love? Who does Rachel love?" Leon demanded of the child with mock ferocity.

"Papa!" she cried and put her arms about his neck.

Sarah watched as Floyd overtook Roman, shoved him in a friendly way and then walked along beside him. After a moment's conversation, he put an arm casually around the boy's shoulders.

Sixteen

There was no frost that morning, but it was chill enough for Leon to go to a window when he got out of bed, to see if there was. He remembered doing so as a boy, sometimes discovering frost on the empty fields like a benediction of snow—or the way he imagined snow, for he had never seen it. He dressed quickly and left Sarah still sleeping when he tiptoed out of their room. The remembrance of boyhood sent him from the house directly, to see if Floyd was up. It was a fine day, so bright and clear, Leon felt, that had it been a jot more so, it would have broken like a piece of too-perfect glass.

As he came into Ezra's back yard, the cabin door opened and Floyd came out, seeing Leon with no surprise. It had happened often since Floyd's return. Each went his own way, but they would meet just as one thought of the other and considered going to find him, as though their thoughts, like magnets, compelled them to meet.

"Morning."

"Morning."

"Thought there might be frost," Leon said.

"I just came out to look."

The kitchen door opened again, and Lovey shook a dishcloth in the air.

"Morning, Lovey," Leon called.

"Morning, boy." Her face softened as she looked at him. To her he would always be a boy, the one she had defended from old Deborah's cold discipline. "Come on in. Coffee's boiling."

"Thought we'd go check on the lines I set last night," Floyd said.

"You got time. That's all you have got. Come on."

Half an hour later they went to the woods, after she had filled them up with batter cakes and fresh-made cane syrup, and coffee so black and hot it might have dissolved a stone.

After checking Floyd's fishing lines and finding no catch, they sat on a log and talked, and then strolled to the higher, drier woods. Leon found chinquapins on the leafy ground and put a few into his pocket to give Rachel later.

They were together more often those days than they had been since childhood. With Bonard gone and Felix less ready to roister than he used to be, Leon had been lonely for man-company. Floyd had been homesick since leaving two years ago. Beulah Land was many things to him: father and mother, and other less tangible roots, one being the childhood he and Leon had lived together.

They walked about, sometimes with direction and object and sometimes not, to the barns, into the woods, over the empty fields, beautiful in their autumn starkness as they were beautiful in their spring awakening and summer abundance. Each of them carried a stick, a habit from boyhood, to prod a goat or cow aside, to whack a weed or dry corn stalk, or together to send the sticks sailing through the air like javelins, for no other reason than idle fancy.

The resumption of friendship had been planned by neither. Neither thought about it beyond knowing he found it good. But Roscoe Elk saw in it deliberation and dark intent, a danger to his position; and his suspicion helped to make it so. Sometimes a stranger observing two people will suppose a relationship between them that does not exist at the time, yet comes to be. Roscoe was no stranger to Leon and Floyd. He had seen their intimacy as a threat when they were boys. That intimacy had been dispelled by Clovis, who had thus put herself in the way of becoming Roscoe's wife.

He suspected that Floyd and Leon would not long be content to repeat their childhood patterns. They would need to share a larger concern, and that could only be the running of Beulah Land. His mind having worked in such manner, he decided that he would not wait for them to act. He would surprise them.

Seventeen

Sarah's favorite sweet was nut and raisin cake with hard
white icing. Sitting in their empty school with Roman beside her, she thought she could pick out the scent of hot
raisins from the other baking and roasting smells that
came across the yard from the kitchens. The children had
been dismissed only minutes ago—they had not been kept
long today—and Roman was playing his flute for their
mutual relaxation and pleasure.

It was afternoon of the day before Thanksgiving. The
aromas of roasting fowl and baking cakes and pies had
sweetened the air for the past three days. After noonday
dinner she had left Aunts Pea and Nell upstairs in the sewing room with Selma and Pauline, the four women
working together on the four sides of a quilting frame.
The many-colored quilt was three-quarters done. They
had worked at it all yesterday and were determined to finish it before nightfall. It was to be a surprise gift for Myrtis to thank her for the extra work she was doing in
preparation for the holiday.

The women worked quietly, for they saw that Penelope
was preoccupied with the news she had received from
Savannah. Yesterday a letter had come from Clarice
saying Uncle Joshua was ill and had taken to his bed, and
that they had even had the doctor. Clarice did not, maddeningly, say what the doctor had told them, nor even
give a name to what ailed the old man. When Penelope
said she must go to him at once, they prevailed upon her
to put off the journey until the day following Thanksgiving, pointing out that Clarice had not asked her to come,
and that the very fact that no name was put to the illness
was an indication that she did not consider it serious.
When they pressed her not to go at all but wait to hear
better news from Clarice, or worse if the Lord so willed,
she declared that she would most certainly not, reminding
them sharply that Uncle Joshua had looked after her all
her life and that she would be derelict in her duty if she
did not now look after him.

Just as Roman finished a piece both he and Sarah liked,
Sharon came running from the house to announce importantly to Sarah that Mr. Rooster Davis waited upon her

and the master in the office, where he had desired to be shown. With a glance at Roman she rose, and telling Sharon to find the master, she went quickly toward the house.

A few minutes later Leon, having been summoned from a crib in one of the barns where he and Ezra and Floyd were examining a strain of corn new to them, entered the office to find Sarah and Rooster sitting silently together. Rooster looked up but made no greeting. "It's best I tell you together," he said.

Leon pulled a chair over to Rooster's and sat down. He and Sarah gave him their attention and let him say what he had to say in his own way, without endeavoring to prompt or comment with question or exclamation.

"I don't know if you know—I haven't been close with the Cokers since Trudy died last November. I never liked Orin, nor considered him a farmer. Found myself riding by even less often when Lester up and left to see what he could find for himself in Mississippi. Orin's always been sorry, good enough long as his ma and pa were alive to tell him to get up of a morning and what to do once up. But not a speck of Lester's judgment had he. Lester should have been first born so he could take over, but he wasn't and that's life. As for Prue and Hattie, I never saw how they could be Trudy's sisters, cowish old maids with clabber where their noodles ought to be. You know what that Orin has done?"

Neither Leon nor Sarah asked.

Rooster nodded affirmatively, as if he had already said what he said next. "Sold up. Sold everything that was left after the debts and a bad crop that wasn't worth taking off the ground. Sold it through our very bank, mine and yours, and that lawyer Guthrie over at Kitesville—sold it to Roscoe Elk."

Sarah and Leon stared at each other as they considered what their friend's news meant. Rooster was silent, studying it over before continuing.

"Blame myself. Should have made it my business to check on Orin. I found out only this morning and went over and charged him with it, asking why if he was up against it he hadn't come to me—or to you all, seeing as his place lay between us. Well, he laughed. —Never know who hates you, by God! —Just laughed. Said he'd heard from Lester and Lester's doing good, got him a spread over close to Jackson, Mississippi, and wrote they could all come on out if they ever felt like it and he'd help them get settled. Asked him again why he didn't come to me or you all. He said he was plain tired of having to act like a poor relation of mine, and wasn't about to come to you either with his hat in his hand to beg a favor when he could deal like a man with the nigger, so eager to deal."

"That means," Leon said slowly, "means Roscoe is going to have—"

"*Has!*" Rooster interrupted. "That's what I'm telling you—has! It's been done. Signed and paid yesterday. They're loading their wagon now and figure to set out tomorrow morning, Thanksgiving Day or no. Roads are hard as iron with the cold and no rain, so they hope to travel fast. Mr. Hooper at the bank told me he figured I knew all about it, Orin and me being brothers-in-law, and hadn't wanted to bail Orin out myself on account of the bad year I've had."

"The new Elk Place," Sarah said, pronouncing the name with controlled anger, "will be big."

"Not big like Oaks and Beulah," Rooster said.

"Sixty acres was the Andersons'. The Cokers' was bigger, say eighty-five or so. Near to a hundred and fifty."

"That nigger!" Rooster exploded.

Sarah looked at him sharply, but her voice was dry when she spoke. "Half Indian, they say—original owners of the country."

"By hell," Leon said, turning to her, glad to have a target for his frustration, "I never thought to hear you take up for Roscoe Elk!"

"I'm not taking up for him," Sarah said.

"Next year," Leon said to Rooster. "Wait till next year when we've had a good crop and prices go back to a decent level and we sell off *this* year's cotton too—then one of us or both together will offer him so much for the Anderson-Coker farms he'll have to take it. Somehow we'll get rid of him, make him pack up and move on."

Rooster blinked at Leon, looked at Sarah sorrowfully, then fixed his gaze on the floor.

"More to tell you," he mumbled in such a way they quieted themselves instantly to listen. "Ten days ago Elk came to see me on business. Haven't told you because haven't seen you." He turned his eyes to Sarah. "Except at the church, and it didn't seem to signify anyhow as regarded you. In fact, it was—I thought and Mama did too—like a godsend, this year being what it was. Roscoe Elk came to see me and talked about the no-good hands he

took over on the Anderson Farm—and we all know what
they are—and how he'd got that new place the other side
of the county he was thinking of grazing cows on. Nothing big, nothing important, to hear him tell it; made it all
seem little and spread thin. He said he'd already talked to
you, and you understood his problem and wished him
well. Said I'd know how you felt and why you'd refused
him; and so I did. It all made such sense, you see, and I
don't share your notions about not buying and selling."

"How many did you sell him?" Leon asked.

"Eight," Rooster said. "Six men, two women."

Eighteen

Leon and Sarah let Thanksgiving pass without confronting
Roscoe, each cautioning the other that they must not
speak or act in haste and heat, but talk to the man, listen
to him, and then be guided by their reasoning together. In
a less festive time their special thoughtfulness might have
been remarked by the gathered family but, excepting Penelope, each of them was so preoccupied with the pleasure
of the season, no question was asked of host and hostess.
All went very much as usual. Nell ate such a lot that even
she did not have to contrive a way to slip to the kitchen
later and eat more without anyone's being the wiser. Felix, revived in health and spirits by the family festivities,
managed a rendezvous with his old friend Stella, a happy
occasion made happier in the privacy of fresh hay.

The following morning Sarah and Leon drove Penelope
and the maid Ricey into Highboro where they took the
stage for Savannah, Sarah begging her aunt to return as
soon as Uncle Joshua was out of danger, to spend Christmas at Beulah Land and stay into the new year of 1838.

It had most often been Roscoe Elk who requested the
formal meetings in the office, but when he and Sarah returned from town, Leon sent word to require his attendance there. Roscoe arrived promptly, looking serious
unto solemn. Sarah was again with Leon, waiting. They'd
had no chance of a thorough discussion of the situation
and had come to no agreement on what to say to Roscoe
Elk, or even how to conduct the meeting.

Protected from surprise by his last experience in the
room, Roscoe's eyes found Sarah as soon as he entered,

and he greeted her before turning to Leon. He did not wait as he had done before to be given license to speak. "I am pleased that you initiated this meeting," he said. "Had you not done, I should have myself. I was only waiting to be certain not to disturb your celebation of the yearly giving of thanks. Although it is not generally, I believe, considered a year of special thanksgiving, yet I shall remember it as one that treated me well."

"Mr. Elk—" Leon interjected.

Roscoe held up a hand with a mild smile. Then having taken a necessary small pause, he went ahead before Leon was able to speak again. "You expressed appreciation on the occasion of our last business talk for my coming to you first to consult you on the purchase of a few slaves. You refused me, but indicated good will for my cause. I therefore went to see our neighbor, Mr. Bruce Davis, who, happily—dare I say even gratefully?—agreed to sell me a few helping hands. It was, of course, an advantage that I have come to know 'his' people almost as well over the years as I know 'yours,' and so I could name the ones I desired to buy. He did not hesitate over any man I named. It was fortunate that this happened so expeditiously for just after that I concluded—somewhat to my surprise, although I will not pretend displeasure—an arrangement whereby I added some acreage to my original property nearby."

"In fact," Leon insisted on interrupting now, "you have managed to get a sizable wedge of land between Beulah Land and Oaks!"

Roscoe spread his hands open, palms up. "I pray you look at it the other way. You and Mr. Davis surround me!" He smiled brilliantly. "We must learn to live together, it seems, which should not be difficult, since we all have known each other so very long."

"I asked you to come here," Leon said, "with the single, simple purpose of knowing how you consider yourself to relate to Beulah Land. You have been Overseer here for many years."

"A happy arrangement for us both, I hope I can say. I grieve that it must now be terminated."

"You've decided to leave us?" Leon's surprise sounded a little foolish after the other man's self-assurance.

"New circumstances indicate that it will be better for your plantation, and for my own small plot, if we sever our long and mutually beneficial business connection."

"I see," Leon said, who did not yet see. He looked to Sarah, but the look she returned gave him no hint on how to proceed. "I see," he repeated. "Your intention then is to 'tend your own garden,' as it were."

"That is felicitously expressed," Roscoe said. "Yes. I shall 'tend my own garden.' But I shall be nearby, and I hope that if ever I may be of service to you in the way of advice, that sort of thing—"

"Thank you," Leon said curtly. "I hope we shall be able to tend our own garden."

"I take relief in the fact then that I shall not be missed, and that you have no cause to regret my going."

Leon looked again at Sarah. She was no help. "Well," Leon said, and then gave an awkward laugh, "that is all we have to say to one another, I suppose."

Roscoe bowed his head as he had often before, but having done it, he did not then move to the door. He said instead, "Not quite, if you please." He turned to look directly at Sarah. "Perhaps Mrs. Kendrick has other matters to claim her? These I now must mention, if not trivial, are only tangential to the more important ones that have been settled."

"Say what you have to say," she declared, and was not sorry that her voice sounded rude, except in that it might gratify the man to know he had upset her.

Roscoe shrugged lightly; his voice was brisk as he turned to Leon. "Over the years a number of your slaves have run up debts to me. I have made them loans of money when there was something they had set their hearts upon and could not afford—a wedding dress, a burying suit, that kind of thing. All small, inconsequential. But the inconsequentialities have accumulated over the long years, and the sum owed me is—not an amount that would seem substantial to you perhaps, but to me, yes. I had not foreseen that accounts would have to be so suddenly closed. But so it is."

"How much are you owed?" Leon said. "I will pay you."

"That is gratifying to be told," Roscoe said.

"Even though," Sarah said, her voice trembling, "it was improper of you to lend money to them. You were not ever authorized to lend them money or demand interest."

"Ah!" Roscoe said, as if taken by surprise at such an attitude. "I did not know. The system began many years before the young Mrs. Kendrick's arrival at Beulah Land. It was known by the old mistress before you. No one said then or has said since that it was wrong—until now." He looked at Leon as if genuinely puzzled.

"How much is it?" Leon said.

"I have no figures with me," Roscoe said, "but I believe it is something over a thousand dollars. Of course, if it is for whatever reason or circumstance inconvenient to pay me in gold, I shall be agreeable to accepting slaves in exchange."

"I shall—try to arrange direct payment to you," Leon said.

"You will want to check my accounting. May I suggest that we set a day that is convenient for both of us and have the debtor slaves brought to our mutual presence and confirm—or deny, if they can—the sum charged against their names?"

"Yes. I agree."

Roscoe bowed and turned as if to go, then turned back. "There is one other thing," he said. "My family is complete with the exception of one—the boy Roman. I want to buy him, as I bought my wife."

"He is not for sale," Sarah said.

Roscoe appeared to ponder the reply. "It is thought to be cruel to break up families, to part a son from his mother. However, if you are determined to keep him as a pet slave, I must submit to your power to do so." For the last time he bowed slowly; for the first time he did not bother to conceal his feelings of triumph.

Nineteen

That evening after supper Leon found Floyd and the two walked away from the buildings into the wide, moonlit fields, so that they might talk in privacy. Leon told Floyd all that had happened and been revealed in the meeting with Rooster the day before Thanksgiving and the meeting with Roscoe today. Then he asked Floyd to take Roscoe's job.

Floyd said, "I will, but I won't be called 'Overseer.' Let Roscoe be the only Overseer that Beulah Land has ever had."

"I don't care what they call you or you call them, just so you take it over and stay here."

"Oh, I'll stay. I tried the leaving. I went a long way and then I turned around and came home."

"I never knew why you left. I spent a while trying to figure it out."

"Does it matter now?"

"No."

"When do you want me to start?"

"Now," Leon said.

"If I catch Roscoe giving even one more order, I'm going to kick his ass all the way over to 'the Elk Place.'"

Both men whooped and roared with laughter. They hit each other on back and shoulders; they bent double and wept and staggered about. And when they had worn out their exuberance, Leon said, "Floyd! Look at it, just look at it all around us. Far as we can see it's Beulah Land— yours and mine!"

"Yours on paper, but mine where it counts, in my bones. You don't know, you can't, no matter how I try to tell you, the way I've thought about this place. I love every goddam privy door and hound dog! When I was gone, I worked mostly as farm hand or sailor. I'd wake in the morning and tell myself: all right, there's work to do, get up and do it. But it was never mine, Leon. I never cared a damn. Not caring what you do can kill your heart. I mean it."

Leon did not understand, and Floyd saw that he did not, but such was their joy on the occasion it did not matter.

Calmer, they shared a few minutes' quiet and then began to talk in detail about the business matters of running the plantation. Shortly, they found themselves in the office with two chairs drawn up to the big desk, record and account books open. Because he could relate every name and figure and brief, inked phrase to actual things on the plantation, Floyd absorbed a great deal of information during the next few hours. When they had been there just under an hour, there was a knock at the door, and Myrtis entered carrying a tray which she set down on a side table. Leon looked at her questioningly. She gave a flustered bob of her head and said, "I didn't know how long you might be being; coffee and cake and cheese and cold biscuits."

"Thank you, Myrtis."

She bobbed a second time and went out. They turned back to the ledgers. As Floyd studied a page, frowning,

BEULAH LAND   331

Leon, who knew what was on it, said more to himself than his companion, "She never brought anything before when I was working here." Louder he said, "By God, Floyd, it's you! She's cocked her bonnet at you, and you'd better watch out. She's tired of widowing and looking for a daddy for her twins!"

"She'll keep on looking," Floyd said so mildly Leon did not press his joke.

No announcement was made to the plantation hands, but Leon and Floyd went about together the next day and the day after it, and people grew used to seeing them together. It was, in any case, only an extension of their old ways. Leon gradually gave fewer orders and directions, and Floyd gave more; together they rode a steady seesaw. Word had circulated about Roscoe's leaving and his new independence. There were some sly looks, but most of the looks were not sly nor eager nor reluctant; they merely waited for what would happen next.

A time was agreed upon for the questioning of the debtor slaves. Sarah was not present, but Roscoe found Floyd with Leon in the office. Leon and Roscoe greeted each other formally; Floyd and Roscoe stared at each other briefly without troubling to dissemble their dislike. Leon and Floyd then took their places in chairs close together. Roscoe sat in a chair which had been set close to theirs, but not as close to theirs as theirs were to each other.

Sugar had been asked to let the men into the room one at a time. All appeared apprehensive, a few frightened, some crafty and amused. The procedure was that the man came into the room, and Roscoe read from his ledger an account of the debt, date and amount, payment made if any, balance due. After he had read out his charge, Leon or Floyd put a question or more to the man, after which he was dismissed and the next man was sent in by Sugar. The full session went on nearly three hours. When the last man had been seen and no serious challenge had been made to Roscoe's accounting, Leon sat down at the desk and drafted a payment note on his bank for eleven hundred and sixty-eight dollars, payable to Roscoe Elk.

Twenty

Penelope arrived at her house on Broughton Street, having traveled without stopping since leaving Highboro. Ricey whined complaints the whole way, until Penelope was so vexed she felt like turning her out of the coach and telling her to walk.

She found Uncle Joshua very low. He had been unable to take nourishment and retain it, and for the last twenty-four hours he had refused it altogether, allowing himself to be given only a spoonful of water now and then. In addition to vomiting, he had fever; his forehead was dry and hot when she put her hand to it. Dr. Lowell Stone, whom she sent Ichabod for immediately, and who had taken it upon himself to call twice a day anyhow, knowing Joshua's importance to his mistress, told her that Joshua had not responded to any of his remedies for fever and vomiting. Only that morning he had been there and confirmed the fear he had entertained last night that the old man's affliction, whatever it was, was now compounded by pneumonia. Considering the patient's age, recovery was too much to hope.

Penelope questioned the doctor anxiously on what could be done, begging to be told something to do, but he said there was nothing she could do other than keep the patient as comfortable as possible, to watch him and to wait. She sent Clarice to bed. She had been up and down for nearly a week, on her feet more hours of the night than on her bed. Ricey, who might have been some use to her mistress, had already crept off to bed after complaining that she just knew she was coming down with something too.

Penelope left the sick man for no more than a minute or so, to step into the kitchen for water, to fetch a towel, to look over her own little stock of medicines in the vain hope of finding something she could believe might help him. She sat close beside his bed, the oil lamp turned low and set on a table the other side of the room so that it would not disturb him. He lay with eyes closed, and his breathing was labored and irregular. At one point he opened his eyes and looked at her, but she could not tell if he knew her. She hoped he did, hoped he knew she was there with him. He was wearing a flannel nightgown with long sleeves. and his arms were outside the covering of sheet and quilt.

She said softly, "It's Pea, Uncle Joshua. Do you know me?"

But he only stared at her without making any sign. She took his hand and held it in hers, praying to herself. His eyes were closed again, and he breathed more and more heavily, the sound becoming a rattling one, something like but not quite like a noisy snore. She realized gradually that it was the thing they called, horribly, "the death rattle."

She had held his hand so long, she had prayed so long, her hand and brain were numb. At some point she realized that the sound of breathing came no more. The hand she held had died. She continued to hold it for another moment or two, and then she set it down gently at his side.

She got up from her chair, looked around the window curtains and saw that it was still dark. Taking a little clock to the lamp she found that its hands read 4:27. When she set the clock down and returned to the bedside, she was startled, thinking she must have been mistaken after all, for the old man's eyes were open a little, the way he had looked at her sometimes when she was a little girl and he disapproved of her words or behavior. Then she understood, and closed the eyes and held them until they remained closed, or almost.

Not wanting to wake Clarice, who needed her rest, she sat down again beside the dead man to wait for it to be day. As she remembered years and occasions long gone, tears rolled down her face, and she hugged herself in her despair and loneliness.

Uncle Joshua had not married, and as far as was known, he had no other family. At the funeral Penelope and Clarice sat in the front row of the church. They were Joshua's family in all that counted except blood.

Ricey sat back somewhere with Ichabod. Joshua would not have approved of Ichabod's giving himself the importance of sitting with the family. So that Ichabod's feelings would not be hurt, Ricey had been persuaded to sit with him.

Penelope had written to Sarah telling her what had happened. Sarah had written to her aunt, at first only about the sorrow on Broughton Street, but then to tell about Roscoe's leaving and Floyd's taking over his function. As soon as she had Penelope's report of the funeral, which had been well attended by white and black, Sarah wrote urging her aunt to join them all again at Beulah Land. After she had signed the letter she added a note saying: *I have long hoped that you would one day choose to make your home with us at Beulah Land, and Leon wants you too. Won't you think of it now?*

Penelope thought about it, but as each day broke and ran its course and became yesterday, she lingered, unable to make up her mind to go or to stay. She had never within her true memory been without Uncle Joshua. It was not what he had done or said that had counted so heavily; it was not even love in the usual sense. It was rather that Uncle Joshua had been an indefinable force in her life, her life's witness. She had forever measured herself and her behavior against what he wanted her to be and do. Even when he hadn't told her, she had known. Without him she was unanchored and adrift. Had he died before her return, she would have blamed herself, but she might still feel his presence and concern. However, she had been there; she had asked, "Do you know me?" And he had not answered her even with a look. His look did not deny her; it did not acknowledge her. For the first time in her life she had seen him concerned not with her but with himself. His intensity was that of a man who must concentrate body and soul on the problem of dying. Ignoring her was only a very incidental part of it.

How could she go to Beulah Land? She could not leave Clarice and Ichabod to tend the house and garden. Who would tell them what to do? They had shared her dependence on Joshua. Then was she never to leave for more than an hour or two; was she, in effect, to seal herself into this house and garden on Broughton Street? Until she decided, there she would abide.

Twenty-One

Peace abided, for once, at Beulah Land. Sarah and Edna spent a mild day together at the cemetery working around their graves. And when the first genuine freeze, one that promised to last several days, came more or less on schedule toward the end of the first week of December, as it

did almost every year, they had their first hog-killing at
Beulah Land and at Oaks and at smaller farms there-
about. Every man and woman lent a hand in that, and
gladly, for the fleshly rewards and the ritual satisfaction
they took in the regular recurrence of the event.

That accomplished, Floyd set some to mending farm
tools, others to repairing ladders and doors and roofs and
rotting floors in cabins and barns that had been let go in
the busier season, or given at most a lick and a promise.
The women made soap and candles, darned old clothes
and quilts and made new ones, ripped open and restuffed
mattresses and pillows with fragrant, fresh corn shucks.

The old ones sat before fires on the low-slung hide seats
of creaking chairs that had settled exactly to their bodies'
requirements and dimensions. The children, including
Rachel and Doreen and Annabel, attended school. Roman
was a man of importance again, his pupils repeating his
words and Sarah's to their parents until they too learned
the lessons. Adam and James had their tutor, Mr. Driscoll
Proctor, and were lofty in the company of their sisters
and Rachel.

Peace abided at Oaks and Beulah Land, but peace did
not abide at the Elk place. Roscoe had taken solid satisfaction in the ownership of new slaves and land. He had set
the grazing farm to rights with his whole team of mules
and workers in four days, and then left Turnip alone there
to tend the barn and a few head of cattle. In the spring,
Roscoe would add more cattle.

Roscoe had made the home farm, the hundred and fifty
acres combined, seem more his by shifting fences and tearing down old ones. He considered plans for winter plowing and speculated on what crops to set in which fields.
His sons, Alonzo and Roscoe Junior, began to help him at
his commanding them. They were lazy boys, but they
knew how to move when their father spoke, and Junior
had inherited something of his father's sharpness of mind.
Clovis trained her new house woman to do things her
way, and she ordered new furnishings where they were
needed.

All these activities gave satisfaction to Roscoe, but as
December wore on, he became aware of an underlying
dissatisfaction. He thought about it and decided that, although he could take pride in himself and his manipula-
tion of events and his old employers, what he had done
had also left them too much and too happy. It was not

enough to make his independence, as he had, at their expense. He must punish them; he would make them unhappy if he could. A bold idea came to him one day with
the force of a sudden clap of thunder.

Twenty-Two

First one and then another, depending on the lightness or
heaviness of the sleeper, woke in the night to a ringing of
bells such as might summon the dead to rise on Resurrection Day. Fumbling, stumbling out of beds and going to
windows and doors, they asked one another the meaning
of the sounds. It was the night before Christmas Eve, and
so first natural thoughts had to do with that celebration.

At their bedroom window Leon looked out. Coming to
stand behind him, Sarah said, "What can it be?"

Leon rapidly donned trousers over his nightshirt, put on
boots without stockings, and snatched a greatcoat from
the wardrobe, arms blindly finding sleeve openings as he
ran into the upper hallway. Sarah flung a robe about her
and followed him into the hall, as Juanita poked her head
anxiously around the opened door of Rachel's room. At
the front end of the hall, walk-through shutters led to a
balcony that afforded a more general view than did the
bedroom windows.

"Look!" Sarah said, but Leon's eyes had already found
the far glow of light. Something in Highboro was burning,
and from the importance given it by the ringing of the
town's church bells, it was something considerable. Fear
sent him back into the hall and down the stairs, racing
through the dark lower floor of the house and out to the
stables.

There he found Floyd, hastily half-dressed as he was,
Plumboy with him. They were saddling two horses, who
stood quivering with nervous excitement until Leon and
Floyd mounted and swung them out of the stable yard,
around the house and into the orchard drive.

From the second-floor balcony Sarah watched them ride
by below her; and as the sound of the horses' hoofs grew
fainter on the hard clay road, she again heard the bells
and turned her face to the glow of light off yonder in the
night. A shutter banged behind her, and Rachel pulled at
her robe sash. "Mama!"

Juanita arrived as Sarah picked the little girl up and held her close, cheek pressed to cheek, as they listened together to the urgent calling of the bells.

"Is it Christmas?" the child asked.

"No, my darling."

Leon and Floyd went at a fast canter through the orchard. The moon had set, but their eyes were quick to adapt to the dark. They saw well enough, and what they could not see, they left to the intuition of the horses. Hitting the main road they broke into a gallop, straining their bodies as they urged the horses to full effort, not knowing why, or if there was any true reason, but all their senses and sinews alerted to the possibility of doom.

Twenty-Three

Having set down on paper "Dear Aunt Pea," Sarah wrote:

It is after midnight of the night after Christmas, the 26th of December, or I should say 27th, shouldn't I? I am alone in the office which you know so well. The others of the household have gone to their rooms, if not to sleep. I hope my dear Leon is asleep at last, for he has not closed his eyes to rest for fully three days and nights.

It is difficult to begin; so much to tell. On the eve of Christmas Eve, early morning of the 24th we discovered when we took a moment to look at a clock, we were all wakened by a great ringing of bells in the direction of Highboro. Leon and Floyd rode immediately to see what was the matter, and the matter, dear Aunt, was great. Our warehouse was afire and subsequently burned to the ground with God only knows how many bales of cotton, our own and those we had undertaken to hold for others. Lost, all lost.

The gin would have gone too except for a favorable wind and the efforts of every man in Highboro. All gave their strength to contain and subdue the blaze.

One man has died: Rex, the one we had set as watchman over the warehouse: he died of burns the following day, in spite of the little-all that could be done. There was not enough soda in all Highboro to cool his poor flesh. Fortunately for him, and may God forgive him for I cannot, he suffered little, they say, for he was already nigh dead of drunkenness. We did not know his weakness, if he had it; it may indeed have been induced that night for a purpose, the very one of having him out of the way for the burning of the warehouse! Oh, it might have been a friend who stopped with him and made him drunk in mistaken celebration of the holy season, and is now afraid to step forward and speak. But it may likelier have been a necessary part, and hence murder, of a plot against us.

Rumors have circulated morbidly. My own first thought, and Leon's, was that Roscoe Elk was behind it, seeking to wreak some revenge upon us. But why? I have already written you what happened between him and us. God knows he has had the best of it and can have no reason to hate us. But when such calamity occurs, our minds search blindly, and hate need have no reason. It cannot have been he, we tell ourselves and each other a thousand times over, for he had nothing to gain.

This is not even the worst. Snatched from sleep in the middle of the night, Uncle Felix rushed to the scene, was one of the first there, directing the attempt to halt the fire. In the midst of pleading for haste he fell to the ground, having had, as we learned subsequently, a stroke of paralysis. He is alive, but he cannot speak, although his lips and eyes move. (Is this a good sign? No one appears to know.) His left side shows no life.

Aunt Nell, who might be thought too frail to bear such a blow, has responded splendidly. She has left his bedside since the tragedy only to take an hour's rest or a little nourishment. She is sensible and not at all hysterical, in a way I confess I envy as well as admire at this juncture, for they, Uncle Felix and Aunt Nell, share our great loss and face possible ruin as we do.

There is insurance on the building but not its contents, and of course the building was worth comparatively little, and the contents considerable. Because of the poor prices this year we have taken cotton to hold for others until prices improve, standing good for supplies the owners need to see them through the winter, acting as their agents.

As I write to you, we are trying to find our way out of this chaos. Leon has rightly committed us to stand good for all that has been lost. In time we may possibly dig our way out, but it will be hard and take long, and the future is a riddle. The immediate problem is ready cash. The very presence of money is a promise, I have learned, as its absence is a threat.

We have committed everything and try now to be calm, but in the prevailing hysteria we are required to show gold. Our mere promise to pay is no longer good.

Edna and Bruce are wonderful. They have gone around pledging themselves as far as they dared to back our promises Because Uncle Felix has been unable even to write his name, Aunt Nell has signed papers that may take the very clothes off their backs if all is indeed lost.

Christmas Day, I will not speak of, other than to say I am glad, dear Aunt, you were spared it. I hope never to see another such. All sat about, either speaking not at all, or all at once. Rachel, who cannot of course understand, would not, still will not play with her new toys. In time she is sure to love the doll you left for her—so prettily dressed, and I showed her how each garment comes off and goes back on—but now she will not look at anything. Dear Roman is the most successful in distracting her. She will walk out with him into the grounds. He tells her stories, and she adds little things to them as he tells them, so it is like a game, you see.

May God bless you and look upon us all with kinder favor in the New Year. Sarah.

One more thing, too awful to tell, yet it belongs to this account. With our anxieties exhausted, we had given no thought to reassuring our own people. It seems that many rumors, all false and spread, I now contend, by a malicious mind—you will know who I mean—have been circulated. One held that Beulah Land would be put for auction-sale and with it the people. A man called Bird, from his nature of hopping about excitedly like a bird in a cage, was teased and told that he would be sold for certain. He was put in such terror that he took a hatchet and chopped off his left hand to make certain none would want to buy him.

Twenty-Four

Within an hour of reading the letter Penelope sat in the private office of the president of her bank, Mr. Ellison Watts, and told him that she wanted him to be ready to convert all assets of her estate into the promise of cash payment.

A man who had trained himself to show nothing but a stoical face no matter what surprising demand or whimsical request was made of him by a client, Mr. Watts nevertheless dropped, if only briefly, in his chair. When he found breath, he asked, "Why?"

Penelope told him, or tried to, and failing to make it clear, simply handed him the letter she had received from her niece. Mr. Watts grasped the situation quickly and entirely then; it was only spoken words that confused his mind; anything written he could fathom. "I see," he said. "I see. I see." And when she put a question or two to him, she saw that he did see.

He wrote a letter on the spot and sent it by stage within the next hour to Leon's bank in Highboro, explaining his own relation to his client, and hers to theirs, and committing his client to stand behind as many promissory understandings as her resources warranted. Having done that, he then scolded her, but in much the same way Judge Truebody had done when he was alive and managed her affairs. Mr. Watts knew Sarah Kendrick, had known her since she was born. He had also dealt with Leon Kendrick and his father before him, and he understood something of what Beulah Land meant to all of them.

The next day found Penelope still active. She signed papers to make all her property negotiable, including the house on Broughton Street. She talked to Clarice and Ricey, and to Ichabod separately, saying that she might soon be leaving Savannah forever, and that if she did, would they choose to stay or go with her? Ichabod elected to stay, and so without a qualm she added him to her list of salable assets held by Mr. Watts. Ricey hemmed and hawed about country living and giving up the city until Clarice slapped her and told Penelope they would remain with her, whatever her future abode, or fortune.

PART FIVE

1845

One

Nell frowned at her image and Bianca's in the mirror that Bianca had set at an angle to best catch the light of the lamp she used to heat her curling irons. Having sat quietly watching Bianca burn curls into her hair, then lift and touch and fluff with light fingers and comb, Nell sighed and said, "That will be enough, Bianca. Who looks at an old woman at a ball?"

Bianca stepped back, staring at Nell's head as self-critically as a painter might examine a work in progress on his easel. She made no remark to comfort or flatter, but when Nell saw her nod her head once, she was satisfied that she would do. She stood, and Bianca shifted the lamp and adjusted the tilt of the mirror so that Nell could best see the whole effect she made. The dark green silk dress she wore was long-sleeved and high-necked, with creamy lace overlay at the cuffs and extending from neckband to bosom, ending there in gentle scallops with just enough space at the cleft for a favorite cameo brooch.

Nell smoothed the wrinkles at the waist, adjusted her lace cuffs, and slipped a jade ring onto the long finger of her left hand, observing it briefly beside her gold wedding band before turning this way and that at the mirror, and then proceeding to the door. "No need for you to stay up after you turn down my bed. I'll manage alone." Bianca nodded, cleaning the curling irons with a rag.

Nell knocked at the door that led from her room to that of her husband. They had found separate rooms more comfortable and convenient since coming to live at Beulah Land two months after Felix was stricken with partial paralysis. Presently, the door was opened by Stella, who took care of Felix. She bobbed a curtsy as Nell swept into the room, putting on a bright smile for the man who lay propped on pillows, looking more indolent and pampered than invalid. The lamp on the table beside his bed was turned high for reading. Nell noted that it was smoking.

"The wick wants trimming, Stella," she observed.

"Never mind, my dear," Felix said, dropping the book he'd been reading face-flat on the bed so that his place was kept, and holding out his good right hand. She took it in both of hers. "You look very fine!" Felix declared admiringly.

She squeezed his hand and smiled. "You are certain I shan't disgrace you?"

He laughed and withdrew his hand. " 'Rich, not gaudy,' " he quoted. "You will be the handsomest lady downstairs."

Nell smiled to thank him and patted his cheek. There was a quick knock outside the open door that led to the hall, and Leon entered a step behind Sarah, who went directly to the bed and kissed her uncle on the forehead.

"Oh, my, my!" Felix exclaimed. "I may get up and walk—you are that miraculous a sight!"

She laughed and kissed him again. Sarah wore a pink and gold brocade gown. Her figure had grown fuller without any hint of heaviness or coarseness; she had merely ripened. Her step, her look, the slightest gesture of hand spoke assurance and ease; there would be no doubting who was hostess and mistress of Beulah Land when she went downstairs.

"Where is Rachel?" Felix asked. "She popped in before she dressed but hasn't since."

"Downstairs," Leon said. "I heard her when I was dressing, chattering to the musicians as they got themselves in tune and acting hostess for her mother."

"What do you have?" Felix asked.

Leon said, "Two fiddlers, the piano, and a clarinet. Mr. Proctor is a clarinetist, you know."

"Oh, the Davis tutor; I had forgot. I never see the man."

"And Roman will play his flute," Sarah said, "where it seems appropriate and he can follow."

"It promises to be a splendid evening altogether," Felix said. "I shall have the best of it. I shall hear your pleasure but not be obliged to think of witty things to say to the ladies."

Sarah said, "Should the noise bother you—"

Felix said, "It won't, I assure you. I have that kind of ear which hears only what and when it pleases."

"But if it should—"

"I shall close my door in any case to discourage visitors," he promised. "I shan't be bothered if your ball turns into a veritable Bacchanalia with a parade of elephants and a bevy of dancing girls from Egypt."

"Do you have laudanum?" Nell asked Stella. "In the event Mr. Kendrick *is* wakeful?"

"Yes, and something better too," Felix said cheerily. His good hand found a bottle of brandy on the floor beside his bed and raised it in the air. The visitors laughed.

Leon said, "I believe I hear a carriage," and went to the window. "Yes."

"Edna said they would be first." Sarah kissed Felix quickly and went out. Leon beamed a smile at his uncle and followed her. Together they went downstairs.

Nell said, "Shall I bring up a plate when supper is set out?"

"Please not, my dear," Felix said. "I shall be long asleep."

She nodded and fussed a little with the top sheet and counterpane which had slipped off his chest. "Well then," she said. "Good night, my love." She pressed dry lips lightly to his forehead.

"Enjoy yourself," he said.

"I go only from a sense of duty," she allowed.

"You are very good," he said seriously and raised her hand and kissed it.

Gratified, she went. In the hall she met Penelope, who had just come out of her room. Penelope wore a simple gray woolen dress she had brought with her when she came to live seven years ago. Seeing Nell, she caught her breath. "That dress surely cost three bales of cotton," she declared.

Sweeping past her to the stairway, Nell said, "Only two, I believe."

"Uncle Joshua said a lady does nothing to draw attention to her person."

As she started down the stairs, Nell said, *"Honi soit qui mal y pense."*

Penelope followed so closely that Nell grasped a banister, as if fearful of being pushed or tripped.

"Vanity, vanity," Penelope whispered as the two olding women came to the foot of the stairs and heard the voices of guests being welcomed in the broad center hall, which would be the main place for dancing. They put on sweet old-lady smiles and went forward.

In his room upstairs Felix had eased his head to the

high pillow tops when his visitors left. He raised it and
spoke to Stella, who waited in the warm shadows beside
the fireplace which all day had burned with a small fire,
for it was still January. "Shut the door," he said. She
moved quickly and did so. "Secure the bolt."

When she had done that, she turned to face him and
leaned her back against the closed door, smiling at the
man. He picked up the book he had put down on the bed,
bent the bottom corner of a page and closed it. Stella
came to the bed and took the book he held out and set it
aside.

He said, "Pour us a glass, girl."

She found glass and brandy and poured. He took the
glass from her, nodded to her as if making a silent toast,
and drank from it. She took the glass from him when he
held it for her, and drank too. She offered it to him again,
but he shook his head with a smile. She set the glass on
the table and then sat herself down on the side of the bed.

"The other door," he murmured.

She rose and slid the bolt softly on the door that led to
Nell's room. As she came back to him, she pulled her
dress over her head and dropped it to the floor beside the
bed. She sat down again, untying the drawstring at the top
of her petticoat. She leaned closer for his convenience,
and his hand slipped into the bodice of her petticoat and
found a breast.

"Stella," he said softly.

She smiled, and her hand reached deep under the bed
covering, then under his nightshirt, and moved along his
leg to his crotch. When she found his old dick and held it,
it livened up. Taking one of her breasts, he got a gentle
grip on its nipple with his teeth, and tickled it caressingly
with his tongue. She held his dick more firmly as it
hardened.

The sound of music began downstairs.

Two

For Floyd there was no separation of work and non-work;
all he did was his life. After he had supper with Lovey
and Roman and Clarice in the servants' dining room off
the kitchen of the main house, the room that had for a
time been Roman's own room, he went out to make the

round of the barns, not to check on anybody's work, for that was seldon necessary now, but simply because he liked looking at the animals in their stalls and pens nighting down. He slapped a flank here, a rump there as he walked through the cow barn.

Lovey went to her old cabin which she shared with Clarice and Ricey, to freshen herself and to put on a black dress with white collar and cuffs before returning to the big house to direct the servants' work during the hours of the ball. As they shared living quarters, Lovey and Clarice also shared the supervision of work in the big house, it being understand that Lovey was the real mistress, after the mistress, and that Clarice was second to her in both the big house and the little cabin. Lovey was a stern woman but not a jealous one. She had welcomed Clarice to the plantation and to a share in her authority, and she spoke her praise generously. There was not one female worker in house or field who did not understand that the two women stood together even as they lived together. There was no getting to or around one of them by way of the other.

Ricey, who had been reluctant to leave Savannah and come to Beulah Land, lived with her mother and Lovey in a state of near hysteria, swearing that she would run away or kill herself unless she were criticized, supervised. and advised less severely. Clarice told her that she might not be happy but that she would, by God, be good. Lovey wished the girl would marry and remove herself from the cabin. She was tired of the young and their problems, most of which had to do with self-concern. So far, however, Ricey, had been too lofty to settle on any of the plantation men who fancied her, and her mother feared that she would stay an old maid.

Roman, after his supper, went to the cabin he shared with Floyd to dress himself appropriately before joining the other musicians in the hall. Floyd lingered for a while in the stabling barn talking to Plumboy, who would have a long night's work supervising the care of the horses and carriages of the guests at the ball, although the critical times were naturally those of arrivals and departures which tended to bunch up together. Plumboy had married Myrtis four years ago in the dining room of the main house, and Otis was now one of his helpers, as Lotus was one of her mother's, along with Sallou and Sharon who still worked in the kitchens and dining room, and were married and had small children of their own.

Sugar walked the first team and carriage around the house. It was a large, closed family coach and had brought the Davises from Oaks—Edna and Bruce, Adam, Annabel, Doreen, and James—to the front door, where Otis now waited to take the next carriage to arrive. As Plumboy and Sugar worked quickly together to settle the Davis horses and carriage, Floyd wandered away. Between them, Plumboy and Sugar had a vast knowledge of the carriage horses of the gentry of the county. For no reason they understood, some horses did not like others, and it was prudent to settle them separately. A horse might rear and flash his eyes and shake his head in the air beside one beast. only to be quiet as a lamb beside another.

Floyd's house was that in which Roscoe Elk had lived with his family, and Roman had taken perverse pleasure in moving back into it when Floyd invited him to. Although Floyd had thought of it himself, it was Sarah who was behind the immediate suggestion and arrangement, for she had seen something inappropriate in Roman's living in the kitchen wing when he became a man and was the acknowledged schoolmaster of Beulah Land.

On his way home, Floyd went a little out of his way, as he so often did, to visit his father's grave. Ezra had died less than a year after Floyd's return, and in spite of his age, both Lovey and Floyd had grieved bitterly. When Leon suggested that he be buried on Beulah Land instead of in the nearby country cemetery where the plantation Negroes were usually buried when they died, Lovey agreed eagerly.

Ezra's was the only grave on Beulah Land. It was near a big oak tree that shaded the washwomen's working area; it was covered with a marble slab and boasted both headstone and footstone, so that it was something like a bed in contour. The carved words on it read: EZRA KENDRICK 1760-1839. WIFE LAVERNE. CHILDREN—FLOYD AND PAULINE. EVER LOVED.

There was no railing around the grave, and it became a sort of focus or meeting place because everyone knew just where it was, like a well in the country or a courthouse in a town. Children played around it; lovers met there before going off into the night to their secret places. Floyd and Leon frequently sat on the grave, smoking pipes or not, talking of any and every thing, large and small. It was more than a year after Ezra died that Leon and Floyd together had bought the marble slab and head- and foot-stones, for the first two years after the fire had been hard ones, in spite of Penelope's generosity, years when every penny was needed to pay off debts.

Tonight Floyd did not sit, for it was cool and getting cold, and he was restless. He squatted briefly, hand on the headstone, both to steady himself and to touch his father. He talked to Ezra often in his mind, not in a sentimental way, although certainly in a loving and trusting one. He would often think: Now, Papa, what do *you* think, what would *you* do? If another thought answered him, fine; if not, fine.

Death and graves were formalities that set limits, but consciousness flew everywhere. Right now he rubbed the headstone on one spot until it took a little warmth from his palm, but his thoughts asked nothing, confided nothing. He got up and went on to his house, where he found Roman in the kitchen shaving. They did not use the room as a kitchen, because both ate in the back dining room of the big house; so their kitchen had become a washing-dressing room.

"Evening, Dude," Floyd said, coming in and banging the back door.

"Mm." Roman held his mouth in a grimace like a silent cry as he shaved his chin and, last thing, his upper lip. Then he rinsed his face in a bowl of fresh water and dried it.

"You and Mr. Proctor got a duet planned for tonight?" Floyd asked, his voice innocent.

Roman whipped the towel he had just used at Floyd, catching him on the forearm. "Ow! That stings."

Roman laughed and rolled his sleeves down, fitting silver links into the cuffs. They had been a gift from Sarah on his twenty-first birthday, along with his official papers of freedom. "You having a little ball of your own?" Roman said.

Floyd smiled. "Thought of it. There's a girl got me on her mind."

"Is she on yours?"

"You know better. Not on my mind's mind. Just on my dick's mind."

"Make her happy and pleasure yourself," Roman said, fitting a tie under his collar and tying a bow.

"Meow when you come in," Floyd said. "If I don't bark back, it means I won't see you till in the morning. This girl is widowed, and she says her bed is cold."

Three

At the door Leon, after welcoming Edna and Bruce with
a handshake, turned to their children-grandchildren with a
smile that was especially gentle as it met Annabel's eyes.
Annabel was fifteen, and the year's seniority she enjoyed
over her sister Doreen showed the difference between
child and young woman. Doreen was all jutting angles;
Annabel was circles and curves. Adam, who did not much
like Leon, watched Annabel smile at the older man like a
bud becoming blossom. As James dutifully helped Doreen
out of her jacket, Adam assisted Annabel more roughly in
removing hers, both of them perfectly aware of the reason.

"How beautiful it all is!" Annabel exclaimed to repair
the awkwardness of the moment, and the whole party
turned faces to look at the way the great hall had been arranged for the evening. Flanking its long sides were chairs
of all descriptions and degrees of comfort, with scarce an
inch between them when not indeed touching. Here and
there the line of chairs was broken by stands of Boston
fern, the ferns having been washed to look fresher, and
the stands sashed in broad bands of colored silks tied with
elaborate bows. Large branches of dark-brown limbed and
dark-green leaved magnolia were set in tin tubs that had
been tinseled over and gave back the light of two hundred
candles that brightened the hall for the dancing to come.

"Yes, it's pretty!" Edna said and squeezed Sarah's hand
just as Annabel decided to clap hers together like a delighted princess. Adam scowled ironically as Leon smiled
appreciation at the girl. Turning her head and seeing what
guests had arrived, Rachel left the musicians, whose place
was at the breezeway end of the hall. The double doors to
the open-sided passage leading to the kitchen wing had
been closed for the evening until fresh air was needed.
With the spontaneity permitted pre-adolescent girls,
Rachel ran to the party to give them her own welcome. As
she ran, the musicians began to play *Drink to Me Only
With Thine Eyes*. Bruce offered his arm to Sarah, and
they promenaded down the hall toward the musicians'
stand, followed by Leon who had given one arm to Edna

and the other to Annabel, who had only just put her tongue back into her mouth after sticking it out at Adam. Taking Leon's arm, she smiled as though she had never known cruder company than that of angels. James and Doreen brought up the rear in a willing but sloppy way, James squirming in the tight collar he hated, and Doreen scratching her behind that suddenly itched. She had fought against woolen drawers, begging to be allowed to leave them off for just that evening, but Edna had told her sharply that she'd rather see her suffer discomfort now than suffer later with a chill and fever.

Adam, no longer sardonic, waited near the door until Rachel came around the others and found him. Nell and Penelope entered then from the office and joined the little procession that proceeded to admire the orchestra. Behind them, Rachel and Adam giggled and whispered with delight and superiority.

Presently, a heavy knocking at the front door at the other end of the hall claimed attention. Sarah and Leon disengaged themselves and went quickly to welcome the new arrivals who were being let in by Lovey, just taking her station.

A hundred had been invited—more than a hundred came in carriage and coach, buggy and barouche and cabriolet, in phaeton and rockaway. It was long enough after Christmas and long enough before spring for a party to be particularly welcome. Before they arrived at Beulah Land the guests had decided they would have a good time. When that is so, there is no skill in entertaining; providing the premises is enough. But more than that was forthcoming. Although no larger than Oaks, Beulah Land ever possessed a drama and richness that Oaks did not. Beulah Land was, indeed, the plantation of the several surrounding counties. The fact that it was known to have endured and survived both scandal and hard times only added to its glamour and romantic aura. Hearing praise on all sides, Nell felt that she had been right to spend extravagantly on her dress.

As for Sarah, the pink and gold brocade hardly deserved her, so radiant was she. She not only looked beautiful, she felt beautiful. When Roman came in, she talked a little with him as he adjusted his mind to the music the other musicians were making and began to think of his flute in relation to them. Having seen him settled, she moved here, there, and yonder with laughter and good humor, and a special sympathetic welcome for the old who, no matter their everyday complaints, had willed themselves into a condition permitting attendance at the ball. If they dropped dead chewing a bit of ham or sipping a glass of wine, why that was still better than farting into a slop jar at home and feeling lonely and left out.

Selma judged her descent to the party precisely. The hall was half filled. Dancing had begun, but only waltzing; the formal sets were not yet being called. There was a general air of coming and going, with the spectators staking jealous claims to the chairs that would afford the best views of the dancing and flirting. The ladies did much traipsing up and down the stairs in the office on the excuse of leaving wraps or repairing hair and faces. The office, as had been intended, was largely given over to the younger members of the party, those too young to participate in the formal dancing sets, but who still might ape and mock among themselves as they practiced the ways of their elders.

At fifteen Annabel was just at a time she might presume to include herself with the adult party, so long as she showed modesty and deference, which she did almost to ostentation; whereas Adam, although sixteen, was still considered a boy and expected to enjoy the company of the younger group in the office. This he was perfectly happy to do, for there he could claim Rachel.

Roman had not been wrong that day of the children's picnic in the grove. Adam had started to love Rachel then, and his love had been steady. For Rachel, Leon had been, was still, the romantic father. Roman was the trusted brother. Even as a child she understood that, although they loved her, she was not the center and mainstay of their lives. But when she was with Adam, she had the exhilarating sense of being exactly the peak of his consciousness. The fact that he was so much older than she—so it seemed to her then—did not matter. Her assurance of his feeling made her proud of herself and a little arrogant with life.

Without anyone's having noticed her descent, such was the traffic on the stairs, Selma was there, sitting in the office by the desk, part of the children's party, in a black gown to be sure, but wearing a double-looped necklace of amethysts that kept her from looking mournful, and a wreath of cloth violets as a crown for her hair. Presently, without anyone's having seen it happen, Pauline was seated beside Selma as if attending her—and no one questioned attendance, even though the Negro woman was not dressed as a servant and did not behave as a servant would have. She sat quietly beside Selma, hands in lap. She answered agreeably those who spoke to her, and kept her peace when she was let alone. She was accepted as a member of the party without anyone's deciding what her place or function of the evening was. Because of her eccentricity, Selma was considered by outsiders to be something like a child, and a Negro woman's presence anywhere was acceptable where there was a child to be seen to. As the evening progressed and the occasional gentleman approached Selma to ask her hand in the dancing, she explained that she was in mourning. For the most part she and her companion kept solemn faces, but now and then, inexplicably to those who observed them, they would burst into a fit of giggling and put their heads together and whisper.

Mr. Driscoll Proctor had not come in the Davis family coach. He had known it would be crowded, but that had not been his reason. He might need the horse the family had made his to ride, if he decided to stop over longer than they did. Proctor had been at Oaks seven years. He had done his best to teach Adam and James as much as they would take from him, and Adam took quite a lot. He had his Uncle Bonard's liveliness of mind. Come autumn, he would go off to attend the University of Virginia; it had been so arranged. Adam was thrilled at the prospect of seeing the larger world, at the same time he thought that the university, in Charlottesville, was a fearful distance from those he loved at Oaks and Beulah Land.

The tutor saw Adam's leaving as a signal for him to leave also, or to think about it; for James was like his father Bruce: his mind and heart were on the land, and the very opening of a book numbed some part of that mind and heart. He was not stupid, no more than Bruce had been. Seeing what the boy was like, Bruce scolded him for his indifference to book learning, at the same time rejoicing in his heart that the boy was truly his son, and would surely be, though the younger son, his successor even as he had been his father Benjamin's.

The tutor had also given certain lessons to the young females, but when fortunes improved, they were sent into Highboro each day to make the acquaintance of other young ladies at the day school Selma had once attended,

and to have lessons with the town's dancing master, Mr.
Midas Mott, who also gave instruction in elocution.

And so, although no one had hinted that he do so,
Driscoll Proctor had turned his mind toward leaving
Oaks. He had engaged to escort Adam to the university
and see him settled there. After that he was free to go on,
on his own, or to return to Oaks. He thought he should
go on. He had acquaintances in several states along the
Eastern coast and had in the adult part of his forty years
been employed as far north as Camden, New Jersey, and
as far south as he now found himself. His deliberate manner—the ladies said "heavy" with a private, condescending
smile—camouflaged an active mind. New books and peri-
odicals arrived for him in nearly every post. His corre-
spondence was large. He knew what was going on in the
world and guessed something of what might come. He
had friends as far north as Boston.

The uncertain factor in Driscoll Proctor's life at this
time was what to do about Roman. When he'd first come
to Oaks, he had heard about the boy, half white, half Negro, who was a sort of schoolmaster at nearby Beulah
Land, and out of curiosity he had made his acquaintance.
And indeed, their early talking had been altogether about
teaching. The mutuality of their calling, on however different levels, prevented any suspicion of unseemliness at-
taching to their further acquaintance. Roman was eager to
listen to and learn from the older man; and presently
Driscoll Proctor knew that he had come to love the young
man.

The discovery was both joyful and frightening. He had
long been aware of his reaction to young men in general.
Indeed, it was, apart from the need to earn a living and
the fact that he knew himself more inclined to scholarly
work than manual, the thing that had turned him to tutoring. Yet until he knew Roman, he had not touched another male with an expression of love. He loved Roman,
and certainly Roman loved him, in however complex a
way, having to do with admiration and gratitude and son-
fathering, no doubt, but love all the same. The question
was: If Proctor left, would Roman go with him; would he
be willing to leave what had been his only home? Proctor
did not know. But he did know that if they left together,
their destination would have to be somewhere north.

For many years Proctor had felt slavery to be wrong.
The major reason for working his way farther and farther

south as he had done was to observe the institution. In doing so he had developed a love for the South at the same time his convictions were strengthened against slavery. He kept his convictions to himself; he knew himself no crusader. Most Negroes, he believed, were not ready for freedom, but they would never be unless their masters trained them for it, and that would not happen. Teaching them even to read and write was breaking the law in most Southern states, although a family as powerful as the Kendricks might ignore the law as they pleased. He thought of these things and of Roman as he rode to the ball.

Arriving at Beulah Land, he trotted his horse around the house to the stables and left him with Plumboy, taking his clarinet case with him. He approached the house from the back, not as a servant, simply because he came from the stables and followed the sound of music. Going along the breezeway he opened one of the double doors to the hall and found himself in the middle of the orchestra. The formal sets of dancing had not yet begun. Proctor caught Roman's eye, and they exchanged greeting smiles, as Roman continued to improvise a note or a phrase for the casual dancing music the others played.

Roman nodded toward the chair he had set out for his friend, and Proctor sat down on it, edging it about until he felt himself part of the ensemble. Then he opened his case, took out the clarinet, fingered it without putting it to his lips in order to test the response of his fingers that had so recently held cold leather reins. Then putting the mouthpiece to his lips, he picked up the tune with the others.

Elizabeth-Ann Clay, who as Elizabeth-Ann Malone had once been Selma's schoolmate and secret love, arrived just then with her husband Sefton, their daughters, Ann-Elizabeth and Margaret-Ella, and a man named Casey Troy. Casey Troy had come to Highboro two months ago with letters of reference and settled himself comfortably in the small hotel, where he had not long to wait for commissions to paint portraits of the local gentry. One of his warmest letters of introduction was to the Clays, from an old Savannah business acquaintance of Sefton Clay's, and he had since his arrival painted a group portrait of the family that had been so enthusiastically received that he had then been given the commission to paint separate portraits of the Misses Clay, and one of Mrs. Clay, Sefton suggesting that the portrait of his wife contain also the family pets, the ginger cat named Amos and the springer spaniel named Rufus. Mr. Troy obliged.

His fame spread locally, as he was accustomed to its doing when he came to a new place. He had three definite commissions for portraits and a dozen eager waverers. Casey Troy enjoyed the life he had made for himself, from no deliberate plan, but from a talent and skill triggered by his need to earn a living and a desire to earn it in the most agreeable way open to him. He was intelligent without being weighty, lively without appearing silly. He had manners and taste, and he paid his way in society with both his talent and his agreeable nature. He enjoyed the company of gentlemen and was discreet in the pleasure he took in the company of ladies. Also, he genuinely liked the work he did. He was not a cynical hack with his brush. He took pride and care in getting a true likeness of a subject, and he was happily able to do it without flattering or offending.

What most often pleased his commissioners was the detail he used in the portraits. He had great skill in rendering clothes and hair and shoes and jewels. One of his happiest knacks was that of being able to see and to set onto canvas with paint the personality of pets. Having caught the dignity and mystery of Amos and the keen affability of Rufus, and by doing so pleasing the husband who would pay for the portraits, he could risk Mrs. Clay's wondering if her mouth was quite that straight in repose and if her eyes were really so small. How was she to complain of such matters when Mr. Clay was laughing delightedly and telling Casey Troy that he had surely caught that devil Rufus to the life!

And so now, as the early music played and the late guests arrived, Casey Troy came in with the Clay family, and Sarah and Leon went to the door to greet them, as Lovey accepted coats and capes and gave them over to other servants to put away. As he was introduced to his host and hostess, Casey automatically made a quick study of their faces, as if he were to paint them—as he firmly intended to do once they thought the idea was their own. Knowing well that the first and most necessary target of approval was the man who would pay him, he was careful to make himself agreeable to Leon. Since he liked and enjoyed men, this part of his work was easy enough, and he and Leon had talked for less than five minutes when Leon told himself that he must see the portraits he had only heard about that had been done of the Clays, and if they bore out his favorable opinion of the good sense of the painter, to ask Mr.

Troy to consider his family as future subjects. Troy knew
from experience the very moment his host made that decision, and turned his attention to his hostess. When he did,
he saw that she had caught his train of thought even as he
had caught Leon's. She smiled at him, not as though she had
found him out, but rather as if her perception was the beginning of friendship. He smiled back at her, at first to hide
a stir of embarrassment, and then because he saw how
lovely she was. This was no common rich farmer's wife.

The musicians finished their tune, and Mr. Midas Mott,
the dancing master, clapped his hands and announced in
his best elocution voice that those engaged for the first
formal set must take their places. Sarah turned to Leon.
They smiled and nodded at the guests around them and
then went off, her hand on his arm, to open the ball.

Four

As Beulah Land had paid off its debts and prospered, with
the combined efforts of Sarah, Leon, and Floyd, and the
added resources of Felix and Nell and Penelope, so too
had Roscoe Elk prospered and his enterprises expanded.
The cattle farm had done well with Turnip's overseeing. It
now supported a hundred head, and used the services of
two male slaves in addition to Turnip, and one female,
Puddy, who had married Turnip because it was convenient for them to have it so, and kept the new house that
had been built around the chimney left over from the old
Ralston house.

Besides the cattle farm, which had been expanded by
further purchase, Roscoe now owned a thousand acres of
good timberland, three business-district properties in
Highboro, and the house that had been Felix and Nell's.
The last had required time and discretion to effect.

Two months after the big fire, in early March 1838,
Nell had decided to give up the house in town. As Felix
began to improve in health and spirits, it became clear
that he would never be fit enough to pursue his old life of
law and business. More and more he talked of Beulah
Land, his mind and stories going back to his boyhood
there with his brother Arnold. Leon, who had always
loved Felix, urged Nell to leave the town and come to live

at Beulah Land. There was room enough and to spare,
even after Penelope came to live; and the visiting back
and forth between town and country was impossible for
Nell and Felix and inconvenient for Sarah and Leon.

Taking only what she prized and sensibly leaving the remainder of its furnishings to be sold with the house, Nell
and Felix made the move—a happy day for both of them,
for although she had responded well to the crisis of her
husband's illness and a drastic change in their fortune,
Nell was tired. She no longer cared about having a house
of her own. Gladly, she gave up domestic management,
selling all her house slaves, excepting Bianca who had for
so long been her personal maid.

The house in town stood by itself at the dead end of its
own little road, because of the extra land Felix had
bought around it for his pride after marrying Nell. The
town had of necessity grown in the other direction. Although the bank posted it for sale, there was no buyer for
more than a year. No one appeared to want it, or if they
did, to have money enough for such a purchase. Then one
afternoon after a long, solemn conference with Woodrow
Saxon, the bank president, Roscoe indicated cautious
willingness to buy the property. Mr. Saxon, who had increasing reason to value Roscoe Elk as a client, then took
the matter up with Leon and Felix and Nell. Leon was ve-
hemently against the sale, but Felix said that attitude was
all pride and prejudice, and Nell said they could not afford to pass over such an offer. The truth was, too, that
neither Felix nor Nell had any great affection for the
place. Their marriage had been successful in its way, but
they had not had children, the memory of whose growing
up might have given the old house a warmer identity for
them. So it was sold, along with the furnishings Nell had
decided to abandon. The money from the sale, or rather,
the sounder credit it gave them with the bank, made Beulah Land that much more secure from failure during its
second year of hard times.

Although he intended to live in it with his family, Roscoe took his time about it. First, he allowed the town to
become accustomed to the fact that he owned the property. He even suggested to Mr. Saxon that he might be
willing to resell the place if a suitable and sound buyer
came forward. None did, although Mr. Saxon dutifully
made currency of Roscoe's offer to sell, which was all Roscoe had wanted him to do anyway.

The new owner neglected the place deliberately. Grass and weeds took over the garden. The screws on the hinges of two front windows were loosened, so that the shutters were left sagging. A fence post rotted and went unrepaired. The brick walkway from the front gate to the doorsteps began to crumble. As deterioration became obvious, boys crept through high Jimson weeds, pretending to trail hostile Indians, and broke window glass with pebbles from their slingshots. The fact that the house was not lived in, added to the fact that it was owned by a Negro, diminished its importance. What is unwanted is unvalued. Just before the place could look derelict, Roscoe set about making repairs, and moved his family into it from what had been the Anderson farm. Even the Elks' moving in was done with a small touch that disarmed any disapproval there might have been.

Clovis had savored the importance that being Roscoe Elk's wife gave her, but after she tired of training and bullying their slaves—and they owned many more now than the half a score they had begun with—she admitted to being restless. As Roscoe acquired business property in town, she thought she saw a way of being interestingly occupied and at the same time gaining a measure of independence. She asked Roscoe to give her one of his empty stores and let her open a dress-making shop. Without discussing it, or even directly answering her, he refused with a shake of his head. But when he decided to move into the house in town, he had a sign painted and himself hammered it into the front yard beside the newly repaired brick walkway. It read: DRESSMAKING. This small touch made it all right for Negroes to live there. That no one came to Clovis to have sewing done made no difference. The suggestion had been made that the house was a place of business, not a mere residence. When the townspeople were used to the Elks living there, Roscoe removed the sign.

His sons were grown men, twenty-two and twenty-three years old. Junior, as his eldest was called, had overcome or lost the laziness of his adolescence and entered usefully into Roscoe's business concerns. But the younger son, Alonzo, was idly inclined, and Roscoe declared that Clovis had babied and spoiled him. When he began to sneak off with low white companions; when his dissolute behavior became more than an occasional wild oat, and the beatings Roscoe had tried were no longer feasible because ot the boy's maturity, Roscoe put him out of the house in town and set him to live on the Anderson Place—no one would call it anything else, and even Roscoe thought of it by its old name—and learn farming. Because it gave him an illusion of freedom, Alonzo went to work, and it began to look as though Roscoe's idea was a sound one.

Clovis elected one of the older women she had trained to be housekeeper for Alonzo. Maude was a motherly seeming soul, who talked more than she worked, and indeed had a thorough understanding of how to make talk pass as work. Once Clovis left her on her own, she complained to Alonzo that she needed someone to help her. He took the comeliest female slave from her barnyard chores, a girl named Geraldine, and she served as old Maude's helper and as Alonzo's mistress. He did not care for her, but she was conveniently there when his flesh felt the need of woman. By alternately consorting in the friendliest way with the people who worked the farm, and then bullying them when he himself had gone too far toward spoiling them with indulgence, he completely confused them and made them despise him.

Easily bored when Roscoe, preoccupied with other projects, forgot to press him, Alonzo envied his older brother's living in town and dealing in business affairs. Looking around for diversion, he found little. There were no free Negroes he might meet even as near-equals. No female he had seen, slave or free, tempted him to marry and begin the production of a family of his own. Educated enough to read and write and figure sums, but not enough to find interest and solace in books and ideas, he fretted in idleness, and his attention drifted inevitably to Oaks and Beulah Land, whose big fields bordered his own lesser ones, making him feel insignificant, reminding him that he did not own even this little patch but was merely his father's steward.

Bruce Davis was stiffly courteous when they met, as they sometimes did, each riding a horse over his land and not too careful to keep to his own boundary lines. Farmers weren't. They felt themselves free to ride anywhere they pleased, particularly when there was no fence to make them pause; and they even ventured where they had to open and close a gate, no one minding as long as gates that were unlatched were latched again. Sometimes Alonzo confronted the Davis children, but not often, for

they had been warned by their father not to go onto Elk
land.

More often, however, Alonzo in his walking or riding
met someone from Beulah Land, usually Leon or Floyd,
or both together. At such meetings Floyd and Leon were
cool and polite, exchanging only the most meager courtesies. Now and then Alonzo encountered the child
Rachel, pretty and proud on the roan mare she had been
given to ride on her eighth birthday a year and a half ago.
Sounding friendly enough, Rachel would call out a quick
greeting and quickly be gone. She too had evidently been
warned to have nothing to do with those on the farm between Oaks and Beulah Land.

The occasional meetings Alonzo came to remember and
think about later were those with Sarah Kendrick. When
they met on foot or horse, she looked at him and greeted
him firmly and directly, with no evasion, no shifting of
eyes or unnatural pitching of voice.

"How do you do, Mr. Elk?" she would enquire in a
way that was not a question.

And he would in unconscious imitation, answer just as
formally, "How do you do?"

He longed for her to say more and knew that she
would not. He understood surprisingly little, and that little
only in the haziest way, of the history of Roscoe Elk and
the owners of Beulah Land. He knew, of course, that he
had been born there and lived his childhood there until
that day he and his brother and his mother had left in
their newly acquired carriage, to the sound of derisive
laughter from the slaves who had hidden to watch them
go. He knew that there was bad feeling, but he did not
know why there was. No one had dared tell him, or even
hint, what had happened between his mother and Leon
Kendrick. He had no reason to know the particular ironies
in the attachment of Roman and Sarah, of Roman and
Rachel.

Whereas Junior had made sly surmises that brought
him close enough to the truth, Alonzo had not even
speculated. He was not a bad young man, only ignorant
and lonely and given to indulging himself when and where
he could. If Sarah had let herself be more than formally
polite on their chance meetings, she might have helped
him toward being better than he had been taught to be, or
he might even have begun to learn by himself. But she
could not, seeing him only as an extension of her enemy

Roscoe Elk. Since she was not friendly, he began to think of her as someone to overcome, someone to be made to see that he was a man and therefore to be dealt with as a man.

Once in the winter past when they met, each alone and on horseback, he drew up, but she cantered her horse past him. In her carelessness and haste to separate herself from him, she lost a glove she had held in her hands as they loosened on the reins of her horse. He dismounted, calling after her to tell her of her loss, but she went on as though she did not hear.

He picked up the brown leather glove from a holly bush where it had caught in falling. The leather was soft as a woman's breast, and when he lifted it to his face, he knew that its scent was Sarah Kendrick's. He stood so for a minute watching her disappear. Then he got back onto his horse and rode home in a fury. Finding Geraldine in the back yard hanging washed clothes on a line, he grabbed her by the wrist and took her into the house and to his bedroom, where he threw her onto his bed and fucked her without removing a stitch of his or her clothes. When he had come, he despised her and drew out of her and sat on the side of the bed. When, still in a sort of confusion, she swung her body to sit on the other side of the bed, they were silent with their backs to each other, until he said, "Get out. You stink. Your body stinks. Get out of here."

Five

The boundaries between Oaks and the Anderson Place were not ruler-straight, but followed topographical variations, and a certain narrow spear of Oaks property was all but surrounded by that of its neighbor. It was woodland just there, scrub and trees making no distinction of lines set down in the records at the county seat. The Oaks land was a glade with a brook cutting through slate and rock. In summer with the trees full-foliaged it was cool and almost dark even with a noon sun overhead. In winter there were enough evergreens to keep the secret look and feeling of the place. Driscoll Proctor had discovered it on a solitary walk his first autumn at Oaks, and when he and Roman became friends, they used it as a meeting place. It was not necessary to meet secretly, but sometimes they did so for privacy.

To get there Roman crossed a piece of the Anderson Place, but since it was wooded and he was wary, he believed he had never been observed. Both men had finished teaching for the day when they met one warm midafternoon in February. Proctor had been there a little while, leaning against a rock that caught a spotlight of sun beside the brook, his hat off, his eyes closed against the glare.

"A very pensive, poetic picture you make," Roman said, stepping out of the darker woods. Proctor smiled before opening his eyes, but they did not shake hands or touch each other in any other way of greeting. "There should be a ruin with vines, and maybe an owl flapping blindly overhead. What were you thinking about, or was your mind dreaming?"

"You."

"Good!"

"How was the school today?" Proctor asked.

"They're just before getting truly restless. It always happens at the end of winter. The very benches seem to get harder; they sit fidgeting and staring, and when I call on one to recite and he doesn't even hear his name, the others giggle and nudge each other. How were yours?"

"James is like you say your lot are. His eyes out the window, his mind on his 'farm.' He begged his father so, Mr. Davis has given him an acre to do with as he wants this year. He's to plow it, plant it, tend it, harvest it. At twelve he already thinks of himself as a farmer like his father." Proctor shrugged, bent to pick up a piece of slate and studied it before dropping it into the brook. "At least he's begun to work at arithmetic—as long as I couch the problems in bushels of corn and gallons of milk and pounds of cotton. Adam is working in a kind of happy fever. He's determined to feel no shame when he goes to the university. Nor will he need to in Latin and algebra and ancient history. But Greek is not his subject."

"Don't mention Greek; I feel ignorant."

"Adam will never know English grammar as well as you do. And how is Miss Sarah?"

"Well." Roman's tone was a little surprised.

"The other ladies?"

"Well too." There was something in this he did not yet comprehend.

"There are so many. And Rachel?"

"At about this minute she'll be getting home from the day school, if she hasn't gone off with Annabel and Doreen. If she's home, she'll be looking for me. She's teaching me French and how to waltz, and she can do a funny imitation of Mr. Midas Mott declaiming Juliet."

Proctor left a long pause while he studied his friend's face. "And you? How are you?"

They touched then, eagerly and clumsily: rubbing hands, patting hands. Then they relaxed and leaned together side by side against the sunny rock, arm in arm, fingers clasped, legs touching, joined and separated by the similar woolen trousers they wore.

"I had a letter by today's post," Proctor said, "from my friend in Philadelphia, Miss Eliza Truman." Roman frowned slightly; this then was the little mystery. He knew her name from past references Proctor had made. "She has succeeded at last in interesting a number of her more prosperous acquaintance in the idea of her school. She is determined to make a beginning by October. A Mr. McLeod has given her the use of some upper rooms of a stable he owns in Chestnut Street, which may serve both as classrooms and as dormitory for certain students who come to her homeless."

Roman held Proctor's hand in a tighter grip. "You have told me about her before."

"Yes, but now her plans are certain."

"She's the 'lady' who would like to help the 'poor Negro,' I believe," Roman said drily.

"Don't make fun."

"Why not? What does she know?"

"She knows a good deal, and she has a good heart."

"By which you mean she's listened to lectures by abolitionists and no doubt subscribes to *The Emancipator.*"

"Don't put on cynicism with me!"

"I'm not putting on anything," Roman said. "This 'lady'—"

"Eliza Truman," Proctor said shortly. "You know her name."

"—is concerned to do something about the ignorant Southern darky when he has escaped from his cruel master and found his way in rags and tears to her door."

"She is going to start a school for free Negroes," Proctor said.

"And for those with Georgia clay still between their toes, who will somehow contrive to crawl north."

"Are you trying to make me angry?"

Roman shook his head. "I don't need her. I'm beyond all that, thank you."

"Do you feel nothing, no pity, no compassion for the—"

"My dear Proctor, I have a foot in each camp, as one might say. My mother, such as she was, was a slave."

"She's now a free woman."

"And my father is master of one of those plantations from which Miss Truman so fervently hopes to recruit future pupils."

"Does that father acknowledge you as his son?"

"You know he cannot."

"I know he won't, not even privately. Hasn't and never will."

"He made me free."

"To soothe his vanity and conscience. Could he let his own flesh stay slave?"

"Many do. In any case, it was Sarah, my beautiful Sarah who set me free."

"I know that. And you know I honor her for it."

"I don't only honor her for it; I adore her for it. She is the best woman that ever lived, the kindest, the most beautiful—the best. I would die for her."

"She is a very rare one, I certainly agree."

"And she did not set me free when she gave me the silver cuff links and a piece of paper on my twenty-first birthday. She made me free when she first touched me and talked to me. I was an ugly child without a friend. No one cared if I lived or died because I was only a deformed embarrassment."

"You've paid her back with devotion, and with the school."

"I can never 'pay her back,' Proctor."

"Don't you think you were owed something, that part of her goodness to you came perhaps from a sense of guilt?"

"If at first—only at first. You can't shake what she did."

"Nor shall I try. That is not my aim." They were silent together a time, not touching. "Well," Proctor said, "what are you going to do?"

"Do? I am doing. I am working and living. Here, now."

"Could you ever think of leaving to make a life with me, somewhere else?"

Roman looked at his friend carefully. "You're not coming back after you take Adam to the university, are you?"

Proctor smiled humorlessly. "To teach James how to farm?"

"There are other families in the county. Your abilities are known. If you put it about that you desired other tutoring, you could live in town and start a school of your own."

"Eliza Truman's letter today is only the last link in the long thinking I've done. She has asked me to join her in starting her school, and she asked me to persuade you to join us."

"Me!"

"Yes."

"Why?"

"I've written her about you, of course, told her about your work here. She wants you to help us."

Roman was quiet, considering it, before his face cleared. "I am to be the first exhibit. You see, ladies and gentlemen, they do not all hang by the tail in trees and eat bananas; some can be taught. Behold! This one is even able to button his clothes and bow and say 'thank you.'"

"Roman—stop, stop."

They stared at each other again, Proctor's look imploring, Roman's betrayed.

"You've decided to go," Roman declared. "Or you wouldn't reject automatically any idea I put forward to persuade you to stay."

"What kind of school could I make here that would have any meaning? Do I want nothing more than to teach a lot of restless farmers' sons to parrot Cicero?"

Roman gripped his friend's arm. "Shh!"

"What?" Proctor looked around.

"I heard someone. I think I did." Roman ran into the brush, and when he returned a minute later said, "It was my half brother, Alonzo. I wonder how long he's been watching us here? We mustn't come here again."

Six

It would never have entered Bruce's head that he needed portraits of his daughters if they had not pressed him. But when their dearest friends—Rachel was too much younger than they to be dignified by the appellation, "dearest friend"—and deadliest rivals at the day school, the Misses Ann-Elizabeth and Margaret-Ella Clay became the subjects of separate portraits, in addition to appearing in the family portrait, thereby being provided with the insufferable advantage of being able to compare one likeness to another, why the Misses Annabel and Doreen Davis demanded of their father that he have Mr. Casey Troy paint their portraits. It was, of course, Annabel principally who led the campaign. Doreen, although she hated the Clay sisters almost as much as did Annabel, would in truth have preferred a new horse. She was bored with the dull, predictable Genesis, who swallowed wind as if it were hay and who had been old when her father made him hers five years ago.

But Annabel's vanity was aggressive and competitive, must be indulged, must prevail. She reasoned that Adam was getting the University of Virginia and that James had his acre of land. She, therefore, must have at the very least her portrait to console her, and not one, if you please, shared by her sister. They must be painted separately, Annabel insisted, so that those who admired only one of them would not be obliged to swallow the other too.

Seeing how things stood, Bruce gave in to Annabel, but he promised Doreen a young horse for her next Christmas present. She might even, he said, go about the county with him and help him choose. Thus rewarded, she would sit peaceably enough for her picture when the time came. Casey Troy was used to young girls who preferred horses to their own painted likenesses and even rather liked them, although he knew well enough it was the Annabels who lined his purse with more than dust.

It was the occasion of a funeral that enabled Annabel to inform her friends Ann-Elizabeth and Margaret-Ella Clay, and indeed everyone else, that she was to be limned on canvas. Old Dr. Chester Porterfield, who had with the help of quantities of biscuit and cheese and brandy seen Deborah Kendrick out of this world and Rachel Kendrick into it, had died four years ago. Today it was his good wife Mamie's turn to be stared at for the last, and perhaps only time, and prayed over before being deposited in the ground.

As the mourners drifted out of the church door onto the church porch, Annabel poked out her rounding bosom and further invited attention by fluttering her shawl in the air like a butterfly exercising his wings.

"It seems to me," Annabel confided with a sigh to Leon whom she had managed to exit beside, "I go nowhere but to funerals and weddings."

Leon smiled sympathetically, his eyes on her young bosom.

Edna, who had not been able to shake off a particularly tenacious chest cold that had racked her for a month, stepped to the edge of the church porch, and hawked and spat into the yard.

Annabel smiled with mortification. "Granny dear, must you?"

"I-be-dogged if I'll swallow pus and corruption when there's a yard to spit in," Edna replied, and hawked and spat again to make her determination clear.

For Annabel's sake, Leon pretended not to have seen or heard, and Annabel fussed up to Sarah. "Aunt Sarah," she said, "you're looking mighty pretty today!"

"Why, thank you, Annabel," Sarah answered, amused and irritated about equally.

"That magnificent ball you gave us last month has perked you up just enormously," Annabel continued.

"I must have allowed myself to droop terribly for the difference now to be so marked."

"Well, I do declare you look perfectly fine these days, really very well!"

Sarah nodded abruptly and turned to Leon who was busy ignoring both of them. Sarah was not a jealous woman in the ordinary way, but she had none of her husband's excuse or reward for ignoring Annabel's silliness. "Where is Rachel?" Sarah asked.

"I believe she has gone ahead into the grave yard," Nell said.

"She loves a funeral," Penelope, beside Nell, said. "Especially the burying part."

Annabel put a hand lightly on Leon's arm as if to ask support. "Is not death a sad thing? Even when it comes to those so full of years, who have all but worn out life's ritual experiences and long since been forced to forego its pleasures."

Leon stared at the young girl as earnestly as she did at him, but his thoughts were not on philosophy. Sarah turned away and found herself face to face with Casey Troy, whom she had not noticed inside the church.

"Mr. Troy!"

He bowed. "Mrs. Kendrick."

"I had not thought to see you here," she said.

He returned her look with seeming gravity. "I hope that means you had given a thought to not seeing me here this afternoon."

"It is most feeling and generous of you to share our country sorrows. Did you portray the deceased?"

"I did not. I merely enjoy convivial occasions of all sorts, particularly when they put me in the way of seeing those who do not make themselves common in town society by showing themselves in regular afternoon promenade."

"What an accomplished flirt you are."

"It is a useful part of my trade." He smiled, but his eyes mocked her a little.

"Of course," she said, feeling a blush begin and trying to stop it. "Miss Annabel Davis has only this morning spread the happy tidings that you are to paint her portrait, news at which we must all rejoice, it seems. She enjoys flirting too—naturally, in an entirely innocent and harmless way."

His eyes followed hers to her husband and the girl. "I admire children only as children and only then if they are admirable."

Sarah could not help warming to the man, while she understood that he was being consciously charming and flattering. "I am told that you also are to paint Miss Doreen Davis, although she speaks more enthusiastically of a horse her father has promised her than of the projected portrait."

"She sounds a most sensible girl. I should like to paint their grandmother, but she won't hear of it. She has an interesting face, beautiful in its own way."

"She is my dearest friend," Sarah declared. "How very perceptive of you to see that beauty of hers."

Casey Troy bowed slightly. "You do not mention that before or after the pair of Davis sisters I am to begin on the ladies of Beulah Land, and that I am to paint the master's portrait as well."

"I would not agree to having my own painted unless he did also. I very much want a portrait of my husband."

"He is a handsome man," Casey said.

"Yes, he is," Sarah agreed. "I shall hang his likeness in the drawing room over the mantel."

"That is usually the place reserved for the mistress of the house."

"Oh, mine may go anywhere; I don't care. In the office over the desk would be perhaps most appropriate."

"Do you spend so much time upon business affairs of the plantation?"

"Oh, yes. Especially these last years. With the price of cotton continuing low, Mr. Kendrick occupies much of his time with our lumber works."

"You have a sawmill."

She nodded.

"I have passed it on my riding about. I very much enjoy the sights of the neighboring country. It is beautiful. I may not, of course, be seen idling about on my horse too often, or my patrons will not feel that I earn my price."

"When you come to Beulah Land to do us—and, pray, not until you have made the Davis sisters happy—you may feel free to ride as much as you like. The quicker the portraits are done, the better pleased I shall be!"

"That sounds most inhospitable!"

"Oh! I am sorry. I did not mean it so. I only mean—I am sure to fidget and be a bad sitter. I am a restless person, I fear. Not nervously so, but there are always so many things I want to do, so many places I think I should be all at once."

"Then when you sit for me, I shall try to keep you still with amusing stories."

"Can you talk and paint?"

"They are done with entirely different parts of the mind, I assure you."

"I should warn you, my Aunts Penelope and Nell are jealous of one another. When you portray them, I hope you are able to give their likenesses equal appeal."

"Thank you! Such hints are invaluable. Your sister-in-law, Mrs. Davis—can you advise me how to proceed there? I have met her just the once, on the occasion of your ball."

Sarah laughed, "Indeed yes. They are already talking of it. Her—companion is a colored person to whom she is devoted. The woman is of a family dear to us all, in fact. My sister-in-law insists that she will ask you to paint them together. Not side by side, mind you, but like a playing card. It is her notion to change the portrait about when she feels like it—one day one face right side up and the other upside down, another day—well, you see."

Casey checked his laughter when a look from Sarah reminded him that they were walking together between two parts of a funeral. "What an original idea! I shall do it."

"Here we are," Sarah said.

They came to the open gate of the grave yard and paused there. Sarah was suddenly self-conscious, realizing how freely she had conversed with Mr. Troy, nearly forgetting the event that had allowed them to meet. She squinted against the glare of afternoon sunlight as she looked for and found Leon. He was just approaching, with Annabel decorous but amiable beside him.

Rachel waited at the side of the open grave. She watched the others entering and wondered why those walking in a grave yard stepped so gingerly. Did they fear the dead would feel their tread?

At the conclusion of the graveside service Edna found Sarah and linked arms with her, steering her to the gate and on toward the grove where their carriages waited.

"We have had a letter from Bonard," Edna said as soon as they passed through the cemetery gateway, as if she could not mention his name inside a holy place.

Sarah did not speak, but looked her eagerness.

"Yes," Edna continued. "They are in California. You have not heard from your sister?"

"Not for more than a year," Sarah said. "They were then still in Texas."

"Our letter is almost three months old. When he wrote it, Bonard was full of praise for that new land out there, and saying it is sure to break away from Mexico and join the United States."

"What did he write of Lauretta?"

"Only 'my wife is well.' "

Sarah's voice was almost apologetic. "Practically speaking, they are husband and wife."

"Legally speaking, they are not." Edna sighed heavily. "He doesn't mention any regular business he is engaged in. I fear me that since leaving us Bonard has made his way by speculation, if not worse. It is as if turning scoundrel he had to go the whole way."

"Do you think we shall ever see them again?"

Edna shook her head. "Almost certainly not, I should think." She looked into her friend's face to read what was there. "Do you hope for your sister's eventual return?"

"I do not." Sarah's tone was as cold as the corpse they

had seen consigned to earth. "It would only make mischief and confusion."

"Rachel thinks herself your child," Edna said, and it was not a question or quite a statement either.

"She is our child. Before she was christened Rachel Kendrick, Uncle Felix started the legal process to make her ours. She was abandoned by her mother, the law says, and says truly. Anyway, ours."

"I think people have forgot she was not born to you."

"I think I have forgot it myself."

Rachel, walking with Adam, came into the grove. They were laughing, and then suddenly they broke off and put their heads together seriously, as Rachel spoke words Sarah and Edna could not hear.

Edna said. "Will you ever tell her the truth?"

Sarah did not answer.

Seven

In spite of the fact that Annabel Davis considered Sarah "an elder," Sarah was generally admired by men. Her appeal was double, that of a virtuous woman who happens also to be physically desirable. Of the men who knew her, Leon was perhaps alone in being unresponsive to her sensual quality. Casey Troy was certainly struck by it, however much Sarah might set aside his compliments as exaggerated good manners and a clever business tactic.

Bruce Davis had long found himself powerfully drawn to her. He was the kind of man who falls in love only once in his life. The unique object had been Trudy Coker, and he had been truly in love with her only during the spring they were briefly engaged and then married. Some men need to be in love and are so all their lives, however often the object of their love changes. Bruce needed not to be, in order to concentrate on the affairs closer to his heart and soul than a woman could be. It was as if nature claimed him for herself, had been able to spare him only briefly from her chores.

Even so, there was a time eight years ago when he daydreamed about Sarah without perhaps being exactly in love. There was nothing in it so conscious as a wish. But he found himself wondering—if Leon died unexpectedly in an epidemic of the fever, say—and if he, Bruce, were to help the widow to manage the large affairs of Beulah Land, would she be receptive to his regard? One day, would he look at her and she look back at him and both understand? It was at this point his daydream always faded discreetly into vagueness; but being honest, Bruce admitted to himself what he had been doing. He had been fantasying adultery with his neighbor's wife. Acknowledging it both shocked and thrilled him. It was at that time some of his own awareness of his feelings must have become evident to Sarah, for it was then she stopped calling him by his childhood nickname of Rooster and began to call him "Bruce." Edna had guessed how things were with her son. There was no one whose funeral, therefore, she might have attended with easier resignation than Leon's, although she did not dislike him in the least. But the prospect of Sarah as a possible daughter-in-law appealed to Edna mightily. Thus do good Christians commit murder casually in their hearts.

Banked fires are none the less fires, but the love Floyd felt for Sarah was subject to such control that even Lovey might pretend to herself that it had burned out during those years of her son's travels away from and back to Beulah Land. He was easy in Sarah's presence. He did not appear to suffer, seeing Sarah and knowing that he could not have her. He even gained by seeing her. His spirit fed on her if his flesh could not. Nor was he one to sublimate desire. He was a healthy man with a healthy mind and body, and he used them. He briefly fancied many women, and enjoyed them as long as he fancied them. Still, he could not bring himself to marry.

He was not unhappy. Happiness does not consist of having all the heart desires, but in realizing capabilities in the best ways open. If the true, long love is beyond grasp, a man may still savor a story, a woman, and a pork chop.

So it was; so it is, confounding the romantics.

Eight

Annabel Davis, who of all his subjects would have most enjoyed lengthy sittings, sketches made and then abandoned with a groan of despair, earnest discussions of the problem of catching her unique lineaments and soul, proved to be the easiest to paint; and Casey Troy completed her portrait in four days. Even he was astonished, and wondered if the picture would be rejected because of the speed with which it had been done.

He need not have feared.

Annabel had not been permitted a glimpse of the work in progress. When she was invited to look upon the completed portrait, she burst into tears of happiness, declaring that it was her very self, Annabel Davis to the life, and that if she had wondered at the rapidity of his work, she had now perceived the truth: he had been inspired. She called to her father and grandmother to come at once and share her pleasure. Happening to be both in the house and in ear shot, they came, and Bruce looked and said that it was indeed a beautiful thing, squinting hard at it to indicate that he knew he looked upon no ordinary work of art and keeping his hands behind him, as if he were afraid it might bite. After giving it a good hard look Edna said, "It flatters you."

An urgent invitation was sent to the Kendricks to ask them please to come and dine that evening, which Sarah and Leon and Rachel did. The viewing of the portrait was, of course, the first order of the impromptu party. Rachel's exclamations were rewarding enough, but Annabel could hardly wait for the Clay sisters to see it. Leon, after studying the picture in something of a rapt trance, turned to the painter and said, "Sir, it is your masterpiece." For a few seconds Annabel lost her aplomb and squealed with true fifteen-year-old delight. She even jumped up and down a couple of times, and rewarded Leon with a kiss on the cheek, which seemed acceptable enough in the heat of the moment.

"An excellent likeness," Sarah agreed, and knowing she was not observed, let her eyes meet those of the painter. Casey Troy laughed out loud, which might have been interpreted as gratification at the enthusiastic reception given his work. In fact, his laughter came because he knew from Sarah's eyes that she had seen exactly what he had done. Certainly the likeness he had painted flattered the sitter. Edna had been the first to see and say that. But Casey had done something more. By the degree he had exaggerated Annabel's beauty, he had mocked it, and the expression he had given the eyes was purest mirror vanity.

"I don't wonder," Sarah said to Annabel, "that you burst into tears when you first saw it. To look upon such—a revelation is not a common experience."

"Oh, Aunt Sarah, what a lovely thing to say!" Annabel cried and made a sort of ritual dart of affection toward the older woman, although their cheeks did not quite touch, and all that really did was Annabel's hand on Sarah's, and that but briefly. "I am certain that Mr. Troy will be able to make something very creditable out of you when your turn comes!"

This effrontery allowed Sarah to smile openly at Casey Troy with a clear conscience.

Casey's portrait of Doreen took him longer than Annabel's had done. She was not an easy subject, although she sat for him quietly, as if, had she spoken or laughed, the finished work would somehow reflect her lack of strict attention, and her father might withhold the promised horse. Doreen was between girl and woman, and that made her difficult for the painter to catch in a way that would not look absurd two years hence. Her facial features had not come clear; they were still disguised in youth-fat, youth-ambiguity. Casey talked to Doreen seriously about horses, and gained her confidence by his knowledge and appreciation of them. When the picture was done, and Casey worked on it for nearly three weeks, Doreen was glad to be released from the chore of sitting. Annabel had followed its progress, not being committed this time to surprise at the finished product.

"He's taking so long." she confided to Ann-Elizabeth Clay. "I suppose he simply doesn't know what to do with the poor thing."

Ann-Elizabeth replied, "It was the same with Margaret-Ella. How boring for a painter with his eye for beauty to be obliged to paint just anyone."

The response of Ann-Elizabeth and Margaret-Ella to Annabel's portrait had been gratifying and made the girls friends again, at any rate for a week or two until some new competition could drive them apart.

Both Bruce and Edna genuinely liked the portrait and said so. Casey listened to their remarks attentively, for the picture was more important to him than Annabel's had been. As for Doreen, the first time she looked at it, she studied it quietly for so long that Casey became a little unnerved, when suddenly she smiled—a smile that grew and spread all over her young-girl face. "Why, I'm going to look like Granny," she said with delight, as if she had just found out who she was. Casey thought he had never had such a gratifying compliment to his work.

Nine

Sarah was later to wonder if her hesitation had been
prompted by some inner warning, even though she
thought that what happened that summer might have happened, if not then and in the same way, at another time,
for the inception of its events lay deep in the past, and
their incubation had been long.

After Leon commissioned portraits of each member of
the family, Sarah put off Casey Troy's coming to them. It
was the wrong time. Everyone was busy, she argued, and
she feared Mr. Troy would only become bored and impatient waiting about while his subjects found time to pose
for him. Yet there was never a really idle time at Beulah
Land; there were only busier and less-busy days and seasons. Every farmer knows how things seem to come all at
once, no matter how carefully he plans ahead, and to require his immediate attention with no possibility of postponement and not even much prospect of giving priority.
This is the result of the infinite unpredictability of
nature—not merely weather, but seed quality, and soil
conditions which vary from hour to hour—and there is no
arguing the point.

As far as order may obtain with such unpredictability,
it did so at Beulah Land. Floyd was in charge of directing
the slaves in their everyday work on the plantation, and
he was in frequent consultation with Leon and Sarah.
Leon's areas of closest personal supervision were the cotton gin and warehouses in Highboro, which was three
miles from Beulah Land, and the lumber works centering
around the sawmill, which was five miles away from Beulah Land in the opposite direction from Highboro. To go
from one to the other, which was often necessary, therefore meant riding or driving eight miles.

Work arrangements were flexible. If the sawmill was especially busy one week, Leon would ask Floyd to shift
some of the Negroes from fields to mill, and if the mill
work was slack, mill hands were given into Floyd's employment as he needed them.

Sarah had the most general knowledge of anyone of
Beulah Land activities, both business and social. She kept
the account books of plantation and sawmill and cotton

gin. Lovey held a tight rein on all house workers, but
Sarah was at least aware of what was being done, and
while she never required anything so formal as an arranged meeting with Lovey or Clarice or Myrtis, they
were in frequent communication as they met or passed in
room and hallway and yard, with the quick exchange of
question and answer.

All special requests and occasional complaints came to
Sarah. A gentle woman, Sarah had yet made it clear that
no one other than she gave orders on the management of
her household. No servant, and certainly not Lovey, was
to be bothered directly. Exceptions to this general understanding were Clarice, who made it her business to be
heedful of Penelope's wants; Bianca, who did nothing but
look after Nell; Stella, who cared for Felix; and, of course,
Pauline, who was not considered a servant at all, but Selma's companion. Juanita, who had been Rachel's nurse,
was now free for other duties because the child needed little attendance, but she still considered Rachel her special
charge and saw to the care of her clothes and her room.
Sarah had no one whose principal function was to attend
her. She liked to do things for herself unless she was ill,
and she was almost never that. She had been brought up to
do for herself, and she enjoyed the privacy it gave her to do
so still, living as she did in the midst of nearly two hundred people, all of whom looked to her either directly or
indirectly.

After allowing himself to be put off and put off again in
what he acknowledged was the pleasantest and most anxious way, Casey Troy finally laughed at Sarah's urging yet
another postponement and said that he had finished all his
commissions in the neighborhood except those to be executed at Beulah Land, and that he must come to them
now or never, for he intended going on to Savannah no
later than September.

"Very well," she said, laughing with him. "Come now
and stay until you have made a whole gallery of Kendrick
portraits! But I warn you, you must catch us all as you
can, for it is the very busiest time."

"What hours would I be most likely to 'catch you' all?"

"No, you mistake me." She shook her head. "I mean
that you must come and stay, of course. I shall see that
you have a comfortable room which you may turn into a
studio, as you like, or set us to pose any other place you
please. We might house a dozen more than we do without

crowding, and there certainly is no sense in you riding
back and forth every day between Beulah Land and your
lodging in town. Do you know what the country heat is
like in summer? The very sight of a corn field can make
you gasp for air."

Casey Troy bowed. "I accept your kindness without
protest. But I shan't mind the heat; I shall enjoy every
hour of my days at Beulah Land!" He bowed again,
smiling, and she smiled too, although she felt a vein in her
temple begin to throb and knew that it was from more
than anticipation at entertaining a pleasant, casual guest.

Ten

And so Casey Troy came, and was comfortably settled
into a room at the back of the second floor. It was a
large, nearly square room with three windows, through
one of which he might step out to a small private balcony
framed and shaded by wisteria vines. The balcony had
been built for the pleasure and convenience of Leon's
great-aunt Prudence, his father Arnold's paternal aunt,
who had been a maiden lady with some weakness of the
chest, it was said, who had lived there until she died in
1793.

Now that Casey was there and ready to begin his work,
Nell and Penelope, both of whom had privately itched
with irritation at Sarah's formerly putting off Mr. Troy's
visit to them, protested that they were "not eager to be
first." Each declared herself to be an impossibly difficult
and unrewarding subject for a painter and hinted that Mr.
Troy must learn all he could of the particular tricks of
light and shadow at Beulah Land before they could feel
easy on his model stand. And so, Selma and Pauline were
the first to sit to him, and they sat more or less at the
same time.

He used no model stand, nor did he suggest a way for
them to dress, hoping by not doing so to gain an insight
into them. He was pleased when Selma invited him to
come into their apartment rather than that they go to his.
For one thing, he knew that Selma was an original and
something of a recluse, and he hoped to find her easier in
her own quarters than she would likely be in his neutral
studio room. Too, her room had its main light from the

north, and although he set less value on this than other
painters might, he was happy to use it when it was offered, because in it he was better able to judge color tone.

When he saw how the women were dressed, he suspected that they were teasing or baiting him, for Selma was
all in black, and Pauline all in white. He made no comment and set them straightaway on chairs facing each
other to pose for preliminary sketches. When Selma protested that they were surely not to be painted in profile, he
told her that he had other reasons for placing them so,
and she did not press him further.

These early sketches, for which they remained fixed at
his command as he moved about, were useful in more
than freeing him in his approach to the pair by showing
him the lines and planes and masses their faces and bodies
made. What he saw in their faces as they sat staring at
each other did not appear in the sketches, but showed in
the finished portrait and made it a successful painting instead of merely a clever trick, although there was an element of that too, as he suspected the women had meant
there to be.

He worked at them alternately after he had set up the
large, stretched canvas and squeezed his colors onto a
newly scraped palette board. Whoever was not sitting
stayed in the room and watched him work; but Casey was
used to all sorts of situations and did not mind as long as
the watcher did not comment. It happened that both
women were quickly sensitive to his serious application of
himself to the project at hand, and the room soon took on
an atmosphere of harmony and mutual respect. No one
else was allowed there to observe. Casey began work in
the middle of June, and July was a third over before he
could look at the double portrait and declare it finished.

The flesh tones of the two women were neither white
nor black, and so the final effect was far from the starkly
obvious comment they had seemed to ask of him by the
way they first dressed: black on white, white on black. He
invented a rich background of floating flowers around
both faces. The faces he kept almost clear; they were little
more than colored drawings. Their expressions were not
mysterious or enigmatic, but deliberately unrevealed.

The element that made the double portrait succeed as a
painting was something Casey could not explain, although
he had certainly intended it as he worked, and felt it first
during the making of the early sketches. Neither face re-

vealed itself by itself, but needed the other, so that a viewer's reaction was to want to turn the picture around as he looked at it to find the second face what he had not discovered in the first.

Selma and Pauline were pleased at the result, and Selma said that without having known what they wanted, it was precisely what they wanted. Other members of the family came in to see it, and it was generally admired, although its oddness made viewers nervous, unused as they were to anything but the most solemn approach to a painting. Nell whispered to Mr. Troy that, when he came to paint her, she hoped he would not find her face so pale as Selma's appeared, and asked if she should apply carmine to her cheeks. Casey assured her that it would not be necessary and that his approach to every sitter was individual.

After the playing-card canvas, he painted Penelope and Nell, in that order, because they had privately decided to have it so. He worked exactly eight days on each picture. Nell chose to wear her ball gown, to get the full use of it and be able always to remember it, she said. Penelope wore her old best gray, but Mr. Troy made it and her look anything but drab. In fact, Penelope's portrait had something in it more innocently girlish than did either of the pictures of the Davis sisters. He gave Nell a more worldly look than she usually wore, although there was a touch of the wistful in her eyes that muted somewhat the richness of the creamy lace and green gown and cameo brooch. Each lady praised the other's likeness extravagantly and secretly preferred her own, believing that Mr. Troy had somehow or other seen her as she really was.

Finding himself less busy for a few days in early August, Leon put himself at Casey's disposal, and Casey quickly set to work. He knew what he wanted, and when he explained his concept to Leon, Leon agreed to it. Casey used a large canvas and painted the master of Beulah Land full figure against a somewhat stylized background that showed the house and some trees and two peacocks. It was a handsome job of work, and everyone said so. Sarah insisted that it be hung over the mantel in the big drawing room even before it was varnished and framed. They could take it down again for that, she said.

It was now late August, and although Casey had made a beginning of his portrait of the nearly ten-year-old Rachel, there was still Sarah, who begged him to be patient, "for it

is our busiest time," and he insisted that he must move on
to Savannah as soon as practicable in September.

During all this summer of art work at Beulah Land, the
other work, the reason for the plantation's being, maintained its pace. The sawmill was all but shut down as every
effort and all hands were put to harvesting the corn
and cotton crops. The gin in Highboro was working seventeen hours a day, and the line of wagons waiting with
cotton to be ginned was constant night and day. Leon
spent most of his time at the gin and warehouses, and often slept in his office in a small hut just by the gin. He
was always saying he must have a proper office and never
doing anything about it.

The weather stayed hot and clear, and the rhythm of
the days was work—work that made men and women
weary, but there was so much to be done there was little
time to rest and none to complain. The work itself became a kind of necessary fever that fed on itself. Even the
animals caught the prevailing mood. Mules left off their
quirkiness and pulled and hauled when they were told to.
The food animals—cattle, hogs, fowl—ate until they could
eat no more, as if they embraced their destiny of growing
fat to feed the men and women who fed and tended them.
They ate and stood stupidly in the shade, if they could
find any, and waited.

There was no time for fishing, but curiously, there were
games, mostly by the children to counterpoint the feverish
work of parents, but sometimes the adults joined briefly in
games too, or someone suddenly appeared with watermelons that had been cooled all day in a well, and someone
else picked up a fiddle or a banjo, and some of the furious, self-propagating energy of the time was used in dancing and clapping hands and laughing—by people who a
moment before would have sworn they hadn't enough energy left to remove their clothes and wash their feet and
drop into bed until four o'clock the next morning.

The kitchens were busy too, cooking to feed the field
hands. Women who usually cooked for their men who
worked in the fields now worked in the fields alongside them
with only a few added to the regular kitchen staff of the big
house to cook for all. No sooner was the breakfast of
fried fatback, flour hoecake and syrup eaten than the
cooks set to work to provide the midday meal. Huge pots
of fresh peas were set to boil with generous hunks of fatback, to be served later with rice and hoe cakes of corn

bread, made of nothing but corn meal, water, and salt and fried thin and crisp, and pot liquor to soak the rice, and as much chopped onion as anybody wanted for seasoning.

Those at the table in the big house ate boiled peas and thin corn bread every day too, but added to it such items of food as sliced tomatoes, squash, snap beans or butter beans, corn cut off the cob and roasted in the oven, and—always—rice. There was also, almost daily, chicken: fried, roasted, or cut up in a pie with dumplings. And after that they ate berry or peach pies, and they drank quantities of tea. As if providing all of this immediately consumed food was not enough, the kitchen women were busy making jellies and jams and preserves and putting up jars of tomatoes and cucumber pickles, and beets and hot peppers and all the other vegetables that lent themselves to preservation in any way for winter use.

Sarah spoke truly when she said it was the busiest time at Beulah Land, and she was in her glory—here, there, everywhere, drunk with all the activity until she felt that she was spinning through the hot days like a whirling dervish and might spin on forever, because it was easier to go on than to stop. Yet in this feverish time when action seemed to beget more action, and energy came from the very heat that sapped them all in tamer times, she found time to keep track of her Aunts Penelope and Nell, her Uncle Felix, to know how Selma and Pauline felt and fared, to spend ten minutes with Roman here, with Rachel there, or more often with both together, for of all the inhabitants of Beulah Land there was least for them to do. Sarah also found time to be hostess to Casey Troy, who himself had little freedom, so busy was he with his commissions.

Sarah, and Leon when he could come home from Highboro, saw Casey mainly at the second and third meals of the day, dinner at noon and supper in the early evening. But sometimes Sarah saw him at odd moments. Although keeping close to the house where his work required him to be, he slipped out now and then to look about the fields and barns. She would see him come back with shirt collar open and shirt struck to his back and arms with sweat, and sweat beads on his eyebrows and mustache and the hair at his temples and around his ears, but he would come back smiling with exhilaration.

No one was sick, no one died. There was no time. Every sense was heightened. The words and laughter of children sounded sweet on the ear. Food tasted good and lay easy in the belly. There was more sexual doing than at

any other time of the year. Everything was used. Everyone was harvested.

Eleven

"And now, you," Casey said after breakfast to Sarah. She
usually had her breakfast in the kitchen with Lovey and
Clarice before anyone else in the big house was up, and
the very fact that this morning she ate in the dining room
with Nell and Penelope and Rachel and Casey Troy was
an indication that her work, while it would doubtless continue heavy for a while yet, had lightened enough for her
to pause and breathe and take personal stock.

"Why, yes," she said, surprising both herself and him.

"Eureka!" he cried like a boy, and they laughed.

"You must finish Rachel first."

"It's done. Well, nearly. I don't need her to pose any
more. I can finish it without her. When will you be
ready?"

"I can see that you mean to finish me off in jig time,"
she said, "and get on the train to Savannah."

"And you with your postponements would keep me here
forever!"

They had spoken only the glib banter of easy society,
but his words made them both smile awkwardly, until
Sarah laughed.

"The mention of Savannah made me remember my sister Lauretta, and suddenly I thought how much she would
have liked you."

He sighed a mockery of despair. "It is discouraging to
hear a lady say one puts her in mind of her sister."

"You would not say so if you saw her."

"Is she as fair as you?"

"Much fairer—although somewhat older." He laughed
with delight. "You are the only person I know who makes
me speak unkindly of other females."

"That makes me take heart again. When will you pose
for me?"

She frowned. "Tomorrow," she said. "I think we may
really talk about it tomorrow and then set aside a time
which, I promise, I shall hold to."

"No more putting off. You always make me joke, but I
am a serious fellow."

"I like your joking."

"Today—ten thirty? The shady side of the house."

"Oh," she said with something like relief, "you plan to paint me out of doors as a companion piece to the portrait of my husband?"

"I've thought of a hundred ways, but this morning, sketches."

"Ten-thirty? I'll try to be there, although—"

Twelve

Although not what could be considered a venal man, Leon had never made much resistance to his desires when gratification of them was available, and some of his easy submissions had resulted in serious consequences, to wit: his brief sexual affairs with Clovis and Lauretta.

Going about now from Beulah Land to the sawmill to the cotton gin, on a horse or in a buggy, he found himself stopping at Oaks often for half or quarter of an hour. Oaks was as busy as Beulah Land, and Leon usually discovered that Bruce Davis was not at home but in the fields with his hands. Edna regularly went into the fields too, to observe for herself the work Bruce would talk about at their noon and evening meals, the only times she had anything like conversation with him during the harvesting. Doreen accompanied her grandmother whenever she caught her setting out, and the old lady took to calling for her as she put a sun bonnet on her head and ventured forth. Young James was busy with his acre, as if the feeding and clothing of a naked, hungry world depended on it. Adam worked long hours every day with Driscoll Proctor.

Leon was only certain, therefore, of finding Annabel at home, usually on the vine-shady porch that ran along two sides of the house, at one end of which might still be seen the ramp that had been built years ago for Benjamin's wheeled chair after his first stroke. It was too hot for Annabel to walk—no bonnet or parasol could protect that fresh, fair complexion from Georgia's summer blaze. Taking little pleasure in reading and none in the working of the house or her mind, Annabel was frequently alone and bored, and she welcomed Leon with the more enthusiasm because she well knew his admiration of her face and form.

Although never missing a chance to address Sarah as "aunt," Annabel dropped the "uncle" in speaking to Leon, using "sir" instead, as a lady of any age might address a gentleman of any age.

"I'm so glad to see you!" Annabel exclaimed whenever Leon hopped off his horse or out of the buggy, securing the reins himself to the railing of the steps to the porch, for in those busy days, no attendant from the stable was provided for visitors. "Hopping" was something Leon did only for Annabel's benefit. At forty, although vigorous enough, he eased himself down from saddle and stirrups, and stepped carefully from a buggy more often than he hopped. But in Annabel's company he felt and hoped to appear younger than he was.

Smiling, he would go up the steps and join her on the porch, bowing and saying formally, "Miss Annabel," before asking if her father was anywhere about the house.

"I expect he's in one of the far fields," was her usual reply. "Is there anything particular you have to see him for? If there is, I'll be glad to send someone—"

"No, nothing you'd call particular, just generally wanting to know how things are going along with his harvesting."

"Well then, sir, you must make do with a visit with me."

She was, he thought, such a very amiable young girl, ready to talk of anything, happy to listen to any scrap of news or anecdote relating to mutual acquaintances. Her appreciation was so very eager and generous. He never saw in her liveliness a reaction against the boredom she had endured immediately before his arrival; instead, he read special regard.

He was always equipped with compliments. They sprang readily to his mind and lips because he could not see her without thinking how pretty she was, how fragrant she smelled, how delightful it would be to touch her in more ways than civil manners allowed. He was able to listen to her chatter about anything, or rather, he looked and did not listen more than to register key words, if there were any, and to murmur whenever she paused, "I do declare!" or "By my soul!"

Of course, sometimes Edna was there, and sometimes even Bruce, and he talked to them, only now and then letting his eyes veer from them to Annabel while she sat back with a secret smile, enjoying his performance and by

the smile letting him know she knew he would have preferred finding her alone.

Annabel progressed from simple flirting, in which she felt
competent and perfectly safe, to chaffing Leon in a familiar way she would not have dared had anyone else been
present. She liked to flirt; it gave her a feeling of importance and even power. She meant no harm; she merely
found it pleasant. And he was there and agreeable, the
first grown man who had noticed her as anything but a
child. Now and then she gave him a small commission to
execute for her in town, for there was little casual traffic
between Oaks and Highboro during those busy days, and
sometimes when he brought the card of embroidery
thread she had needed, he added a little present to it to
surprise her.

Most recently, he had brought a tiny bottle of French
perfume, and when she saw it, her eyes got large, and she
said, "Oh!" as if in the grip of the tenderest passion, and
then she held it out firmly for him to take back. "I
mustn't. You let Miss Sarah have it."

Leon blushed. "I'm sure she buys for herself whatever
she wants in this sort of line," he said.

"I know Granny would tell me no, but all the same I'm
tempted."

"Keep it, and don't tell your grandmother. You don't tell
her everything anyway, do you?"

"No." She laughed and held the bottle tighter in her
hand. "I shall do as you suggest, and I shall open it only
when I am alone, and use a drop of it before I go to bed at
night to make me think of pretty things and sleep happy."

Imagining the scene, Leon squirmed in his chair.

The next time he came to Oaks, Doreen was on the
porch with Annabel and immediately ran to fetch her
grandmother from the kitchen where Edna was watching
the women there boil up blackberries for jam and shell
peas for supper. It was midafternoon.

Edna was glad to see Leon, as she would have been
glad to see any visitor, and proceeded to ask him detailed
questions concerning Sarah's activities, to which he gave
vague answers because he seldom noticed how Sarah occupied herself. Then they spoke of crops, comparing their
yield by acre of corn and cotton, each knowing the qualities of the other's various fields as well as he did his own.
Doreen listened eagerly to her grandmother and the visitor, little inclined to join in, being at a particular stage of

shyness with men. Annabel sat back in her chair with the secret smile, feeling superior to everyone and amused by the situation, because Leon was so obviously put out at not finding her alone.

"Doreen!" Edna said, turning to the younger girl. "What was it I was trying to remember last night at the supper table, and your daddy couldn't tell me?—I know." She faced Leon again. "What was the name of that red-headed woman used to live, before she died, two doors over from Upton Cooks's dry goods? Had a goiter big as my two fists—now surely you know who I mean."

"I do, Miss Edna, but I can't recall her name."

"No more could I." She nodded rapidly, as if fortified by his not being able to remember either. "That'll worry me till I find out—you know how you get some bitty thing on your mind and can't let it go till you finish with it. I'll ask Lovey next time I see her. She remembers everything and everybody. She's better than a family tree in a Bible. Sarah wouldn't because it was before she came."

Annabel and Doreen in one of their occasional collusions then all but exploded and collapsed with laughter they had held in. They were both at a time when they found their grandmother funny, although Doreen's amusement was loving and Annabel's was patronizing.

"What?" Edna exclaimed in surprise. "So silly! Silly, silly!" She spoke more quietly when she turned back to Leon. "They think everything that happened before they were born of absolutely no consequence, and everybody that died before they were born might just as well never have lived. My only comfort is knowing they'll get older."

Together the girls cried, "Grandma" Doreen conciliating, Annabel protesting.

Leon, who was old enough to appreciate the old, found himself turning to his Uncle Felix more than he had recently done. Always an adaptable man, Felix had wasted no time feeling sorry for himself when he was struck down, but thanked the Lord he was left with some capacity to enjoy himself, although knowing the frustration of not being able to get about according to his own will and on his own legs. He rejected the suggestion of a wheeled chair. He had hated and pitied the sight of Benjamin Davis in his. So he decided that he would stay in his room. With Stella's help he could dress and propel himself from bed to chair when he wanted to, but he generally preferred to remain in bed. If he could not walk and ride where he pleased, he could at least choose to rest comfortably.

Sarah came and went two or three times a day. Rachel paid him countless visits when his door was open. Penelope did not often come in, but she stopped at the door when she saw it open to enquire how he felt and if there was anything he wanted done that she could do. He liked Penelope well enough but never had much to say to her. "No, no, my dear cousin," he would usually answer, although she was not his cousin; but that was the way of Southerners, to give a kinship word to someone close but not kin. Nell came to see him regularly, for which he was thankful, because her regularity let him know when she was pretty certain to be absent.

But now he had these slightly disquieting visits from Leon. He'd always loved the boy, and—oh, for a long time—they had been good companions, they with each other and both with Bonard. He sighed with pleasure at the memory of the times they'd had together, not all of them good, but all worth remembering. Now, however, Leon came and sat and talked and looked at his uncle as if he expected Felix to give him answers to questions he never quite put. Felix tried to guess what was in Leon's mind and answer the unasked question rather than the vague ones posed. In matters having to do with the law or commercial affairs, Felix, was brisk and helpful. His physical incapacity had not blunted his mind's ability to judge business matters.

When Leon seemed hesitant and unsure of himself one day and gave Felix the sense of wanting to know if he should follow the laws of convention or personal inclination, Felix, assuming that some woman was on his mind, said, "Dear boy, so long as I wasn't hurting anybody or confounding public morality I've always done what I wanted to do. I don't think I've been sorry for anything I've done, but now that I'm not able to be immoral on any really ambitious scale, I do sometimes regret pieces of mischief I used to want to try and hung back from because of—oh, timidity, I suppose. Don't do it. Have the courage of your desires, for God's sake, or the Devil's, perhaps I should say."

Another time, in answer to a fumbled near-question, Felix said testily, not liking the role of mentor, "The choices we make are usually accidental, and then we spend the rest of our lives making the best or the worst of them." He smiled to soften the acerbity he had heard in his tone. "Look at your own life. Did you plan it that way?"

"In other words," Leon said, "you are saying it doesn't matter."

"Not at all. Whatever 'it' is always matters damnably. Now then, I'm tired of being uncle for the day and answering questions I don't understand anyway. Is she pretty, hm? No offense, only jesting, my boy. Stella! Where are you?" She was there, of course. She was almost always there, but his consciousness admitted her or denied her as he wanted or did not want her. Turning back to Leon, Felix spoke his own vague suggestion. "If you don't mind, I think I—"

"I'm just going, Uncle." He left, and Stella closed the door after him.

Felix had long found it useful to suggest in such a way that he was tired, or that he felt the need to perform a private function, when he was merely bored for the moment with whoever was present and wanted to be alone. More and more he preferred his own company, and Stella's, to that of any others. He thanked God for the accident that had brought him and Stella together.

The next time Leon stopped at Oaks, he was in his buggy, and he had come directly from the sawmill and hadn't made up his mind whether or not to drive on to Highboro and the gin, or to go home and let things at the gin sort themselves, as he knew they would if he were not there. It was the middle of a hot afternoon at the beginning of September, and he found Annabel alone on the porch, dressed in a pretty new frock as if she had been waiting for him, or for someone.

"Miss Annabel, you look like a lady about to go off to a party. Are you expecting company?"

"I wish I were," she complained wistfully. "I haven't been to a party in I-can't-even-remember when. This summer will never end, will it? They'll go on picking cotton and making hay and fodder, and I shall die of very boredom!"

Leon laughed softly. "For whatever company I may provide, I offer myself to your command." As he bowed over her, he caught her scent. "You have used the perfume. Did you guess I would come today?"

"Of course not!" She tossed her head as she had seen older girls do with men they were only pretending to

check with a rebuke. But then she smiled conspiratorially.
"Do you truly mean you are mine to command?"

"Entirely."

"Take me for a drive in your rig!"

"Now?"

"Yes!"

"Just us, alone?"

'Why not?'

"No reason not, of course, but—"

"I can see your offer was only one of words, sir!"

"Not at all—but is your grandmother home? Perhaps
you should just step in and tell her, so she won't wonder
where you are."

"Everyone is in the confounded fields!"

"Then come!"

"You mean you will?"

"Certainly."

"Oh!" She sprang up from her chair and sashayed
across the porch, and tripped down the steps. He followed
her quickly, and at the side of the buggy held her arm to
help her in, she pulling her skirt tight with her free hand
so that its freshness would not be soiled by the wheels,
which he'd had no opportunity to turn out of her way.
Loosening the reins, he hopped up to the driver's seat on
the other side of her, and off they went.

They did not speak until they were well clear of the
house.

"Oh!" she cried then, with much the same happy moan
she had made when she received his gift of perfume. "I
feel like I'm eloping!"

Leon grinned, looking straight ahead and urging the
horse into a faster trot. He did not register the fact that
she'd said "I" instead of "we."

"Do let us go on and on! I want to ride forever! I don't
care where!" The next minute as the horse was trotted
faster and faster, and then broke into a gallop, she cried
in contradiction, "Please! Not so fast! Where are we going?"

"Will Boiling Springs do as a beginning?"

"Oh, yes, I dearly love it!"

Boiling Springs was a wooded picnicking grove that
took its name from a particularly strong spring there that
sent water gushing up to the surface of what had come to
be a small lake. Sometimes gentlemen bathed in it, although it was considered dangerous for the ladies, and so

they could only trail their fingers in it and marvel at its coldness.

Leon had checked the horse to a trot again, and they were at their destination in little more than a quarter of an hour. He slowed them to a walk as they came into the grove of trees. Even the rutted trail was sprinkled with fragrant, fresh-fallen pine needles atop the older brown ones. Bringing the buggy to a stop, Leon whipped the reins about the post at the side of the foot rest and hopped down, going quickly to the other side to help Annabel alight.

Holding his hand, she stepped out of the buggy like a princess arrived at a ball. "Ah—" She breathed the piny air. "How cool. How pretty it is. I'm so glad you came when you did. I was about ready to die from having nothing to do or think about!" She walked away from the buggy before turning and curtsying to him. "I thank you, sir, for rescuing this maiden from the Demons of Boredom!"

"What would you have done had I not come just then?"

What she had been considering before his arrival was going to her room and examining her ribbons and hats and dresses, a pastime that never failed to give her some pleasure, no matter how familiar all her things were. "Expired! Oh yes, I would surely have expired. You saved my life."

"That gives me a claim on it, don't you think?"

She was suddenly aware that they were alone, together and alone in a way she had never before felt with anyone. She walked from the buggy toward the small lake made by the spring, and he followed, breathing her fragrance, the scent of the gift perfume only faintly there in her own aroma and that of the pine woods.

He came up behind her as she stood at the bank, looking down at the water a foot away from her shoes. Bewitched by the spell her youth had cast upon him, he put his hands on her waist, turning her to him and embracing her, clamping his mouth on hers before she could cry out or retreat in surprise.

After one stunned moment Annabel wrenched away with more energy than she had ever perhaps done anything, almost falling into the lake as a result. He let her go, as alarmed by her total and brutal rejection as she had been by his sudden attack.

"What are you doing, Uncle Leon? You are being awful!" These were no longer the words and inflections of the flirting young woman he had recently known, but the outrage of a shocked child.

He managed to mumble only, "I meant no—but you led me to think—"

She burst into tears, and dropping herself down on a stump, howled with fury. He let her entirely alone for a little bit, and then he said, "Come, Annabel, you mustn't carry on so."

Stopping her weeping midbreath, she looked up at him. "What is that?" she asked in surprised interest.

"That," he might have told her, was a hard-on bulging up in his loose-fitting trousers, but there was no need to explain, because the physical manifestation of his desire for her rapidly subsided under the barrage of her teary innocence.

"There now," he said ineffectually. "I'm sorry if I frightened you. I did not mean to do it."

She stood. "How dare you touch me in such a rough manner?"

He could not help it; he smiled at the sudden realization of the absurdity of the whole episode. "I am sorry," he said.

Believing from his smile that he found her somehow ridiculous, she turned instinctively vindictive. "What would Aunt Sarah say if I told her?"

"Oh, God."

"Never fear, sir!" she said in a sneering tone. "I see that you are at heart a coward."

"Every man is at heart a coward. I think though that I must tell your grandmother privately what happened and apologize to her, as I have just done to you."

"You will most certainly do no such thing! I implore you. For she would only blame me!" Her tone of outrage turned to whimpering accusation. "How could you, Uncle Leon? Just because I talked to you—because nobody else was there—because you gave me little presents. Well, you may have them all back. Whatever could you have thought? I mean, look at you. Your clothes are all covered with sawdust from the mill—"

He quickly began to dust and beat at his clothing. Bending, he slapped larger bits of sawdust that clung to the bottoms of his trouser legs.

"And you're old!"

He left off slapping his trouser legs and slowly lifted his head and straightened his body. He wanted to slap her. In-

stead, after a moment, he managed to lift his hands and indicate the buggy. "If you please, I shall take you home
now."

"Do you promise you won't say anything to Granny?"

He nodded.

"If you drive fast, we'll be back before anyone is there.
If they are, I'll think of something."

As they came to the buggy, the horse arched his tail
and shat with obvious satisfaction. She burst into tears
again, and he was rescued from his anger by laughter.
"Oh, get in, child, and let me take you home."

She got into the buggy unassisted, and he pulled himself
up to the driver's seat with a grunt. They did not talk as
they left the grove and made their return. But as they
came into the driveway to Oaks, she said, "I feel ever so
much older than when we left."

"So do I," he replied.

Thirteen

Since their quarrel in early spring, Roman and Proctor
had not resolved their differences, or managed to see them
as unimportant. They made, or took advantage of, opportunities to come together physically, without being able to
achieve any understanding of minds. The mind is more
fastidious and less realistic than the body. They were glad
of each other; there was no one else as close to either. But
pride and what they called principle made them watchful
in their encounters and prevented their acknowledging
even to themselves, let alone to each other, that the sum
of their love was greater than its subtractions. If there had
been urgent need of it, pride and principle would have
tumbled or been compromised, but Proctor's days were
full helping Adam prepare himself for the University of
Virginia; and Roman had Rachel. He was the only one of
her three favorites always available to her that summer,
and the differences in their ages was so large it made no
difference at all.

On the neighboring farm, Alonzo continued to oversee
his fields with more of conscious application than commit-
ment of heart and spirit. He was up early each morning to
rouse his slaves and set them to work for an hour or two
before Maude and Geraldine were ready to provide break-

fast for them. Summoned by the lackadaisical ringing of a hand bell, they would leave the fields and gather around the back steps to eat from tin plates, their bare feet still wet with the morning dew, and sandy earth clinging to the soles and sides.

Alonzo ate alone at the kitchen table while they fed outside. He was always finished before they were and waiting to witness their return to work. His assiduity resulted from boredom that seeks relief in any activity. Boredom also made him impatient with lazy, muttering old Maude and her bad cooking and worse housekeeping. He complained to his mother about Maude on one of her visits to the farm, and after scolding the woman, who responded only with biggety cackles, Clovis made up her mind to stay at the farm and see Alonzo through the harvest season.

Roscoe made no objection when she told him; he was glad to be rid of her. Her body had long since ceased to give him any pleasure—for that he sought and found elsewhere—and he would have laughed if anybody had suggested that Clovis or any other woman had a mind. During the last two years she had taken to drinking more than she ought, and several times during recent months he had come home from overseeing his various land holdings and business dealings to find her drunk and abusive, or drunk and weeping, or drunk and snoring, often as not on the floor. Beating her effected no correction in her behavior. He had not tried to talk to her, but then he never had done that.

In any event, he was glad to see her go, and she was glad to leave him. What did a house in town matter, if all she could do was sit in it alone?

Clovis was a woman of energy; she liked having things to do. It was the not having and not being needed that had set her to careless drinking. After observing Maude for a day and suffering her jabber, she struck her and sent her off to take care of the slave cabins and the yards. Clovis knew that Geraldine went to bed with her son when it pleased him to take her, and she didn't care one way or another. She did not, however, consider that this fact gave Geraldine any privileges. She told the young woman what housework to do and showed her how to do it. When Geraldine alternately balked and feigned simplicity, Clovis smacked her on the head and showed her again. By the end of the second day Clovis and Geraldine had come to understand each other, and they were not displeased with their understanding either. Clovis continued to drink, but in moderation now and for pleasure. Her days followed a routine of activities. She had been born to farm work, and she found herself slipping into the first real contentment she had known since she was a girl. Town had not suited her, she decided. Here, she could be Clovis, instead of Roscoe Elk's wife.

Alonzo was well pleased too. He talked to his mother and slept alone, not allowing Geraldine to stay in his bed after his need of her was satisfied. She was cleaner; the house was sensibly kept; meals were better prepared, and he did not have to listen to stupid, self-important old Maude. Without saying so, he was grateful to Clovis for the order she had brought to his life. He had always been a little resentful and shy of her, because he thought she favored his brother Roscoe over him. But since Roscoe, called Junior, had become more like his father in his arrogant self-assurance, assuming that everyone else, including his mother and brother, was stupid or weak or both Clovis had begun to look to her younger son for whatever familiar comfort she might hope to find.

Alonzo did not forget what he had seen and heard of his brother Roman and the white man who taught the Davis boys. Indeed, he regularly returned to the glade to see if he could catch them. But they had not come there again that he knew, and gradually his frequenting the place made it seem like his own, and instead of going there to spy, he began to go there to be alone and private when he grew bored with the farm and thinking of weather and weeds and crop yield.

He did not forget Sarah Kendrick either, although he did not see her now. But he knew they were all of them at Beulah Land busy, as was he, with no time for idle riding or walking about. When they and he had leisure, he would pick up observing and meeting them again. Brought up to resent the Kendricks, he had not remembered the reasons. By now his resentment had been replaced largely by curiosity. Sometimes, standing on the farthest edges of his land nearest Beulah Land, he would see Floyd walking about among the field hands. There were so many of them the work seemed none too hard or pressing. And sometimes, to his surprise, they would sing, for no reason he could guess, their beginning cued by no signal he had seen or heard. Like a flock of birds they would suddenly begin

all together and continue until moved to stop. He saw that
Floyd was easy with the men and women, and they with
him. There was easy laughing and joking, or they would
all stop briefly and just stand there resting themselves and
looking about, whereas his own people, when he was with
them anyway, worked with their faces toward the ground.

Monotonous though being a farmer was to him, Alonzo
was glad enough to have a place he could think of as his
own, in spite of the regular visits of his father and Junior
to see how things were going, to be critical and nagging,
no matter how well he had done, never to smile and com-
mend. But real life, good life, was over there at Beulah
Land, he thought, across the invisible and invincible border line that ringed the big plantation as effectively as a
Great Wall. Over there they were happy, or seemed so.
Over here they were not.

He sent his cotton to the Kendrick gin. Family hatred
did not keep Roscoe from using what was convenient and
cheapest, in spite of the bit of profit accruing to his old
enemies. When the corn was dry, Alonzo sent it to the
mill to be ground into meal, which was used more as a
staple for bread than flour was. Alonzo took the first
wagon with its sacks of shelled corn to the mill himself,
for the change and adventure of leaving the farm even for
a little while, and he came home covered with a fine, light
dusting of corn meal that made him look, Clovis told him
when he came in the door, like a spook.

As harvest work dwindled to the last scattered corn and
cotton to be picked from the fields, Alonzo went back to
the glade now and then, not expecting to find anyone, but
in a reflective, questing mood, nonetheless. One day as he
rested against the rock he had seen Driscoll Proctor use
for the same purpose, he heard someone approaching and
quickly left, but stopped and waited as soon as he was
hidden, to see who came.

The man was a stranger. Staring at him through foliage,
Alonzo finally placed him. He had seen him two or three
times on the sidewalk outside the old stage and post office.
He was the man who painted portraits of people. Alonzo
had heard of his painting the Davis family and now being
at Beulah Land to paint the Kendricks. He watched for a
little while, but the man did nothing other than sit down
by the brook and look into it, so Alonzo left him to it—
with some resentment, for he had come to think of the
glade as his own.

Making his way to his own land, the fancy came to him

that perhaps he should turn back and tell the man who he was, and ask him to come to his house when he had fulfilled his obligations at Beulah Land. He could paint drunken Mama, sloppy Maude, Geraldine—even himself, master of the farm, just as Leon Kendrick was master of Beulah Land. At first the fancy amused him, but by the time he reached home he was angry, and he did not know why.

Fourteen

The Central Railroad linking Savannah and Macon had been completed in 1843. The wail of train whistle and racket of boxcars carried far over the quiet countryside, and the line of smoke from the engine stack was still a sight that caused people to lift their heads from their work and marvel.

Highboro had the fortune to be directly on the line, and for several years Leon had sent his cotton and lumber to Savannah by rail. The sudden ease of travel did not, however, do very much to encourage those at Beulah Land to make more frequent trips to Savannah than they had done before. Their society was, if not self-contained, then bounded roughly by the county lines.

Penelope wrote to friends in Savannah, but had returned to visit only once, three years ago. When she came back, she declared that the old city had "gone down," and was growing much too rapidly for her taste, and that she had actually been introduced to people she had not even heard of before she came to live at Beulah Land.

It was customary for anyone going from Highboro to Savannah to carry with him commissions for friends and relatives. During autumn, though, a number of men and a few women went on the train to Savannah to sell their crops and to buy goods they did not produce and could not find in the home town. Leon was one of these. He left home a few days after the buggy ride with Annabel Davis to Boiling Springs, glad to put a little time and distance between that episode and the future. He expected to be in Savannah two or three weeks, and he had lists of errands and purchases for every female in the family, including Selma who, having so much withdrawn from the world, yet craved a few of its goods not available in Highboro stores.

In spite of her promises to Casey Troy, Sarah was not ready to give him much of her time until Leon had gone. Then she declared herself to be quite at his beck and call. For two afternoons he made quick drawings of her. At her suggestion he drew her wearing an ordinary day dress at the desk in the office. At his suggestion she put on the pink and gold brocade gown she'd had made for the late winter ball, the dress and occasion of his first seeing her. None of the drawings pleased him or gave him the necessary conviction of a specific idea for her portrait.

As she sat and as he worked, she developed a new respect for the painter, as happens sometimes when one sees another engrossed in his work. Until then, their encounters had been pleasant, but all in the same genial, bantering key. Now she saw him unsmiling, making no effort to amuse her, concentrated on the work of his mind and hands. True, she was at present the center of that work, but being so made her feel anonymous for the first time with him. As he studied her, trying to catch a clue to her inner self as well as her physiognomy, so did she study him.

She knew him to be handsome, but handsome features are not always those that best please. Now she saw and responded to something under the surface look of the man, and wanted to reach out to it. Disturbed, she set her gaze beyond him, over his shoulder, then at the point between his eyes, which was like not seeing him at all. But always she came back to him, to the way the bone ridge just above the eyes jutted; on his left cheek an inch from the tip of his mustache a pimple that looked to have been aggravated by careless shaving; the red, wet tip of his tongue held between his teeth to fix concentration; the dark, curling hair on the back of his hands.

He put down his crayon and sketch pad and said quietly. "It's wrong. It doesn't come the right way."

"You mean I'm a bad sitter," she said, falling into her joking way with him.

"I don't mean anything of the sort," he said. "It's nothing to do with you." He sat without saying more, frowning as he considered the problem. Seeing that he no longer looked at her, she relaxed.

They remained so for five minutes. His frown turned darker, harder, and more private; and then at last his eyes began to lighten, and his face muscles relaxed a little. He looked at her. "Will you do something—try something, I mean to say? It may not work either, but I have to listen to instinct when I'm not getting forward; and I'm not."

"Of course," she said. "The fault is mine, I venture.
I've put you off so many times that whatever ideas you
might have had are now dissipated."

"I found a place—" He paused to correct himself. "I
know a place. I found it during a walk when I was staying
at Oaks. The tutor—Mr. Proctor?—a kind man, guided me
to it one day and said no one went there except him, and
he wouldn't for a while, for he was busy with young—"

When he paused again, she said, "Adam."

He nodded. "And I needn't fear that either of the
young ladies would go there, because Miss Annabel didn't
walk, and Miss Doreen walked only about the fields and
barn yards with her grandmother and her brother James."

She began to frown now, wondering where his thoughts
led. Seeing her uncertainty, he smiled and shrugged. "It's
just a place. Wooded. Rocks and a little stream. But it has
a feeling, and I can see you there."

"It seems an elaborate procedure for us to go to Oaks.
We have plenty of woods and a creek here. If you like—"

"No, no. We wouldn't have to go to Oaks. I've learned
the way from here. Last week when I was—waiting. I
went walking and found it again. I'd like you to see it.
That is all."

She smiled. "I am not to pose in my brocaded gown
then."

"No. Come with me tomorrow. I may be wrong about
it. But let us see what happens."

Fifteen

With the harvest in Clovis made no move to return to
town. Roscoe did not tell her to come back, nor did
Alonzo urge her to stay on the farm. Nevertheless, she
stayed. She went into Highboro only once, to buy materials for two winter dresses and cloth to make half a dozen
shirts for Alonzo. Sewing was a thing she had always liked
to do, and now she spent her days at it, cutting paper patterns and then the cloth under the paper shapes she had
pinned and trimmed. She knew just how a sleeve should
be joined and how a collar was made to fit flat and neat.

Under her guidance Geraldine had turned into a tolerable cook, and Clovis wondered if it might be a good
thing for Alonzo to make her his wife. She was not a bad

girl, only ignorant and needing a firm hand. She half hoped Geraldine would become pregnant, and indeed wondered why she had not.

Alonzo had never been one to express himself to others, but seeing Geraldine in the kitchen, and smelling the food she cooked for them, he was not unaware of the fact that his mother's discipline had given the girl some pride in herself and her work. This both pleased and worried him. It was pleasanter to eat good food than bad, to touch a clean woman rather than a malodorous one; but the changes in Geraldine seemed to suggest to him a feeling of responsibility for her he did not like. But it was not a pressing matter.

In a freer, easier way he enjoyed, without saying anything about it, his mother's revival. She was busy and cheerful and, he thought, almost pretty again. Her eyes had lost their muddy, vacant look and were clear and alive. Even when she drank, and she did so still, she did not slur and confuse her thoughts and words. A glass of whiskey made her cheerful now, instead of bitter and abusive.

She sang—well, not quite, but she almost sang. He had never known her to do that. But as she worked away, shoulders hunched cozily over sewing in her lap, eyes steady and purposeful, she hummed vague stretches of melody that were not any songs he knew but were an expression of a peaceful spirit.

He began to make jokes with her—nothing anyone would actually laugh at—but references that turned on a sly word or thought, and she, while she did not laugh, would pause and get a sweeter, smoother look about her eyes and mouth, which encouraged him to speak to her more often.

Then, just as he was beginning to feel content, even something like happy, his father or his brother would stop by with suspicious questions and glum, hard attitudes toward the work he was having done on the farm. Nothing was ever good. Nothing good would come. He must work harder, prod the slaves to greater effort. They were eating too much. The price of cotton was still low. The place didn't pay. Jesus God!

After such a visit, Alonzo would find himself filled with resentment and anger that he had not dared direct toward Roscoe or Junior, and no longer felt inclined to take out on Geraldine or his mother. It turned in on him, bled what little pride he had, annulled contentment, rubbed out any budding ambition he had begun to nurture. After such a time with either one or both of them, he did not want to see or speak to his mother or Geraldine. He shouted at, even cursed them when they, knowing or guessing something of what he felt, tried to make comments to comfort and ameliorate.

He hated them all then; he rejected them all. His mind flew over to Beulah Land where the people were beautiful and mannerly even when they looked at him with dislike, where the slaves walked like men and their women sang of joy as well as sorrow. And he would find himself back at the glade, just over his own boundaries on Oaks property, as if only there could he believe there was a gentler, happier world than that he lived in.

In such a mood of impotent anger and need did he go one day and discover Sarah Kendrick and Casey Troy. He almost stepped into the open area that led to the brook before he saw them, for they made no sound at all. Alonzo froze, did not even breathe again until he had stepped back into the cover of the dark trees.

The woman leaned on the big rock by the brook, a look of calm thought on her face. She might have been about to smile or about to frown. It was as though he caught her at the dead center of an unfinished thought. Her hands were held one by the other loosely in front of her. The skin of her throat and neck glowed moistly. Her hair was not orderly nor disorderly, but looked free and alive; tendrils of it around her face, soft as baby hair, moved in the gentle breeze.

The man stood six or seven feet away from her. His body was fully alert, as was evidenced by the muscular stance of his wide-apart legs. One arm firmly cradled the large sketch pad as the other swung both freely and meticulously over the paper with dark crayon that, too, seemed to be alive. The man's neck was taut with his intentness. His eyes moved quickly between paper and woman.

Alonzo watched for a quarter of an hour as the two continued so: the man rigid of body but with alertly moving eyes and drawing hand, the woman still except for the steady rising and falling of her breast as she breathed and lived.

Presently, the man relaxed and glanced at his drawing briefly before stopping work altogether and putting down the sketch pad and crayon on a stump as casually as he would have set them on a table indoors. When he approached the woman, she remained still in her reverie until he was quite near her. She looked at him for a moment startled, then with eyes that understood, accepted, asked.

There was no protesting, no pretending surprise, no turning away. He took her hand, held it in his briefly, then placed its open palm on his cheek. She bent forward to meet his lips with hers. They held each other and kissed harder.

Alonzo stared at them astounded. This, the woman who had sat her horse and looked at him coolly—spoke to him with deliberate courtesy—dropped her glove as she rode away, unheeding his call? This woman was pressing herself against the man as if she were the man and he the woman to be taken.

Alonzo held his breath in a kind of amazement. He must go—he must stay. He had to stay and see. He watched as they kissed and held and drew apart; then as they removed or opened their clothes to effect direct contact. He saw glowing flesh put to flesh, and heard their cries. Only then, seeing and hearing and hating the joy of their conjunction, did he go. When he was at a distance where he could no longer hear them, on what he called his own land, he began to cry. It was as if the woman had betrayed him. He despised her for her falseness even as he exulted in it. She was no better than Geraldine! For all her fine airs, she was not beautiful nor good; she had given herself as loosely as a sow in season.

But what had all that to do with him?

Everything!

Day after day Alonzo returned to the glade, but the lovers never came there again. He put his hand on the warm, sunny rock where she had leaned. He stood where the man had stood drawing the woman, and tried to imagine he saw her there before him. He knelt on the leaves where they had lain locked in their loving, as if he hoped to find some proof or denial there of his own witnessing.

Sixteen

During the daytime when she sat for him as he stood behind his easel and worked on the portrait; when they met, as they did at meals; or even when they strolled the grounds together in brief recess from the work of the portrait—their attitudes and behavior were as unremarkable as if the roles they played were true. Their discretion was not deceptive so much as considerate. Privately, they gloried in their love, but they had none of that youthful temptation to show it off to others. Their days were public and proper. But at night, when Sarah judged the house to be sleeping, with all its members safe in their rooms, she would leave hers and go to Casey's.

She did it without sneaking and with no feeling of guilt. She carried no lighted candle because she needed none. Her eyes were keen even in the dark, but she could have found her way had she been totally blind, so well did her other senses know every bit of the house.

Sarah was happy in her love, although she knew it would end when Casey left Beulah Land. All that she had speculated upon and anticipated as a girl, all that she had missed as a woman, was revealed to her during the nights with Casey. There was little need of talk for either of them. The intensity of their encounter was such as required no wording, and certainly not the reassurance of words. No one seeing a hungry man devour a full banquet has to ask if he is satisfied or hungry still.

During the nights Sarah did not think, but during the days when she was occupied in various ways, she marveled that the love of Casey, the love for Casey, could be—was, without her ever willing it to be—so separate and private a part of her experience. It had no precedent, it would have no future. It was to be lived fully now, and that is what she did and how she did it.

It was Casey who voiced regret when it had to end. The night of the day he finished the portrait was the last they spent together; and if it seemed their best night, that was doubtless because they both knew it to be their last.

His flesh to hers and hers to him had never been as familiar and dear and responsive; their pauses to rest, or merely to catch breath, never more mutual, their completion never more tremblingly balanced between birth and death. When toward morning they were finally, finally done with each other, he lighted a candle, and they lay side by side in his bed like friends, and talked.

"Will you stay in Savannah all the winter?"

"I expect to. I have some tentative commissions."

"Which will surely secure you more." She smiled. "You'll do it all over again, won't you?"

"Yes," he said.

"And this will happen again," she said without co-
quetry.

"Yes. Not this, but something like it. 'This' has not happened to me before, but something like it has, and something like it surely will again."

After a pause Sarah said, "Will you ever marry?"

"I want no wife, and I have no home to offer one."

"You want no children either?"

"My children are my pictures. Painters say that. For me
it is true. I want to keep on making pictures for as long as
I can. And when I cannot, I hope to die—in some quick,
easy, painless way, of course."

"I have no children," Sarah said.

For the first time since he had known her, Casey
laughed at Sarah. "You're married to Beulah Land. You
have two hundred children—two hundred thousand. Not
only the people, but every cricket, tadpole, bee; every butterfly, every boll of cotton and ear of corn, every stalk of
sugar cane and okra pod is Sarah's child."

"If you were not my lover, I'd ask you to stay and be
my friend."

"If you were not my lover," he said, "I'd ask you to go
with me and be mine."

"Casey! You are a sweet, good man!"

Quickly, as friends, they kissed. Sarah got out of bed
and put on her night robe. "Sugar or Plumboy will drive
you into town to the depot in plenty of time for the train."

He got out of bed and, naked, accompanied her to the
door.

"You look funny," she said. "It doesn't go with a sad
face."

"Go back to bed."

"Not for long. It's almost day."

"Good night," she said.

"Goodbye."

Her smile loved him and thanked him for letting it be
this way. "God be with you always."

She closed the door with no furtiveness. She was the
mistress of Beulah Land and might go anywhere at any
time. Casey had said she was married to Beulah Land.
Thinking of it she smiled as she went down the long hallway to her own room.

Seventeen

Driscoll Proctor said, "We leave Monday."

"Monday is a good day to start a journey," Roman said.

"I had a letter again this week from Miss Eliza Truman urging me to urge you once more—"

"I am gratified," Roman said glacially, "but I need none of Miss Eliza's patronage."

"Stop being arrogant and superior with me! I'm asking you not as one of those sentimental abolitionists you say you hate, but as your friend!" Proctor paused to collect himself. He had not meant to get angry.

"And I thank you. Will I see you before you go finally?"

"Come with me, I beg. I beg."

Roman was silent, but when Proctor looked at him as though he judged Roman to be reconsidering his earlier decision, Roman said, "No, Proctor. I'm not thinking about it. I have my school. My school has me."

"It needs somebody, but not necessarily you," Proctor said.

"Will I see you again?" Roman asked with less flippancy than he had before.

Roman had ridden into Highboro with Sugar, who drove Casey Troy and his luggage in to catch the train to Savannah. Roman had known Proctor would be there on errands, and so had invented some of his own. They'd met, as if by accident, in the post office after the train left and the mail was being sorted.

"I don't know," Proctor said in answer. "I want to be with you forever, but I don't think I want to see you again for half an hour."

Eighteen

It would stay warm for another six to eight weeks, but Nell and Penelope, and even Selma and Pauline, talked of the winter things they had asked Leon to buy for them in Savannah. Among these were toiletries Highboro did not afford, presents they meant to give at Christmas, and dress

materials. The instructions for the last of these had been
precise, and Leon had been cautioned not to deviate from
them—for what does a man know of design and material?
If it were absolutely necessary to make substitutions, he
was to ask the advice of some respectable older female if
one happened to be in the store when he was there; but
on no account was he to take the advice of sales clerks,
for they would try to take advantage of his being a man
and knowing nothing of what he was about.

All during Leon's absence Nell and Penelope, and
sometimes even Sarah when she had a moment to sit
down, discussed these matters tirelessly as they rocked
back and forth in their personal chairs on the cool,
columned front porch. Both older women had become enthusiastic rockers, and a couple of years back Leon had
given them identical chairs, which they had immediately
taken pains to differentiate. Nell filled hers with back and
seat cushions and small pillows in pretty colors. Penelope
contented herself with scarlet velvet ribbons on the two
back posts and with a single thin quilted cushion for the
seat. Each treated the other's additions with kindly sneers.

Penelope in particular came to use the rocking chair to
express her variations of temper. When she was content,
she would sit moving only a little, or for minutes together,
not at all. If she were in a happy mood, she rocked freely
back and forth, giving herself little pushes with her small,
child's feet when they touched the floor on the forward
rock. If she were angry, or merely "put out"—usually
with Nell, for she focused most of her resentments on the
other old woman—why then she would rock furiously
back and forth holding the chair arms grimly and looking
straight ahead with tight lips until someone took the trouble to humor her. She read there, she took occasional
naps there, she sewed there, but most of all she sat there
and made verbal her opinions of the world and its inhabitants. The chair was her forum, her pew, her haven, her
only final, absolute claim to property. No one else, not
even a cat, dared sit in it.

It was two days after Casey Troy's departure that Sarah
found a quiet half hour to look at her portrait seriously
for the first time. She'd seen it, of course, and listened to
the comments made by others in the household. Although
no one came right out and said so, no one liked it; it
made them uneasy and resentful. As she now studied the
portrait, she began to find their reasons. Casey had paint-

ed her in the glade, although they had been there together only one time; so the outdoors and the simple dress
she was wearing gave the portrait a casual look. Nell expressed it for all of them when she said it lacked the authority and dignity they knew her to have, and which
should be apparent in a likeness of the mistress of Beulah
Land. That, she supposed, was as near to it as they could
come.

It was indeed not a portrait of the mistress of Beulah
Land, but a portrait of Sarah. It showed more of her than
they were accustomed to see and an aspect of her Casey
had reason to know and they did not. As a child finds it
impossible to entertain the idea of a parent's sexuality, so
was Sarah's family inclined to deny hers and set the artist's suggestion of it down to misinterpretation. There was
nothing obvious, of course, but there was a shine on her
lips and eyes, a tilt of the head that hinted invitation, a
sensual languor in the repose of the arms.

Sarah smiled. He had painted the portrait for her and
so that she would always—as if she needed a picture—
remember their time together. Reminded now, she felt her
first regret at Casey's leaving and decided to go to the
glade, where she might think of him as privately as she
pleased, with no one to interrupt her reverie.

The clock showed nearer four than three. It was really
too late in the afternoon for such a walk, for the days
were drawing in. But she would do it now while she
thought of it, for if she postponed it, the gesture would
seem too calculated for her to enjoy. She picked up a
shawl from the back of a chair in the office where she had
sat examining the portrait. Not needing it yet, she folded
it over her arm and then slipped through and out of the
house the back way, hoping no one, not even Rachel or
Roman, would see her and ask to go along, for then it
would not be right for her to do. When she knew she had
got away, she laughed, feeling as free as a girl.

Roscoe and Junior had come together to the farm that
afternoon, and they had just left Alonzo in a fuming rage,
after declaring that even Clarence Anderson had got more
bales of cotton per acre than Alonzo had. (They had no
way of knowing this, but Alonzo never disputed what they
stated as fact.) They were also critical of the looks of the
cows. The bag of one of them was blue and shriveled; another's coat was rough. As a parting insult, Junior said,

"See you still haven't got around to new hinges for this saggy barn door." He gave it a rude kick and mounted his horse.

Already mounted, Roscoe looked down at his younger son and said, "Time for you to get your finger out of your ass and amount to something."

He watched them ride away and then went into the house. Stepping from the back porch into the kitchen, he found his mother and Geraldine, one of them sifting flour to make supper biscuits, the other washing new turnip greens. They broke off talking when they saw him.

"They gone?" Clovis said.

He nodded.

She sighed relief. "Thank God for that."

Alonzo went to the round dining table and picked up a cold baked sweet potato left from the noon meal. Pinching off the end he peeled it carefully and began to eat it.

Clovis had turned back to Geraldine. "Finish telling me about the cake." She added buttermilk to the bowl of sifted flour.

Geraldine laughed comfortably. "Well. While it was still light, Mama sent me out to cut some fat lighter wood so she could start the stove next morning. That was Mrs. Considine's old house, you remember." Clovis nodded. "Well, I passed the table where that chocolate cake sat, the icing just hardening, and it looked so good I said, 'Mama, can't I have me a piece of that cake?' And she said no, not till after suppertime and we'd see what they left over, if any. Seemed like I never wanted anything much as I wanted that cake that minute, but I went out like she told me and on to the woodpile and started to cut the wood.

"I had to stop to pick a splinter out of my hand; you know how splintery lighter wood is, but it didn't bleed hardly at all because it was in the hard part of my hand, from hoeing. Oh, yes'm, even that young I hoed.

"On the sudden I smelled fire. Then I turnt and saw it, and it wasn't but minutes till the whole place roared up and was gone. Didn't save a stick of furniture, but everybody got out—"

"Thank the Lord!" Clovis murmured.

"Yes'm. Even the old tomcat named Abraham. Well, I couldn't think of nothing but that cake and how it had sat there on the table, and I'd wanted me a piece of it, and now it was all burnt up with the rest."

Both women were thoughtful. "What we remember," Clovis said, shaking her head.

Finished with the potato, Alonzo dropped its limp, sticky skin on the table and went out the door.

"Where you going?" Clovis called.

"Wander about," Alonzo said.

"Don't get too far and forget your supper."

Alonzo went into the yard and to the barn. He kicked the door lightly, then went close to examine the hinges. One would have to be replaced. The other needed only a big nail or two hammered in part way and bent over. He'd do it tomorrow—maybe. He grimaced with the first return to feeling himself again. Going into the barn, he rummaged in a box of nails and old fish hooks and hinges until he saw that he had what he needed and would not have to make a special trip to town. Then he came out of the barn, stretched his arms upward, and looked around.

With the part of his mind and vision that was ever alert to the sector of land leading to the glade, he saw a woman's figure going along the edge of a field, and knew it was Sarah Kendrick. Sarah Kendrick, alone. He'd heard at the post office that the artist had taken the train to Savannah. As he watched, she turned into the woods. She was going to the place he had seen her with the artist, where another time he had seen Roman with the Oaks tutor.

Not consciously deciding to do so, he set off to follow her. He used caution only as he came near the glade, meaning no more than to see what the woman was up to. Maybe the man he'd seen her with had not gone away, but had merely gone to stay with another family nearby, and they'd made an arrangement to meet here today.

It took him five minutes to steal the last hundred feet into a position that gave him a clear view of the glade. Sarah would not have heard him if he had moved without stealth, because she was not expecting anyone. His cunning served no purpose other than to quicken the tension in him to trigger sharpness. As he turned aside the last leafy branch to reveal the glade, he was in the near-darkness of the trees, and she was in shadow deep enough for him to have to narrow his eyes to find and read her face.

She leaned against the big rock just as she had that day the artist stood a little away from her making rapid sketches. She had been thoughtful then; now her eyes were closed, and a smile curved her lips.

He studied her and waited, but nothing happened; no one came. Gradually, he realized that she was not expecting the man. She had returned there simply to do what she was doing. He bent to the ground, found a small chip of slate, and threw it so that it dropped near her feet, hitting the side of the big rock. She did not open her eyes, and she surely would have done so if she had been expecting anyone. He let a long minute go by, and then he found a dry pine cone on the ground near him and tossed that. It hit her shoes and bounced away from her.

Frowning, she opened her eyes and looked up, as though thinking the cone had fallen from one of the trees whose branches spread high over her head and made the glade darker as the sun went down. Then she looked around her slowly, without expectation or apprehension. But belying her air of assurance, she began to shiver. Shaking out the shawl she had brought with her, she threw it around her shoulders and tied it loosely where its ends crossed her bosom. Folding her arms to hug herself as she felt the chill of the coming night, she looked about her and drew in a slow, deep breath.

She was about to leave, he realized.

He would not let her—not without her learning he was here; and not, his next thought told him, without her knowing this place was his as much as hers, being the property of neither, that he had as much right here as she, and that he had not only been here before her, and after, but had seen her here too.

He stepped out of the shadow of the woods into the glade. Her exclamation of surprise gratified him.

"Who—?"

He found himself bowing to the woman, low and deep, in a mockery of the manners of gentle folk. When he raised his body and head and looked at her again, her face had set into the formal mold it had always assumed when he had met her riding or walking.

"You are Roscoe Elk's—"

"I am Alonzo Elk," he said in a tone that matched and mocked her own formality.

"This isn't your land. Is it? I was told—"

"Nor yours!" he said. He was surprised at the roughness of his tone, but somehow reassured by it too.

"No," she said. "It is part of Oaks, I believe."

He stepped twice in her direction before her voice halted him. "What are you doing here?"

He stared at her, astonished to see fear in her face. "I come here too sometimes," he said and knew that his tone was now too gentle. She would think him afraid of her.

"You say you come here *too*."

"I have seen you here."

"I've been only once before."

"Yes," He smiled, and as the fear in her face increased, so did the deliberate suggestion of his smile. "I saw you then." He took more steps toward her.

"Stop! Please—"

He continued to smile, feeling stronger with every step he took. "I saw you with the man. On the ground there."

"Don't come any closer!"

What she said gave him the clue to his next action. He'd had no conscious intentions toward her, until what she told him not to do put them into his head. He was compelled to perform the positive of every negative command she gave. It was a matter of self-assertion more than defiance, a result of being rubbed raw in his pride by Roscoe and Junior's telling him what to do, what not to do, how worthless he was.

"Don't touch me—"

He took one of her wrists, and when she tried to break away, he grabbed the other. She kicked him, and he pulled her to him so that she would have no room in which to kick again.

Struggling, she declared, "You are evil like your father!"

He tossed his head as if to clear it. "No."

"Let me go!" As she made a greater effort to pull away, she dropped the shawl, and her dress split from neck to right shoulder.

He stared at her, still without purpose until she gave it to him. She began to scream, and he held her close to him with one arm so that the hand of the other might close her mouth. As she struggled harder and he worked to hold her, their bodies grew warmer, and he became more aware of the feel and smell of her. Another part of her dress ripped, the result of her own twisting. She shook her head free and cried, "No! No " as if he had harmed her, and he had not, or had not meant to. She began to weep and to plead. "Please don't—Don't hurt me!—Have mercy, do!—Oh, have mercy!"

Her weakness made him powerful. It was not her struggling that excited him, but his own. He could, he discovered, resist. He did not have to yield when told to yield. He was not his father's nor his brother's servant; he was not this woman's dog to be commanded. He would conquer her—and then all who thought him weak.

He gripped her in his arms, and she could only bleat and beg: "Have mercy! Have mercy on me!" Then suddenly, shockingly, she was no longer weak, but a force that fought back and might overcome him, "God damn you!" she cried. "God damn you, Roscoe Elk!"

He struck her with his fist, and she fell. He fell on her; and when she began to revive, he held her on the ground and struck her face again and again until she lay still. Then he drew back from her and gripping the hem of her skirt ripped it up to her breasts. Supporting his own weight. he let himself gently down upon her. She was so soft: she was so clean. What had disarmed her husband's desire gave heat to Alonzo's. As if he were a puppet in a play that had been written long ago, of which he had no knowledge and over which he had no control, he took her then as his prize, although there was no glory in it for him, for she lay as if dead. As he thrust himself into her below, he clamped his mouth over her slack, sleeping lips, and dropped tears of lust and terror on her face.

Nineteen

She came to herself, hearing the barking of dogs.

She was cold.

She was on the ground.

Why was she on the ground?

Automatically, she reached to pull her clothes about her, and so discovered that they were in rags. As she sat up and tried to gather herself and her clothes together, she began to remember what had happened, and she began to scream.

Roman was the one to find her. Hearing her, he ran into the clearing, a lantern swinging from one hand, the other hand shielding his eyes from the lantern that had lighted his way and now prevented him from seeing her. She was crouched over her knees, suddenly quiet.

The lantern he set down on the ground beside her showed him the state of her clothes. He threw the quilt he carried around her, and she drew it tight before she looked up and recognized him. "Roman."

"We missed you hours ago—we've all been looking everywhere!"

Her arms reached for him, losing the quilt, and he dropped to his knees and held her. "Are you hurt, my Sarah?"

In a raw, quick jumble of words she told him what had happened. The barking of the dogs came louder, and presently they were surrounded by men from Oaks and Beulah Land. Floyd was there, and a minute later Bruce Davis and Driscoll Proctor. Proctor tried to quiet the dogs. Bruce called for his horse to be brought up, and when it was, he mounted, and Sarah was lifted by Floyd to ride in front of the saddle. Then Floyd led the horse out of the clearing and back toward Beulah Land. Sarah, who had been given a large drink of brandy, lay limp against Bruce and the horse, making no effort to speak.

Roman walked with Floyd and whispered to him what Sarah had said in the few moments they were by themselves before the larger party came.

Floyd nodded, and then nodded more grimly. "Soon as we get her into the house, I'm going to town."

"Town!" Roman said.

"To get Sheriff Byrne and Roscoe Elk and go to the farm and arrest Alonzo—"

"Arrest Alonzo! Everybody will know—"

"You keep out of it," Floyd warned. "Leon's not here. I'm doing the best thing."

"Think of her! If there's ever a trial—"

"You be still!" Floyd said angrily, and Roman subsided, without understanding, as well as he knew Floyd, that his friend's rage was not toward him but toward what had happened.

As they went on to Beulah Land, they gathered more and more followers, so that when they arrived at the house, there was a mob of men serving as escort. Rachel screamed when she saw her mother, and Edna Davis, who was waiting on the porch, grabbed her and handed her to Juanita, telling the woman to take her to Felix's room. Then Edna and Lovey led the way into the house and up the stairs to Sarah's room, Edna guiding, Lovey calling orders and threats right and left. Floyd and Bruce stopped in the office, and Driscoll Proctor stayed with the men outside and talked to them to quiet them. The lady had been found. She appeared to have suffered no very serious injury, but the doctor would be sent for. They were all to go home and go to bed. The trouble was over.

In the office Bruce and Floyd made a quick plan. The women would see to Sarah. Together, they would ride into town and send out to Beulah Land Dr. Theodore Platt, who had come to Highboro as Dr. Porterfield's replacement when that placid, greedy man died. Then they would get Sheriff Byrne and after acquainting him with the details of Sarah's calamity, the three would ask Roscoe Elk to ride with them to the Anderson Place to arrest Alonzo and take him to jail, for his own safety as well as to serve the cause of law and justice. They would be as quiet about it as they could be, but the main line of events was bound to become known, and it would be better to discourage speculation by telling as much of the truth as seemed necessary.

They went upstairs together and found Nell policing Sarah's door, keeping all out who were not needed. She had already, to her considerable satisfaction, managed to insult both Penelope and Selma by telling them the best thing they could do was to go to their rooms and stay there. She had stepped briefly into her husband's room to acquaint him and Rachel with the gist of the episode before taking her stand outside Sarah's room. However languid she appeared to be in the ordinary way, Nell's mind was quick and efficient when circumstances required it to be.

Nell told Bruce and Floyd that Edna was busy with Sarah and could not be called out, so they explained their plan to her, and she promised to relay it to Edna and Lovey. How, she asked, were they going to tell Leon? Bruce said he would go to Savannah on the next train and bring Leon home.

When they came downstairs and went out through the breezeway, they found Driscoll Proctor still talking to the men, most of whom remained. Driscoll said, "Where is Roman?" They shook their heads and went to the barn for their horses.

Twenty

"What ails you?" Clovis asked fretfully, coming into the room where Alonzo sat alone in front of the fireplace in which no fire burned. "Come dragging yourself home after we-all had our supper and then wouldn't eat or say where you'd been—"

"Told you I wasn't hungry."

"You sick?"

"No."

"Look funny. Where you been to?"

"Never mind."

"That sweet potato you ate disagreed. I told Geraldine they was too green and stringy to bake good; they got to age first. But she say you like baked, and you'll get baked as long as she does your cooking."

"Mama, you got any whiskey?"

She looked at him closely; her face relaxed in relief. "Best thing for you, you got the upset stomach and nerves. I'll get it." She went off to her bedroom.

When she returned with a jug, she found him just as she had left him, but Geraldine stood beside him holding a shawl over one arm. "Look what I found," Geraldine said. Alonzo kept his eyes on the dead fireplace, but Clovis looked and saw a shawl that was red with a dark blue binding, and in good condition except that it was dirty. "'Tisn't mine," she said.

"Well, whose is it?" Geraldine asked. "I never had nothing so good."

"You bring the liquor, Mama?" Alonzo asked.

"Here." She held out the jug and a glass. He uncorked the jug and poured whiskey into the glass. When he had drunk half of what he poured, he looked at the shawl for the first time.

"Where you find that?" he asked.

Geraldine said, "In the yard when I went to draw a bucket of water. I thought there was enough, but then I looked and there wasn't. I stepped on it in the yard in the dark. First, I thought it was a dead bird, but it was this."

He looked at it. "Give it to me."

"You know whose it is?" Clovis asked.

"I dropped it," he said, taking the shawl in his hands

and holding it to his face to smell it before dropping it
into his lap with a shrug of helplessness.

"Where you get such a thing?" Clovis asked roughly, to
hide the fear that stirred in her like nausea.

Alonzo drank from the glass again, half of what was
now left in it.

"Somebody coming." Geraldine cocked her head, listening.

"What?" Clovis said.

"Thought I heard somebody."

"Maybe one of our people," Clovis suggested.

"They don't come to the front."

Alonzo seemed uninterested.

Then they heard footsteps crossing the porch, and the
door from it was opened without a preceding knock.
When thus unannounced, the man walked into the room,
the three already there stared at him with equal surprise.

"What do you want here?" Clovis asked angrily.

Roman ignored her, his eyes on the man who sat in the
chair before the dark fireplace, a woman's shawl on his
lap.

"That's hers," Roman said. He reached under his coat
and brought forth a large pistol. Geraldine screeched but
did not move. Alonzo raised the shawl to his face as if he
could hide in it, but Roman, holding the heavy pistol
steady with both hands, aimed it at his brother and fired.

Twenty-One

Two days later four men met in the small jailhouse that
had only one cell, and it seldom used. They were Leon
Kendrick, Roscoe Elk, Sheriff Charles Byrne, and Judge
Fulton Maynard who had been summoned from the
county seat.

Sheriff Byrne and Judge Maynard had already been to
Beulah Land where they had talked at length and sepa-
rately to Sarah Kendrick and to Roman Elk. They had
been to the Anderson Place where they questioned Clovis
Elk. They had met and talked with Roscoe Elk and with
Leon Kendrick, with Bruce and Edna Davis, and with Dr.
Theodore Platt. Everyone knew how the affair was to be
settled; it only remained to do it.

Judge Maynard presided. He said, "Does anyone question the fact that rape occurred?"

Roscoe turned his head deliberately to look at Leon. "From the doctor's report I have no doubt that my son Alonzo raped Mrs. Leon Kendrick. As to what may have led up to the act—"

Leon said nothing; his face was like stone.

"Nor," the judge continued after a hard look at Roscoe, "does there appear to be any doubt that Roman Elk, who was devoted to Mrs. Kendrick because she had befriended him, took a pistol from Leon Kendrick's desk and went to what is hereabouts known as the 'Anderson Place' and shot his brother Alonzo Elk—he, Roman Elk, having been told by Mrs. Kendrick the name of the man who attacked her."

No one spoke in assent or dissent.

"The dead man has been buried. A vile wrong has been avenged. If this were a case in court, with the facts presented as I have learned them, I as Judge of Court would dismiss the case as already having been settled. If it were tried, the verdict would most certainly be that the killing was justified. There will be no trial of Roman Elk, and no judgment against him this side of Judgment Day. Any further airing of the events would serve no purpose of justice and would only distress the lady who has already suffered greatly and who deserves our every consideration. Is there any objection to this settlement, any further comment, or are we in agreement?"

"Agreed," Leon said.

The others looked at Roscoe Elk. After holding them with one of his long pauses, he spoke at last. "However grieved I may be at the—you must allow me to say—principal victim of these circumstances, my son Alonzo Elk, I have the hope that he has found forgiveness and understanding with the Lord God Jehovah." The three white men stared down at their hands, frowning. "As for my wife's son, Roman, I move, I recommend, I urge—with consideration given to the fact that I am no ordinary 'free colored person,' but one of substantial properties and thus deserving the law's consideration—I urge that the man carrying the name of Roman Elk be banished not only from the plantation called Beulah Land and the town of Highboro, but the State of Georgia, for so long as he may live."

Judge Maynard and Leon looked at each other, startled at this proposal. But the judge had some experience reading men's faces; reading Leon's now, and wanting to finish the case and go home, he asked, "Have you any objection?"

For the first time in his life Leon felt grateful to Roscoe. "I have none," he said.

Driscoll Proctor waited with Bruce and Adam Davis outside the jailhouse to hear from Leon when he emerged what had transpired inside. Proctor then made known the invitation that had been extended to Roman by his friend, Miss Eliza Truman, in Philadelphia. It was received by all as an excellent solution to the situation.

And so, after arrangements had been made, Roman was told that he was to leave Beulah Land and go with Driscoll Proctor to Philadelphia to try his fortune there. On Monday he would leave on the train with Proctor and his other charge, Adam Davis, going first to Savannah, then by coastal steamer to Norfolk. There he would wait for Proctor to see Adam properly installed at the university in Charlottesville and return. He and Proctor then would proceed, by boat again, to Philadelphia. Leon brought him a trunk and traveling bags, and gave five hundred dollars into Driscoll Proctor's keeping. He was to use whatever was necessary for Roman's traveling expenses, and to give him the remainder, which would certainly be the major portion of it, to start life in the strange city.

Roman's mind was a jumble. He had no feeling of guilt or regret over killing a man, even though that man was his half brother. The kinship they shared derived from one who did not love him; the other half of Alonzo was from a man Roman hated and who hated him. The only important thing to Roman was the fact that Sarah had been violated. His rage had little to do with the specifically sexual nature of the act; he'd have felt the same way if her attacker had merely touched her person with violent intention. He could have killed him a thousand times without feeling that the scales had been balanced.

As to going away, his initial resentment of the coercion involved was very soon assuaged by the prospect of travel and change, of having the company of his old idol Adam Davis for a part of the journey, and then of going on to a place he knew himself to be welcome, with the friend whose love he hoped never to exhaust. Lovey packed his clothes and books into the trunk and cases Leon had bought. For the first time since his birth Lovey approved of Roman and treated him with respect and consideration.

To her, he had with one action justified having been mis-
begotten and having lived what she considered to be a
useless, pampered life.

Sarah stayed in her room for only a day after the attack. She would not have whispering and worried speculation among her people. When she went among them, they
saw her bruises, but after their initial shock of pity and
anger, they ignored her appearance even as she did. She
did not, however, venture beyond the grounds immediately around the house. When she realized that she was
afraid to do so, she set out to walk into the fields and
woods. During her walk she thought of Clovis Elk. She
had always disliked the woman, and resented and envied
her for bearing a child of Leon's, when she could not. But
she realized for the first time, and was immediately
ashamed that it had not occurred to her before, that
Clovis must have loved Alonzo, and that she must grieve
for him. She remembered the day long ago she had seen
Clovis with her two younger sons, and her obvious affection for them, even when she was trying to be rude to
Sarah.

On the instant, she turned out of the woods and headed
straight toward the house on the Anderson Place. Alonzo
had been buried two days ago, but she had overheard
kitchen gossip indicating that Clovis had not gone back to
live in town. Walking with determination she arrived at
the house in a quarter of an hour. She found Clovis sitting alone in a low straight chair on the front porch. She
held a half-filled glass in both hands on her lap, and there
was a jug on the floor beside her chair. Her eyes were
open, but otherwise she might have been asleep, so still
did she sit, and so empty was her face of expression.

Sarah did not go onto the porch, but stopped at its edge
in the yard, directly in front of Clovis.

"I am sorry for you," Sarah said. "I am sorry for everything."

She had begun to think the woman hadn't heard her
when Clovis said thickly, "Get off my land."

On the day Roman left, Proctor came for him from
Oaks with the driver on a wagon that was to carry them
and all the traveling bags and trunks and boxes to the
train station. Adam was being driven in the family coach
by his father and with his sisters and grandmother. The
wagon was slow; it had started out much earlier from

Oaks than the carriage, and would be overtaken by the
carriage before it arrived in Highboro.

Having said goodbye to Floyd, Roman had been with
Sarah privately for the last hour, during which they had
not talked of the past but of Roman's future in the North.
He promised her that he would write frequently, and she
said, although neither of them really believed it, that one
day she'd come to Philadelphia, and that he and Mr.
Proctor would show her the city. He said he was worried
about his school, but she assured him that she would keep
it going and that furthermore she had decided to—not
ask—but insist that Selma become its principal teacher. It
was precisely what Selma needed to stop her from further
wasting her life.

Roman said, "And Pauline can keep order with a
peach-tree switch." They smiled at the picture the two
companions thus would make.

It was at that point Lovey came to say the wagon was
waiting at the front of the house. The three went out and
found that Sugar had loaded Roman's cases and trunk.
Lovey stayed on the porch, her presence enough compliment to the occasion; but Sarah went down the steps to
the wagon and greeted Proctor. Then suddenly, and at the
same moment, Sarah and Roman knew this was farewell
and turned to each other in panic and grief. Sarah threw
her arms around Roman, and they held each other, their
bodies quaking with tears. When they broke apart, she
kissed him. He turned blindly to the wagon, set his foot
on one of the wheel spokes and climbed up. Proctor gave
quick instructions to the driver, and they rolled away.
Sarah followed a few steps and then stopped, waving her
hand high until Roman, standing in the back of the wagon
facing her and waving, was lost to her as the driveway
through the orchard widened and curved out to the main
road. On the little porch that led off the hallway of the
upper floor, Rachel, who had said she would not watch
him leave, sat numb with her grief and watched.

Twenty-Two

In early November, Sarah knew that she was pregnant.
For a day after deciding that it was so, she felt an exhilaration, a soaring of soul she had never before in her life

experienced. But on the second day she made herself think practically about it, and immediately began to doubt and speculate. She decided that she would have to talk with someone she could trust, of whom she might ask advice. But who was there? Edna was her closest friend, but this was not something they would be able to talk about. There was no other woman. Oddly enough, Lauretta, she thought, would have been the one to listen and advise her. After her initial delight in the "drama" of the dilemma, Lauretta would have settled down to think about it and would have given sensible advice. For all her romantic nature, she was practical and clear-thinking about everyone but herself. It could not be Nell. Certainly not Selma. Nor Lovey.

No woman then.

It must be Felix. His mind was his own; he did not think in tidy, closed boxes, nor speak in platitudes. She waited until after breakfast the next morning. After bathing and feeding him and making him comfortable for the day, Stella went downstairs with his dishes and bath water and generally stayed gossiping with the kitchen women for an hour or more.

Sarah found his door open, tapped on it as she entered, and then closed it behind her.

Felix closed his book. "Good morning, my dear."

"Good morning, Uncle." She went to the bed and kissed his cheek.

Glancing over her shoulder at the closed door he said, "Are we to have secrets?"

"Yes, if you please."

"Sit down." She drew a chair close to the bed. "I am flattered that you come to me."

"Only you can advise me."

He threw up his hand. "My dear Sarah! Please not. You have come to the wrong person. I am not qualified to advise anybody, and certainly no one as good and bright as you."

"You must, Uncle."

He sighed and looked at her intently.

"I'm going to have a child."

He let a moment pass. "I am right, I trust, in believing you have always longed for children of your own?"

"Yes."

"Well, then! Oh God. Yes. It may not be Leon's. That's what you mean, of course."

"Not 'may not.' It cannot be his."

He said slowly, "I had imagined you were not close in that way."

"Not of my own wishing."

"Oh?"

"I have no complaint of Leon—"

Felix smiled tiredly and took her hand. "Nor I of your aunt. Some people—well, it doesn't take them right. I don't know why, but we mustn't blame them." After a brief pause he nodded his head vigorously. "Then it is the black man's doing, and you must have the doctor out immediately. No one need know, not even Leon, if you prefer not to tell him. Every doctor understands it. No white woman can be allowed to bear a colored baby. Surely you know that?"

"Uncle, I cannot believe it will be colored. How could that one violent time—? I'm sure it will be white."

His mouth opened in surprise. "The artist?" She did not answer. "Now, be still, don't pull away."

"Was there whispering when he was here?" she wanted to know.

"Not that I heard. But when I saw the portrait, my dear, for just a moment I did wonder. I have a wicked mind, or at any rate I'm not as innocent as the remainder of this household."

"You are not shocked?"

"No." He frowned.

"But you condemn me."

He thought about it before he answered. "I don't think I do—not in the personal way, I mean to say. If the fact of it makes me uneasy, I think it has to do with Beulah Land rather than you. But never mind that. Whoever the father, you must do as I suggest. Have the doctor out and get rid of it. At once, and no more thinking about it."

Without making a sound, she began to cry. "I want my child."

He held both of her hands close against his body to comfort her. "No, Sarah."

"It will be mine, only mine."

"It will be heir to Beulah Land, and no Kendrick. You are not a common farmer's wife who can mix in a little outside blood with her own brood without anyone's thinking the worse of her for it. Whatever child you have will one day inherit this place. I was born here. I grew up here. I shall die here. It's home, and more than home.

One of the reasons I have always loved you, Sarah, is that I knew from the very beginning, before you married and came here to live, that you felt the way I did about it. You are not a private woman who belongs to herself. You belong to Beulah Land."

She stopped crying and sat still. The tears began to dry on her face without her attending them. They did not look at each other, and neither of them spoke for a long time. At last she rose from her chair. "I shall send for Dr. Platt," she said and went out of the room walking like an old woman.

PART SIX

1853

One

Before daybreak on a cold morning in January, Leon rose and dressed quickly in the rough, heavy clothes Sarah had laid out for him. Not bothering to light a candle he crept down the stairs to the office. There he found the gun he had cleaned the night before in the cabinet that held all his guns. Going through the wide hall and breezeway, he discovered Floyd in the big kitchen, his gun propped against the back of a straight chair.

The two men did not speak, but nodded in greeting. Floyd set two tumblers on the table and poured three fingers of whiskey into each from a stone jug he took from the bottom shelf of a food safe. Each raised a glass and drank.

"Ah," they said together, experiencing the same shock of pleasure.

"That'll warm us," Floyd said.

Leon lifted the cloth that covered a pan of cold biscuits on the back of the stove. He took half of one with one bite and handed another to Floyd, who began to eat it. When they had chewed and swallowed, they stuffed the remaining biscuits inside their shirts against their bodies to warm and soften them. Then they finished their whiskey, took up their guns, and went out the back door, finding Joe-Tom by the old fig tree with two of the best hunting hounds, Brutus and Molly.

Joe-Tom was a skinny boy fourteen years old, son of Sallou who, with Sharon and Lotus, still worked in the kitchens with Myrtis. The boy had a passion for dogs and hunting. No one had trained him to it. He had made a job out of his own inclinations, as often happened on the plantation. He took care of all the dogs, putting them through their early training and recommending the likeliest to Leon and Floyd when they hunted, depending on what the quarry was to be. Floyd and Leon were the only ones on the place who hunted. Neither cared for shooting as sport, but they liked to go about the woods and fields together as they had done ever since they were boys. Now and then someone in the big house would voice boredom with the sameness of the table meats—mostly pork and domestic fowl, sometimes beef—or simply express a longing for game; and then off Leon and Floyd would go, as they were doing this morning.

"Howdy, Joe-Tom," Floyd said.

"Howdy!" the boy said eagerly. He had been waiting and was not as warmly dressed as they were. He wore trousers that were too short for him, a heavy woolen shirt and stocking cap. He never wore more, no matter how severe the weather, preferring the freedom of easy movement to comfort. His hands were cold, and he had been rubbing them together without generating much warmth in them. He would be all right when they got going; it was only the waiting he minded.

"Howdy, Joe-Tom," Leon said.

"Howdy!"

"Dogs ready?"

"Yes, sir!"

Molly wagged her tail at the sight of men and guns that meant doing the work she loved, and Leon bent to rub her head. Brutus lifted a leg to the base of the fig tree, and his urine steamed in the cold air.

"We ready then?" Floyd said, reaching into his shirt for a biscuit which he handed the boy.

"Yes, sir!" Joe-Tom was more interested in hunting than food at the moment, but he ate half of the biscuit and tore the other half into two parts to throw to Molly and Brutus, who caught and swallowed them automatically and then trotted ahead through the back yard, past the clothes-washing area with its tables and tubs and black pots and the stump for pounding dirt out of clothes after they had soaked. They always set off in the same direction, however they varied their route as they went along. The first light of day showed as they crossed the fields covered with heavy frost. The earth was frozen and crunched under their feet. Circling ahead, the dogs were followed by Joe-Tom, who let them lead him; and he was followed by Leon and Floyd, who let the boy and dogs lead them.

In an hour and a half they took a dozen squirrels, enough to make a big stew for noon dinner, and broth to flavor a gruel for Felix, if he were able to eat it. Felix had suffered a light stroke of paralysis on Christmas Day, and although he had appeared to be rallying, yesterday he'd taken a turn for the worse.

But that was forgotten now as men and boy and dogs sat in a clearing in the woods, dogs on the ground, the men side by side on a log, the boy astride a low stump. They shared the remainder of the biscuits, and the dogs trotted into the brush, their hunting fever undiminished.

Joe-Tom was humming to himself when Floyd turned to him and said solemnly, "Joe-Tom, what's this I hear about you can gobble like a wild turkey?"

The boy smirked. This was the way hunts always ended. They waited, and presently he did indeed gobble like a turkey in such an accurate manner that the dogs came running to investigate.

The men laughed, and the dogs sat again, looking puzzled.

With a straight face Floyd said, "Joe-Tom, can you give us some bird calls?"

Joe-Tom obliged, sometimes working with his fingers, more often only with lips and teeth and tongue. The dogs stood wagging their tails, on to the joke now, barking pleasure and protest.

When Joe-Tom finished his repertory, they all laughed again. Leon slapped his thighs and stood and stretched. "Let's go home and get some breakfast!"

Leon and Floyd set off briskly, then broke into a run, racing each other as they had done in childhood with no signal to start or stop other than either's inclination. The boy, laden with guns now as well as the morning kill, followed more slowly, and the dogs dropped back to keep him company.

They were still in high spirits when they came to the kitchen door where they were met by Lovey.

"I heard the shooting; what'd you get?"

"Big mess of squirrels," Leon said.

"You tell Joe-Tom to take them to the barn to skin and gut. I don't want them in this kitchen for Myrtis to deal with."

Floyd said, "He knows that, Mama."

She scowled at the two cheerful men. Without turning she said, "Myrtis! They've come. Start." To the men she said, "Scrape your shoes before you come in." They obeyed her and entered the kitchen where Myrtis was breaking eggs into a skillet. A plate of fried ham stood warming on the back of the stove, and grits were cooked and ready in a pot. "You'll eat here," Lovey said, indicating the round table where she and Floyd and Clarice always ate.

Sharon poured warm water into a tin basin, and they washed their hands. Sallou set plates and cutlery down and then fetched jars of plum jam and fig preserves, which she knew they both particularly fancied. Presently all was ready, and they ate, exchanging a word, a phrase as they did so. They knew each other so well there was seldom need for whole sentences between them; often a nod or glance sufficed for communication more complete than others make with words.

They had finished the gifts and ham and gravy and sopped up the last of the egg yoke from their plates when Sarah came in. She looked tired and preoccupied. Her face had lost flesh and her chin and nose appeared more angular than they had when she was younger. Although there was no sagging under her chin, her neck had accumulated wrinkles. There were lines around her eyes, and others held her mouth in parentheses.

"Good morning," Leon said.

It was only then she noticed the men. "Oh. Good morning. Did you go hunting?"

Leon nodded and said, "Got some squirrels."

Sarah had not waited for his answer; she was speaking to Lovey. "Tell Otis to saddle a horse, and then come to me in the offices. I want to send him to town directly."

"How is Uncle Felix?" Leon asked.

She said, "I want Otis to go for Dr. Platt."

Leon stood. "What can I do?"

Before he finished saying the words Sarah had left them.

Floyd rose from the table. "I'll go tell Otis, Mama." He went out.

"Where are the others?" Leon said to Lovey.

"Miss Nell up with Mister Felix. Miss Pea, Miss Selma in the dining room finishing their breakfast. Mister Adam Davis rode over while ago like he happened by and begged Miss Rachel to ride with him." She grunted. "Planned it between them, you ask me. Off she went without her breakfast. Foolishness." When he stepped to the back door, she said, "Now where you going to?"

"Out to the barn."

The frost had melted away, and a row of icicles suspended from the rope pulley over the well nearest the big house dripped in an almost steady flow. Leon found Joe-Tom outside the cow barn. He helped the boy finish dressing the squirrels, and he tried a joke or two with him, but the pleasure had gone out of the morning. When he drew guts from the body of a squirrel and threw them over the fence into the chicken run, a big red rooster came running to claim them, and the hens scattered out of his way, squawking simulated alarm.

Two

Their ride had taken them to the very glade which Roman and Proctor had once used as a private meeting place, where Sarah and Casey Troy had become lovers, and where Sarah had been attacked by Alonzo Elk, now more than seven years in his grave. They did not know, of course, what had happened there and, indeed, considered that they had discovered it. Dismounted, they strolled hand in hand, Rachel holding Adam's tightly, her fingers alternating with his.

"Can you really wait until I'm eighteen in October?" she said, not for the first or the tenth or the last time.

"Well—" He frowned, seeming to consider it. "I must, mustn't I? They've said you have to be eighteen before we can marry."

"I don't know why!" Rachel exclaimed. "Lots of girls marry at fifteen and sixteen. Annabel was just seventeen when she married Blair Saxon."

"Annabel was said to be exceptionally mature for her age."

"I admit only that she was as silly and vain at seventeen as she is today."

Adam whooped with laughter. "I shall tell her you said so!"

"Don't bother. I shall tell her myself one day, but not until I am married, and we are equals at last."

"That won't make you equal, you know. She's already a mother twice over."

"So shall I be—and more times too."

"Her children will always be older than yours."

"Ours will be smarter and better looking." He smiled.

"Did you hear what I said? I said *ours*. *Our* children!
Doesn't that raise goose bumps?"

He shrugged and tried not to smile again, although all
that she said and did pleased him. "Everyone has children,
so I suppose we shall too."

She pulled her hand from his. "You are hateful! You
have no more feeling than a flea!"

"Are you so certain fleas are not swept by passion too?"

"Do you think they are?"

They both laughed then at their absurdity.

"I only wish," she said, seeming to grow serious again;
"I only wish you were not so even-tempered and reasonable."

"Lawyers must be reasonable. It would not do if we
burst into tears or shouted with laughter in the midst of
arguing a case. No one would respect or trust us."

She waved a hand imperiously. "I want you to burn for
me and swear you cannot wait until October!"

"Oh," he said drily, "I burn for you."

"Do you?" she said doubtfully. "Tell me how."

"I—burn. That's all."

She took his hand and kissed the back of it. "And I for
you."

"That's improper. Girls are supposed to be cool and
'unawakened.' "

"Well, I'm fully awake, I'm happy to tell you. Kiss me,
Adam?"

His lips touched hers lightly, but no other part of him
touched her.

"I've seen you kiss Aunt Edna with more fervor."

He laughed. "Well, you see—she's my granny, and
that's proper."

"You are far too proper!" she declared.

"Upon my soul! You describe me as hateful and prim,
unfeeling and cold. I wonder that you're willing to marry
me at all."

"I guess it's because I don't know anyone else."

"You know everyone in the county."

"Perhaps then it's because I saw you first and got used
very early to the idea that you are perfect. You are not
perfect. You are sorely flawed."

"Of course I am, and so are you."

"How can you say so! You must consider me a paragon
of every virtue!"

"But you're not. You are a spoiled young girl."

"Am I?" she wailed.

"No," he said quickly. "You are a paragon of—every other virtue. That must satisfy you—and now we must be going."

"Not yet, please."

"I'm to be in court at ten o'clock."

"That's hours away."

"It isn't, and I must go over the case again in my mind."

"What is the case about?"

"Do you really want to know?"

"Yes!"

"My client, Orin Swerdlow, claims that one Peter Constable allows his cattle to trespass on his, Orin Swerdlow's, land and that—"

"No, don't tell me."

"You see?" He walked back toward the horses, both of whom had begun to shift their weight and stamp their feet, impatient of standing about in the cold. She ran after him and grabbed him from behind and began to tickle him on the ribs. Laughing, he pulled free. "Stop! Mercy! Stop—"

"Kiss me." He did so. "No. Kiss me really, and then I shall let you go." He kissed her again. She slipped her arms about his waist and held him. "Adam, you are sweet. Only do not be too 'reasonable' with me." He kissed her again slowly, and they held each other until he made a sudden effort to part them. "No!" she said, holding on to him.

He grabbed her hands and forced her to let him go.

She appeared to yield, but as soon as he freed her hands, one of them darted back and touched him. "You're hard!" she whispered triumphantly. "Oh, Adam! You do burn for me, don't you?"

"You're a silly creature," he declared, his face going red as he turned from her and threw the bridle reins over his horse's head.

"Very well," she said meekly. "I'll be proper—a paragon of every virtue. But oh, it goes against the grain!"

He led her horse to her, and then crouched and cupped his hands to help her mount. She leaned forward quickly and kissed him on the brow. "You see," she said, looking down at him when she had mounted. "I can be as proper as you please." He mounted, and they walked the horses out of the glade.

"Such a pretty place," she said as they left it. In silence they trotted their horses out of the woods and along the edge of a field. Presently Rachel said, "Look, there she is."

"Clovis Elk?"

"She sees us!"

"It's all right," he said.

They looked deliberately away from the woman who stood in the distance by a fenced pen near the barn. Her arms were folded, and she stared in their direction.

"Just to see her makes me shiver," Rachel said. "She's like a witch. Mama says never to cross over to her land."

"We're only on the edge of it," Adam said reasonably. "She can't mind that, can she?"

"She hates us because of what happened," Rachel said. "It scares me to think of anyone hating us." She urged her horse to a gallop, and he galloped after her; and a few minutes later they came in sight of the big house on Beulah Land.

Three

He had slept all day, or appeared to, his eyes closed, chest rising and falling irregularly, his breath whistling in throat and lungs and then rattling eerily like dry seeds in a gourd. He had taken nothing to eat and only a little water from a spoon, most of it dribbling from his lips onto his high-collared night shirt. Then all of a sudden, at the moment after supper when all of the household had tiptoed quietly into the invalid's room to pay anxious respects, Felix opened his eyes, stared at them and seemed for a moment to be his own old lucid self. As his gaze passed from Sarah to Leon, and to Penelope and Rachel and Selma in a kind of angry wondering, his eyes then settled on Nell's face. He tried to raise himself in bed, until Stella caught him to support him, and he said protestingly, "Come to watch me die! Get away! For God's sake, Nellie, make them go!"

He fell back against Stella, who eased him onto the pillows and pulled the bed covering over his arms and tucked it under his neck. His eyes were closed; he might have been sleeping again, except that tears gathered under his lids and oozed from the corners of his eyes.

Silently, without looking at one another, everyone left

except Nell and Stella. The last to leave, Sarah closed the door softly behind her, making no sound; but he had sensed that they were private again and relaxed, or rather, he had given what energies were left to him to the difficulty of simply breathing.

Felix had pneumonia and was dying. No one had said so, but everyone had thought it. Dr. Platt had come to see him twice today, although there was nothing he could do beyond putting his ear to the old man's chest, and listening, and looking grave. There is a moment on such occasions when everyone accepts the presence and inevitability of death. An awareness of that's having happened was what had roused Felix to protest; but now that he had been left alone with Nell and Stella, he got on as well as he could with the sorry business of dying.

Nell and Stella had been with him all of last night and today. They had drunk coffee and now and then a little brandy, but they had not felt like eating. With a sad shake of her head Penelope had said during noon dinner, "Poor Nell is particularly fond of a good squirrel stew." Lovey and Pauline came and went in the sick room, but there was nothing they could do that made any difference, although Pauline tried earnestly and in vain to remember Ezra's remedies for ailments of the lungs.

Sarah came in just before midnight with fresh coffee and begged Nell: "Do go to bed. Let me sit. I'll call you if there's any change."

Nell did not answer, and after standing quietly a little while and seeing the coffee she had brought grow cold, Sarah left. Stella and Nell sat on either side of the bed, not speaking to each other, but not unfriendly either. There was a time of special fatigue that came to them in the early hours of the morning when they both silently, selfishly wished that he would die and let them go. Simple, brutal thoughts occur at such times about those we love.

Then came the time of night when both women so longed for day they could imagine light seeping around the edges of curtains, but it continued night, and Felix continued to breathe somehow, even though his body now quaked with the effort of it.

One candle burned low on the mantelpiece. The fire in the fireplace glowed dull red under gray ash-cover. It could have been revived in an instant with a poke and another log, but both women sat on, concentrated on the dying man. Suddenly his hands thrashed up and free of the bed covering, and each caught and held one. So joined, the three of them tensed with the awful effort of his dying.

She could not have dozed, she told herself, but some time later she came out of a kind of numb-mindedness when she heard Stella say, "He's gone." Nell was still holding his right hand, as Stella held his left. His hand was dry and claw-like but warm, or it may have been her own warmth that made his seem so. "He's gone," Stella said again. "I know this man, and he's gone from us."

Nell did not know what to do with his hand, so after a minute she put it carefully under the bed covering again before she looked at his face. His mouth was open a little; his eyes blessedly were not. It was not he so much as the hair on his head and the stubble on his face that seemed lifeless.

Nell was presently aware that Stella had dropped her head down onto the bed against Felix's side. The poor woman was exhausted, of course. She had attended him ever since they came to live at Beulah Land shortly after his first stroke of paralysis; she had nursed him lovingly and made his life tolerable.

Familiarity expels horror, and so the two women sat on beside the dead man for another hour before Nell noticed that light—real not hoped-for daylight—showed around the curtains at the windows; and she heard faint sounds from downstairs at the back of the house. Myrtis, or Sharon or Sallou or Lotus, had started a fire in the kitchen stove; soon there would be warmth and a smell of food cooking.

Nell got up from the chair where she had sat for so long and went around the bed to the other side. Fully awake, Stella lifted her head from Felix's side and said, "I don't want nobody to touch this man but me. I'll wash him and dress him. I promised him to do that. When you go downstairs, you tell one of them in the kitchen to bring me up a kettle of hot water."

Nell acknowledged the words with a nod and went to the door and out. She found Sallou and Lotus in the kitchen and told Lotus to heat a kettle of water and take it up to Stella in her husband's room. Lotus hastened to do so. Nell turned to Sallou. "I'm hungry," she said.

"You didn't eat all yesterday, Miss Nell," Sallou said. "Was there any of that squirrel stew left?"

"No'm."

"I was afaid not. I thought about it. Well, fry me some eggs, and if there's any cold biscuits from last night's supper—"

"Yes'm, there is."

"Cut them in two and butter them the way Myrtis does for me sometimes and put them in the oven to heat up."

Sallou nodded. "I will do that."

Nell sat down at Lovey's dining table to wait. "After I eat I'm going to bed and sleep. You tell them when they get up Mister Felix is dead, and they are to make arrangements as they see fit; only don't bother me. I want to sleep and sleep. After I eat."

"Yes'm."

Nell got up and went to the back door and looked out. It was another frosty morning. "I'm a widow," she said, without self-pity.

"Yes'm," Sallou agreed uneasily, as Lotus took a kettle of hot water from the stove and a tin basin and hurried out.

"Are my eggs ready?" Nell said.

"No'm. I just—"

"Do make haste. I'm about to perish with hunger."

Four

For the time of year the funeral was well attended. Most of his adult life Felix had engaged in commerce and the law in Highboro, and almost every family there was represented at the church service by one or more of its members. Quite apart from his business and professional pursuits, Felix had gained the affection of many people, because he had been kind and generous. Without ever having thought of himself as "a good man," he had been one. Nobody, black or white, poor and in trouble with the law or his fellow man, had been refused his advice and help. Denied children of his own, he had been sympathetic to the wants of others' children. More than one middle-aged man could have placed the blame for his rotting teeth on the candies Felix had bought and distributed with a free hand to children as he went about from home to office to courtroom to post office; and a large number of middle-aged matrons, both the plain and the still-pretty, remembered with wistful gratitude his flattering looks and com-

pliments when they were awkward young girls. So they
came, every man and woman and child of them feeling
that theirs had been a special, private, shared affection
with the man whose body lay in its coffin on trestles before the pulpit.

There had been another earlier service at Beulah Land,
where all the Negros, who if they were old had known
him all his life, and who if they were young had known
him all theirs, paid their last respects, not from any sense
of duty but with freely given affection. Heroes are seldom
mourned as genuinely as men with feet of clay.

At the last brief graveside service there was only the
family: Nell, Leon and Sarah, Penelope, Selma, Rachel,
Lovey and Stella. Felix's last will and testament had given
Stella her freedom and a thousand dollars. Since his death
she had stayed with Lovey and Clarice in the little house
they shared. Clarice's daughter Ricey had married five
years ago, to her mother's exasperated relief, the tinker-
blacksmith of Oaks and gone there to live. Leon offered
Stella a home forever or for as long as she pleased to stay
at Beulah Land, but she was still only in her forties, and
healthy and adventurous besides, and so she elected to go
and live in Savannah, Penelope giving her copious references to friends and acquaintances, should she decide to
seek work as a nurse.

The earth will fill holes made in it; air merges with air
and flows on, missing nothing and no one that has been
subtracted from the landscape. But after Felix died and
was buried, there remained and continued in people's
memory thoughts of the man. In Leon's life particularly
Felix's death left a space not filled by earth or air, a space
that would always remain vacant and make him a little
lonely. Felix, although uncle to him, was part of his youth
and manhood. If Floyd had been and was his "good"
friend, then Felix and Bonard had been his "bad"
friends—perhaps even more necessary than the former because they understood and shared his weaknesses.

In the real sense they had both been lost to him since
Bonard went off with Lauretta and Felix suffered the first
stroke of paralysis on the occasion of the burning of the
warehouses nearly fifteen years ago. But whereas their
special function as "bad" friends had not for some time
been exercised, they had been alive; and now they were
dead, both of them.

Last October Sarah had received a letter from Lauretta

who then was living in San Francisco. In part Lauretta
had written:

> You will be surprised to learn that I am no longer
> Mrs. Bonard Davis [*She forgot, or chose to ig-
> nore, the fact that she could not ever have been le-
> gally Mrs. Bonard Davis.*] You will have heard of
> the gold fever that has made this coast populous.
> Bonard, my late husband, did not, alas, "strike it
> lucky" in the gold fields. He did, however, have con-
> siderable luck at the gaming tables which were, as he
> himself always said, more to his fancy than the "don-
> key and the pick and the pan" of the prospector!
> However, his luck seemingly ran out a little more
> than a month ago. He was accused of cheating at
> cards—a lie, of course! He was too clever and skill-
> ful to need to cheat at any game. But that can be nei-
> ther here nor there. His accusor, who was said to be
> drunk at the time, left the gaming room and
> presently returned with a gun and shot him through
> the heart. He died instantly, the hand of cards he was
> holding (and, I was told, a winning hand!—but that
> may have been in sentimental kindness to me) falling
> face down on the table.
>
> I was, as you will conceive, inconsolable. However,
> Fate walks in through strange doors, and we never
> know what will happen next! Well! Bonard was no
> more than laid to rest when—but I shall spare you
> the suspenseful details! Let me say immediately that
> before the month was out, in fact only five days ago,
> I consented to become the wife of a Mr. Robb Quale
> Tilly!—whose (to some) amusing name is given dig-
> nity by the fact that he is a rich man. He is, my dear
> Sarah, *very* rich, and *I* am very rich! Don't you envy
> me?

There had been more, much more, but Leon's mind
when he read the letter retained only the fact that Bonard
was dead. Now Felix was dead too. He thought over all
the years his uncle had been understanding of and amused
by his peccadilloes, and the memory of one incident leading back to the one preceding it, he finally arrived at the
time of their first complicity—and Felix had not even
known of it! He wished he had told him at some moment
when they were drinking and laughing together; it would

have added to their merriment. It was the summer of
1820 when he and Clovis—when he and Floyd and Clovis
had at first met together—then he and Clovis alone. She
had asked for a reward, and he'd finally given her the
gold piece Felix had given him the Christmas before.

How long ago it was. How young they all—even Felix—had been.

Thinking of Clovis as she was when young, sassy and
hot bodied, led him to think of her as she was now. She
lived still on the Anderson Place, although no one ever
mentioned her, and she was seldom seen by any except
the slaves who worked the farm. After Alonzo's death,
Roscoe brought Turnip and his wife back from the hilly
cattle farm he had superintended to manage the Anderson
Place. Turnip's wife Puddy was pleased to be so near
town; she began to wear shoes in summer and learned the
pleasure of dipping snuff.

Five

Roscoe Elk was richer, and therefore more powerful, than
ever. He and Junior were a successful team. As Junior
had developed judgment and skill in business dealings, Roscoe had been wise enough to give him further scope and
even in some projects autonomy. On his side Junior
served his father's interests well, and was himself clever
enough to see how much he did not yet know and to realize that his father was a better teacher than any other he
might have found had he gone looking. Junior understood
that the way an ambitious Negro got ahead was not the
same way an ambitious white would take. Besides, Roscoe
was sixty-three; one day Junior would have it all his way.
The future belonged to him.

They lived quietly but well in the by now soberly and
richly furnished house Roscoe had bought from Felix
Kendrick. Geraldine had been moved to the house in
town soon after Alonzo's death, when Roscoe began to notice her as a result of Clovis's having taught her some
manners and hygiene. Her position there was discreetly
ambiguous. She was not the cook, nor officially the housekeeper. Rather she "helped keep house," it was said. She
ate in the kitchen with the cook and other house slaves.
And she understood that whenever Roscoe was at home

she was to attend to him constantly unless he ordered her to go away and leave him alone. A part of the discreet ambiguity of her position was the result of the fact that Roscoe felt himself too important a man to openly flaunt an ignorant slave-mistress; and it was partly out of deference to Junior's wife Dorothy.

Their marriage had elements of a business-power arrangement, although the young woman was certainly pretty, almost beautiful; and she had been educated. She was from Savannah. Her mother was dark brown and married to a man as near black as a man can be. Dorothy was a sallow, coffee-with-milk color, and it was known that her father was a married white banker. He had seen to her mother's marriage and subsequent prosperity, and he had arranged for Dorothy's education. He had conceived a strong affection for the girl when she was still a small child, had even entertained a romantic dream of sending her North to live and be educated, where she might one day make a sensible and dignified marriage.

But the girl was delicate—or such was the reason given for the fact that any plan to educate her along ambitious lines was doomed to failure because she did not have the character and mental capacity to flourish and grow in an intellectual way.

Roscoe, who knew the white father, having dealt with him in Savannah for several years, knew the truth about the mulatto child. She was sometimes even brought to the bank by her mother to see her true father, and had been there one day when Roscoe was closeted with the man on business. Roscoe began to think of the possible advantages of marriage between Junior and the young girl. He waited to suggest the matter until he knew the father to be sufficiently discouraged with his own dream of his daughter's future and imagined he might welcome a safe and respectable alliance for the girl. And so it turned out. Junior was quick to see the possibilities of the union in his future dealings in Savannah; and Dorothy was compliant even to weakness. They were married in Savannah, an occasion not attended by Clovis. Junior brought her home. She bore two children in three years, a girl who died before she was a year old, and a boy they named Roscoe. The fat solemn baby looked shrewd in his grandfather's way even in his cradle.

Clovis had been left very much to herself. No one con-

sulted her about anything to do with the farm, because
she was so often vague and weak with drinking. Having
once tried to reform her with his fists, Roscoe now left her
alone. He didn't want her in town. He gave her just
enough money to keep her in whiskey. He had tried denying her that, but she would sell or bargain anything she
could lay her hands on in order to buy her pacifier.

Leon's thinking of her made him curious to see her. He
spoke hints, made seemingly casual speculations that encouraged answers, without learning any more than was
common knowledge. Without deliberately setting out to
do it, he rode his horse on several rainy days in February
when there was little work at the sawmill and on the plantation, along the perimeters of the Anderson Place, hoping
to catch a glimpse of her.

And then one day he simply said out loud, "Hell and
damnation!" and acknowledged that he was curious to see
her. Feeling better and free to act natural because of his
honesty, he rode his horse along the little road to the
front door of the farmhouse of the Anderson Place. He
did not get down to knock at the door; he did not call
out. He saw no one, but he did not leave. He knew that
eventually someone would discover his presence. The rain
was a mere drizzle, but it was cold, Nevertheless, he
waited.

Presently, a woman opened the door and bumbled out.
He would not at first have recognized her as Clovis except
that gossip had prepared him for her drunken appearance.
Her hair looked as if it had not been properly dressed in
days; it was every-which-way but the right one. Her dress
was not quite disgusting, but it showed stains, the result of
her drinking and eating carelessly. The shawl she must
have picked up to throw over her shoulders before coming
out into the damp, chilly weather of the porch was—Leon
recognized it with astonishment—the very one Sarah had
carried the day she was attacked, and that Alonzo, according to Roman's report, had held like a veil in front of
his face when Roman had raised the pistol to kill him.

She came to the edge of the porch and held a wooden
column for support as she squinted her eyes to make out
who the visitor was. When recognition came, she said, "I
know you. Go away."

He made no answer, and when the horse, disturbed by
the woman's tone and appearance, went tense—Leon
could feel the body tensing with the inside of his thighs—
he sat still, holding the reins a little more firmly than he

had, and looking back at the woman to make her feel that, although hers had been the last reaction, it was yet up to her to make the next move.

"I told you—get away from here!"

Finally he said, afraid she would simply leave him, "Clovis?"

"You remember my name, do you?"

He made no reply.

She said after a pause, "I know yours too. Leon Kendrick."

He made no move, no reply.

"Your son Roman," she continued after a moment, "came here and killed my son Alonzo!" She drew out the syllables of the last word, making of them a kind of howled curse.

Still he sat, making no reply.

She drew the shawl from her shoulders with a grab and a snatch. "You see this thing?" She held it up. "There's blood on it! It looks like rust now, but it was blood! *I* never let it be washed. You know whose?"

He turned his horse then and began to walk him away, but when he heard her laughing in a taunting, childish, triumphant way, he turned the puzzled horse again and walked him back to the position they had held before. "Clovis?" he said.

She had stopped laughing surprised at his return. She supported herself against the column.

"Clovis?" he repeated.

Holding tight to the column she said, "Yes—*boy?*"

He sat and stared at her. The horse shifted his feet nervously. She looked back at Leon. When again he said, "Clovis?" she stumbled and groped her way back into the house.

Leon stayed where he was for a little time, until it began to rain harder, and then he turned up the collar of his coat, pulled his hat down, and rode away, feeling as he went that she was watching him from the window, her eyes held on his back like a pointed gun.

Six

He came again, but she did not come out to meet him, although he sat on his horse in her front yard for half an hour, feeling more aimless and foolish by the minute. She watched him all the time from the side shadows of the front window. When he finally pressed his heels into the horse's sides, and turned his head with the reins, and went down the little road, she felt that she had won something, and then was immediately sorry she had not gone out to speak to him, because such was the tedium of her life that even the unexplained appearance of the man was an event not to be wasted—better than sitting and having nothing happen at all.

One day she found herself waiting for him, for no reason other than the fact that it was four days after his second visit, and that had been four days after the first. He did not appear, and as the day waned, she began to drink more heavily than usual. She ate nothing but drank herself into unconsciousness in the early evening. Turnip dragged her off to her bed when he came in from his work. Puddy was afraid of her when she was drunk and would not go near her unless commanded.

Clovis slept until midnight. Waking then, she had a severe chill and couldn't stop herself from shaking until she drank a half glass of whiskey. Feeling gradually better, she built up the fire in the sitting room and drank slowly the rest of the night, as Clarence Anderson had done before her in the same room. The longer she drank and thought about things, the clearer they became. She found that her mind was really very quick and clever; it explained all of the past to her, and showed her how one thing had led to another, until her whole life had been spun out based on nothing better than mistaken impulses of her youth. Still sitting in the chair, she slept again. Waking cold an hour or so later, she did not bother to resurrect the fire but went off to bed in her clothes, removing only her shoes, giggling as she wrapped the old shawl of Sarah's around her feet to warm them.

When she woke again, it was midmorning, and she felt miserable. There was no more whiskey in her jug, and it was the last one she had. She had drunk it up too quickly. What she had meant to last two more days, the earliest time at which Roscoe might ride out and give her a little money, was gone, and she would have to shake and suffer. *Do, God,* she thought to herself. She went to the kitchen and was thankful Puddy was not there. She made herself eat a cold biscuit, although she felt that every bite she chewed and swallowed was like to choke her. There was a piece of leftover fried fatback, congealed in its own grease. She wiped the white lard off on her dress and bit into it. Its greasy saltiness almost made her vomit; and then contrarily, when she swallowed it, she felt better and steadier. She ate the rest of it with another cold biscuit. Puddy came in from the back yard, her arm heavy with a load of stove wood, and asked her if she wanted anything. She said no and went into the sitting room to get away from the woman and her curious, fearful stare.

She heard a horse then and wondered if Roscoe had come early. It had not rained for several days, and the earth of the front yard had hardened so that the horse's hoofs sounded as loud as they would have on a baked clay road. She went to the window and saw that it was Leon Kendrick, and that he had stopped at the same spot he had on the two earlier occasions he had come. Without thinking how she looked, and she looked like a crazed witch, she stepped out on the porch.

Seeing her, Leon nodded his head. "Clovis," he said, as easily as he might have pronounced the name of any casual acquaintance he greeted at train depot or post office.

Her need conquering her uncertainty, she called to him hoarsely, "You got any liquor?"

"What?" He cupped a hand over one ear and tilted that side of his head in her direction.

"I say: you got any drinking whiskey with you?"

He shook his head. "No."

"Oh." One of her hands made a fist and kneaded her stomach. "I got this ache in my gut and thought a little liquor might ease it some."

"Oh," he said and thought about that. "I don't have any with me, but I can get you some."

"Well—" She sounded doubtful but vaguely, politely hopeful. "I had some myself, but seem like I don't know where it got to."

"It wouldn't take me long to go and come back," he said.

"I don't want to trouble you—"

"No trouble. I'm not doing anything. You wait. I'll be back in half an hour's time." He slapped the reins lightly on the horse's neck and turned.

"Hey!" she called. "Wait a minute—"

He paused, standing in the stirrups and craning his head around to her.

"I don't want everybody knowing my business. Don't come back here. You see that little copse yonder twixt your fields and mine?" He nodded. "I'll be there."

He rode away, first at a trot, then abandoning the road
and galloping over the fields toward Beulah Land.

She was in the copse when he returned twenty minutes
later. She wore a man's coat, one of Alonzo's, for
warmth, but she still shook a little. She got up from the
log where she had sat when he rode up, but she sat down
again when he got off the horse and unstoppered the jug
he had brought. She reached for the jug and drank directly from it, he helping her to hold it steady. When she
raised her head and took a breath, he set the jug down on
the ground beside her and stepped a little way apart, from
courtesy.

When the whiskey had warmed her, she looked up at
him. She examined his face critically, and finding no scorn
or pious reproval in it, nor gawking pity either, only an
open, calm look, she relaxed. "Seem like my guts bubble
and thresh about, less they got liquor to hold onto."

He nodded. "It's happened to me like that."

She seized on this as a pleasantry. "Has it now!"

"Oh, yes," Leon said.

She touched the jug with the toe of her shoe. "You
want some, you go ahead. Only I got no glass with me.
You can wipe off the lip good."

"Not right now," he said, his tone suggesting politely
that he might want and take a swallow a minute later.

"Well," she said, "I think I will." He moved to help
her. "No, I can do it now." After drinking she set the jug
down and leaned her head against a bare branch that
forked off the log. "I thought about it," she said.

"You have?" He squatted near her so that their heads
were more nearly level, and waited.

"I thought and thought about it, and it seem to me to
all go back to that day—you remember?" He nodded.
"Hot as the soles of the devil's feet. I was washing clothes.
I can see you and Floyd now, sawing wood and then slipping off to go fishing. And pretty soon I followed you."
Her chin jutted; the flesh of her face firmed with the intensity of her thinking. "Seem to me it all goes back to
that day and them that followed. Everything. You think
about it." He blinked and waited. "Still and all, I don't
blame you; I blame God. You spect there is a God? He
ever hold your hand or pat your shoulder? He never, mine."
She rested her head against the jutting branch again, closing her eyes. A minute later she began to snore. She snored

four times lightly and the fifth time heavily and raspingly.

Leon moved to her and shook her arm gently. Waking, she pulled Alonzo's old coat close about her, her face blankly content.

Leon said, "Shouldn't you go home? I'll walk you over."

She shook her head. "I be all right. Just let me rest here. You don't need to stay." She closed her eyes.

He looked at her for a minute or two, but she seemed to be comfortable and easy enough where she was, so he decided to go. He put the stopper in the jug so that it would not spill its contents if she happened to kick it while she slept. He looked at the sky and saw no sign of rain. Quiet as a mother leaving the nursery after getting her child to sleep, he put his foot into the left stirrup and swung his body onto the horse. Stroking the horse's neck to make him gentle, he turned and went out of the copse.

Seven

Doreen was in love with her brother James, and because she was, she knew—and she was the only one besides James who did know—that he was in love with Rachel.

At twenty James was a husky young man with face and hands weathered red; he was serious in his ways, already a true farmer. He seldom left Oaks except on business matters to do with the land and its animals and its crops. Doreen, who was only two years his senior, looked thirty. She was a sturdy, plain woman with a strong-featured face, and large hands and feet. They were the country children, James and Doreen, as Annabel and Adam were the town children. Adam lived at home but rode each day into Highboro to attend to his law practice, and talked of building a house there when he married. Nothing, however, had been settled as to that, because Rachel loved country living, and he would have to persuade her to accept a life in town.

Annabel, on the other hand, had taken to town living with enthusiasm. At seventeen she'd married the banker's elder son, Blair Saxon, and Mr. Woodrow Saxon had given them a house to live in. It would do very well for their "first" house, Annabel said, having her eye already on the grander house of her parents-in-law. She had set about buying furnishings as costly as Blair would allow, in

deadly competition with her old friends Ann-Elizabeth
and Margaret-Ella (no longer Clay) who married on the
same day in a double ceremony—Annabel declaring it
"too tacky and done to save money"—less than a month
before Annabel's wedding.

So far, Annabel was ahead. Her silver was heavier, and
her drawing room boasted an Aubusson carpet. Also, she
had two children to their one each; hers were boys, and
theirs, girls. Blair Junior was six and Bonard was four.
They were fat and frequently ill, alternately spoiled and
slapped. Young as they were, both were accomplished
liars and audacious petty thieves. Annabel proclaimed to
one and all that she loved them to distraction, whereas
they often dreamed of seeing her eaten by a crocodile.

There was a drawing of one of the fearsome creatures
in a book their father had given Blair Junior—or Little
Blair as he was called, to his worthy disgust—the past
Christmas. It was young Bonard who, staring at the
likeness of the creature with its horrendous jaws gaping
wide, had said, "Oh, what if it ate Mama!" Both little
boys had laughed merrily at the notion and Annabel, entering the room just then where they sprawled on the floor
before the fire with picture books about them, had
reached down and slapped her younger son on suspicion.
To make up for the slap she allowed him to have two
large pieces of fruit cake with his supper, which he later
threw up on her Aubusson carpet, thus evening scores
with her. After a fit of hysteria Annabel took to her bed
and would not get up until late the following afternoon
when word came to her by the servant grapevine that
Ann-Elizabeth and Margaret-Ella had returned on the
train from a shopping trip to Savannah where they had
bought "several new gowns and bonnets suitable for summer wearing and in the latest mode." Blair Saxon was
much praised for the earnestness with which he applied
himself to his work at the bank, his father Woodrow often boasting, "I have to order him to go home at night!"

Both Edna and Bruce were well content with James and
Doreen. Although they had used to tease Doreen a little
about becoming an old maid, they were not sorry to have
her remain at home. There is always something flattering
to a father's feelings in a daughter's remaining under the
family roof. Casey Troy had been shrewd in his portrait
of Doreen; she looked more and more like her grandmother. The two women, the young one, the other now in

her seventies, were calm, good friends. Between them
there was affection and trust.

Few young men had made an effort to know Doreen.
She was not beautiful. Being the second daughter in a
family of two sons, she would not be rich. But most telling of the reasons she had not married: she did not want
to. Without her being unfriendly, her indifference to the
young men who approached her on social occasions in
town discouraged further pursuit. She needed no man
other than her father and brothers.

James was her heart. She felt something of a mother's,
something of a lover's, more than a sister's pride and joy
in him as she saw him give himself to the service of the
land and animals, as she shared his concern over weather,
and anticipated his needs when she could. He repaid her
devotion with devotion; but it was Rachel he thought of
in the night.

Doreen wanted to hate Rachel for holding the hearts of
both her brothers, but she could not, for Rachel was so
genuinely fond of all the Davises, so gay and warm a
companion, and so sensibly admiring of both the Davis
brothers, although it was Adam she adored. She loved
Edna too, and that spring for the first time she and
Doreen went along with Edna and Sarah for the day of
work on the family graves, the younger women doing
most of the low, kneeling chores, Sarah and Edna strolling
among the graves and reviewing family history. Felix's
grave had still a new and vulnerable look, and they cared
for it with special gentleness. When they were two together, Doreen had naught but affectionate feelings for the
younger girl. When they were all together and she saw the
anguished love in James's eyes as he looked at Rachel and
Adam, then Doreen wished for impossible things, such as
James's finding her own love enough, and not minding
that he could never have Rachel too.

One day two of the girls who were old enough to quit
school for good but had begged to stay on because of
their extravagant affection for Selma, brought her a bunch
of violets they had just picked in the woods. Selma put
them in a glass of water and kept them on her desk all
day. And they all knew it was spring.

Selma had become a dedicated teacher. As a child she
had felt a special affinity for the Negroes on the plantation, and now after her years of comparative isolation, she

took them into her life again, and they made her bloom
and blossom. Sarah had been right to say that she would
make a good teacher. Shy or indifferent with most of her
peers, she came alive when she saw the young children of
the slaves before her, themselves shy and at first afraid of
school. To tell them, to show them, to teach them, to see
them learn, became her sustaining joy. She loved their innocence, and she administered to their ignorance in such
an unforcing way that the cleverest of them advanced
quickly, like baby birds learning to fly on the first try, and
having been led by her into learning, subsequently led her
into whole new skies of the mind and heart.

As Sarah had been right about Selma, so too had Roman been right about Pauline: she became an excellent
disciplinarian. Pauline had a precise, just mind that enjoyed making judgments. She punished, she praised; and
she was never uncertain of which to do, nor the extent of
the doing. She liked the children, but she was not sentimental about them as Selma tended to be. Her precaution-
ary suspicion made them respect her even as it amused
them, although they would never love her as they did
Selma.

Roman wrote to Sarah every month, sometimes oftener.
The school in Philadelphia that had been founded by Miss
Eliza Truman had flourished and now occupied two
houses near the waterfront. Roman and Proctor lived in
one and superintended the classrooms and dormitory
there. Eliza and another white teacher, her protégé, a
Miss Felicity Chapman, lived in the other house and supervised the girls' dormitory. The boys and girls mingled
in the classrooms of both buildings. Besides these four res-
ident teachers, various artisans were employed by patrons
of the school to teach manual trades to those pupils who
might become self-supporting by such training.

Both Roman and Proctor belonged to a small orchestra,
and so still enjoyed making music. Roman wrote to Sarah
of performances they attended at the theatre, of public
lectures, and sent her clippings from newspapers and
other journals he thought might interest her. Roman also
wrote to Rachel, but less often as the years went by, and
finally not at all. For him, Sarah was Beulah Land. Rachel
began to fade, until she was like a part of Sarah; and as
her life filled with new people and other loves, she let him
go too. Sometimes Roman had difficulty remembering who
the people were Sarah referred to in her letters—she was

apt to assume that he remembered every living soul there, and he did not, and had to say to himself, "Let me see; that must be Pecora's child." But he read every scrap of her news with interest. It was all part of the great ferment into which he had been born, although specially born, and of which he would always be a part.

After violets, other flowers and grass and trees grew. The fields were planted. Winter silence and closed doors gave way to spring and summer openness and noise. Nell and Penelope put their rocking chairs on the front porch, and rocked and gossiped and laughed, and now and then quarreled and despised each other. They had nothing else to do.

Eight

The long, columned porch was not merely a shady retreat for the old ladies that summer; it was a lively junction much trafficked by casual visitors, as well as by the residents of Beulah Land. Nell and Penelope were original settlers; their claims were held inviolate. One morning Selma set a chair carefully away from the older women, where she was presently joined by Pauline and a gangly girl of eleven, who seemed all eyes, awkward hands, long legs. Her name was Lilac. She had been so quick to learn last winter—she'd shown no signs of such quickness before—they could not bear to leave her mind idle during the summer when the school was closed; and so they had offered to give her special lessons in reading and grammar, if her parents would spare her for an hour or two a day.

That trio became a regular grouping each morning from nine o'clock until near noon, and when lessons were done, Selma and Pauline usually remained, thereby gradually establishing that end of the porch as their special place, just as the other end of it was acknowledged to belong to Penelope and Nell. The latter, assured that their rights were respected, were not averse to being amused by company and ceased talking altogether when lessons were in progress.

Although certain general rules and customs were observed, it was not a formal household, and impromptu conferences were frequently held on the porch. If Lovey

found Sarah there, resting or even pausing briefly, and
wanted to decide a question, she did so. Others were sent
to Sarah there, or to Lovey when she drew up a chair beside Sarah and extended her stay.

Although it was not to be until the middle of October,
Rachel's wedding cast a long backward shadow into the
summer. There were a thousand details to settle, and the
front porch was the coolest convenient place for such
matters. There Sarah and Rachel had preliminary discussions with the minister and the choirmaster, with dress-
makers, with advisers of every sort, long known or previously unknown, who seem to spring up from nowhere
around such events to give advice that sounds more like a
laying down of laws.

Not much real law was practiced in summer, and so
Adam was often hanging about Rachel when it was too
hot for them to seek privacy by walking or riding to the
glade. There was no division between the business and the
social; this merging was a part of the easy democracy of
the South in those days. If someone suddenly suggested it,
watermelons were brought from the bricked artesian well
and set on the floor of the porch. Adam or Leon—the
job, although it required neither strength nor special skill
with a knife, usually fell to a man—found himself standing in the front yard and using the porch as a table, as he
cut watermelons into sections for Rachel, and a lace merchant—a popular alto singer of love songs who was to
help provide a suitable mood after the wedding when everyone would be congratulating everyone else and eating
and drinking—a fancy-confections maker, and Nell, and
Penelope, and Sarah, and Selma, and Pauline, and anyone
else who happened to be present.

It was a relaxed, and cheerful time when melons were
cut and sections passed around, with salt for those who
liked it that way, and in the hot weather some seemed to
want salt on everything; but half an hour later when the
melons had been eaten and the rinds collected in one spot
on the porch but not yet taken away to the hog pens, flies
gathered to sit in the sticky juice and grow drunk on
sweetness. People drifted away into the house if they were
of the household, to wash hands or merely to avoid the
flies, and back to town if they were business people who
had happened to be there when refreshment was offered.
At such times Rachel and Adam would slip away, and
going from shade to shade as they had quickly learned to
do, managed to avoid the worst of the open afternoon

heat and to achieve the privacy of their glade.

On the first Sunday in August, before the frenzied activity of full harvest began, there was a spend-the-day party at Beulah Land for the family from Oaks. There had been no question of anyone's going to church in Highboro that day; the logistics of transport alone would have been far too complicated. Both families agreed to "taking it easily." The Davises were asked to come when they pleased—"but the sooner the better and stay forever," Rachel had urged when issuing the invitation.

Everyone of the two families at Oaks and Beulah Land was up at daybreak to bathe and shave, or crimp hair and primp faces, and to try to remember all the things they meant to tell each other and were always forgetting in the hurried meetings of the busy summer season. ("Aunt Pea, please remind me to tell Edna—now what was it?")

To live is complex enough; to live and react to each other with anything like grace can demand anything from the most natural, effortless behavior to the greatest heroism. In our dreams we are hunted and threatened, hurt and shamed—glorified, all but deified. We know in familiar ways people we have never seen before, or have merely known about; we act in what seems to be a manner contrary to our nature. The sleeping state makes acceptable those encounters that would be the subject of the most grisly fantasy at midday. All is possible, and sometimes an odd impulse from a forgotten dream surfaces during waking hours to astonish us.

Nell, being unthreatened by any personal demand, and suddenly panicked at the realization that nothing more would ever be asked of her in life, could slip into a reverie where today she looked at young James with his innocent physicality and felt a positive lust to put her hands to his red cheeks and taste his lips.

Selma, who was forty-five years old and spoiled by her pupils even as she spoiled them, looked across the dining table at the troubled, plain, beautiful Doreen, half her age, and wanted to reach and touch her and say, "Whatever it is that makes you tremble and frown, it will end. I understand."

Sarah and Bruce talked mainly to each other at one end of the table, and Leon and Edna talked mainly to each other at the other. In between there were Doreen and James, Nell and Penelope and Selma, Rachel and Adam.

They talked. They talked.

Sarah had a moment in which, although her face kept its mild look, she thought: "I don't know anybody." She remembered Roman far away and almost wept from missing him.

After the big noon dinner, lying down was suggested, and those who wanted to rest quietly alone drifted up the stairs, while others wandered out to the front porch to sit idly, now and then to talk with animation for a few minutes and then lapse abruptly into silence again.

Adam and Rachel went into the grounds in front of the porch, and, after looking back at the house and seeming to study it a few moments without speaking, they proceeded to walk slowly to and fro. Only James of the group on the porch watched them as they went off toward the orchard. Although not hungry, they could not resist the bright reds and yellows of late-ripening plums on one tree. Adam picked a few, and they rubbed them to a shine between their hands and ate them.

On the porch Bruce and Leon had gone to sleep in their chairs. Edna, Nell, Penelope, and Selma were upstairs resting. Now Sarah rose to go to her room. She was followed by Doreen who had watched James as his eyes followed the lovers strolling away into the orchard. She touched his arm without speaking as she passed him and went into the house behind Sarah. James's were the only eyes to see the young lovers as they circled the house without coming near it and went off toward the back fields.

Within half an hour they reached the glade, not hurrying, content to be anywhere as long as they were together, but the love in both urging them to the place they always felt most private. Talking progressed to talking and touching, and then kissing quickly, and then kissing slowly. When Adam endeavored to pull back, it was too late; Rachel would not have it so.

They gave themselves, and took each other; and both wept with relief when completion came. They lay together, still for a while, marveling. After resting, their bodies touched and joined more wisely and confidently than they had done before. It was late afternoon when they reminded themselves and each other that they must go back to the house. After cooling the heat of their faces in the brook, they walked for a little time without touching. Finally, they looked each other over critically to make certain neither showed signs of the momentous oc-

currence of the afternoon. It was the first unselfish gesture
they had together made toward society. Happy and sure
of themselves, they did not want to disturb the equanimity
of those they loved. When each was satisfied with the
other's appearance, they left the glade.

"I shall always remember," Rachel said. "I am so glad
this place belongs to Oaks. It will be ours forever."

He said, "Do you suppose nobody found it before us? I
swear no one can have!"

"Oh," she said with easy arrogance, "who do we know
who could have wanted so private a place as we do?"

Nine

"Dear *darling* Sarah!"

Wheeling around in surprise from the mantelpiece, having just given the clock its weekly winding, Sarah saw
Lauretta. Without thinking, she slapped her as hard as she
could, and they both burst into tears.

Clarice, who had quietly let Lauretta into Sarah's room
after Lauretta's requesting that she not knock on the door,
fled.

Catching her sister by the arms Sarah said, "Oh, how
you frightened me!"

"I only meant to surprise you!" Lauretta cried.

"And so you did! I don't believe I have ever had a
pleasant surprise in my life!"

"What a welcome!"

"Well, my dear, you come without ceremony—even as
you left us. Did you not meet Leon on the porch? And
Bruce, James?"

"There was no one. I came from Savannah on the train
and hired a man at the livery stable to bring me on here.
My trunks are still at the depot."

"But—why are you here? I mean to say, where do you
come from, and where is Mr.—Robb Quale Tilly? Do I
have it right?"

"You have it right, and where he is may be the concern
of the Devil, but it is not mine!"

"Whatever can you mean?"

Lauretta shook her head firmly. "That can wait."

Not yet over her shock, Sarah babbled. "I cannot believe no one was on the porch. Why, someone is always

there. And we are having a spend-the-day. The Davises are here. Edna and Bruce—Doreen and Adam and James."

"The Davis children? I remember. They're doubtless off playing somewhere, you know."

" 'The children' you remember are quite grown up. In fact, one of them is to marry—" She stopped herself, but Lauretta did not note her sudden caution.

Lauretta said, "People marry too young nowadays, without knowing each other well enough."

Sarah laughed nervously. "That, from you. I remember—"

"Please do not begin remembering things, or we shall be all day and the rest of the week too. I am a little tired. May we sit down?"

"I am sorry!" Sarah led her to a chaise lounge at the foot of her bed and drew up a chair for herself. Lauretta sat down, slipped her bonnet off and dropped it to the floor beside the chaise. "Do you want anything? Tea? A glass of wine? Something to eat?"

Lauretta shook her head. "Just let me sit a little and get used to being here."

"Of course, my dear. Tired or not, you're looking very well."

Lauretta sighed and rolled her eyes. "I take care of my looks—but I'm forty, and today I feel it."

"You are forty-four, Lauretta, and I am forty-two."

Lauretta stared intently at Sarah. "*You* haven't taken care of yourself. All faded, not a bit pretty, I used to think you pretty. You had such a fresh and girlish appearance, quite disarming, I assure you."

"Well," Sarah said simply, "I'm not a girl any longer."

"Life is hard!" Lauretta exclaimed. Tears came into her eyes, and her lip trembled. "Life has used both of us hardly, sister!"

"It has done nothing of the kind—to me anyway. I do just about as I please—but, you see, there is so very much to do!"

"I'm sure you work too much; it shows in the lines of your face. I shall speak to Leon about you."

"No, you shall not. I am quite happy."

"Do you mean to say you believe yourself happy?" Lauretta said incredulously.

"I am at any rate not *un*happy. That is enough."

"For you perhaps. You were never one to ask for

much. But I—I wanted the world!" Lauretta burst into tears again, holding her face in her hands.

Sitting down beside her on the chaise, Sarah put an arm around her shoulders and rocked her gently, without offering words of comfort.

But as though she had, Lauretta suddenly drew herself up, stopped crying and blew her nose. "You are right. I mustn't cry. It will make me look too dreary. Tears are a luxury women our age may indulge only at a price!" She got up from the chaise and went quickly to Sarah's dressing table, first looking critically at herself in the mirror, then fluffing her hair out at the sides. She glanced at the objects on the table, her hands playing over brush and comb as if they were her own. "You certainly don't have much, do you? A thin box of face powder and one tiny bottle of perfume. No wonder you look so wan. I shall lend you some of my own little helpers. One of the hardships of California was that there was no really good hair dye."

"Come and sit down again and talk to me. You have told me nothing yet of yourself."

Lauretta turned and smiled brightly. "Are you glad to see me?"

"I don't know, but you're welcome anyhow. Now come." Lauretta returned and sat down meekly in the chair beside the chaise where Sarah had remained. "To work backward—you are here." She nodded, and Lauretta nodded agreement. "You come from Savannah."

"A clipper ship brought me from San Francisco, of course. How I do loathe and despise the ocean! It is so very unreasonable. Though Captain Slocum declared over and over again that it was a lucky trip for weather, I was ill for more than half the voyage."

"You show no sign of it," Sarah said.

"I am resilient."

"That is certainly true." Lauretta giggled as if she were a child successfully teasing an adult. "How came you to make the voyage alone? The last word I had from you was that Bonard had died—"

"Poor dear Bonard! Do not remind me—"

"—and that you had married a wealthy Mr. Tilly?"

"Was ever woman more deceived!"

"Please explain what you mean, Lauretta."

"I mean that yes, I married Robb Quale Tilly—ridiculous name!—and yes, he was immensely rich. We had

been married but seven weeks when the most hideous vi-
rago—fat and with no style or beauty at all—arrived in
San Francisco by clipper ship and came direct to the hotel
where we were lodged. We had not yet begun to build a
house, although Robb spoke of doing so every day! In the
meantime we stayed at the hotel for comfort and convenience. This caustic shrew, capable of playing any or all
of the weird sisters in *Macbeth,* arrived at the hotel and
announced to me that *she,* if you please, was Mrs. Robb
Quale Tilly!"

"And what did Mr. Tilly say to that?" Sarah asked.

"He said to her, 'I did not expect you so soon, my
love.' He made then as if to kiss her warty cheek, this
man with whom I had lived seven weeks believing myself
to be his wife, and she boxed his ears. There occurred, indeed, the most appalling scene, right there in the public
sitting room of the hotel. I don't know which of us was
the angrier. Poor Robb had a bad half hour."

"I should reckon so," Sarah said. They looked at each
other, looked quickly away, then back at each other. At
the same instant they burst into laughter. Rising from their
seats, they embraced, still laughing; and when they subsided a little, Sarah said, "Yes, you are welcome, Lauretta,
and I *am* glad to see you! You are such a fool you make
me feel quite sane. It is your saving grace."

"Well, I hoped for a politer, more sympathetic reception—" Lauretta complained, and then shrugged and
smiled at her sister. "It is my romantic nature. I believe
everyone, you see, especially men—and especially those
who say I am beautiful. I can't think what I shall do when
I grow old." She shuddered. "Wretched thought."

Sarah stood back from her and marveled. "Three times
a wife and never married at all!"

"Ah well," Lauretta said as if she were accepting a
compliment, "I dare say there are women who've had dull-
er lives."

"I dare say there are," Sarah agreed. "What followed
the dramatic scene in the hotel sitting room?"

"Half of San Francisco was laughing at me while the
other half pitied and despised me. The newly arrived Mrs.
Tilly moved into rooms at the hotel, and Robb ran back
and forth between us for half a day, until an arrangement
was made. The 'lawful' Mrs. Tilly insisted that I leave San
Francisco, and I confess I had little desire to remain after
what had happened. So I agreed to go on the very first

clipper ship for the East Coast, with my passage paid, of course, and a little something besides."

Sarah shook her head and smiled. "As you say—you are resilient."

"I hate vulgarity, and I have learned the right time to leave a party. I have my share of vanity, but only the rich can afford pride. The rest of us must scramble to catch whatever moonbeams we may."

"From the richness of your gown it's more than moon-beams you caught."

Lauretta took her sister's hand and sat down on the chaise again, drawing Sarah down beside her. "But for you life hasn't been so romantic, has it?"

Sarah said carefully, "I wouldn't have wanted it to be more than it has been."

"That is because you are good." Lauretta sighed. "And I am not. But that's my nature. How is Leon?"

"He's well. Uncle Felix died."

"Oh?"

"They all came here to live after our big trouble. I wrote you—the warehouse fire in town—everything."

Lauretta looked vague. "Oh yes. You did write me about that, I believe. Leon's uncle and aunt, and our Aunt Penelope."

"Without Aunt Pea we might have lost Beulah Land."

"As bad as that, was it?"

"Everything is all right now," Sarah assured her to change the tack the conversation had taken, seeing that Lauretta remembered and cared nothing about what had happened.

"Oh, I'm glad. I hate hardship. But with so many, do you have room for me?"

"Of course."

"You're good." She squeezed Sarah's hand. "And I'm tired. I'd like to stay with you a little while and get my breath."

"Do you have plans for the future?" Sarah said.

"I?" Lauretta said. "You know I never plan. Things happen to me. I've thought of returning to the stage. I'm not too old. A woman may be any age and play Shakespeare's ladies—except Juliet, of course; and I've seen some essay even that role who were on the *grave* side of fifty!" She laughed. "There used to be a Negro boy who followed you about everywhere—adored you. Do you have him still?"

"No, he's a man now and free. He lives in Philadelphia where he teaches in a school."

"My goodness! And do you still work at your own little school?"

"Not much, I look in once in a while, but Selma has taken it over, and Pauline helps her."

"Selma." Lauretta frowned.

"Leon's sister," Sarah said as though she were making an introduction. "Bonard's wife."

"I hope she did not think harshly of me—"

"Selma lives in her own world, and I don't believe she minded that you and Bonard went off together. It clarified the situation for her, in a way."

"Yes, I thought it would," Lauretta said eagerly. "You might even say she has me to thank."

"If I were you, I shouldn't expect expressions of gratitude."

"I suppose you—you never wrote about it, not one word. But you must have hated me for what I told you—" She paused, but Sarah remained silent. "We haven't spoken of, even mentioned—" For the first time both women were embarrassed and cautious. "You never wrote about her. It *was* a girl? Yes, I remember, certainly it was. I let you name her."

"Rachel."

"Did she live?"

"Yes."

"I have a child! How very odd that seems to me. Where is she? Have someone bring her to us!"

"She is out walking with Adam Davis. They are to be married in October after she becomes eighteen."

"Eighteen years! Can you believe it?"

"Yes," Sarah said. "I have lived them here."

"Is she at all like me?" Sarah did not reply. "Like her father then? Is she plain or pretty, sensible like you or romantic like me?"

Sarah's voice faltered when she spoke. "I don't compare her. I only think of her as herself."

"You say she is to marry Adam Davis. How does he stand in the line of the family?"

"He is the elder son, twenty-four years old, a lawyer of promise, it is said. He attended the University of Virginia at Charlottesville. He had appeared to love her ever since they were children, but we thought that would change when he spent four years away from her. It did not."

"Well, *he* at any rate would seem to be romantic! Is he delicate or robust?"

"Adam is a healthy young man," Sarah allowed, "if not perhaps as hearty as his father and brother."

"My daughter will be mistress of a great plantation!"

"You overlook the fact that Adam's father Bruce is the master of Oaks and likely to be so for twenty or thirty years longer—and Bruce's mother—Adam's grandmother, is very much mistress of Oaks."

"I remember her, a crude woman. She must be terribly old by now. Surely she can't count for anything."

"I should not like her to hear you say so."

"And they are all here for your spend-the-day?"

Sarah nodded. "They are."

"What a lucky thing I came on instead of resting longer in Savannah!" Lauretta exclaimed. "Something must have told me. Oh, how I cried when I saw Aunt Penelope's house. Strangers living there—how could she let them? I did not dare knock and tell them who I was. To have looked inside would have broken my heart."

"Well, Lauretta—"

"But that is all past. I shall get to know everyone again at supper! I suppose they are staying for that?"

Sarah hesitated before she answered. "Lauretta, you go too fast. Pause and consider, I beg you." Lauretta waited, looking quizzically at her sister. "To begin—I ask you to remember that eighteen years ago you—to everyone's surprise—went away with Bruce's brother, Edna's son, Selma's husband. You cannot—really, you cannot simply appear and expect everyone to say 'howdy-do' as if nothing had happened."

"I'm sure I don't know what you think I've done to cause offense to anyone!" Lauretta stood and flounced across the room to a window, feeling that she had lost a little of her advantage in the interview. Looking out, she exclaimed, "There's a girl walking with a young man! Oh, I know they are the young lovers—Rachel with her husband-to-be who is master-to-be of Oaks!"

Sarah went hastily to join Lauretta as she spoke, knowing her to be quite capable of calling down from the window to whoever was there. She looked out and breathed relief. "That is James Davis and his sister Doreen. Bruce's younger girl. The elder one married the son of our town's banker, Mr. Saxon."

"What a sweet thing for her to have done." Lauretta said. "It appears to be a clever family my daughter is to join!"

"Lauretta—" Sarah took her by the hand and drew her away from the window, back to a chair. She sat her down firmly on it and stood looking at her for a moment. Shaking her head, she then drew another chair close to Lauretta's and dropped into it. "You really do beat all!"

"What have I done?" Lauretta wailed, accusing and defensive at the same time.

"You've done what you always have done—plunged ahead with no thought of anyone but yourself!"

Lauretta tossed her head. "If I'm not welcome, of course—"

"Oh, shut up, shut up!" Sarah stood and paced back and forth, Lauretta watching her uncertainly. When she stopped in front of Lauretta, Sarah said, "Do you remember the letter you left for me when you went away?"

"Oh, Sarah, forget those old jealousies and complaints!"

"Be still, I say! In that letter you told me Rachel was Leon's daughter and said that was why you could leave her. In that letter you gave the child to me."

"Gave her into your safe keeping—of course. What else was I to do?"

"You gave her to me. I still have the letter."

"Oh!" Lauretta declared. "It is so very wrong to keep old letters!"

"That letter was the basis of our legally adopting Rachel. Uncle Felix saw to the whole thing. Rachel is *my* child."

Lauretta started to rise, fell back into the chair, her hand flying to her cheek as if she had been struck. She closed her eyes, squeezed a tear or two from them and opened them again. "What a cruel thing to say to me. How can she be yours when she is mine?"

"It is you, Lauretta, who gave her away."

"What else could I have done?"

"I took her and learned to be grateful for the gift."

Lauretta remained silent for a little, and then asked, "What does she think of all this? Has she never put questions to you about her real mother?"

"She considers me her mother," Sarah said.

Lauretta laughed, not wickedly, but as though it were all a kind of family joke.

"You are welcome to stay here," Sarah said, "but only

if you agree to let Rachel alone—and not to shock her with any of the dramatic revelations I can see leaping onto your mind's stage even now!"

Lauretta stood taller. "You ask me to remain a stranger to my own child?"

"Cease dramatizing! Is nothing real to you? Can you think of no one but yourself?"

"You have grown hard and cruel. That is what has faded you, no doubt, put lines in your face and neck—"

"Lauretta, you may stay or you may go, but if you stay, you must promise to remain silent on the subject of your—motherhood."

Lauretta blinked her eyes at Sarah. "I am a lone creature without friends. I suppose I must be silent."

"I said no dramatizing—"

"Very well," Lauretta said crossly. "I shall be quiet and good—for the time being. Yes, I agree. I can see that I do everyone a favor by keeping my own counsel. But, that you can blame me after what I've been through is inconceivable."

Sarah studied her face briefly, then nodded. "You have promised."

Lauretta nodded back at her, but vaguely, as if what they had been talking about was suddenly boring to her. She walked to the fireplace and looked up at the portrait that hung over the mantel. "Why, it's you!" she exclaimed, and turned to Sarah. Then looking back at the portrait, she studied it closely, with growing surprise. "Sarah!" she said, more as if she thought aloud than as if she were speaking to the woman beside her. "You were beautiful, my dear. Whatever happened?"

Ten

Otis was dispatched with a wagon to fetch Lauretta's trunks from the depot in Highboro. Sarah led her sister to the room she would occupy during her stay and left her there to rest, Lauretta having declared that she would like a little time to collect herself before seeing the others. Downstairs, Sarah asked Clarice to have one of the kitchen girls carry hot water to the new guest in an hour's time; and then she went out onto the front porch where family and friends had begun to come together again.

Quickly, she acquainted them with news of Lauretta'a arrival.

Alone, Lauretta lay down on top of the bed without bothering to undress. Having by then fully registered Sarah's exhortation to "cease dramatizing" she gave herself a consideration of what her immediate tactics might be. Late in the afternoon Sarah knocked at the door; Lauretta invited her to enter; Sarah did so and said, "Are you ready to join us?"

Lauretta allowed that she was. She had changed into a simple frock with no adornment, and she had removed all traces of "little helpers" from her face, so that she appeared now to be the wan one. She had brushed her hair and caught it in a bun at the back of her neck, and she had removed her rings.

Together they went downstairs and found the others on the porch, waiting. Excepting Edna, the company rose, as if on command. Penelope kissed her, but briefly, dutifully, without warmth. Nell and Edna nodded only, observing her through narrowed eyes. Bruce, James, and Adam bowed formally. Leon shook her hand, flushing and telling her that she was welcome again at Beulah Land. Doreen made a quick, awkward, bobbing gesture; and then, seeming to realize that it was childish, shook hands. Rachel met her eyes calmly, although Sarah could see curiosity behind the reserved manner, and then shook her hand.

Lauretta seemed to hesitate, then quickly darted her head forward and kissed Rachel's cheek. "I must do more," she said, "than shake hands with my—sister's child."

Selma stepped up and bowed like a man. When Lauretta turned to her with a gentle look, Selma said, "Sarah has told us that you married after my husband was murdered, but that is all over too. How are you now known and what are we to call you, ma'am?"

With meek voice to match her face, Lauretta replied, "I hope, my dear, that you will call me Lauretta, and I ask to be known only as Sarah Kendrick's sister, come to visit after a long absence, with a sad heart and the desire for no more than a tranquil future existence, if it be God's will."

Selma's face, and the faces of the men, softened at this utterance, but the faces of the other women went blank with caution.

"Well!" Sarah said brightly. "Let us all sit down."

Lauretta moved toward the chair beside Penelope's, but Nell announced, "That is my chair," and every man present immediately made as if to lift or drag his own chair to the place Lauretta had indicated she wished to be. She accepted Adam's offer, apparently at random, although she gave him an intimate, grateful smile and murmured, "I thank you sir."

Until they were called in to supper, Lauretta held her audience with a recital of the hazards of her long sea voyage, making something more of a hero of Captain Slocum than she had done in her earlier report to Sarah. Everyone listened to her; there were no separate conversations, and when now and then a question was put, the voice of the questioner was as sober and hushed as that of the narrator.

Edna said, after having kept silent the entire time, "What of California? You have not spoken a word of it."

Lauretta waited a moment before answering and then said, so quietly the others found themselves leaning forward to catch the words, "It is not a place for gentlewomen, ma'am. I may say more to you at a private time, but innocent young ears are now present."

With an actor's instinct she had timed that modest, teasing remark perfectly. Her lips were hardly still when Lotus arrived to say that supper was on the table, and that, "Mama would be obliged if you all come right now while the biscuits are hot."

They sat down twelve together. Lauretta ate heartily, which gained her a certain respect in Nell's eyes. Observing her, the others, who had pretty much sated themselves at the heavy noon meal, pitied, forgave, and accepted her—as people will do those who seem to be in need. Not a one slept that night without having last kind thoughts about the poor woman who had come back into their midst that day.

Lauretta's presence was soon taken for granted in the subsequent heat of harvesting activity that began the day after her arrival. Her behavior was a model of propriety and thoughtfulness. Quelling her natural disposition to step out first and to assume the crown in every situation, she became a follower, a little hesitant, ever polite. She never joined a chatting twosome or group without asking if she might do so.

She flattered Selma and Pauline, who were idle now

that Lilac was required to work in the harvest, asking a thousand questions about their winter school, and even appearing to listen to the answers. She was a welcome addition to Nell and Penelope's querulous duet, entertaining them with amusing lies about her life in the West. When Sarah and Rachel engaged in wedding talk, as they did now almost constantly—there were only two topics at Beulah Land: crops and the wedding—Lauretta sat by silently, a wistful smile on her lips, as if remembering her own youth without venturing to speak of it. She was even considerate of the servants, and mutely deferential in Lovey's presence, which did little, however, to advance her in Lovey's esteem.

For the first time Lovey and Clarice almost quarreled. "She sure has changed," Clarice said. "I have known her just about all of her life, and she has changed, I tell you. She is nothing like the girl that used to stamp her foot at me and say I'd ironed the ruffles wrong."

"She may be older, but she's the same," Lovey declared. "Snake may shed one skin, but got another ready underneath. Still the same snake."

Neither spoke to the other for the remainder of that day.

Rachel was courteous without being warm or even relaxed with her in the way she usually was with people. Sarah marked that as something to think about when she had a minute, but she was always too busy to explore her observation further. It was easy enough for Leon to avoid Lauretta except at meals, and during the harvesting he often took his meals alone, earlier or later than the others, sometimes at the sawmill from the general mess, more frequently with Floyd at the table in the big kitchen. If the kitchen was too hot for comfort, as happened when Myrtis and her helpers were boiling fruit and vegetables for preserving, they took plates and forks in hand and stepped outside to eat and talk in the shade of the fig tree.

Only Floyd knew that Leon rode or walked over to the Anderson Place every few days to see Clovis. Leon had not spoken about it, and Floyd had not spied; but the two men knew each other in ways that went beyond confidences or directly observed behavior. Floyd worried about those visits, wondering what would happen if Leon and Roscoe met over there one day, wondering too why Leon went and what he and Clovis had to say to each other when they met.

One day Bruce who, when he came visiting at all in this busy season, generally rode over the back way through the fields to see how Leon and his hands were getting along with their work, happened instead to come by the front road, having been into Highboro to the post office and the cotton gin. Lauretta was alone on the porch, and Bruce halted his horse near her, meaning no more than to say a civil word or two before continuing around the house. But half an hour later, without his knowing how it happened or even actually realizing that it had, he had dismounted and was sitting on the edge of the porch, holding the horse's reins, his body twisted around to converse with Lauretta.

At that moment Sarah came out of the hallway and, without hearing a word of their conversation, for they were talking in low voices, she was immediately on her guard. At the very sight of them she was, perhaps illogically, annoyed with Bruce. He had once pined after her; she had known and enjoyed it without encouraging him, and without his pining having hurt anyone.

But Lauretta was a different kettle of fish altogether. Innocence was not a quality she could claim. Sarah suddenly remembered the day of her sister's arrival when Lauretta had been thrilled at the notion of her daughter's being mistress of Oaks; and Sarah had told her that eventuality would be long deferred, because Bruce Davis would surely be master of Oaks for another twenty or thirty years. Was it possible that Lauretta had thought over that remark and was even now attempting to plant and nourish the idea of *her* being mistress of Oaks?

Yes, it was possible.

Eleven

"I'm seventy-eight, you're seventy-nine," Posie said to Buttercup.

"No. You're seventy-nine, I'm seventy-eight," Buttercup said to Posie.

The two old women did no regular work nowadays. They kept a few chickens and piddled a bit in a patch of garden they called theirs; but mainly they sat dozing in the shade of a chinaberry tree, wearing long, clean, stiffly starched dresses with sun bonnets in matching material on their heads. If anyone stopped with them, they woke up and prattled in a bragging way about the one's having been nurse to "Massa Leon" and the other, nurse to "Missy Selma."

Leon and Selma were good about coming regularly to see and sit with them, asking how they were and what they needed, bringing little gifts of sugar and snuff and such. Their quarrel about ages was the only spark of conflict, even of interest, left them, and they made as much of it as they could. In truth, neither remembered how old she was, and they might have been twins for all the difference there was between them.

But one night after the familiar quarrel, they went to bed without making up. The next morning Posie discovered that Buttercup had died in the night, and when she stumbled into the yard, still in her nightgown, to call for help, she dropped dead too. The two who had shared the same bed, not having married, for thirty thousand nights were now buried side by side in the little country cemetery favored by the slaves of the neighborhood, where their mortal remains might rest, or not, through all eternity.

Roscoe continued to ride out to the Anderson Place once a week to look over the crops and to give Clovis a little money, but that made no less welcome Leon's frequent gifts of whiskey on his own visits. It simply meant that she could drink all she wanted, and the more she drank the more she needed to achieve the desired nirvana. Leon did not ask himself why he visited Clovis; he only knew he was drawn to do it. Perhaps it was the memory of shared youth, or merely that she reminded him of his own—an instinct of kindness or guilt, or both together. Sometimes they talked, their expressions polite and formal, but never did they talk in a personal way. One day, however, when he found her there in the patch of woods between their fields, and they sat down on the log and drank from the jug one after the other, each wiping the opening after drinking, she closed her eyes for five minutes. He thought nothing of it; it was a thing she often did. She might have been sleeping or merely "studying." Then she opened her eyes, and their intense expression showed that she had been not asleep but thinking, and she said, "I bet you want to know if he did it."

"If who did it?" he said vaguely, not sure he had heard her right.

She nodded, still busy with her own thought. "Well, he did. He had to tell somebody. Told me, nobody but me; that I know."

"Who?"

"Roscoe," she said.

"Roscoe did it?" he repeated in a puzzled tone. "What?"

"Got the watchman drunk and set the fire."

He did not answer, but sat blinking at her and remembering the night he and Floyd had ridden wildly into Highboro, their eyes on a dreadful glow in the sky.

"You understand?" she asked.

"Yes."

She laughed with a snorting sound. "You can't prove it."

"No."

"I'd say I never told you nothing."

"It's a long time ago," he said.

She brooded over that. "Everything is."

When he left her, he wondered if what she had said was true, and decided that it no longer mattered anyhow.

Lauretta was still a pretty woman, and since her first stark appearance at the spend-the-day party, she had modified the severity of her appearance, dressing her hair in a softer style and using some of her subtler artifices to improve her looks without giving evidence of altering the work of God's hand. But her appeal to Bruce—and in spite of his preoccupation with weather and harvesting, he found that Lauretta was often in his thoughts—was not limited to mechanical aids. She had mastered the tricks of sitting and walking in modest but seductive ways, of listening, of speaking—above all, speaking with her eyes—in a manner that had caught and held the attention of more worldly men than Bruce Davis.

He began to sprinkle his mealtime conversation with references to her that he considered casual, but that Edna noted, and that caused even the unsuspicious Doreen to smile at James in a mysterious way. These references became more frequent and more extravagant, although they were received with neither comment nor encouragement. Edna kept a discreet silence, considering her son's fancy to be a passing one. But at a certain noon dinner he made bold to say, "Though she be past her youth, yet I declare she is all the better for it. She would make a fine wife for any man!"

Adam and James and Doreen were embarrassed to hear
their father reveal his inclination so badly, and began to
speak quickly among themselves. Adam was to go the day
after tomorrow to Savannah on business of the plantation.
Like his Uncle Bonard before him, he had little or nothing to do directly with the land, but was happy to make
himself useful in town and city matters having to do with
the plantation.

It was the middle of September. The harvest was mostly
in, although Bruce and James, as well as Edna and
Doreen, still found many things to do and would stay
busy from now until Adam's wedding a month hence. So
they talked of Savannah, Doreen reminding Adam of two
or three personal commissions he had offered to execute
for her there. After a little while, the brothers and their
sister excused themselves from the table, leaving Edna and
Bruce alone.

They had always been comfortable together, but now
Bruce found his mother staring at him balefully. "Whatever is the matter?" he asked.

"Do you mean what you said about that woman?"

He affected perplexity. "Miss Lauretta?"

She nodded shortly. "If she were any other than Sarah
Kendrick's sister, I would not sit in the same room with
her."

"Mama, you surprise me!"

"And you surprise me!"

"But—my son is marrying her daughter."

"I consider Rachel to be Sarah's child. She has brought
her up and is responsible for making her the dear girl she
is to all of us. I shall welcome *her* with joy."

"Then you must see you cannot cut her mother."

"She doesn't know Lauretta is her mother."

"Are you certain of that?" Bruce said.

"Insofar as I may be. But that is neither here nor there.
What is more to the point is your speaking of her in a
way that would be absurd even in a callow innocent—and
you are not that. Can you actually tell me you hold a high
regard for that woman?"

Bruce fiddled with his tumbler, making prints on the ta-
blecloth with its moist bottom. "I find her pretty and her
company agreeable. I have said no more than that."

"I hope you have said less than that to her."

"She certainly knows that I admire her."

"Then you must henceforth contain your admiration,
for I will not allow it!"

"Mama!" he cried in protest, sounding more like a boy than a man nearer fifty than forty.

"No, sir!" she said emphatically. "I will not! She is a wanton creature without a thought for anyone but herself. When I see them together, I find it hard to credit that she is Sarah's blood kin."

"You surely are very hard on her, Mama!"

"Hard or not, that is how I feel, and I shall not change. If you have any idea—even the remotest beginning of such an idea as making her your wife, you must forget it. I will not—I *will* not allow it! I would set fire to this house before letting her step across its threshold as mistress."

"Mama, you are shocking! And you overexcite yourself. I have only said I think her nice."

"*Nice?* That bawd of Beelzebub?"

"Mama, please!—if you please! They'll hear you in the kitchen."

"And I shan't mind if they hear me at Beulah Land, as they most certainly will if you make one further move toward that sly, scheming, wicked creature—who abandoned her child, who took your brother and my son from his hearth and home and had him murdered in a brawling frontier town!"

Bruce strove for dignity. "I am sure I have no intention of—of paying serious court to Miss Lauretta."

"I am glad to hear you say so."

He slapped the table suddenly in exasperation. "However, Mama! I won't have you telling me what I may do in personal matters."

"Have I ever tried to do so?" Edna replied in wounded astonishment. "I, my son? Why, I would sooner walk out of this house and live the rest of my days, which cannot be many, in one of the darky cabins than to interfere with any personal arrangement you wish to make. If you were to find a suitable woman and decide to marry again, I'm sure I should make no objection." She sighed heavily. "I cannot live forever, and I understand that you will want someone to keep you comfortable. Of course, Doreen as yet shows no sign of marrying—and may not; and Rachel will soon be here as bride. I cannot imagine a finer future mistress of Oaks than Rachel Kendrick when she is Rachel Davis."

"I have no plans to remarry," Bruce said stiffly.

"Well, you must suit yourself as to that, as I have made clear."

Bruce pushed his chair back from the table and stood.
"They're picking scatter-cotton in the high west field.
They hate doing it, so I have to keep them at it."

She nodded and pushed her own chair away from the
table. "And I must help Doreen. We're working in Bonard's old room and intend to have everything fresh and
new as a surprise when it becomes the bridal chamber."

And so, although she was unaware of it, Lauretta's
hope of being mistress of Oaks was to grow no wings.

Twelve

The following day, an hour after Floyd had ridden back
from town bringing with him the day's mail, having
waited for it to be sorted at the post office when the train
from Savannah had come and gone, Rachel rode forth
from Beulah Land as fast as she could to Oaks. Arriving
there, she stopped her horse and flew from his back as
easily as a bird, ran up the steps and into the house calling, "Adam! Adam, you cannot go! Where are you?"

Doreen ran down the stairs and into the hall from what
had been Bonard's room, where she had been working
with her grandmother. Edna, made curious by the clamorous arrival, followed Doreen more slowly down the stairs
to learn what was the matter.

"It is this letter!" Rachel exclaimed, holding a page in
one hand as evidence of what she spoke. "It tells of the
fever in Savannah!"

"I'll find Adam," Doreen said as Edna arrived. Edna
led Rachel into the small visiting parlor off the larger
drawing room. "Calm yourself, my dear child. Whatever
is wrong may always be set right again. Agitation only
burns itself up and leaves a hard cinder. What is this letter, and who is it from?"

"Oh—" Rachel sat down on a short settee beside the
older woman. "I am sorry if I have made a hullabaloo. I
quite startled Aunt Pea, I'm sure. This is her letter, you
see, from a friend of hers in Savannah, who lives on the
very same Broughton Street where Mama lived as a girl.
It says that the yellow fever is worse than it has been
since the epidemic of 1820! I have heard Mama speak of
that, though she was a child at the time, and Aunt Pea
took them all into the country to wait until it was over!
Oh, you see, do you not? We must not let Adam go. He

must be persuaded to cancel or at any rate postpone his going."

Adam entered, followed by Doreen, who had found him in the office with James, the two of them evaluating and discussing accounts. "Rachel?" he said and went to her and took her hands as she rose from the settee. Rachel could not at first speak. Her mind, having raced ahead to invent calamity, needed a moment to return to the present and accept him as he was, healthy and well.

"She is unhappy," Edna explained, without letting herself seem to patronize the girl's apprehensions, "about a letter Miss Penelope has had from a friend in Savannah."

"Is that all?" Adam laughed relief. "I had thought from the racket and Doreen's urgent summons to find tragedy waiting on the doorstep."

Rachel thrust the letter out to him.

"You are asking me to read another's letter?" he said.

She took it back and unfolded the sheet. "I shall read it to you, and then you will not think me silly." She smoothed the sheet of paper where she had crumpled it, and held it up to catch daylight from the window behind her. "I shall read only the passage about the fever. Aunt Pea was reading it to herself, and when she came to that part, she exclaimed and began to read aloud, knowing your plan." Rachel's eyes ran along the lines to find what she wanted. Then she began to read aloud, making a strong effort to hold her voice steady.

" 'The epidemic is a severe one. Folks say there has been no worse since 1820. It is rumored that more than half our population of 15,000 have gone into the country from panic, to escape the noxious humors of the city. Not a single, solitary bell rang for church last Sunday, so preoccupied were those remaining with the sick and the dying and dead—' " Rachel broke off with a sob and held out the letter. "You see, Adam, why you must not go."

"My dear child!" Edna took the young girl in her arms to comfort her, while Adam took the letter from Rachel's hand and scanned it. After a moment he added his soothing sounds to Edna's, and Doreen, feeling unneeded and a little jealous for James's sake, went out of the parlor and back to the office to be with him.

But when she entered and told him what had taken Adam from the business that had engaged the two brothers, James frowned seriously, and closed the ledger he held in his hands. He went out and through the hallway, Doreen following, and arrived at the open front door in

time to see Adam and Rachel go down the steps and into
the grounds. James watched them, frowning more deeply,
and Doreen watched James, her throat and eyeballs
aching with the tears she knew she must not show him.

"Now now now now now now now now—"

She went from muffled weeping to gasping laughter in a
moment. "Stop!—oh, do! You sound like someone calling
cows."

He took advantage of her laughter to make a conscious
joke of it, saying again, "Now now now now—"

She then stopped his lips with her hand, and as he lifted
a leafy vine in the arbor they had come to and so entered,
he took the middle finger of her reprimanding hand with
his lips and teeth and began to suck on it. She pressed
herself against him when they were in the shadows of the
vines, drew her breath in sharply and held it. Not breathing at all, she strained her body against him. His teeth released her fingertip; his lips reached for her lips, and met
them reaching for his. They clung and kissed like starve-
lings. When they had to break off or suffocate, they
laughed at themselves, and Adam laughed again when she
remained still, looking at him.

"How can we marry and live together?" he said. "I
shall want to be holding you and loving you every instant!
We shall starve for not thinking to eat, smother from kissing and forgetting to breathe!"

"Adam—you will not go?"

"Someone must. Should I ask my brother or father to
go for me? They do not ask me to do their work."

"It can surely wait—"

"No, dearest. This is not a matter of whim or convenience. It is business, the life and breath of Oaks—and
Beulah Land too. I act as cotton agent for your father too
on this trip."

"I'll tell him not to let you go!"

He held her by both wrists. "Rachel!—I love you!—I
love you! But you must not ever use that fact to get your
way with me, do you hear?"

"It is not a question of getting my way— You read the
letter."

"Yes, and I have read and heard other reports and
rumors too. There are a thousand."

"This is not rumor, it is direct from Broughton Street!"

"Those in the very eye of the storm cannot see when it
is passing. Now, come. I love you for being concerned for

me, but I am going only for a day or so, three at most, and I have had word that the worst of the fever is over. I shall do what I go to do. I shall keep clear of the danger, if there still is any. And I shall return, and we shall smile over this anxiety together, you and I."

"The letter said—oh, it sounds so very dreadful, Adam—that the gas works had failed from the hurricane, and the city was in darkness."

"I shall do my work only in daylight hours."

"Don't make fun of me—"

"That I do not, and never shall do. Rachel, I don't think you foolish, dearest love—but only a little overanxious—because I am your dearest love. But I shall go."

"Adam! I want, I want—"

He pulled her to him and closed her mouth with his.

Thirteen

Lauretta fretted with a piece of embroidery as she sat on the porch between Nell and Penelope, who had gone to sleep slumped in their rocking chairs. It was the worst time of day: the middle of the afternoon. Rain was needed. Trees and grass looked heavy and dull with dust, and the air was thick with dust motes. Pursing her lips, Lauretta looked down at her piece of embroidery and decided that she had used the wrong shade of thread for the bird's breast feathers. She disengaged the circular wooden hoops that held the picture tracing taut, managing to drop one of the hoops which bounced lightly on the floor before rolling off the porch into the yard. She would have cursed but that she did not wish to wake her companions. Her solicitude was not, however, for them; it was for herself. She had nothing ready to say to them, no smile to warm their chill boredom. She rose from her chair silently and tiptoed until she was safely in the yard.

She found the vagrant hoop easily enough and slipped it over her hand and wrist. It was like a bracelet, only too large. She pushed it up on the sleeve of her dress where it held for a moment and then dropped down. Safely out of sight of the porch now, she sailed the silly hoop through the air, watching with satisfaction as it landed in a rose bush, shaking petals loose from an overblown rose, abjectly surrendering to the end of summer. Let someone

find it there and wonder what in hell's name it was! Two
embroidery hoops were easy enough to identify, fitting as
they did neatly one inside the other. But one hoop needed
explaining, provided a puzzle.

"De de de de-de-dum," she hummed, then stopped and
looked about her, hating the dusty grass and live oaks, the
drying, dying orchard she saw in the distance down
the drive; and when she turned her head back, hating the
house—that big, ugly, comfortable house that held them
all in their smug satisfaction, that house that ever smelled
of cooking food and of Negroes, that house with all its
comings and goings, and none of it to do with her.

She turned full around and put her hands on her hips
as she looked squarely at the house, adversary to adversary. The house was the very heart of Beulah Land, moth-
ering as it did the people whose will and ambition and
conscience meant its continuance. Her anger made fists of
her hands. Fists on hips, feet apart, she stood like a mocking gypsy, until her thinking released the knotted anger in
her heart, and that released the muscles of her body, making fists hands again, allowing arms to droop and fold
comfortably into each other, legs to relax, shoulders to
round.

She knew suddenly what was wrong with her, because
her angry boredom had given her a picture of what would
draw her out of boredom: the arrival of an admirer—of
Bruce Davis, in whose power it lay to turn her life in a
new direction. He was, God knows, a dull man, but she
was—not old enough, but of an age to be ready to appreciate the tamer currents of certainty and abandon the
rushing uncertainty of the rapids.

He had been interested—more than lightly involved,
nearly hers. Then something had happened. Something
certainly had happened—oh, she knew it without knowing
what it was. Yesterday when he had stopped with the first
report of his son Adam, in Savannah to arrange the final
sale and shipping of the cotton of both Oaks and Beulah
Land, she had looked at him when he had finished the
business side of his report; she had looked at him with a
sympathetic, intimate, we-two, half smile—and he had got
the look in his eyes of a bolting rabbit. Well, hoppety,
hoppety, hop! And goodbye, rabbit stew.

Even as she thought of him, she saw him. She had continued walking away from the house at an angle that
presently gave her a partial view of the yards at the back

of the house. And there he was, standing near the back door, still holding the reins of his horse—he must have just then arrived—and talking to Rachel. Lauretta was too far away from them to hear even the murmur of voices, and they could not see her because she was in the shade of the live oaks. Not that they appeared to be looking for her!

Lauretta decided that she would stroll on in the most aimless-seeming way, and then that she would suddenly "discover" them. It would be a splendid opportunity to blush, and that always charmed a man and made him feel strong and protective. Oh, if only she *could* still blush! Well, she would try. Concentrating, she endeavored to remember the most embarrassing incidents of her past life—but, alas, thinking of them, and there had been many, only made her smile. Perhaps laughter would do as well. She could almost always summon laughter, because the world usually struck her as absurd. And men liked laughter almost as well as blushes. Quite mistakenly they considered that it evidenced good nature. And it relaxed them, as long as it was not at all hinting at ridicule.

When she allowed herself to look at the pair again, she saw that Bruce was about to mount his horse. So, he had come the back way on purpose to avoid her, supposing that she would be either indoors or on the front porch, but never at the back of the house. The sight of him now in his saddle set her anger raging again.

She was ignored; she was neglected; she was passed over; she was allowed only to companion old ladies! She had been too good; that was ever the way of it. Even Sarah, when enjoining her to a discretion which amounted to a lie, had agreed that she did them all a great favor—that, indeed, they were all in her debt.

After bowing from the saddle, Bruce turned his horse and walked him a little way, then trotted him, and was soon gone. If the master of Oaks was lost to her, there was still the girl who humiliated her with her indifferent manner. How quickly would that casual calm fall away if she knew the truth of their relationship!

Keeping to the shadows, Lauretta hurried now, although there was no need, for the girl did not go into the house, but stood still, apparently considering the matter of her visit from Bruce Davis. So deep in thought was she, she showed little reaction when Lauretta stepped up to her

and said, "Was that our good neighbor, Mr. Bruce Davis
who just rode away?"

"Yes," Rachel said.

"Perhaps he enquired after me? There was a certain
matter of no importance that I asked him to look into—"

"No, ma'am, he made no mention of it, or of you."

"And did he have news for you from Savannah?"

"None that I had not received by letter myself."

(Confound the girl—would she give nothing away?)
"And I hope that news tells of a quick return of a certain
party who is missed!"

Stepping over to the gnarled fig tree by the back door,
Rachel made no comment on Lauretta's hope, but touched
a dusty leaf, then a hard branch, her fingers tracing its
surface like a blind man's hand searching another's face in
order to "see" it. Presently, she turned to Lauretta. "The
tree has been here such a long time, it seems to give a little of its life to me when I touch it."

Puzzled, Lauretta tried an understanding simper, with
indifferent results. "A pretty fancy, I'm sure."

"I touch it and make a wish, sometimes." Rachel began
to walk away into the yard, and Lauretta stepped off beside her, as if they had decided to walk together. Finding
herself so companioned, Rachel asked politely, as the first
thing that came into her head, "Have you ever been told
about the tree, ma'am?"

"Why, what is there to tell?"

"Lovey says that when they were babies, Papa and Uncle Floyd both nursed her—together, one on either side,
at the same time—"

"Revolting! No one is old enough to dispute her, I suppose."

"—and when the babies were fed, she swaddled them in
pillow cases, and Uncle Ezra hung the cases from a stout
branch of the fig tree, so that they swung to and fro when
the wind blew."

"Old servants tell such tales. It is their solace, and one
humors them."

"Oh, I know it was so! Only I find it so very hard to
think of Papa and Uncle Floyd as babies!"

"Yes, I suppose you must," Lauretta agreed amiably
enough and took the girl's arm so that, should Sarah be
looking out from any window. she might wonder at the
intimate picture they made together.

But Rachel said, "Are you tired, ma'am?"

"Well, I had been walking about a little time before I met you. I am not tired, only disposed to rest a moment here if you will stay with me." They had come to a seat built around the base of an oak tree. Lauretta sat and gently pulled the girl down beside her. When Rachel had disengaged her hand, firmly but not rudely, Lauretta said, "I declare! It is so very peaceful here. It has done me a world of good to visit with you all after the ordeal of my journey from California. You have been so very kind and hospitable."

"I am sure that you are welcome, Ma'am."

"How sweet of you to say so." That seemed to Lauretta to get them very little further. After a pause she ventured, "I have been here before, of course, but not for many years."

"So I understand."

"Indeed—in fact—I was here eighteen years ago when you were born." Rachel made no reply or comment, and Lauretta, staring at her earnestly, said, "Have you never felt when we were together a—special bond of intimacy?"

"I cannot say I have, ma'am."

Lauretta needed only a moment to summon the appropriate emotion. "Rachel—you are my child!" she exclaimed and burst into tears, expecting to be held and questioned tenderly. When nothing of the kind occurred, Lauretta let her tears subside, but gradually, making an artful effort of regaining control of herself, not risking a look yet toward her companion. When she felt that she could manage a tone of some dignity, she said, "Perhaps you did not understand what I said. I hope you did not. I—gave way. It is certainly not my desire to cause unhappiness to another. You must please forgive me. I am a woman of sensitive feeling, and I fear that for a moment I gave way to a—maternal feeling. Oh, I should not say that! I pray you forget everything that has just passed between us."

"Very well, ma'am."

Lauretta could not resist a direct look at her now. "There," she said and blew her nose again, this time with a sort of delicate finality. "I am so very glad there is no harm done and that you have not guessed my secret."

"Oh, I am perfectly aware that you bore me, ma'am."

Back came the tears; up flew the arms. "My child!"

Rachel edged discreetly away.

Lauretta caught and held her breath, then allowed her

lip to tremble, and felt with satisfaction the dropping of tears from her lashes to her cheek. "You deny a kind word, a touch for your mother?"

"I acknowledge that you bore me, madam, but not that you are my mother. Mama is my mother."

Lauretta, not knowing how to go forward, veered. "They all suppose you so innocent!"

"People imagine children to be unnoticing, and they are not. There were so many little hints and nudges. One day I asked Aunt Selma. and Aunt Selma told me. She and Aunt Pauline told me together. They said they thought I ought to know. I was very glad to have the mystery explained. That was some years ago."

"But you have never told Sarah that you know?"

"No, ma'am, I have not. Since she did not tell me herself. I considered that she might have her reasons—an understandable pride perhaps."

"Pride? How do you mean that?"

"Would it be easy for her to acknowledge to me that her husband and her sister had deceived her? Surely you see how she might have felt?"

Lauretta sighed and tried to draw the drifting mood back to herself. "It was in Charleston, South Carolina. Charleston is such a pretty, romantic city, you know. I was appearing there on the stage in a play by Shakespeare. We were—Leon and I—consumed by an irresistible passion"

"Poor Papa."

"How dare you!"

"I do not mean to offend you, ma'am. Only Papa must have been so very confused and unhappy about it all."

Lauretta laughed ironically. "And I—I who am your mother—am I not to be pitied at all?"

"I tried to think of it this way: you and Mama were sisters. The same flesh and blood, so to say. I settled that you bore me for her when she could not."

"I call that most accommodating of me!" Lauretta declared furiously.

"I dare say it was, madam. And having performed that sisterly function, you then—and I do not blame you—abandoned the child you had borne."

"That is heartless of you to say!"

"I am sorry that you feel it so, madam, but that is no real concern of mine."

"Would you have preferred me to take you along?"

"When you eloped with Uncle Bonard, you mean?"

"For God's sake, stop calling everyone Uncle and Aunt! That Southern custom is too absurd! Uncle Floyd! Aunt Pauline! Uncle Ezra!"

"It cannot be denied, ma'am, that Uncle Bonard was my uncle—twice my uncle, you might say, since he was married to my father's sister before he became the supposed husband of my mother's sister. If that doesn't make him my uncle, then nothing could. And you are my Aunt Lauretta."

"Was not my leaving you here with your father doing you a better service than taking you along with me?"

"Leaving me was certainly doing me the better service," Rachel agreed. "But you must not pretend that my welfare weighed heavily in your decision. A squalling brat in the arms must surely take away something of the romance of an elopement."

Lauretta yet strove to keep a shred of command and dignity. "Your best welfare and my own requirements happened to coincide."

"How happy then for both of us." Rachel stood. "And that surely makes us quits. I shall leave you now, ma'am, with your feelings—and I shall attend to my own, whose concern is somewhat different at the moment."

"You will not," Lauretta began hopefully, "you will not tell your—tell Sarah of this conversation?"

"I think it best not, don't you?" Rachel said.

Lauretta did not answer.

Rachel left the grounds near the house and walked into the fields and woods, thinking her thoughts. When she returned late in the afternoon, she found Sarah alone at her desk in the office. She came up behind her and put her arms around her. Turning in surprise, Sarah's wrinkled neck creased the more deeply, but the lines of her face smoothed away in the smile she turned on Rachel. Dropping to her knees Rachel managed to say only, "Mama, I love you!" before she broke into a fit of weeping, her head on Sarah's knees. Sarah stroked her head and hugged and rocked her, and her own tears when they fell on the girl's head were like a happy benediction. "My child, my dear child!"

Fourteen

"Go to the glade, go to the glade—"

The words repeated themselves again and again in what Rachel recognized as her own inner voice, although she felt that it was directed by some will beyond hers. The command sounded at first faintly, and she dismissed it as romantic fancy. It persisted, growing stronger as the day wore on.

"Go to the glade—"

At noon dinner she sat with the others, eating little, aware of the general conversation around her but taking no part in it except when addressed directly. As soon as she could do so without discourtesy and without raising questions about her health or disposition, she excused herself and slipped out of the house, pausing only to pick up a shawl she had dropped that morning in the office. Although the day was warm, the glade would be shady.

She managed to get away without anyone's noticing her, no small achievement in so large a household with its many individual habits: and that seemed important to her, because a smaller voice, beyond the commanding one that had spoken, commended her to secrecy and solitariness.

She ran the last quarter mile, so anxious was she to be there, and when at last she arrived, she was panting for breath. After the briefest look around, she leaned against the big rock by the brook and rested, bunching the shawl into a cushion for her head. She closed her eyes and listened to the sounds she knew so well. There was the light sweet rush of water over rocks, a trembling and sighing of leaves as the wind stirred them, and a way off a dog barked and then was quiet.

Another inner command: and she opened her eyes. Another: she turned her head. And there he was.

He was just then stepping into the glade. He came so silently, and the look of his face was so remote from anything she had ever seen there, it struck her at once that it was not Adam, but his ghost. She screamed and continued screaming until he ran to her and caught and held her, crying: "Rachel! My darling!"

Then she knew he was no ghost and wept with relief and joy. "You're home. You are here!"

"Sh-sh. It's all right. All right, my darling. Hush—"

"I was forlorn! Is it you?"

He laughed and held her away from him a moment so that they might look on each other.

"It is, it is you!"

"Yes!"

"It is you!"

"Sh-sh, hush—"

"Home!"

"Yes!"

"And well?"

"Thank God."

"Oh, dear God, I thank you, thank you—" Alternately reassured and newly anxious, she had to touch him, hold him, kiss him, feel his hands and arms and lips and cheeks, look into his eyes, weep and laugh and say a hundred times and more that she loved him.

When they had grown a little used to being together again, she told him of the remarkable experience of the inner voice commanding her to come to the glade. He told her of returning by train late that morning, and going home from Highboro—no one was at the depot to meet him because he had not said he was coming, so he'd caught a ride home on a wagon from a farm beyond Oaks that had come in for mail and supplies—and of getting home and setting off again almost at once because he had to be with her. He had not waited for his horse to be saddled, but had come on foot the quicker back way, which had brought him to the glade.

Together they declared the wonder of it, deciding that their love had blessed them with a special knowledge of each other's heart.

Adam walked Rachel home late in the afternoon, leaving her at the door to make his own way back to Oaks without going in to greet her family because he was, he said, beginning to feel the strain of his journey, now that it was over.

He was in a shaking fever by the time he reached Oaks, delirious by midnight, and dead before the next noon.

Fifteen

That Rachel was brought down with the yellow fever too was not an unmixed misfortune; for it put off for a time her learning of Adam's death. His funeral was a hurried affair, sparsely attended, fearful superstition as well as medical opinion urging quick burial of victims of the fever. Leon was there; Sarah was not. Sarah stayed at Rachel's bedside day and night until Dr. Platt could assure her that the girl was no longer in mortal danger. When she feared no more, Sarah went to bed herself and slept a whole night through and most of the following morning.

Waking at eleven, she dressed, took coffee with Lovey who had come in to apprise her briefly of the household situation, and then went straight to Rachel's room to find Juanita brushing out the girl's hair as well as she could with Rachel's head still resting on her pillow.

Rachel's first words to Sarah were: "What has happened, Mama? No one will tell me."

Sarah took her hand, and Juanita withdrew into a corner. "You have been ill, but now you are better."

"What of? I know I have not been myself."

"The fever," Sarah said.

"Has Adam had the fever too? Tell me!"

"Yes, my dearest; he has."

That seemed almost to satisfy her. "Then that is why he has not come."

Sarah nodded and touched her forehead, finding it cool and dry.

"You will tell him I ask for him?"

After brief hesitation Sarah again nodded.

"What a gift he has brought us from Savannah! I shall scold him."

"You must not tire yourself with so much talking."

Rachel's face relaxed. "Will you stay with me?"

"Yes," Sarah said, and kissed her cheek. "And if you sleep, I shall be here when you wake. I promise."

Rachel closed her eyes.

The next day she was stronger and again asked for Adam.

"You remember: I told you he has been ill," Sarah answered.

"But Adam is so strong," Rachel protested. "Surely he is recovering as quickly as I. I wish he would write to me. A word would do. Will you tell him, Mama?" Sarah could not answer. "Mama, bring paper and pen to me so that I may write a sentence to him."

"Not now, darling. You are not strong yet. Rest."

"Please, Mama."

"In a little while perhaps."

Rachel lay silent for a time, but her eyes were open, and worry made lines between them. Sarah fussed at tidying articles on a small table nearby; but that seemed heartless and evasive to her, and so presently she returned to the bedside, drawing a chair close. Rachel did not look at her, but she knew she had returned, for she said, "Mama, you have always told me the truth." Sarah waited in silent dread. "Is Adam alive?"

Sarah knelt by the bed and took Rachel's hands, holding them to her lips, wordless. When she dared to look at Rachel's face, she saw that it was vacant of expression. Rachel had fainted. Sarah revived her with spirits of ammonia while Juanita stroked her forehead with a hand moistened in camphor water.

Rachel looked at no one, but as she continued to think, her expression grew more firm, and she said, "He is alive. I know it." And for the time Sarah was willing to leave it at that.

In her weakness Rachel slept much of the next several days. Dr. Platt came once instead of twice a day, and then not at all, asking that he be summoned only if the patient's condition worsened, which he did not anticipate its doing.

Lauretta chose this time to take her leave. "Now that I know the Angel of Death has flown away," she whispered to Sarah with a meaningful quaver. Her trunks were packed and off she went, her destination Atlanta. She was vague as to her plans. "Things happen to me, you know."

Rachel took nourishment. She did not speak often, and when she did, she did not say Adam's name. Sarah was at first thankful, but then she began to worry, for when she was not sleeping, Rachel appeared to spend her time altogether in deep thought. She never asked for food, but when it was brought to her, she ate a little; when water was offered, she drank a swallow or two. She sat up in bed if pillows were propped to support her. She smiled a little at family members when Sarah allowed them to enter the room for short visits. But she seemed glad only to see Sarah and Leon, and she had little to say to them.

One morning—it was now middle October—Sarah went into Rachel's room to find that Juanita had bathed her and helped her to dress, and that Rachel was sitting in a chair by a window looking out.

"Good morning, Mama," Rachel said.

Sarah bent and kissed her. "Good morning, Rachel. Did you rest well?"

"Yes. Today is a special day, isn't it?"

"You remember?" Sarah said happily.

"Oh yes," Rachel said. "I asked Juanita to bring me my book and tell me the days that have gone. I am eighteen today. And now I may marry!"

"Rachel!"

The girl looked out the window. "You speak so sharply, Mama. What is the matter?"

"It is past time we talk of Adam."

Rachel continued to look out the window.

Sarah brought a chair close to the girl's and sat down, dismissing Juanita with a nod. She yearned to touch Rachel, to take her hand or stroke her cheek, but she was afraid Rachel would not want her to. So she sat still and calmed herself before she said, "Dr. Platt tells us you are nearly well. It is time for you to understand—and try to accept the fact that Adam is dead. He died of the fever."

Rachel frowned slightly, but her gaze held to whatever in the distant view had fixed it.

Sarah continued. "Adam came back from Savannah believing he was well, but he was not. After meeting with you he went home and was ill when he arrived there. While he was still himself he told his father and grandmother that he had come upon our Stella by accident in Savannah. She was nursing a family, all of them sick, and had only left them to fetch lemons and calomel. Adam helped her with her errands, then left her. She was perfectly well, he said. But he had contracted the fever. You caught it from him before he knew he had it. His was a desperate case, and he died."

Rachel continued to look out of the window, her expression gentle, untragic. "I know you think so, Mama."

"It is true, my Rachel!"

"No, Mama. I do not accept it."

"You must!"

"No."

"Rachel!" Sarah's voice was sharp as it had never been before when she addressed the girl. "You shall acknowledge it to yourself—if I have to hitch a buggy and drive you to the cemetery in Highboro and show you his grave. You must accept what happened, or you will be ill again."

Rachel shook her head. "You might show me a dozen graves, but I would still know Adam is alive."

"How can you say so?" Sarah demanded in angry solicitude.

Rachel smiled. "Because I carry his child inside me. So, he is alive, you see."

"Do you think it is so?" Edna said.

"Yes, I do," Sarah said. "I questioned her further. Dr. Platt talked with her, and he is certain of it too. She is nothing like deranged, as I first feared. They came together, she says, for the first time on the day of our spend-the-day, before the harvesting began."

"It was early August. Well, what are we to do? What are we to do? Doreen?"

"Yes, Grandmama?" Sarah had almost forgotten her, so quietly had the young woman sat as Sarah and Edna talked. "Tell Violet to bring us some coffee and a piece of that light fruit cake she baked as a test for Thanksgiving."

"Yes, Grandmama."

Doreen left the little parlor and went straight to the office where she found James and told him what she had heard.

"She must marry me," James said.

Sixteen

The trouble with the idea of a marriage between Rachel Kendrick and James Davis was that it became immediately too popular. Its supporters were ignorant of James's true feelings—and forgot Rachel's in considering the practical aspects of the solution to a problem that had seemed insoluble.

James and Adam had been brothers; therefore, Adam's child would be, properly, a Davis.

The adjoining plantations would one day be united. With James and Rachel married, their double inheritance would eventually go to their sons.

Rachel would not be an unmarried "widow"; her child would be no orphan.

Propriety, so often the victim of the Kendrick family passions, would at last be observed.

With everything so perfectly logical, who could object? Rachel could, and did.

Having started wrong, the thing continued wrong. On the evening of the day of Sarah's visit to Oaks with her news of Rachel's pregnancy, Doreen—acting, she thought, for the best—haltingly confided James's declaration to Edna, who talked it over with Bruce. An hour after supper Edna and Bruce took a buggy ride to Beulah Land where they had an earnest but happily agreeable hour's consultation with Sarah and Leon, in the office so as not to involve the other ladies of the household. Sarah was, of course, delegated to present the plan to Rachel, which she did the following morning in the gentlest way she could. But even as she spoke, she could hear how brutally "practical" the thing sounded.

When at last Rachel, white-faced with shock rather than from her recent illness, found words to reply, they were these: "I never heard anything so cold-blooded in my life. No, I will not be a party to it. My own life is over. I shall not ruin James's. I shall have my child and live quietly here, if you will let me, in whatever disgrace the county decrees. I do not care what people say. I am only sorry if I hurt you, Mama. But I am not sorry that Adam and I loved each other. That I can never be; I can only thank God for it."

Both were quiet for minutes then, sitting together, each with her own thoughts.

"You know, Mama—when you came in and began to speak about 'a plan,' my fear was that you would ask me to get rid of my child somehow with the connivance of Dr. Platt."

Sarah went to the girl and took her hands, drawing her up from her chair and into her arms. "I could never ask you to do that!"

And so James, without having been allowed to speak for himself, was told later that day that his proposal was refused. That usually gentle and sober young man was thunderstruck when Bruce and Edna spoke with him.

"What right had you to act for me? And without even my knowing what you were doing?"

"But Doreen told us that you—"

"I spoke privately to her. Papa, how dared you! Grandmama, you have all done wrong!"

He strode from the room, ran from the house to the barn where he saddled a horse, and then galloped as fast as he could to Beulah Land.

Sarah was just having a word with Otis in the back yard when James arrived. Dismounting even as he rode around the house, he threw the reins to Otis. "Aunt Sarah, where is Rachel?"

"Why, in her room, James!"

He had gone into the house and through the breezeway when Sarah ran after him. "James! You cannot see her! She is not yet well! What do you want? She is not to be disturbed!"

At the foot of the stairs he turned. "Aunt Sarah, it seems to me I can't make any more of a mess of things than you all together have already made. I intend to see Rachel alone, and I will thank you, ma'am, to keep out of it until I have had my say!"

As he bounded up the stairs, taking them two and three at a time, Sarah stared after him, not knowing what she should do and not moving to deter him further. But when she heard him pounding his fist on a door and calling, "Rachel!" she climbed the stairs and waited to see what would happen.

Her door closed to discourage visitors, Rachel had sat through the afternoon at a window of her room. Open on her lap was Hawthorne's *The House of the Seven Gables*, which had been among the books belonging to Felix that Nell had offered to beguile the invalid's idle hours. Although she was well into the book, Rachel found herself not attending it closely today, her mind suddenly quivering at the remembrance of Sarah's suggestion.

Expecting no visitor, not even one of her own family, she was startled to hear James's voice outside her door calling her name and demanding to be let in. She had not seen James since Adam's departure for Savannah, and that seemed an age ago. Without thinking, she said, "Come in."

James flung the door open and entered, going straight to the seated girl, who in her surprise dropped her book to the floor and left it there, her hands tugging the shawl closer about her shoulders as if to shield herself from attack.

"Look here, Rachel," James said. "I'm sorry they went

about it so badly, and I've come to apologize to you!"

"You did not know of the proposal before it was made?" she said wonderingly.

"Indeed no. Doreen overheard something I said to myself, that is all, and it grew from that without my knowledge. I was very angry when I found out what they had done."

"I can see that you would be!" Rachel declared.

"They take me too much for granted. They still treat me like the boy they gave an acre of land to till. I'm not; I'm a man, you see. I will not any longer be treated like a boy—I will not any longer be passed over and ignored because I was the second son!" She stared at him, moved by his warmth and vehemence to look at him newly. "It was crude and unfeeling of them to come at you as they did—and so I have come to see you myself and to say that, in spite of their crudeness, you must marry me."

She shrank into her chair. "I cannot!"

"Why?"

She swallowed and struggled for words. "I—I do not love you—as I must love to become a wife."

"Pish! Tush!" he cried. "You are thinking only of yourself."

"No, I am not—"

"You are most certainly! By your stubbornness you choose to have a child born a bastard who has every right to be legitimate!"

Her eyes glowed with scorn. "You think that reason enough for me to marry?"

"Indeed I do, but it goes further. What of the child's claim on Oaks? You must protect that. What of the inheritance of Beulah Land?"

"I understand," she said quietly. "You are thinking of property."

"I thought you cared about Beulah Land as I do for Oaks—"

"Not in the same way, it seems."

"And what do you mean by that?" he demanded to know.

"Only that my feelings and ideals of honor are not to be bartered like a bale of cotton or a stack of timber! As to that, I wonder that you hold yourself so lightly you can consider marrying without love."

"I cannot expect you to love me yet; it is too soon. But one day you will; I know it."

"Why so? Because it is convenient for Oaks and Beulah Land?"

"No! Because I love you so much." He paused then, seeing tears come into her eyes. "Forgive me. I have been as thoughtless and blundering as they. You will, of course, do as you please and as your heart directs. Only—I have loved you forever, Rachel. Even knowing it hopeless, knowing you were promised to Adam, I could not stop myself from loving you. I have been tormented by guilt because of it, for it seemed disloyal—and I loved Adam too. Not only because he was my brother, but because he was Adam. I reject what you are doing, for Adam's sake as much as my own. You have no right to let Adam's child be born a bastard when I who love both of you offer you my heart and my hand! Oh, Rachel, you don't have to pretend to love me. Only say you don't hate me for what I propose. And be my wife, because without you there is nothing ahead for me but loneliness."

"You say you love me for myself?" Her voice trembled as she said the words.

"Yes, damn it! Have I not spoken plain enough?"

She almost smiled. "Yes, you have spoken plain. If you mean all that you say—"

"How can you doubt me?"

"Then I shall marry you."

"Thank God! You *do* mean it?"

"I mean it."

The tears were now in his eyes. "Oh, my dearest Rachel! How I have longed to call you that, and called you so in my dreams." She held out her hands to him; he took them and pulled her to her feet. "I am too rough and awkward. But I love you, Rachel, you know I do." He kissed her hands. She hesitated and then kissed him gently on the cheek. When she drew her head back to look at him seriously, she suddenly smiled her first real smile since her illness. "James, I hope it will not ever be necessary, but should it fall to you to propose again, don't do it any differently."

"What on earth do you mean?"

And so there was a wedding at Beulah Land, although with a change of one of the principals, and not as soon as had been expected. The county society which Rachel had been ready to offend was satisfied as to the event, although not allowed to witness it.

Stewart Throckmorton was the new rector of St. Thomas's, having succeeded the Reverend Curtis Lamont on the death of that worthy man, and came out from Highboro to perform the ceremony on Thanksgiving Day. It was a quietly happy occasion with only the family attending. The one indiscreet, mean remark that was made, and it caused Blair Saxon to blush, was Annabel's to Rachel: "I declare I never saw such a lucky girl—to capture both my brothers!—Blair Junior! Bonard! If you love me, don't run about so—it is a solemn event. Didn't Mama tell you before we came to *behave?*"

James and Rachel sat down to dinner with the whole family after the marriage was performed just at noon. The couple then drove alone to Oaks in James's buggy. They spent the remainder of the daylight hours in a long, slow walk about the grounds of Oaks, talking quietly, Rachel looking at everything in a new way, knowing that one day she would be mistress there. They supped alone by candlelight with only Violet to attend them, and retired to the room Edna and Doreen had prepared for Rachel and Adam.

When Bruce and Edna and Doreen went home to Oaks after a late supper at Beulah Land, rain had started. It come on harder as the night passed. Rachel and James lay without touching on the big bed in what had once been Bonard's room and Selma's bridal chamber. Neither slept. They had not spoken to each other since getting into bed, but lay listening to the sound of the pounding rain outside.

After a while James pretended to sleep, breathing in a regular way, hoping thereby to quiet whatever anxieties Rachel might have. But when she began to cry, he knew it, although she made little noise, not wanting to disturb him. He supposed she wept for the wedding night Adam's death had denied her. His throat ached with love and pity, but he dared not turn and offer comfort.

Seventeen

Others than Rachel and James lay awake that night and listened to the rain.

Selma remembered her own wedding night twenty-five years ago and turned to her friend, who guessed the drift of her thinking and was waiting to comfort her.

Nell thought of Felix; she did when it rained in the night—she did not know why. In her mind she saw the cemetery with its oak and willow trees shiny wet, the poor graves soaking the water in and down to the defenseless corpses with their moldy clothes and cold bones. Near sleep but with something of her mind still held by the sound of the rain, she mused: "If only I could put dry stockings on his feet"—waking herself with the thought and shuddering with relief that she was alive and warm in her own bed, finally falling into real sleep, the sound of rain in her ears but fainter now, and she dreaming that Myrtis would take it into her head to make sweet potato biscuits for breakfast to cheer the damp morning.

Edna found comfort in the rain and in the knowledge that James and Rachel lay together. To her, rain on earth meant sprouting seed; in time James and Rachel's lying together would provide sons and daughters to fill the house and tend the land. Edna never thought of the cemetery when it rained at night. The dead were dead. Come day, she might be moved to go and brush the leaves from Benjamin's grave and set straight the border of single bricks the storm had disordered. But now she rested, and comfortably belched away the gas of pumpkin pie, and went to sleep peaceful.

In her bed Doreen lay stiff as a corpse for a long time, until she cried out, "Oh, God. I wish it was me!" And when she had wept a while to ease herself, she asked God to forgive her and to bless the union that had been formed that day.

Tired and relieved, Sarah listened to the rain, and then felt shame for her relief, for was it not echo and variation of the memory of Casey Troy? Where was he now? she wondered. Whose country wife did he please tonight? She thrashed in her bed with an unhappy itching and turned, throwing the covers off, then shivered and drew them over her again.

Leon had not even dozed when he heard Sarah moving about in her bed. He lay still, not wanting to talk to her. Sometimes when she knew him to be awake, she asked a question or made a comment on an event of the day past, and then they would lie in their two beds talking companionably across the dark room to one another. But today, although he had spent it with relatives and friends, he had been master of Beulah Land, *their* Leon Kendrick, not for a moment any of his own private selves, and so tonight he needed to feel alone in his mind. He let himself remember Lauretta, not the painted, posing creature going to flab who had recently been in residence at Beulah Land, but the independent, laughing, charmingly greedy woman he had loved a night or two in Charleston those many years ago, the two of them making a child that had grown to be Rachel. From that his mind slipped further back to Floyd and their boyhood, to the hot summer days of tall, heavyheaded sunflowers, and the creekbank (his mind rejecting any memory of Roman) with the sly, voluptuous Clovis—as she had been then.

In the morning it still rained. Whether independently or by transference of thought, Myrtis had seen fit to provide sweet potato biscuits which they ate with fresh butter and new cane syrup. As Nell enjoyed a hearty meal, Penelope picked at a soggy bit of milk toast and said something about the Lord and gluttony, but nobody minded her.

After breakfast Leon put on boots and spent the rest of the morning in the barns with Floyd, poking about corn cribs and hay lofts and animal stalls. Floyd had set some of the men to sharpening hoes and plows. They worked cheerfully enough after yesterday's feast, saying in only a half-joking way that they were tired of turkey and: "Won't it be good when it turns cold enough to kill hogs?"

After noon dinner most of the population of Beulah Land found time to lie down and sleep a while, but Leon was restless. The rain had eased to drizzle when he saddled a horse and turned him toward the Anderson Place. He had not seen Clovis for a week. When he got there, it occurred to him that it was like the first time he had gone, and he sat on his horse in the front yard waiting to be noticed. Presently, he heard a dog bark, and a minute later Clovis emerged from indoors and called, "Get down and come in."

He had never before been invited by her to enter the house. Always before they had met in the copse or some other remote part of the grounds, but the weather now would keep Clovis indoors. "Is it all right?" he asked.

"He come the day before yesterday. This time of year he don't be back for a week."

Leon swung down from his horse, led him over to the porch, looped the bridle reins loosely around a bannister post at the top of the steps, and followed Clovis into the house. There was a fire in the sitting room, a rocking chair before it which she had occupied. A full-grown hound sprawled flat on his belly beside the chair.

"Sit and get warm," she said and left the room. When Leon went to the fire and opened his hands to it, front and back, the dog raised his head from the floor and gave him a full, serious look. "Hey there, old boy," Leon said. The dog lazily rose to his feet, stretching his hind legs to their full length behind him and yawning. Then he wagged his tail slowly and went to the man. Leon took the dog's ears in both hands and tugged and scratched them, and the dog keened his pleasure. "What's this?" Leon said. He had found a deep indentation in one ear.

Clovis came back with glasses and a jug which she set down on a round table, moving a table scarf she had been sewing. "See you made friends," she said, pouring whiskey into the glasses. "Only thing on this place I can abide. Only thing that can abide me." The hound left Leon and went to Clovis, butting her thigh with his head.

"What happened to his ear?" Leon said.

"That Turnip—was it last winter or the one before? I don't know. Don't matter. Two or three my hogs broke out and went wild in the woods back yonder. Early spring Turnip took Sunup there to round 'em up. They did, all right, but not before a crazy sow got a piece of his ear and crippled him some in the left back leg. Like to bled to death, Sunup did. Here." She held a glass to Leon which he took and drank from. She sat down with her glass and said, "Pull a chair to the fire." He found another rocking chair and brought it over, setting it at an angle to hers so that they might glance at each other as they pleased without having to confront each other directly. "Since," she went on as the old dog put his head on her knee, "Sunup elected hisself the house dog. Won't go outdoors 'cept to pee and so on. Scared." She ran her hand lightly over his muzzle and head. "Never mind, Sunup, it's you and me."

They sat before the fire sipping whiskey, talking a little but mainly keeping quiet in a companionable way. When Leon got up to go home, it was nearly dark. Clovis and Sunup went to the door with him. Clovis squinted to judge the weather as Leon mounted. "Is it drizzly still?" she called, more to be sociable than to get an answer.

"Nearly stopped," Leon said. He turned his horse, and when he was halfway across the yard, twisted in the saddle to wave. She and the dog were still in the doorway,

the fire behind them showing them in silhouette. Leon
walked the horse all the way home, peaceful and calm.

Turnip and Puddy had often talked of Leon's visits, and
they had argued about them, the question being whether
or not they should tell Roscoe. If they didn't and he found
out, they would be blamed and beaten, perhaps sold; and
they preferred to go on as they were rather than risk the
uncertainties of life with another master. But if they told
him, they knew they would still be faulted somehow. They
reckoned finally that no harm was done and they could
pretend not to see and know, and so kept quiet as long as
Clovis and Leon met away from the house. But Leon's
coming in today had changed things. While Leon and
Clovis rocked themselves before the fire, the dog on the
floor between them, Turnip went to town to Roscoe.

He had only stumblingly got through the introduction
to his story when Roscoe without a word to him went out
and got on the horse that Turnip had ridden into town
and trotted away. Panicked now, doubting that he had
done right, Turnip begged Junior the loan of a mule and
followed Roscoe a few minutes later riding bareback, having put only a bridle on the mule.

Roscoe had needed to hear no more of Turnip's tale
than: "Master Leon of Beulah Land—Miss Clovis—drinking together—" to set him off. What he felt was more in
the way of cold irritation than hot anger. Certainly jealousy had little to do with it. He gave not a damn for
Clovis as she was, and whatever jealousy he felt was for
the distant past, for the fact that Leon had fucked her before he did, and made the bastard Roman, who had grown
to manhood and killed *his* son Alonzo.

When he arrived at the farm, he slowed the horse and
picked his way through the darkness around the house to
the barn. The horse was property to be taken care of. One
of the field hands was in the barn and came to meet Roscoe. Roscoe gave the horse to him, ignoring the man's nervous jibber-jabber.

When he opened the back door to the kitchen, Puddy
was at the stove cooking lye hominy. She dropped her
spoon and cowered beside the box of stove wood. As if he
had not seen her Roscoe went on through the dining room
into the sitting room. Clovis was in her chair, her back to
him, rocking slowly, the piece of sewing on her lap. She
was not aware of Roscoe's presence until Sunup flattened

himself on the floor and growled. Turning in her chair she saw him and exclaimed, "What you come creeping up on me like that for?" She rose, lighted a straw from the fireplace, and with the burning straw lighted a candle on the table.

Emboldened by her tone and movement the dog rose too and growled again, hackles rising. Without haste Roscoe walked to the dog and kicked him in the side. Sunup yelped and scuttled out of the room.

"Keep your foot off my dog!" Clovis said.

"You shut your mouth till I tell you to open it." Roscoe stood with his back to the fire looking at her. She sat again and made a little business of taking the sewing into her lap, pulling the candle closer as if she meant to go on working.

"I see you been drinking," he said.

"I been drinking for years," she answered.

"Dainty of you to use two glasses."

She frowned at her work, held it closer to the light and pursed her lips as if considering some small detail.

"I didn't know you entertained visitors out of my liquor. Maybe that's why you use so much."

She took careful small stitches in the hem of the table scarf she had already embroidered.

His hands opened and closed behind his back, a sign of his anger she could not see. "Who's been here?"

She continued sewing even when he stepped toward her. His slap spun the chair and almost knocked her out of it. She tried to stand. He pushed her down. "I asked you a question."

"You told me to keep my mouth shut."

"Until I told you to open it. Open it and speak, woman. Who was here?"

She drew herself back in the chair and flared with a show of bravery she did not feel. "How long you sneak around to spy on me?"

"I don't have to spy."

"Others do it for you?"

"I asked you something."

"Didn't your spies give you the answer?"

"Don't you dare me, woman. Answer straight."

Clovis got up from the chair carefully, and he did not move to stop her. She stepped to the table, took the cork from the jug and poured a glass half full of whiskey. He waited until she had taken a swallow of it.

"Who?" he said.

She grinned falsely, not at him, but toward vacancy as if she was alone. "Did the wind blow?"

Another slap of his hand flung the glass she held crashing into the fireplace. She looked at the sizzling fire briefly and then slowly, deliberately poured whiskey from the jug into the other glass, filling it to the rim. She drank from it without spilling a drop, to show him how steady her hand was and that she was not afraid. Then she set the glass down on the table and said, "Leon Kendrick was here. Now what about it? I live here. You live in town. You may be big, but you not big enough to keep Leon Kendrick from coming if he wants to come and I let him. Me and him's—neighbors like."

"What do you talk about—Alonzo? You drink my whiskey together and go over again how your white bastard killed Alonzo?"

"No!"

He let her take up the glass again and drink from it and set it down. "You're too old and ugly for him to want to fuck, so why does he come?"

"What do you care?" she said dully. "Nothing to do with you. You got Geraldine. She's more pussy than you can handle, your age."

"I asked you why he comes. What do you say together?"

"Maybe we talk about—days of youth when we used to fuck!"

"Don't you sass and jive me, you whore-bitch!"

She gripped the chair back for support. "I'm tired. I don't want you here. Go home: go back to town."

"You sit together in these two chairs—or does he sit and you wait on him like you're still his mama's slave?"

"I wish to God I was."

Roscoe shook his head. "I don't remember I ever sat down with him. He was always sitting on his ass while I stood. He asked. I answered."

"Yeah, I bet!" she jeered. "Don't make yourself out some meek darky bobbing his head to the white folks. You don't say nothing about stealing from him."

"I stood, but you sit. You and him sit. Together, like you both white or both black. That so?"

"You don't know nothing about it," she said.

"I'm trying to find out," Roscoe said.

"Go home. Let me be."

"You say I'm not big enough to keep him from coming here long as he pleases and you let him?"

"Never mind what I say. Go on home."

"Maybe you talk about other things, you and him?" Clovis marched out of the room, through the dining room, to the kitchen. He did not go after her. There was nowhere she could go he could not find her if he wanted to.

In the kitchen Clovis saw that Turnip was now there with Puddy, but she did not make any sign that she saw either of them. She went to a cabinet and opened a drawer and took a long knife out of it. Puddy and Turnip froze where they stood, and Clovis went back into the sitting room.

Holding the knife high with her arm raised straight and stiff, she advanced toward the fireplace where Roscoe stood, but stopped a few feet before she reached him. "You get out."

"Be careful. You could hurt yourself with that."

"Are you going?"

Roscoe sighed. "What do you and him *talk* about?"

She lowered the hand that held the knife, but kept it still pointed toward him. Controlling her voice so that she spoke as evenly as he did, she said, "We talk about this and that. How you burnt down the warehouses and tried to burn down the cotton gin after killing that fool watchman. Then we talk about how if you ever make a funny sound to me or to him, your ass will rot in jail the rest of your life—if he decides not to kill you instead. That's what we talk about."

In the kitchen Turnip and Puddy hovered together, listening at the door. They heard Clovis's voice rise as she spoke, and then they heard her scream. There was a scuffle and a sound of falling, a light, whining noise like a dog makes, and then nothing. They stood as if petrified during the silence that followed. When Turnip could move, he took Puddy by the arm and drew her as far toward the back door as they could go. They were standing together, eyes big and mouths open, when Roscoe came in from the dining room.

He looked at them, and they did not breathe. He went to a nail on the wall and took down a dish rag and wiped his hands clean of blood. They stared at him. "Your mistress has cut her throat in a drunk fit," he said. "She was saying she was going to, and that's why you come to town to get me. Remember that, Turnip." The slave managed one nod of his head. "I come out and tried to calm her, but it wasn't any use. You saw her run in here and get a butcher knife, didn't you, Puddy?" Puddy gave a cry at being directly addressed, then clapped a hand over her mouth and nodded dumbly. Roscoe looked back at Turnip. "You go to town and tell Junior that's what happened. Tell him to get the sheriff and come out. You got it clear, what to say?"

"Yassah."

"Then go. I'll stay with the missus."

Turnip hurried out the back door, and when presently Roscoe heard him riding away, he ordered Puddy: "Get hold of yourself," and went out of the kitchen, back to the sitting room. There he looked around the room carefully before he sat down in one of the rocking chairs and stared into the fire, ignoring the dead woman at his feet, her eyes glazing open in her head, her throat still bleeding.

Eighteen

Sheriff Byrne saw the new tragedy as a continuance of a curse begun with the suicide of Clarence Anderson. Roscoe Elk's story was generally accepted as truth, the nervous distraction of Puddy and Turnip merely giving weight to what had been testified. Clovis died on Friday and was buried on Saturday, with scant formality and a short service, the allegation of suicide excusing haste and brevity. Of those who may have doubted the official account of the event, only Leon was certain that Clovis had been murdered, and there was nothing he could do about it. He could not go forward and say that he had sat and talked with her an hour before her death and that she had appeared to be—for her, anyway—in good enough spirits. He could not say that he visited her often and that he certainly knew her as well as anybody, without reviving the old scandal of their youthful encounter.

He kept silent except to talk once to Floyd when they first heard of her death on Saturday morning. Floyd offered to go to the funeral, seeing Leon's anxiety and knowing that Leon could not go without an explanation he was unwilling to give. Lovey went with Floyd. When they returned, they went together to the office where they found Sarah and Leon and gave them a report of the ceremony. Clovis had not been taken into church at all. The Bible was read over her mortal remains at the side of her grave. There were only a dozen people, themselves included. Roscoe and Junior were there, but not Junior's wife and child. The Elks had not acknowledged the presence of Lovey and Floyd in any way.

Lovey said now, "He buried her in the cheapest box he could buy."

Sarah said, "Poor thing."

Leon said, "She wouldn't care."

Angry and grieved, and with no one he could talk to about it, Leon walked alone on Sunday morning in the woods. He could not say he had loved Clovis in a way anyone else would understand, but there are kinds and degrees of love. Certainly during the last year they had shared a bond based on early error, if error it had been, and middle-aged disappointment of life. However it was, he felt anger and regret.

It had turned colder, and Leon walked with a quick, stiff-legged stride. Mist lay close over the creek, and his breath steamed in the air. With his thoughts what they were, it was natural for him to go to the creek bank at what he remembered as the place he and Floyd had first encountered Clovis on that day thirty-three years ago. As he stood, he heard a movement in the dry brush behind him, and turning saw a hound dog emerge from the cover of woods. The dog whined as if he knew or at least needed him; and then he knew the dog. The animal looked wild and lost as he staggered into the clearing. When Leon went toward him, the dog stopped, and then came on again, every step an effort. Leon touched his head, found the ragged ear, and said, "Sunup?"

The dog whimpered and fell exhausted to the ground. Leon knelt and examined him. His coat had a few breaks in the skin, and some burrs and dry mud, but he was otherwise whole. The dog gave a whine of relief as Leon scooped him up in his arms. He trembled, but he was no longer afraid, for he turned his eyes to see the man's face. Leon held the dog close to him all the way back to Beulah Land.

In a couple of days, with regular feeding, a warm place to sleep, and the broken places on his coat treated with some of Pauline's special salve made from one of Ezra's recipes, Sunup recovered. Leon gave him into Joe-Tom's keeping, but the dog would be no one's but Leon's. Not allowed into the big house at first, he waited at the door for Leon to emerge, and when he did, followed him everywhere. Gradually, it became an accepted thing for him to go with Leon into and about the house. He was well-behaved, making no fuss or games indoors, but he would not leave the man; he even slept on the floor beside Leon's bed. Leon never said where he had come from.

Nineteen

Christmas would be soon, and as people will do at the end of a year, those at Beulah Land, especially the older women, weighed the character of the year, Penelope speaking perhaps for all of them when she observed that it had truly been a year the Angel of Death had hovered over them.

No day passed without a visit from Rachel. At first pleased, Sarah began to wonder if it was not a bad thing, indicating as it did the girl's lack of acceptance of her life at Oaks. When she and James were together with others, they were polite and quiet with one another, but the exuberance that had won Rachel as wife had deserted James when they settled down to every day. For all his appearance of heartiness, James was a shy man, unsure of himself in close relationships, and the more so with Rachel, knowing as he did that she continued to grieve for Adam.

In the middle of December they attended a large party at Annabel's house in Highboro, but that was a rather stiff affair, since Annabel had no gift for making people welcome and comfortable, but had only asked them to admire her and what was hers, and poor Blair had been bullied by her and their children into the kind of bland silence that people call seriousness, not amiss in a young banker.

There were other parties, and simple gatherings that were not called that. Sarah and Floyd went one day into the woods and cut a young pine tree, which Floyd brought back over his shoulder, and which Sarah decorated with help from Selma and Pauline, and suggestions from Nell and Penelope. With all the comings-together Sarah grew more and more troubled at the evidence that

Rachel and James had not yet accepted each other as husband and wife.

Rachel was perfectly aware of how things stood. Although they slept in the same bed, she and James never touched each other once they had got into it. On the day he'd proposed marriage to her she had felt a first flicker of interest in him as a man, as opposed to her having known him as neighbor, friend, and near-brother. But married to him, something perverse in her made her want to punish him. It was as though, having satisfied convention and the two families, she rejected what she had done, for Adam's sake.

She knew that James wanted to love her, and that knowledge made her despise him a little, gave her a feeling of unhappy superiority. With Adam she had been eager to please; with James, it did not matter. She thought of Adam and of his child that she would bear; and that was enough for her, and encouraged her to a sort of selfishness, or self-containment, pregnant women often feel.

They never quarreled, but sometimes he looked at her, unhappy and disappointed. When he did, she felt glad, and was both shocked and proud at the feeling, for it seemed to keep Adam alive for her. She was in essence saying to Adam: I am true to you. And then again, she would observe James in his uncertainty that made him awkward, and feel sorry for him, but not enough to change the way she behaved toward him.

Doreen was out of her depth during this time, for while a part of her exulted over the fact that Rachel was no more wife to James than she was—indeed not as much, since Doreen did so many things to make his life agreeable and comfortable—still, another part of her wept to witness his discontent and lack of fulfillment.

Edna brooded, but she knew that, for once, she must keep silent.

On Christmas Eve both families traveled into Highboro in various equipages to attend services at St. Thomas's. In the church, lighted by a hundred candles, there was a hushed, expectant feeling as the congregation gathered. Leon sat in his pew with Sarah and Nell and Penelope. Selma sat upstairs with Pauline. In the Davis pew directly in front of the Kendricks', Bruce sat with Edna on his right, and Edna with Doreen on hers. Next to Doreen, Rachel sat with James. Rachel wore a calm "church" expression, doing what was required of her, but seeming detached from the event and from those beside and around her.

However, when the choir began to sing, her attention came back from exile to the present moment. She smelled the pine boughs and burning candles. She felt the presence of the people around her. It was as though she had been long away and was now come home. Here they were, beside her, behind her, those she loved. They had waited for her. The choir sang:

> "Silent night, holy night,
> All is calm, all is bright
> Round yon Virgin Mother and Child
> Holy Infant so tender and mild,
> Sleep in heavenly peace,
> Sleep in heavenly peace."

As the pure, sweet sound of the words and music flooded her being, Rachel let Adam go. She gave no voice to her feeling, but tears filled her eyes, and she reached blindly for James. And James was there.

PART SEVEN

1861

One

The weather was rainy that winter, with many suffering from colds and worse, but Sarah and Edna contrived to pick a clement day early in January to clean and tend their family graves.

At eighty-one Edna admitted that her eyes were not as good as they had been and gave up driving her own trap; but today's excursion called for a larger vehicle, anyway. Doreen drove the new six-seat barouche, and beside her sat Rachel's son Benjamin Bruce, called B.B. He and Doreen had been particular friends almost since his birth in April of 1854. Rachel and James were fond and proud of him too, but James fairly doted on his daughter Deborah Jane, called Jane, who had been born in June 1855.

So, on the driver's seat sat B.B. and Doreen, with Doreen occasionally giving in to B.B.'s pleas to let him hold the horses' reins, although to his disgust she insisted on putting her arms loosely about his in order to take the reins from him should there be sudden necessity. On the back seat facing front were Edna and Rachel, with Jane chewing her bonnet strings on the seat facing them, because she said she liked to ride backwards and alone, although her real reason was that she anticipated sitting there beside Sarah, whom she called Other-Mama instead of Grandmother.

Rein-slapping the horses into a fast trot, Doreen quickly covered the length of the driveway to Beulah Land and guided the team around the house into the back yards where the washerwomen were also taking advantage of the fair weather to work at their pots and tubs. Almost before the carriage stopped Jane had scrambled out and was running toward the kitchen door where Sarah, emerging, stooped and caught the child to lift and kiss her. By the time she had walked to the carriage to greet the others, Rachel had stepped down. After kissing Sarah and, as if on impulse, Jane too, she looked at Sarah severely and said, "Between you and James she's certain to be spoiled."

"*You* can say that after your father and I—!" Sarah laughed and let the squirming child slide over her hip to the ground. Turning to the carriage she said good morning to Edna and Doreen and hugged B.B. who had hopped off the driver's seat.

"I drove, Grandma!" B.B. bragged.

"Did you!" To Edna she said, "My lunch baskets are ready. You don't have to get down at all. Edna, what is it?"

"I wish you'd tell me," Edna said. "What in the name of God are they doing over yonder?"

Sarah followed the line of Edna's gaze, and seeing the sight that baffled her, laughed, "Selma and Pauline are teaching the school children to march. They have a recess when they grow dull from sitting too long, and instead of running about at games—now they march."

"Are those real muskets the women carry?" Edna demanded in amazement.

"No!" Sarah laughed again. "Floyd cut musket shapes out of old boards for them, and the children carry only sticks—but they insist on carrying something!"

"Well, I don't like to think about it all," Edna said. "Now, come on—everybody get in and off we'll go."

"Did you forget anything?" Edna fretted as Sarah checked the tools on the floor of the carriage. "Rake, hoe, shears—"

"It's all there," Edna said. "I think it's too bold of Selma! Pleasing herself if you want my opinion, prancing about like a Zouave."

"Jane! B.B.! Come back here or we'll leave you!" Doreen called, but the children had joined the marchers and pretended not to hear.

"Never you mind," Sarah said to Edna. "Here comes Lotus with the picnic baskets. I thought she'd go with us today if there's room."

Lotus, now a stout, capable woman who was gradually assuming her mother Myrtis's dominion over the kitchen, had stepped out the back door, kicking it to behind her. In each hand she carried a large deep basket; and strong though she was, her shoulders sloped with the weight of the load.

Doreen and Sarah shifted the work tools to make room for the food baskets. When shouted threats failed to bring the children, Rachel ran to fetch them. A little time was then required to decide the placing of the party. Edna and Sarah sat on the rear seat facing forward, with Jane demanding a place between them, forgetting her earlier preference for riding backwards. Rachel and Lotus occupied the back-facing seat. Doreen and B.B. again shared the driver's position. As Doreen turned the carriage in a large circle, the sound of Selma's cadenced commands to the children came to them: "Left, right, up, down! They were right to hang John Brown!"

Edna rested on a backless stone bench between the Davis and Kendrick burial grounds as the others worked. The sun shone feebly for a while and then was gradually blotted out by thickening clouds. Sarah, wiping sweat from her face with her dress sleeve, joined Edna and said, "I can't do as much as I used to. It's the bending. Oh, I can bend right enough, but then it's hard straightening up!" She laughed at herself and arched her back until bones snapped.

"While I sit here doing nothing," Edna observed broodingly.

"You've done more in your life than all of us together ever shall, and don't you forget it."

"Even if true, it wouldn't make up for my not being able to do now." She paused, thinking, her face gradually showing surprise. "I don't understand it, I declare I don't. In my head I feel I can do as much as any of you; then when I start to, I hear this awful sound and realize it's me, breathing."

"You go about it too fast," Sarah said equably.

"It's hard to admit you're old and good for nothing."

"Stop feeling sorry for yourself," Sarah scolded her mildly, "and help me with the victuals. Lotus! Take those filthy children to the well back of the church and wash their hands. Then bring the baskets and help us get ready, you hear?"

"If I move off this bench, we can use it to set things out on." Edna put her hands on her knees and rose stiffly.

Presently Lotus returned with the children, each trying to help carry the baskets on either side of her. Rachel and Doreen had done most of the morning's work and now wandered off to the well to wash their faces and hands. When they came back, Doreen, who had lately taken to public praying, spoke a short blessing over the food. All stood and ate together, cheerful enough in spite of the setting. Then Lotus took the children to the carriage to lie down while she watched them, although they were too full of giggles to sleep, Jane setting B.B. off into a new fit of mirth every time he became quiet.

Rachel and Doreen turned to work, much of it accomplished on hands and knees, the sort of labor neither did any other time or place, but did here as an act of piety and family regard. They were too young to think of their being one day put here for their final rest, with Jane perhaps doing the work that presently engaged them.

But Sarah, having packed empty dishes into the baskets, sat on the bench beside Edna and thought of the time that would certainly come when she would be here forever. "Only please, God, not soon!" she asked silently.

Edna said, "I wish I was dead."

"And I was just saying to myself I want to live forever."

"So you should say at your age."

"Anybody who can eat fruit cake and boiled ham the way you did awhile ago surely isn't contemplating life on a cloud playing a harp." They were silent a few moments until Sarah said, "I can't see you and me flying around heaven on wings, can you?"

"They'd have to be bigger wings than I ever saw on a bird to keep my old butt in the air!" Laughing, Sarah turned and hugged Edna. "You're good to me," Edna said.

"I don't know what I'd have done without you." Sarah shook her head. "There've been times I felt you were the only friend I had."

Edna brooded quietly a little while. "I meant it, what I said. There's going to be a war, Sarah."

After brief hesitation Sarah said, "I surely hope not!"

Edna nodded. "South Carolina has led the way. Rooster says the rest of us Southerners will secede soon."

"So does Leon," Sarah admitted. "Still and all—"

"There's no 'still' any more. It will come. I just wish I had got myself out of the way and was lying over there by my Benjamin. I've had a life. I want nothing to do with what they all say will happen. One says the Union will let us go peaceful. But others say they'll fight to hold us. Why can't they just leave us alone? What we do is none of their business. We're not a Union any more, we're different kinds of people. And that ugly Lincoln and his vulgar wife! Black Republicans!" Edna spat on the ground, then shivered and drew closer to Sarah. "To think I'd ever spit in a graveyard."

"A lot of people up North and some down here say slavery is wrong."

Edna bridled. "They didn't say so as long as they sailed their ships back and forth to Africa selling us the slaves in the first place! *Now* they talk morality! Oh, there's nothing lower than a Yankee, and you know it. More and more they go against us, and all for money you can bet, no matter how they tell it. But Rooster says we'll never let them force us to anything!"

Sarah waited a minute before speaking. "Edna, they think they're every bit as right as we think we are. Roman writes me regularly, and he says—"

"He's a Nigra, a *Northern* Nigra by now."

"He's Roman and part of us wherever he is, and in his heart he's suffering the way we do. He loves it down here, but he can't come home, you know that. Not as long as the Elk family is here, and it looks like they grow stronger by the year. Roman says rumors in Philadelphia are just ridiculous, but that plenty of ignorant people, and some not so ignorant, believe them. It's being said by the abolitionists—"

"Lying hypocrites!"

"They claim they have secretly supplied our people with arsenic and strychnine to kill us when the time comes!"

"They who say so ought to be tarred and feathered! Stripped and dipped in boiling tar and feathered, I say! When I think of my people—Can you see Lovey poisoning you?"

"Roman says they're ridiculous, but they believe it because they want to. They're listened to now even by decent people."

"If there are any such north of the Mason-Dixon—"

"And they've begun to think of us down here as traitors and—unnatural monsters!"

"It's all those ideas they talk," Edna said. "I can't argue worth a shoot; I just get mad. Anybody can make me look a fool talking *ideas*. Still, I know right and wrong. They use words that don't have anything to do with the actual way we live and do things. Don't you go listening to them and getting mixed up with their ideas. Rooster says that's what they want, to turn us against each other. Doreen! Rachel!"

The two younger women had finished their work and stood pensively side by side, their arms resting lightly about each other's waist as they stared at Benjamin's headstone, now dark with time, and thought of the dead around them, those they had known and those they had only been told about. Hearing Edna, they turned their heads.

'I'm tired, and it's going to rain," Edna said. "Gather our things and let's go home."

Two

The rain came and continued to fall off and on for a week, but it did not keep the two families from going into Highboro for church services on Sunday. The uncertainties of that time and of future time made them want to gather with other county families to exchange news and rumors, to reassure one another that whatever happened they would stand together.

At the end of his sermon the Reverend Stewart Throckmorton asked the congregation to pray with him "That our Overruling and Heavenly Father may still avert this unjust and unholy war the North is determined to thrust upon us."

Afterwards, as Annabel and Blair Saxon talked on the church porch with the adult Kendricks and Davises, Blair Junior and his brother Bonard chased B.B. and Jane around the graveyard, aiming index fingers at them and calling out, "You're the Yankees, and we aim to kill you! Bang! Bang! Bang! Bang!"

Annabel stopped the conversation to say how cute the boys were and how staunchly patriotic to the South, until the game was broken up by Jane's climbing a memorial stone and whacking her Bible as hard as she could on their heads, which sent them both squalling to their mother, who slapped them and told Rachel that her children were savages.

Penelope had news to offer from friends in Savannah. "Rosalie Pernell wrote me there was prayer meeting every day. But she says after Georgia seceded there was less of a demonstration than the great torchlight parade when South Carolina bravely set the example."

"Surely there was an illumination?" Annabel queried.

"Oh, yes, I believe so." Penelope agreed vaguely.

Annabel laughed. "Well, I swanee, I'm going to leave the speeches and fighting to the men and just enjoy things while I can. In spite of the rain, last Tuesday, I and Ann-Elizabeth and Margaret-Ella got into my carriage and went out to the camp grounds where Captain Buck Jordan is drilling his company. It's just the most amusing thing you ever saw, those men marching back and forth. You must go too, Auntie Sarah." Sarah shook her head. "You mean you don't plan to? Oh, I'm certain it would take your mind off things and make you laugh, as it did us!"

Edna said, "You were a silly child, and you are a silly woman."

Nearby the men talked: Bruce and Leon, James and Blair. After a glance at his wife Blair said, "If it comes to war, and it surely will, I'll not wait to be called. I'll go on the instant, won't you, James?"

James said, "I'll go only when I have to go."

Blair flushed. "That'll set the wrong example to others, you know. They look to us to see what we'll do because of our position. I had reckoned you'd be exactly of my mind about it."

James shook his head. "I'll only go if there's no other way."

Blair turned stiffly to Leon and Bruce. "At your age you won't be expected to march off at the head of a column, but James can surely be spared from the plantation."

Looking pointedly at Annabel who was laughing merrily because she couldn't open her umbrella, James said, "I don't have the strong incentive you do to run off to war."

By the end of January, Louisiana, Mississippi, Alabama, Florida, and Georgia had voted in legislature to follow South Carolina out of the Union. Nell and Penelope drove to the camp grounds with Selma and Pauline one day, and all four returned to Beulah Land full of excitement. "If only I were a man!" Selma exclaimed, and Pauline nodded vigorous sympathy. After that the older women, Nell now using a cane to help her about the grounds, attended the marching drills in which Selma and Pauline led the children. When their enthusiasm for the martial spirit spilled over at meal times and they tried to engage Sarah in the conversation, Sarah said, "It's all for nothing, for nothing will happen here. We're not big enough, thank the Lord. We're just a dot on the map between Atlanta and Savannah. What I'm going to do is try to live as we've always lived at Beulah Land." As she looked down the table at Leon, he gave her one of his rare, happy smiles.

Three

Given to a certain melancholy all his life. Leon had over
the last years become oddly isolated as well. He made his
usual rounds of the plantation, knowing it was unnecessary, for Floyd as Overseer was as firm and knowledgeable as he was just. At the sawmill Leon spoke to the men
as he went about observing them at work, but the mill
was run by a foreman who knew the work and the men
better now than Leon did.

At Beulah Land, Sarah paid attention to the running of
the house, but Lovey and Clarice were formidable collab-
orators, and required no supervision. Old as she was,
Lovey commanded respect amounting to terror from all
the house workers, more because of her legend than any
severity she exerted. It had always under Sarah been a
steady sort of household; there were few quarrels among
the servants, and none between them and those who superintended them. Easily bored with her female relatives,
Sarah spent much of her time in the office attending to
records and accounts, work that she had learned thor-
oughly during the lean years that had followed the big
fire.

And so Leon, not lazy but not one to make work either,
was often idle; and there were no companions left to
share his idleness. Floyd was busy. Even their fishing and
hunting together became special experiences because they
were not common any more. Leon's former companions
in idleness, Bonard and Felix—and finally, Clovis—were
dead and gone. Leon was too young to accept the idea of
growing old, and he was too old to hope that life held
anything new and wonderful for him in the future.

Then, there was the eager talk of coming war, a war
Leon did not understand the reasons for. But he did understand enough to know that if it came, the way he lived
was doomed and done, whatever the outcome. The convention that met at Montgomery on February 4 had
created the Confederate States of America with Jefferson
Davis as its President. White-haired old Buchanan fumbled through his last weeks as President of the United
States, and Lincoln traveled about making speeches before
his Inaugural on March 4. One of the jokes Leon over-

heard at the depot was: "If the USA is called Uncle Sam, will the CSA be called Uncle Sambo?"

Leon had never leaned to politics. If he was largely ignorant of government affairs, it was because he was not interested. His concerns had always been personal. No more than Edna could he argue and care about "ideas." He cared about his family and Beulah Land. He had lost Rachel when she married James. He had long ago accepted as fact the notion that Sarah had married not him but Beulah Land. Had he been different, she might have married both, but he was Leon.

His happiest hours were spent nowadays with Jane. From the first he had found himself courting her, and she, although surrounded by those who loved her, including her own doting father, was not satiated and complacent, but recognized in Leon's love a special offer, an inexhaustible abundance. From infancy she cared little for women other than Sarah. For her own mother Jane's feeling was more cool than not, and Rachel was conscious of being jealous of her daughter when she saw her with James or Leon. Oh, she knew they loved her too, even as they had loved her first; but she understood that she was no longer the delightful surprise to them Jane was. Jane knew it too. At five she was as old as Lilith.

Sarah was Other-Mama, Leon was Other-Papa; but the way Jane used the terms, each pronounced as one word as if it were a name rather than a designation, never had conveyed anything like "second" for "other." Leon rode over every day to Oaks to see her, even when he was sure of seeing her through other circumstances later in a day. He often brought her presents, but that was not why she loved him. He took her into town with him, in his rig or riding in his arms in front of the saddle. Neither was happier than when they were together.

On one of those days he left his horse at the hitching rail behind the post office, and they crossed the railroad tracks to the depot to wait for the train to arrive from Savannah with the day's mail. Leon stood with a group of men who were chewing tobacco and spitting and talking as usual of Davis and Lincoln and war. Jane ran after a black and white cat that had stepped prissily out of the telegraph room on the platform and stared at her coldly before hopping off the platform and turning to see if she was still observed. It was not in Jane to refuse such a dare.

The talk of the men continued until the whistle of the train, not yet in sight, wailed and shrilled distantly. Hearing it, the men broke off their talk. Jane heard it and abandoned the chase of the cat, clambering up the wooden steps to the platform and running full force toward Leon who saw and caught and held her up even before she could command, as she always did: "Hold me up high so I can see!"

And then it happened: the miracle of the train's arrival. No faint and distant sound now, but the hard braking of iron and hissing of steam and bucketing of boxcars knocking against their joinings when the engine stopped. Among the men there was a general sigh of satisfaction. Jane turned in Leon's arms, and they looked at each other with an excitement that never lessened, as often as they had seen this together. She butted his chin with her head, and he threw her into the air, shouting, "Jane can fly!" Catching her again as she shrieked her delight, he set her down on the platform. She took his hand and pulled him toward the engine of the train. And there Leon saw Roscoe and his grandson; they had come too, to watch the train's arrival. The boy Roscoe was nine years old; a stout, bold, black fellow, he stared at the engine. Jane called up to the engineer who knew her and took off his cap and waved to her. Leon and Roscoe looked directly at each other, but only for a moment before each turned to his grandchild. For the first time Leon thought of Roscoe as mortal, because he looked old and unwell.

Four

On an afternoon soon after Lincoln's Inaugural, which had been much discussed with little consequence other than to establish the fact that everyone agreed that war was now inevitable, Leon retreated to the office at Beulah Land, knowing that no one would follow him there other than Sarah, and knowing that she had gone to one of the cabins to doctor a woman with severe toothache. He was sitting idle at his desk, although a ledger was open before him when there was a knock at the door. Opening it when bidden to, Lovey announced with as much surprise as Leon heard the words: "Roscoe Elk is here."

"What does he want?" The name still had the power to

summon in Leon a kind of panic he had known in his youth.

"He says: to see you alone."

"Well, bring him."

Leon was standing beside his chair when Roscoe entered, Lovey closing the door behind him and leaving the two men alone. They looked at each other without any greeting until Roscoe said, "I have come to finish it."

Observing him, Leon remembered that Roscoe must be more than seventy years old. The straight hair that had appeared to give substance to the rumor of Indian blood was as black as ever, and he stood as straight as he ever had; but it seemed to be deliberate now, not the automatic arrogance of his younger years. His face was thinner than Leon remembered, but Leon might have been mistaken about that, for one seldom looks closely at a face one hates.

"We finished with each other long ago," Leon said.

"No, it goes on." Roscoe's voice was thin and dry but steady, and his eyes were piercing.

Leon sat down in the chair at the desk he had earlier occupied and waved a hand. "Sit if you please."

"I do not please. I have always stood in this room, and I shall now."

Leon shrugged and waited. Roscoe looked about him slowly, as if seeking something. When he saw the portrait of Sarah over the mantel, he smiled slightly with his lips, although his eyes did not change. "The mistress of Beulah Land."

"Painted some years ago," Leon said.

"Yes," Roscoe said. "The year my son Alonzo was murdered."

Leon looked at him sharply. "That was all settled then."

Roscoe continued to inspect the room, moving his body not at all and his head minimally. "It is a room in which money has been discussed much, and handled." Leon nodded curtly. "It is where I bought and paid for my first slave: Clovis."

Leon sat very still.

"You remember her, of course!" Roscoe said with sudden force that was just short of obvious anger.

"I remember her—of course," Leon said.

"You paid her the compliment of visiting her, I believe, in the last year of her life when her residence was the farm next to yours."

"Did she tell you that?"

"I knew," Roscoe answered without answering. "That was only your late acquaintance. Your earlier acquaintance, if I may call it that, resulted in the birth of the cripple named Roman, whom your wife much fancied and adopted as a pet. It was, indeed, the result of his conception that I came to marry the woman. Your mother would not tolerate illegitimate issue, and I obliged—everyone, I may say—on that occasion. Your mother was grateful. It was then, in this room, she gave me the title of 'Overseer.' It seemed important to me then, but that is all so long ago."

Leon acknowledged Roscoe's remarks with a slight frown. "I know all this, but I don't know why you are recounting it."

Roscoe raised both hands, as if to ask patience, and then lowered them. "In time." He paused to think about it. "You will know in a little time." Almost imperceptibly he shifted his weight from one leg to the other, and Leon thought again that he looked not only old, but frail, although the dark strength of his eyes belied any appearance of weakness. "You did not come to her funeral."

"Our families," Leon said carefully, "are not on those terms."

Roscoe nodded with deliberate irony. "It is so. The areas of intimacy and formality between black and white are complex matters, surely enough; and suicide makes for a certain alarm and discomfort. People do not like anything to do with it, so I understand why you would ignore the affair. And yet—I was with her when she died, and she had only just spoken of you; so you see you were in her thoughts."

"You've waited a long time to bring her message. What did she say?"

"She told me that you visited her, and that there was nothing I might do to stop you."

Leon stirred in his chair, then leaned forward with decision, clasping his hands together, elbows on his knees. "I am not a boy for you to make uneasy with your suggestive rhetoric. And we are both too old to play at cat and mouse. I have, I may as well say, long been certain that you killed her. I had been with her too the day she died. We talked as we sometimes did in those days; and I know that she was not thinking of killing herself!"

"If you are, as you say, certain that murder and not suicide was done, why did you not accuse me?"

Leon leaned back in his chair to study the man's face. "I could not have proven it."

Roscoe nodded reasonably. "Intimacy with Negroes so often stops short of the law." He nodded again, as if in sympathy with Leon's discretion. "It was a worthless life she had, except to bear two sons of mine, one of whom survives—and will, to say the least of it, continue to survive."

"I understand," Leon said, "that you have done well in various business ventures."

"That is so. But the thing I wanted most I did not get. You know what that was."

"You wanted Beulah Land," Leon said.

"I wanted Beulah Land," Roscoe agreed. "I didn't get it, but my son will."

Leon cut short an exclamation and tried to curb his anger before he spoke again. "You had better go because I feel like killing you."

"You won't do that, and I won't go until I have said all that I came to say."

"I'll have you thrown out, old as you are, unless you go now."

"You would have it done, but you would not soil your hands by doing it yourself. Although other parts of your body you have not been so nice as to keep unsoiled by contact with black flesh."

His face burning with embarrassment and rage, Leon still managed to speak in a voice that was almost normal. "Say quickly what you came for, and go."

Roscoe paused to consider. "We have not done with Clovis. I wonder if what she declared was true?" Leon waited. "That she had told you I was responsible for the fire that very nearly ruined you."

"She told me. And that you killed the watchman."

"He was of no account."

"Nevertheless, his death makes you twice a murderer, at least."

"But only of Negroes, and they do not really count, do they?" The sarcasm of his tone was deliberate and taunting.

"You move with the times, I see, in matters of conscience. You did not always, I believe, disapprove of slave holding."

"I move with no time but my own," Roscoe said. "I don't care at all that blacks are enslaved, and I intend to hold the slaves I own as long as the law allows. I am, however, a man to see an advantage. There will be war, and the North will win, because they will blockade your ports. You will not be able to sell your cotton and timber, and you cannot manufacture the tools you need for war." Roscoe paused thoughtfully. "I see that you do not contradict me with talk of courage—and the popular claim that the fighting arm of one Confederate soldier is worth ten of the Union's!"

"I don't pretend to know how it will go," Leon said.

"It will go as I have said. Maybe quick, maybe slow. But when it ends, my son and his son will rise in this county and state in ways you do not dream. When that comes, they will have Beulah Land. They won't even have to buy it."

"Or steal it?" Leon said. "As you stole from Beulah Land and its slaves to make your beginning toward money and power?"

"They will have it as a gift," Roscoe said. "And whoever here survives will be turned out to beg—and to starve, because all the others like them will be begging too."

"Old as you are and powerful as you think you are, you would be lucky to live until sundown if I told in town half of what you have said here today."

"But you will not tell," Roscoe said.

"Why shouldn't I?"

"Because of a thing I know and have told no one, but shall tell you now."

"More?" Leon asked with irony.

"I think you will think it more. Yes." Roscoe shifted his weight again and turned his head to the portrait of Sarah. "It is a fine thing," he said, nodding. "I have no knowledge of art, but I can see that it is no ordinary piece of workmanship, but rather—a labor of love. I never saw the mistress looking that way, and I wonder"—Roscoe swung his gaze from the portrait to Leon's face—"I wonder if you ever did."

"We will not speak of Mrs. Kendrick!"

Roscoe put on a look of dismay. "But that is the very reason I have come."

"What has the painting, or Mrs. Kendrick, got to do with you?"

Roscoe's voice gathered strength, no longer teased and insinuated. "I am familiar with the place used as background for the picture. It is easily recognizable to anyone who has seen it. It is the place your wife was found after she said she had been raped by my son."

The silence between them had the cadence of a beating heart.

"You will not ever have heard of a woman named Geraldine."

Leon made no answer, but continued to look astounded.

"She lives in my house and attends to me. She used to do the same for my son Alonzo. She was there the night your crippled bastard went there with your pistol and killed him. Clovis was there too, but she was drunk and got drunker, and only Geraldine heard and remembered the words. Having fired the pistol, the murderer left. My son lived long enough to say he had seen the mistress of Beulah Land and the artist-man Casey Troy fucking on the ground like dogs in that very place."

Leon sat so still in his chair he might have been dead, except that presently he began to tremble and then to shake, his head and body quivering as if with malarial chill, so that he had to hold on to the arms of the chair.

Roscoe continued. "It was nearly a year after Alonzo died that Geraldine told me, and even then she was frightened to say it all until I made her. Later, I asked questions about the man who lived for a time in your house as honored guest and artist. What happened between him and your woman was not an uncommon occurrence. Slaves see, and they talk—and can be made to talk when they will not—however little their masters credit them with the ability to see and understand what they have evidence of. Alonzo did certainly lie with your woman, but only after her cunt had been greased with slime of another than you!"

Leon stopped trembling but did not rise from his chair.

"That is what I came to tell you. That is what was unfinished between us." Roscoe made a slight bow as he had done in times past. Then he turned and went to the door, but as he came to it, Leon found his voice.

"Why have you chosen to tell me these things?"

Without turning, Roscoe said in an even voice that might have conveyed nothing more important than the time of day, "I am dying of the consumption. I have known it for some time. When I saw you at the depot that day, I decided that I could not die without your knowing what I knew. And by way of parting, I may tell you that my grandson thought your granddaughter a pretty little thing."

Roscoe opened the door and went out.

Five

Annabel had never been happier than she was with the
opportunities given her by the preparations for war. Shallow, vain, and energetic, she was perfectly equipped for
the role she now assumed. Hearing from Penelope that
the ladies of Savannah had begun to organize themselves
to make the fullest patriotic effort, she clapped her hands
together and went instantly to call on Ann-Elizabeth and
Margaret-Ella. Although the latter were to complain behind her back of her bossiness, they were happy enough
to be lieutenants to her captaining of committees of townswomen who were soon making bandages and preparing
lint, cutting and sewing flannel shirts, finally—and this
was to Annabel the most thrilling activity of all—preparing cartridges for muskets and cannon. There was so very
much to be done. At last, here was occupation worthy of
her! Holding the flag of patriotism, she could bully those
about her to her heart's content. All was not, however,
work. There were parties and balls. Indeed, the smallest
event provided an excuse for festivity.

James withdrew B.B. from the town school when he
learned that even the young boys were taking part in drill
and marching. In truth, they went at it eagerly, as boys
will at any activity that allows them to imitate men. Annabel said that B.B's withdrawal was a scandal and that she
was ashamed to admit that she was his aunt. She thanked
God that her own beloved sons were eager to drill. She
was proud of her little Confederate soldiers, she declared,
and should the war be a long one, she would not draw
back from the mother's ultimate sacrifice of them to the
battlefield of "our Noble Cause."

Penelope and Nell offered their services, but Annabel
told them that at eighty-one and seventy-nine they were
too old to be of much use. She asked for Selma instead.
So Selma left the plantation school to Pauline while she
went into Highboro to take part in the women's work.
Even Doreen joined them two days a week, Annabel had
so bullied her. Only Sarah and Edna and Rachel resisted
her chivvying. They had their work at Oaks and Beulah
Land, they said; and so they did.

There was so much to do and see to as spring went on,

Sarah did not pay much attention to Leon's further with-drawal from all of them. She found him one morning in the office staring at the portrait of her, but when she came in, he went out immediately. No one spoke of his coming to the dinner and supper table smelling of whiskey. He had always enjoyed a drink or two; only now he drank more than that and seemed not to enjoy it at all. He made no kind of scenes, but his eyes were often moist and vague. When others talked, he kept silent. He left off going about the fields with Floyd to oversee the men at their work.

Jane more than anyone else saw the change in him, but she was a child to whom adult ways, even Other-Papa's, were not matters to be questioned. He no longer went to see her every day; but when he did go, she tried to amuse him in the old ways. She made even more of him and his visits than she had done before. Once, however, when he had come and gone, she had a fit of crying which had never happened before. Alarmed, Rachel took the child onto her lap and tried to soothe her, begging to know what ailed her.

Finally Jane shrieked, "Why is Other-Papa sad!"

"He isn't, dear child—he is only a little worried about the way things are going."

"Why?" Jane wailed.

"Well, because there may be war—and times are not good, you see."

"Why?"

"Now, stop it. Stop crying. It isn't good for you, and I won't have it." The child stopped crying, but disengaged herself and slid from her mother's lap and ran away. "Jane, come back!" Rachel called, but she did not go after her. She had her own fears and worries now, concerning James.

From being a bride who, if not reluctant, was certainly little more than resigned, Rachel had grown into a loving wife. Hers was such a warm and passionate nature she could not and did not hold herself back from James's love. Whenever she thought of Adam now, it was as "that dear young boy," but her woman's love was for the man James. And James, in spite of his stubborn refusal to ac-knowledge the fact that war was coming, would, when it came, go. She knew he would, and when she thought of it, she thought that she would not be able to bear it. The thought of living without James sent silent screams through her mind, sickened her body with dread.

And then, what they had all talked of for so long, happened. The only major forts in the Confederate States still manned by Union forces were Sumter in Charleston Harbor and Pickens in Pensacola Bay. Lincoln decided not to abandon them. The Confederate Secretary of War in Montgomery ordered Brigadier General P. G. T. Beauregard in Charleston to demand the surrender of Sumter. Major Robert Anderson, who commanded the fort, replied that he would evacuate it of his troops unless supplies and new orders were received. Lincoln sent the supplies and made known his determination not to surrender the fort to the Southerners. At 4:30 on the morning of April 12 the forces of General Beauregard opened fire on Fort Sumter. The war had begun.

On hearing the news, Leon left the house and walked alone into the woods he had known and loved all his life. When he returned he went into the main stock barn and hanged himself. Joe-Tom found him later that day (Leon had chosen a room seldom used) and ran to find Floyd. Floyd returned with Joe-Tom and, unbelieving, cut the rope that freed his friend. Before going to tell Sarah, he settled Leon gently against a pile of hay, and then holding him in his arms, wept bitterly.

Six

In late April, James joined the county's Volunteer Rifle Regiment and went to the camp grounds every day to drill. A month later the regiment was ordered to Savannah where it would be assigned positions along the coast to guard. Savannah was already blockaded by a Union ship, the *Harriet Lane*.

When he returned to Oaks on the day the orders reached the regiment, James told Rachel.

"And so you will go," she said. "As I always knew you would."

"I hate to, Rachel. All I want is you and our young ones, and to work the land. I don't give a damn about the rest of it. But I have to go. If the war was fought only by men who loved fighting, who'd fight it?"

Beginning to cry, she shook her head and seemed to shrivel as she closed in on herself. He all but enfolded her with his arms and body as she said, "I'll do the best I can, only don't expect me to be brave, for I'm not. I can't let you go the way Annabel let Blair, laughing and waving. I'll probably scream my head off, and they'll have to hold me back from boarding the train when you get on it!"

In the event, that did not occur.

Edna would not go into town; she was too old for public displays, she said, and she asked for the children to be left with her. B.B. would not agree to stay until Doreen said she would stay too. Sarah came over to Oaks that day and she and Bruce sat on the driver's seat together, leaving James and Rachel alone behind them. Or so it had been planned. But when James made his home farewells, Jane would not be torn away from him. Although she had promised to remain with the others, it was decided to let her go as the easiest thing. She rode quietly enough on her father's lap. James and Rachel's hands were clasped together, and they were quiet too, the whole distance into Highboro.

Bruce found a place for the carriage near the depot. James then quickly said his goodbyes to them and joined the regiment that was forming ranks in front of the post office. The whole town had assembled there, and when the whistle of the coming train sounded in the distance, the band began to play *Dixie* and the regiment marched raggedly the short way to the station, followed by all the crowd. Children danced and pranced to the music, screaming with excitement; and dogs barked and ran with them.

First one, then another broke from the ranks to give a last kiss to a wife or mother, to hold a child another time. Every woman had brought with her a bouquet of flowers, which she pressed into the hands of a soldier she loved, or merely knew; and so most of the men carried flowers in one hand and a rifle in the other.

Bruce and Sarah remained in the carriage, Sarah holding Jane by force so that Rachel and James might have the time alone.

"Try not to worry about me, honey. I'll be all right, I swear I will. I'm going to be the least daring soldier this army has got."

Rachel's laugh was forced. "Promise me," she said. "Promise me you'll be a coward!"

"Don't you doubt it, and don't you fear. For I'll be back, and soon, and we'll go on just like before. Nothing can stop us, my honey darling, this side of God Himself."

When James boarded the train, Rachel looked so forlorn that Sarah yielded to Jane's demand and let her run
to join her mother. Then after a minute, fearing that Jane
would be a bother for Rachel, Sarah left Bruce in the carriage and went onto the station platform. A whistle blew,
bells clanged, the big wheels of the engine turned. The
train moved slowly, then faster, and soon was gone.

All about them women held and comforted women,
some weeping, others not. Gradually, these began to drift
away, leaving Rachel, who had refused Sarah's embrace,
standing alone. Sarah and Jane waited a little apart from
her. The three, who still wore black for Leon, lingered until all was vacant and silent on the platform; and then at a
movement from Rachel they drew together and went back
to the carriage to go home.

Seven

In the office Sarah and Floyd had been working and
worrying over accounts since suppertime. It was now
nearly ten o'clock, and Sarah had heard the other family
members go off to their rooms a good while ago. She sat
at the desk, Floyd at a table he had pulled up near her.
Each used a tallow candle to work by; wax and lamp oil
had become luxuries.

Sarah drew breath in deeply and slowly to try to calm
herself; failing to do so, she let it out in a groan and
pushed her ledger back on the desk. "Let's stop. I'm too
tired for any more of it tonight," she said.

Floyd looked over at her, his mind still on the figures
he had been checking. When his sight registered her, his
face relaxed. He nodded. "Go to bed," he said. "It won't
seem so bad in the morning."

"It will seem just as bad in the morning," she said 'irritably. "And I don't want to go to bed, for I shan't sleep
much anyway." She rose from her chair and went to a
sideboard that held glasses, a couple of stone jugs, and
several decanters. "Have a glass of wine with me, unless
you want to go. I know you're tired too, and with more
reason than I, for you've been in the fields all day."

"I'll have a glass," he said.

She poured claret generously into two glasses, handing

one to Floyd and sitting down with the other on the desk before her. After a glance at the ledger, she closed it. "A dollar for three pounds of rice! Coffee not to be had, and flour out of sight! And the war going for only two months. What will we do if it lasts a year?"

"We'll get used to corn bread with everything. 'It crumbles and don't sop the syrup good as biscuits do!' But it's filling."

"Who were you imitating?" she asked sharply.

"All of them." He sipped from his glass.

"The people don't understand it." She shrugged. "I don't either. Ships run the blockade into Savannah every day, but ordinary provisions are hard to find and too dear to buy when you can find them."

Floyd took a folding knife from his pocket, opened a small blade and began to whittle a turkey quill. "We'll manage. Remember, England wants our cotton, so England will keep the ports open."

She sighed and drank from her glass. "I wish I were over there right now, or anywhere but here!"

He laughed. "No, you don't. Give you your choice of the world, and you'd pick this little wart on it."

She relaxed in her chair, crossed her legs comfortably and swung her free foot. "It's good to talk. Just talk, I mean. Not about what we need and can't afford, nor about all the others' complaints. You're the only one I talk to, except Edna. Even mama complains about 'the way it used to be; the way it's supposed to be.' " He nodded. "The others I don't talk to; I try to soothe and placate, when what I feel like doing is shaking them." She turned her head, and looking directly at him, showed surprise. "Why, you're getting old, Floyd!" She shook her head. "I don't mean it. Only, we don't look at each other, we're so used to seeing each other. And I just looked at you and remembered you're not young any longer."

"I'm fifty-five," he said drily.

"I always think of you as the young man who, the first day I came to Beulah Land—Leon was driving the carriage that brought us out from town—do you remember?"

He nodded.

"And there you came to ride alongside; and then you broke out laughing and rode ahead of us through the orchard shouting, 'Company's coming!' "

"Oh, I remember." He smiled.

"Those were good days," she said.

"A lot of them have been."

"Yes," she agreed. They were quiet for a minute, sipping wine. Suddenly, she laughed at herself. "I said you're no longer young, and look at me. Last week some time, I forget when, I was busy thinking about something else when I stopped and said to myself: 'Who is that haggard old woman?' Of course, it was me. I was looking in the mirror in the upstairs hall without knowing where I was or who I was."

After smiling with her he said, "I always think of you as that pretty young girl in the carriage the day you came. I remember how we all wanted you to stay."

"Well, I did—and that's nice to hear, Floyd." She stood and went to the sideboard. "I want another glass, and this one I'll drink slower or I'll get the hiccups. Will you have another?" He nodded. She filled both glasses from the decanter, and when she came back and sat down, she said, "I complain, whereas I should go about with a patient, sweet face the way they say we're supposed to do. But I am not that kind of a woman."

"Thank God," he said. "My work's hard enough as it is."

She had not heard him; she was occupied with another thought. "The only thing though that ever frightens me is when I wake sometimes at night and think: What if Floyd leaves?"

"Have no fear of that kind," he said.

She studied his face. "Beulah Land means as much to you as it does to me."

"It's been my home longer," he reminded her.

"And that's why you came back, the time you left."

He thought about it a minute. "You could say so."

"I know you came back on Lovey's account, and Ezra's, but are you suggesting there was another reason? I was so glad to see you I never thought about it."

"I came back," he said with deliberation, "for the same reason I left."

"That sounds like a conundrum."

"No, it's only the truth."

She paused, considering what he had said. "Will you tell me?"

He took a swallow of wine that nearly emptied his glass. When he spoke, the words came slowly. It was important to him to use the right ones. "I left here because I found out—Mama guessed, by the way, though we only

talked about it a little that one time. I had found out that
I cared about you in a way I must not." She continued to
look at him steadily. "I came back because I kept on feeling that way." He nodded. "I was right to. Living here,
working on the land together, seeing you live your life
and living my own, the feeling I'd had changed. Or no; it
grew in a different way. I said while ago I think of you as
the young girl arriving in the carriage that first day. Well,
I do, but I see you other ways too. I've heard you curse,
and I've seen you with sweat running down your face and
your hair all every way and your hands chapped and
dirty. You just won't remember you're a lady!" She hid
one hand in her lap as the other went to find her hair.
"I've seen you with tears running down your face and
your face like a grieving stone angel's in the cemetery.
You're the mistress of Beulah Land. You're the widow of
my friend. But if everything had been different, I'd have
tried to have you for my own. As the thing works out, I'll
never leave Beulah Land. Because of you, and Leon, and
me. It's all come to be one thing."

"Do you think we might have another glass of wine?"
she asked after a moment.

"Why not?" he said. "Aren't you the mistress of this
plantation?"

"Of course I am!" Laughing, she rose and, mocking the
movements of a sashaying belle, fetched the decanter and
poured wine into their glasses, slopping a little over the
side of his glass. "I'm sorry."

He licked his wet fingers. "It's only generosity."

"I'm not drunk. Only tired, and it's good to talk." She
closed her eyes, and they sat quietly. Eyes still closed, she
began to speak again. "Do you remember? Of course, you
don't; you weren't here. It was the morning after you left,
the day after Thanksgiving. I went out in the back yard
and found Uncle Felix there, and he told me you'd gone."

"He helped me; that's right."

"He had just told Lovey and Ezra. I couldn't believe
him. I got very upset. Enough to surprise him. Then we
found out my sister Lauretta had run away with Bonard
Davis, and everything got mixed together, and I never
thought about why I was upset. I missed you, but then
you came home. And when I saw you, I knew you were
one of the family dearest to me. You and Leon and
Rachel and Roman." She frowned into her glass. "I
haven't heard from Roman since they cut off the mails in

April. And won't, I guess, until this is over. I want him home, but that's selfish of me. He's better off where he is. Only it's hard, not to get his letters."

Floyd was silent for a time, and then he said, "Did Leon ever say anything about Roscoe's visit that day?"

She shook her head. "Not a word, and when I asked, he just stared at me. What happened we'll never know, except that it had something—not all, but something surely—to do with his death."

"In town they say Roscoe won't live another month."

"Have you seen him?"

Floyd shook his head. "He doesn't leave the house now."

"Let's have another glass—to Roscoe's dying!" She walked steadily to the sideboard for the decanter and poured wine into their glasses. Then raising hers, she said, "To the death of Roscoe Elk!"

They drank. She hiccupped. "I should never swallow when I'm thinking bad things. I'm glad he's dying, but it's evil to gloat over anyone's dying."

"Hold your breath and count to ten."

She tried, but presently another hiccup sounded. She shook her head, annoyed with herself, and then reached for her glass. After drinking from it, she belched and waited. A minute later when she was sure, she said, "Gone now. And the little too much has made me sober instead of drunk."

He finished his glass. "Well, it's made me a little drunk. If not drunk, quiet enough to sleep."

"Go to bed and leave me here." When he frowned, she added, "I'm all right." She stood, moved a step and stopped in a listening attitude. "This big house that has seen so much and so many—is now only the domicile of women left behind! It's true; think about it. There's no man at Beulah Land; there isn't even a boy. We're a bunch of old women snapping and nattering at each other." He looked at her with tired worry. She smiled. "Having a friendly ear has spoiled me. I'll walk you to the door." She blew out her candle. He carried his in its holder to light their way, cupping its flame against the air currents. They went through the hall and the breezeway, on to the back door. There he handed her the holder. She took it and blew the candle out. Its burnt tallow smell hung briefly on the warm, moist air and then dissolved. "I'll find my way in the dark. I know every board of this house."

"Sarah?"

She trembled and, dropping the candle holder, did not bother to retrieve it. He saw her hand reach out. He put his arms around her; she put hers on him. They held each other close and wept for what had been, and what had not been, and what would never be. Parting, they spoke in whispers, although there was no one to hear them.

"I'll see you in the morning," he said.

"As long as you say that, my world survives. You and I are the survivors, Floyd!"

"We're only the stewards and the slaves of Beulah Land. Good night, Sarah."

"Tomorrow."

Eight

Nell woke abruptly and shouted, "Tippecanoe and Tyler too!"

Penelope, in the rocking chair alongside her, frowned and drew her lips up pursily. Closing her ivory fan with a click, she used it to prod Nell's fat thigh protruding from the open side of her chair. "Old fool," she said. "That was a long time ago. Now it's 'Do not tread on me!' *Noli me tangere!*"

"Oh, I know it; I was dreaming."

"If you didn't eat so much, you wouldn't sleep so much," Penelope said. "Uncle Joshua used to say: 'Enough is a plenty.' You're not much company. If it wasn't for your gassiness I wouldn't know you were alive, sometimes."

The day was Monday, July 29, and the two old women had sat together since noon dinner, rocking in their chairs, scolding each other. A little way down the porch from them sat Selma and Pauline, working on flannel shirts for the soldiers.

"Am I still dreaming?" Nell said. "Who is that coming? Is it—?"

Suspiciously, Penelope followed the direction of Nell's gaze and saw the solitary figure of a woman, shoulders drooping, making her way slowly—exhaustedly, if appearance were true—toward the house through the orchard. Penelope rose, as if standing would afford her a clearer view. "Well, dear Lord above us, it is!" she exclaimed. "It is Lauretta!"

"You see!" Nell declared triumphantly, as if vindicated of some doubt or aspersion. With the help of her cane, she too stood.

Penelope called, "Selma, will you look there who's coming up the drive!"

Selma stood, and then Pauline, so that the four women all were standing staring at the woman approaching them with her head bowed. She did not acknowledge that she saw them until she reached the short brick walk directly in front of the porch. Covered with dust, trembling with fatigue or emotion, or possibly both, she then raised her eyes and looked at them.

"Yes, it is I," Lauretta said as they continued to stare. "A refugee from the North. Cast out from there. Penniless and near to—" She did not finish, for she fainted. At any rate she closed her eyes and collapsed in a heap, and Selma and Pauline dropped their sewing, which they had continued to hold when they rose from their chairs, and ran to lift her and support her up the steps to the porch. At that moment Sarah emerged from the center hallway and saw her sister. "Oh, dear God!" she exclaimed, and then burst into laughter.

Ruffled feathers smoothed, dress, corset, and shoes removed, face and hands washed, Lauretta lay on the chaise longue in Sarah's room. Her energies had been somewhat revived by her drinking three glasses of wine and eating a plate of cold fried chicken and pickled peaches which Myrtis herself had brought up out of curiosity, when food was ordered. So far, Lauretta had spoken only sketchily of how she happened to come there, and Sarah had not pressed her. But now, satisfied that Lauretta was not ill, had been fed, and appeared no longer to be unduly fatigued, Sarah drew a chair close to the chaise and sat down on it.

Lauretta turned her head to meet her sister's eyes and said meekly, "You are good to me. And what a lot of sorrow and suffering I have seen since we parted! Just yesterday when I arrived in Savannah there was a funeral for which the entire city had apparently turned out into the streets. I asked whose it was and was told that it was the funeral of 'Colonel Bartow, hero of Manassas.' Have you heard of him?" Sarah nodded. "Well," Lauretta continued, "it was a very grand affair. The way was thronged with black as well as white faces. And then I arrived here today and was standing on the platform at the depot, having ordered my trunk—I have only one now; will you send someone for it?—to be taken inside; and I was wondering what to do next, for I hadn't money to hire a trap to bring me out here, when another funeral procession passed before my very eyes. It seemed such a solemn, somehow, although not large, *important* event, I asked who might be dead and was told— Now I declare!" She frowned and shrugged with vexation, having forgot the name.

Sarah supplied it. "Roscoe Elk."

"Yes! But wasn't he a Negro?"

"A very substantial 'free person of color,' " Sarah said slowly.

"And isn't he the man who—?"

Sarah's nod filled the new pause. "He is the man."

"I thought so!" Lauretta exclaimed as though she had been clever. "Two funerals in two places in two days— well, you understand how it depressed my spirit. I felt like a goose had stepped over my grave."

"And then? Surely you did not walk all the way from town; it's nearly three miles."

"Well, no." Lauretta admitted. "Only from the main road. I begged a ride in a wagon headed for Oaks, driven by one of their people. How are they at Oaks?"

"Well enough. Rachel married James."

"But he died—"

"That was Adam. James was his brother."

" Good gracious! I wish you had written to me."

"You never sent a mailing address."

"Well, I was moving around, you know. But I did write to you."

"You did; three times in eight years. Rachel has two children, a boy and a girl."

"I'm a grandmother!" Lauretta discovered. "I! And my daughter is mistress of a great plantation!"

"Not yet," Sarah said. "Bruce Davis is still master of Oaks."

"Do you mean to say he's married again?"

"No, but he has a daughter—"

"Daughters don't count."

"And his mother is still very much alive."

"Is she!" Lauretta said as though affronted by the news. "That old woman seems determined to live forever!"

"I wish she could." Sarah said.

"How is dear Bruce? Perhaps you did not know it, but I had every reason to believe he was about to offer himself to me when I left Beulah Land—"

Stifling a smile Sarah said, "James is no longer at home. He has gone to war with his regiment."

"And you haven't said—how is Leon?"

After a moment's hesitation Sarah said, "Leon is dead and buried these three and a half months."

"Ah!" Lauretta wailed in despair. "I should have guessed it! You in black; but somehow I associated it with the war. And they were all in black on the porch too. Oh, it is a sad, cruel time. My poor Leon!" Lauretta cried.

Ignoring her tears Sarah said quietly, "Now, what of you, my dear? You have not told me how you happen to be here."

Lauretta wept the harder for another minute or so, and Sarah waited as patiently as she could. When Lauretta had composed herself, she said calmly enough, "When I left you, *nearly* eight years ago—"

Sarah interrupted. "My dear Lauretta, I have ten gallons of cucumbers boiling to make pickles. If we start with eight years ago, we shall be at it all day and well into the night. Pick up a little closer to the present, do."

"Surely Myrtis knows how to make cucumber pickles!" Lauretta protested tartly.

"She likes me to test them. Proceed, if you will; otherwise I must leave you for a while."

"I returned to acting and appeared with various companies under my old name, Mrs. Lauretta Savage. I had to give Shakespeare up because I couldn't seem to remember all the lines exactly as he wrote them, and people in the audience know the plays so well they will even venture to correct one during a performance—" As she saw a look of impatience sweep Sarah's face, she went on quickly. "I've acted, and to much acclaim, in contemporary comedies, American and English. There have been very nice parts for me since I forsook the ingenue roles. Well, since the war began—and I realize now for several months before that—there have been difficulties. I am Southern; my voice has what they call the Southern accent." She paused, thinking. "Of course, I put down a large part of what happened in Philadelphia to the jealousy of another actress in the company whose husband had begun to pay more than casual attentions to me—unwelcome and unencouraged, I assure you. But one does not like to be cruel or rude.

Well, one night ten days ago we were performing at the Walnut Street Theatre a play called *Fashion* by Anna Cora Mowatt. I had entered the scene but two minutes, and spoken my speeches on the proper cues, when there was a cry from the gallery: 'She is a Southern spy!' That woman I spoke of had hired someone to do it, of course. We tried to go on with the play. But in the middle of my next speech there came again the self-same cry from the gallery: 'Southern spy!' I paused, not knowing whether to go back and take the speech over again or— Then someone else took up the cry, and then another, until the entire gallery seemed to be hissing and roaring: 'Southern spy! Spy! Spy! Spy!' The play could not continue. The curtain was brought down, the theatre by then a savage mob. It was all the policemen could do to keep them from pouring backstage. I had scarcely reached my dressing room when the company manager arrived to say I was discharged."

"Monstrous! Hateful!"

"Well, I don't know," Lauretta said in a suddenly reasonable tone. "I could not entirely blame him. Feelings were high, and there had been an occasional mutter before we played in Philadelphia. What about your pickles?"

"Never mind," Sarah said. "Myrtis will go on with them if I do not come."

Lauretta continued. "I was sitting alone when there was a knock at the door. At first I thought it was that woman come to jeer at me, but when I asked who was there, a voice said, 'Roman Kendrick!' "

"Roman!"

"Yes. Roman Kendrick, he said. Of course, they take the name of their masters when they go free, don't they?"

"Roman has every right to the name of Kendrick," Sarah said. "He is Leon's son."

"But he's a darky."

"Does it shock you to know you were not Leon's first—diversion?" Sarah said.

"But with a Negress! I call that disgusting! I declare, Sarah, you have put up with the most—"

"Oh, shut up, and tell me about my dear Roman! The mails have stopped coming, and I have had no news of him for three months now!"

"He was a perfect gentleman, if a darky can be called that, and my very savior in that hard hour. When I let him in, he explained who he was. He was very well dressed, very well mannered; yes, quite the gentleman.

Handsome even, if a darky may— He had been in the audience and knew all. He had recognized me, although he had not seen my name on the posters. We talked for an hour, until they locked the theatre for the night. He offered to help me. I wanted nothing, I told him, but to leave the North and return to my own people. He told me briefly about the school he was about to leave—"

"Leave the school!" Sarah exclaimed.

"Yes, he had decided he wanted to be part of the war, but not the fighting part, so he was leaving the school to his friends and going to Washington to work in the army hospital, however they needed him. He offered me shelter at the school—I dared not stay in my old lodgings with the other actors—until he was ready to leave, a couple of days later. On his way to Washington he escorted me to Baltimore and arranged passage for me on a sloop that was running blockade into Norfolk, Virginia. And from there I made my way to Charleston. From there to Savannah. Savannah, here. I have a letter for you from Roman Kendrick if I can remember where I put it."

"A letter from Roman!"

"He gave it to me only minutes before we sailed from Baltimore." Shaking her head, she said to herself, "Now where did I put it?"

"Please do look for it!" Sarah urged.

"Yes, well, I don't like leaving this blessed resting place. However—" Lauretta pulled herself to a sitting position and bent to rub a knotted muscle in her right calf. "Since you set such store by it, I'll look." In the middle of the room she paused to consider. "I certainly didn't put it into my trunk." She went to Sarah's dressing table, found her handbag and opened it. "Abracadabra, and here it is!" she said triumphantly.

Sarah all but snatched it from her, and then stood hesitating, not wanting to read it in the company of her sister. "Perhaps you would like to sleep a little."

"No, I'm quite awake now, thank you."

"I really ought to go down to the kitchen. Is there anything you want before I go?"

Lauretta took Sarah's hand and held it tightly for a moment. "There is something I want most desperately!" she said.

"What is it, my dear Lauretta?" Sarah said, alarmed at the other's vehemence.

"Your promise to let me abide here."

"You are certainly welcome to stay as long as you please."

"No, I don't mean in the social way of a visit; I don't mean that at all. I mean to say I am—" She turned her face away. "Well, I always thought I was strong enough to ricochet from one droll disaster to another, getting plenty of fun out of life's absurdities and even sometimes a little profit. But now I'm confused. I don't know how to live in this new world of war. Everyone is so deadly serious. I don't understand people's hating someone they don't even know. How can that be? I have been very angry with a great many—for five minutes or even five days at a time—but I have never hated anyone. Your Roman talked to me quite a lot—nicely, too. But he really took me seriously as a person, something that has seldom happened to me. And so when I bade him farewell, I continued to think of myself seriously. And oh, I did not enjoy it! I may be trivial, but I am not a fool. I stood outside myself, as it were, and I saw that however delightful the world might even now find a young and pretty Lauretta, there is no place in it for an aging and frightened Lauretta. I beg of you—a haven. If there is any way I may be of use or help or service, please direct me. Only do not—I pray you: do not make me go!"

Sarah took her sister tenderly into her arms and held her a long moment. "You are welcome, and we probably *shall* find a use for you! As for 'haven,' yours is here for as long as you want it and as long as Beulah Land can offer it to any of us."

"I thank you, sister!"

"Now I must get to work!" Sarah said. "But unless you are very tired, why don't you just throw your dress over your head without bothering with the corset and go down to sit and talk with the others? They're all breathless to hear your adventures, I know they are."

"Do you think they'd be truly interested?"

"I'm certain of it. They're lonely. I don't have much time to give them. They need your wit and liveliness. And I'll tell you what— I'll send over to Oaks to ask Bruce and Rachel to join us here for supper this very night. Edna won't go out at night any more, and Doreen stays with her—"

"Oh, that would be nice, a little party!" Lauretta clapped her hands. "Only, I beg you: wait until tomorrow, when I've had time to rest, and shake out a pretty dress, and maybe put a curl into this poor old dyed hair!"

They laughed together, hands in hands. "Very well,"
Sarah said, "but do go downstairs and relieve their curiosity!" She kissed Lauretta's cheek and left her.

Sarah picked at the sealing wax with both thumbnails as
she descended the stairs and went into the office, closing
its door behind her in order to read her letter in privacy.
It was a short one, written in haste; but when she finished
it, she ached with longing for the actual presence of her
beloved Roman.

He had written in part, and this she read again to herself:

> I must tell you a particular dream I had. Do you be-
> lieve dreams? I don't, unless they tell me something I
> want to believe. Well, Sarah! In this dream Leon ap-
> peared. Not as I had known him, but young and
> smiling and happy as I never saw him. Still, I knew
> who he was. He was laughing. He called me by my
> name in an easy—I might even say—affectionate
> way; and he said, "Tell Sarah I love her." Now, is
> that not odd and interesting? Considering my age—
> forty, you know!—it may be strange of me to say it,
> but for the first time in my life I felt that I had a fa-
> ther. I must seal this and give it to your sister, for
> she is ready to leave. I know you will be good to her,
> because she needs you. I love you always, my Beauty!
> Roman.

Sarah sat with the letter in her lap for a little while, until sounds of the household began to reach her, and consciousness of obligations beyond this room reminded her
to get up and go out, show herself and say sensible things.
Tomorrow or the day after they would begin picking cotton and taking it into Highboro to be ginned.

Suddenly, as if she could hear it, she imagined the flinging of shovelfuls of earth into the crevices around the coffin in the grave of Roscoe Elk. Roscoe was dead, but his
son and grandson lived on, and were strong. Well, so was
she; and Beulah Land had never been more beautiful than
it was now in the fullness of its ripening harvest. She must
go and find Floyd, wherever he was in the barns or fields,
and read him that part of Roman's letter telling of Leon
and the dream.

As she left the office, the sound of Lauretta's voice

from the porch made her pause and listen. Lauretta was making an adventure of her escape from Philadelphia. Sarah went to the open doorway, but without showing herself.

There they were, a line of old ladies in their rocking chairs, rocking back and forth: Selma and Pauline and Penelope and Nell—and now Lauretta, who had paused in the telling of her story. With a belligerent glare, and gripping the arms of her chair, Nell cried: *"Noli me tangere!"* The others nodded their heads and took up the warning cry.

"Noli me tangere!"

"Noli me tangere!"

Turning her back on them Sarah went through the broad center hall, through the breezeway; and when she stepped out into the yard, she began to run, calling, "Floyd! Floyd! Where are you?"

BESTSELLERS FROM DELL

fiction